Detec[...]
and
Young Adventurers

The Complete
Short Stories

C000245134

Books by Agatha Christie

The ABC Murders
The Adventure of the Christmas
   Pudding
After the Funeral
And Then There Were None
Appointment with Death
At Bertram's Hotel
The Big Four
The Body in the Library
By the Pricking of My Thumbs
Cards on the Table
A Caribbean Mystery
Cat Among the Pigeons
The Clocks
Crooked House
Curtain: Poirot's Last Case
Dead Man's Folly
Death Comes as the End
Death in the Clouds
Death on the Nile
Destination Unknown
Dumb Witness
Elephants Can Remember
Endless Night
Evil Under the Sun
Five Little Pigs
4.50 from Paddington
Hallowe'en Party
Hercule Poirot's Christmas
Hickory Dickory Dock
The Hollow
The Hound of Death
The Labours of Hercules
The Listerdale Mystery
Lord Edgware Dies
The Man in the Brown Suit
The Mirror Crack'd from Side to
Side
Miss Marple's Final Cases
The Moving Finger
Mrs McGinty's Dead
The Murder at the Vicarage
Murder in Mesopotamia
Murder in the Mews
A Murder is Announced
Murder is Easy
The Murder of Roger Ackroyd
Murder on the Links
Murder on the Orient Express
The Mysterious Affair at Styles
The Mysterious Mr Quin
The Mystery of the Blue Train

Nemesis
N or M?
One, Two, Buckle My Shoe
Ordeal by Innocence
The Pale Horse
Parker Pyne Investigates
Partners in Crime
Passenger to Frankfurt
Peril at End House
A Pocket Full of Rye
Poirot Investigates
Poirot's Early Cases
Postern of Fate
Problem at Pollensa Bay
Sad Cypress
The Secret Adversary
The Secret of Chimneys
The Seven Dials Mystery
The Sittaford Mystery
Sleeping Murder
Sparkling Cyanide
Taken at the Flood
They Came to Baghdad
They Do It With Mirrors
Third Girl
The Thirteen Problems
Three-Act Tragedy
Towards Zero
While the Light Lasts
Why Didn't They Ask Evans?

Plays adapted into novels

Black Coffee
Spider's Web
The Unexpected Guest

*Novels under the Nom de Plume
of 'Mary Westmacott'*

Absent in the Spring
The Burden
A Daughter's A Daughter
Giant's Bread
The Rose and the Yew Tree
Unfinished Portrait

Memoirs

Come, Tell Me How You Live
An Autobiography

Agatha Christie

Detectives
and
Young Adventurers

The Complete
Short Stories

HARPER

HARPER

An Imprint of HarperCollins*Publishers*
77–85 Fulham Palace Road
Hammersmith, London W6 8JB
www.harpercollins.co.uk

This collection first published 2008
3

*The publishers would like to acknowledge the help of Karl Pike
in the preparation of this volume.*

ISBN 978 0 00 728419 1

Typeset by Palimpsest Book Production Limited,
Grangemouth, Stirlingshire

Printed and bound in Great Britain by
Clays Ltd, St Ives plc

Contents

PART THREE

PARKER PYNE, INVESTIGATOR

PART FOUR

HERCULE POIROT: BELGIAN DETECTIVE

POSTSCRIPT
THE CHRISTMAS STORIES

APPENDIX

Part One

Tommy & Tuppence:
Young Adventurers Ltd

Author's Foreword

I published a book of short stories called *Partners in Crime*. Each story here was written in the manner of some particular detective of the time. Some of them by now I cannot even recognize. I remember Thornley Colton, the blind detective – Austin Freeman, of course; Freeman Wills Croft with his wonderful timetables; and inevitably Sherlock Holmes. It is interesting in a way to see who of the twelve detective story writers that I chose are still well known – some are household names, others have more or less perished in oblivion. They all seemed to me at the time to write well and entertainingly in their different fashions. *Partners in Crime* featured in it my two young sleuths, Tommy and Tuppence, who had been the principal characters in my second book, *The Secret Adversary*. It was fun to get back to them for a change.

AGATHA CHRISTIE

from *An Autobiography*, 1977

A Fairy in the Flat

'A Fairy in the Flat' and 'A Pot of Tea', the two opening chapters of the 1929 book *Partners in Crime*, were first published together as 'Publicity' in *The Sketch*, 24 September 1924. It set the scene for a continuous run of twelve Tommy and Tuppence stories, in which Agatha Christie parodied well-known literary detectives.

Mrs Thomas Beresford shifted her position on the divan and looked gloomily out of the window of the flat. The prospect was not an extended one, consisting solely of a small block of flats on the other side of the road. Mrs Beresford sighed and then yawned.

'I wish,' she said, 'something would happen.'

Her husband looked up reprovingly.

'Be careful, Tuppence, this craving for vulgar sensation alarms me.'

Tuppence sighed and closed her eyes dreamily.

'So Tommy and Tuppence were married,' she chanted, 'and lived happily ever afterwards. And six years later they were still living together happily ever afterwards. It is extraordinary,' she said, 'how different everything always is from what you think it is going to be.'

'A very profound statement, Tuppence. But not original. Eminent poets and still more eminent divines have said it before – and if you will excuse me saying so, have said it better.'

'Six years ago,' continued Tuppence, 'I would have sworn that with sufficient money to buy things with, and with you for a husband, all life would have been one grand sweet song, as one of the poets you seem to know so much about puts it.'

'Is it me or the money that palls upon you?' inquired Tommy coldly.

'Palls isn't exactly the word,' said Tuppence kindly. 'I'm used to my blessings, that's all. Just as one never thinks what a boon it is to be able to breathe through one's nose until one has a cold in the head.'

'Shall I neglect you a little?' suggested Tommy. 'Take other women about to night clubs. That sort of thing.'

'Useless,' said Tuppence. 'You would only meet me there with other men. And I should know perfectly well that you didn't care for the other women, whereas you would never be quite sure that I didn't care for the other men. Women are so much more thorough.'

'It's only in modesty that men score top marks,' murmured her husband. 'But what is the matter with you, Tuppence? Why this yearning discontent?'

'I don't know. I want things to happen. Exciting things. Wouldn't you like to go chasing German spies again, Tommy? Think of the wild days of peril we went through once. Of course I know you're more or less in the Secret Service now, but it's pure office work.'

'You mean you'd like them to send me into darkest Russia disguised as a Bolshevik bootlegger, or something of that sort?'

'That wouldn't be any good,' said Tuppence. 'They wouldn't let me go with you and I'm the person who wants something to do so badly. Something to do. That is what I keep saying all day long.'

'Women's sphere,' suggested Tommy, waving his hand.

'Twenty minutes' work after breakfast every morning keeps the flag going to perfection. You have nothing to complain of, have you?'

'Your housekeeping is so perfect, Tuppence, as to be almost monotonous.'

'I do like gratitude,' said Tuppence.

'You, of course, have got your work,' she continued, 'but tell me, Tommy, don't you ever have a secret yearning for excitement, for things to *happen*?'

'No,' said Tommy, 'at least I don't think so. It is all very well to want things to happen – they might not be pleasant things.'

'How prudent men are,' sighed Tuppence. 'Don't you ever have a wild secret yearning for romance – adventure – life?'

'What *have* you been reading, Tuppence?' asked Tommy.

'Think how exciting it would be,' went on Tuppence, 'if we heard a wild rapping at the door and went to open it and in staggered a dead man.'

'If he was dead he couldn't stagger,' said Tommy critically.

'You know what I mean,' said Tuppence. 'They always stagger in just before they die and fall at your feet, just gasping out a few enigmatic words. "The Spotted Leopard", or something like that.'

'I advise a course of Schopenhauer or Emmanuel Kant,' said Tommy.

'That sort of thing would be good for you,' said Tuppence. 'You are getting fat and comfortable.'

'I am not,' said Tommy indignantly. 'Anyway you do slimming exercises yourself.'

'Everybody does,' said Tuppence. 'When I said you were getting fat I was really speaking meta-phorically, you are getting prosperous and sleek and comfortable.'

'I don't know what has come over you,' said her husband.

'The spirit of adventure,' murmured Tuppence. 'It is better than a longing for romance anyway. I have that sometimes too. I think of meeting a man, a really handsome man –'

'You have met me,' said Tommy. 'Isn't that enough for you?'

'A brown, lean man, terrifically strong, the kind of man who can ride anything and lassoes wild horses –'

'Complete with sheepskin trousers and a cowboy hat,' interpolated Tommy sarcastically.

'– and has lived in the Wilds,' continued Tuppence. 'I should like him to fall simply madly in love with me. I should, of course, rebuff him virtuously and be true to my marriage vows, but my heart would secretly go out to him.'

'Well,' said Tommy, 'I often wish that I may meet a really beautiful girl. A girl with corn coloured hair who will fall desperately in love with me. Only I don't think I rebuff her – in fact I am quite sure I don't.'

'That,' said Tuppence, 'is naughty temper.'

'What,' said Tommy, 'is really the matter with you, Tuppence? You have never talked like this before.'

'No, but I have been boiling up inside for a long time,' said Tuppence. 'You see it is very dangerous to have everything you want – including enough money to buy things. Of course there are always hats.'

'You have got about forty hats already,' said Tommy, 'and they all look alike.'

'Hats are like that,' said Tuppence. 'They are not really alike. There are *nuances* in them. I saw rather a nice one in Violette's this morning.'

'If you haven't anything better to do than going on buying hats you don't need –'

'That's it,' said Tuppence, 'that's exactly it. If I had something better to do. I suppose I ought to take up good works. Oh, Tommy, I do wish something exciting would happen. I feel – I really do feel it would be good for us. If we could find a fairy –'

'Ah!' said Tommy. 'It is curious your saying that.'

He got up and crossed the room. Opening a drawer of the writing table he took out a small snapshot print and brought it to Tuppence.

'Oh!' said Tuppence, 'so you have got them developed. Which is this, the one you took of this room or the one I took?'

'The one I took. Yours didn't come out. You under exposed it. You always do.'

'It is nice for you,' said Tuppence, 'to think that there is one thing you can do better than me.'

'A foolish remark,' said Tommy, 'but I will let it pass for the moment. What I wanted to show you was this.'

He pointed to a small white speck on the photograph.

'That is a scratch on the film,' said Tuppence.

'Not at all,' said Tommy. 'That, Tuppence, is a fairy.'

'Tommy, you idiot.'

'Look for yourself.'

He handed her a magnifying glass. Tuppence studied the print attentively through it. Seen thus by a slight stretch of fancy the scratch on the film could be imagined to represent a small winged creature on the fender.

'It has got wings,' cried Tuppence. 'What fun, a real live fairy in our flat. Shall we write to Conan Doyle about it? Oh, Tommy. Do you think she'll give us wishes?'

'You will soon know,' said Tommy. 'You have been wishing hard enough for something to happen all the afternoon.'

At that minute the door opened, and a tall lad of fifteen who seemed undecided as to whether he was a butler or a page boy inquired in a truly magnificent manner.

'Are you at home, madam? The front-door bell has just rung.'

'I wish Albert wouldn't go to the Pictures,' sighed Tuppence, after she had signified her assent, and Albert had withdrawn. 'He's copying a Long Island butler now. Thank goodness I've cured him of asking for people's cards and bringing them to me on a salver.'

The door opened again, and Albert announced: 'Mr Carter,' much as though it were a Royal title.

'The Chief,' muttered Tommy, in great surprise.

Tuppence jumped up with a glad exclamation, and greeted a tall grey-haired man with piercing eyes and a tired smile.

'Mr Carter, I *am* glad to see you.'

'That's good, Mrs Tommy. Now answer me a question. How's life generally?'

'Satisfactory, but dull,' replied Tuppence with a twinkle.

'Better and better,' said Mr Carter. 'I'm evidently going to find you in the right mood.'

'This,' said Tuppence, 'sounds exciting.'

Albert, still copying the Long Island butler, brought in tea. When this operation was completed without mishap and the door had closed behind him Tuppence burst out once more.

'You did mean something, didn't you, Mr Carter? Are you going to send us on a mission into darkest Russia?'

'Not exactly that,' said Mr Carter.

'But there is something.'

'Yes – there is something. I don't think you are the kind who shrinks from risks, are you, Mrs Tommy?'

Tuppence's eyes sparkled with excitement.

'There is certain work to be done for the Department – and I fancied – I just fancied – that it might suit you two.'

'Go on,' said Tuppence.

'I see that you take the *Daily Leader*,' continued Mr Carter, picking up that journal from the table.

He turned to the advertisement column and indicating a certain advertisement with his finger pushed the paper across to Tommy.

'Read that out,' he said.

Tommy complied.

The International Detective Agency, Theodore Blunt, Manager. Private Inquiries. Large staff of confidential and highly skilled Inquiry Agents. Utmost discretion. Consultations free. 118 Haleham St, W.C.'

He looked inquiringly at Mr Carter. The latter nodded. 'That detective agency has been on its last legs for some time,' he murmured. 'Friend of mine acquired it for a mere song. We're thinking of setting it going again – say, for a six months' trial. And during that time, of course, it will have to have a manager.'

'What about Mr Theodore Blunt?' asked Tommy.

'Mr Blunt has been rather indiscreet, I'm afraid. In fact, Scotland Yard have had to interfere. Mr Blunt is being detained at Her Majesty's expense, and he won't tell us half of what we'd like to know.'

'I see, sir,' said Tommy. 'At least, I think I see.'

'I suggest that you have six months leave from the office. Ill health. And, of course, if you like to run a Detective Agency under the name of Theodore Blunt, it's nothing to do with me.'

Tommy eyed his Chief steadily.

'Any instructions, sir?'

'Mr Blunt did some foreign business, I believe. Look out for blue letters with a Russian stamp on them. From a ham merchant anxious to find his wife who came as a refugee to this country some years ago. Moisten the stamp and you'll find the number 16 written underneath. Make a copy of these letters and send the originals on to me. Also if any one comes to the office and makes a reference to the number 16, inform me immediately.'

'I understand, sir,' said Tommy. 'And apart from these instructions?'

Mr Carter picked up his gloves from the table and prepared to depart.

'You can run the Agency as you please. I fancied' – his eyes twinkled a little – 'that it might amuse Mrs Tommy to try her hand at a little detective work.'

A Pot of Tea

Mr and Mrs Beresford took possession of the offices of the International Detective Agency a few days later. They were on the second floor of a somewhat dilapidated building in Bloomsbury. In the small outer office, Albert relinquished the role of a Long Island butler, and took up that of office boy, a part which he played to perfection. A paper bag of sweets, inky hands, and a tousled head was his conception of the character.

From the outer office, two doors led into inner offices. On one door was painted the legend 'Clerks'. On the other 'Private'. Behind the latter was a small comfortable room furnished with an immense businesslike desk, a lot of artistically labelled files, all empty, and some solid leather-seated chairs. Behind the desk sat the pseudo Mr Blunt trying to look as though he had run a Detective Agency all his life. A telephone, of course, stood at his elbow. Tuppence and he had rehearsed several good telephone effects, and Albert also had his instructions.

In the adjoining room was Tuppence, a typewriter, the necessary tables and chairs of an inferior type to those in the room of the great Chief, and a gas ring for making tea.

Nothing was wanting, in fact, save clients.

Tuppence, in the first ecstasies of initiation, had a few bright hopes.

'It will be too marvellous,' she declared. 'We will hunt down murderers, and discover the missing family jewels, and find people who've disappeared and detect embezzlers.'

At this point Tommy felt it his duty to strike a more discouraging note.

'Calm yourself, Tuppence, and try to forget the cheap fiction you are in the habit of reading. Our clientèle, if we have any clientèle at all – will consist solely of husbands who want their wives shadowed, and wives who want their husbands shadowed. Evidence for divorce is the sole prop of private inquiry agents.'

'Ugh!' said Tuppence, wrinkling a fastidious nose. 'We shan't touch divorce cases. We must raise the tone of our new profession.'

'Ye-es,' said Tommy doubtfully.

And now a week after installation they compared notes rather ruefully.

'Three idiotic women whose husbands go away for weekends,' sighed Tommy. 'Anyone come whilst I was out at lunch?'

'A fat old man with a flighty wife,' sighed Tuppence sadly. 'I've read in the papers for years that the divorce evil was growing, but somehow I never seemed to realise it until this last week. I'm sick and tired of saying, "We don't undertake divorce cases."'

'We've put it in the advertisements now,' Tommy reminded her. 'So it won't be so bad.'

'I'm sure we advertise in the most tempting way too,' said Tuppence in a melancholy voice. 'All the same, I'm not going to be beaten. If necessary, I shall commit a crime myself, and you will detect it.'

'And what good would that do? Think of my feelings when I bid you a tender farewell at Bow Street – or is it Vine Street?'

'You are thinking of your bachelor days,' said Tuppence pointedly.

'The Old Bailey, that is what I mean,' said Tommy.

'Well,' said Tuppence, 'something has got to be done about it. Here we are bursting with talent and no chance of exercising it.'

'I always like your cheery optimism, Tuppence. You seem to have no doubt whatever that you have talent to exercise.'

'Of course,' said Tuppence, opening her eyes very wide.

'And yet you have no expert knowledge whatever.'

'Well, I have read every detective novel that has been published in the last ten years.'

'So have I,' said Tommy, 'but I have a sort of feeling that that wouldn't really help us much.'

'You always were a pessimist, Tommy. Belief in oneself – that is the great thing.'

'Well, you have got it all right,' said her husband.

'Of course it is easy in detective stories,' said Tuppence thoughtfully, 'because one works backwards. I mean if one knows the solution one can arrange the clues. I wonder now –'

She paused wrinkling her brows.

'Yes?' said Tommy inquiringly.

'I have got a sort of idea,' said Tuppence. 'It hasn't quite come yet, but it's coming.' She rose resolutely. 'I think I shall go and buy that hat I told you about.'

'Oh, God!' said Tommy, 'another hat!'

'It's a very nice one,' said Tuppence with dignity.

She went out with a resolute look on her face.

Once or twice in the following days Tommy inquired curiously about the idea. Tuppence merely shook her head and told him to give her time.

And then, one glorious morning, the first client arrived, and all else was forgotten.

There was a knock on the outer door of the office and Albert, who had just placed an acid drop between his lips, roared out an indistinct 'Come in.' He then swallowed the acid drop whole in his surprise and delight. For this looked like the Real Thing.

A tall young man, exquisitely and beautifully dressed, stood hesitating in the doorway.

'A toff, if ever there was one,' said Albert to himself. His judgement in such matters was good.

The young man was about twenty-four years of age, had beautifully slicked back hair, a tendency to pink rims round the eyes, and practically no chin to speak of.

In an ecstasy, Albert pressed a button under his desk and almost immediately a perfect fusilade of typing broke out from the direction of 'Clerks'. Tuppence had rushed to the post of duty. The effect of this hum of industry was to overawe the young man still further.

'I say,' he remarked. 'Is this the whatnot – detective agency – Blunt's Brilliant Detectives? All that sort of stuff, you know? Eh?'

'Did you want, sir, to speak to Mr Blunt himself?' inquired Albert, with an air of doubts as to whether such a thing could be managed.

'Well – yes, laddie, that was the jolly old idea. Can it be done?'

'You haven't an appointment, I suppose?'

The visitor became more and more apologetic.

'Afraid I haven't.'

'It's always wise, sir, to ring up on the phone first. Mr Blunt is so terribly busy. He's engaged on the telephone at the moment. Called into consultation by Scotland Yard.'

The young man seemed suitably impressed.

Albert lowered his voice, and imparted information in a friendly fashion.

'Important theft of documents from a Government Office. They want Mr Blunt to take up the case.'

'Oh! really. I say. He must be no end of a fellow.'

'The Boss, sir,' said Albert, 'is It.'

The young man sat down on a hard chair, completely unconscious of the fact that he was being subjected to keen scrutiny by two pairs of eyes looking through cunningly contrived peep-holes – those of Tuppence, in the intervals of frenzied typing, and those of Tommy awaiting the suitable moment.

Presently a bell rang with violence on Albert's desk.

'The Boss is free now. I will find out whether he can see you,' said Albert, and disappeared through the door marked 'Private'.

He reappeared immediately.

'Will you come this way, sir?'

The visitor was ushered into the private office, and a pleasant faced young man with red hair and an air of brisk capability rose to greet him.

'Sit down. You wish to consult me? I am Mr Blunt.'

'Oh! Really. I say, you're awfully young, aren't you?'

'The day of the Old Men is over,' said Tommy, waving his hand. 'Who caused the war? The Old Men. Who is responsible for the present state of unemployment? The Old Men. Who is responsible for every single rotten thing that has happened? Again I say, the Old Men!'

'I expect you are right,' said the client, 'I know a fellow who is a poet – at least he says he is a poet – and he always talks like that.'

'Let me tell you this, sir, not a person on my highly trained staff is a day over twenty-five. That is the truth.'

Since the highly trained staff consisted of Tuppence and Albert, the statement was truth itself.

'And now – the facts,' said Mr Blunt.

'I want you to find someone that's missing,' blurted out the young man.

'Quite so. Will you give me the details?'

'Well, you see, it's rather difficult. I mean, it's a frightfully delicate business and all that. She might be frightfully waxy about it. I mean – well, it's so dashed difficult to explain.'

He looked helplessly at Tommy. Tommy felt annoyed. He had been on the point of going out to lunch, but he foresaw that getting the facts out of this client would be a long and tedious business.

'Did she disappear of her own free will, or do you suspect abduction?' he demanded crisply.

'I don't know,' said the young man. 'I don't know anything.'

Tommy reached for a pad and pencil.

'First of all,' he said, 'will you give me your name? My office boy is trained never to ask names. In that way consultations can remain completely confidential.'

'Oh! rather,' said the young man. 'Jolly good idea. My name – er – my name's Smith.'

'Oh! no,' said Tommy. 'The real one, please.'

His visitor looked at him in awe.

'Er – St Vincent,' he said. 'Lawrence St Vincent.'

'It's a curious thing,' said Tommy, 'how very few people there are whose real name is Smith. Personally, I don't know anyone called Smith. But nine men out of ten who wish to conceal their real name give that of Smith. I am writing a monograph upon the subject.'

At that moment a buzzer purred discreetly on his desk. That meant that Tuppence was requesting to take hold. Tommy, who wanted his lunch, and who felt profoundly unsympathetic towards Mr St Vincent, was only too pleased to relinquish the helm.

'Excuse me,' he said, and picked up the telephone.

Across his face there shot rapid changes – surprise, consternation, slight elation.

'You don't say so,' he said into the phone. 'The Prime Minister himself? Of course, in that case, I will come round at once.'

He replaced the receiver on the hook, and turned to his client.

'My dear sir, I must ask you to excuse me. A most urgent summons. If you will give the facts of the case to my confidential secretary, she will deal with them.'

He strode to the adjoining door.

'Miss Robinson.'

Tuppence, very neat and demure with smooth black head and dainty collars and cuffs, tripped in. Tommy made the necessary introductions and departed.

'A lady you take an interest in has disappeared, I understand, Mr St Vincent,' said Tuppence, in her soft voice, as she sat down and took up Mr Blunt's pad and pencil. 'A young lady?'

'Oh! rather,' said St Vincent. 'Young – and – and – awfully good-looking and all that sort of thing.'

Tuppence's face grew grave.

'Dear me,' she murmured. 'I hope that –'

'You don't think anything's really happened to her?' demanded Mr St Vincent, in lively concern.

'Oh! we must hope for the best,' said Tuppence, with a kind of false cheerfulness which depressed Mr St Vincent horribly.

'Oh! look here, Miss Robinson. I say, you must do something. Spare no expense. I wouldn't have anything happen to her for the world. You seem awfully sympathetic, and I don't mind telling you in confidence that I simply worship the ground that girl walks on. She's a topper, an absolute topper.'

'Please tell me her name and all about her.'

'Her name's Jeanette – I don't know her second name. She works in a hat shop – Madame Violette's in Brook Street – but she's as straight as they make them. Has ticked me off no end of times – I went round there yesterday – waiting for her to come out – all the others came, but not her. Then I found that she'd never turned up that morning to work at all – sent no message either – old Madame was furious about it. I got the address of her lodgings, and I went round there. She hadn't come home the night before, and they didn't know where she was. I was simply frantic. I thought of going to the police. But I knew that Jeanette would be absolutely furious with me for doing that if she were really all right and had gone off on her own. Then I remembered that she herself had pointed out your advertisement to me one day in the paper and told me that one of the women who'd been in buying hats had simply raved about your ability and discretion and all that sort of thing. So I toddled along here right away.'

'I see,' said Tuppence. 'What is the address of her lodgings?'

The young man gave it to her.

'That's all, I think,' said Tuppence reflectively. 'That is to say – am I to understand that you are engaged to this young lady?'

Mr St Vincent turned a brick red.

'Well, no – not exactly. I never said anything. But I can tell you this, I mean to ask her to marry me as soon as ever I see her – if I ever do see her again.'

Tuppence laid aside her pad.

'Do you wish for our special twenty-four hour service?' she asked in business-like tones.

'What's that?'

'The fees are doubled, but we put all our available staff on to the case. Mr St Vincent, if the lady is alive, I shall be able to tell you where she is by this time tomorrow.'

'What? I say, that's wonderful.'

'We only employ experts – and we guarantee results,' said Tuppence crisply.

'But I say, you know. You must have the most topping staff.'

'Oh! we have,' said Tuppence. 'By the way, you haven't given me a description of the young lady.'

'She's got the most marvellous hair – sort of golden but very deep, like a jolly old sunset – that's it, a jolly old sunset. You know, I never noticed things like sunsets until lately. Poetry too, there's a lot more in poetry than I ever thought.'

'Red hair,' said Tuppence unemotionally, writing it down. 'What height should you say the lady was?'

'Oh! tallish, and she's got ripping eyes, dark blue, I think. And a sort of decided manner with her – takes a fellow up short sometimes.'

Tuppence wrote down a few words more, then closed her notebook and rose.

'If you will call here tomorrow at two o'clock, I think we shall have news of some kind for you,' she said. 'Good-morning, Mr St Vincent.'

When Tommy returned Tuppence was just consulting a page of Debrett.

'I've got all the details,' she said succinctly. 'Lawrence St Vincent is the nephew and heir of the Earl of Cheriton. If we pull this through we shall get publicity in the highest places.'

Tommy read through the notes on the pad.

'What do you really think has happened to the girl?' he asked.

'I think,' said Tuppence, 'that she has fled at the dictates of her heart, feeling that she loves this young man too well for her peace of mind.'

Tommy looked at her doubtfully.

'I know they do it in books,' he said, 'but I've never known any girl who did it in real life.'

'No?' said Tuppence. 'Well, perhaps you're right. But I dare say Lawrence St Vincent will swallow that sort of slush. He's full of romantic notions just now. By the way, I guaranteed results in twenty-four hours – our special service.'

'Tuppence – you congenital idiot, what made you do that?'

'The idea just came into my head. I thought it sounded rather well. Don't you worry. Leave it to mother. Mother knows best.'

She went out leaving Tommy profoundly dissatisfied.

Presently he rose, sighed, and went out to do what could be done, cursing Tuppence's over-fervent imagination.

When he returned weary and jaded at half-past four, he found Tuppence extracting a bag of biscuits from their place of concealment in one of the files.

'You look hot and bothered,' she remarked. 'What have you been doing?'

Tommy groaned.

'Making a round of the hospitals with that girl's description.'

'Didn't I tell you to leave it to me?' demanded Tuppence.

'You can't find that girl single-handed before two o'clock tomorrow.'

'I can – and what's more, I have!'

'You have? What do you mean?'

'A simple problem, Watson, very simple indeed.'

'Where is she now?'

Tuppence pointed a hand over her shoulder.

'She's in my office next door.'

'What is she doing there?'

Tuppence began to laugh.

'Well,' she said, 'early training will tell, and with a kettle, a gas ring, and half a pound of tea staring her in the face, the result is a foregone conclusion.

'You see,' continued Tuppence gently. 'Madame Violette's is where I go for my hats, and the other day I ran across an old pal of hospital days amongst the girls there. She gave up nursing after the war and started a hat shop, failed, and took this job at Madame Violette's. We fixed up the whole thing between us. She was to rub the advertisement well into young

St Vincent, and then disappear. Wonderful efficiency of Blunt's Brilliant
Detectives. Publicity for us, and the necessary fillip to young St Vincent
to bring him to the point of proposing. Janet was in despair about it.'

'Tuppence,' said Tommy. 'You take my breath away! The whole thing
is the most immoral business I ever heard of. You aid and abet this young
man to marry out of his class –'

'Stuff,' said Tuppence. 'Janet is a splendid girl – and the queer thing
is that she really adores that week-kneed young man. You can see with
half a glance what *his* family needs. Some good red blood in it. Janet will
be the making of him. She'll look after him like a mother, ease down the
cocktails and the night clubs and make him lead a good healthy country
gentleman's life. Come and meet her.'

Tuppence opened the door of the adjoining office and Tommy followed
her.

A tall girl with lovely auburn hair, and a pleasant face, put down the
steaming kettle in her hand, and turned with a smile that disclosed an
even row of white teeth.

'I hope you'll forgive me, Nurse Cowley – Mrs Beresford, I mean. I
thought that very likely you'd be quite ready for a cup of tea yourself.
Many's the pot of tea you've made for me in the hospital at three o'clock
in the morning.'

'Tommy,' said Tuppence. 'Let me introduce you to my old friend,
Nurse Smith.'

'Smith, did you say? How curious!' said Tommy shaking hands. 'Eh?
Oh! nothing – a little monograph that I was thinking of writing.'

'Pull yourself together, Tommy,' said Tuppence.

She poured him out a cup of tea.

'Now, then, let's drink together. Here's to the success of the International Detective Agency. Blunt's Brilliant Detectives! May they never
know failure!'

The Affair of the Pink Pearl

'The Affair of the Pink Pearl' was first published in *The Sketch*,
1 October 1924. Dr John Thorndyke was created by
Richard Austin Freeman (1862–1943).

'What on earth are you doing?' demanded Tuppence, as she entered the
inner sanctum of the International Detective Agency – (Slogan – Blunt's
Brilliant Detectives) and discovered her lord and master prone on the
floor in a sea of books.

Tommy struggled to his feet.

'I was trying to arrange these books on the top shelf of that cupboard,'
he complained. 'And the damned chair gave way.'

'What are they, anyway?' asked Tuppence, picking up a volume. '*The
Hound of the Baskervilles*. I wouldn't mind reading that again some time.'

'You see the idea?' said Tommy, dusting himself with care. 'Half-hours
with the Great Masters – that sort of thing. You see, Tuppence, I can't
help feeling that we are more or less amateurs at this business – of course
amateurs in one sense we cannot help being, but it would do no harm
to acquire the technique, so to speak. These books are detective stories
by the leading masters of the art. I intend to try different styles, and
compare results.'

'H'm,' said Tuppence. I often wonder how these detectives would have
got on in real life.' She picked up another volume. 'You'll find a difficulty
in being a Thorndyke. You've no medical experience, and less legal, and
I never heard that science was your strong point.'

'Perhaps not,' said Tommy. 'But at any rate I've bought a very good
camera, and I shall photograph footprints and enlarge the negatives and
all that sort of thing. Now, *mon ami*, use your little grey cells – what does
this convey to you?'

He pointed to the bottom shelf of the cupboard. On it lay a somewhat futuristic dressing-gown, a turkish slipper, and a violin.

'Obvious, my dear Watson,' said Tuppence.

'Exactly,' said Tommy. 'The Sherlock Holmes touch.'

He took up the violin and drew the bow idly across the strings, causing Tuppence to give a wail of agony.

At that moment the buzzer rang on the desk, a sign that a client had arrived in the outer office and was being held in parley by Albert, the office boy.

Tommy hastily replaced the violin in the cupboard and kicked the books behind the desk.

'Not that there's any great hurry,' he remarked. 'Albert will be handing them out the stuff about my being engaged with Scotland Yard on the phone. Get into your office and start typing, Tuppence. It makes the office sound busy and active. No, on second thoughts you shall be taking notes in shorthand from my dictation. Let's have a look before we get Albert to send the victim in.'

They approached the peephole which had been artistically contrived so as to command a view of the outer office.

The client was a girl of about Tuppence's age, tall and dark with a rather haggard face and scornful eyes.

'Clothes cheap and striking,' remarked Tuppence. 'Have her in, Tommy.'

In another minute the girl was shaking hands with the celebrated Mr Blunt, whilst Tuppence sat by with eyes demurely downcast, and pad and pencil in hand.

'My confidential secretary, Miss Robinson,' said Mr Blunt with a wave of his hand. 'You may speak freely before her.' Then he lay back for a minute, half closed his eyes and remarked in a tired tone: 'You must find travelling in a bus very crowded at this time of day.'

'I came in a taxi,' said the girl.

'Oh!' said Tommy aggrieved. His eyes rested reproachfully on a blue bus ticket protruding from her glove. The girl's eyes followed his glance, and she smiled and drew it out.

'You mean this? I picked it up on the pavement. A little neighbour of ours collects them.'

Tuppence coughed, and Tommy threw a baleful glare at her.

'We must get to business,' he said briskly. 'You are in need of our services, Miss –?'

'Kingston Bruce is my name,' said the girl. 'We live at Wimbledon. Last night a lady who is staying with us lost a valuable pink pearl. Mr St Vincent was also dining with us, and during dinner he happened to mention your firm. My mother sent me off to you this morning to ask you if you would look into the matter for us.'

The girl spoke sullenly, almost disagreeably. It was clear as daylight that she and her mother had not agreed over the matter. She was here under protest.

'I see,' said Tommy, a little puzzled. 'You have not called in the police?'

'No,' said Miss Kingston Bruce, 'we haven't. It would be idiotic to call in the police and then find the silly thing had rolled under the fireplace, or something like that.'

'Oh!' said Tommy. 'Then the jewel may only be lost after all?'

Miss Kingston Bruce shrugged her shoulders.

'People make such a fuss about things,' she murmured. Tommy cleared his throat.

'Of course,' he said doubtfully. 'I am extremely busy just now –'

'I quite understand,' said the girl, rising to her feet. There was a quick gleam of satisfaction in her eyes which Tuppence, for one, did not miss.

'Nevertheless,' continued Tommy. 'I think I can manage to run down to Wimbledon. Will you give me the address, please?'

'The Laurels, Edgeworth Road.'

'Make a note of it, please, Miss Robinson.'

Miss Kingston Bruce hesitated, then said rather ungraciously.

'We'll expect you then. Good-morning.'

'Funny girl,' said Tommy when she had left. 'I couldn't quite make her out.'

'I wonder if she stole the thing herself,' remarked Tuppence meditatively. 'Come on, Tommy, let's put away these books and take the car and go down there. By the way, who are you going to be, Sherlock Holmes still?'

'I think I need practice for that,' said Tommy. 'I came rather a cropper over that bus ticket, didn't I?'

'You did,' said Tuppence. 'If I were you I shouldn't try too much on that girl – she's as sharp as a needle. She's unhappy too, poor devil.'

'I suppose you know all about her already,' said Tommy with sarcasm, 'simply from looking at the shape of her nose!'

'I'll tell you my idea of what we shall find at The Laurels,' said Tuppence, quite unmoved. 'A household of snobs, very keen to move in the best society; the father, if there is a father, is sure to have a military title. The girl falls in with their way of life and despises herself for doing so.'

Tommy took a last look at the books now neatly arranged upon the shelf.

'I think,' he said thoughtfully, 'that I shall be Thorndyke today.'

'I shouldn't have thought there was anything medicolegal about this case,' remarked Tuppence.

'Perhaps not,' said Tommy. 'But I'm simply dying to use that new camera of mine! It's supposed to have the most marvellous lens that ever was or could be.'

'I know those kind of lenses,' said Tuppence. 'By the time you've adjusted the shutter and stopped down and calculated the exposure and kept your eye on the spirit level, your brain gives out, and you yearn for the simple Brownie.'

'Only an unambitious soul is content with the simple Brownie.'

'Well, I bet I shall get better results with it than you will.'

Tommy ignored the challenge.

'I ought to have a "Smoker's Companion",' he said regretfully. 'I wonder where one buys them?'

'There's always the patent corkscrew Aunt Araminta gave you last Christmas,' said Tuppence helpfully.

'That's true,' said Tommy. 'A curious-looking engine of destruction I thought it at the time, and rather a humorous present to get from a strictly teetotal aunt.'

'I,' said Tuppence, 'shall be Polton.'

Tommy looked at her scornfully.

'Polton indeed. You couldn't begin to do one of the things that he does.'

'Yes, I can,' said Tuppence. 'I can rub my hands together when I'm pleased. That's quite enough to get on with. I hope you're going to take plaster casts of footprints?'

Tommy was reduced to silence. Having collected the corkscrew they went round to the garage, got out the car and started for Wimbledon.

The Laurels was a big house. It ran somewhat to gables and turrets, had an air of being very newly painted and was surrounded with neat flower beds filled with scarlet geraniums.

A tall man with a close-cropped white moustache, and an exaggeratedly martial bearing opened the door before Tommy had time to ring.

'I've been looking out for you,' he explained fussily. 'Mr Blunt, is it not? I am Colonel Kingston Bruce. Will you come into my study?'

He let them into a small room at the back of the house.

'Young St Vincent was telling me wonderful things about your firm. I've noticed your advertisements myself. This guaranteed twenty-four hours' service of yours – a marvellous notion. That's exactly what I need.'

Inwardly anathematising Tuppence for her irresponsibility in inventing this brilliant detail, Tommy replied: 'Just so, Colonel.'

'The whole thing is most distressing, sir, most distressing.'

'Perhaps you would kindly give me the facts,' said Tommy, with a hint of impatience.

'Certainly I will – at once. We have at the present moment staying with us a very old and dear friend of ours, Lady Laura Barton. Daughter of the late Earl of Carrowway. The present earl, her brother, made a striking speech in the House of Lords the other day. As I say, she is an old and dear friend of ours. Some American friends of mine who have just come over, the Hamilton Betts, were most anxious to meet her. "Nothing easier," I said. "She is staying with me now. Come down for the weekend." You know what Americans are about titles, Mr Blunt.'

'And others beside Americans sometimes, Colonel Kingston Bruce.'

'Alas! only too true, my dear sir. Nothing I hate more than a snob. Well, as I was saying, the Betts came down for the weekend. Last night – we were playing bridge at the time – the clasp of a pendant Mrs Hamilton Betts was wearing broke, so she took it off and laid it down on a small table, meaning to take it upstairs with her when she went. This, however, she forgot to do. I must explain, Mr Blunt, that the pendant consisted of two small diamond wings, and a big pink pearl depending from them. The pendant was found this morning lying where Mrs Betts had left it, but the pearl, a pearl of enormous value, had been wrenched off.'

'Who found the pendant?'

'The parlourmaid – Gladys Hill.'

'Any reason to suspect her?'

'She has been with us some years, and we have always found her perfectly honest. But, of course, one never knows –'

'Exactly. Will you describe your staff, and also tell me who was present at dinner last night?'

'There is the cook – she has been with us only two months, but then she would have no occasion to go near the drawing-room – the same applies to the kitchenmaid. Then there is the housemaid, Alice Cummings. She also has been with us for some years. And Lady Laura's maid, of course. She is French.'

Colonel Kingston Bruce looked very impressive as he said this. Tommy, unaffected by the revelation of the maid's nationality, said: 'Exactly. And the party at dinner?'

'Mr and Mrs Betts, ourselves – my wife and daughter – and Lady Laura. Young St Vincent was dining with us, and Mr Rennie looked in after dinner for a while.'

'Who is Mr Rennie?'

'A most pestilential fellow – an arrant socialist. Good looking, of course, and with a certain specious power of argument. But a man, I don't mind telling you, whom I wouldn't trust a yard. A dangerous sort of fellow.'

'In fact,' said Tommy drily, 'it is Mr Rennie whom you suspect?'

'I do, Mr Blunt. I'm sure, holding the views he does, that he can have no principles whatsoever. What could have been easier for him than to have quietly wrenched off the pearl at a moment when we were all absorbed in our game? There were several absorbing moments – a redoubled no trump hand, I remember, and also a painful argument when my wife had the misfortune to revoke.'

'Quite so,' said Tommy. 'I should just like to know one thing – what is Mrs Betts's attitude in all this?'

'She wanted me to call in the police,' said Colonel Kingston Bruce reluctantly. 'That is, when we had searched everywhere in case the pearl had only dropped off.'

'But you dissuaded her?'

'I was very averse to the idea of publicity and my wife and daughter backed me up. Then my wife remembered young St Vincent speaking about your firm at dinner last night – and the twenty-four hours' special service.'

'Yes,' said Tommy, with a heavy heart.

'You see, in any case, no harm will be done. If we call in the police tomorrow, it can be supposed that we thought the jewel merely lost and were hunting for it. By the way, nobody has been allowed to leave the house this morning.'

'Except your daughter, of course,' said Tuppence, speaking for the first time.

'Except my daughter,' agreed the Colonel. 'She volunteered at once to go and put the case before you.'

Tommy rose.

'We will do our best to give you satisfaction, Colonel,' he said. 'I should like to see the drawing-room, and the table on which the pendant was laid down. I should also like to ask Mrs Betts a few questions. After that, I will interview the servants – or rather my assistant, Miss Robinson, will do so.'

He felt his nerve quailing before the terrors of questioning the servants.

Colonel Kingston Bruce threw open the door and led them across the hall. As he did so, a remark came to them clearly through the open door of the room they were approaching and the voice that uttered it was that of the girl who had come to see them that morning.

'You know perfectly well Mother,' she was saying, 'that she *did* bring home a teaspoon in her muff.'

In another minute they were being introduced to Mrs Kingston Bruce, a plaintive lady with a languid manner. Miss Kingston Bruce acknowledged their presence with a short inclination of the head. Her face was more sullen than ever.

Mrs Kingston Bruce was voluble.

'– but I know who *I* think took it,' she ended. 'That dreadful socialist young man. He loves the Russians and the Germans and hates the English – what else can you expect?'

'He never touched it,' said Miss Kingston Bruce fiercely. 'I was watching him – all the time. I couldn't have failed to see if he had.'

She looked at them defiantly with her chin up.

Tommy created a diversion by asking for an interview with Mrs Betts. When Mrs Kingston Bruce had departed accompanied by her husband and daughter to find Mrs Betts, he whistled thoughtfully.

'I wonder,' he said gently, 'who it was who had a teaspoon in her muff?'

'Just what I was thinking,' replied Tuppence.

Mrs Betts, followed by her husband, burst into the room. She was a big woman with a determined voice. Mr Hamilton Betts looked dyspeptic and subdued.

'I understand, Mr Blunt, that you are a private inquiry agent, and one who hustles things through at a great rate?'

'Hustle,' said Tommy, 'is my middle name, Mrs Betts. Let me ask you a few questions.'

Thereafter things proceeded rapidly. Tommy was shown the damaged pendant, the table on which it had lain, and Mr Betts emerged from his taciturnity to mention the value, in dollars, of the stolen pearl.

And withal, Tommy felt an irritating certainty that he was not getting on.

'I think that will do,' he said, at length. 'Miss Robinson, will you kindly fetch the special photographic apparatus from the hall?'

Miss Robinson complied.

'A little invention of my own,' said Tommy. 'In appearance, you see, it is just like an ordinary camera.'

He had some slight satisfaction in seeing that the Betts were impressed.

He photographed the pendant, the table on which it had lain, and took several general views of the apartment. Then 'Miss Robinson' was delegated to interview the servants, and in view of the eager expectancy on the faces of Colonel Kingston Bruce and Mrs Betts, Tommy felt called upon to say a few authoritative words.

'The position amounts to this,' he said. 'Either the pearl is still in the house, or it is not still in the house.'

'Quite so,' said the Colonel with more respect than was, perhaps, quite justified by the nature of the remark.

'If it is not in the house, it may be anywhere – but if it is in the house, it must necessarily be concealed somewhere –'

'And a search must be made,' broke in Colonel Kingston Bruce. 'Quite so. I give you carte blanche, Mr Blunt. Search the house from attic to cellar.'

'Oh! Charles,' murmured Mrs Kingston Bruce tearfully, 'do you think that is wise? The servants won't *like* it. I'm sure they'll leave.'

'We will search their quarters last,' said Tommy soothingly. 'The thief is sure to have hidden the gem in the most unlikely place.'

'I seem to have read something of the kind,' agreed the Colonel.

'Quite so,' said Tommy. 'You probably remember the case of Rex v Bailey, which created a precedent.'

'Oh – er – yes,' said the Colonel, looking puzzled.

'Now, the most unlikely place is in the apartment of Mrs Betts,' continued Tommy.

'My! Wouldn't that be too cute?' said Mrs Betts admiringly.

Without more ado she took him up to her room, where Tommy once more made use of the special photographic apparatus.

Presently Tuppence joined him there.

'You have no objection, I hope, Mrs Betts, to my assistant's looking through your wardrobe?'

'Why, not at all. Do you need me here any longer?'

Tommy assured her that there was no need to detain her, and Mrs Betts departed.

'We might as well go on bluffing it out,' said Tommy. 'But personally I don't believe we've a dog's chance of finding the thing. Curse you and your twenty-four hours' stunt, Tuppence.'

'Listen,' said Tuppence. 'The servants are all right, I'm sure, but I managed to get something out of the French maid. It seems that when Lady Laura was staying here a year ago, she went out to tea with some friends of the Kingston Bruces, and when she got home a teaspoon fell out of her muff. Everyone thought it must have fallen in by accident. But, talking about similar robberies, I got hold of a lot more. Lady Laura is always staying about with people. She hasn't got a bean, I gather, and she's out for comfortable quarters with people to whom a title still means something. It may be a coincidence – or it may be something more, but five distinct thefts have taken place whilst she has been staying in various houses, sometimes trivial things, sometimes valuable jewels.'

'Whew!' said Tommy, and gave vent to a prolonged whistle. 'Where's the old bird's room, do you know?'

'Just across the passage.'

'Then I think, I rather think, that we'll just slip across and investigate.'

The room opposite stood with its door ajar. It was a spacious apartment, with white enamelled fitments and rose pink curtains. An inner door led to a bathroom. At the door of this appeared a slim, dark girl, very neatly dressed.

Tuppence checked the exclamation of astonishment on the girl's lips.

'This is Elise, Mr Blunt,' she said primly. 'Lady Laura's maid.'

Tommy stepped across the threshold of the bathroom, and approved inwardly its sumptuous and up-to-date fittings. He set to work to dispel the wide stare of suspicion on the French girl's face.

'You are busy with your duties, eh, Mademoiselle Elise?'

'Yes, Monsieur, I clean Milady's bath.'

'Well, perhaps you'll help me with some photography instead. I have a special kind of camera here, and I am photographing the interiors of all the rooms in this house.'

He was interrupted by the communicating door to the bedroom banging suddenly behind him. Elise jumped at the sound.

'What did that?'

'It must have been the wind,' said Tuppence.

'We will come into the other room,' said Tommy.

Elise went to open the door for them, but the door knob rattled aimlessly.

'What's the matter?' said Tommy sharply.

'Ah, Monsieur, but somebody must have locked it on the other side.' She caught up a towel and tried again. But this time the door handle turned easily enough, and the door swung open.

'*Voilà ce qui est curieux.* It must have been stuck,' said Elise.

There was no one in the bedroom.

Tommy fetched his apparatus. Tuppence and Elise worked under his orders. But again and again his glance went back to the communicating door.

'I wonder,' he said between his teeth – 'I wonder why that door stuck?'

He examined it minutely, shutting and opening it. It fitted perfectly.

'One picture more,' he said with a sigh. 'Will you loop back that rose curtain, Mademoiselle Elise? Thank you. Just hold it so.'

The familiar click occurred. He handed a glass slide to Elise to hold, relinquished the tripod to Tuppence, and carefully readjusted and closed the camera.

He made some easy excuse to get rid of Elise, and as soon as she was out of the room, he caught hold of Tuppence and spoke rapidly.

'Look here, I've got an idea. Can you hang on here? Search all the rooms – that will take some time. Try and get an interview with the old bird – Lady Laura – but don't alarm her. Tell her you suspect the parlour-maid. But whatever you do don't let her leave the house. I'm going off in the car. I'll be back as soon as I can.'

'All right,' said Tuppence. 'But don't be too cocksure. You've forgotten one thing.

'The girl. There's something funny about that girl. Listen, I've found out the time she started from the house this morning. It took her two hours to get to our office. That's nonsense. Where did she go before she came to us?'

'There's something in that,' admitted her husband. 'Well, follow up any old clue you like, but don't let Lady Laura leave the house. What's that?'

His quick ear had caught a faint rustle outside on the landing. He strode across to the door, but there was no one to be seen.

'Well, so long,' he said, 'I'll be back as soon as I can.'78

Tuppence watched him drive off in the car with a faint misgiving. Tommy was very sure – she herself was not so sure. There were one or two things she did not quite understand.

She was still standing by the window, watching the road, when she saw a man leave the shelter of a gateway opposite, cross the road and ring the bell.

In a flash Tuppence was out of the room and down the stairs. Gladys Hill, the parlourmaid, was emerging from the back part of the house, but Tuppence motioned her back authoritatively. Then she went to the front door and opened it.

A lanky young man with ill-fitting clothes and eager dark eyes was standing on the step.

He hesitated a moment, and then said:

'Is Miss Kingston Bruce in?'

'Will you come inside?' said Tuppence.

She stood aside to let him enter, closing the door.

'Mr Rennie, I think?' she said sweetly.

He shot a quick glance at her.

'Er – yes.'

'Will you come in here, please?'

She opened the study door. The room was empty, and Tuppence entered it after him, closing the door behind her. He turned on her with a frown.

'I want to see Miss Kingston Bruce.'

'I am not quite sure that you can,' said Tuppence composedly.

'Look here, who the devil are you?' said Mr Rennie rudely.

'International Detective Agency,' said Tuppence succinctly – and noticed Mr Rennie's uncontrollable start.

'Please sit down, Mr Rennie,' she went on. 'To begin with, we know all about Miss Kingston Bruce's visit to you this morning.'

It was a bold guess, but it succeeded. Perceiving his consternation, Tuppence went on quickly.

'The recovery of the pearl is the great thing, Mr Rennie. No one in this house is anxious for – publicity. Can't we come to some arrangement?'

The young man looked at her keenly.

'I wonder how much you know,' he said thoughtfully. 'Let me think for a moment.'

He buried his head in his hands – then asked a most unexpected question.

'I say, is it really true that young St Vincent is engaged to be married?'

'Quite true,' said Tuppence. 'I know the girl.'

Mr Rennie suddenly became confidential.

'It's been hell,' he confided. 'They've been asking her morning, noon and night – chucking Beatrice at his head. All because he'll come into a title some day. If I had my way –'

'Don't let's talk politics,' said Tuppence hastily. 'Do you mind telling me, Mr Rennie, why you think Miss Kingston Bruce took the pearl?'

'I – I don't.'

'You do,' said Tuppence calmly. 'You wait to see the detective, as you think, drive off and the coast clear, and then you come and ask for her. It's obvious. If you'd taken the pearl yourself, you wouldn't be half so upset.'

'Her manner was so odd,' said the young man. 'She came this morning and told me about the robbery, explaining that she was on her way to a firm of private detectives. She seemed anxious to say something, and yet not able to get it out.'

'Well,' said Tuppence. 'All I want is the pearl. You'd better go and talk to her.'

But at that moment Colonel Kingston Bruce opened the door.

'Lunch is ready, Miss Robinson. You will lunch with us, I hope. The –'

Then he stopped and glared at the guest.

'Clearly,' said Mr Rennie, 'you don't want to ask me to lunch. All right, I'll go.'

'Come back later,' whispered Tuppence, as he passed her.

Tuppence followed Colonel Kingston Bruce, still growling into his moustache about the pestilential impudence of some people, into a massive dining-room where the family was already assembled. Only one person present was unknown to Tuppence.

'This, Lady Laura, is Miss Robinson, who is kindly assisting us.'

Lady Laura bent her head, and then proceeded to stare at Tuppence through her pince-nez. She was a tall, thin woman, with a sad smile, a gentle voice, and very hard shrewd eyes. Tuppence returned her stare, and Lady Laura's eyes dropped.

After lunch Lady Laura entered into conversation with an air of gentle curiosity. How was the inquiry proceeding? Tuppence laid suitable stress on the suspicion attaching to the parlourmaid, but her mind was not really on Lady Laura. Lady Laura might conceal teaspoons and other articles in her clothing, but Tuppence felt fairly sure that she had not taken the pink pearl.

Presently Tuppence proceeded with her search of the house. Time was going on. There was no sign of Tommy, and, what mattered far more to Tuppence, there was no sign of Mr Rennie. Suddenly Tuppence came out of a bedroom and collided with Beatrice Kingston Bruce, who was going downstairs. She was fully dressed for the street.

'I'm afraid,' said Tuppence, 'that you mustn't go out just now.'

The other girl looked at her haughtily.

'Whether I go out or not is no business of yours,' she said coldly.

'It is my business whether I communicate with the police or not, though,' said Tuppence.

In a minute the girl had turned ashy pale.

'You mustn't – you mustn't – I won't go out – but don't do that.' She clung to Tuppence beseechingly.

'My dear Miss Kingston Bruce,' said Tuppence, smiling, 'the case has been perfectly clear to me from the start – I –'

But she was interrupted. In the stress of her encounter with the girl, Tuppence had not heard the front-door bell. Now, to her astonishment, Tommy came bounding up the stairs, and in the hall below she caught sight of a big burly man in the act of removing a bowler hat.

'Detective Inspector Marriot of Scotland Yard,' he said with a grin.

With a cry, Beatrice Kingston Bruce tore herself from Tuppence's grasp and dashed down the stairs, just as the front door was opened once more to admit Mr Rennie.

'Now you *have* torn it,' said Tuppence bitterly.

'Eh?' said Tommy, hurrying into Lady Laura's room. He passed on into the bathroom and picked up a large cake of soap which he brought out in his hands. The Inspector was just mounting the stairs.

'She went quite quietly,' he announced. 'She's an old hand and knows when the game is up. What about the pearl?'

'I rather fancy,' said Tommy, handing him the soap, 'that you'll find it in here.'

The Inspector's eyes lit up appreciatively.

'An old trick, and a good one. Cut a cake of soap in half, scoop out a place for the jewel, clap it together again, and smooth the join well over with hot water. A very smart piece of work on your part, sir.'

Tommy accepted the compliment gracefully. He and Tuppence

descended the stairs. Colonel Kingston Bruce rushed at him and shook him warmly by the hand.

'My dear sir, I can't thank you enough. Lady Laura wants to thank you also –'

'I am glad we have given you satisfaction,' said Tommy. 'But I'm afraid I can't stop. I have a most urgent appointment. Member of the Cabinet.'

He hurried out to the car and jumped in. Tuppence jumped in beside him.

'But Tommy,' she cried. 'Haven't they arrested Lady Laura after all?'

'Oh!' said Tommy. 'Didn't I tell you? They've not arrested Lady Laura. They've arrested Elise.'

'You see,' he went on, as Tuppence sat dumbfounded, 'I've often tried to open a door with soap on my hands myself. It can't be done – your hands slip. So I wondered what Elise could have been doing with the soap to get her hands as soapy as all that. She caught up a towel, you remember, so there were no traces of soap on the handle afterwards. But it occurred to me that if you were a professional thief, it wouldn't be a bad plan to be maid to a lady suspected of kleptomania who stayed about a good deal in different houses. So I managed to get a photo of her as well as of the room, induced her to handle a glass slide and toddled off to dear old Scotland Yard. Lightning development of negative, successful identification of finger-prints – and photo. Elise was a long lost friend. Useful place, Scotland Yard.'

'And to think,' said Tuppence, finding her voice, 'that those two young idiots were only suspecting each other in that weak way they do it in books. But why didn't you tell me what you were up to when you went off?'

'In the first place, I suspected that Elise was listening on the landing, and in the second place –'

'Yes?'

'My learned friend forgets,' said Tommy. 'Thorndyke never tells until the last moment. Besides, Tuppence, you and your pal Janet Smith put one over on me last time. This makes us all square.'

The Adventure of the Sinister Stranger

'The Adventure of the Sinister Stranger' was first published in
The Sketch, 22 October 1924. The brothers Desmond and Major
Okewood were created by Valentine Williams (1183–1946),
writing as Douglas Valentine.

'It's been a darned dull day,' said Tommy, and yawned widely.

'Nearly tea time,' said Tuppence and also yawned.

Business was not brisk in the International Detective Agency. The eagerly expected letter from the ham merchant had not arrived and *bona fide* cases were not forthcoming.

Albert, the office boy, entered with a sealed package which he laid on the table.

'The Mystery of the Sealed Packet,' murmured Tommy. 'Did it contain the fabulous pearls of the Russian Grand Duchess? Or was it an infernal machine destined to blow Blunt's Brilliant Detectives to pieces?'

'As a matter of fact,' said Tuppence, tearing open the package. 'It's my wedding present to Francis Haviland. Rather nice, isn't it?'

Tommy took a slender silver cigarette case from her outstretched hand, noted the inscription engraved in her own handwriting, *'Francis from Tuppence,'* opened and shut the case, and nodded approvingly.

'You do throw your money about, Tuppence,' he remarked. 'I'll have one like it, only in gold, for my birthday next month. Fancy wasting a thing like that on Francis Haviland, who always was and always will be one of the most perfect asses God ever made!'

'You forget I used to drive him about during the war, when he was a General. Ah! those were the good old days.'

'They were,' agreed Tommy. 'Beautiful women used to come and squeeze my hand in hospital, I remember. But I don't send them all wedding presents. I don't believe the bride will care much for this gift of yours, Tuppence.'

'It's nice and slim for the pocket, isn't it?' said Tuppence, disregarding his remarks.

Tommy slipped it into his own pocket.

'Just right,' he said approvingly. 'Hullo, here is Albert with the afternoon post. Very possibly the Duchess of Perthshire is commissioning us to find her prize Peke.'

They sorted through the letters together. Suddenly Tommy gave vent to a prolonged whistle and held up one of them in his hand.

'A blue letter with a Russian stamp on it. Do you remember what the Chief said? We were to look out for letters like that.'

'How exciting,' said Tuppence. 'Something has happened at last. Open it and see if the contents are up to schedule. A ham merchant, wasn't it? Half a minute. We shall want some milk for tea. They forgot to leave it this morning. I'll send Albert out for it.'

She returned from the outer office, after despatching Albert on his errand, to find Tommy holding the blue sheet of paper in his hand.

'As we thought, Tuppence,' he remarked. 'Almost word for word what the Chief said.'

Tuppence took the letter from him and read it.

It was couched in careful stilted English, and purported to be from one Gregor Feodorsky, who was anxious for news of his wife. The International Detective Agency was urged to spare no expense in doing their utmost to trace her. Feodorsky himself was unable to leave Russia at the moment owing to a crisis in the pork trade.

'I wonder what it really means,' said Tuppence thoughtfully, smoothing out the sheet on the table in front of her.

'Code of some kind, I suppose,' said Tommy. 'That's not our business. Our business is to hand it over to the Chief as soon as possible. Better just verify it by soaking off the stamp and seeing if the number 16 is underneath.'

'All right,' said Tuppence. 'But I should think –'

She stopped dead, and Tommy, surprised by her sudden pause, looked up to see a man's burly figure blocking the doorway.

The intruder was a man of commanding presence, squarely built, with a very round head and a powerful jaw. He might have been about forty-five years of age.

'I must beg your pardon,' said the stranger, advancing into the room, hat in hand. 'I found your outer office empty and this door open, so I ventured to intrude. This is Blunt's International Detective Agency, is it not?'

'Certainly it is.'

'And you are, perhaps, Mr Blunt? Mr Theodore Blunt?'

'I am Mr Blunt. You wish to consult me? This is my secretary, Miss Robinson.'

Tuppence inclined her head gracefully, but continued to scrutinise the stranger narrowly through her downcast eyelashes. She was wondering how long he had been standing in the doorway, and how much he had seen and heard. It did not escape her observation that even while he was talking to Tommy, his eyes kept coming back to the blue paper in her hand.

Tommy's voice, sharp with a warning note, recalled her to the needs of the moment.

'Miss Robinson, please, take notes. Now, sir, will you kindly state the matter on which you wish to have my advice?'

Tuppence reached for her pad and pencil.

The big man began in rather a harsh voice.

'My name is Bower. Dr Charles Bower. I live in Hampstead, where I have a practice. I have come to you, Mr Blunt, because several rather strange occurrences have happened lately.'

'Yes, Dr Bower?'

'Twice in the course of the last week I have been summoned by telephone to an urgent case – in each case to find that the summons has been a fake. The first time I thought a practical joke had been played upon me, but on my return the second time I found that some of my private papers had been displaced and disarranged, and now I believe that the same thing had happened the first time. I made an exhaustive search and came to the conclusion that my whole desk had been thoroughly ransacked, and the various papers replaced hurriedly.'

Dr Bower paused and gazed at Tommy.

'Well, Mr Blunt?'

'Well, Dr Bower,' replied the young man, smiling.

'What do you think of it, eh?'

'Well, first I should like the facts. What do you keep in your desk?'

'My private papers.'

'Exactly. Now, what do those private papers consist of? What value are they to the common thief – or any particular person?'

'To the common thief I cannot see that they would have any value at all, but my notes on certain obscure alkaloids would be of interest to anyone possessed of technical knowledge of the subject. I have been making a study of such matters for the last few years. These alkaloids are deadly and virulent poisons, and are in addition, almost untraceable. They yield no known reactions.'

'The secret of them would be worth money, then?'

'To unscrupulous persons, yes.'

'And you suspect – whom?'

The doctor shrugged his massive shoulders.

'As far as I can tell, the house was not entered forcibly from the outside. That seems to point to some member of my household, and yet I cannot believe –' He broke off abruptly, then began again, his voice very grave.

'Mr Blunt, I must place myself in your hands unreservedly. I dare not go to the police in the matter. Of my three servants I am almost entirely sure. They have served me long and faithfully. Still, one never knows. Then I have living with me my two nephews, Bertram and Henry. Henry is a good boy – a very good boy – he has never caused me any anxiety, an excellent hard-working young fellow. Bertram, I regret to say, is of quite a different character – wild, extravagant, and persistently idle.'

'I see,' said Tommy thoughtfully. 'You suspect your nephew Bertram of being mixed up in this business. Now I don't agree with you. I suspect the good boy – Henry.'

'But why?'

'Tradition. Precedent.' Tommy waved his hand airily. 'In my experience, the suspicious characters are always innocent – and vice versa, my dear sir. Yes, decidedly, I suspect Henry.'

'Excuse me, Mr Blunt,' said Tuppence, interrupting in a deferential tone. 'Did I understand Dr Bower to say that these notes on – er – obscure alkaloids – are kept in the desk with the other papers?'

'They are kept in the desk, my dear young lady, but in a secret drawer, the position of which is known only to myself. Hence they have so far defied the search.'

'And what exactly do you want me to do, Dr Bower?' asked Tommy. 'Do you anticipate that a further search will be made?'

'I do, Mr Blunt. I have every reason to believe so. This afternoon I received a telegram from a patient of mine whom I ordered to Bournemouth a few weeks ago. The telegram states that my patient is in a critical condition, and begs me to come down at once. Rendered suspicious by the events I have told you of, I myself despatched a telegram, prepaid, to the patient in question, and elicited the fact that he was in good health and had sent no summons to me of any kind. It occurred to me that if I pretended to have been taken in, and duly departed to Bournemouth, we should have a very good chance of finding the miscreants at work. They – or he – will doubtless wait until the household has retired to bed before commencing operations. I suggest that you should meet me outside my house at eleven o'clock this evening, and we will investigate the matter together.'

'Hoping, in fact, to catch them in the act.' Tommy drummed thoughtfully on the table with a paper-knife. 'Your plan seems to me an excellent one, Dr Bower. I cannot see any hitch in it. Let me see, your address is –?'

'The Larches, Hangman's Lane – rather a lonely part, I am afraid. But we command magnificent views over the Heath.'

'Quite so,' said Tommy.

The visitor rose.

'Then I shall expect your tonight, Mr Blunt. Outside The Larches at – shall we say, five minutes to eleven – to be on the safe side?'

'Certainly. Five minutes to eleven. Good-afternoon, Dr Bower.'

Tommy rose, pressed a buzzer on his desk, and Albert appeared to show the client out. The doctor walked with a decided limp, but his powerful physique was evident in spite of it.

'An ugly customer to tackle,' murmured Tommy to himself. 'Well, Tuppence, old girl, what do you think of it?'

'I'll tell you in one word,' said Tuppence. '*Clubfoot!*'

'What?'

'I said Clubfoot! My study of the classics has not been in vain. Tommy, this thing's a plant. Obscure alkaloids indeed – I never heard a weaker story.'

'Even I did not find it very convincing,' admitted her husband.

'Did you see his eyes on the letter? Tommy, he's one of the gang. They've got wise to the fact that you're not the real Mr Blunt, and they're out for our blood.'

'In that case,' said Tommy, opening the side cupboard and surveying his rows of books with an affectionate eye, 'our role is easy to select. We are the brothers Okewood! And I am Desmond,' he added firmly.

Tuppence shrugged her shoulders.

'All right. Have it your own way. I'd as soon be Francis. Francis was much the more intelligent of the two. Desmond always gets into a mess, and Francis turns up as the gardener or something in the nick of time and saves the situation.'

'Ah!' said Tommy, 'but I shall be a super Desmond. When I arrive at the Larches –'

Tuppence interrupted him unceremoniously.

'You're not going to Hampstead tonight?'

'Why not?'

'Walk into a trap with your eyes shut!'

'No, my dear girl, walk into a trap with my eyes open. There's a lot of difference. I think our friend, Dr Bower, will get a little surprise.'

'I don't like it,' said Tuppence. 'You know what happens when Desmond disobeys the Chief's orders and acts on his own. Our orders were quite clear. To send on the letters at once and to report immediately on anything that happened.'

'You've not got it quite right,' said Tommy. 'We were to report immediately if any one came in and mentioned the number 16. Nobody has.'

'That's a quibble,' said Tuppence.

'It's no good. I've got a fancy for playing a lone hand. My dear old Tuppence, I shall be all right. I shall go armed to the teeth. The essence of the whole thing is that I shall be on my guard and they won't know it. The Chief will be patting me on the back for a good night's work.'

'Well,' said Tuppence. 'I don't like it. That man's as strong as a gorilla.'

'Ah!' said Tommy, 'but think of my blue-nosed automatic.'

The door of the outer office opened and Albert appeared. Closing the door behind him, he approached them with an envelope in his hand.

'A gentleman to see you,' said Albert. 'When I began the usual stunt of saying you were engaged with Scotland Yard, he told me he knew all about that. Said he came from Scotland Yard himself! And he wrote something on a card and stuck it up in this envelope.'

Tommy took the envelope and opened it. As he read the card, a grin passed across his face.

'The gentleman was amusing himself at your expense by speaking the truth, Albert,' he remarked. 'Show him in.'

He tossed the card to Tuppence. It bore the name Detective Inspector Dymchurch, and across it was scrawled in pencil – 'A friend of Marriot's.'

In another minute the Scotland Yard detective was entering the inner office. In appearance, Inspector Dymchurch was of the same type as Inspector Marriot, short and thick set, with shrewd eyes.

'Good-afternoon,' said the detective breezily. 'Marriot's away in South Wales, but before he went he asked me to keep an eye on you two, and on this place in general. Oh, bless you, sir,' he went on, as Tommy seemed about to interrupt him, 'we know all about it. It's not our department and we don't interfere. But somebody's got wise lately to the fact that all is not what it seems. You've had a gentleman here this afternoon. I don't know what he called himself, and I don't know what his real name is, but I know just a little about him. Enough to want to know more. Am I right in assuming that he made a date with you for some particular spot this evening?'

'Quite right.'

'I thought as much. 16 Westerham Road, Finsbury Park – was that it?'

'You're wrong there,' said Tommy with a smile. 'Dead wrong. The Larches, Hampstead.'

Dymchurch seemed honestly taken aback. Clearly he had not expected this.

'I don't understand it,' he muttered. 'It must be a new layout. The Larches, Hampstead, you said?'

'Yes. I'm to meet him there at eleven o'clock tonight.'

'Don't you do it, sir.'

'There!' burst from Tuppence.

Tommy flushed.

'If you think, Inspector –' he began heatedly.

But the Inspector raised a soothing hand.

'I'll tell you what I think, Mr Blunt. The place you want to be at eleven o'clock tonight is here in this office.'

'What?' cried Tuppence, astonished.

'Here in this office. Never mind how I know – departments overlap sometimes – but you got one of those famous "Blue" letters today. Old what's-his-name is after that. He lures you up to Hampstead, makes quite sure of your being out of the way, and steps in here at night when all the building is empty and quiet to have a good search round at his leisure.'

'But why should he think the letter would be here? He'd know I should have it on me or else have passed it on.'

'Begging your pardon, sir, that's just what he wouldn't know. He may have tumbled to the fact that you're not the original Mr Blunt, but he probably thinks that you're a *bona fide* gentleman who's bought the business. In that case, the letter would be all in the way of regular business and would be filed as such.'

'I see,' said Tuppence.

'And that's just what we've got to let him think. We'll catch him red-handed here tonight.'

'So that's the plan, is it?'

'Yes. It's the chance of a lifetime. Now, let me see, what's the time? Six o'clock. What time do you usually leave here, sir?'

'About six.'

'You must seem to leave the place as usual. Actually we'll sneak back to it as soon as possible. I don't believe they'll come here till about eleven, but of course they might. If you'll excuse me, I'll just go and take a look round outside and see if I can make out anyone watching the place.'

Dymchurch departed, and Tommy began an argument with Tuppence.

It lasted some time and was heated and acrimonious. In the end Tuppence suddenly capitulated.

'All right,' she said. 'I give in. I'll go home and sit there like a good little girl whilst you tackle crooks and hobnob with detectives – but you wait, young man. I'll be even with you yet for keeping me out of the fun.'

Dymchurch returned at that moment.

'Coast seems clear enough,' he said. 'But you can't tell. Better seem to leave in the usual manner. They won't go on watching the place once you've gone.'

Tommy called Albert and gave him instructions to lock up.

Then the four of them made their way to the garage near by where the car was usually left. Tuppence drove and Albert sat beside her. Tommy and the detective sat behind.

Presently they were held up by a block in the traffic. Tuppence looked over her shoulder and nodded. Tommy and the detective opened the right hand door and stepped out into the middle of Oxford Street. In a minute or two Tuppence drove on.

'Better not go in just yet,' said Dymchurch as he and Tommy hurried into Haleham Street. 'You've got the key all right?'

Tommy nodded.

'Then what about a bite of dinner? It's early, but there's a little place here right opposite. We'll get a table by the window, so that we can watch the place all the time.'

They had a very welcome little meal, in the manner the detective had suggested. Tommy found Inspector Dymchurch quite an entertaining companion. Most of his official work had lain amongst international spies, and he had tales to tell which astonished his simple listener.

They remained in the little restaurant until eight o'clock, when Dymchurch suggested a move.

'It's quite dark now, sir,' he explained. 'We shall be able to slip in without any one being the wiser.'

It was, as he said, quite dark. They crossed the road, looked quickly up and down the deserted street, and slipped inside the entrance. Then they mounted the stairs, and Tommy inserted his key in the lock of the outer office.

Just as he did so, he heard, as he thought, Dymchurch whistle beside him.

'What are you whistling for?' he asked sharply.

'*I* didn't whistle,' said Dymchurch, very much astonished. 'I thought *you* did.'

'Well, some one –' began Tommy.

He got no further. Strong arms seized him from behind, and before he could cry out, a pad of something sweet and sickly was pressed over his mouth and nose.

He struggled valiantly, but in vain. The chloroform did its work. His head began to whirl and the floor heaved up and down in front of him. Choking, he lost consciousness . . .

He came to himself painfully, but in full possession of his faculties. The chloroform had been only a whiff. They had kept him under long enough to force a gag into his mouth and ensure that he did not cry out.

When he came to himself, he was half-lying, half-sitting, propped against the wall in a corner of his own inner office. Two men were busily turning out the contents of the desk and ransacking the cupboards, and as they worked they cursed freely.

'Swelp me, guv'nor,' said the taller of the two hoarsely, 'we've turned the whole b—y place upside down and inside out. It's not there.'

'It must be here,' snarled the other. 'It isn't on him. And there's no other place it can be.'

As he spoke he turned, and to Tommy's utter amazement he saw that the last speaker was none other than Inspector Dymchurch. The latter grinned when he saw Tommy's astonished face.

'So our young friend is awake again,' he said. 'And a little surprised – yes, a little surprised. But it was so simple. We suspect that all is not as it should be with the International Detective Agency. I volunteer to find out if that is so, or not. If the new Mr Blunt is indeed a spy, he will be suspicious, so I send first my dear old friend, Carl Bauer. Carl is told to act suspiciously and pitch an improbable tale. He does so, and then I appear on the scene. I used the name of Inspector Marriot to gain confidence. The rest is easy.'

He laughed.

Tommy was dying to say several things, but the gag in his mouth prevented him. Also, he was dying to *do* several things – mostly with his hands and feet – but alas, that too had been attended to. He was securely bound.

The thing that amazed him most was the astounding change in the man standing over him. As Inspector Dymchurch the fellow had been a typical Englishman. Now, no one could have mistaken him for a moment for anything but a well-educated foreigner who talked English perfectly without a trace of accent.

'Coggins, my good friend,' said the erstwhile Inspector, addressing his rufflanly-looking associate, 'take your life-preserver and stand by the prisoner. I am going to remove the gag. You understand, my dear Mr Blunt, do you not, that it would be criminally foolish on your part to cry out? But I am sure you do. For your age, you are quite an intelligent lad.'

Very deftly he removed the gag and stepped back.

Tommy eased his stiff jaws, rolled his tongue round his mouth, swallowed twice – and said nothing at all.

'I congratulate you on your restraint,' said the other. 'You appreciate the position, I see. Have you nothing at all to say?'

'What I have to say will keep,' said Tommy. 'And it won't spoil by waiting.'

'Ah! What I have to say will not keep. In plain English, Mr Blunt, where is that letter?'

'My dear fellow, I don't know,' said Tommy cheerfully. 'I haven't got it. But you know that as well as I do. I should go on looking about if I were you. I like to see you and friend Coggins playing hide-and-seek together.'

The other's face darkened.

'You are pleased to be flippant, Mr Blunt. You see that square box over there. That is Coggins's little outfit. In it there is vitriol . . . yes, vitriol . . . and irons that can be heated in the fire, so that they are red hot and burn . . .'

Tommy shook his head sadly.

'An error in diagnosis,' he murmured. 'Tuppence and I labelled this adventure wrong. It's not a Clubfoot story. It's a Bull-dog Drummond, and you are the inimitable Carl Peterson.'

'What is this nonsense you are talking,' snarled the other.

'Ah!' said Tommy. 'I see you are unacquainted with the classics. A pity.'

'Ignorant fool! Will you do what we want or will you not? Shall I tell Coggins to get out his tools and begin?'

'Don't be so impatient,' said Tommy. 'Of course I'll do what you want, as soon as you tell me what it is. You don't suppose I want to be carved up like a filleted sole and fried on a gridiron? I loathe being hurt.'

Dymchurch looked at him in contempt.

'Gott! What cowards are these English.'

'Common sense, my dear fellow, merely common sense. Leave the vitriol alone and let us come down to brass tacks.'

'I want the letter.'

'I've already told you I haven't got it.'

'We know that – we also know who must have it. The girl.'

'Very possibly you're right,' said Tommy. 'She may have slipped it into her handbag when your pal Carl startled us.'

'Oh, you do not deny. That is wise. Very good, you will write to this Tuppence, as you call her, bidding her bring the letter here immediately.'

'I can't do that,' began Tommy.

The other cut in before he had finished the sentence.

'Ah! You can't? Well, we shall soon see. Coggins!'

'Don't be in such a hurry,' said Tommy. 'And do wait for the end of the sentence. I was going to say that I can't do that unless you untie my arms. Hang it all, I'm not one of those freaks who can write with their noses or their elbows.'

'You are willing to write, then?'

'Of course. Haven't I been telling you so all along? I'm all out to be pleasant and obliging. You won't do anything unkind to Tuppence, of course. I'm sure you won't. She's such a nice girl.'

'We only want the letter,' said Dymchurch, but there was a singularly unpleasant smile on his face.

At a nod from him the brutal Coggins knelt down and unfastened Tommy's arms. The latter swung them to and fro.

'That's better,' he said cheerfully. 'Will kind Coggins hand me my fountain pen? It's on the table, I think, with my other miscellaneous property.'

Scowling, the man brought it to him, and provided a sheet of paper.

'Be careful what you say,' Dymchurch said menacingly. 'We leave it to you, but failure means – death – and slow death at that.'

'In that case,' said Tommy, 'I will certainly do my best.'

He reflected a minute or two, then began to scribble rapidly.

'How will this do?' he asked, handing over the completed epistle.

Dear Tuppence,
   Can you come along at once and bring that blue letter with you? We want to decode it here and now.
   In haste,
      Francis.

'Francis?' queried the bogus Inspector, with lifted eyebrows. 'Was that the name she called you?'

'As you weren't at my christening,' said Tommy, 'I don't suppose you can know whether it's my name or not. But I think the cigarette case you took from my pocket is a pretty good proof that I'm speaking the truth.'

The other stepped over to the table and took up the case, read 'Francis from Tuppence' with a faint grin and laid it down again.

'I am glad to find you are behaving so sensibly,' he said. 'Coggins, give that note to Vassilly. He is on guard outside. Tell him to take it at once.'

The next twenty minutes passed slowly, the ten minutes after that more slowly still. Dymchurch was striding up and down with a face that grew darker and darker. Once he turned menacingly on Tommy.

'If you have dared to double-cross us,' he growled.

'If we'd had a pack of cards here, we might have had a game of picquet to pass the time,' drawled Tommy. 'Women always keep one waiting. I hope you're not going to be unkind to little Tuppence when she comes?'

'Oh, no,' said Dymchurch. 'We shall arrange for you to go to the same place – together.'

'Will you, you swine,' said Tommy under his breath.

Suddenly there was a stir in the outer office. A man whom Tommy had not yet seen poked his head in and growled something in Russian.

'Good,' said Dymchurch. 'She is coming – and coming alone.'

For a moment a faint anxiety caught at Tommy's heart.

The next minute he heard Tuppence's voice.

'Oh! there you are, Inspector Dymchurch. I've brought the letter. Where is Francis?'

With the last words she came through the door, and Vassilly sprang on her from behind, clapping his hand over her mouth. Dymchurch tore the handbag from her grasp and turned over its contents in a frenzied search.

Suddenly he uttered an ejaculation of delight and held up a blue envelope with a Russian stamp on it. Coggins gave a hoarse shout.

And just in that minute of triumph the other door, the door into Tuppence's own office, opened noiselessly and Inspector Marriot and two men armed with revolvers stepped into the room, with the sharp command: 'Hands up.'

There was no fight. The others were taken at a hopeless disadvantage. Dymchurch's automatic lay on the table, and the two others were not armed.

'A very nice little haul,' said Inspector Marriot with approval, as he snapped the last pair of handcuffs. 'And we'll have more as time goes on, I hope.'

White with rage, Dymchurch glared at Tuppence.

'You little devil,' he snarled. 'It was you put them on to us.'

Tuppence laughed.

'It wasn't all my doing. I ought to have guessed, I admit, when you brought in the number sixteen this afternoon. But it was Tommy's note clinched matters. I rang up Inspector Marriot, got Albert to meet him with the duplicate key of the office, and came along myself with the empty blue envelope in my bag. The letter I forwarded according to my instructions as soon as I had parted with you two this afternoon.'

But one word had caught the other's attention.

'*Tommy?*' he queried.

Tommy, who had just been released from his bonds, came towards them.

'Well done, brother Francis,' he said to Tuppence, taking both her hands in his. And to Dymchurch: 'As I told you, my dear fellow, you really ought to read the classics.'

Finessing the King

'Finessing the King', combining the later book chapter 'The
Gentleman Dressed in Newspaper', was first published in
The Sketch, 8 October 1924. McCarty and Riordan were created
by Isobel Ostrander (1885–1924).

It was a wet Wednesday in the offices of the International Detective
Agency. Tuppence let the *Daily Leader* fall idly from her hand.

'Do you know what I've been thinking, Tommy?'

'It's impossible to say,' replied her husband. 'You think of so many
things, and you think of them all at once.'

'I think it's time we went dancing again.'

Tommy picked up the *Daily Leader* hastily.

'Our advertisement looks well,' he remarked, his head on one side.
'Blunt's Brilliant Detectives. Do you realise, Tuppence, that you and you
alone are Blunt's Brilliant Detectives? There's glory for you, as Humpty
Dumpty would say.'

'I was talking about dancing.'

'There's a curious point that I have observed about newspapers. I
wonder if you have ever noticed it. Take these three copies of the *Daily
Leader*. Can you tell me how they differ one from the other?'

Tuppence took them with some curiosity.

'It seems fairly easy,' she remarked witheringly. 'One is today's, one is
yesterday's, and one is the day before's.'

'Positively scintillating, my dear Watson. But that was not my meaning.
Observe the headline, "Daily Leader." Compare the three – do you see
any difference between them?'

'No, I don't,' said Tuppence, 'and what's more, I don't believe there
is any.'

Tommy sighed and brought the tips of his fingers together in the most
approved Sherlock Holmes fashion.

'Exactly. Yet you read the papers as much – in fact, more than I do. But I have observed and you have not. If you will look at today's *Daily Leader*, you will see that in the middle of the downstroke of the D is a small white dot, and there is another in the L of the same word. But in yesterday's paper the white dot is not in DAILY at all. There are two white dots in the L of LEADER. That of the day before again has two dots in the D of DAILY. In fact, the dot, or dots, are in a different position every day.'

'Why?' asked Tuppence.

'That's a journalistic secret.'

'Meaning you don't know, and can't guess.'

'I will merely say this – the practice is common to all newspapers.'

'Aren't you clever?' said Tuppence. 'Especially at drawing red herrings across the track. Let's go back to what we were talking about before.'

'What were we talking about?'

'The Three Arts Ball.'

Tommy groaned.

'No, no, Tuppence. Not the Three Arts Ball. I'm not young enough. I assure you I'm not young enough.'

'When I was a nice young girl,' said Tuppence, 'I was brought up to believe that men – especially husbands – were dissipated beings, fond of drinking and dancing and staying up late at night. It took an exceptionally beautiful and clever wife to keep them at home. Another illusion gone! All the wives I know are hankering to go out and dance, and weeping because their husbands will wear bedroom slippers and go to bed at half-past nine. And you do dance so nicely, Tommy dear.'

'Gently with the butter, Tuppence.'

'As a matter of fact,' said Tuppence, 'it's not purely for pleasure that I want to go. I'm intrigued by this advertisement.'

She picked up the *Daily Leader* again and read it out.

'I should go three hearts. 12 tricks. Ace of Spades. Necessary to finesse the King.'

'Rather an expensive way of learning bridge,' was Tommy's comment.

'Don't be an ass. That's nothing to do with bridge. You see, I was lunching with a girl yesterday at the Ace of Spades. It's a queer little underground den in Chelsea, and she told me that it's quite the fashion at these big shows to trundle round there in the course of the evening for bacon and eggs and Welsh rarebits – Bohemian sort of stuff. It's got screened-off booths all around it. Pretty hot place, I should say.'

'And your idea is –?'

'Three hearts stands for the Three Arts Ball, tomorrow night, 12 tricks is twelve o'clock, and the Ace of Spades is the Ace of Spades.'

'And what about its being necessary to finesse the King?'

'Well, that's what I thought we'd find out.'

'I shouldn't wonder if you weren't right, Tuppence,' said Tommy magnanimously. 'But I don't quite see why you want to butt in upon other people's love affairs.'

'I shan't butt in. What I'm proposing is an interesting experiment in detective work. We *need* practice.'

'Business is certainly not too brisk,' agreed Tommy. 'All the same, Tuppence, what you want is to go to the Three Arts Ball and dance! Talk of red herrings.'

Tuppence laughed shamelessly.

'Be a sport, Tommy. Try and forget you're thirty-two and have got one grey hair in your left eyebrow.'

'I was always weak where women were concerned,' murmured her husband. 'Have I got to make an ass of myself in fancy dress?'

'Of course, but you can leave that to me. I've got a splendid idea.'

Tommy looked at her with some misgiving. He was always profoundly mistrustful of Tuppence's brilliant ideas.

When he returned to the flat on the following evening, Tuppence came flying out of her bedroom to meet him.

'It's come,' she announced.

'What's come?'

'The costume. Come and look at it.'

Tommy followed her. Spread out on the bed was a complete fireman's kit with shining helmet.

'Good God!' groaned Tommy. 'Have I joined the Wembley fire brigade?'

'Guess again,' said Tuppence. 'You haven't caught the idea yet. Use your little grey cells, *mon ami*. Scintillate, Watson. Be a bull that has been more than ten minutes in the arena.'

'Wait a minute,' said Tommy. 'I begin to see. There is a dark purpose in this. What are you going to wear, Tuppence?'

'An old suit of your clothes, an American hat and some horn spectacles.'

'Crude,' said Tommy. 'But I catch the idea. McCarty incog. And I am Riordan.'

'That's it. I thought we ought to practise American detective methods as well as English ones. Just for once I am going to be the star, and you will be the humble assistant.'

'Don't forget,' said Tommy warningly, 'that it's always an innocent remark by the simple Denny that puts McCarty on the right track.'

But Tuppence only laughed. She was in high spirits.

It was a most successful evening. The crowds, the music, the fantastic dresses – everything conspired to make the young couple enjoy themselves. Tommy forgot his role of the bored husband dragged out against his will.

At ten minutes to twelve they drove off in the car to the famous – or infamous – Ace of Spades. As Tuppence had said, it was an underground den, mean and tawdry in appearance, but it was nevertheless crowded with couples in fancy dress. There were closed-in booths round the walls, and Tommy and Tuppence secured one of these. They left the doors purposely a little ajar so that they could see what was going on outside.

'I wonder which they are – our people, I mean,' said Tuppence. 'What about that Columbine over there with the red Mephistopheles?'

'I fancy the wicked Mandarin and the lady who calls herself a Battleship – more of a fast Cruiser, I should say.'

'Isn't he witty?' said Tuppence. 'All done on a little drop of drink! Who's this coming in dressed as the Queen of Hearts – rather a good get-up, that.'

The girl in question passed into the booth next to them, accompanied by her escort, who was 'the gentleman dressed in newspaper' from *Alice in Wonderland*. They were both wearing masks – it seemed to be rather a common custom at the Ace of Spades.

'I'm sure we're in a real den of iniquity,' said Tuppence with a pleased face. 'Scandals all round us. What a row everyone makes.'

A cry, as of protest, rang out from the booth next door and was covered by a man's loud laugh. Everybody was laughing and singing. The shrill voices of the girls rose above the booming of their male escorts.

'What about that shepherdess?' demanded Tommy. 'The one with the comic Frenchman. They might be our little lot.'

'Any one might be,' confessed Tuppence. 'I'm not going to bother. The great thing is that we are enjoying ourselves.'

'I could have enjoyed myself better in another costume,' grumbled Tommy. 'You've no idea of the heat of this one.'

'Cheer up,' said Tuppence. 'You look lovely.'

'I'm glad of that,' said Tommy. 'It's more than you do. You're the funniest little guy I've ever seen.'

'Will you keep a civil tongue in your head, Denny, my boy. Hullo, the gentleman in newspaper is leaving his lady alone. Where's he going, do you think?'

'Going to hurry up the drinks, I expect,' said Tommy. 'I wouldn't mind doing the same thing.'

'He's a long time doing it,' said Tuppence, when four or five minutes had passed. 'Tommy, would you think me an awful ass –' She paused.

Suddenly she jumped up.

'Call me an ass if you like. I'm going in next door.'

'Look here, Tuppence – you can't –'

'I've a feeling there's something wrong. I *know* there is. Don't try and stop me.'

She passed quickly out of their own booth, and Tommy followed her. The doors of the one next door were closed. Tuppence pushed them apart and went in, Tommy on her heels.

The girl dressed as the Queen of Hearts sat in the corner leaning up against the wall in a queer huddled position. Her eyes regarded them steadily through her mask, but she did not move. Her dress was carried out in a bold design of red and white, but on the left hand side the pattern seemed to have got mixed. There was more red than there should have been . . .

With a cry Tuppence hurried forward. At the same time, Tommy saw what she had seen, the hilt of a jewelled dagger just below the heart. Tuppence dropped on her knees by the girl's side.

'Quick, Tommy, she's still alive. Get hold of the manager and make him get a doctor at once.'

'Right. Mind you don't touch the handle of that dagger, Tuppence.'

'I'll be careful. Go quickly.'

Tommy hurried out, pulling the doors to behind him. Tuppence passed her arm round the girl. The latter made a faint gesture, and Tuppence realised that she wanted to get rid of the mask. Tuppence unfastened it gently. She saw a fresh, flower-like face, and wide starry eyes that were full of horror, suffering, and a kind of dazed bewilderment.

'My dear,' said Tuppence, very gently. 'Can you speak at all? Will you tell me, if you can, who did this?'

She felt the eyes fix themselves on her face. The girl was sighing, the deep palpitating sighs of a failing heart. And still she looked steadily at Tuppence. Then her lips parted.

'Bingo did it –' she said in a strained whisper.

Then her hands relaxed, and she seemed to nestle down on Tuppence's shoulder.

Tommy came in, two men with him. The bigger of the two came forward with an air of authority, the word doctor written all over him.

Tuppence relinquished her burden.

'She's dead, I'm afraid,' she said with a catch in her voice.

The doctor made a swift examination.

'Yes,' he said. 'Nothing to be done. We had better leave things as they are till the police come. How did the thing happen?'

Tuppence explained rather haltingly, slurring over her reasons for entering the booth.

'It's a curious business,' said the doctor. 'You heard nothing?'

'I heard her give a kind of cry, but then the man laughed. Naturally I didn't think –'

'Naturally not,' agreed the doctor. 'And the man wore a mask you say. You wouldn't recognise him?'

'I'm afraid not. Would you, Tommy?'

'No. Still there is his costume.'

'The first thing will be to identify this poor lady,' said the doctor. 'After that, well, I suppose the police will get down to things pretty quickly. It ought not to be a difficult case. Ah, here they come.'

The Gentleman Dressed in Newspaper

It was after three o'clock when, weary and sick at heart, the husband and wife reached home. Several hours passed before Tuppence could sleep. She lay tossing from side to side, seeing always that flower-like face with the horror-stricken eyes.

The dawn was coming in through the shutters when Tuppence finally dropped off to sleep. After the excitement, she slept heavily and dreamlessly. It was broad daylight when she awoke to find Tommy, up and dressed, standing by the bedside, shaking her gently by the arm.

'Wake up, old thing. Inspector Marriot and another man are here and want to see you.'

'What time is it?'

'Just on eleven. I'll get Alice to bring you your tea right away.'

'Yes, do. Tell Inspector Marriot I'll be there in ten minutes.'

A quarter of an hour later, Tuppence came hurrying into the sitting-room. Inspector Marriot, who was sitting looking very straight and solemn, rose to greet her.

'Good-morning, Mrs Beresford. This is Sir Arthur Merivale.'

Tuppence shook hands with a tall thin man with haggard eyes and greying hair.

'It's about this sad business last night,' said Inspector Marriot. 'I want Sir Arthur to hear from your own lips what you told me – the words the poor lady said before she died. Sir Arthur has been very hard to convince.'

'I can't believe,' said the other, 'and I won't believe, that Bingo Hale ever hurt a hair of Vere's head.'

Inspector Marriot went on.

'We've made some progress since last night, Mrs Beresford,' he said. 'First of all we managed to identify the lady as Lady Merivale. We communicated with Sir Arthur here. He recognised the body at once, and was horrified beyond words, of course. Then I asked him if he knew anyone called Bingo.'

'You must understand, Mrs Beresford,' said Sir Arthur, 'that Captain Hale, who is known to all his friends as Bingo, is the dearest pal I have. He practically lives with us. He was staying at my house when they arrested him this morning. I cannot but believe that you have made a mistake – it was not his name that my wife uttered.'

'There is no possibility of mistake,' said Tuppence gently. 'She said, "Bingo did it –"'

'You see, Sir Arthur,' said Marriot.

The unhappy man sank into a chair and covered his face with his hands.

'It's incredible. What earthly motive could there be? Oh, I know your idea, Inspector Marriot. You think Hale was my wife's lover, but even if that were so – which I don't admit for a moment – what motive was there for killing her?'

Inspector Marriot coughed.

'It's not a very pleasant thing to say, sir. But Captain Hale has been paying a lot of attention to a certain young American lady of late – a young lady with a considerable amount of money. If Lady Merivale liked to turn nasty, she could probably stop his marriage.'

'This is outrageous, Inspector.'

Sir Arthur sprang angrily to his feet. The other calmed him with a soothing gesture.

'I beg your pardon, I'm sure, Sir Arthur. You say that you and Captain Hale both decided to attend this show. Your wife was away on a visit at the time, and you had no idea that she was to be there?'

'Not the least idea.'

'Just show him that advertisement you told me about, Mrs Beresford.'

Tuppence complied.

'That seems to me clear enough. It was inserted by Captain Hale to catch your wife's eye. They had already arranged to meet there. But you only made up your mind to go the day before, hence it was necessary to warn her. That is the explanation of the phrase, "Necessary to finesse the King." You ordered your costume from a theatrical firm at the last minute, but Captain Hale's was a home-made affair. He went as the Gentleman dressed in Newspaper. Do you know, Sir Arthur, what we found clasped in the dead lady's hand? A fragment torn from a newspaper. My men have orders to take Captain Hale's costume away with them from your house. I shall find it at the Yard when I get back. If there's a tear in it corresponding to the missing piece – well, it'll be the end of the case.'

'You won't find it,' said Sir Arthur. 'I know Bingo Hale.'

Apologising to Tuppence for disturbing her, they took their leave.

Late that evening there was a ring at the bell, and somewhat to the astonishment of the young pair Inspector Marriot once more walked in.

'I thought Blunt's Brilliant Detectives would like to hear the latest developments,' he said, with a hint of a smile.

'They would,' said Tommy. 'Have a drink?'

He placed materials hospitably at Inspector Marriot's elbow.

'It's a clear case,' said the latter, after a minute or two. 'Dagger was the lady's own – the idea was to have made it look like suicide evidently, but thanks to you two being on the spot, that didn't come off. We've found plenty of letters – they'd been carrying on together for some time, that's clear – without Sir Arthur tumbling to it. Then we found the last link –'

'The last what?' said Tuppence sharply.

'The last link in the chain – that fragment of the *Daily Leader*. It was torn from the dress he wore – fits exactly. Oh, yes, it's a perfectly clear case. By the way, I brought round a photograph of those two exhibits – I thought they might interest you. It's very seldom that you get such a perfectly clear case.'

'Tommy,' said Tuppence, when her husband returned from showing the Scotland Yard man out, 'why do you think Inspector Marriot keeps repeating that it's a perfectly clear case?'

'I don't know. Smug satisfaction, I suppose.'

'Not a bit of it. He's trying to get us irritated. You know, Tommy, butchers, for instance, know something about meat, don't they?'

'I should say so, but what on earth –'

'And in the same way, greengrocers know all about vegetables, and fishermen about fish. Detectives, professional detectives, must know all about criminals. They know the real thing when they see it – and they know when it isn't the real thing. Marriot's expert knowledge tells him that Captain Hale isn't a criminal – but all the facts are dead against him. As a last resource Marriot is egging us on, hoping against hope that some little detail or other will come back to us – something that happened last night – which will throw a different light on things. Tommy, why shouldn't it be suicide, after all?'

'Remember what she said to you.'

'I know – but take that a different way. It was Bingo's doing – his conduct that drove her to kill herself. It's just possible.'

'Just. But it doesn't explain that fragment of newspaper.'

'Let's have a look at Marriot's photographs. I forgot to ask him what Hale's account of the matter was.'

'I asked him that in the hall just now. Hale declared he had never spoken to Lady Merivale at the show. Says somebody shoved a note into his hand which said, 'Don't try and speak to me tonight. Arthur suspects.' He couldn't produce the piece of paper, though, and it doesn't sound a very likely story. Anyway, you and I *know* he was with her at the Ace of Spades, because we saw him.'

Tuppence nodded and pored over the two photographs.

One was a tiny fragment with the legend DAILY LE – and the rest torn off. The other was the front sheet of the *Daily Leader* with the small round tear at the top of it. There was no doubt about it. Those two fitted together perfectly.

'What are all those marks down the side?' asked Tommy.

'Stitches,' said Tuppence. 'Where it was sewn to the others, you know.'

'I thought it might be a new scheme of dots,' said Tommy. Then he gave a slight shiver. 'My word, Tuppence, how creepy it makes one feel. To think that you and I were discussing dots and puzzling over that advertisement – all as lighthearted as anything.'

Tuppence did not answer. Tommy looked at her and was startled to observe that she was staring ahead of her, her mouth slightly open, and a bewildered expression on her face.

'Tuppence,' said Tommy gently, shaking her by the arm, 'what's the matter with you? Are you just going to have a stroke or something?'

But Tuppence remained motionless. Presently she said in a faraway voice:

'Denis Riordan.'

'Eh?' said Tommy, staring.

'It's just as you said. One simple innocent remark! Find me all this week's *Daily Leaders*.'

'What are you up to?'

'I'm being McCarty. I've been worrying round, and thanks to you, I've got a notion at last. This is the front sheet of Tuesday's paper. I seem to remember that Tuesday's paper was the one with two dots in the L of LEADER. This has a dot in the D of DAILY – and one in the L too. Get me the papers and let's make sure.'

They compared them anxiously. Tuppence had been quite right in her remembrance.

'You see? This fragment wasn't torn from Tuesday's paper.'

'But Tuppence, we can't be sure. It may merely be different editions.'

'It may – but at any rate it's given me an idea. It can't be coincidence – that's certain. There's only one thing it can be if I'm right in my idea. Ring up Sir Arthur, Tommy. Ask him to come round here at once. Say I've got important news for him. Then get hold of Marriot. Scotland Yard will know his address if he's gone home.'

Sir Arthur Merivale, very much intrigued by the summons, arrived at the flat in about half an hour's time. Tuppence came forward to greet him.

'I must apologise for sending for you in such a peremptory fashion,' she said. 'But my husband and I have discovered something that we think you ought to know at once. Do sit down.'

Sir Arthur sat down, and Tuppence went on.

'You are, I know, very anxious to clear your friend.'

Sir Arthur shook his head sadly.

'I was, but even I have had to give in to the overwhelming evidence.'

'What would you say if I told you that chance has placed in my hands a piece of evidence that will certainly clear him of all complicity?'

'I should be overjoyed to hear it, Mrs Beresford.'

'Supposing,' continued Tuppence, 'that I had come across a girl who was actually dancing with Captain Hale last night at twelve o'clock – the hour when he was supposed to be at the Ace of Spades.'

'Marvellous!' cried Sir Arthur. 'I knew there was some mistake. Poor Vere must have killed herself after all.'

'Hardly that,' said Tuppence. 'You forget the other man.'

'What other man?'

'The one my husband and I saw leave the booth. You see, Sir Arthur, there must have been a second man dressed in newspaper at the ball. By the way, what was your own costume?'

'Mine? I went as a seventeenth century executioner.'

'How very appropriate,' said Tuppence softly.

'Appropriate, Mrs Beresford. What do you mean by appropriate?'

'For the part you played. Shall I tell you my ideas on the subject, Sir Arthur? The newspaper dress is easily put on over that of an executioner. Previously a little note has been slipped into Captain Hale's hand, asking him not to speak to a certain lady. But the lady herself knows nothing of that note. She goes to the Ace of Spades at the appointed time and sees the figure she expects to see. They go into the booth. He takes her in his arms, I think, and kisses her – the kiss of a Judas, and as he kisses he strikes with the dagger. She only utters one faint cry and he covers that with a laugh. Presently he goes away – and to the last, horrified and bewildered, she believes her lover is the man who killed her.

'But she has torn a small fragment from the costume. The murderer notices that – he is a man who pays great attention to detail. To make the case absolutely clear against his victim the fragment must seem to have been torn from Captain Hale's costume. That would present great difficulties unless the two men happened to be living in the same house. Then, of course, the thing would be simplicity itself. He makes an exact duplicate of the tear in Captain Hale's costume – then he burns his own and prepares to play the part of the loyal friend.'

Tuppence paused.

'Well, Sir Arthur?'

Sir Arthur rose and made her a bow.

'The rather vivid imagination of a charming lady who reads too much fiction.'

'You think so?' said Tommy.

'And a husband who is guided by his wife,' said Sir Arthur. 'I do not fancy you will find anybody to take the matter seriously.'

He laughed out loud, and Tuppence stiffened in her chair.

'I would swear to that laugh anywhere,' she said. 'I heard it last in the Ace of Spades. And you are under a little misapprehension about us both. Beresford is our real name, but we have another.'

She picked up a card from the table and handed it to him. Sir Arthur read it aloud.

'International Detective Agency . . .' He drew his breath sharply. 'So that is what you really are! That was why Marriot brought me here this morning. It was a trap –'

He strolled to the window.

'A fine view you have from here,' he said. 'Right over London.'

'Inspector Marriot,' cried Tommy sharply.

In a flash the Inspector appeared from the communicating door in the opposite wall.

A little smile of amusement came to Sir Arthur's lips.

'I thought as much,' he said. 'But you won't get me this time, I'm afraid, Inspector. I prefer to take my own way out.'

And putting his hands on the sill, he vaulted clean through the window.

Tuppence shrieked and clapped her hands to her ears to shut out the sound she had already imagined – the sickening thud far beneath. Inspector Marriot uttered an oath.

'We should have thought of the window,' he said. 'Though, mind you, it would have been a difficult thing to prove. I'll go down and – and – see to things.'

'Poor devil,' said Tommy slowly. 'If he was fond of his wife –'

But the Inspector interrupted him with a snort.

'Fond of her? That's as may be. He was at his wits' end where to turn for money. Lady Merivale had a large fortune of her own, and it all went to him. If she'd bolted with young Hale, he'd never have seen a penny of it.'

'That was it, was it?'

'Of course, from the very start, I sensed that Sir Arthur was a bad lot, and that Captain Hale was all right. We know pretty well what's what at the Yard – but it's awkward when you're up against facts. I'll be going down now – I should give your wife a glass of brandy if I were you, Mr Beresford – it's been upsetting like for her.'

'Greengrocers,' said Tuppence in a low voice as the door closed behind the imperturbable Inspector, 'butchers, fishermen, detectives. I was right, wasn't I? He knew.'

Tommy, who had been busy at the sideboard, approached her with a large glass.

'Drink this.'

'What is it? Brandy?'

'No, it's a large cocktail – suitable for a triumphant McCarty. Yes, Marriot's right all round – that was the way of it. A bold finesse for game and rubber.'

Tuppence nodded.

'But he finessed the wrong way round.'

'And so,' said Tommy, 'exit the King.'

The Case of the Missing Lady

'The Case of the Missing Lady' was first published in *The Sketch*,
15 October 1924. Sherlock Holmes was created by
Sir Arthur Conan Doyle (1859–1930).

The buzzer on Mr Blunt's desk – International Detective Agency, Manager, Theodore Blunt – uttered its warning call. Tommy and Tuppence both flew to their respective peepholes which commanded a view of the outer office. There it was Albert's business to delay the prospective client with various artistic devices.

'I will see, sir,' he was saying. 'But I'm afraid Mr Blunt is very busy just at present. He is engaged with Scotland Yard on the phone just now.'

'I'll wait,' said the visitor. 'I haven't got a card with me, but my name is Gabriel Stavansson.'

The client was a magnificent specimen of manhood, standing over six foot high. His face was bronzed and weatherbeaten, and the extraordinary blue of his eyes made an almost startling contrast to the brown skin.

Tommy swiftly made up his mind. He put on his hat, picked up some gloves and opened the door. He paused on the threshold.

'This gentleman is waiting to see you, Mr Blunt,' said Albert.

A quick frown passed over Tommy's face. He took out his watch.

'I am due at the Duke's at a quarter to eleven,' he said. Then he looked keenly at the visitor. 'I can give you a few minutes if you will come this way.'

The latter followed him obediently into the inner office, where Tuppence was sitting demurely with pad and pencil.

'My confidential secretary, Miss Robinson,' said Tommy. 'Now, sir, perhaps you will state your business? Beyond the fact that it is urgent, that you came here in a taxi, and that you have lately been in the Arctic – or possibly the Antarctic, I know nothing.'

The visitor stared at him in amazement.

'But this is marvellous,' he cried. 'I thought detectives only did such things in books! Your office boy did not even give you my name!'

Tommy sighed deprecatingly.

'Tut, tut, all that was very easy,' he said. 'The rays of the midnight sun within the Arctic circle have a peculiar action upon the skin – the actinic rays have certain properties. I am writing a little monograph on the subject shortly. But all this is wide of the point. What is it that has brought you to me in such distress of mind?'

'To begin with, Mr Blunt, my name is Gabriel Stavansson –'

'Ah! of course,' said Tommy. 'The well-known explorer. You have recently returned from the region of the North Pole, I believe?'

'I landed in England three days ago. A friend who was cruising in northern waters brought me back on his yacht. Otherwise I should not have got back for another fortnight. Now I must tell you, Mr Blunt, that before I started on this last expedition two years ago, I had the great good fortune to become engaged to Mrs Maurice Leigh Gordon –'

Tommy interrupted.

'Mrs Leigh Gordon was, before her marriage –?'

'The Honourable Hermione Crane, second daughter of Lord Lanchester,' reeled off Tuppence glibly.

Tommy threw her a glance of admiration.

'Her first husband was killed in the war,' added Tuppence.

Gabriel Stavansson nodded.

'That is quite correct. As I was saying, Hermione and I became engaged. I offered, of course, to give up this expedition, but she wouldn't hear of such a thing – bless her! She's the right kind of woman for an explorer's wife. Well, my first thought on landing was to see Hermione. I sent a telegram from Southampton, and rushed up to town by the first train. I knew that she was living for the time being with an aunt of hers, Lady Susan Clonray, in Pont Street, and I went straight there. To my great disappointment, I found that Hermy was away visiting some friends in Northumberland. Lady Susan was quite nice about it, after getting over her first surprise at seeing me. As I told you, I wasn't expected for another fortnight. She said Hermy would be returning in a few days' time. Then I asked for her address, but the old woman hummed and hawed – said Hermy was staying at one or two different places and that she wasn't quite sure what order she was taking them in. I may as well tell you, Mr Blunt, that Lady Susan and I have never got on very well. She's one of those fat women with double chins. I loathe fat women – always have – fat women and fat dogs are an abomination unto the Lord – and unfortunately they so often go together! It's an idiosyncrasy of mine, I know – but there it is – I never can get on with a fat woman.'

'Fashion agrees with you, Mr Stavansson,' said Tommy dryly. 'And every one has their own pet aversion – that of the late Lord Roberts was cats.'

'Mind you, I'm not saying that Lady Susan isn't a perfectly charming woman – she may be, but I've never taken to her. I've always felt, deep down, that she disapproved of our engagement, and I feel sure that she would influence Hermy against me if that were possible. I'm telling you this for what it's worth. Count it out as prejudice if you like. Well, to go on with my story, I'm the kind of obstinate brute who likes his own way. I didn't leave Pont Street until I'd got out of her the names and addresses of the people Hermy was likely to be staying with. Then I took the mail train north.'

'You are, I perceive, a man of action, Mr Stavansson,' said Tommy, smiling.

'The thing came upon me like a bombshell. Mr Blunt, none of these people had seen a sign of Hermy. Of the three houses, only one had been expecting her – Lady Susan must have made a bloomer over the other two – and she had put off her visit there at the last moment by telegram. I returned post haste to London, of course, and went straight to Lady Susan. I will do her the justice to say that she seemed upset. She admitted that she had no idea where Hermy could be. All the same, she strongly negatived any idea of going to the police. She pointed out that Hermy was not a silly young girl, but an independent woman who had always been in the habit of making her own plans. She was probably carrying out some idea of her own.

'I thought it quite likely that Hermy didn't want to report all her movements to Lady Susan. But I was still worried. I had that queer feeling one gets when something is wrong. I was just leaving when a telegram was brought to Lady Susan. She read it with an expression of relief and handed it to me. It ran as follows: '*Changed my plans. Just off to Monte Carlo for a week. – Hermy.*'

Tommy held out his hand.

'You have got the telegram with you?'

'No, I haven't. But it was handed in at Maldon, Surrey. I noticed that at the time, because it struck me as odd. What should Hermy be doing at Maldon. She'd no friends there that I had ever heard of.'

'You didn't think of rushing off to Monte Carlo in the same way that you had rushed north?'

'I thought of it, of course. But I decided against it. You see, Mr Blunt, whilst Lady Susan seemed quite satisfied by that telegram, I wasn't. It struck me as odd that she should always telegraph, not write. A line or two in her own handwriting would have set all my fears at rest. But anyone can sign a telegram "Hermy." The more I thought it over, the more uneasy I got. In the end I went down to Maldon. That was yesterday afternoon. It's a fair-sized place – good links there and all that – two hotels. I inquired everywhere I could think of, but there wasn't a sign that Hermy had ever been there. Coming back in the train I read your advertisement and I thought I'd put it up to you. If Hermy has really gone off to Monte Carlo, I don't want to set the police on her track and make a scandal, but I'm not going to be sent off on a wild goose chase myself. I stay here in London, in case – in case there's been foul play of any kind.'

Tommy nodded thoughtfully.

'What do you suspect exactly?'

'I don't know. But I feel there's something wrong.'

With a quick movement, Stavansson took a case from his pocket and laid it open before them.

'That is Hermione,' he said. 'I will leave it with you.'

The photograph represented a tall, willowy woman, no longer in her first youth, but with a charming frank smile and lovely eyes.

'Now, Mr Stavansson,' said Tommy, 'there is nothing you have omitted to tell me?'

'Nothing whatever.'

'No detail, however small?'

'I don't think so.'

Tommy sighed.

'That makes the task harder,' he observed. 'You must often have noticed, Mr Stavansson, in reading of crime, how one small detail is all the great detective needs to set him on the track. I may say that this case presents some unusual features. I have, I think, partially solved it already, but time will show.'

He picked up a violin which lay on the table and drew the bow once or twice across the strings. Tuppence ground her teeth, and even the explorer blenched. The performer laid the instrument down again.

'A few chords from Mosgovskensky,' he murmured. 'Leave me your address, Mr Stavansson, and I will report progress to you.'

As the visitor left the office, Tuppence grabbed the violin, and putting it in the cupboard turned the key in the lock.

'If you must be Sherlock Holmes,' she observed, 'I'll get you a nice little syringe and a bottle labelled cocaine, but for God's sake leave that violin alone. If that nice explorer man hadn't been as simple as a child, he'd have seen through you. Are you going on with the Sherlock Holmes touch?'

'I flatter myself that I have carried it through very well so far,' said Tommy with some complacence. 'The deductions were good, weren't they? I had to risk the taxi. After all, it's the only sensible way of getting to this place.'

'It's lucky I had just read the bit about his engagement in this morning's *Daily Mirror*,' remarked Tuppence.

'Yes, that looked well for the efficiency of Blunt's Brilliant Detectives. This is decidedly a Sherlock Holmes case. Even you cannot have failed to notice the similarity between it and the disappearance of Lady Frances Carfax.'

'Do you expect to find Mrs Leigh Gordon's body in a coffin?'

'Logically, history should repeat itself. Actually – well, what do you think?'

'Well,' said Tuppence. 'The most obvious explanation seems to be that for some reason or other, Hermy, as he calls her, is afraid to meet her fiancé, and that Lady Susan is backing her up. In fact, to put it bluntly, she's come a cropper of some kind, and has got the wind up about it.'

'That occurred to me also,' said Tommy. 'But I thought we'd better make pretty certain before suggesting that explanation to a man like Stavansson. What about a run down to Maldon, old thing? And it would do no harm to take some golf clubs with us.'

Tuppence agreeing, the International Detective Agency was left in the charge of Albert.

Maldon, though a well-known residential place, did not cover a large area. Tommy and Tuppence, making every possible inquiry that ingenuity could suggest, nevertheless drew a complete blank. It was as they were returning to London that a brilliant idea occurred to Tuppence.

'Tommy, why did they put Maldon, Surrey, on the telegram?'

'Because Maldon is in Surrey, idiot.'

'Idiot yourself – I don't mean that. If you get a telegram from – Hastings, say, or Torquay, they don't put the county after it. But from Richmond, they do put Richmond, Surrey. That's because there are two Richmonds.'

Tommy, who was driving, slowed up.

'Tuppence,' he said affectionately, 'your idea is not so dusty. Let us make inquiries at yonder post office.'

They drew up before a small building in the middle of a village street. A very few minutes sufficed to elicit the information that there were two Maldons. Maldon, Surrey, and Maldon, Sussex, the latter, a tiny hamlet but possessed of a telegraph office.

'That's it,' said Tuppence excitedly. 'Stavansson knew Maldon was in Surrey, so he hardly looked at the word beginning with S after Maldon.'

'Tomorrow,' said Tommy, 'we'll have a look at Maldon, Sussex.'

Maldon, Sussex, was a very different proposition to its Surrey namesake. It was four miles from a railway station, possessed two public houses, two small shops, a post and telegraph office combined with a sweet and picture postcard business, and about seven small cottages. Tuppence took on the shops whilst Tommy betook himself to the Cock and Sparrow. They met half an hour later.

'Well?' said Tuppence.

'Quite good beer,' said Tommy, 'but no information.'

'You'd better try the King's Head,' said Tuppence. 'I'm going back to the post office. There's a sour old woman there, but I heard them yell to her that dinner was ready.'

She returned to the place and began examining postcards. A fresh-faced girl, still munching, came out of the back room.

'I'd like these, please,' said Tuppence. 'And do you mind waiting whilst I just look over these comic ones?'

She sorted through a packet, talking as she did so.

'I'm ever so disappointed you couldn't tell me my sister's address. She's staying near here and I've lost her letter. Leigh Gordon, her name is.'

The girl shook her head.

'I don't remember it. And we don't get many letters through here either – so I probably should if I'd seen it on a letter. Apart from the Grange, there isn't many big houses round about.'

'What is the Grange?' asked Tuppence. 'Who does it belong to?'

'Dr Horriston has it. It's turned into a nursing home now. Nerve cases mostly, I believe. Ladies that come down for rest cures, and all that sort of thing. Well, it's quiet enough down here, heaven knows.' She giggled.

Tuppence hastily selected a few cards and paid for them.

'That's Doctor Horriston's car coming along now,' exclaimed the girl.

Tuppence hurried to the shop door. A small two-seater was passing. At the wheel was a tall dark man with a neat black beard and a powerful unpleasant face. The car went straight on down the street. Tuppence saw Tommy crossing the road towards her.

'Tommy, I believe I've got it. Doctor Horriston's nursing home.'

'I heard about it at the King's Head, and I thought there might be something in it. But if she's had a nervous breakdown or anything of that sort, her aunt and her friends would know about it surely.'

'Ye-es. I didn't mean that. Tommy, did you see that man in the two-seater?'

'Unpleasant-looking brute, yes.'

'That was Doctor Horriston.'

Tommy whistled.

'Shifty looking beggar. What do you say about it, Tuppence? Shall we go and have a look at the Grange?'

They found the place at last, a big rambling house, surrounded by deserted grounds, with a swift mill stream running behind the house.

'Dismal sort of abode,' said Tommy. 'It gives me the creeps, Tuppence. You know, I've a feeling this is going to turn out a far more serious matter than we thought at first.'

'Oh, don't. If only we are in time. That woman's in some awful danger; I feel it in my bones.'

'Don't let your imagination run away with you.'

'I can't help it. I mistrust that man. What shall we do? I think it would be a good plan if I went and rang the bell alone first and asked boldly for Mrs Leigh Gordon just to see what answer I get. Because, after all, it may be perfectly fair and above board.'

Tuppence carried out her plan. The door was opened almost immediately by a manservant with an impassive face.

'I want to see Mrs Leigh Gordon, if she is well enough to see me.'

She fancied that there was a momentary flicker of the man's eyelashes, but he answered readily enough.

'There is no one of that name here, madam.'

'Oh, surely. This is Doctor Horriston's place, The Grange, is it not?'

'Yes, madam, but there is nobody of the name of Mrs Leigh Gordon here.'

Baffled, Tuppence was forced to withdraw and hold a further consultation with Tommy outside the gate.

'Perhaps he was speaking the truth. After all, we don't *know*.'

'He wasn't. He was lying. I'm sure of it.'

'Wait until the doctor comes back,' said Tommy. 'Then I'll pass myself off as a journalist anxious to discuss his new system of rest cure with him. That will give me a chance of getting inside and studying the geography of the place.'

The doctor returned about half an hour later. Tommy gave him about five minutes, then he in turn marched up to the front door. But he too returned baffled.

'The doctor was engaged and couldn't be disturbed. And he never sees journalists. Tuppence, you're right. There's something fishy about this place. It's ideally situated – miles from anywhere. Any mortal thing could go on here, and no one would ever know.'

'Come on,' said Tuppence, with determination.

'What are you going to do?'

'I'm going to climb over the wall and see if I can't get up to the house quietly without being seen.'

'Right. I'm with you.'

The garden was somewhat overgrown and afforded a multitude of cover. Tommy and Tuppence managed to reach the back of the house unobserved.

Here there was a wide terrace with some crumbling steps leading down from it. In the middle some french windows opened on to the terrace, but they dared not step out into the open, and the windows where they were crouching were too high for them to be able to look in. It did not seem as though their reconnaissance would be much use, when suddenly Tuppence tightened her grasp of Tommy's arm.

Someone was speaking in the room close to them. The window was open and the fragment of conversation came clearly to their ears.

'Come in, come in, and shut the door,' said a man's voice irritably. 'A lady came about an hour ago, you said, and asked for Mrs Leigh Gordon?'

Tuppence recognised the answering voice as that of the impassive manservant.

'Yes, sir.'

'You said she wasn't here, of course?'

'Of course, sir.'

'And now this journalist fellow,' fumed the other.

He came suddenly to the window, throwing up the sash, and the two outside, peering through a screen of bushes, recognised Dr Horriston.

'It's the woman I mind most about,' continued the doctor. 'What did she look like?'

'Young, good-looking, and very smartly dressed, sir.'

Tommy nudged Tuppence in the ribs.

'Exactly,' said the doctor between his teeth, 'as I feared. Some friend of the Leigh Gordon woman's. It's getting very difficult. I shall have to take steps –'

He left the sentence unfinished. Tommy and Tuppence heard the door close. There was silence.

Gingerly Tommy led the retreat. When they had reached a little clearing not far away, but out of earshot from the house, he spoke.

'Tuppence, old thing, this is getting serious. They mean mischief. I think we ought to get back to town at once and see Stavansson.'

To his surprise Tuppence shook her head.

'We must stay down here. Didn't you hear him say he was going to take steps – That might mean anything.'

'The worst of it is we've hardly got a case to go to the police on.'

'Listen, Tommy. Why not ring up Stavansson from the village? I'll stay around here.'

'Perhaps that is the best plan,' agreed her husband. 'But I say – Tuppence –'

'Well?'

'Take care of yourself – won't you?'

'Of course I shall, you silly old thing. Cut along.'

It was some two hours later that Tommy returned. He found Tuppence awaiting him near the gate.

'Well?'

'I couldn't get on to Stavansson. Then I tried Lady Susan. She was out too. Then I thought of ringing up old Brady. I asked him to look up Horriston in the Medical Directory or whatever the thing calls itself.'

'Well, what did Dr Brady say?'

'Oh, he knew the name at once. Horriston was once a *bona fide* doctor, but he came a cropper of some kind. Brady called him a most unscrupulous quack, and said he, personally, wouldn't be surprised at anything. The question is, what are we to do now?'

'We must stay here,' said Tuppence instantly. 'I've a feeling they mean something to happen tonight. By the way, a gardener has been clipping ivy round the house. Tommy, *I saw where he put the ladder.*'

'Good for you, Tuppence,' said her husband appreciatively. 'Then tonight –'

'As soon as it's dark –'

'We shall see –'

'What we shall see.'

Tommy took his turn at watching the house whilst Tuppence went to the village and had some food.

Then she returned and they took up the vigil together. At nine o'clock they decided that it was dark enough to commence operations. They were now able to circle round the house in perfect freedom. Suddenly Tuppence clutched Tommy by the arm.

'Listen.'

The sound she had heard came again, borne faintly on the night air. It was the moan of a woman in pain. Tuppence pointed upward to a window on the first floor.

'It came from that room,' she whispered.

Again that low moan rent the stillness of the night.

The two listeners decided to put their original plan into action. Tuppence led the way to where she had seen the gardener put the ladder. Between them they carried it to the side of the house from which they had heard the moaning. All the blinds of the ground floor rooms were drawn, but this particular window upstairs was unshuttered.

Tommy put the ladder as noiselessly as possible against the side of the house.

'I'll go up,' whispered Tuppence. 'You stay below. I don't mind climbing ladders and you can steady it better than I could. And in case the doctor should come round the corner you'd be able to deal with him and I shouldn't.'

Nimbly Tuppence swarmed up the ladder and raised her head cautiously to look in at the window. Then she ducked it swiftly, but after a minute or two brought it very slowly up again. She stayed there for about five minutes. Then she descended again.

'It's her,' she said breathlessly and ungrammatically. 'But, oh, Tommy, it's horrible. She's lying there in bed, moaning, and turning to and fro – and just as I got there a woman dressed as a nurse came in. She bent over her and injected something in her arm and then went away again. What shall we do?'

'Is she conscious?'

'I think so. I'm almost sure she is. I fancy she may be strapped to the bed. I'm going up again, and if I can I'm going to get into that room.'

'I say, Tuppence –'

'If I'm in any sort of danger, I'll yell for you. So long.'

Avoiding further argument Tuppence hurried up the ladder again. Tommy saw her try the window, then noiselessly push up the sash. Another second and she had disappeared inside.

And now an agonising time came for Tommy. He could hear nothing at first. Tuppence and Mrs Leigh Gordon must be talking in whispers if they were talking at all. Presently he did hear a low murmur of voices and drew a breath of relief. But suddenly the voices stopped. Dead silence.

Tommy strained his ears. Nothing. What could they be doing?

Suddenly a hand fell on his shoulder.

'Come on,' said Tuppence's voice out of the darkness.

'Tuppence! How did you get here?'

'Through the front door. Let's get out of this.'

'Get out of this?'

'That's what I said.'

'But – Mrs Leigh Gordon?'

In a tone of indescribable bitterness Tuppence replied:

'Getting thin!'

Tommy looked at her, suspecting irony.

'What do you mean?'

'What I say. Getting thin. Slinkiness. Reduction of weight. Didn't you hear Stavansson say he hated fat women? In the two years he's been away, his Hermy has put on weight. Got a panic when she knew he was coming back and rushed off to do this new treatment of Dr Horriston's. It's injections of some sort, and he makes a deadly secret of it, and charges through the nose. I dare say he is a quack – but he's a damned successful one!

Stavansson comes home a fortnight too soon, when she's only beginning the treatment. Lady Susan has been sworn to secrecy and plays up. And we come down here and make blithering idiots of ourselves!'

Tommy drew a deep breath.

'I believe, Watson,' he said with dignity, 'that there is a very good concert at the Queen's Hall tomorrow. We shall be in plenty of time for it. And you will oblige me by not placing this case upon your records. It has absolutely *no* distinctive features.'

Blindman's Buff

'Blindman's Buff' was first published as 'Blind Man's Buff' in *The Sketch*, 26 November 1924. Thornley Colton was created by Clinton H. Stagg (1890–1916).

'Right,' said Tommy, and replaced the receiver on its hook.

Then he turned to Tuppence.

'That was the Chief. Seems to have got the wind up about us. It appears that the parties we're after have got wise to the fact that I'm not the genuine Mr Theodore Blunt. We're to expect excitements at any minute. The Chief begs you as a favour to go home and stay at home, and not mix yourself up in it any more. Apparently the hornet's nest we've stirred up is bigger than anyone imagined.'

'All that about my going home is nonsense,' said Tuppence decidedly. 'Who is going to look after you if I go home? Besides, I like excitement. Business hasn't been very brisk just lately.'

'Well, one can't have murders and robberies every day,' said Tommy. 'Be reasonable. Now, my idea is this. When business is slack, we ought to do a certain amount of home exercises every day.'

'Lie on our backs and wave our feet in the air? That sort of thing?'

'Don't be so literal in your interpretation. When I say exercises, I mean exercises in the detective art. Reproductions of the great masters. For instance –'

From the drawer beside him Tommy took out a formidable dark green eyeshade, covering both eyes. This he adjusted with some care. Then he drew a watch from his pocket.

'I broke the glass this morning,' he remarked. 'That paved the way for its being the crystalless watch which my sensitive fingers touch so lightly.'

'Be careful,' said Tuppence. 'You nearly had the short hand off then.'

'Give me your hand,' said Tommy. He held it, one finger feeling for the pulse. 'Ah! the keyboard of silence. This woman has *not* got heart disease.'

'I suppose,' said Tuppence, 'that you are Thornley Colton?'

'Just so,' said Tommy. 'The blind Problemist. And you're thingummy-bob, the black haired, apple-cheeked secretary –'

'The bundle of baby clothes picked up on the banks of the river,' finished Tuppence.

'And Albert is the Fee, alias Shrimp.'

'We must teach him to say, "Gee,"' said Tuppence. 'And his voice isn't shrill. It's dreadfully hoarse.'

'Against the wall by the door,' said Tommy, 'you perceive the slim hollow cane which held in my sensitive hand tells me so much.'

He rose and cannoned into a chair.

'Damn!' said Tommy. 'I forgot that chair was there.'

'It must be beastly to be blind,' said Tuppence with feeling.

'Rather,' agreed Tommy heartily. 'I'm sorrier for all those poor devils who lost their eyesight in the war than for anyone else. But they say that when you live in the dark you really do develop special senses. That's what I want to try and see if one couldn't do. It would be jolly handy to train oneself to be some good in the dark. Now, Tuppence, be a good Sydney Thames. How many steps to that cane?'

Tuppence made a desperate guess.

'Three straight, five left,' she hazarded.

Tommy paced it uncertainly, Tuppence interrupting with a cry of warning as she realised that the fourth step left would take him slap against the wall.

'There's a lot in this,' said Tuppence. 'You've no idea how difficult it is to judge how many steps are needed.'

'It's jolly interesting,' said Tommy. 'Call Albert in. I'm going to shake hands with you both, and see if I know which is which.'

'All right,' said Tuppence, 'but Albert must wash his hands first. They're sure to be sticky from those beastly acid drops he's always eating.'

Albert, introduced to the game, was full of interest.

Tommy, the handshakes completed, smiled complacently.

'The keyboard of silence cannot lie,' he murmured. 'The first was Albert, the second, you, Tuppence.'

'Wrong!' shrieked Tuppence. 'Keyboard of silence indeed! You went by my dress ring. And I put that on Albert's finger.'

Various other experiments were carried out, with indifferent success.

'But it's coming,' declared Tommy. 'One can't expect to be infallible straight away. I tell you what. It's just lunch time. You and I will go to

the Blitz, Tuppence. Blind man and his keeper. Some jolly useful tips to
be picked up there.'

'I say, Tommy, we shall get into trouble.'

'No, we shan't. I shall behave quite like the little gentleman. But I bet
you that by the end of luncheon I shall be startling you.'

All protests being thus overborne, a quarter of an hour later saw
Tommy and Tuppence comfortably ensconced at a corner table in the
Gold Room of the Blitz.

Tommy ran his fingers lightly over the Menu.

'Pilaff de homar and grilled chicken for me,' he murmured.

Tuppence also made her selection, and the waiter moved away.

'So far, so good,' said Tommy. 'Now for a more ambitious venture.
What beautiful legs that girl in the short skirt has – the one who has just
come in.'

'How was that done, Thorn?'

'Beautiful legs impart a particular vibration to the floor, which is
received by my hollow cane. Or, to be honest, in a big restaurant there
is nearly always a girl with beautiful legs standing in the doorway looking
for her friends, and with short skirts going about, she'd be sure to take
advantage of them.'

The meal proceeded.

'The man two tables from us is a very wealthy profiteer, I fancy,' said
Tommy carelessly. 'Jew, isn't he?'

'Pretty good,' said Tuppence appreciatively. 'I don't follow that one.'

'I shan't tell you how it's done every time. It spoils my show. The head
waiter is serving champagne three tables off to the right. A stout woman
in black is about to pass our table.'

'Tommy, how can you –'

'Aha! You're beginning to see what I can do. That's a nice girl in brown
just getting up at the table behind you.'

'Snoo!' said Tuppence. 'It's a young man in grey.'

'Oh!' said Tommy, momentarily disconcerted.

And at that moment two men who had been sitting at a table not far
away, and who had been watching the young pair with keen interest, got
up and came across to the corner table.

'Excuse me,' said the elder of the two, a tall, well-dressed man with
an eyeglass, and a small grey moustache. 'But you have been pointed out
to me as Mr Theodore Blunt. May I ask if that is so?'

Tommy hesitated a minute, feeling somewhat at a disadvantage. Then
he bowed his head.

'That is so. I am Mr Blunt!'

'What an unexpected piece of good fortune! Mr Blunt, I was going to call at your offices after lunch. I am in trouble – very grave trouble. But – excuse me – you have had some accident to your eyes?'

'My dear sir,' said Tommy in a melancholy voice, 'I'm blind – completely blind.'

'What?'

'You are astonished. But surely you have heard of blind detectives?'

'In fiction. Never in real life. And I have certainly never heard that you were blind.'

'Many people are not aware of the fact,' murmured Tommy. 'I am wearing an eyeshade today to save my eyeballs from glare. But without it, quite a host of people have never suspected my infirmity – if you call it that. You see, my eyes cannot mislead me. But, enough of all this. Shall we go at once to my office, or will you give me the facts of the case here? The latter would be best, I think.'

A waiter brought up two extra chairs, and the two men sat down. The second man who had not yet spoken, was shorter, sturdy in build, and very dark.

'It is a matter of great delicacy,' said the older man dropping his voice confidentially. He looked uncertainly at Tuppence. Mr Blunt seemed to feel the glance.

'Let me introduce my confidential secretary,' he said. 'Miss Ganges. Found on the banks of the Indian river – a mere bundle of baby clothes. Very sad history. Miss Ganges is my eyes. She accompanies me everywhere.'

The stranger acknowledged the introduction with a bow.

'Then I can speak out. Mr Blunt, my daughter, a girl of sixteen, has been abducted under somewhat peculiar circumstances. I discovered this half an hour ago. The circumstances of the case were such that I dared not call in the police. Instead, I rang up your office. They told me you were out to lunch, but would be back by half-past two. I came in here with my friend, Captain Harker –'

The short man jerked his head and muttered something.

'By the greatest good fortune you happened to be lunching here also. We must lose no time. You must return with me to my house immediately.'

Tommy demurred cautiously.

'I can be with you in half an hour. I must return to my office first.'

Captain Harker, turning to glance at Tuppence, may have been surprised to see a half smile lurking for a moment at the corners of her mouth.

'No, no, that will not do. You must return with me.' The grey-haired man took a card from his pocket and handed it across the table. 'That is my name.'

Tommy fingered it.

'My fingers are hardly sensitive enough for that,' he said with a smile, and handed it to Tuppence, who read out in a low voice: 'The Duke of Blairgowrie.'

She looked with great interest at their client. The Duke of Blairgowrie was well known to be a most haughty and inaccessible nobleman who had married as a wife, the daughter of a Chicago pork butcher, many years younger than himself, and of a lively temperament that augured ill for their future together. There had been rumours of disaccord lately.

'You will come at once, Mr Blunt?' said the Duke, with a tinge of acerbity in his manner.

Tommy yielded to the inevitable.

'Miss Ganges and I will come with you,' he said quietly. 'You will excuse my just stopping to drink a large cup of black coffee? They will serve it immediately. I am subject to very distressing headaches, the result of my eye trouble, and the coffee steadies my nerves.'

He called a waiter and gave the order. Then he spoke to Tuppence.

'Miss Ganges – I am lunching here tomorrow with the French Prefect of Police. Just note down the luncheon, and give it to the head waiter with instructions to reserve me my usual table. I am assisting the French police in an important case. *The fee*' – he paused – 'is considerable. Are you ready, Miss Ganges.'

'Quite ready,' said Tuppence, her stylo poised.

'We will start with that special salad of shrimps that they have here. Then to follow – let me see, *to follow* – Yes, Omelette Blitz, and perhaps a couple of *Tournedos à l'Etranger*.'

He paused and murmured apologetically:

'You will forgive me, I hope. Ah! yes, *Souffle en surprise*. That will conclude the repast. A most interesting man, the French Prefect. You know him, perhaps?'

The other replied in the negative, as Tuppence rose and went to speak to the head waiter. Presently she returned, just as the coffee was brought.

Tommy drank a large cup of it, sipping it slowly, then rose.

'My cane, Miss Ganges? Thank you. Directions, please?'

It was a moment of agony for Tuppence.

'One right, eighteen straight. About the fifth step, there is a waiter serving the table on your left.'

Swinging his cane jauntily, Tommy set out. Tuppence kept close beside him, and endeavoured unobtrusively to steer him. All went well until they were just passing out through the doorway. A man entered rather hurriedly, and before Tuppence could warn the blind Mr Blunt, he had barged right into the newcomer. Explanations and apologies ensued.

At the door of the Blitz, a smart landaulette was waiting. The Duke himself aided Mr Blunt to get in.

'Your car here, Harker?' he asked over his shoulder.

'Yes. Just round the corner.'

'Take Miss Ganges in it, will you.'

Before another word could be said, he had jumped in beside Tommy, and the car rolled smoothly away.

'A very delicate matter,' murmured the Duke. 'I can soon acquaint you with all the details.'

Tommy raised his hand to his head.

'I can remove my eyeshade now,' he observed pleasantly. 'It was only the glare of artificial light in the restaurant necessitated its use.'

But his arm was jerked down sharply. At the same time he felt something hard and round being poked between his ribs.

'No, my dear Mr Blunt,' said the Duke's voice – but a voice that seemed suddenly different. 'You will not remove that eyeshade. You will sit perfectly still and not move in any way. You understand? I don't want this pistol of mine to go off. You see, I happen not to be the Duke of Blairgowrie at all. I borrowed his name for the occasion, knowing that you would not refuse to accompany such a celebrated client. I am something much more prosaic – a ham merchant who has lost his wife.'

He felt the start the other gave.

'That tells you something,' he laughed. 'My dear young man, you have been incredibly foolish. I'm afraid – I'm very much afraid that your activities will be curtailed in future.'

He spoke the last words with a sinister relish.

Tommy sat motionless. He did not reply to the other's taunts.

Presently the car slackened its pace and drew up.

'Just a minute,' said the pseudo Duke. He twisted a handkerchief deftly into Tommy's mouth, and drew up his scarf over it.

'In case you should be foolish enough to think of calling for help,' he explained suavely.

The door of the car opened and the chauffeur stood ready. He and his master took Tommy between them and propelled him rapidly up some steps and in at the door of a house.

The door closed behind them. There was a rich oriental smell in the air. Tommy's feet sank deep into velvet pile. He was propelled in the same fashion up a flight of stairs and into a room which he judged to be at the back of the house. Here the two men bound his hands together. The chauffeur went out again, and the other removed the gag.

'You may speak freely now,' he announced pleasantly. 'What have you to say for yourself, young man?'

Tommy cleared his throat and eased the aching corners of his mouth.

'I hope you haven't lost my hollow cane,' he said mildly. 'It cost me a lot to have that made.'

'You have nerve,' said the other, after a minute's pause. 'Or else you are just a fool. Don't you understand that I have got you – got you in the hollow of my hand? That you're absolutely in my power? That no one who knows you is ever likely to see you again.'

'Can't you cut out the melodrama?' asked Tommy plaintively. 'Have I got to say, "You villain, I'll foil you yet"? That sort of thing is so very much out of date.'

'What about the girl?' said the other, watching him. 'Doesn't that move you?'

'Putting two and two together during my enforced silence just now,' said Tommy. 'I have come to the inevitable conclusion that that chatty lad Harker is another of the doers of desperate deeds, and that therefore my unfortunate secretary will shortly join this little tea party.'

'Right as to one point, but wrong on the other. Mrs Beresford – you see, I know all about you – Mrs Beresford will not be brought here. That is a little precaution I took. It occurred to me that just probably your friends in high places might be keeping you shadowed. In that case, by dividing the pursuit, you could not both be trailed. I should still keep one in my hands. I am waiting now –'

He broke off as the door opened. The chauffeur spoke.

'We've not been followed, sir. It's all clear.'

'Good. You can go, Gregory.'

The door closed again.

'So far, so good,' said the 'Duke.' 'And now what are we to do with you, Mr Beresford Blunt?'

'I wish you'd take this confounded eyeshade off me,' said Tommy.

'I think not. With it on, you are truly blind – without it you would see as well as I do – and that would not suit my little plan. For I have a plan. You are fond of sensational fiction, Mr Blunt. This little game that you and your wife were playing today proves that. Now I, too, have arranged a little game – something rather ingenious, as I am sure you will admit when I explain it to you.

'You see, this floor on which you are standing is made of metal, and here and there on its surface are little projections. I touch a switch – so.' A sharp click sounded. 'Now the electric current is switched on. To tread on one of those little knobs now means – death! You understand? If you could see . . . but you cannot see. You are in the dark. That is the game – Blindman's Buff with death. If you can reach the door in safety – freedom! But I think that long before you reach it you will have

trodden on one of the danger spots. And that will be very amusing –
for me!'

He came forward and unbound Tommy's hands. Then he handed him
his cane with a little ironical bow.

'The blind Problemist. Let us see if he will solve this problem. I shall
stand here with my pistol ready. If you raise your hands to your head to
remove that eyeshade, I shoot. Is that clear?'

'Perfectly clear,' said Tommy. He was rather pale, but determined. 'I
haven't a dog's chance, I suppose?'

'Oh! that –' the other shrugged his shoulders.

'Damned ingenious devil, aren't you?' said Tommy. 'But you've
forgotten one thing. May I light a cigarette by the way? My poor little
heart's going pit-a-pat.'

'You may light a cigarette – but no tricks. I am watching you, remember,
with the pistol ready.'

'I'm not a performing dog,' said Tommy. 'I don't do tricks.' He extracted
a cigarette from his case, then felt for a match box. 'It's all right. I'm not
feeling for a revolver. But you know well enough that I'm not armed. All
the same, as I said before, you've forgotten one thing.'

'What is that?'

Tommy took a match from the box, and held it ready to strike.

'I'm blind and you can see. That's admitted. The advantage is with
you. But supposing we were both in the dark – eh? Where's your advantage then?'

He struck the match.

'Thinking of shooting at the switch of the lights? Plunging the room
into darkness? It can't be done.'

'Just so,' said Tommy. 'I can't give you darkness. But extremes meet,
you know. What about *light*?'

As he spoke, he touched the match to something he held in his hand,
and threw it down upon the table.

A blinding glare filled the room.

Just for a minute, blinded by the intense white light, the 'Duke' blinked
and fell back, his pistol hand lowered.

He opened his eyes again to feel something sharp pricking his
breast.

'Drop that pistol,' ordered Tommy. 'Drop it quick. I agree with you
that a hollow cane is a pretty rotten affair. So I didn't get one. A good
sword stick is a very useful weapon, though. Don't you think so? Almost
as useful as magnesium wire. *Drop that pistol.*'

Obedient to the necessity of that sharp point, the man dropped it.
Then, with a laugh, he sprang back.

'But I still have the advantage,' he mocked. 'For I can see, and you cannot.'

'That's where you're wrong,' said Tommy. 'I can see perfectly. The eyeshade's a fake. I was going to put one over on Tuppence. Make one or two bloomers to begin with, and then put in some perfectly marvellous stuff towards the end of lunch. Why, bless you, I could have walked to the door and avoided all the knobs with perfect ease. But I didn't trust you to play a sporting game. You'd never have let me get out of this alive. Careful now –'

For, with his face distorted with rage, the 'Duke' sprang forward, forgetting in his fury to look where he put his feet.

There was a sudden blue crackle of flame, and he swayed for a minute, then fell like a log. A faint odour of singed flesh filled the room, mingling with a stronger smell of ozone.'

'Whew,' said Tommy.

He wiped his face.

Then, moving gingerly, and with every precaution, he reached the wall, and touched the switch he had seen the other manipulate.

He crossed the room to the door, opened it carefully, and looked out. There was no one about. He went down the stairs and out through the front door.

Safe in the street, he looked up at the house with a shudder, noting the number. Then he hurried to the nearest telephone box.

There was a moment of agonising anxiety, and then a well-known voice spoke.

'Tuppence, thank goodness!'

'Yes, I'm all right. I got all your points. The Fee, Shrimp, Come to the Blitz and follow the two strangers. Albert got there in time, and when we went off in separate cars, followed me in a taxi, saw where they took me, and rang up the police.'

'Albert's a good lad,' said Tommy. 'Chivalrous. I was pretty sure he'd choose to follow you. But I've been worried, all the same. I've got lots to tell you. I'm coming straight back now. And the first thing I shall do when I get back is to write a thumping big cheque for St Dunstan's. Lord, it must be awful not to be able to see.'

The Man in the Mist

'The Man in the Mist' was first published in *The Sketch*, 3 December 1924. Father Brown was created by G. K. Chesterton (1874–1936).

Tommy was not pleased with life. Blunt's Brilliant Detectives had met with a reverse, distressing to their pride if not to their pockets. Called in professionally to elucidate the mystery of a stolen pearl necklace at Adlington Hall, Adlington, Blunt's Brilliant Detectives had failed to make good. Whilst Tommy, hard on the track of a gambling Countess, was tracking her in the disguise of a Roman Catholic priest, and Tuppence was 'getting off' with the nephew of the house on the golf links, the local Inspector of Police had unemotionally arrested the second footman who proved to be a thief well known at headquarters, and who admitted his guilt without making any bones about it.

Tommy and Tuppence, therefore, had withdrawn with what dignity they could muster, and were at the present moment solacing themselves with cocktails at the Grand Adlington Hotel. Tommy still wore his clerical disguise.

'Hardly a Father Brown touch, that,' he remarked gloomily. 'And yet I've got just the right kind of umbrella.'

'It wasn't a Father Brown problem,' said Tuppence. 'One needs a certain atmosphere from the start. One must be doing something quite ordinary, and then bizarre things begin to happen. That's the idea.'

'Unfortunately,' said Tommy, 'we have to return to town. Perhaps something bizarre will happen on the way to the station.'

He raised the glass he was holding to his lips, but the liquid in it was suddenly spilled, as a heavy hand smacked him on the shoulder, and a voice to match the hand boomed out words of greeting.

'Upon my soul, it is! Old Tommy! And Mrs Tommy too. Where did you blow in from? Haven't seen or heard anything of you for years.'

'Why, it's Bulger!' said Tommy, setting down what was left of the

cocktail, and turning to look at the intruder, a big square-shouldered man
of thirty years of age, with a round red beaming face, and dressed in
golfing kit. 'Good old Bulger!'

'But I say, old chap,' said Bulger (whose real name, by the way, was
Marvyn Estcourt), 'I never knew you'd taken orders. Fancy you a blinking
parson.'

Tuppence burst out laughing, and Tommy looked embarrassed. And
then they suddenly became conscious of a fourth person.

A tall, slender creature, with very golden hair and very round blue
eyes, almost impossibly beautiful, with an effect of really expensive black
topped by wonderful ermines, and very large pearl earrings. She was
smiling. And her smile said many things. It asserted, for instance, that
she knew perfectly well that she herself was the thing best worth looking
at, certainly in England, and possibly in the whole world. She was not vain
about it in any way, but she just knew, with certainty and confidence,
that it was so.

Both Tommy and Tuppence recognised her immediately. They had
seen her three times in *The Secret of the Heart*, and an equal number of
times in that other great success, *Pillars of Fire*, and in innumerable other
plays. There was, perhaps, no other actress in England who had so firm
a hold on the British public, as Miss Gilda Glen. She was reported to
be the most beautiful woman in England. It was also rumoured that she
was the stupidest.

'Old friends of mine, Miss Glen,' said Estcourt, with a tinge of apology
in his voice for having presumed, even for a moment, to forget such a
radiant creature. 'Tommy and Mrs Tommy, let me introduce you to Miss
Gilda Glen.'

The ring of pride in his voice was unmistakable. By merely being seen
in his company, Miss Glen had conferred great glory upon him.

The actress was staring with frank interest at Tommy.

'Are you really a priest?' she asked. 'A Roman Catholic priest, I mean?
Because I thought they didn't have wives.'

Estcourt went off in a boom of laughter again.

'That's good,' he exploded. 'You sly dog, Tommy. Glad he hasn't
renounced you, Mrs Tommy, with all the rest of the pomps and vanities.'

Gilda Glen took not the faintest notice of him. She continued to stare
at Tommy with puzzled eyes.

'Are you a priest?' she demanded.

'Very few of us are what we seem to be,' said Tommy gently. 'My
profession is not unlike that of a priest. I don't give absolution – but I
listen to confessions – I –'

'Don't you listen to him,' interrupted Estcourt. 'He's pulling your leg.'

'If you're not a clergyman, I don't see why you're dressed up like one,' she puzzled. 'That is, unless –'

'Not a criminal flying from justice,' said Tommy. 'The other thing.'

'Oh!' she frowned, and looked at him with beautiful bewildered eyes.

'I wonder if she'll ever get that,' thought Tommy to himself. 'Not unless I put it in words of one syllable for her, I should say.'

Aloud he said:

'Know anything about the trains back to town, Bulger? We've got to be pushing for home. How far is it to the station?'

'Ten minutes' walk. But no hurry. Next train up is the 6.35 and it's only about twenty to six now. You've just missed one.'

'Which way is it to the station from here?'

'Sharp to the left when you turn out of the hotel. Then – let me see – down Morgan's Avenue would be the best way, wouldn't it?'

'Morgan's Avenue?' Miss Glen started violently, and stared at him with startled eyes.

'I know what you're thinking of,' said Estcourt, laughing. 'The Ghost. Morgan's Avenue is bounded by the cemetery on one side, and tradition has it that a policeman who met his death by violence gets up and walks on his old beat, up and down Morgan's Avenue. A spook policeman! Can you beat it? But lots of people swear to having seen him.'

'A policeman?' said Miss Glen. She shivered a little. 'But there aren't really any ghosts, are there? I mean – there aren't such things?'

She got up, folding her wrap tighter round her.

'Goodbye,' she said vaguely.

She had ignored Tuppence completely throughout, and now she did not even glance in her direction. But, over her shoulder, she threw one puzzled questioning glance at Tommy.

Just as she got to the door, she encountered a tall man with grey hair and a puffy face, who uttered an exclamation of surprise. His hand on her arm, he led her through the doorway, talking in an animated fashion.

'Beautiful creature, isn't she?' said Estcourt. 'Brains of a rabbit. Rumour has it that she's going to marry Lord Leconbury. That was Leconbury in the doorway.'

'He doesn't look a very nice sort of man to marry,' remarked Tuppence.

Estcourt shrugged his shoulders.

'A title has a kind of glamour still, I suppose,' he said. 'And Leconbury is not an impoverished peer by any means. She'll be in clover. Nobody knows where she sprang from. Pretty near the gutter, I dare say. There's something deuced mysterious about her being down here anyway. She's not staying at the hotel. And when I tried to find out where she was staying, she snubbed me – snubbed me quite crudely, in the only way she knows. Blessed if I know what it's all about.'

He glanced at his watch and uttered an exclamation.

'I must be off. Jolly glad to have seen you two again. We must have a bust in town together some night. So long.'

He hurried away, and as he did so, a page approached with a note on a salver. The note was unaddressed.

'But it's for you, sir,' he said to Tommy. 'From Miss Gilda Glen.'

Tommy tore it open and read it with some curiosity. Inside were a few lines written in a straggling untidy hand.

I'm not sure, but I think you might be able to help me. And you'll be going that way to the station. Could you be at The White House, Morgan's Avenue, at ten minutes past six?
   Yours sincerely,
   Gilda Glen.

Tommy nodded to the page, who departed, and then handed the note to Tuppence.

'Extraordinary!' said Tuppence. 'Is it because she still thinks you're a priest?'

'No,' said Tommy thoughtfully. 'I should say it's because she's at last taken in that I'm not one. Hullo! what's this?'

'This,' was a young man with flaming red hair, a pugnacious jaw, and appallingly shabby clothes. He had walked into the room and was now striding up and down muttering to himself.

'Hell!' said the red-haired man, loudly and forcibly. 'That's what I say – Hell!'

He dropped into a chair near the young couple and stared at them moodily.

'Damn all women, that's what I say,' said the young man, eyeing Tuppence ferociously. 'Oh! all right, kick up a row if you like. Have me turned out of the hotel. It won't be for the first time. Why shouldn't we say what we think? Why should we go about bottling up our feelings, and smirking, and saying things exactly like everyone else. I don't feel pleasant and polite. I feel like getting hold of someone round the throat and gradually choking them to death.'

He paused.

'Any particular person?' asked Tuppence. 'Or just anybody?'

'One particular person,' said the young man grimly.

'This is very interesting,' said Tuppence. 'Won't you tell us some more?'

'My name's Reilly,' said the red-haired man. 'James Reilly. You may have heard it. I wrote a little volume of Pacifist poems – good stuff, although I say so.'

'*Pacifist poems?*' said Tuppence.

'Yes – why not?' demanded Mr Reilly belligerently.

'Oh! nothing,' said Tuppence hastily.

'I'm for peace all the time,' said Mr Reilly fiercely. 'To Hell with war. And women! Women! Did you see that creature who was trailing around here just now? Gilda Glen, she calls herself. Gilda Glen! God! how I've worshipped that woman. And I'll tell you this – if she's got a heart at all, it's on my side. She cared once for me, and I could make her care again. And if she sells herself to that muck heap, Leconbury – well, God help her. I'd as soon kill her with my own hands.'

And on this, suddenly, he rose and rushed from the room.

Tommy raised his eyebrows.

'A somewhat excitable gentleman,' he murmured. 'Well, Tuppence, shall we start?'

A fine mist was coming up as they emerged from the hotel into the cool outer air. Obeying Estcourt's directions, they turned sharp to the left, and in a few minutes they came to a turning labelled Morgan's Avenue.

The mist had increased. It was soft and white, and hurried past them in little eddying drifts. To their left was the high wall of the cemetery, on their right a row of small houses. Presently these ceased, and a high hedge took their place.

'Tommy,' said Tuppence. 'I'm beginning to feel jumpy. The mist – and the silence. As though we were miles from anywhere.'

'One does feel like that,' agreed Tommy. 'All alone in the world. It's the effect of the mist, and not being able to see ahead of one.'

Tuppence nodded.

'Just our footsteps echoing on the pavement. What's that?'

'What's what?'

'I thought I heard other footsteps behind us.'

'You'll be seeing the ghost in a minute if you work yourself up like this,' said Tommy kindly. 'Don't be so nervy. Are you afraid the spook policeman will lay his hands on your shoulder?'

Tuppence emitted a shrill squeal.

'Don't, Tommy. Now you've put it into my head.'

She craned her head back over her shoulder, trying to peer into the white veil that was wrapped all round them.

'There they are again,' she whispered. 'No, they're in front now. Oh! Tommy, don't say you can't hear them?'

'I do hear something. Yes, it's footsteps behind us. Somebody else walking this way to catch the train. I wonder –'

He stopped suddenly, and stood still, and Tuppence gave a gasp.

For the curtain of mist in front of them suddenly parted in the most
artificial manner, and there, not twenty feet away, a gigantic policeman
suddenly appeared, as though materialised out of the fog. One minute
he was not there, the next minute he was – so at least it seemed to the
rather superheated imaginations of the two watchers. Then as the mist
rolled back still more, a little scene appeared, as though set on a stage.

The big blue policeman, a scarlet pillar box, and on the right of the
road the outlines of a white house.

'Red, white, and blue,' said Tommy. 'It's damned pictorial. Come on,
Tuppence, there's nothing to be afraid of.'

For, as he had already seen, the policeman was a real policeman. And,
moreover, he was not nearly so gigantic as he had at first seemed looming
up out of the mist.

But as they started forward, footsteps came from behind them. A man
passed them, hurrying along. He turned in at the gate of the white house,
ascended the steps, and beat a deafening tattoo upon the knocker. He
was admitted just as they reached the spot where the policeman was
standing staring after him.

'There's a gentleman seems to be in a hurry,' commented the policeman.

He spoke in a slow reflective voice, as one whose thoughts took some
time to mature.

'He's the sort of gentleman always would be in a hurry,' remarked
Tommy.

The policeman's stare, slow and rather suspicious, came round to rest
on his face.

'Friend of yours?' he demanded, and there was distinct suspicion now
in his voice.

'No,' said Tommy. 'He's not a friend of mine, but I happen to know
who he is. Name of Reilly.'

'Ah!' said the policeman. 'Well, I'd better be getting along.'

'Can you tell me where the White House is?' asked Tommy.

The constable jerked his head sideways.

'This is it. Mrs Honeycott's.' He paused, and added, evidently with
the idea of giving them valuable information, 'Nervous party. Always
suspecting burglars is around. Always asking me to have a look around
the place. Middle-aged women get like that.'

'Middle-aged, eh?' said Tommy. 'Do you happen to know if there's a
young lady staying there?'

'A young lady,' said the policeman, ruminating. 'A young lady. No, I
can't say I know anything about that.'

'She mayn't be staying here, Tommy,' said Tuppence. 'And anyway, she mayn't be here yet. She could only have started just before we did.'

'Ah!' said the policeman suddenly. 'Now that I call it to mind, a young lady did go in at this gate. I saw her as I was coming up the road. About three or four minutes ago it might be.'

'With ermine furs on?' asked Tuppence eagerly.

'She had some kind of white rabbit round her throat,' admitted the policeman.

Tuppence smiled. The policeman went on in the direction from which they had just come, and they prepared to enter the gate of the White House.

Suddenly, a faint, muffled cry sounded from inside the house, and almost immediately afterwards the front door opened and James Reilly came rushing down the steps. His face was white and twisted, and his eyes glared in front of him unseeingly. He staggered like a drunken man.

He passed Tommy and Tuppence as though he did not see them, muttering to himself with a kind of dreadful repetition.

'My God! My God! Oh, my God!'

He clutched at the gatepost, as though to steady himself, and then, as though animated by sudden panic, he raced off down the road as hard as he could go in the opposite direction from that taken by the policeman.

Tommy and Tuppence stared at each other in bewilderment.

'Well,' said Tommy, 'something's happened in that house to scare our friend Reilly pretty badly.'

Tuppence drew her finger absently across the gatepost.

'He must have put his hand on some wet red paint somewhere,' she said idly.

'H'm,' said Tommy. 'I think we'd better go inside rather quickly. I don't understand this business.'

In the doorway of the house a white-capped maid-servant was standing, almost speechless with indignation.

'Did you ever see the likes of that now, Father,' she burst out, as Tommy ascended the steps. 'That fellow comes here, asks for the young lady, rushes upstairs without how or by your leave. She lets out a screech like a wild cat – and what wonder, poor pretty dear, and straightaway he comes rushing down again, with the white face on him, like one who's seen a ghost. What will be the meaning of it all?'

'Who are you talking with at the front door, Ellen?' demanded a sharp voice from the interior of the hall.

'Here's Missus,' said Ellen, somewhat unnecessarily.

She drew back, and Tommy found himself confronting a grey-haired, middle-aged woman, with frosty blue eyes imperfectly concealed by pince-nez, and a spare figure clad in black with bugle trimming.

'Mrs Honeycott?' said Tommy. 'I came here to see Miss Glen.'

'Mrs Honeycott gave him a sharp glance, then went on to Tuppence and took in every detail of her appearance.

'Oh, you did, did you?' she said. 'Well, you'd better come inside.'

She led the way into the hall and along it into a room at the back of the house, facing on the garden. It was a fair-sized room, but looked smaller than it was, owing to the large amount of chairs and tables crowded into it. A big fire burned in the grate, and a chintz-covered sofa stood at one side of it. The wallpaper was a small grey stripe with a festoon of roses round the top. Quantities of engravings and oil paintings covered the walls.

It was a room almost impossible to associate with the expensive personality of Miss Gilda Glen.

'Sit down,' said Mrs Honeycott. 'To begin with, you'll excuse me if I say I don't hold with the Roman Catholic religion. Never did I think to see a Roman Catholic priest in my house. But if Gilda's gone over to the Scarlet Woman, it's only what's to be expected in a life like hers – and I dare say it might be worse. She mightn't have any religion at all. I should think more of Roman Catholics if their priests were married – I always speak my mind. And to think of those convents – quantities of beautiful young girls shut up there, and no one knowing what becomes of them – well, it won't bear thinking about.'

Mrs Honeycott came to a full stop, and drew a deep breath.

Without entering upon a defence of the celibacy of the priesthood or the other controversial points touched upon, Tommy went straight to the point.

'I understand, Mrs Honeycott, that Miss Glen is in this house.'

'She is. Mind you, I don't approve. Marriage is marriage and your husband's your husband. As you make your bed, so you must lie on it.'

'I don't quite understand –' began Tommy, bewildered.

'I thought as much. That's the reason I brought you in here. You can go up to Gilda after I've spoken my mind. She came to me – after all these years, think of it! – and asked me to help her. Wanted me to see this man and persuade him to agree to a divorce. I told her straight out I'd have nothing whatever to do with it. Divorce is sinful. But I couldn't refuse my own sister shelter in my house, could I now?'

'Your sister?' exclaimed Tommy.

'Yes, Gilda's my sister. Didn't she tell you?'

Tommy stared at her openmouthed. The thing seemed fantastically impossible. Then he remembered that the angelic beauty of Gilda Glen had been in evidence for many years. He had been taken to see her act as quite a small boy. Yes, it was possible after all. But what a piquant contrast. So it was from this lower middle-class respectability that Gilda Glen had sprung. How well she had guarded her secret!

'I am not yet quite clear,' he said. 'Your sister is married?'

'Ran away to be married as a girl of seventeen,' said Mrs Honeycott succinctly. 'Some common fellow far below her in station. And our father a reverend. It was a disgrace. Then she left her husband and went on the stage. Play-acting! I've never been inside a theatre in my life. I hold no truck with wickedness. Now, after all these years, she wants to divorce the man. Means to marry some big wig, I suppose. But her husband's standing firm – not to be bullied and not to be bribed – I admire him for it.'

'What is his name?' asked Tommy suddenly.

'That's an extraordinary thing now, but I can't remember! It's nearly twenty years ago, you know, since I heard it. My father forbade it to be mentioned. And I've refused to discuss the matter with Gilda. She knows what I think, and that's enough for her.'

'It wasn't Reilly, was it?'

'Might have been. I really can't say. It's gone clean out of my head.'

'The man I mean was here just now.'

'That man! I thought he was an escaped lunatic. I'd been in the kitchen giving orders to Ellen. I'd just got back into this room, and was wondering whether Gilda had come in yet (she has a latchkey), when I heard her. She hesitated a minute or two in the hall and then went straight upstairs. About three minutes later all this tremendous rat-tatting began. I went out into the hall, and just saw a man rushing upstairs. Then there was a sort of cry upstairs, and presently down he came again and rushed out like a madman. Pretty goings on.'

Tommy rose.

'Mrs Honeycott, let us go upstairs at once. I am afraid –'

'What of?'

'Afraid that you have no red wet paint in the house.'

Mrs Honeycott stared at him.

'Of course I haven't.'

'That is what I feared,' said Tommy gravely. 'Please let us go to your sister's room at once.'

Momentarily silenced, Mrs Honeycott led the way. They caught a glimpse of Ellen in the hall, backing hastily into one of the rooms.

Mrs Honeycott opened the first door at the top of the stairs. Tommy and Tuppence entered close behind her.

Suddenly she gave a gasp and fell back.

A motionless figure in black and ermine lay stretched on the sofa. The face was untouched, a beautiful soulless face like a mature child asleep. The wound was on the side of the head, a heavy blow with some blunt instrument had crushed in the skull. Blood was dripping slowly on to the floor, but the wound itself had long ceased to bleed . . .

Tommy examined the prostrate figure, his face very white.

'So,' he said at last, 'he didn't strangle her after all.'

'What do you mean? Who?' cried Mrs Honeycott. 'Is she dead?'

'Oh, yes, Mrs Honeycott, she's dead. Murdered. The question is – by whom? Not that it is much of a question. Funny – for all his ranting words, I didn't think the fellow had got it in him.'

He paused a minute, then turned to Tuppence with decision.

'Will you go out and get a policeman, or ring up the police station from somewhere?'

Tuppence nodded. She too, was very white. Tommy led Mrs Honeycott downstairs again.

'I don't want there to be any mistake about this,' he said. 'Do you know exactly what time it was when your sister came in?'

'Yes, I do,' said Mrs Honeycott. 'Because I was just setting the clock on five minutes as I have to do every evening. It loses just five minutes a day. It was exactly eight minutes past six by my watch, and that never loses or gains a second.'

Tommy nodded. That agreed perfectly with the policeman's story. He had seen the woman with the white furs go in at the gate, probably three minutes had elapsed before he and Tuppence had reached the same spot. He had glanced at his own watch then and had noted that it was just one minute after the time of their appointment.

There was just the faint chance that some one might have been waiting for Gilda Glen in the room upstairs. But if so, he must still be hiding in the house. No one but James Reilly had left it.

He ran upstairs and made a quick but efficient search of the premises. But there was no one concealed anywhere.

Then he spoke to Ellen. After breaking the news to her, and waiting for her first lamentations and invocations to the saints to have exhausted themselves, he asked a few questions.

Had any one else come to the house that afternoon asking for Miss Glen? No one whatsoever. Had she herself been upstairs at all that evening? Yes she'd gone up at six o'clock as usual to draw the curtains – or it might have been a few minutes after six. Anyway it was just before that wild fellow came breaking the knocker down. She'd run downstairs to answer the door. And him a black-hearted murderer all the time.

Tommy let it go at that. But he still felt a curious pity for Reilly, and unwillingness to believe the worst of him. And yet there was no one else who could have murdered Gilda Glen. Mrs Honeycott and Ellen had been the only two people in the house.

He heard voices in the hall, and went out to find Tuppence and the policeman from the beat outside. The latter had produced a notebook, and a rather blunt pencil, which he licked surreptitiously. He went upstairs and surveyed the victim stolidly, merely remarking that if he was to touch anything the Inspector would give him beans. He listened to all Mrs Honeycott's hysterical outbursts and confused explanations, and occasionally he wrote something down. His presence was calming and soothing.

Tommy finally got him alone for a minute or two on the steps outside ere he departed to telephone headquarters.

'Look here,' said Tommy, 'you saw the deceased turning in at the gate, you say. Are you sure she was alone?'

'Oh! she was alone all right. Nobody with her.'

'And between that time and when you met us, nobody came out of the gate?'

'Not a soul.'

'You'd have seen them if they had?'

'Of course I should. Nobody come out till that wild chap did.'

The majesty of the law moved portentously down the steps and paused by the white gatepost, which bore the imprint of a hand in red.

'Kind of amateur he must have been,' he said pityingly. 'To leave a thing like that.'

Then he swung out into the road.

It was the day after the crime. Tommy and Tuppence were still at the Grand Hotel, but Tommy had thought it prudent to discard his clerical disguise.

James Reilly had been apprehended, and was in custody. His solicitor, Mr Marvell, had just finished a lengthy conversation with Tommy on the subject of the crime.

'I never would have believed it of James Reilly,' he said simply. 'He's always been a man of violent speech, but that's all.'

Tommy nodded.

'If you disperse energy in speech, it doesn't leave you too much over for action. What I realise is that I shall be one of the principal witnesses against him. That conversation he had with me just before the crime was particularly damning. And, in spite of everything, I like the man, and if there was anyone else to suspect, I should believe him to be innocent. What's his own story?'

The solicitor pursed up his lips.

'He declares that he found her lying there dead. But that's impossible, of course. He's using the first lie that comes into his head.'

'Because, if he happened to be speaking the truth, it would mean that the garrulous Mrs Honeycott committed the crime – and that is fantastic. Yes, he must have done it.'

'The maid heard her cry out, remember.'

'The maid – yes –'

Tommy was silent a moment. Then he said thoughtfully.

'What credulous creatures we are, really. We believe evidence as though it were gospel truth. And what is it really? Only the impression conveyed to the mind by the senses – and suppose they're the wrong impressions?'

The lawyer shrugged his shoulders.

'Oh! we all know that there are unreliable witnesses, witnesses who remember more and more as time goes on, with no real intention to deceive.'

'I don't mean only that. I mean all of us – we say things that aren't really so, and never know that we've done so. For instance, both you and I, without doubt, have said some time or other, "There's the post," when what we really meant was that we'd heard a double knock and the rattle of the letter-box. Nine times out of ten we'd be right, and it would be the post, but just possibly the tenth time it might be only a little urchin playing a joke on us. See what I mean?'

'Ye-es,' said Mr Marvell slowly. 'But I don't see what you're driving at?'

'Don't you? I'm not so sure that I do myself. But I'm beginning to see. It's like the stick, Tuppence. You remember? One end of it pointed one way – but the other end always points the opposite way. It depends whether you get hold of it by the right end. Doors open – but they also shut. People go upstairs, but they also go downstairs. Boxes shut, but they also open.'

'What *do* you mean?' demanded Tuppence.

'It's so ridiculously easy, really,' said Tommy. 'And yet it's only just come to me. How do you know when a person's come into the house. You hear the door open and bang to, and if you're expecting any one to come in, you will be quite sure it is them. But it might just as easily be someone going *out*.'

'But Miss Glen didn't go out?'

'No, I know *she* didn't. But some one else did – the murderer.'

'But how did she get in, then?'

'She came in whilst Mrs Honeycott was in the kitchen talking to Ellen. They didn't hear her. Mrs Honeycott went back to the drawing-room, wondered if her sister had come in and began to put the clock right, and then, as she thought, she heard her come in and go upstairs.'

'Well, what about that? The footsteps going upstairs?'

'That was Ellen, going up to draw the curtains. You remember, Mrs Honeycott said her sister paused before going up. That pause was just the time needed for Ellen to come out from the kitchen into the hall. She just missed seeing the murderer.'

'But, Tommy,' cried Tuppence. 'The cry she gave?'

'That was James Reilly. Didn't you notice what a high-pitched voice he has? In moments of great emotion, men often squeal just like a woman.'

'But the murderer? We'd have seen him?'

'We *did* see him. We even stood talking to him. Do you remember the sudden way that policeman appeared? That was because he stepped out of the gate, just after the mist cleared from the road. It made us jump, don't you remember? After all, though we never think of them as that, policemen are men just like any other men. They love and they hate. They marry . . .

'I think Gilda Glen met her husband suddenly just outside that gate, and took him in with her to thrash the matter out. He hadn't Reilly's relief of violent words, remember. He just saw red – and he had his truncheon handy . . .'

The Crackler

'The Crackler' was first published as 'The Affair of the Forged Notes' in *The Sketch*, 19 November 1924. The Busies were created by Edgar Wallace (1875–1932).

'Tuppence,' said Tommy. 'We shall have to move into a much larger office.'

'Nonsense,' said Tuppence. 'You mustn't get swollen-headed and think you are a millionaire just because you solved two or three twopenny half-penny cases with the aid of the most amazing luck.'

'What some call luck, others call skill.'

'Of course, if you really think you are Sherlock Holmes, Thorndyke, McCarty and the Brothers Okewood all rolled into one, there is no more to be said. Personally I would much rather have luck on my side than all the skill in the world.'

'Perhaps there is something in that,' conceded Tommy. 'All the same, Tuppence, we do need a larger office.'

'Why?'

'The classics,' said Tommy. 'We need several hundreds of yards of extra bookshelf if Edgar Wallace is to be properly represented.'

'We haven't had an Edgar Wallace case yet.'

'I'm afraid we never shall,' said Tommy. 'If you notice he never does give the amateur sleuth much of a chance. It is all stern Scotland Yard kind of stuff – the real thing and no base counterfeit.'

Albert, the office boy, appeared at the door.

'Inspector Marriot to see you,' he announced.

'The mystery man of Scotland Yard,' murmured Tommy.

'The busiest of the Busies,' said Tuppence. 'Or is it "Noses"? I always get mixed between Busies and Noses.'

The Inspector advanced upon them with a beaming smile of welcome.

'Well, and how are things?' he asked breezily. 'None the worse for our little adventure the other day?'

'Oh, rather not,' said Tuppence. 'Too, too marvellous, wasn't it?'

'Well, I don't know that I would describe it exactly that way myself,' said Marriot cautiously.

'What has brought you here today, Marriot?' asked Tommy. 'Not just solicitude for our nervous systems, is it?'

'No,' said the Inspector. 'It is work for the brilliant Mr Blunt.'

'Ha!' said Tommy. 'Let me put my brilliant expression on.'

'I have come to make you a proposition, Mr Beresford. What would you say to rounding up a really big gang?'

'Is there such a thing?' asked Tommy.

'What do you mean, is there such a thing?'

'I always thought that gangs were confined to fiction – like master crooks and super criminals.'

'The master crook isn't very common,' agreed the Inspector. 'But Lord bless you, sir, there's any amount of gangs knocking about.'

'I don't know that I should be at my best dealing with a gang,' said Tommy. 'The amateur crime, the crime of quiet family life – that is where I flatter myself that I shine. Drama of strong domestic interest. That's the thing – with Tuppence at hand to supply all those little feminine details which are so important, and so apt to be ignored by the denser male.'

His eloquence was arrested abruptly as Tuppence threw a cushion at him and requested him not to talk nonsense.

'Will have your little bit of fun, won't you, sir?' said Inspector Marriot, smiling paternally at them both. 'If you'll not take offence at my saying so, it's a pleasure to see two young people enjoying life as much as you two do.'

'Do we enjoy life?' said Tuppence, opening her eyes very wide. 'I suppose we do. I've never thought about it before.'

'To return to that gang you were talking about,' said Tommy. 'In spite of my extensive private practice – duchesses, millionaires, and all the best charwomen – I might, perhaps, condescend to look into the matter for you. I don't like to see Scotland Yard at fault. You'll have the *Daily Mail* after you before you know where you are.'

'As I said before, you must have your bit of fun. Well, it's like this.' Again he hitched his chair forward. 'There's any amount of forged notes going about just now – hundreds of 'em! The amount of counterfeit Treasury notes in circulation would surprise you. Most artistic bit of work it is. Here's one of 'em.'

He took a one pound note from his pocket and handed it to Tommy. 'Looks all right, doesn't it?'

Tommy examined the note with great interest.

'By Jove, I'd never spot there was anything wrong with that.'

'No more would most people. Now here's a genuine one. I'll show you the differences – very slight they are, but you'll soon learn to tell them apart. Take this magnifying glass.'

At the end of five minutes' coaching both Tommy and Tuppence were fairly expert.

'What do you want us to do, Inspector Marriot?' asked Tuppence. 'Just keep our eyes open for these things?'

'A great deal more than that, Mrs Beresford. I'm pinning my faith on you to get to the bottom of the matter. You see, we've discovered that the notes are being circulated from the West End. Somebody pretty high up in the social scale is doing the distributing. They're passing them the other side of the Channel as well. Now there's a certain person who is interesting us very much. A Major Laidlaw – perhaps you've heard the name?'

'I think I have,' said Tommy. 'Connected with racing, isn't that it?'

'Yes. Major Laidlaw is pretty well known in connection with the Turf. There's nothing actually against him, but there's a general impression that he's been a bit too smart over one or two rather shady transactions. Men in the know look queer when he's mentioned. Nobody knows much of his past or where he came from. He's got a very attractive French wife who's seen about everywhere with a train of admirers. They must spend a lot of money, the Laidlaws, and I'd like to know where it comes from.'

'Possibly from the train of admirers,' suggested Tommy.

'That's the general idea. But I'm not so sure. It may be coincidence, but a lot of notes have been forthcoming from a certain very smart little gambling club which is much frequented by the Laidlaws and their set. This racing, gambling set get rid of a lot of loose money in notes. There couldn't be a better way of getting it into circulation.'

'And where do we come in?'

'This way. Young St Vincent and his wife are friends of yours, I understand? They're pretty thick with the Laidlaw set – though not as thick as they were. Through them it will be easy for you to get a footing in the same set in a way that none of our people could attempt. There's no likelihood of their spotting you. You'll have an ideal opportunity.'

'What have we got to find out exactly?'

'Where they get the stuff from, if they *are* passing it.'

'Quite so,' said Tommy. 'Major Laidlaw goes out with an empty suit-case. When he returns it is crammed to the bursting point with Treasury notes. How is it done? I sleuth him and find out. Is that the idea?'

'More or less. But don't neglect the lady, and her father, M. Heroulade. Remember the notes are being passed on both sides of the Channel.'

'My dear Marriot,' exclaimed Tommy reproachfully, 'Blunt's Brilliant Detectives do not know the meaning of the word neglect.'

The Inspector rose.

'Well, good luck to you,' he said, and departed.

'Slush,' said Tuppence enthusiastically.

'Eh?' said Tommy, perplexed.

'Counterfeit money,' explained Tuppence. 'It is always called slush. I know I'm right. Oh, Tommy, we have got an Edgar Wallace case. At last we are Busies.'

'We are,' said Tommy. 'And we are out to get the Crackler, and we will get him good.'

'Did you say the Cackler or the Crackler?'

'The Crackler.'

'Oh, what is a Crackler?'

'A new word that I have coined,' said Tommy. 'Descriptive of one who passes false notes into circulation. Banknotes crackle, therefore he is called a crackler. Nothing could be more simple.'

'That is rather a good idea,' said Tuppence. 'It makes it seem more real. I like the Rustler myself. Much more descriptive and sinister.'

'No,' said Tommy, 'I said the Crackler first, and I stick to it.'

'I shall enjoy this case,' said Tuppence. 'Lots of night clubs and cocktails in it. I shall buy some eyelash-black tomorrow.'

'Your eyelashes are black already,' objected her husband.

'I could make them blacker,' said Tuppence. 'And cherry lipstick would be useful too. That ultra-bright kind.'

'Tuppence,' said Tommy, 'you're a real rake at heart. What a good thing it is that you are married to a sober steady middle-aged man like myself.'

'You wait,' said Tuppence. 'When you have been to the Python Club a bit, you won't be so sober yourself.'

Tommy produced from a cupboard various bottles, two glasses, and a cocktail shaker.

'Let's start now,' he said. 'We are after you, Crackler, and we mean to get you.'

Making the acquaintance of the Laidlaws proved an easy affair. Tommy and Tuppence, young, well-dressed, eager for life, and with apparently money to burn, were soon made free of that particular coterie in which the Laidlaws had their being.

Major Laidlaw was a tall, fair man, typically English in appearance, with a hearty sportsmanlike manner, slightly belied by the hard lines round his eyes and the occasional quick sideways glance that assorted oddly with his supposed character.

He was a very dexterous card player, and Tommy noticed that when the stakes were high he seldom rose from the table a loser.

Marguerite Laidlaw was quite a different proposition. She was a charming creature, with the slenderness of a wood nymph and the face of a Greuze picture. Her dainty broken English was fascinating, and Tommy felt that it was no wonder most men were her slaves. She seemed to take a great fancy to Tommy from the first, and playing his part, he allowed himself to be swept into her train.

'My Tommee,' she would say; 'but positively I cannot go without my Tommee. His 'air, eet ees the colour of the sunset, ees eet not?'

Her father was a more sinister figure. Very correct, very upright, with his little black beard and his watchful eyes.

Tuppence was the first to report progress. She came to Tommy with ten one pound notes.

'Have a look at these. They're wrong 'uns, aren't they?'

Tommy examined them and confirmed Tuppence's diagnosis.

'Where did you get them from?'

'That boy, Jimmy Faulkener. Marguerite Laidlaw gave them to him to put on a horse for her. I said I wanted small notes and gave him a tenner in exchange.'

'All new and crisp,' said Tommy thoughtfully. 'They can't have passed through many hands. I suppose young Faulkener is all right?'

'Jimmy? Oh, he's a dear. He and I are becoming great friends.'

'So I have noticed,' said Tommy coldly. 'Do you really think it is necessary?'

'Oh, it isn't business,' said Tuppence cheerfully. 'It's pleasure. He's such a nice boy. I'm glad to get him out of that woman's clutches. You've no idea of the amount of money she's cost him.'

'It looks to me as though he were getting rather a pash for you, Tuppence.'

'I've thought the same myself sometimes. It's nice to know one's still young and attractive, isn't it?'

'Your moral tone, Tuppence, is deplorably low. You look at these things from the wrong point of view.'

'I haven't enjoyed myself so much for years,' declared Tuppence shamelessly. 'And anyway, what about you? Do I ever see you nowadays? Aren't you always living in Marguerite Laidlaw's pocket?'

'Business,' said Tommy crisply.

'But she is attractive, isn't she?'

'Not my type,' said Tommy. 'I don't admire her.'

'Liar,' laughed Tuppence. 'But I always did think I'd rather marry a liar than a fool.'

'I suppose,' said Tommy, 'that there's no absolute necessity for a husband to be either?'

But Tuppence merely threw him a pitying glance and withdrew.

Amongst Mrs Laidlaw's train of admirers was a simple but extremely wealthy gentleman of the name of Hank Ryder.

Mr Ryder came from Alabama, and from the first he was disposed to make a friend and confidant of Tommy.

'That's a wonderful woman, sir,' said Mr Ryder following the lovely Marguerite with reverential eyes. 'Plumb full of civilisation. Can't beat *la gaie France*, can you? When I'm near her, I feel as though I was one of the Almighty's earliest experiments. I guess he'd got to get his hand in before he attempted anything so lovely as that perfectly lovely woman.'

Tommy agreeing politely with these sentiments, Mr Ryder unburdened himself still further.

'Seems kind of a shame a lovely creature like that should have money worries.'

'Has she?' asked Tommy.

'You betcha life she has. Queer fish, Laidlaw. She's skeered of him. Told me so. Daren't tell him about her little bills.'

'Are they *little* bills?' asked Tommy.

'Well – when I say little! After all, a woman's got to wear clothes, and the less there are of them the more they cost, the way I figure it out. And a pretty woman like that doesn't want to go about in last season's goods. Cards too, the poor little thing's been mighty unlucky at cards. Why, she lost fifty to me last night.'

'She won two hundred from Jimmy Faulkener the night before,' said Tommy drily.

'Did she indeed? That relieves my mind some. By the way, there seems to be a lot of dud notes floating around in your country just now. I paid in a bunch at my bank this morning, and twenty-five of them were down-and-outers, so the polite gentleman behind the counter informed me.'

'That's rather a large proportion. Were they new looking?'

'New and crisp as they make 'em. Why, they were the ones Mrs Laidlaw paid over to me, I reckon. Wonder where she got 'em from. One of these toughs on the racecourse as likely as not.'

'Yes,' said Tommy. 'Very likely.'

'You know, Mr Beresford, I'm new to this sort of high life. All these swell dames and the rest of the outfit. Only made my pile a short while back. Came right over to Yurrop to see life.'

Tommy nodded. He made a mental note to the effect that with the aid of Marguerite Laidlaw, Mr Ryder would probably see a good deal of life and that the price charged would be heavy.

Meantime, for the second time, he had evidence that the forged notes were being distributed pretty near at hand, and that in all probability Marguerite Laidlaw had a hand in their distribution.

On the following night he himself was given a proof.

It was at that small select meeting place mentioned by Inspector Marriot. There was dancing there, but the real attraction of the place lay behind a pair of imposing folding doors. There were two rooms there with green baize-covered tables, where vast sums changed hands nightly.

Marguerite Laidlaw, rising at last to go, thrust a quantity of small notes into Tommy's hands.

'They are so bulkee, Tommee – you will change them, yes? A beeg note. See my so sweet leetle bag, it bulges him to distraction.'

Tommy brought her the hundred pound note she asked for. Then in a quiet corner he examined the notes she had given him. At least a quarter of them were counterfeit.

But where did she get her supplies from? To that he had as yet no answer. By means of Albert's cooperation, he was almost sure that Laidlaw was not the man. His movements had been watched closely and had yielded no result.

Tommy suspected her father, the saturnine M. Heroulade. He went to and fro to France fairly often. What could be simpler than to bring the notes across with him? A false bottom to the trunk – something of that kind.

Tommy strolled slowly out of the Club, absorbed in these thoughts, but was suddenly recalled to immediate necessities. Outside in the street was Mr Hank P. Ryder, and it was clear at once that Mr Ryder was not strictly sober. At the moment he was trying to hang his hat on the radiator of a car, and missing it by some inches every time.

'This goddarned hatshtand, this goddamed hatshtand,' said Mr Ryder tearfully. 'Not like that in the Shtates. Man can hang up his hat every night – every night, sir. You're wearing two hatshs. Never sheen a man wearing two hatshs before. Must be effect – climate.'

'Perhaps I've got two heads,' said Tommy gravely.

'Sho you have,' said Mr Ryder. 'Thatsh odd. Thatsh remarkable fac'. Letsh have a cocktail. Prohibition – probishun thatsh whatsh done me in. I guess I'm drunk – constootionally drunk. Cocktailsh – mixed 'em – Angel's Kiss – that's Marguerite – lovely creature, fon o' me too. Horshes Neck, two Martinis – three Road to Ruinsh – no, roadsh to roon – mixed 'em all – in a beer tankard. Bet me I wouldn't – I shaid – to hell, I shaid –'

Tommy interrupted.

'That's all right,' he said soothingly. 'Now what about getting home?'

'No home to go to,' said Mr Ryder sadly, and wept.

'What hotel are you staying at?' asked Tommy.

'Can't go home,' said Mr Ryder. 'Treasure hunt. Swell thing to do. She did it. Whitechapel – white heartsh, white headsn shorrow to the grave –'

But Mr Ryder became suddenly dignified. He drew himself erect and attained a sudden miraculous command over his speech.

'Young man, I'm telling you. Margee took me. In her car. Treasure hunting. English aristocrashy all do it. Under the cobblestones. Five hundred poundsh. Solemn thought, *'tis* solemn thought. I'm *telling* you, young man. You've been kind to me. I've got your welfare at heart, sir, at heart. We Americans –'

Tommy interrupted him this time with even less ceremony.

'What's that you say? Mrs Laidlaw took you in a car?'

The American nodded with a kind of owlish solemnity.

'To Whitechapel?' Again that owlish nod.

'And you found five hundred pounds there?'

Mr Ryder struggled for words.

'S-she did,' he corrected his questioner. 'Left me outside. Outside the door. Always left outside. It's kinder sad. Outside – always outside.'

'Would you know your way there?'

'I guess so. Hank Ryder doesn't lose his bearings –'

Tommy hauled him along unceremoniously. He found his own car where it was waiting, and presently they were bowling eastward. The cool air revived Mr Ryder. After slumping against Tommy's shoulder in a kind of stupor, he awoke clear-headed and refreshed.

'Say, boy, where are we?' he demanded.

'Whitechapel,' said Tommy crisply. 'Is this where you came with Mrs Laidlaw tonight?'

'It looks kinder familiar,' admitted Mr Ryder, looking round. 'Seems to me we turned off to the left somewhere down here. That's it – that street there.'

Tommy turned off obediently. Mr Ryder issued directions.

'That's it. Sure. And round to the right. Say, aren't the smells awful. Yes, past that pub at the corner – sharp round, and stop at the mouth of that little alley. But what's the big idea? Hand it to me. Some of the oof left behind? Are we going to put one over on them?'

'That's exactly it,' said Tommy. 'We're going to put one over on them. Rather a joke, isn't it?'

'I'll tell the world,' assented Mr Ryder. 'Though I'm just a mite hazed about it all,' he ended wistfully.

Tommy got out and assisted Mr Ryder to alight also. They advanced into the alley way. On the left were the backs of a row of dilapidated

houses, most of which had doors opening into the alley. Mr Ryder came
to a stop before one of these doors.

'In here she went,' he declared. 'It was this door – I'm plumb certain
of it.'

'They all look very alike,' said Tommy. 'Reminds me of the story of
the soldier and the Princess. You remember, they made a cross on the
door to show which one it was. Shall we do the same?'

Laughing, he drew a piece of white chalk from his pocket and made
a rough cross low down on the door. Then he looked up at various dim
shapes that prowled high on the walls of the alley, one of which was
uttering a blood-curdling yawl.

'Lots of cats about,' he remarked cheerfully.

'What is the procedure?' asked Mr Ryder. 'Do we step inside?'

'Adopting due precautions, we do,' said Tommy.

He glanced up and down the alley way, then softly tried the door. It
yielded. He pushed it open and peered into a dim yard.

Noiselessly he passed through, Mr Ryder on his heels.

'Gee,' said the latter, 'there's someone coming down the alley.'

He slipped outside again. Tommy stood still for a minute, then hearing
nothing went on. He took a torch from his pocket and switched on the
light for a brief second. That momentary flash enabled him to see his
way ahead. He pushed forward and tried the closed door ahead of him.
That too gave, and very softly he pushed it open and went in.

After standing still a second and listening, he again switched on the
torch, and at that flash, as though at a given signal, the place seemed to
rise round him. Two men were in front of him, two men were behind
him. They closed in on him and bore him down.

'Lights,' growled a voice.

An incandescent gas burner was lit. By its light Tommy saw a circle
of unpleasing faces. His eyes wandered gently round the room and noted
some of the objects in it.

'Ah!' he said pleasantly. 'The headquarters of the counterfeiting
industry, if I am not mistaken.'

'Shut your jaw,' growled one of the men.

The door opened and shut behind Tommy, and a genial and well-
known voice spoke.

'Got him, boys. That's right. Now, Mr Busy, let me tell you you're up
against it.'

'That dear old word,' said Tommy. 'How it thrills me. Yes. I am the
Mystery Man of Scotland Yard. Why, it's Mr Hank Ryder. This is a
surprise.'

'I guess you mean that too. I've been laughing fit to bust all this evening

– leading you here like a little child. And you so pleased with your clever-ness. Why, sonny, I was on to you from the start. You weren't in with that crowd for your health. I let you play about for a while, and when you got real suspicious of the lovely Marguerite, I said to myself: "Now's the time to lead him to it." I guess your friends won't be hearing of you for some time.'

'Going to do me in? That's the correct expression, I believe. You have got it in for me.'

'You've got a nerve all right. No, we shan't attempt violence. Just keep you under restraint, so to speak.'

'I'm afraid you're backing the wrong horse,' said Tommy. 'I've no inten-tion of being "kept under restraint," as you call it.'

Mr Ryder smiled genially. From outside a cat uttered a melancholy cry to the moon.

'Banking on that cross you put on the door, eh, sonny?' said Mr Ryder. 'I shouldn't if I were you. Because I know that story you mentioned. Heard it when I was a little boy. I stepped back into the alleyway to enact the part of the dog with eyes as big as cart-wheels. If you were in that alley now, you would observe that every door in the alley is marked with an identical cross.'

Tommy dropped his head despondently.

'Thought you were mighty clever, didn't you?' said Ryder.

As the words left his lips a sharp rapping sounded on the door.

'What's that?' he cried, starting.

At the same time an assault began on the front of the house. The door at the back was a flimsy affair. The lock gave almost immediately and Inspector Marriot showed in the doorway.

'Well done, Marriot,' said Tommy. 'You were quite right as to the district. I'd like you to make the acquaintance of Mr Hank Ryder who knows all the best fairy tales.

'You see, Mr Ryder,' he added gently, 'I've had my suspicions of you. Albert (that important-looking boy with the big ears is Albert) had orders to follow on his motorcycle if you and I went off joy-riding at any time. And whilst I was ostentatiously marking a chalk cross on the door to engage your attention, I also emptied a little bottle of valerian on the ground. Nasty smell, but cats love it. All the cats in the neighbourhood were assembled outside to mark the right house when Albert and the police arrived.'

He looked at the dumbfounded Mr Ryder with a smile, then rose to his feet.

'I said I would get you Crackler, and I have got you,' he observed.

'What the hell are you talking about?' asked Mr Ryder. 'What do you mean – Crackler?'

'You will find it in the glossary of the next criminal dictionary,' said Tommy. 'Etymology doubtful.'

He looked round him with a happy smile.

'And all done without a nose,' he murmured brightly. 'Good-night, Marriot. I must go now to where the happy ending of the story awaits me. No reward like the love of a good woman – and the love of a good woman awaits me at home – that is, I hope it does, but one never knows nowadays. This has been a very dangerous job, Marriot. Do you know Captain Jimmy Faulkener? His dancing is simply too marvellous, and as for his taste in cocktails –! Yes, Marriot, it has been a very dangerous job.'

The Sunningdale Mystery

'The Sunningdale Mystery' was first published as 'The Sunninghall Mystery' in *The Sketch*, 19 October 1924. The Old Man in the Corner was created by Baroness Orczy (1865–1947).

'Do you know where we are going to lunch today, Tuppence?'

Mrs Beresford considered the question.

'The Ritz?' she suggested hopefully.

'Think again.'

'That nice little place in Soho?'

'No.' Tommy's tone was full of importance. 'An ABC shop. This one, in fact.'

He drew her deftly inside an establishment of the kind indicated, and steered her to a corner marble-topped table.

'Excellent,' said Tommy with satisfaction, as he seated himself. 'Couldn't be better.'

'Why has this craze for the simple life come upon you?' demanded Tuppence.

'*You see, Watson, but you do not observe.* I wonder now whether one of these haughty damsels would condescend to notice us? Splendid, she drifts this way. It is true that she appears to be thinking of something else, but doubtless her sub-conscious mind is functioning busily with such matters as ham and eggs and pots of tea. Chop and fried potatoes, please, miss, and a large coffee, a roll and butter, and a plate of tongue for the lady.'

The waitress repeated the order in a scornful tone, but Tuppence leant forward suddenly and interrupted her.

'No, not a chop and fried potatoes. This gentleman will have a cheese-cake and a glass of milk.'

'A cheesecake and a milk,' said the waitress with even deeper scorn, if that were possible. Still thinking of something else, she drifted away again.

'That was uncalled for,' said Tommy coldly.

'But I'm right, aren't I? You are the Old Man in the Corner? Where's your piece of string?'

Tommy drew a long twisted mesh of string from his pocket and proceeded to tie a couple of knots in it.

'Complete to the smallest detail,' he murmured.

'You made a small mistake in ordering your meal, though.'

'Women are so literal-minded,' said Tommy. 'If there's one thing I hate it's milk to drink, and cheese-cakes are always so yellow and bilious-looking.'

'Be an artist,' said Tuppence. 'Watch me attack my cold tongue. Jolly good stuff, cold tongue. Now then, I'm all ready to be Miss Polly Burton. Tie a large knot and begin.'

'First of all,' said Tommy, 'speaking in a strictly unofficial capacity, let me point out this. Business is not too brisk lately. If business does not come to us, we must go to business. Apply our minds to one of the great public mysteries of the moment. Which brings me to the point – the Sunningdale Mystery.'

'Ah!' said Tuppence, with deep interest. 'The Sunningdale Mystery!'

Tommy drew a crumpled piece of newspaper from his pocket and laid it on the table.

'That is the latest portrait of Captain Sessle as it appeared in the *Daily Leader.*'

'Just so,' said Tuppence. 'I wonder someone doesn't sue these news-papers sometimes. You can see it's a man and that's all.'

'When I said the Sunningdale Mystery, I should have said the so-called Sunningdale Mystery,' went on Tommy rapidly.

'A mystery to the police perhaps, but not to an intelligent mind.'

'Tie another knot,' said Tuppence.

'I don't know how much of the case you remember,' continued Tommy quietly.

'All of it,' said Tuppence, 'but don't let me cramp your style.'

'It was just over three weeks ago,' said Tommy, 'that the gruesome discovery was made on the famous golf links. Two members of the club, who were enjoying an early round, were horrified to find the body of a man lying face downwards on the seventh tee. Even before they turned him over they had guessed him to be Captain Sessle, a well-known figure on the links, and who always wore a golf coat of a peculiarly bright blue colour.

'Captain Sessle was often seen out on the links early in the morning, practising, and it was thought at first that he had been suddenly over-come by some form of heart disease. But examination by a doctor revealed the sinister fact that he had been murdered, stabbed to the heart with a significant object, *a woman's hatpin*. He was also found to have been dead at least twelve hours.

'That put an entirely different complexion on the matter, and very soon some interesting facts came to light. Practically the last person to see Captain Sessle alive was his friend and partner, Mr Hollaby of the Porcupine Assurance Co, and he told his story as follows:

'Sessle and he had played a round earlier in the day. After tea the other suggested that they should play a few more holes before it got too dark to see. Hollaby assented. Sessle seemed in good spirits, and was in excellent form. There is a public footpath that crosses the links, and just as they were playing up to the sixth green, Hollaby noticed a woman coming along it. She was very tall, and dressed in brown, but he did not observe her particularly, and Sessle, he thought, did not notice her at all.

'The footpath in question crossed in front of the seventh tee,' continued Tommy. 'The woman had passed along this and was standing at the farther side, as though waiting. Captain Sessle was the first to reach the tee, as Mr Hollaby was replacing the pin in the hole. As the latter came towards the tee, he was astonished to see Sessle and the woman talking together. As he came nearer, they both turned abruptly, Sessle calling over his shoulder: "Shan't be a minute."

'The two of them walked off side by side, still deep in earnest conversation. The footpath there leaves the course, and, passing between the two narrow hedges of neighbouring gardens, comes out on the road to Windlesham.

'Captain Sessle was as good as his word. He reappeared within a minute or two, much to Hollaby's satisfaction, as two other players were coming up behind them, and the light was failing rapidly. They drove off, and at once Hollaby noticed that something had occurred to upset his companion. Not only did he foozle his drive badly, but his face was worried and his forehead creased in a big frown. He hardly answered his companion's remarks, and his golf was atrocious. Evidently something had occurred to put him completely off his game.

'They played that hole and the eighth, and then Captain Sessle declared abruptly that the light was too bad and that he was off home. Just at that point there is another of those narrow "slips" leading to the Windlesham road, and Captain Sessle departed that way, which was a short cut to his home, a small bungalow on the road in question. The other two players came up, a Major Barnard and Mr Lecky, and to them Hollaby mentioned Captain Sessle's sudden change of manner. They also had seen him speaking to the woman in brown, but had not been near enough to see her face. All three men wondered what she could have said to upset their friend to that extent.

'They returned to the clubhouse together, and as far as was known at the time, were the last people to see Captain Sessle alive. The day was a Wednesday, and on Wednesday cheap tickets to London are issued. The man and wife who ran Captain Sessle's small bungalow were up in town, according to custom, and did not return until the late train. They entered the bungalow as usual, and supposed their master to be in his room asleep. Mrs Sessle, his wife, was away on a visit.

'The murder of the Captain was a nine days' wonder. Nobody could suggest a motive for it. The identity of the tall woman in brown was eagerly discussed, but without result. The police were, as usual, blamed for their supineness – most unjustly, as time was to show. For a week later, a girl called Doris Evans was arrested and charged with the murder of Captain Anthony Sessle.

'The police had had little to work upon. A strand of fair hair caught in the dead man's fingers and a few threads of flame-coloured wool caught on one of the buttons of his blue coat. Diligent inquiries at the railway station and elsewhere had elicited the following facts.

'A young girl dressed in a flame-coloured coat and skirt had arrived by train that evening about seven o'clock and had asked the way to Captain Sessle's house. The same girl had reappeared again at the station, two hours later. Her hat was awry and her hair tousled, and she seemed in a state of great agitation. She inquired about the trains back to town, and was continually looking over her shoulder as though afraid of something.

'Our police force is in many ways very wonderful. With this slender evidence to go upon, they managed to track down the girl and identify her as one Doris Evans. She was charged with murder and cautioned that anything she might say would be used against her, but she never-theless persisted in making a statement, and this statement she repeated again in detail, without any subsequent variation, at the subsequent proceedings.

'Her story was this. She was a typist by profession, and had made friends one evening, in a cinema, with a well-dressed man, who declared he had taken a fancy to her. His name, he told her, was Anthony, and he suggested that she should come down to his bungalow at Sunningdale. She had no idea then, or at any other time, that he had a wife. It was arranged between them that she should come down on the following Wednesday – the day, you will remember, when the servants would be absent and his wife away from home. In the end he told her his full name was Anthony Sessle, and gave her the name of his house.

'She duly arrived at the bungalow on the evening in question, and was greeted by Sessle, who had just come in from the links. Though he professed himself delighted to see her, the girl declared that from the first his manner was strange and different. A half-acknowledged fear sprang up in her, and she wished fervently that she had not come.

'After a simple meal, which was all ready and prepared, Sessle suggested going out for a stroll. The girl consenting, he took her out of the house, down the road, and along the "slip" on to the golf course. And then suddenly, just as they were crossing the seventh tee, he seemed to go completely mad. Drawing a revolver from his pocket, he brandished it in the air, declaring that he had come to the end of his tether.

'"Everything must go! I'm ruined – done for. And you shall go with me. I shall shoot you first – then myself. They will find our bodies here in the morning side by side – together in death."

'And so on – a lot more. He had hold of Doris Evans by the arm, and she, realising she had to do with a madman, made frantic efforts to free herself, or failing that to get the revolver away from him. They struggled together, and in that struggle he must have torn out a piece of her hair and got the wool of her coat entangled on a button.

'Finally, with a desperate effort, she freed herself, and ran for her life across the golf links, expecting every minute to be shot down with a revolver bullet. She fell twice, tripping over the heather, but eventually regained the road to the station and realised that she was not being pursued.

'That is the story that Doris Evans tells – and from which she has never varied. She strenuously denies that she ever struck at him with a hatpin in self-defence – a natural enough thing to do under the circumstances, though – and one which may well be the truth. In support of her story, a revolver has been found in the furze bushes near where the body was lying. It had not been fired.

'Doris Evans has been sent for trial, but the mystery still remains a mystery. If her story is to be believed, who was it who stabbed Captain Sessle? The other woman, the tall woman in brown, whose appearance so upset him? So far no one has explained her connection with the case. She appears out of space suddenly on the footpath across the links, she disappears along the slip, and no one ever hears of her again. Who was she? A local resident? A visitor from London? If so, did she come by car or by train? There is nothing remarkable about her except her height; no one seems to be able to describe her appearance. She could not have been Doris Evans, for Doris Evans is small and fair, and moreover was only just then arriving at the station.'

'The wife?' suggested Tuppence. 'What about the wife?'

'A very natural suggestion. But Mrs Sessle is also a small woman, and besides, Mr Hollaby knows her well by sight, and there seems no doubt

that she was really away from home. One further development has come
to light. The Porcupine Assurance Co is in liquidation. The accounts
reveal the most daring misappropriation of funds. The reasons for Captain
Sessle's wild words to Doris Evans are now quite apparent. For some
years past he must have been systematically embezzling money. Neither
Mr Hollaby nor his son had any idea of what was going on. They are
practically ruined.

'The case stands like this. Captain Sessle was on the verge of discovery
and ruin. Suicide would be a natural solution, but the nature of the wound
rules that theory out. Who killed him? Was it Doris Evans? Was it the
mysterious woman in brown?'

Tommy paused, took a sip of milk, made a wry face, and bit cautiously
at the cheesecake.

'Of course,' murmured Tommy, 'I saw at once where the hitch in this
particular case lay, and just where the police were going astray.'

'Yes?' said Tuppence eagerly.

Tommy shook his head sadly.

'I wish I did. Tuppence, it's dead easy being the Old Man in the Corner
up to a certain point. But the solution beats me. Who did murder the
beggar? I don't know.'

He took some more newspaper cuttings out of his pocket.

'Further exhibits – Mr Hollaby, his son, Mrs Sessle, Doris Evans.'

Tuppence pounced on the last and looked at it for some time.

'She didn't murder him anyway,' she remarked at last. 'Not with a
hatpin.'

'Why this certainty?'

'A lady Molly touch. She's got bobbed hair. Only one woman in twenty
uses hatpins nowadays, anyway – long hair or short. Hats fit tight and
pull on – there's no need for such a thing.'

'Still, she might have had one by her.'

'My dear boy, we don't keep them as heirlooms! What on earth should
she have brought a hatpin down to Sunningdale for?'

'Then it must have been the other woman, the woman in brown.'

'I wish she hadn't been tall. Then she could have been the wife. I
always suspect wives who are away at the time and so couldn't have had
anything to do with it. If she found her husband carrying on with that
girl, it would be quite natural for her to go for him with a hatpin.'

'I shall have to be careful, I see,' remarked Tommy.

But Tuppence was deep in thought and refused to be drawn.

'What were the Sessles like?' she asked suddenly. 'What sort of things
did people say about them?'

'As far as I can make out, they were very popular. He and his wife were supposed to be devoted to one another. That's what makes the business of the girl so odd. It's the last thing you'd have expected of a man like Sessle. He was an ex-soldier, you know. Came into a good bit of money, retired, and went into this Insurance business. The last man in the world, apparently, whom you would have suspected of being a crook.'

'It is absolutely certain that he was the crook? Couldn't it have been the other two who took the money?'

'The Hollabys? They say they're ruined.'

'Oh, they say! Perhaps they've got it all in a bank under another name. I put it foolishly, I dare say, but you know what I mean. Suppose they'd been speculating with the money for some time, unbeknownst to Sessle, and lost it all. It might be jolly convenient for them that Sessle died just when he did.'

Tommy tapped the photograph of Mr Hollaby senior with his fingernail.

'So you're accusing this respectable gentleman of murdering his friend and partner? You forget that he parted from Sessle on the links in full view of Barnard and Lecky, and spent the evening in the Dormy House. Besides, there's the hatpin.'

'Bother the hatpin,' said Tuppence impatiently. 'That hatpin, you think, points to the crime having been committed by a woman?'

'Naturally. Don't you agree?'

'No. Men are notoriously old-fashioned. It takes them ages to rid themselves of preconceived ideas. They associate hatpins and hairpins with the female sex, and call them "women's weapons." They may have been in the past, but they're both rather out of date now. Why, I haven't had a hatpin or a hairpin for the last four years.'

'Then you think –?'

'That it was a *man* killed Sessle. The hatpin was used to make it seem a woman's crime.'

'There's something in what you say, Tuppence,' said Tommy slowly. 'It's extraordinary how things seem to straighten themselves out when you talk a thing over.'

Tuppence nodded.

'Everything must be logical – if you look at it the right way. And remember what Marriot once said about the amateur point of view – that it had the *intimacy*. We know something about people like Captain Sessle and his wife. We know what they're likely to do – and what they're not likely to do. And we've each got our special knowledge.'

Tommy smiled.

'You mean,' he said, 'that you are an authority on what people with bobbed and shingled heads are likely to have in their possession, and that you have an intimate acquaintance with what wives are likely to feel and do?'

'Something of the sort.'

'And what about me? What is my special knowledge? Do husbands pick up girls, etc?'

'No,' said Tuppence gravely. 'You know the course – you've been on it – not as a detective searching for clues, but as a golfer. You know about golf, and what's likely to put a man off his game.'

'It must have been something pretty serious to put Sessle off his game. His handicap's two, and from the seventh tee on he played like a child, so they say.'

'Who say?'

'Barnard and Lecky. They were playing just behind him, you remember.'

'That was after he met the woman – the tall woman in brown. They saw him speaking to her, didn't they?'

'Yes – at least –'

Tommy broke off. Tuppence looked up at him and was puzzled. He was staring at the piece of string in his fingers, but staring with the eyes of one who sees something very different.

'Tommy – what is it?'

'Be quiet, Tuppence. I'm playing the sixth hole at Sunningdale. Sessle and old Hollaby are holing out on the sixth green ahead of me. It's getting dusk, but I can see that bright blue coat of Sessle's clearly enough. And on the footpath to the left of me there's a woman coming along. She hasn't crossed from the ladies' course – that's on the right – I should have seen her if she had done so. And it's odd I didn't see her on the footpath before – from the fifth tee, for instance.'

He paused.

'You said just now I knew the course, Tuppence. Just behind the sixth tee there's a little hut or shelter made of turf. Any one could wait in there until – the right moment came. They could change their appearance there. I mean – tell me, Tuppence, this is where your special knowledge comes in again – would it be very difficult for a man to look like a woman, and then change back to being a man again? Could he wear a skirt over plus-fours, for instance?'

'Certainly he could. The woman would look a bit bulky, that would be all. A longish brown skirt, say a brown sweater of the kind both men and women wear, and a woman's felt hat with a bunch of side curls attached each side. That would be all that was needed – I'm speaking, of course, of what would pass at a distance, which I take to be what you are driving at. Switch off the skirt, take off the hat and curls, and put on a man's cap which you can carry rolled up in your hand, and there you'd be – back as a man again.'

'And the time required for the transformation?'

'From woman to man, a minute and a half at the outside, probably a good deal less. The other way about would take longer, you'd have to arrange the hat and curls a bit, and the skirt would stick getting it on over the plus fours.'

'That doesn't worry me. It's the time for the first that matters. As I tell you, I'm playing the sixth hole. The woman in brown has reached the seventh tee now. She crosses it and waits. Sessle in his blue coat goes towards her. They stand together a minute, and then they follow the path round the trees out of sight. Hollaby is on the tee alone. Two or three minutes pass. I'm on the green now. The man in the blue coat comes back and drives off, foozling badly. The light's getting worse. I and my partner go on. Ahead of us are those two, Sessle slicing and topping and doing everything he shouldn't do. At the eighth green, I see him stride off and vanish down the slip. What happened to him to make him play like a different man?'

'The woman in brown – or the man, if you think it was a man.'

'Exactly, and where they were standing – out of sight, remember, of those coming after them – there's a deep tangle of furze bushes. You could thrust a body in there, and it would be pretty certain to lie hidden until the morning.'

'Tommy! You think it was *then*. – But someone would have heard –'

'Heard what? The doctors agreed death must have been instantaneous. I've seen men killed instantaneously in the war. They don't cry out as a rule – just a gurgle, or a moan – perhaps just a sigh, or a funny little cough. Sessle comes towards the seventh tee, and the woman comes forward and speaks to him. He recognises her, perhaps, as a man he knows masquerading. Curious to learn the why and wherefore, he allows himself to be drawn along the footpath out of sight. One stab with the deadly hatpin as they walk along. Sessle falls – dead. The other man drags his body into the furze bushes, strips off the blue coat, then sheds his own skirt and the hat and curls. He puts on Sessle's well-known blue coat and cap and strides back to the tee. Three minutes would do it. The others behind can't see his face, only the peculiar blue coat they know so well. They never doubt that it's Sessle – *but he doesn't play Sessle's brand of golf.* They all say he played like a different man. Of course he did. He *was* a different man.'

'But –'

'Point No. 2. His action in bringing the girl down there was the action of *a different man*. It wasn't Sessle who met Doris Evans at a cinema and induced her to come down to Sunningdale. It was a man *calling* himself Sessle. Remember, Doris Evans wasn't arrested until a fortnight after the time. *She never saw the body.* If she had, she might have bewildered everyone by declaring that that wasn't the man who took her out on the golf links that night and spoke so wildly of suicide. It was a carefully laid plot. The girl invited down for Wednesday when Sessle's house would be empty, then the hatpin which pointed to its being a woman's doing. The murderer meets the girl, takes her into the bungalow and gives her supper, then takes her out on the links, and when he gets to the scene of the crime, brandishes his revolver and scares the life out of her. Once she has taken to her heels, all he has to do is to pull out the body and leave it lying on the tee. The revolver he chucks into the bushes. Then he makes a neat parcel of the skirt and – now I admit I'm guessing – in all probability walks to Woking, which is only about six or seven miles away, and goes back to town from there.'

'Wait a minute,' said Tuppence. 'There's one thing you haven't explained. What about Hollaby?'

'Hollaby?'

'Yes. I admit that the people behind couldn't have seen whether it was really Sessle or not. But you can't tell me that the man who was playing with him was so hypnotised by the blue coat that he never looked at his face.'

'My dear old thing,' said Tommy. 'That's just the point. Hollaby knew all right. You see, I'm adopting your theory – that Hollaby and his son were the real embezzlers. The murderer's got to be a man who knew Sessle pretty well – knew, for instance, about the servants being always out on a Wednesday, and that his wife was away. And also someone who was able to get an impression of Sessle's latch key. I think Hollaby junior would fulfil all these requirements. He's about the same age and height as Sessle, and they were both clean-shaven men. Doris Evans probably saw several photographs of the murdered man reproduced in the papers, but as you yourself observed – one can just see that it's a man and that's about all.'

'Didn't she ever see Hollaby in Court?'

'The son never appeared in the case at all. Why should he? He had no evidence to give. It was old Hollaby, with his irreproachable alibi, who stood in the limelight throughout. Nobody has ever bothered to inquire what his son was doing that particular evening.'

'It all fits in,' admitted Tuppence. She paused a minute and then asked: 'Are you going to tell all this to the police?'

'I don't know if they'd listen.'

'They'd listen all right,' said an unexpected voice behind him.

Tommy swung round to confront Inspector Marriot. The Inspector was sitting at the next table. In front of him was a poached egg.

'Often drop in here to lunch,' said Inspector Marriot. 'As I was saying, we'll listen all right – in fact I've been listening. I don't mind telling you that we've not been quite satisfied all along over those Porcupine figures. You see, we've had our suspicions of those Hollabys, but nothing to go upon. Too sharp for us. Then this murder came, and that seemed to upset all our ideas. But thanks to you and the lady, sir, we'll confront young Hollaby with Doris Evans and see if she recognises him. I rather fancy she will. That's a very ingenious idea of yours about the blue coat. I'll see that Blunt's Brilliant Detectives get the credit for it.'

'You *are* a nice man, Inspector Marriot,' said Tuppence gratefully.

'We think a lot of you two at the Yard,' replied that stolid gentleman. 'You'd be surprised. If I may ask you, sir, what's the meaning of that piece of string?'

'Nothing,' said Tommy, stuffing it into his pocket. 'A bad habit of mine. As to the cheesecake and the milk – I'm on a diet. Nervous dyspepsia. Busy men are always martyrs to it.'

'Ah!' said the detective. 'I thought perhaps you'd been reading – well, it's of no consequence.'

But the Inspector's eyes twinkled.

The House of Lurking Death

'The House of Lurking Death' was first published in *The Sketch*,
5 November 1924. Inspector Hanaud was created by
A. E. W. Mason (1865–1948).

'What –' began Tuppence, and then stopped.

She had just entered the private office of Mr Blunt from the adjoining one marked 'Clerks,' and was surprised to behold her lord and master with his eye riveted to the private peep-hole into the outer office.

'Ssh,' said Tommy warningly. 'Didn't you hear the buzzer? It's a girl – rather a nice girl – in fact she looks to me a frightfully nice girl. Albert is telling her all that tosh about my being engaged with Scotland Yard.'

'Let *me* see,' demanded Tuppence.

Somewhat unwillingly, Tommy moved aside. Tuppence in her turn glued her eye to the peep-hole.

'She's not bad,' admitted Tuppence. 'And her clothes are simply the lastest shout.'

'She's perfectly lovely,' said Tommy. 'She's like those girls Mason writes about – you know, frightfully sympathetic, and beautiful, and distinctly intelligent without being too saucy. I think, yes – I certainly think – I shall be the great Hanaud this morning.'

'H'm,' said Tuppence. 'If there is one detective out of all the others whom you are most unlike – I should say it was Hanaud. Can you do the lightning changes of personality? Can you be the great comedian, the little gutter boy, the serious and sympathetic friend – all in five minutes?'

'I know this,' said Tommy, rapping sharply on the desk, 'I am the Captain of the Ship – and don't you forget it, Tuppence. I'm going to have her in.'

He pressed the buzzer on his desk. Albert appeared ushering in the client.

The girl stopped in the doorway as though undecided. Tommy came forward.

'Come in, mademoiselle,' he said kindly, 'and seat yourself here.'

Tuppence choked audibly and Tommy turned upon her with a swift change of manner. His tone was menacing.

'You spoke, Miss Robinson? Ah, no, I thought not.'

He turned back to the girl.

'We will not be serious or formal,' he said. 'You will just tell me about it, and then we will discuss the best way to help you.'

'You are very kind,' said the girl. 'Excuse me, but are you a foreigner?'

A fresh choke from Tuppence. Tommy glared in her direction out of the corner of his eye.

'Not exactly,' he said with difficulty. 'But of late years I have worked a good deal abroad. My methods are the methods of the Sûreté.'

'Oh!' The girl seemed impressed.

She was, as Tommy had indicated, a very charming girl. Young and slim, with a trace of golden hair peeping out from under her little brown felt hat, and big serious eyes.

That she was nervous could be plainly seen. Her little hands were twisting themselves together, and she kept clasping and unclasping the catch of her lacquered handbag.

'First of all, Mr Blunt, I must tell you that my name is Lois Hargreaves. I live in a great rambling old-fashioned house called Thurnly Grange. It is in the heart of the country. There is the village of Thurnly nearby, but it is very small and insignificant. There is plenty of hunting in winter, and we get tennis in summer, and I have never felt lonely there. Indeed I much prefer country to town life.

'I tell you this so that you may realise that in a country village like ours, everything that happens is of supreme importance. About a week ago, I got a box of chocolates sent through the post. There was nothing inside to indicate who they came from. Now I myself am not particularly fond of chocolates, but the others in the house are, and the box was passed round. As a result, everyone who had eaten any chocolates was taken ill. We sent for the doctor, and after various inquiries as to what other things had been eaten, he took the remains of the chocolates away with him, and had them analysed. Mr Blunt, those chocolates contained arsenic! Not enough to kill anyone, but enough to make anyone quite ill.'

'Extraordinary,' commented Tommy.

'Dr Burton was very excited over the matter. It seems that this was the third occurrence of the kind in the neighbourhood. In each case a big house was selected, and the inmates were taken ill after eating the mysterious chocolates. It looked as though some local person of weak intellect was playing a particularly fiendish practical joke.'

'Quite so, Miss Hargreaves.'

'Dr Burton put it down to Socialist agitation – rather absurdly, I thought. But there are one or two malcontents in Thurnly village, and it seemed possible that they might have had something to do with it. Dr Burton was very keen that I should put the whole thing in the hands of the police.'

'A very natural suggestion,' said Tommy. 'But you have not done so, I gather, Miss Hargreaves?'

'No,' admitted the girl. 'I hate the fuss and the publicity that would ensue – and you see, I know our local Inspector. I can never imagine him finding out anything! I have often seen your advertisements, and I told Dr Burton that it would be much better to call in a private detective.'

'I see.'

'You say a great deal about discretion in your advertisement. I take that to mean – that – that – well, that you would not make anything public without my consent?'

Tommy looked at her curiously, but it was Tuppence who spoke.

'I think,' she said quietly, 'that it would be as well if Miss Hargreaves told us *everything*.'

She laid especial stress upon the last word, and Lois Hargreaves flushed nervously.

'Yes,' said Tommy quickly, 'Miss Robinson is right. You must tell us everything.'

'You will not –' she hesitated.

'Everything you say is understood to be strictly in confidence.'

'Thank you. I know that I ought to have been quite frank with you. I have a reason for not going to the police. Mr Blunt, that box of chocolates was sent by someone in our house!'

'How do you know that, mademoiselle?'

'It's very simple. I've got a habit of drawing a little silly thing – three fish intertwined – whenever I have a pencil in my hand. A parcel of silk stockings arrived from a certain shop in London not long ago. We were at the breakfast table. I'd just been marking something in the newspaper, and without thinking, I began to draw my silly little fish on the label of the parcel before cutting the string and opening it. I thought no more about the matter, but when I was examining the piece of brown paper in which the chocolates had been sent, I caught sight of the corner of the original label – most of which had been torn off. My silly little drawing was on it.'

Tommy drew his chair forward.

'That is very serious. It creates, as you say, a very strong presumption that the sender of the chocolates is a member of your household. But you will forgive me if I say that I still do not see why that fact should render you indisposed to call in the police?'

Lois Hargreaves looked him squarely in the face.

'I will tell you, Mr Blunt. I may want the whole thing hushed up.'

Tommy retired gracefully from the position.

'In that case,' he murmured, 'we know where we are. I see, Miss Hargreaves, that you are not disposed to tell me who it is you suspect?'

'I suspect no one – but there are possibilities.'

'Quite so. Now will you describe the household to me in detail?'

'The servants, with the exception of the parlourmaid, are all old ones who have been with us many years. I must explain to you, Mr Blunt, that I was brought up by my aunt, Lady Radclyffe, who was extremely wealthy. Her husband made a big fortune, and was knighted. It was he who bought Thurnly Grange, but he died two years after going there, and it was then that Lady Radclyffe sent for me to come and make my home with her. I was her only living relation. The other inmate of the house was Dennis Radclyffe, her husband's nephew. I have always called him cousin, but of course he is really nothing of the kind. Aunt Lucy always said openly that she intended to leave her money, with the exception of a small provision for me, to Dennis. It was Radclyffe money, she said, and it ought to go to a Radclyffe. However, when Dennis was twenty-two, she quarrelled violently with him – over some debts that he had run up, I think. When she died, a year later, I was astonished to find that she had made a will leaving all her money to me. It was, I know, a great blow to Dennis, and I felt very badly about it. I would have given him the money if he would have taken it, but it seems that kind of thing can't be done. However, as soon as I was twenty-one, I made a will leaving it all to him. That's the least I can do. So if I'm run over by a motor, Dennis will come into his own.'

'Exactly,' said Tommy. 'And when were you twenty-one, if I may ask the question?'

'Just three weeks ago.'

'Ah!' said Tommy. 'Now will you give me fuller particulars of the members of your household at this minute?'

'Servants – or – others?'

'Both.'

'The servants, as I say, have been with us some time. There is old Mrs Holloway, the cook, and her niece Rose, the kitchenmaid. Then there are two elderly housemaids, and Hannah who was my aunt's maid and who has always been devoted to me. The parlourmaid is called Esther Quant, and seems a very nice quiet girl. As for ourselves, there is Miss Logan, who was Aunt Lucy's companion, and who runs the house for me, and Captain Radclyffe – Dennis, you know, whom I told you about, and there is a girl called Mary Chilcott, an old school friend of mine who is staying with us.'

Tommy thought for a moment.

'That all seems fairly clear and straightforward, Miss Hargreaves,' he said after a minute or two. 'I take it that you have no special reason for attaching suspicion more to one person than another? You are only afraid it might prove to be – well – not a servant, shall we say?'

'That's it exactly, Mr Blunt. I have honestly no idea who used that piece of brown paper. The handwriting was printed.'

'There seems only one thing to be done,' said Tommy. 'I must be on the spot.'

The girl looked at him inquiringly.

Tommy went on after a moment's thought.

'I suggest that you prepare the way for the arrival of – say, Mr and Miss Van Dusen – American friends of yours. Will you be able to do that quite naturally?'

'Oh, yes. There will be no difficulty at all. When will you come down – tomorrow – or the day after?'

'Tomorrow, if you please. There is no time to waste.'

'That is settled then.'

The girl rose and held out her hand.

'One thing, Miss Hargreaves, not a word, mind, to anyone – anyone at all, that we are not what we seem.'

'What do you think of it, Tuppence?' he asked, when he returned from showing the visitor out.

'I don't like it,' said Tuppence decidedly. 'Especially I don't like the chocolates having so little arsenic in them.'

'What *do* you mean?'

'Don't you see? All those chocolates being sent round the neighbourhood were a blind. To establish the idea of a local maniac. Then, when the girl was really poisoned, it would be thought to be the same thing. You see, but for a stroke of luck, no one would ever have guessed that the chocolates were actually sent by someone in the house itself.'

'That was a stroke of luck. You're right. You think it's a deliberate plot against the girl herself?'

'I'm afraid so. I remember reading about old Lady Radclyffe's will. That girl has come into a terrific lot of money.'

'Yes, and she came of age and made a will three weeks ago. It looks bad – for Dennis Radclyffe. He gains by her death.'

Tuppence nodded.

'The worst of it is – that she thinks so too! That's why she won't have the police called in. Already she suspects him. And she must be more than half in love with him to act as she has done.'

'In that case,' said Tommy thoughtfully, 'why the devil doesn't he marry her? Much simpler and safer.'

Tuppence stared at him.

'You've said a mouthful,' she observed. 'Oh, boy! I'm getting ready to be Miss Van Dusen, you observe.'

'Why rush to crime, when there is a lawful means near at hand?'

Tuppence reflected for a minute or two.

'I've got it,' she announced. 'Clearly he must have married a barmaid whilst at Oxford. Origin of the quarrel with his aunt. That explains everything.'

'Then why not send the poisoned sweets to the barmaid?' suggested Tommy. 'Much more practical. I wish you wouldn't jump to these wild conclusions, Tuppence.'

'They're deductions,' said Tuppence, with a good deal of dignity. 'This is your first *corrida*, my friend, but when you have been twenty minutes in the arena –'

Tommy flung the office cushion at her.

'Tuppence, I say, Tuppence, come here.'

It was breakfast time the next morning. Tuppence hurried out of her bedroom and into the dining-room. Tommy was striding up and down, the open newspaper in his hand.

'What's the matter?'

Tommy wheeled round, and shoved the paper into her hand, pointing to the headlines.

MYSTERIOUS POISONING CASE
DEATHS FROM FIG SANDWICHES

Tuppence read on. This mysterious outbreak of ptomaine poisoning had occurred at Thurnly Grange. The deaths so far reported were those of Miss Lois Hargreaves, the owner of the house, and the parlourmaid, Esther Quant. A Captain Radclyffe and a Miss Logan were reported to be seriously ill. The cause of the outbreak was supposed to be some fig paste used in sandwiches, since another lady, a Miss Chilcott, who had not partaken of these was reported to be quite well.

'We must get down there at once,' said Tommy. 'That girl! That perfectly ripping girl! Why the devil didn't I go straight down there with her yesterday?'

'If you had,' said Tuppence, 'you'd probably have eaten fig sandwiches too for tea, and then you'd have been dead. Come on, let's start at once. I see it says that Dennis Radclyffe is seriously ill also.'

'Probably shamming, the dirty blackguard.'

They arrived at the small village of Thurnly about midday. An elderly woman with red eyes opened the door to them when they arrived at Thurnly Grange.

'Look here,' said Tommy quickly before she could speak. 'I'm not a reporter or anything like that. Miss Hargreaves came to see me yesterday, and asked me to come down here. Is there anyone I can see?'

'Dr Burton is here now, if you'd like to speak to him,' said the woman doubtfully. 'Or Miss Chilcott. She's making all the arrangements.'

But Tommy had caught at the first suggestion.

'Dr Burton,' he said authoritatively. 'I should like to see him at once if he is here.'

The woman showed them into a small morning-room. Five minutes later the door opened, and a tall, elderly man with bent shoulders and a kind, but worried face, came in.

'Dr Burton,' said Tommy. He produced his professional card. 'Miss Hargreaves called on me yesterday with reference to those poisoned chocolates. I came down to investigate the matter at her request – alas! too late.'

The doctor looked at him keenly.

'You are Mr Blunt himself?'

'Yes. This is my assistant, Miss Robinson.'

The doctor bowed to Tuppence.

'Under the circumstances, there is no need for reticence. But for the episode of the chocolates, I might have believed these deaths to be the result of severe ptomaine poisoning – but ptomaine poisoning of an unusually virulent kind. There is gastro-intestinal inflammation and haemorrhage. As it is, I am taking the fig paste to be analysed.'

'You suspect arsenic poisoning?'

'No. The poison, if a poison has been employed, is something far more potent and swift in its action. It looks more like some powerful vegetable toxin.'

'I see. I should like to ask you, Dr Burton, whether you are thoroughly convinced that Captain Radclyffe is suffering from the same form of poisoning?'

The doctor looked at him.

'Captain Radclyffe is not suffering from any sort of poisoning now.'

'Aha,' said Tommy. 'I –'

'Captain Radclyffe died at five o'clock this morning.'

Tommy was utterly taken aback. The doctor prepared to depart.

'And the other victim, Miss Logan?' asked Tuppence.

'I have every reason to hope that she will recover since she has survived so far. Being an older woman, the poison seems to have had less effect on her. I will let you know the result of the analysis, Mr Blunt. In the meantime, Miss Chilcott, will, I am sure, tell you anything you want to know.'

As he spoke, the door opened, and a girl appeared. She was tall, with a tanned face, and steady blue eyes.

Dr Burton performed the necessary introductions.

'I am glad you have come, Mr Blunt,' said Mary Chilcott. 'This affair seems too terrible. Is there anything you want to know that I can tell you?'

'Where did the fig paste come from?'

'It is a special kind that comes from London. We often have it. No one suspected that this particular pot differed from any of the others. Personally I dislike the flavour of figs. That explains my immunity. I cannot understand how Dennis was affected, since he was out for tea. He must have picked up a sandwich when he came home, I suppose.'

Tommy felt Tuppence's hand press his arm ever so slightly.

'What time did he come in?' he asked.

'I don't really know. I could find out.'

'Thank you, Miss Chilcott. It doesn't matter. You have no objection, I hope, to my questioning the servants?'

'Please do anything you like, Mr Blunt. I am nearly distraught. Tell me – you don't think there has been – foul play?'

Her eyes were very anxious, as she put the question.

'I don't know what to think. We shall soon know.'

'Yes, I suppose Dr Burton will have the paste analysed.'

Quickly excusing herself, she went out by the window to speak to one of the gardeners.

'You take the housemaids, Tuppence,' said Tommy, 'and I'll find my way to the kitchen. I say, Miss Chilcott may feel very distraught, but she doesn't look it.'

Tuppence nodded assent without replying.

Husband and wife met half an hour later.

'Now to pool results,' said Tommy. 'The sandwiches came out for tea, and the parlourmaid ate one – that's how she got it in the neck. Cook is positive Dennis Radclyffe hadn't returned when tea was cleared away. Query – how did *he* get poisoned?'

'He came in at a quarter to seven,' said Tuppence. 'Housemaid saw him from one of the windows. He had a cocktail before dinner – in the library. She was just clearing away the glass now, and luckily I got it from her before she washed it. It was after that that he complained of feeling ill.'

'Good,' said Tommy. 'I'll take that glass along to Burton, presently. Anything else?'

'I'd like you to see Hannah, the maid. She's – she's queer.'

'How do you mean – queer?'

'She looks to me as though she were going off her head.'

'Let me see her.'

Tuppence led the way upstairs. Hannah had a small sitting-room of her own. The maid sat upright on a high chair. On her knees was an open Bible. She did not look towards the two strangers as they entered. Instead she continued to read aloud to herself.

'Let hot burning coals fall upon them, let them be cast into the fire and into the pit, that they never rise up again.'

'May I speak to you a minute?' asked Tommy.

Hannah made an impatient gesture with her hand.

'This is no time. The time is running short, I say. *I will follow upon mine enemies and overtake them, neither will I turn again till I have destroyed them.* So it is written. The word of the Lord has come to me. I am the scourge of the Lord.'

'Mad as a hatter,' murmured Tommy.

'She's been going on like that all the time,' whispered Tuppence.

Tommy picked up a book that was lying open, face downwards on the table. He glanced at the title and slipped it into his pocket.

Suddenly the old woman rose and turned towards them menacingly.

'Go out from here. The time is at hand! I am the flail of the Lord. The wind bloweth where it listeth – so do I destroy. The ungodly shall perish. This is a house of evil – of evil, I tell you! Beware of the wrath of the Lord whose handmaiden I am.'

She advanced upon them fiercely. Tommy thought it best to humour her and withdrew. As he closed the door, he saw her pick up the Bible again.

'I wonder if she's always been like that,' he muttered.

He drew from his pocket the book he had picked up off the table.

'Look at that. Funny reading for an ignorant maid.'

Tuppence took the book.

'Materia Medica,' she murmured. She looked at the flyleaf, 'Edward Logan. It's an old book. Tommy, I wonder if we could see Miss Logan? Dr Burton said she was better.'

'Shall we ask Miss Chilcott?'

'No. Let's get hold of a housemaid, and send her in to ask.'

After a brief delay, they were informed that Miss Logan would see them. They were taken into a big bedroom facing over the lawn. In the bed was an old lady with white hair, her delicate face drawn by suffering.

'I have been very ill,' she said faintly. 'And I can't talk much, but Ellen tells me you are detectives. Lois went to consult you then? She spoke of doing so.'

'Yes, Miss Logan,' said Tommy. 'We don't want to tire you, but perhaps you can answer a few questions. The maid, Hannah, is she quite right in her head?'

Miss Logan looked at them with obvious surprise.

'Oh, yes. She is very religious – but there is nothing wrong with her.'

Tommy held out the book he had taken from the table.

'Is this yours, Miss Logan?'

'Yes. It was one of my father's books. He was a great doctor, one of the pioneers of serum therapeutics.'

The old lady's voice rang with pride.

'Quite so,' said Tommy. 'I thought I knew his name.' he added mendaciously. 'This book now, did you lend it to Hannah?'

'To Hannah?' Miss Logan raised herself in bed with indignation. 'No, indeed. She wouldn't understand the first word of it. It is a highly technical book.'

'Yes. I see that. Yet I found it in Hannah's room.'

'Disgraceful,' said Miss Logan. 'I will not have the servants touching my things.'

'Where ought it to be?'

'In the bookshelf in my sitting-room – or – stay, I lent it to Mary. The dear girl is very interested in herbs. She has made one or two experiments in my little kitchen. I have a little place of my own, you know, where I brew liqueurs and make preserves in the old-fashioned way. Dear Lucy, Lady Radclyffe, you know, used to swear by my tansy tea – a wonderful thing for a cold in the head. Poor Lucy, she was subject to colds. So is Dennis. Dear boy, his father was my first cousin.'

Tommy interrupted these reminiscences.

'This kitchen of yours? Does anyone else use it except you and Miss Chilcott?'

'Hannah clears up there. And she boils the kettle there for our early morning tea.'

'Thank you, Miss Logan,' said Tommy. 'There is nothing more I want to ask you at present. I hope we haven't tired you too much.'

He left the room and went down the stairs, frowning to himself.

'There is something here, my dear Mr Ricardo, that I do not understand.'

'I hate this house,' said Tuppence with a shiver. 'Let's go for a good long walk and try to think things out.'

Tommy complied and they set out. First they left the cocktail glass at the doctor's house, and then set off for a good tramp across the country, discussing the case as they did so.

'It makes it easier somehow if one plays the fool,' said Tommy. 'All this Hanaud business. I suppose some people would think I didn't care. But I do, most awfully. I feel that somehow or other we ought to have prevented this.'

'I think that's foolish of you,' said Tuppence. 'It is not as though we advised Lois Hargreaves not to go to Scotland Yard or anything like that. Nothing would have induced her to bring the police into the matter. If she hadn't come to us, she would have done nothing at all.'

'And the result would have been the same. Yes, you are right, Tuppence. It's morbid to reproach oneself over something one couldn't help. What I would like to do is to make good now.'

'And that's not going to be easy.'

'No, it isn't. There are so many possibilities, and yet all of them seem wild and improbable. Supposing Dennis Radclyffe put the poison in the sandwiches. He knew he would be out to tea. That seems fairly plain sailing.'

'Yes,' said Tuppence, 'that's all right so far. Then we can put against that the fact that he was poisoned himself – so that seems to rule him out. There is one person we mustn't forget – and that is Hannah.'

'Hannah?'

'People do all sorts of queer things when they have religious mania.'

'She is pretty far gone with it too,' said Tommy. 'You ought to drop a word to Dr Burton about it.'

'It must have come on very rapidly,' said Tuppence. 'That is if we go by what Miss Logan said.'

'I believe religious mania does,' said Tommy. 'I mean, you go on singing hymns in your bedroom with the door open for years, and then you go suddenly right over the line and become violent.'

'There is certainly more evidence against Hannah than against anybody else,' said Tuppence thoughtfully. 'And yet I have an idea –' She stopped.

'Yes?' said Tommy encouragingly.

'It is not really an idea. I suppose it is just a prejudice.'

'A prejudice against someone?'

Tuppence nodded.

'Tommy – did *you* like Mary Chilcott?'

Tommy considered.

'Yes, I think I did. She struck me as extremely capable and business-like – perhaps a shade too much so – but very reliable.'

'You didn't think it was odd that she didn't seem more upset?'

'Well, in a way that is a point in her favour. I mean, if she had done anything, she would make a point of being upset – lay it on rather thick.'

'I suppose so,' said Tuppence. 'And anyway there doesn't seem to be any motive in her case. One doesn't see what good this wholesale slaughter can do her.'

'I suppose none of the servants are concerned?'

'It doesn't seem likely. They seem a quiet, reliable lot. I wonder what Esther Quant, the parlourmaid, was like.'

'You mean, that if she was young and good-looking there was a chance that she was mixed up in it some way.'

'That is what I mean,' Tuppence sighed. 'It is all very discouraging.'

'Well, I suppose the police will get down to it all right,' said Tommy.

'Probably. I should like it to be us. By the way, did you notice a lot of small red dots on Miss Logan's arm?'

'I don't think I did. What about them?'

'They looked as though they were made by a hypodermic syringe,' said Tuppence.

'Probably Dr Burton gave her a hypodermic injection of some kind.'

'Oh, very likely. But he wouldn't give her about forty.'

'The cocaine habit,' suggested Tommy helpfully.

'I thought of that,' said Tuppence, 'but her eyes were all right. You could see at once if it was cocaine or morphia. Besides, she doesn't look that sort of old lady.'

'Most respectable and God-fearing,' agreed Tommy.

'It is all very difficult,' said Tuppence. 'We have talked and talked and we don't seem any nearer now than we were. Don't let's forget to call at the doctor's on our way home.'

The doctor's door was opened by a lanky boy of about fifteen.

'Mr Blunt?' he inquired. 'Yes, the doctor is out, but he left a note for you in case you should call.'

He handed them the note in question and Tommy tore it open.

Dear Mr Blunt,
There is reason to believe that the poison employed was Ricin, a vegetable toxalbumose of tremendous potency. Please keep this to yourself for the present.

Tommy let the note drop, but picked it up quickly.

'Ricin,' he murmured. 'Know anything about it, Tuppence? You used to be rather well up in these things.'

'Ricin,' said Tuppence, thoughtfully. 'You get it out of castor oil, I believe.'

'I never did take kindly to castor oil,' said Tommy. 'I am more set against it than ever now.'

'The oil's all right. You get Ricin from the seeds of the castor oil plant. I believe I saw some castor oil plants in the garden this morning – big things with glossy leaves.'

'You mean that someone extracted the stuff on the premises. Could Hannah do such a thing?'

Tuppence shook her head.

'Doesn't seem likely. She wouldn't know enough.'

Suddenly Tommy gave an exclamation.

'That book. Have I got it in my pocket still? Yes.' He took it out, and turned over the leaves vehemently. 'I thought so. Here's the page it was open at this morning. Do you see, Tuppence? Ricin!'

Tuppence seized the book from him.

'Can you make head or tail of it? I can't.'

'It's clear enough to me,' said Tuppence. She walked along, reading busily, with one hand on Tommy's arm to steer herself. Presently she shut the book with a bang. They were just approaching the house again.

'Tommy, will you leave this to me? Just for once, you see, I am the bull that has been more than twenty minutes in the arena.'

Tommy nodded.

'You shall be the Captain of the Ship, Tuppence,' he said gravely. 'We've got to get to the bottom of this.'

'First of all,' said Tuppence as they entered the house, 'I must ask Miss Logan one more question.'

She ran upstairs. Tommy followed her. She rapped sharply on the old lady's door and went in.

'Is that you, my dear?' said Miss Logan. 'You know you are much too young and pretty to be a detective. Have you found out anything?'

'Yes,' said Tuppence. 'I have.'

Miss Logan looked at her questioningly.

'I don't know about being pretty,' went on Tuppence, 'but being young, I happened to work in a hospital during the War. I know something about serum therapeutics. I happen to know that when Ricin is injected in small doses hypodermically, immunity is produced, antiricin is formed. That fact paved the way for the foundation of serum therapeutics. You knew that, Miss Logan. You injected Ricin for some time hypodermically into yourself. Then you let yourself be poisoned with the rest. You helped your father in his work, and you knew all about Ricin and how to obtain it and extract it from the seeds. You chose a day when Dennis Radclyffe was out for tea. It wouldn't do for him to be poisoned at the same time – he might die before Lois Hargreaves. So long as she died first, he inherited her money, and at his death it passes to you, his next-of-kin. You remember, you told us this morning that his father was your first cousin.'

The old lady stared at Tuppence with baleful eyes.

Suddenly a wild figure burst in from the adjoining room. It was Hannah. In her hand she held a lighted torch which she waved frantically.

'Truth has been spoken. That is the wicked one. I saw her reading the book and smiling to herself and I knew. I found the book and the page – but it said nothing to me. But the voice of the Lord spoke to me. She hated my mistress, her ladyship. She was always jealous and envious. She hated my own sweet Miss Lois. But the wicked shall perish, the fire of the Lord shall consume them.'

Waving her torch she sprang forward to the bed.

A cry arose from the old lady.

'Take her away – take her away. It's true – but take her away.'

Tuppence flung herself upon Hannah, but the woman managed to set fire to the curtains of the bed before Tuppence could get the torch from her and stamp on it. Tommy, however, had rushed in from the landing outside. He tore down the bed hangings and managed to stifle the flames with a rug. Then he rushed to Tuppence's assistance, and between them they subdued Hannah just as Dr Burton came hurrying in.

A very few words sufficed to put him *au courant* of the situation.

He hurried to the bedside, lifted Miss Logan's hand, then uttered a sharp exclamation.

'The shock of fire has been too much for her. She's dead. Perhaps it is as well under the circumstances.'

He paused, and then added, 'There was Ricin in the cocktail glass as well.'

'It's the best thing that could have happened,' said Tommy, when they had relinquished Hannah to the doctor's care, and were alone together. 'Tuppence, you were simply marvellous.'

'There wasn't much Hanaud about it,' said Tuppence.

'It was too serious for play-acting. I still can't bear to think of that girl. I won't think of her. But, as I said before, you were marvellous. The honours are with you. To use a familiar quotation, "It is a great advantage to be intelligent and not to look it."'

'Tommy,' said Tuppence, 'you're a beast.'

The Unbreakable Alibi

'The Unbreakable Alibi' was originally the last Tommy and Tuppence story, appearing in *Holly Leaves* (published by Illustrated Sporting and Dramatic News), 1 December 1928. Inspector French was created by Freeman Wills Croft (1879–1957).

Tommy and Tuppence were busy sorting correspondence. Tuppence gave an exclamation and handed a letter across to Tommy.

'A new client,' she said importantly.

'Ha!' said Tommy. 'What do we deduce from this letter, Watson? Nothing much, except the somewhat obvious fact that Mr – er – Montgomery Jones is not one of the world's best spellers, thereby proving that he has been expensively educated.'

'Montgomery Jones?' said Tuppence. 'Now what do I know about a Montgomery Jones? Oh, yes, I have got it now. I think Janet St Vincent mentioned him. His mother was Lady Aileen Montgomery, very crusty and high church, with gold crosses and things, and she married a man called Jones who is immensely rich.'

'In fact the same old story,' said Tommy. 'Let me see, what time does this Mr M. J. wish to see us? Ah, eleven-thirty.'

At eleven-thirty precisely, a very tall young man with an amiable and ingenuous countenance entered the outer office and addressed himself to Albert, the office boy.

'Look here – I say. Can I see Mr – er – Blunt?'

'Have you an appointment, sir?' said Albert.

'I don't quite know. Yes, I suppose I have. What I mean is, I wrote a letter –'

'What name, sir?'

'Mr Montgomery Jones.'

'I will take your name in to Mr Blunt.'

He returned after a brief interval.

'Will you wait a few minutes please, sir. Mr Blunt is engaged on a very important conference at present.'

'Oh – er – yes – certainly,' said Mr Montgomery Jones.

Having, he hoped, impressed his client sufficiently Tommy rang the buzzer on his desk, and Mr Montgomery Jones was ushered into the inner office by Albert.

Tommy rose to greet him, and shaking him warmly by the hand motioned towards the vacant chair.

'Now, Mr Montgomery Jones,' he said briskly. 'What can we have the pleasure of doing for you?'

Mr Montgomery Jones looked uncertainly at the third occupant of the office.

'My confidential secretary, Miss Robinson,' said Tommy. 'You can speak quite freely before her. I take it that this is some family matter of a delicate kind?'

'Well – not exactly,' said Mr Montgomery Jones.

'You surprise me,' said Tommy. 'You are not in trouble of any kind yourself, I hope?'

'Oh, rather not,' said Mr Montgomery Jones.

'Well,' said Tommy, 'perhaps you will – er – state the facts plainly.'

That, however, seemed to be the one thing that Mr Montgomery Jones could not do.

'It's a dashed odd sort of thing I have got to ask you,' he said hesitatingly. 'I – er – I really don't know how to set about it.'

'We never touch divorce cases,' said Tommy.

'Oh Lord, no,' said Mr Montgomery Jones. 'I don't mean that. It is just, well – it's a deuced silly sort of a joke. That's all.'

'Someone has played a practical joke on you of a mysterious nature?' suggested Tommy.

But Mr Montgomery Jones once more shook his head.

'Well,' said Tommy, retiring gracefully from the position, 'take your own time and let us have it in your own words.'

There was a pause.

'You see,' said Mr Jones at last, 'it was at dinner. I sat next to a girl.'

'Yes?' said Tommy encouragingly.

'She was a – oh well, I really can't describe her, but she was simply one of the most sporting girls I ever met. She's an Australian, over here with another girl, sharing a flat with her in. Clarges Street. She's simply game for anything. I absolutely can't tell you the effect that girl had on me.'

'We can quite imagine it, Mr Jones,' said Tuppence.

She saw clearly that if Mr Montgomery Jones's troubles were ever to be extracted a sympathetic feminine touch was needed, as distinct from the businesslike methods of Mr Blunt.

'We can understand,' said Tuppence encouragingly.

'Well, the whole thing came as an absolute shock to me,' said Mr Montgomery Jones, 'that a girl could well – knock you over like that. There had been another girl – in fact two other girls. One was awfully jolly and all that, but I didn't much like her chin. She danced marvellously though, and I have known her all my life, which makes a fellow feel kind of safe, you know. And then there was one of the girls at the "Frivolity." Frightfully amusing, but of course there would be a lot of ructions with the matter over that, and anyway I didn't really want to marry either of them, but I was thinking about things, you know, and then – slap out of the blue – I sat next to this girl and –'

'The whole world was changed,' said Tuppence in a feeling voice.

Tommy moved impatiently in his chair. He was by now somewhat bored by the recital of Mr Montgomery Jones's love affairs.

'You put it awfully well,' said Mr Montgomery Jones. 'That is absolutely what it was like. Only, you know, I fancy she didn't think much of me. You mayn't think it, but I am not terribly clever.'

'Oh, you mustn't be too modest,' said Tuppence.

'Oh, I do realise that I am not much of a chap,' said Mr Jones with an engaging smile. 'Not for a perfectly marvellous girl like that. That is why I just feel I have got to put this thing through. It's my only chance. She's such a sporting girl that she would never go back on her word.'

'Well, I am sure we wish you luck and all that,' said Tuppence kindly. 'But I don't exactly see what you want us to do.'

'Oh Lord,' said Mr Montgomery Jones. 'Haven't I explained?'

'No,' said Tommy, 'you haven't.'

'Well, it was like this. We were talking about detective stories. Una – that's her name – is just as keen about them as I am. We got talking about one in particular. It all hinges on an alibi. Then we got talking about alibis and faking them. Then I said – no, she said – now which of us was it that said it?'

'Never mind which of you it was,' said Tuppence.

'I said it would be a jolly difficult thing to do. She disagreed – said it only wanted a bit of brain work. We got all hot and excited about it and in the end she said, "I will make you a sporting offer. What do you bet that I can produce an alibi that nobody can shake?"'

'"Anything you like," I said, and we settled it then and there. She was frightfully cocksure about the whole thing. "It's an odds on chance for me," she said. "Don't be so sure of that," I said. "Supposing you lose and I ask you for anything I like?" She laughed and said she came of a gambling family and I could.'

'Well?' said Tuppence as Mr Jones came to a pause and looked at her appealingly.

'Well, don't you see? It is up to me. It is the only chance I have got of getting a girl like that to look at me. You have no idea how sporting she is. Last summer she was out in a boat and someone bet her she wouldn't jump overboard and swim ashore in her clothes, and she did it.'

'It is a very curious proposition,' said Tommy. 'I am not quite sure I yet understand it.'

'It is perfectly simple,' said Mr Montgomery Jones. 'You must be doing this sort of thing all the time. Investigating fake alibis and seeing where they fall down.'

'Oh – er – yes, of course,' said Tommy. 'We do a lot of that sort of work.'

'Someone has got to do it for me,' said Montgomery Jones. 'I shouldn't be any good at that sort of thing myself. You have only got to catch her out and everything is all right. I dare say it seems rather a futile business to you, but it means a lot to me and I am prepared to pay – er – all necessary whatnots, you know.'

'That will be all right,' said Tuppence. 'I am sure Mr Blunt will take this case on for you.'

'Certainly, certainly,' said Tommy. 'A most refreshing case, most refreshing indeed.'

Mr Montgomery Jones heaved a sigh of relief, pulled a mass of papers from his pocket and selected one of them. 'Here it is,' he said. 'She says, "I am sending you proof I was in two distinct places at one and the same time. According to one story I dined at the Bon Temps Restaurant in Soho by myself, went to the Duke's Theatre and had supper with a friend, Mr le Marchant, at the Savoy – *but* I was also staying at the Castle Hotel, Torquay, and only returned to London on the following morning. You have got to find out which of the two stories is the true one and how I managed the other."'

'There,' said Mr Montgomery Jones. 'Now you see what it is that I want you to do.'

'A most refreshing little problem,' said Tommy. 'Very naive.'

'Here is Una's photograph,' said Mr Montgomery Jones. 'You will want that.'

'What is the lady's full name?' inquired Tommy.

'Miss Una Drake. And her address is 180 Clarges Street.'

'Thank you,' said Tommy. 'Well, we will look into the matter for you, Mr Montgomery Jones. I hope we shall have good news for you very shortly.'

'I say, you know, I am no end grateful,' said Mr Jones, rising to his feet and shaking Tommy by the hand. 'It has taken an awful load off my mind.'

Having seen his client out, Tommy returned to the inner office. Tuppence was at the cupboard that contained the classic library.

'Inspector French,' said Tuppence.

'Eh?' said Tommy.

'Inspector French, of course,' said Tuppence. 'He always does alibis. I know the exact procedure. We have to go over everything and check it. At first it will seem all right and then when we examine it more closely we shall find the flaw.'

'There ought not to be much difficulty about that,' agreed Tommy. 'I mean, knowing that one of them is a fake to start with makes the thing almost a certainty, I should say. That is what worries me.'

'I don't see anything to worry about in that.'

'I am worrying about the girl,' said Tommy. 'She will probably be let in to marry that young man whether she wants to or not.'

'Darling,' said Tuppence, 'don't be foolish. Women are never the wild gamblers they appear. Unless that girl was already perfectly prepared to marry that pleasant, but rather empty-headed young man, she would never have let herself in for a wager of this kind. But, Tommy, believe me, she will marry him with more enthusiasm and respect if he wins the wager than if she has to make it easy for him some other way.'

'You do think you know about everything,' said her husband.

'I do,' said Tuppence.

'And now to examine our data,' said Tommy, drawing the papers towards him. 'First the photograph – h'm – quite a nice looking girl – and quite a good photograph, I should say. Clear and easily recognisable.'

'We must get some other girls' photographs,' said Tuppence.

'Why?'

'They always do,' said Tuppence. 'You show four or five to waiters and they pick out the right one.'

'Do you think they do?' said Tommy – 'pick out the right one, I mean.'

'Well, they do in books,' said Tuppence.

'It is a pity that real life is so different from fiction,' said Tommy. 'Now then, what have we here? Yes, this is the London lot. Dined at the Bon Temps seven-thirty. Went to Duke's Theatre and saw *Delphiniums Blue*. Counterfoil of theatre ticket enclosed. Supper at the Savoy with Mr le Marchant. We can, I suppose, interview Mr le Marchant.'

'That tells us nothing at all,' said Tuppence, 'because if he is helping her to do it he naturally won't give the show away. We can wash out anything he says now.'

'Well, here is the Torquay end,' went on Tommy. 'Twelve o'clock from Paddington, had lunch in the Restaurant Car, receipted bill enclosed. Stayed at Castle Hotel for one night. Again receipted bill.'

'I think this is all rather weak,' said Tuppence. 'Anyone can buy a theatre ticket, you need never go near the theatre. The girl just went to Torquay and the London thing is a fake.'

'If so, it is rather a sitter for us,' said Tommy. 'Well, I suppose we might as well go and interview Mr le Marchant.'

Mr le Marchant proved to be a breezy youth who betrayed no great surprise on seeing them.

'Una has got some little game on, hasn't she?' he asked. 'You never know what that kid is up to.'

'I understand, Mr le Marchant,' said Tommy, 'that Miss Drake had supper with you at the Savoy last Tuesday evening.'

'That's right,' said Mr le Marchant, 'I know it was Tuesday because Una impressed it on me at the time and what's more she made me write it down in a little book.'

With some pride he showed an entry faintly pencilled. 'Having supper with Una. Savoy. Tuesday 19th.'

'Where had Miss Drake been earlier in the evening? Do you know?'

'She had been to some rotten show called *Pink Peonies* or something like that. Absolute slosh, so she told me.'

'You are quite sure Miss Drake was with you that evening?'

Mr le Marchant stared at him.

'Why, of course. Haven't I been telling you.'

'Perhaps she asked you to tell us,' said Tuppence.

'Well, for a matter of fact she did say something that was rather dashed odd. She said – what was it now? "You think you are sitting here having supper with me, Jimmy, but really I am having supper two hundred miles away in Devonshire." Now that was a dashed odd thing to say, don't you think so? Sort of astral body stuff. The funny thing is that a pal of mine, Dicky Rice, thought he saw her there.'

'Who is this Mr Rice?'

'Oh, just a friend of mine. He had been down in Torquay staying with an aunt. Sort of old bean who is always going to die and never does. Dicky had been down doing the dutiful nephew. He said, "I saw that Australian girl one day – Una something or other. Wanted to go and talk to her, but my aunt carried me off to chat with an old pussy in a bath chair." I said: "When was this?" and he said, "Oh, Tuesday about tea time." I told him, of course, that he had made a mistake, but it was odd, wasn't it? With Una saying that about Devonshire that evening?'

'Very odd,' said Tommy. 'Tell me, Mr le Marchant, did anyone you know have supper near you at the Savoy?'

'Some people called Oglander were at the next table.'

'Do they know Miss Drake?'

'Oh yes, they know her. They are not frightful friends or anything of that kind.'

'Well, if there's nothing more you can tell us, Mr le Marchant, I think we will wish you good-morning.'

'Either that chap is an extraordinarily good liar,' said Tommy as they reached the street, 'or else he is speaking the truth.'

'Yes,' said Tuppence, 'I have changed my opinion. I have a sort of feeling now that Una Drake was at the Savoy for supper that night.'

'We will now go to the Bon Temps,' said Tommy. 'A little food for starving sleuths is clearly indicated. Let's just get a few girls' photographs first.'

This proved rather more difficult than was expected. Turning into a photographers and demanding a few assorted photographs, they were met with a cold rebuff.

'Why are all the things that are so easy and simple in books so difficult in real life,' wailed Tuppence. 'How horribly suspicious they looked. What do you think they thought we wanted to do with the photographs? We had better go and raid Jane's flat.'

Tuppence's friend Jane proved of an accommodating disposition and permitted Tuppence to rummage in a drawer and select four specimens of former friends of Jane's who had been shoved hastily in to be out of sight and mind.

Armed with this galaxy of feminine beauty they proceeded to the Bon Temps where fresh difficulties and much expense awaited them. Tommy had to get hold of each waiter in turn, tip him and then produce the assorted photographs. The result was unsatisfactory. At least three of the photographs were promising starters as having dined there last Tuesday. They then returned to the office where Tuppence immersed herself in an A.B.C.

'Paddington twelve o'clock. Torquay three thirty-five. That's the train and le Marchant's friend, Mr Sago or Tapioca or something saw her there about tea time.'

'We haven't checked his statement, remember,' said Tommy. 'If, as you said to begin with, le Marchant is a friend of Una Drake's he may have invented this story.'

'Oh, we'll hunt up Mr Rice,' said Tuppence. 'I have a kind of hunch that Mr le Marchant was speaking the truth. No, what I am trying to get at now is this. Una Drake leaves London by the twelve o'clock train, possibly takes a room at a hotel and unpacks. Then she takes a train back to town arriving in time to get to the Savoy. There is one at four-forty gets up to Paddington at nine-ten.'

'And then?' said Tommy.

'And then,' said Tuppence frowning, 'it is rather more difficult. There is a midnight train from Paddington down again, but she could hardly take that, that would be too early.'

'A fast car,' suggested Tommy.

'H'm,' said Tuppence. 'It is just on two hundred miles.'

'Australians, I have always been told, drive very recklessly.'

'Oh, I suppose it could be done,' said Tuppence. 'She would arrive there about seven.'

'Are you supposing her to have nipped into her bed at the Castle Hotel without being seen? Or arriving there explaining that she had been out all night and could she have her bill, please?'

'Tommy,' said Tuppence, 'we are idiots. She needn't have gone back to Torquay at all. She has only got to get a friend to go to the hotel there and collect her luggage and pay her bill. Then you get the receipted bill with the proper date on it.'

'I think on the whole we have worked out a very sound hypothesis,' said Tommy. 'The next thing to do is to catch the twelve o'clock train to Torquay tomorrow and verify our brilliant conclusions.'

Armed with a portfolio of photographs, Tommy and Tuppence duly established themselves in a first-class carriage the following morning, and booked seats for the second lunch.

'It probably won't be the same dining car attendants,' said Tommy. 'That would be too much luck to expect. I expect we shall have to travel up and down to Torquay for days before we strike the right ones.'

'This alibi business is very trying,' said Tuppence. 'In books it is all passed over in two or three paragraphs. Inspector Something then boarded the train to Torquay and questioned the dining car attendants and so ended the story.'

For once, however, the young couple's luck was in. In answer to their question the attendant who brought their bill for lunch proved to be the same one who had been on duty the preceding Tuesday. What Tommy called the ten-shilling touch then came into action and Tuppence produced the portfolio.

'I want to know,' said Tommy, 'if any of these ladies had lunch on this train on Tuesday last?'

In a gratifying manner worthy of the best detective fiction the man at once indicated the photograph of Una Drake.

'Yes, sir, I remember that lady, and I remember that it was Tuesday, because the lady herself drew attention to the fact, saying it was always the luckiest day in the week for her.'

'So far, so good,' said Tuppence as they returned to their compartment. 'And we will probably find that she booked at the hotel all right. It is going to be more difficult to prove that she travelled back to London, but perhaps one of the porters at the station may remember.'

Here, however, they drew a blank, and crossing to the up platform Tommy made inquiries of the ticket collector and of various porters. After the distribution of half-crowns as a preliminary to inquiring, two of the porters picked out one of the other photographs with a vague remembrance that someone like that travelled to town by the four-forty that afternoon, but there was no identification of Una Drake.

'But that doesn't prove anything,' said Tuppence as they left the station. 'She may have travelled by that train and no one noticed her.'

'She may have gone from the other station, from Torre.'

'That's quite likely,' said Tuppence, 'however, we can see to that after we have been to the hotel.'

The Castle Hotel was a big one overlooking the sea. After booking a room for the night and signing the register, Tommy observed pleasantly.

'I believe you had a friend of ours staying here last Tuesday. Miss Una Drake.'

The young lady in the bureau beamed at him.

'Oh, yes, I remember quite well. An Australian young lady, I believe.'

At a sign from Tommy, Tuppence produced the photograph.

'That is rather a charming photograph of her, isn't it?' said Tuppence.

'Oh, very nice, very nice indeed, quite stylish.'

'Did she stay here long?' inquired Tommy.

'Only the one night. She went away by the express the next morning back to London. It seemed a long way to come for one night, but of course I suppose Australian ladies don't think anything of travelling.'

'She is a very sporting girl,' said Tommy, 'always having adventures. It wasn't here, was it, that she went out to dine with some friends, went for a drive in their car afterwards, ran the car into a ditch and wasn't able to get home till morning?'

'Oh, no,' said the young lady. 'Miss Drake had dinner here in the hotel.'

'Really,' said Tommy, 'are you sure of that? I mean – how do you know?'

'Oh, I saw her.'

'I asked because I understood she was dining with some friends in Torquay,' explained Tommy.

'Oh, no, sir, she dined here.' The young lady laughed and blushed a little. 'I remember she had on a most sweetly pretty frock. One of those new flowered chiffons all over pansies.'

'Tuppence, this tears it,' said Tommy when they had been shown upstairs to their room.

'It does rather,' said Tuppence. 'Of course that woman may be mistaken. We will ask the waiter at dinner. There can't be very many people here just at this time of year.'

This time it was Tuppence who opened the attack.

'Can you tell me if a friend of mine was here last Tuesday?' she asked the waiter with an engaging smile. 'A Miss Drake, wearing a frock all over pansies, I believe.' She produced a photograph. 'This lady.'

The waiter broke into immediate smiles of recognition.

'Yes, yes, Miss Drake, I remember her very well. She told me she came from Australia.'

'She dined here?'

'Yes. It was last Tuesday. She asked me if there was anything to do afterwards in the town.'

'Yes?'

'I told her the theatre, the Pavilion, but in the end she decided not to go and she stayed here listening to our orchestra.'

'Oh, damn!' said Tommy, under his breath.

'You don't remember what time she had dinner, do you?' asked Tuppence.

'She came down a little late. It must have been about eight o'clock.'

'Damn, Blast, and Curse,' said Tuppence as she and Tommy left the dining-room. 'Tommy, this is all going wrong. It seemed so clear and lovely.'

'Well, I suppose we ought to have known it wouldn't all be plain sailing.'

'Is there any train she could have taken after that, I wonder?'

'Not one that would have landed her in London in time to go to the Savoy.'

'Well,' said Tuppence, 'as a last hope I am going to talk to the chambermaid. Una Drake had a room on the same floor as ours.'

The chambermaid was a voluble and informative woman. Yes, she remembered the young lady quite well. That was her picture right enough. A very nice young lady, very merry and talkative. Had told her a lot about Australia and the kangaroos.

The young lady rang the bell about half-past nine and asked for her bottle to be filled and put in her bed, and also to be called the next morning at half-past seven – with coffee instead of tea.

'You did call her and she was in her bed?' asked Tuppence.

'Why, yes, Ma'am, of course.'

'Oh, I only wondered if she was doing exercises or anything,' said Tuppence wildly. 'So many people do in the early morning.'

'Well, that seems cast-iron enough,' said Tommy when the chambermaid had departed. 'There is only one conclusion to be drawn from it. It is the London side of the thing that *must* be faked.'

'Mr le Marchant must be a more accomplished liar than we thought,' said Tuppence.

'We have a way of checking his statements,' said Tommy. 'He said there were people sitting at the next table whom Una knew slightly. What was their name – Oglander, that was it. We must hunt up these Oglanders, and we ought also to make inquiries at Miss Drake's flat in Clarges Street.'

The following morning they paid their bill and departed somewhat crestfallen.

Hunting out the Oglanders was fairly easy with the aid of the telephone book. Tuppence this-time took the offensive and assumed the character of a representative of a new illustrated paper. She called on Mrs Oglander, asking for a few details of their 'smart' supper party at the Savoy on Tuesday evening. These details Mrs Oglander was only too willing to supply. Just as she was leaving Tuppence added carelessly. 'Let me see, wasn't Miss Drake sitting at the table next to you? Is it really true that she is engaged to the Duke of Perth? You know her, of course.'

'I know her slightly,' said Mrs Oglander. 'A very charming girl, I believe. Yes, she was sitting at the next table to ours with Mr le Marchant. My girls know her better than I do.'

Tuppence's next port of call was the flat in Clarges Street. Here she was greeted by Miss Marjory Leicester, the friend with whom Miss Drake shared a flat.

'Do tell me what all this is about?' asked Miss Leicester plaintively. 'Una has some deep game on and I don't know what it is. Of course she slept here on Tuesday night.'

'Did you see her when she came in?'

'No, I had gone to bed. She has got her own latch key, of course. She came in about one o'clock, I believe.'

'When did you see her?'

'Oh, the next morning about nine – or perhaps it was nearer ten.'

As Tuppence left the flat she almost collided with a tall gaunt female who was entering.

'Excuse me, Miss, I'm sure,' said the gaunt female.

'Do you work here?' asked Tuppence.

'Yes, Miss, I come daily.'

'What time do you get here in the morning?'

'Nine o'clock is my time, Miss.'

Tuppence slipped a hurried half-crown into the gaunt female's hand.
'Was Miss Drake here last Tuesday morning when you arrived?'

'Why, yes, Miss, indeed she was. Fast asleep in her bed and hardly woke up when I brought her in her tea.'

'Oh, thank you,' said Tuppence and went disconsolately down the stairs.

She had arranged to meet Tommy for lunch in a small restaurant in Soho and there they compared notes.

'I have seen that fellow Rice. It is quite true he did see Una Drake in the distance at Torquay.'

'Well,' said Tuppence, 'we have checked these alibis all right. Here, give me a bit of paper and a pencil, Tommy. Let us put it down neatly like all detectives do.'

1.30	Una Drake seen in Luncheon Car of train.
4 o'clock	Arrives at Castle Hotel.
5 o'clock	Seen by Mr Rice.
8 o'clock	Seen dining at hotel.
9.30	Asks for hot water bottle.
11.30	Seen at Savoy with Mr le Marchant.
7.30 a.m.	Called by chambermaid at Castle Hotel.
9 o'clock	Called by charwoman at flat at Clarges Street.

They looked at each other.

'Well, it looks to me as if Blunt's Brilliant Detectives are beat,' said Tommy.

'Oh, we mustn't give up,' said Tuppence. 'Somebody *must* be lying!'

'The queer thing is that it strikes me nobody was lying. They all seemed perfectly truthful and straightforward.'

'Yet there must be a flaw. We know there is. I think of all sorts of things like private aeroplanes, but that doesn't really get us any forwarder.'

'I am inclined to the theory of an astral body.'

'Well,' said Tuppence, 'the only thing to do is to sleep on it. Your sub-conscious works in your sleep.'

'H'm,' said Tommy. 'If your sub-conscious provides you with a perfectly good answer to this riddle by tomorrow morning, I take off my hat to it.'

They were very silent all that evening. Again and again Tuppence reverted to the paper of times. She wrote things on bits of paper. She murmured to herself, she sought perplexedly through Rail Guides. But in the end they both rose to go to bed with no faint glimmer of light on the problem.

'This is very disheartening,' said Tommy.

'One of the most miserable evenings I have ever spent,' said Tuppence.

'We ought to have gone to a Music Hall,' said Tommy. 'A few good jokes about mothers-in-law and twins and bottles of beer would have done us no end of good.'

'No, you will see this concentration will work in the end,' said Tuppence. 'How busy our sub-conscious will have to be in the next eight hours!' And on this hopeful note they went to bed.

'Well,' said Tommy next morning. 'Has the subconscious worked?'

'I have got an idea,' said Tuppence.

'You have. What sort of an idea?'

'Well, rather a funny idea. Not at all like anything I have ever read in detective stories. As a matter of fact it is an idea that *you* put into my head.'

'Then it must be a good idea,' said Tommy firmly. 'Come on, Tuppence, out with it.'

'I shall have to send a cable to verify it,' said Tuppence. 'No, I am not going to tell you. It's a perfectly wild idea, but it's the only thing that fits the facts.'

'Well,' said Tommy, 'I must away to the office. A roomful of disappointed clients must not wait in vain. I leave this case in the hands of my promising subordinate.'

Tuppence nodded cheerfully.

She did not put in an appearance at the office all day. When Tommy returned that evening about half-past five it was to find a wildly exultant Tuppence awaiting him.

'I have done it, Tommy. I have solved the mystery of the alibi. We can charge up all these half-crowns and ten-shilling notes and demand a substantial fee of our own from Mr Montgomery Jones and he can go right off and collect his girl.'

'What is the solution?' cried Tommy.

'A perfectly simple one,' said Tuppence. '*Twins.*'

'What do you mean? – Twins?'

'Why, just that. Of course it is the only solution. I will say you put it into my head last night talking about mothers-in-law, twins, and bottles of beer. I cabled to Australia and got back the information I wanted. Una has a twin sister, Vera, who arrived in England last Monday. That is why she was able to make this bet so spontaneously. She thought it would be a frightful rag on poor Montgomery Jones. The sister went to Torquay and she stayed in London.'

'Do you think she'll be terribly despondent that she's lost?' asked Tommy.

'No,' said Tuppence, 'I don't. I gave you my views about that before.

She will put all the kudos down to Montgomery Jones. I always think respect for your husband's abilities should be the foundation of married life.'

'I am glad to have inspired these sentiments in you, Tuppence.'

'It is not a really satisfactory solution,' said Tuppence. 'Not the ingenious sort of flaw that Inspector French would have detected.'

'Nonsense,' said Tommy. 'I think the way I showed these photographs to the waiter in the restaurant was exactly like Inspector French.'

'He didn't have to use nearly so many half-crowns and ten-shilling notes as we seem to have done,' said Tuppence.

'Never mind,' said Tommy. 'We can charge them all up with additions to Mr Montgomery Jones. He will be in such a state of idiotic bliss that he would probably pay the most enormous bill without jibbing at it.'

'So he should,' said Tuppence. 'Haven't Blunt's Brilliant Detectives been brilliantly successful? Oh, Tommy, I do think we are extraordinarily clever. It quite frightens me sometimes.'

'The next case we have shall be a Roger Sheringham case, and you, Tuppence, shall be Roger Sheringham.'

'I shall have to talk a lot,' said Tuppence.

'You do that naturally,' said Tommy. 'And now I suggest that we carry out my programme of last night and seek out a Music Hall where they have plenty of jokes about mothers-in-law, bottles of beer, *and Twins*.'

The Clergyman's Daughter

'The Clergyman's Daughter', combining the later book chapter
'The Red House', was first published as 'The First Wish' in *Grand Magazine*
in December 1923, before all the other stories in *The Sketch*.
Roger Sherringham was created by Anthony Berkeley (1893–1971).

'I wish,' said Tuppence, roaming moodily round the office, 'that we could befriend a clergyman's daughter.'

'Why?' asked Tommy.

'You may have forgotten the fact, but I was once a clergyman's daughter myself. I remember what it was like. Hence this altruistic urge – this spirit of thoughtful consideration for others – this –'

'You are getting ready to be Roger Sheringham, I see,' said Tommy. 'If you will allow me to make a criticism, you talk quite as much as he does, but not nearly so well.'

'On the contrary,' said Tuppence. 'There is a feminine subtlety about my conversation, a *je ne sais quoi* that no gross male could ever attain to. I have, moreover, powers unknown to my prototype – do I mean prototype? Words are such uncertain things, they so often sound well, but mean the opposite of what one thinks they do.'

'Go on,' said Tommy kindly.

'I was. I was only pausing to take breath. Touching these powers, it is my wish today to assist a clergyman's daughter. You will see, Tommy, the first person to enlist the aid of Blunt's Brilliant Detectives will be a clergyman's daughter.'

'I'll bet you it isn't,' said Tommy.

'Done,' said Tuppence. 'Hist! To your typewriters, Oh! Israel. One comes.'

Mr Blunt's office was humming with industry as Albert opened the door and announced:

'Miss Monica Deane.'

A slender, brown-haired girl, rather shabbily dressed, entered and stood hesitating. Tommy came forward.

'Good-morning, Miss Deane. Won't you sit down and tell us what we can do for you? By the way, let me introduce my confidential secretary, Miss Sheringham.'

'I am delighted to make your acquaintance, Miss Deane,' said Tuppence. 'Your father was in the Church, I think.'

'Yes, he was. But how *did* you know that?'

'Oh! we have our methods,' said Tuppence. 'You mustn't mind me rattling on. Mr Blunt likes to hear me talk. He always says it gives him ideas.'

The girl stared at her. She was a slender creature, not beautiful, but possessing a wistful prettiness. She had a quantity of soft mouse-coloured hair, and her eyes were dark blue and very lovely, though the dark shadows round them spoke of trouble and anxiety.

'Will you tell me your story, Miss Deane?' said Tommy.

The girl turned to him gratefully.

'It's such a long rambling story,' said the girl. 'My name is Monica Deane. My father was the rector of Little Hampsley in Suffolk. He died three years ago, and my mother and I were left very badly off. I went out as a governess, but my mother became a confirmed invalid, and I had to come home to look after her. We were desperately poor, but one day we received a lawyer's letter telling us that an aunt of my father's had died and had left everything to me. I had often heard of this aunt, who had quarrelled with my father many years ago, and I knew that she was very well off, so it really seemed that our troubles were at an end. But matters did not turn out quite as well as we had hoped. I inherited the house she had lived in, but after paying one or two small legacies, there was no money left. I suppose she must have lost it during the war, or perhaps she had been living on her capital. Still, we had the house, and almost at once we had a chance of selling it at quite an advantageous price. But, foolishly perhaps, I refused the offer. We were in tiny, but expensive lodgings, and I thought it would be much nicer to live in the Red House, where my mother could have comfortable rooms and take in paying guests to cover our expenses.

'I adhered to this plan, notwithstanding a further tempting offer from the gentleman who wanted to buy. We moved in, and I advertised for paying guests. For a time, all went well, we had several answers to our advertisement; my aunt's old servant remained on with us, and she and I between us did the work of the house. And then these unaccountable things began to happen.'

'What things?'

'The queerest things. The whole place seemed bewitched. Pictures fell down, crockery flew across the room and broke; one morning we came down to find all the furniture moved round. At first we thought someone was playing a practical joke, but we had to give up that explanation. Sometimes when we were all sitting down to dinner, a terrific crash would be heard overhead. We would go up and find no one there, but a piece of furniture thrown violently to the ground.'

'A *poltergeist*,' cried Tuppence, much interested.

'Yes, that's what Dr O'Neill said – though I don't know what it means.'

'It's a sort of evil spirit that plays tricks,' explained Tuppence, who in reality knew very little about the subject, and was not even sure that she had got the word *poltergeist* right.

'Well, at any rate, the effect was disastrous. Our visitors were frightened to death, and left as soon as possible. We got new ones, and they too left hurriedly. I was in despair, and, to crown all, our own tiny income ceased suddenly – the Company in which it was invested failed.'

'You poor dear,' said Tuppence sympathetically. 'What a time you have had. Did you want Mr Blunt to investigate this "haunting" business?'

'Not exactly. You see, three days ago, a gentleman called upon us. His name was Dr O'Neill. He told us that he was a member of the Society for Physical Research, and that he had heard about the curious manifestations that had taken place in our house and was much interested. So much so, that he was prepared to buy it from us, and conduct a series of experiments there.'

'Well?'

'Of course, at first, I was overcome with joy. It seemed the way out of all our difficulties. But –'

'Yes?'

'Perhaps you will think me fanciful. Perhaps I am. But – oh! I'm sure I haven't made a mistake. It was the same man!'

'What same man?'

'The same man who wanted to buy it before. Oh! I'm sure I'm right.'

'But why shouldn't it be?'

'You don't understand. The two men were quite different, different name and everything. The first man was quite young, a spruce, dark young man of thirty odd. Dr O'Neill is about fifty, he has a grey beard and wears glasses and stoops. But when he talked I saw a gold tooth one side of his mouth. It only shows when he laughs. The other man had a tooth in just the same position, and then I looked at his ears. I had noticed the other man's ears, because they were a peculiar shape with hardly any lobe. Dr O'Neill's were just the same. Both things couldn't be a coincidence, could they? I thought and thought and finally I wrote and said I would let him know in a week. I had noticed Mr Blunt's advertisement some time ago – as a matter of fact in an old paper that lined one of the kitchen drawers. I cut it out and came up to town.'

'You were quite right,' said Tuppence, nodding her head with vigour. 'This needs looking into.'

'A very interesting case, Miss Deane,' observed Tommy.

'We shall be pleased to look into this for you – eh, Miss Sheringham?'

'Rather,' said Tuppence, 'and we'll get to the bottom of it too.'

'I understand, Miss Deane,' went on Tommy, 'that the household consists of you and your mother and a servant. Can you give me any particulars about the servant?'

'Her name is Crockett. She was with my aunt about eight or ten years. She is an elderly woman, not very pleasant in manner, but a good servant. She is inclined to give herself airs because her sister married out of her station. Crockett has a nephew whom she is always telling us is "quite the gentleman".'

'H'm,' said Tommy, rather at a loss how to proceed.

Tuppence had been eyeing Monica keenly, now she spoke with sudden decision.

'I think the best plan would be for Miss Deane to come out and lunch with me. It's just one o'clock. I can get full details from her.'

'Certainly, Miss Sheringham,' said Tommy. 'An excellent plan.'

'Look here,' said Tuppence, when they were comfortably ensconced at a little table in a neighbouring restaurant, 'I want to know: Is there any special reason why you want to find out about all this?'

Monica blushed.

'Well, you see –'

'Out with it,' said Tuppence encouragingly.

'Well – there are two men who – who – want to marry me.'

'The usual story, I suppose? One rich, one poor, and the poor one is the one you like!'

'I don't know how you know all these things,' murmured the girl.

'That's a sort of law of Nature,' explained Tuppence. 'It happens to everybody. It happened to me.'

'You see, even if I sell the house, it won't bring us in enough to live on. Gerald is a dear, but he's desperately poor – though he's a very clever engineer; and if only he had a little capital, his firm would take him into partnership. The other, Mr Partridge, is a very good man, I am sure – and well off, and if I married him, it would be an end to all our troubles. But – but –'

'I know,' said Tuppence sympathetically. 'It isn't the same thing at all. You can go on telling yourself how good and worthy he is, and adding up his qualities as though they were an addition sum – and it all has a simply refrigerating effect.'

Monica nodded.

'Well,' said Tuppence, 'I think it would be as well if we went down to the neighbourhood and studied matters upon the spot. What is the address?'

'The Red House, Stourton-in-the-Marsh.'

Tuppence wrote down the address in her notebook.

'I didn't ask you,' Monica began – 'about terms –' she ended, blushing a little.

'Our payments are strictly by results,' said Tuppence gravely. 'If the secret of the Red House is a profitable one, as seems possible from the anxiety displayed to acquire the property, we should expect a small percentage, otherwise – nothing!'

'Thank you very much,' said the girl gratefully.

'And now,' said Tuppence, 'don't worry. Everything's going to be all right. Let's enjoy lunch and talk of interesting things.'

The Red House

'Well,' said Tommy, looking out of the window of the Crown and Anchor, 'here we are at Toad in the Hole – or whatever this blasted village is called.'

'Let us review the case,' said Tuppence.

'By all means,' said Tommy. 'To begin with, getting my say in first, *I* suspect the invalid mother!'

'Why?'

'My dear Tuppence, grant that this *poltergeist* business is all a put-up job, got up in order to persuade the girl to sell the house, someone must have thrown the things about. Now the girl said everyone was at dinner – but if the mother is a thoroughgoing invalid, she'd be upstairs in her room.'

'If she was an invalid she could hardly throw furniture about.'

'Ah! but she wouldn't be a real invalid. She'd be shamming.'

'Why?'

'There you have me,' confessed her husband. 'I was really going on the well-known principle of suspecting the most unlikely person.'

'You always make fun of everything,' said Tuppence severely. 'There must be *something* that makes these people so anxious to get hold of the house. And if you don't care about getting to the bottom of this matter, I do. I like that girl. She's a dear.'

Tommy nodded seriously enough.

'I quite agree. But I never can resist ragging you, Tuppence. Of course, there's something queer about the house, and whatever it is, it's something that's difficult to get at. Otherwise a mere burglary would do the trick. But to be willing to buy the house means either that you've got to take up floors or pull down walls, or else that there's a coal mine under the back garden.'

'I don't want it to be a coal mine. Buried treasure is much more romantic.'

'H'm,' said Tommy. 'In that case I think that I shall pay a visit to the local Bank Manager, explain that I am staying here over Christmas and probably buying the Red House, and discuss the question of opening an account.'

'But why –?'

'Wait and see.'

Tommy returned at the end of half an hour. His eyes were twinkling.

'We advance, Tuppence. Our interview proceeded on the lines indicated. I then asked casually whether he had had much gold paid in, as is often the case nowadays in these small country banks – small farmers who hoarded it during the war, you understand. From that we proceeded quite naturally to the extraordinary vagaries of old ladies. I invented an aunt who on the outbreak of war drove to the Army and Navy Stores in a four-wheeler, and returned with sixteen hams. He immediately mentioned a client of his own, who had insisted on drawing out every penny of money she had – in gold as far as possible, and who also insisted on having her securities, bearer bonds and such things, given into her own custody. I exclaimed on such an act of folly, and he mentioned casually that she was the former owner of the Red House. You see, Tuppence? She drew out all this money, and she hid it somewhere. You remember that Monica Deane mentioned that they were astonished at the small amount of her estate? Yes, she hid it in the Red House, and someone knows about it. I can make a pretty good guess who that someone is too.'

'Who?'

'What about the faithful Crockett? She would know all about her mistress's peculiarities.'

'And that gold-toothed Dr O'Neill?'

'The gentlemanly nephew, of course! That's it. But whereabouts did she hide it. You know more about old ladies than I do, Tuppence. Where do they hide things?'

'Wrapped up in stockings and petticoats, under mattresses.'

Tommy nodded.

'I expect you're right. All the same, she can't have done that because it would have been found when her things were turned over. It worries me – you see, an old lady like that can't have taken up floors or dug holes in the garden. All the same it's there in the Red House somewhere. Crockett hasn't found it, but she knows it's there, and once they get the house to themselves, she and her precious nephew, they can turn it upside down until they find what they're after. We've got to get ahead of them. Come on, Tuppence. We'll go to the Red House.'

Monica Deane received them. To her mother and Crockett they were represented as would-be purchasers of the Red House, which would account for their being taken all over the house and grounds. Tommy did not tell Monica of the conclusions he had come to, but he asked her various searching questions. Of the garments and personal belongings of the dead woman, some had been given to Crockett and the others sent to various poor families. Everything had been gone through and turned out.

'Did your aunt leave any papers?'

'The desk was full, and there were some in a drawer in her bedroom, but there was nothing of importance amongst them.'

'Have they been thrown away?'

'No, my mother is always very loath to throw away old papers. There were some old-fashioned recipes among them which she intends to go through one day.'

'Good,' said Tommy approvingly. Then, indicating an old man who was at work upon one of the flower beds in the garden, he asked: 'Was that old man the gardener here in your aunt's time?'

'Yes, he used to come three days a week. He lives in the village. Poor old fellow, he is past doing any really useful work. We have him just once a week to keep things tidied up. We can't afford more.'

Tommy winked at Tuppence to indicate that she was to keep Monica with her, and he himself stepped across to where the gardener was working. He spoke a few pleasant words to the old man, asked him if he had been there in the old lady's time, and then said casually.

'You buried a box for her once, didn't you?'

'No, sir, I never buried naught for her. What should she want to bury a box for?'

Tommy shook his head. He strolled back to the house frowning. It was to be hoped that a study of the old lady's papers would yield some clue – otherwise the problem was a hard one to solve. The house itself was old fashioned, but not old enough to contain a secret room or passage.

Before leaving, Monica brought them down a big cardboard box tied with string.

'I've collected all the papers,' she whispered. 'And they're in here. I thought you could take it away with you, and then you'll have plenty of

time to go over them – but I'm sure you won't find anything to throw
light on the mysterious happenings in this house –'

Her words were interrupted by a terrific crash overhead. Tommy ran
quickly up the stairs. A jug and a basin in one of the front rooms was
lying on the ground broken to pieces. There was no one in the room.

'The ghost up to its tricks again,' he murmured with a grin.

He went downstairs again thoughtfully.

'I wonder, Miss Deane, if I might speak to the maid, Crockett, for a
minute.'

'Certainly. I will ask her to come to you.'

Monica went off to the kitchen. She returned with the elderly maid
who had opened the door to them earlier.

'We are thinking of buying this house,' said Tommy pleasantly, 'and
my wife was wondering whether, in that case, you would care to remain
on with us?'

Crockett's respectable face displayed no emotion of any kind.

'Thank you, sir,' she said. 'I should like to think it over if I may.'

Tommy turned to Monica.

'I am delighted with the house, Miss Deane. I understand that there
is another buyer in the market. I know what he has offered for the house,
and I will willingly give a hundred more. And mind you, that is a good
price I am offering.'

Monica murmured something noncommittal, and the Beresfords took
their leave.

'I was right,' said Tommy, as they went down the drive, 'Crockett's in
it. Did you notice that she was out of breath? That was from running
down the backstairs after smashing the jug and basin. Sometimes, very
likely, she has admitted her nephew secretly, and he has done a little
poltergeisting, or whatever you call it, whilst she has been innocently with
the family. You'll see Dr O'Neill will make a further offer before the day
is out.'

True enough, after dinner, a note was brought. It was from Monica.

'I have just heard from Dr O'Neill. He raises his previous offer by
£150.'

'The nephew must be a man of means,' said Tommy thoughtfully.
'And I tell you what, Tuppence, the prize he's after must be well worth
while.'

'Oh! Oh! Oh! if only we could find it!'

'Well, let's get on with the spade work.'

They were sorting through the big box of papers, a wearisome affair,
as they were all jumbled up pell mell without any kind of order or method.
Every few minutes they compared notes.

'What's the latest, Tuppence?'

'Two old receipted bills, three unimportant letters, a recipe for preserving new potatoes and one for making lemon cheesecake. What's yours?'

'One bill, a poem on Spring, two newspaper cuttings: "Why Women buy Pearls – a sound investment", and "Man with Four Wives – Extraordinary Story", and a recipe for Jugged Hare.'

'It's heart-breaking,' said Tuppence, and they fell to once more. At last the box was empty. They looked at each other.

'I put this aside,' said Tommy, picking up a half sheet of notepaper, 'because it struck me as peculiar. But I don't suppose it's got anything to do with what we're looking for.'

'Let's see it. Oh! it's one of these funny things, what do they call them? Anagrams, charades or something.' She read it:

> *My first you put on glowing coal*
> *And into it you put my whole;*
> *My second really is the first;*
> *My third mislikes the winter blast.*

'H'm,' said Tommy critically. 'I don't think much of the poet's rhymes.'

'I don't see what you find peculiar about it, though,' said Tuppence. 'Everybody used to have a collection of these sort of things about fifty years ago. You saved them up for winter evenings round the fire.'

'I wasn't referring to the verse. It's the words written below it that strike me as peculiar.'

'St Luke, xi, 9,' she read. 'It's a text.'

'Yes. Doesn't that strike you as odd? Would an old lady of a religious persuasion write a text just under a charade?'

'It is rather odd,' agreed Tuppence thoughtfully.

'I presume that you, being a clergyman's daughter, have got your Bible with you?'

'As a matter of fact, I have. Aha! you didn't expect that. Wait a sec.'

Tuppence ran to her suitcase, extracted a small red volume and returned to the table. She turned the leaves rapidly. 'Here we are. Luke, chapter xi, verse 9. Oh! Tommy, look.'

Tommy bent over and looked where Tuppence's small finger pointed to a portion of the verse in question.

'Seek and ye shall find.'

'That's it,' cried Tuppence. 'We've got it! Solve the cryptogram and the treasure is ours – or rather Monica's.'

'Well, let's get to work on the cryptogram, as you call it. "*My first* you put on glowing coal." What does that mean, I wonder? Then – "My *second* really is the first." That's pure gibberish.'

'It's quite simple, really,' said Tuppence kindly. 'It's just a sort of knack. Let *me* have it.'

Tommy surrendered it willingly. Tuppence ensconced herself in an armchair, and began muttering to herself with bent brows.

'It's quite simple, really,' murmured Tommy when half an hour had elapsed.

'Don't crow! We're the wrong generation for this. I've a good mind to go back to town tomorrow and call on some old pussy who would probably read it as easy as winking. It's a knack, that's all.'

'Well, let's have one more try.'

'There aren't many things you can put on glowing coal,' said Tuppence thoughtfully. 'There's water, to put it out, or wood, or a kettle.'

'It must be one syllable, I suppose? What about *wood*, then?'

'You couldn't put anything *into* wood, though.'

'There's no one syllable word instead of *water*, but there must be one syllable things you can put on a fire in the kettle line.'

'Saucepans,' mused Tuppence. 'Frying pans. How about *pan?* or *pot?* What's a word beginning pan or pot that is something you cook?'

'Pottery,' suggested Tommy. 'You bake that in the fire. Wouldn't that be near enough?'

'The rest of it doesn't fit. Pancakes? No. Oh! bother.'

They were interrupted by the little serving-maid, who told them that dinner would be ready in a few minutes.

'Only Mrs Lumley, she wanted to know if you like your potatoes fried, or boiled in their jackets? She's got some of each.'

'Boiled in their jackets,' said Tuppence promptly. 'I love potatoes –' She stopped dead with her mouth open.

'What's the matter, Tuppence? Have you seen a ghost?'

'Tommy,' cried Tuppence. 'Don't you see? That's it! The word, I mean. *Potatoes!* "My first you put on glowing coal" – that's pot. "And into it you put my *whole*." "My *second* really is the first." That's A, the first letter of the alphabet. "My *third* mislikes the wintry blast" – cold *toes* of course!'

'You're right, Tuppence. Very clever of you. But I'm afraid we've wasted an awful lot of time over nothing. Potatoes don't fit in at all with missing treasure. Half a sec, though. What did you read out just now, when we were going through the box? Something about a recipe for New Potatoes. I wonder if there's anything in that.'

He rummaged hastily through the pile of recipes.

'Here it is. "To KEEP NEW POTATOES. Put the new potatoes into tins and bury them in the garden. Even in the middle of winter, they will taste as though freshly dug."

'We've got it,' screamed Tuppence. 'That's it. The treasure is in the garden, buried in a tin.'

'But I asked the gardener. He said he'd never buried anything.'

'Yes, I know, but that's because people never really answer what you say, they answer what they think you mean. He knew he'd never buried anything out of the common. We'll go tomorrow and ask him where he buried the potatoes.'

The following morning was Christmas Eve. By dint of inquiry they found the old gardener's cottage. Tuppence broached the subject after some minutes' conversation.

'I wish one could have new potatoes at Christmas time,' she remarked. 'Wouldn't they be good with turkey? Do people round here ever bury them in tins? I've heard that keeps them fresh.'

'Ay, that they do,' declared the old man. 'Old Miss Deane, up to the Red House, she allus had three tins buried every summer, and as often as not forgot to have 'em dug up again!'

'In the bed by the house, as a rule, didn't she?'

'No, over against the wall by the fir tree.'

Having got the information they wanted, they soon took their leave of the old man, presenting him with five shillings as a Christmas box.

'And now for Monica,' said Tommy.

'Tommy! You have no sense of the dramatic. Leave it to me. I've got a beautiful plan. Do you think you could manage to beg, borrow or steal a spade?'

Somehow or other, a spade was duly produced, and that night, late, two figures might have been seen stealing into the grounds of the Red House. The place indicated by the gardener was easily found, and Tommy set to work. Presently his spade rang on metal, and a few seconds later he had unearthed a big biscuit tin. It was sealed round with adhesive plaster and firmly fastened down, but Tuppence, by the aid of Tommy's knife, soon managed to open it. Then she gave a groan. The tin was full of potatoes. She poured them out, so that the tin was completely empty, but there were no other contents.

'Go on digging, Tommy.'

It was some time before a second tin rewarded their search. As before, Tuppence unsealed it.

'Well?' demanded Tommy anxiously.

'Potatoes again!'

'Damn!' said Tommy, and set to once more.

'The third time is lucky,' said Tuppence consolingly.

'I believe the whole thing's a mare's nest,' said Tommy gloomily, but he continued to dig.

At last a third tin was brought to light.

'Potatoes aga –' began Tuppence, then stopped. 'Oh, Tommy, we've got it. It's only potatoes on top. Look!'

She held up a big old-fashioned velvet bag.

'Cut along home,' cried Tommy. 'It's icy cold. Take the bag with you. I must shovel back the earth. And may a thousand curses light upon your head, Tuppence, if you open that bag before I come!'

'I'll play fair. Ouch! I'm frozen.' She beat a speedy retreat.

On arrival at the inn she had not long to wait. Tommy was hard upon her heels, perspiring freely after his digging and the final brisk run.

'Now then,' said Tommy, 'the private inquiry agents make good! Open the loot, Mrs Beresford.'

Inside the bag was a package done up in oil silk and a heavy chamois leather bag. They opened the latter first. It was full of gold sovereigns. Tommy counted them.

'Two hundred pounds. That was all they would let her have, I suppose. Cut open the package.'

Tuppence did so. It was full of closely folded banknotes. Tommy and Tuppence counted them carefully. They amounted to exactly twenty thousand pounds.

'Whew!' said Tommy. 'Isn't it lucky for Monica that we're both rich and honest? What's that done up in tissue paper?'

Tuppence unrolled the little parcel and drew out a magnificent string of pearls, exquisitely matched.

'I don't know much about these things,' said Tommy slowly. 'But I'm pretty sure that those pearls are worth another five thousand pounds at least. Look at the size of them. Now I see why the old lady kept that cutting about pearls being a good investment. She must have realised all her securities and turned them into notes and jewels.'

'Oh, Tommy, isn't it wonderful? Darling Monica. Now she can marry her nice young man and live happily ever afterwards, like me.'

'That's rather sweet of you, Tuppence. So you *are* happy with me?'

'As a matter of fact,' said Tuppence, 'I am. But I didn't mean to say so. It slipped out. What with being excited, and Christmas Eve, and one thing and another –'

'If you really love me,' said Tommy, 'will you answer me one question?'

'I hate these catches,' said Tuppence, 'but – well – all right.'

'Then how did you know that Monica was a clergyman's daughter?'

'Oh, that was just cheating,' said Tuppence happily. 'I opened her letter making an appointment, and a Mr Deane was father's curate once, and he had a little girl called Monica, about four or five years younger than me. So I put two and two together.'

'You are a shameless creature,' said Tommy. 'Hullo, there's twelve o'clock striking. Happy Christmas, Tuppence.'

'Happy Christmas, Tommy. It'll be a Happy Christmas for Monica too – and all owing to US. I am glad. Poor thing, she has been so miserable. Do you know, Tommy, I feel all queer and choky about the throat when I think of it.'

'Darling Tuppence,' said Tommy.

'Darling Tommy,' said Tuppence. 'How awfully sentimental we are getting.'

'Christmas comes but once a year,' said Tommy sententiously. 'That's what our great-grandmothers said, and I expect there's a lot of truth in it still.'

The Ambassador's Boots

'The Ambassador's Boots' was first published as 'The Matter of
the Ambassador's Boots' in *The Sketch*, 12 November 1924.
Reggie Fortune was created by H. C. Bailey (1878–1961)

'My dear fellow, my dear fellow,' said Tuppence, and waved a heavily
buttered muffin.

Tommy looked at her for a minute or two, then a broad grin spread
over his face and he murmured.

'We do have to be so very careful.'

'That's right,' said Tuppence, delighted. 'You guessed. I am the famous
Dr Fortune and you are Superintendent Bell.'

'Why are you being Reginald Fortune?'

'Well, really because I feel like a lot of hot butter.'

'That is the pleasant side of it,' said Tommy. 'But there is another. You
will have to examine horribly smashed faces and very extra dead bodies
a good deal.'

In answer Tuppence threw across a letter. Tommy's eyebrows rose in
astonishment.

'Randolph Wilmott, the American Ambassador. I wonder what he
wants.'

'We shall know tomorrow at eleven o'clock.'

Punctually to the time named, Mr Randolph Wilmott, United States
Ambassador to the Court of St James, was ushered into Mr Blunt's office.
He cleared his throat and commenced speaking in a deliberate and
characteristic manner.

'I have come to you, Mr Blunt – By the way, it is Mr Blunt himself
to whom I am speaking, is it not?'

'Certainly,' said Tommy. 'I am Theodore Blunt, the head of the firm.'

'I always prefer to deal with heads of departments,' said Mr Wilmott.
'It is more satisfactory in every way. As I was about to say, Mr Blunt,

this business gets my goat. There's nothing in it to trouble Scotland Yard about – I'm not a penny the worse in any way, and it's probably all due to a simple mistake. But all the same, I don't see just how that mistake arose. There's nothing criminal in it, I dare say, but I'd like just to get the thing straightened out. It makes me mad not to see the why and wherefore of a thing.'

'Absolutely,' said Tommy.

Mr Wilmott went on. He was slow and given to much detail. At last Tommy managed to get a word in.

'Quite so,' he said, 'the position is this. You arrived by the liner *Nomadic* a week ago. In some way your kitbag and the kitbag of another gentleman, Mr Ralph Westerham, whose initials are the same as yours, got mixed up. You took Mr Westerham's kitbag, and he took yours. Mr Westerham discovered the mistake immediately, sent round your kitbag to the Embassy, and took away his own. Am I right so far?'

'That is precisely what occurred. The two bags must have been practically identical, and with the initials R. W. being the same in both cases, it is not difficult to understand that an error might have been made. I myself was not aware of what had happened until my valet informed me of the mistake, and that Mr Westerham – he is a Senator, and a man for whom I have a great admiration – had sent round for his bag and returned mine.'

'Then I don't see –'

'But you will see. That's only the beginning of the story. Yesterday, as it chanced, I ran up against Senator Westerham, and I happened to mention the matter to him jestingly. To my great surprise, he did not seem to know what I was talking about, and when I explained, he denied the story absolutely. He had not taken my bag off the ship in mistake for his own – in fact, he had not travelled with such an article amongst his luggage.'

'What an extraordinary thing!'

'Mr Blunt, it *is* an extraordinary thing. There seems no rhyme or reason in it. Why, if any one wanted to steal my kitbag, he could do so easily enough without resorting to all this roundabout business. And anyway, it was *not* stolen, but returned to me. On the other hand, if it were taken by mistake, why use Senator Westerham's name? It's a crazy business – but just for curiosity I mean to get to the bottom of it. I hope the case is not too trivial for you to undertake?'

'Not at all. It is a very intriguing little problem, capable as you say, of many simple explanations, but nevertheless baffling on the face of it. The first thing, of course, is the *reason* of the substitution, if substitution it was. You say nothing was missing from your bag when it came back into your possession?'

'My man says not. He would know.'

'What was in it, if I may ask?'

'Mostly boots.'

'Boots,' said Tommy, discouraged.

'Yes,' said Mr Wilmott. 'Boots. Odd, isn't it?'

'You'll forgive my asking you,' said Tommy, 'but you didn't carry any secret papers, or anything of that sort sewn in the lining of a boot or screwed into a false heel?'

The Ambassador seemed amused by the question.

'Secret diplomacy hasn't got to that pitch, I hope.'

'Only in fiction,' said Tommy with an answering smile, and a slightly apologetic manner. 'But you see, we've got to account for the thing somehow. Who came for the bag – the other bag, I mean?'

'Supposed to be one of Westerham's servants. Quite a quiet, ordinary man, so I understand. My valet saw nothing wrong with him.'

'Had it been unpacked, do you know?'

'That I can't say. I presume not. But perhaps you'd like to ask the valet a few questions? He can tell you more than I can about the business.'

'I think that would be the best plan, Mr Wilmott.'

The Ambassador scribbled a few words on a card and handed it to Tommy.

'I opine that you would prefer to go round to the Embassy and make your inquiries there? If not, I will have the man, his name is Richards, by the way – sent round here.'

'No, thank you, Mr Wilmott. I should prefer to go to the Embassy.'

The Ambassador rose, glancing at his watch.

'Dear me, I shall be late for an appointment. Well, goodbye, Mr Blunt. I leave the matter in your hands.'

He hurried away. Tommy looked at Tuppence, who had been scribbling demurely on her pad in the character of the efficient Miss Robinson.

'What about it, old thing?' he asked. 'Do you see, as the old bird put it, any rhyme or reason in the proceedings?'

'None whatever,' replied Tuppence cheerily.

'Well, that's a start, anyway! It shows that there is really something very deep at the back of it.'

'You think so?'

'It's a generally accepted hypothesis. Remember Sherlock Holmes and the depth the butter had sunk into the parsley – I mean the other way round. I've always had a devouring wish to know all about that case. Perhaps Watson will disinter it from his notebook one of these days. Then I shall die happy. But we must get busy.'

'Quite so,' said Tuppence. 'Not a quick man, the esteemed Wilmott, but sure.'

'She knows men,' said Tommy. 'Or do I say *he* knows men. It is so confusing when you assume the character of a male detective.'

'Oh, my dear fellow, my dear fellow!'

'A little more action, Tuppence, and a little less repetition.'

'A classic phrase cannot be repeated too often,' said Tuppence with dignity.

'Have a muffin,' said Tommy kindly.

'Not at eleven o'clock in the morning, thank you. Silly case, this. Boots – you know. Why boots?'

'Well,' said Tommy. 'Why not?'

'It doesn't fit. Boots.' She shook her head. 'All wrong. Who wants other people's boots? The whole thing's mad.'

'Possibly they got hold of the wrong bag,' suggested Tommy.

'That's possible. But if they were after papers, a despatch case would be more likely. Papers are the only things one thinks of in connection with ambassadors.'

'Boots suggest footprints,' said Tommy thoughtfully. 'Do you think they wanted to lay a trail of Wilmott's footsteps somewhere?'

Tuppence considered the suggestion, abandoning her role, then shook her head.

'It seems wildly impossible,' she said. 'No, I believe we shall have to resign ourselves to the fact that the boots have nothing to do with it.'

'Well,' said Tommy with a sigh, 'the next step is to interview friend Richards. He may be able to throw some light on the mystery.'

On production of the Ambassador's card, Tommy was admitted to the Embassy, and presently a pale young man, with a respectful manner and a subdued voice, presented himself to undergo examination.

'I am Richards, sir. Mr Wilmott's valet. I understood you wished to see me?'

'Yes, Richards. Mr Wilmott called on me this morning, and suggested that I should come round and ask you a few questions. It is this matter of the kitbag.'

'Mr Wilmott was rather upset over the affair, I know, sir. I can hardly see why, since no harm was done. I certainly understood from the man who called for the other bag that it belonged to Senator Westerham, but of course, I may have been mistaken.'

'What kind of man was he?'

'Middle-aged. Grey hair. Very good class, I should say – most respectable. I understood he was Senator Westerham's valet. He left Mr Wilmott's bag and took away the other.'

'Had it been unpacked at all?'

'Which one, sir?'

'Well, I meant the one you brought from the boat. But I should like to know about the other as well – Mr Wilmott's own. Had that been unpacked, do you fancy?'

'I should say not, sir. It was just as I strapped it up on the boat. I should say the gentleman – whoever he was – just opened it – realised it wasn't his, and shut it up again.'

'Nothing missing? No small article?'

'I don't think so, sir. In fact, I'm quite sure.'

'And now the other one. Had you started to unpack that?'

'As a matter of fact, sir, I was just opening it at the very moment Senator Westerham's man arrived. I'd just undone the straps.'

'Did you open it at all?'

'We just unfastened it together, sir, to be sure no mistake had been made this time. The man said it was all right, and he strapped it up again and took it away.'

'What was inside? Boots also?'

'No, sir, mostly toilet things, I fancy. I know I saw a tin of bath salts.'

Tommy abandoned that line of research.

'You never saw anyone tampering with anything in your master's cabin on board ship, I suppose?'

'Oh, no, sir.'

'Never anything suspicious of any kind?'

'And what do I mean by that, I wonder,' he thought to himself with a trace of amusement. 'Anything suspicious – just words!'

But the man in front of him hesitated.

'Now that I remember it –'

'Yes,' said Tommy eagerly. 'What?'

'I don't think it could have anything to do with it. But there was a young lady.'

'Yes? A young lady, you say, what was she doing?'

'She was taken faint, sir. A very pleasant young lady. Miss Eileen O'Hara, her name was. A dainty looking lady, not tall, with black hair. Just a little foreign looking.'

'Yes?' said Tommy, with even greater eagerness.

'As I was saying, she was taken queer. Just outside Mr Wilmott's cabin. She asked me to fetch the doctor. I helped her to the sofa, and then went off for the doctor. I was some time finding him, and when I found him and brought him back, the young lady was nearly all right again.'

'Oh!' said Tommy.

'You don't think, sir –'

'It's difficult to know what to think,' said Tommy noncommittally. 'Was this Miss O'Hara travelling alone?'

'Yes, I think so, sir.'

'You haven't seen her since you landed?'

'No, sir.'

'Well,' said Tommy, after a minute or two spent in reflection. 'I think that's all. Thank you, Richards.'

'Thank *you*, sir.'

Back at the office of the Detective Agency, Tommy retailed his conversation with Richards to Tuppence, who listened attentively.

'What do you think of it, Tuppence?'

'Oh, my dear fellow, we doctors are always sceptical of a sudden faintness! So very convenient. And Eileen as well as O'Hara. Almost too impossibly Irish, don't you think?'

'It's something to go upon at last. Do you know what I am going to do, Tuppence? Advertise for the lady.'

'What?'

'Yes, any information respecting Miss Eileen O'Hara known to have travelled such and such a ship and such and such a date. Either she'll answer it herself if she's genuine, or someone may come forward to give us information about her. So far, it's the only hope of a clue.'

'You'll also put her on her guard, remember.'

'Well,' said Tommy, 'one's got to risk something.'

'I still can't see any sense in the thing,' said Tuppence, frowning. 'If a gang of crooks get hold of the Ambassador's bag for an hour or two, and then send it back, what possible good can it do them. Unless there are papers in it they want to copy, and Mr Wilmott swears there was nothing of the kind.'

Tommy stared at her thoughtfully.

'You put these things rather well, Tuppence,' he said at last. 'You've given me an idea.'

It was two days later. Tuppence was out to lunch. Tommy, alone in the austere office of Mr Theodore Blunt, was improving his mind by reading the latest sensational thriller.

The door of the office opened and Albert appeared.

'A young lady to see you, sir. Miss Cicely March. She says she has called in answer to an advertisement.'

'Show her in at once,' cried Tommy, thrusting his novel into a convenient drawer.

In another minute, Albert had ushered in the young lady. Tommy had just time to see that she was fair haired and extremely pretty, when the amazing occurrence happened.

The door through which Albert had just passed out was rudely burst open. In the doorway stood a picturesque figure – a big dark man, Spanish in appearance, with a flaming red tie. His features were distorted with rage, and in his hand was a gleaming pistol.

'So this is the office of Mr Busybody Blunt,' he said in perfect English. His voice was low and venomous. 'Hands up at once – or I shoot.'

It sounded no idle threat. Tommy's hands went up obediently. The girl, crouched against the wall, gave a gasp of terror.

'This young lady will come with me,' said the man. 'Yes, you will, my dear. You have never seen me before, but that doesn't matter. I can't have my plans ruined by a silly little chit like you. I seem to remember that you were one of the passengers on the *Nomadic*. You must have been peering into things that didn't concern you – but I've no intention of letting you blab any secrets to Mr Blunt here. A very clever gentleman, Mr Blunt, with his fancy advertisements. But as it happens, I keep an eye on the advertisement columns. That's how I got wise to his little game.'

'You interest me exceedingly,' said Tommy. 'Won't you go on?'

'Cheek won't help you, Mr Blunt. From now on, you're a marked man. Give up this investigation, and we'll leave you alone. Otherwise – God help you! Death comes swiftly to those who thwart our plans.'

Tommy did not reply. He was staring over the intruder's shoulder as though he saw a ghost.

As a matter of fact he was seeing something that caused him far more apprehension than any ghost could have done. Up to now, he had not given a thought to Albert as a factor in the game. He had taken for granted that Albert had already been dealt with by the mysterious stranger. If he had thought of him at all, it was as one lying stunned on the carpet in the outer office.

He now saw that Albert had miraculously escaped the stranger's attention. But instead of rushing out to fetch a policeman in good sound British fashion, Albert had elected to play a lone hand. The door behind the stranger had opened noiselessly, and Albert stood in the aperture enveloped in a coil of rope.

An agonised yelp of protest burst from Tommy, but too late. Fired with enthusiasm, Albert flung a loop of rope over the intruder's head, and jerked him backwards off his feet.

The inevitable happened. The pistol went off with a roar and Tommy felt the bullet scorch his ear in passing, ere it buried itself in the plaster behind him.

'I've got him, sir,' cried Albert, flushed with triumph. 'I've lassoed him. I've been practising with a lasso in my spare time, sir. Can you give me a hand? He's very violent.'

Tommy hastened to his faithful henchman's assistance, mentally determining that Albert should have no further spare time.

'You damned idiot,' he said. 'Why didn't you go for a policeman? Owing to this fool's play of yours, he as near as anything plugged me through the head. Whew! I've never had such a near escape.'

'Lassoed him in the nick of time, I did,' said Albert, his ardour quite undamped. 'It's wonderful what those chaps can do on the prairies, sir.'

'Quite so,' said Tommy, 'but we're not on the prairies. We happen to be in a highly civilised city. And now, my dear sir,' he added to his prostrate foe. 'What are we going to do with you?'

A stream of oaths in a foreign language was his only reply.

'Hush,' said Tommy. 'I don't understand a word of what you're saying, but I've got a shrewd idea it's not the kind of language to use before a lady. You'll excuse him, won't you, Miss – do you know, in the excitement of this little upset, I've quite forgotten your name?'

'March,' said the girl. She was still white and shaken. But she came forward now and stood by Tommy looking down on the recumbent figure of the discomfited stranger. 'What are you going to do with him?'

'I could fetch a bobby now,' said Albert helpfully.

But Tommy, looking up, caught a very faint negative movement of the girl's head, and took his cue accordingly.

'We'll let him off this time,' he remarked. 'Nevertheless I shall give myself the pleasure of kicking him downstairs – if it's only to teach him manners to a lady.'

He removed the rope, hauled the victim to his feet, and propelled him briskly through the outer office.

A series of shrill yelps was heard and then a thud. Tommy came back, flushed but smiling.

The girl was staring at him with round eyes.

'Did you – hurt him?'

'I hope so,' said Tommy. 'But these dagoes make a practice of crying out before they're hurt – so I can't be quite sure about it. Shall we come back into my office, Miss March, and resume our interrupted conversation? I don't think we shall be interrupted again.'

'I'll have my lasso ready, sir, in case,' said the helpful Albert.

'Put it away,' ordered Tommy sternly.

He followed the girl into the inner office and sat down at his desk, whilst she took a chair facing him.

'I don't quite know where to begin,' said the girl. 'As you heard that man say, I was a passenger on the *Nomadic*. The lady you advertised about, Miss O'Hara, was also on board.'

'Exactly,' said Tommy. 'That we know already but I suspect you must

know something about her doings on board that boat, or else that picturesque gentleman would not have been in such a hurry to intervene.'

'I will tell you everything. The American Ambassador was on board.
One day, as I was passing his cabin, I saw this woman inside, and she
was doing something so extraordinary that I stopped to watch. She had
a man's boot in her hand –'

'A boot?' cried Tommy excitedly. 'I'm sorry, Miss March, go on.'

'With a little pair of scissors, she was slitting up the lining. Then she
seemed to push something inside. Just at that minute the doctor and
another man came down the passage, and immediately she dropped back
on the couch and groaned. I waited, and I gathered from what was being
said that she had pretended to feel faint. I say *pretended* – because when
I first caught sight of her, she was obviously feeling nothing of the kind.'

Tommy nodded.

'Well?'

'I rather hate to tell you the next part. I was – curious. And also, I'd
been reading silly books, and I wondered if she'd put a bomb or a poisoned
needle or something like that in Mr Wilmott's boot. I know it's absurd –
but I did think so. Anyway, next time I passed the empty cabin, I slipped
in and examined the boot. I drew out from the lining a slip of paper. Just
as I had it in my hand, I heard the steward coming, and I hurried out
so as not to be caught. The folded paper was still in my hand. When I
got into my own cabin I examined it. Mr Blunt, it was nothing but some
verses from the Bible.'

'Verses from the Bible?' said Tommy, very much intrigued.

'At least I thought so at the time. I couldn't understand it, but I thought
perhaps it was the work of a religious maniac. Anyway, I didn't feel it
was worth while replacing it. I kept it without thinking much about it until
yesterday when I used it to make into a boat for my little nephew to sail
in his bath. As the paper got wet, I saw a queer kind of design coming
out all over it. I hastily took it out of the bath, and smoothed it out flat
again. The water had brought out the hidden message. It was a kind of
tracing – and looked like the mouth of a harbour. Immediately after that
I read your advertisement.'

Tommy sprang from his chair.

'But this is most important. I see it all now. That tracing is probably
the plan of some important harbour defences. It had been stolen by this
woman. She feared someone was on her track, and not daring to conceal
it amongst her own belongings, she contrived this hiding-place. Later,
she obtained possession of the bag in which the boot was packed – only
to discover that the paper had vanished. Tell me, Miss March, you have
brought this paper with you?'

The girl shook her head.

'It's at my place of business. I run a beauty parlour in Bond Street. I am really an agent for the "Cyclamen" preparations in New York. That is why I had been over there. I thought the paper might be important, so I locked it up in the safe before coming out. Ought not Scotland Yard to know about it?'

'Yes, indeed.'

'Then shall we go there now, get it out, and take it straight to Scotland Yard?'

'I am very busy this afternoon,' said Tommy, adopting his professional manner and consulting his watch. 'The Bishop of London wants me to take up a case for him. A very curious problem, concerning some vestments and two curates.'

'Then in that case,' said Miss March, rising, 'I will go alone.'

Tommy raised a hand in protest.

'As I was about to say,' he said, 'the Bishop must wait. I will leave a few words with Albert. I am convinced, Miss March, that until that paper has been safely deposited with Scotland Yard you are in active danger.'

'Do you think so?' said the girl doubtfully.

'I don't think so, I'm sure. Excuse me.' He scribbled some words on the pad in front of him, then tore off the leaf and folded it.

Taking his hat and stick, he intimated to the girl that he was ready to accompany her. In the outer office he handed the folded paper to Albert with an air of importance.

'I am called out on an urgent case. Explain that to his lordship if he comes. Here are my notes on the case for Miss Robinson.'

'Very good, sir,' said Albert, playing up. 'And what about the Duchess's pearls?'

Tommy waved his hand irritably.

'That must wait also.'

He and Miss March hurried out. Half-way down the stairs they encountered Tuppence coming up. Tommy passed her with a brusque: 'Late again, Miss Robinson. I am called out on an important case.'

Tuppence stood still on the stairs and stared after them. Then, with raised eyebrows, she went on up to the office.

As they reached the street, a taxi came sailing up to them. Tommy, on the point of hailing it, changed his mind.

'Are you a good walker, Miss March?' he asked seriously.

'Yes, why? Hadn't we better take that taxi? It will be quicker.'

'Perhaps you did not notice. That taxi driver has just refused a fare a little lower down the street. He was waiting for us. Your enemies are on the look-out. If you feel equal to it, it would be better for us to walk to

Bond Street. In the crowded streets they will not be able to attempt much against us.'

'Very well,' said the girl, rather doubtfully.

They walked westwards. The streets, as Tommy had said, were crowded, and progress was slow. Tommy kept a sharp look out. Occasionally he drew the girl to one side with a quick gesture, though she herself had seen nothing suspicious.

Suddenly glancing at her, he was seized with compunction.

'I say, you look awfully done up. The shock of that man. Come into this place and have a good cup of strong coffee. I suppose you wouldn't hear of a nip of brandy.'

The girl shook her head, with a faint smile.

'Coffee be it then,' said Tommy. 'I think we can safely risk its being poisoned.'

They lingered some time over their coffee, and finally set off at a brisker pace.

'We've thrown them off, I think,' said Tommy, looking over his shoulder.

Cyclamen Ltd was a small establishment in Bond Street, with pale pink taffeta curtains, and one or two jars of face cream and a cake of soap decorating the window.

Cicely March entered, and Tommy followed. The place inside was tiny. On the left was a glass counter with toilet preparations. Behind this counter was a middle-aged woman with grey hair and an exquisite complexion, who acknowledged Cicely March's entrance with a faint inclination of the head before continuing to talk to the customer she was serving.

This customer was a small dark woman. Her back was to them and they could not see her face. She was speaking in slow difficult English. On the right was a sofa and a couple of chairs with some magazines on a table. Here sat two men – apparently bored husbands waiting for their wives.

Cicely March passed straight on through a door at the end which she held ajar for Tommy to follow her. As he did so, the woman customer exclaimed, 'Ah, but I think that is an *amico* of mine,' and rushed after them, inserting her foot in the door just in time to prevent its closing. At the same time the two men rose to their feet. One followed her through the door, the other advanced to the shop attendant and clapped his hand over her mouth to drown the scream rising to her lips.

In the meantime, things were happening rather quickly beyond the swing door. As Tommy passed through a cloth was flung over his head, and a sickly odour assailed his nostrils. Almost as soon however, it was jerked off again, and a woman's scream rang out.

Tommy blinked a little and coughed as he took in the scene in front of him. On his right was the mysterious stranger of a few hours ago, and busily fitting handcuffs upon him was one of the bored men from the shop parlour. Just in front of him was Cicely March wrestling vainly to free herself, whilst the woman customer from the shop held her firmly pinioned. As the latter turned her head, and the veil she wore unfastened itself and fell off, the well-known features of Tuppence were revealed.

'Well done, Tuppence,' said Tommy, moving forward. 'Let me give you a hand. I shouldn't struggle if I were you, Miss O'Hara – or do you prefer to be called Miss March?'

'This is Inspector Grace, Tommy,' said Tuppence. 'As soon as I read the note you left I rang up Scotland Yard, and Inspector Grace and another man met me outside here.'

'Very glad to get hold of this gentleman,' said the Inspector, indicating his prisoner. 'He's wanted badly. But we've never had cause to suspect this place – thought it was a genuine beauty shop.'

'You see,' explained Tommy gently, 'we do have to be so very careful! Why should anyone want the Ambassador's bag for an hour or so? I put the question the other way round. Supposing it was the other bag that was the important one. Someone wanted that bag to be in the Ambassador's possession for an hour or so. Much more illuminating! Diplomatic luggage is not subjected to the indignities of a Customs examination. Clearly smuggling. But smuggling of what? Nothing too bulky. At once I thought of drugs. Then that picturesque comedy was enacted in my office. They'd seen my advertisement and wanted to put me off the scent – or failing that, out of the way altogether. But I happened to notice an expression of blank dismay in the charming lady's eyes when Albert did his lasso act. That didn't fit in very well with her supposed part. The stranger's attack was meant to assure my confidence in her. I played the part of the credulous sleuth with all my might – swallowed her rather impossible story and permitted her to lure me here, carefully leaving behind full instructions for dealing with the situation. Under various pretexts I delayed our arrival, so as to give you all plenty of time.'

Cicely March was looking at him with a stony expression.

'You are mad. What do you expect to find here?'

'Remembering that Richards saw a tin of bath salts, what do you say about beginning with the bath salts, eh, Inspector?'

'A very sound idea, sir.'

He picked up one of the dainty pink tins, and emptied it on the table. The girl laughed.

'Genuine crystals, eh?' said Tommy. 'Nothing more deadly than carbonate of soda?'

'Try the safe,' suggested Tuppence.

There was a small wall safe in the corner. The key was in the lock. Tommy swung it open and gave a shout of satisfaction. The back of the safe opened out into a big recess in the wall, and that recess was stacked with the same elegant tins of bath salts. Rows and rows of them. He took one out and prised up the lid. The top showed the same pink crystals, but underneath was a fine white powder.

The Inspector uttered an ejaculation.

'You've got it, sir. Ten to one, that tin's full of pure cocaine. We knew there was a distributing area somewhere round here, handy to the West End, but we haven't been able to get a clue to it. This is a fine coup of yours, sir.'

'Rather a triumph for Blunt's Brilliant Detectives,' said Tommy to Tuppence, as they emerged into the street together. 'It's a great thing to be a married man. Your persistent schooling has at last taught me to recognise peroxide when I see it. Golden hair has got to be the genuine article to take me in. We will concoct a business-like letter to the Ambassador, informing him that the matter has been dealt with satisfactorily. And now, my dear fellow, what about tea, and lots of hot buttered muffins?'

The Man Who Was No. 16

'The Man Who Was No.16' was first published as 'The Man Who Was Number Sixteen' in *The Sketch*, 10 December 1924. To end the continuous run of Tommy and Tuppence stories, Agatha Christie parodied her own Hercule Poirot.

Tommy and Tuppence were closeted with the Chief in his private room. His commendation had been warm and sincere.

'You have succeeded admirably. Thanks to you we have laid our hands on no less than five very interesting personages, and from them we have received much valuable information. Meanwhile I learn from a creditable source that headquarters in Moscow have taken alarm at the failure of their agents to report. I think that in spite of all our precautions they have begun to suspect that all is not well at what I may call the distributing centre – the office of Mr Theodore Blunt – the International Detective Bureau.'

'Well,' said Tommy, 'I suppose they were bound to tumble to it some time or other, sir.'

'As you say, it was only to be expected. But I am a little worried – about Mrs Tommy.'

'I can look after her all right, sir,' said Tommy, at exactly the same minute as Tuppence said, 'I can take care of myself.'

'H'm,' said Mr Carter. 'Excessive self-confidence was always a characteristic of you two. Whether your immunity is entirely due to your own superhuman cleverness, or whether a small percentage of luck creeps in, I'm not prepared to say. But luck changes, you know. However, I won't argue the point. From my extensive knowledge of Mrs Tommy, I suppose it's quite useless to ask her to keep out of the limelight for the next week or two?'

Tuppence shook her head very energetically.

'Then all I can do is to give you all the information that I can. We have reason to believe that a special agent has been despatched from Moscow to this country. We don't know what name he is travelling under, we don't know when he will arrive. But we do know something about him. He is a man who gave us great trouble in the war, an ubiquitous kind of fellow who turned up all over the place where we least wanted him. He is a Russian by birth, and an accomplished linguist – so much so that he can pass as half a dozen other nationalities, including our own. He is also a past-master in the art of disguise. And he has brains. It was he who devised the No. 16 code.

'When and how he will turn up, I do not know. But I am fairly certain that he *will* turn up. We do know this – he was not personally acquainted with the real Mr Theodore Blunt. I think that he will turn up at your office, on the pretext of a case which he will wish you to take up, and will try you with the pass words. The first, as you know, is the mention of the number sixteen – which is replied to by a sentence containing the same number. The second, which we have only just learnt, is an inquiry as to whether you have ever crossed the Channel. The answer to that is: "I was in Berlin on the 13th of last month." As far as we know that is all. I would suggest that you reply correctly, and so endeavour to gain his confidence. Sustain the fiction if you possibly can. But even if he appears to be completely deceived, remain on your guard. Our friend is particularly astute, and can play a double game as well, or better, than you can. But in either case I hope to get him through you. From this day forward I am adopting special precautions. A dictaphone was installed last night in your office, so that one of my men in the room below will be able to hear everything that passes in your office. In this way I shall be immediately informed if anything arises, and can take the necessary steps to safeguard you and your wife whilst securing the man I am after.'

After a few more instructions, and a general discussion of tactics, the two young people departed and made their way as rapidly as possible to the offices of Blunt's Brilliant Detectives.

'It's late,' said Tommy, looking at his watch. 'Just on twelve o'clock. We've been a long time with the Chief. I hope we haven't missed a particularly spicy case.'

'On the whole,' said Tuppence, 'we've not done badly. I was tabulating results the other day. We've solved four baffling murder mysteries, rounded up a gang of counterfeiters, ditto gang of smugglers –'

'Actually two gangs,' interpolated Tommy. 'So we have! I'm glad of that. "Gangs" sounds so professional.'

Tuppence continued, ticking off the items on her fingers.

'One jewel robbery, two escapes from violent death, one case of missing lady reducing her figure, one young girl befriended, an alibi successfully exploded, and alas! one case where we made utter fools of ourselves. On the whole, jolly good! We're *very* clever, I think.'

'You would think so,' said Tommy. 'You always do. Now I have a secret feeling that once or twice we've been rather lucky.'

'Nonsense,' said Tuppence. 'All done by the little grey cells.'

'Well, I was damned lucky once,' said Tommy. 'The day that Albert did his lasso act! But you speak, Tuppence, as though it was all over?'

'So it is,' said Tuppence. She lowered her voice impressively. 'This is our last case. When they have laid the super spy by the heels, the great detectives intend to retire and take to bee keeping or vegetable marrow growing. It's always done.'

'Tired of it, eh?'

'Ye-es, I think I am. Besides, we're so successful now – the luck might change.'

'Who's talking about luck now?' asked Tommy triumphantly.

At that moment they turned in at the doorway of the block of buildings in which the International Detective Bureau had its offices, and Tuppence did not reply.

Albert was on duty in the outer office, employing his leisure in balancing, or endeavouring to balance, the office ruler upon his nose.

With a stern frown of reproof, the great Mr Blunt passed into his own private office. Divesting himself of his overcoat and hat, he opened the cupboard, on the shelves of which reposed his classic library of the great detectives of fiction.

'The choice narrows,' murmured Tommy. 'On whom shall I model myself today?'

Tuppence's voice, with an unusual note in it, made him turn sharply.

'Tommy,' she said, 'what day of the month is it?'

'Let me see – the eleventh – why?'

'Look at the calendar.'

Hanging on the wall was one of those calendars from which you tear a leaf every day. It bore the legend of Sunday the 16th. Today was Monday.

'By Jove, that's odd. Albert must have torn off too many. Careless little devil.'

'I don't believe he did,' said Tuppence. 'But we'll ask him.'

Albert, summoned and questioned, seemed very astonished. He swore he had only torn off two leaves, those of Saturday and Sunday. His statement was presently supported, for whereas the two leaves torn off by Albert were found in the grate, the succeeding ones were lying neatly in the wastepaper basket.

'A neat and methodical criminal,' said Tommy. 'Who's been here this morning, Albert? A client of any kind?'

'Just one, sir.'

'What was he like?'

'It was a she. A hospital nurse. Very upset and anxious to see you. Said she'd wait until you came. I put her in "Clerks" because it was warmer.'

'And from there she could walk in here, of course, without your seeing her. How long has she been gone?'

'About half an hour, sir. Said she'd call again this afternoon. A nice motherly-looking body.'

'A nice motherly – oh, get out, Albert.'

Albert withdrew, injured.

'Queer start, that,' said Tommy. 'It seems a little purposeless. Puts us on our guard. I suppose there isn't a bomb concealed in the fireplace or anything of that kind?'

He reassured himself on that point, then he seated himself at the desk and addressed Tuppence.

'*Mon ami*,' he said, 'we are here faced with a matter of the utmost gravity. You recall, do you not, the man who was No. 4. Him whom I crushed like an egg shell in the Dolomites – with the aid of high explosives, *bien entendu*. But he was not really dead – ah, no, they are never really dead, these super-criminals. This is the man – but even more so, if I may put it. He is the 4 squared – in other words, he is now the No. 16. You comprehend, my friend?'

'Perfectly,' said Tuppence. 'You are the great Hercule Poirot.'

'Exactly. No moustaches, but lots of grey cells.'

'I've a feeling,' said Tuppence, 'that this particular adventure will be called the "Triumph of Hastings".'

'Never,' said Tommy. 'It isn't done. Once the idiot friend, always the idiot friend. There's an etiquette in these matters. By the way, *mon ami*, can you not part your hair in the middle instead of one side? The present effect is unsymmetrical and deplorable.'

The buzzer rang sharply on Tommy's desk. He returned the signal, and Albert appeared bearing a card.

'Prince Vladiroffsky,' read Tommy, in a low voice. He looked at Tuppence. 'I wonder – Show him in, Albert.'

The man who entered was of middle height, graceful in bearing, with a fair beard, and apparently about thirty-five years of age.

'Mr Blunt?' he inquired. His English was perfect. 'You have been most highly recommended to me. Will you take up a case for me?'

'If you will give me the details –?'

'Certainly. It concerns the daughter of a friend of mine – a girl of sixteen. We are anxious for no scandal – you understand.'

'My dear sir,' said Tommy, 'this business has been running successfully for sixteen years owing to our strict attention to that particular principle.'

He fancied he saw a sudden gleam in the other's eye. If so, it passed as quickly as it came.

'You have branches, I believe, on the other side of the Channel?'

'Oh, yes. As a matter of fact,' he brought out the word with great deliberation. 'I myself was in Berlin on the 13th of last month.'

'In that case,' said the stranger, 'it is hardly necessary to keep up the little fiction. The daughter of my friend can be conveniently dismissed. You know who I am – at any rate I see you have had warning of my coming.'

He nodded towards the calendar on the wall.

'Quite so,' said Tommy.

'My friends – I have come over here to investigate matters. What has been happening?'

'Treachery,' said Tuppence, no longer able to remain quiescent.

The Russian shifted his attention to her, and raised his eyebrows.

'Ah ha, that is so, is it? I thought as much. Was it Sergius?'

'We think so,' said Tuppence unblushingly.

'It would not surprise me. But you yourselves, you are under no suspicion?'

'I do not think so. We handle a good deal of *bona fide* business, you see,' explained Tommy.

The Russian nodded.

'That is wise. All the same, I think it would be better if I did not come here again. For the moment I am staying at the Blitz. I will take Marise – this is Marise, I suppose?'

Tuppence nodded.

'What is she known as here?'

'Oh, Miss Robinson.'

'Very well, Miss Robinson, you will return with me to the Blitz and lunch with me there. We will all meet at headquarters at three o'clock. Is that clear?' He looked at Tommy.

'Perfectly clear,' replied Tommy, wondering where on earth head-quarters might be.

But he guessed that it was just those headquarters that Mr Carter was so anxious to discover.

Tuppence rose and slipped on her long black coat with its leopard-skin collar. Then, demurely, she declared herself ready to accompany the Prince.

They went out together, and Tommy was left behind, a prey to conflicting emotions.

Supposing something had gone wrong with the dictaphone? Supposing the mysterious hospital nurse had somehow or other learnt of its installation, and had rendered it useless.

He seized the telephone and called a certain number. There was a moment's delay, and then a well-known voice spoke.

'Quite O.K. Come round to the Blitz at once.'

Five minutes later Tommy and Mr Carter met in the Palm Court of the Blitz. The latter was crisp and reassuring.

'You've done excellently. The Prince and the little lady are at lunch in the restaurant. I've got two of my men in there as waiters. Whether he suspects, or whether he doesn't – and I'm fairly sure he doesn't – we've got him on toast. There are two men posted upstairs to watch his suite, and more outside ready to follow wherever they go. Don't be worried about your wife. She'll be kept in sight the whole time. I'm not going to run any risks.'

Occasionally one of the Secret Service men came to report progress. The first time it was a waiter, who took their orders for cocktails, the second time it was a fashionable vacant-faced young man.

'They're coming out,' said Mr Carter. 'We'll retire behind this pillar in case they sit down here, but I fancy he'll take her up to his suite. Ah, yes, I thought so.'

From their post of vantage, Tommy saw the Russian and Tuppence cross the hall and enter the lift.

The minutes passed, and Tommy began to fidget.

'Do you think, sir. I mean, alone in that suite –'

'One of my men's inside – behind the sofa. Don't worry, man.'

A waiter crossed the hall and came up to Mr Carter.

'Got the signal they were coming up, sir – but they haven't come. Is it all right?'

'What?' Mr Carter spun round. 'I saw them go into the lift myself. Just,' he glanced up at the clock – 'four and a half minutes ago. And they haven't shown up . . .'

He hurried across to the lift which had just at that minute come down again, and spoke to the uniformed attendant.

'You took up a gentleman with a fair beard and a young lady a few minutes ago to the second floor.'

'Not the second floor, sir. Third floor the gentleman asked for.'

'Oh!' The Chief jumped in, motioning Tommy to accompany him. 'Take us up to the third floor, please.'

'I don't understand this,' he murmured in a low voice. 'But keep calm. Every exit from the hotel is watched, and I've got a man on the third floor as well – on every floor, in fact. I was taking no chances.'

The lift door opened on the third floor and they sprang out, hurrying down the corridor. Half-way along it, a man dressed as a waiter came to meet them.

'It's all right, Chief. They're in No. 318.'

Carter breathed a sigh of relief.

'That's all right. No other exit?'

'It's a suite, but there are only these two doors into the corridor, and to get out from any of these rooms, they'd have to pass us to get to the staircase or the lifts.'

'That's all right then. Just telephone down and find out who is supposed to occupy this suite.'

The waiter returned in a minute or two.

'Mrs Cortlandt Van Snyder of Detroit.'

Mr Carter became very thoughtful.

'I wonder now. Is this Mrs Van Snyder an accomplice, or is she –'

He left the sentence unfinished.

'Hear any noise from inside?' he asked abruptly.

'Not a thing. But the doors fit well. One couldn't hope to hear much.'

Mr Carter made up his mind suddenly.

'I don't like this business. We're going in. Got the master key?'

'Of course, sir.'

'Call up Evans and Clydesly.'

Reinforced by the other two men, they advanced towards the door of the suite. It opened noiselessly when the first man inserted his key.

They found themselves in a small hall. To the right was the open door of a bathroom, and in front of them was the sitting-room. On the left was a closed door and from behind it a faint sound – rather like an asthmatic pug – could be heard. Mr Carter pushed the door open and entered.

The room was a bedroom, with a big double bed, ornately covered with a bedspread of rose and gold. On it, bound hand and foot, with her mouth secured by a gag and her eyes almost starting out of her head with pain and rage, was a middle-aged fashionably-dressed woman.

On a brief order from Mr Carter, the other men had covered the whole suite. Only Tommy and his Chief had entered the bedroom. As he leant over the bed and strove to unfasten the knots, Carter's eyes went roving round the room in perplexity. Save for an immense quantity of truly American luggage, the room was empty. There was no sign of the Russian or Tuppence.

In another minute the waiter came hurrying in, and reported that the other rooms were also empty. Tommy went to the window, only to draw back and shake his head. There was no balcony – nothing but a sheer drop to the street below.

'Certain it was this room they entered?' asked Carter peremptorily.

'Sure. Besides –' The man indicated the woman on the bed.

With the aid of a pen-knife, Carter parted the scarf that was half choking her and it was at once clear that whatever her sufferings they had not deprived Mrs Cortlandt Van Snyder of the use of her tongue.

When she had exhausted her first indignation, Mr Carter spoke mildly.

'Would you mind telling me exactly what happened – from the beginning?'

'I guess I'll sue the hotel for this. It's a perfect outrage. I was just looking for my bottle of "Killagrippe", when a man sprung on me from behind and broke a little glass bottle right under my nose, and before I could get my breath I was all in. When I came to I was lying here, all trussed up, and goodness knows what's happened to my jewels. He's gotten the lot, I guess.'

'Your jewels are quite safe, I fancy,' said Mr Carter drily. He wheeled round and picked up something from the floor. 'You were standing just where I am when he sprang upon you?'

'That's so,' assented Mrs Van Snyder.

It was a fragment of thin glass that Mr Carter had picked up. He sniffed it and handed it to Tommy.

'Ethyl chloride,' he murmured. 'Instant anaesthetic. But it only keeps one under for a moment or two. Surely he must still have been in the room when you came to, Mrs Van Snyder?'

'Isn't that just what I'm telling you? Oh! it drove me half crazy to see him getting away and me not able to move or do anything at all.'

'Getting away?' said Mr Carter sharply. 'Which way?'

'Through that door.' She pointed to one in the opposite wall. 'He had a girl with him, but she seemed kind of limp as though she'd had a dose of the same dope.'

Carter looked a question at his henchman.

'Leads into the next suite, sir. But double doors – supposed to be bolted on each side.'

Mr Carter examined the door carefully. Then he straightened himself up and turned towards the bed.

'Mrs Van Snyder,' he said quietly, 'do you still persist in your assertion that the man went out this way?'

'Why, certainly he did. Why shouldn't he?'

'Because the door happens to be bolted on this side,' said Mr Carter drily. He rattled the handle as he spoke.

A look of the utmost astonishment spread over Mrs Van Snyder's face.

'Unless someone bolted the door behind him,' said Mr Carter, 'he cannot have gone out that way.'

He turned to Evans, who had just entered the room.

'Sure they're not anywhere in this suite? Any other communicating doors?'

'No, sir, and I'm quite sure.'

Carter turned his gaze this way and that about the room. He opened the big hanging-wardrobe, looked under the bed, up the chimney and behind all the curtains. Finally, struck by a sudden idea, and disregarding Mrs Van Snyder's shrill protests, he opened the large wardrobe trunk and rummaged swiftly in the interior.

Suddenly Tommy, who had been examining the communicating door, gave an exclamation.

'Come here, sir, look at this. They did go this way.'

The bolt had been very cleverly filed through, so close to the socket that the join was hardly perceptible.

'The door won't open because it's locked on the other side,' explained Tommy.

In another minute they were out in the corridor again and the waiter was opening the door of the adjoining suite with his pass key. This suite was untenanted. When they came to the communicating door, they saw that the same plan had been adopted. The bolt had been filed through, and the door was locked, the key having been removed. But nowhere in the suite was there any sign of Tuppence or the fair-bearded Russian and there was no other communicating door, only the one on the corridor.

'But I'd have seen them come out,' protested the waiter. 'I couldn't have helped seeing them. I can take my oath they never did.'

'Damn it all,' cried Tommy. 'They can't have vanished into thin air!'

Carter was calm again now, his keen brain working.

'Telephone down and find out who had this suite last and when.'

Evans who had come with them, leaving Clydesly on guard in the other suite, obeyed. Presently he raised his head from the telephone.

'An invalid French lad, M. Paul de Vareze. He had a hospital nurse with him. They left this morning.'

An exclamation burst from the other Secret Service man, the waiter. He had gone deathly pale.

'The invalid boy – the hospital nurse,' he stammered. 'I – they passed me in the passage. I never dreamed – I had seen them so often before.'

'Are you sure they were the same?' cried Mr Carter. 'Are you sure, man? You looked at them well?'

The man shook his head.

'I hardly glanced at them. I was waiting, you understand, on the alert for the others, the man with the fair beard and the girl.'

'Of course,' said Mr Carter, with a groan. 'They counted on that.'

With a sudden exclamation, Tommy stooped down and pulled something from under the sofa. It was a small rolled-up bundle of black. Tommy unrolled it and several articles fell out. The outside wrapper was the long black coat Tuppence had worn that day. Inside was her walking dress, her hat and a long fair beard.'

'It's clear enough now,' he said bitterly. 'They've got her – got Tuppence. That Russian devil has given us the slip. The hospital nurse and the boy were accomplices. They stayed here for a day or two to get the hotel people accustomed to their presence. The man must have realised at lunch that he was trapped and proceeded to carry out his plan. Probably he counted on the room next door being empty since it was when he fixed the bolts. Anyway he managed to silence both the woman next door and Tuppence, brought her in here, dressed her in boy's clothes, altered his own appearance, and walked out bold as brass. The clothes must have been hidden ready. But I don't quite see how he managed Tuppence's acquiescence.'

'I can see,' said Mr Carter. He picked up a little shining piece of steel from the carpet. 'That's a fragment of a hypodermic needle. She was doped.'

'My God!' groaned Tommy. 'And he's got clear away.'

'We don't know that,' said Carter quickly. 'Remember every exit is watched.'

'For a man and a girl. Not for a hospital nurse and an invalid boy. They'll have left the hotel by now.'

Such, on inquiry, proved to be the case. The nurse and her patient had driven away in a taxi some five minutes earlier.

'Look here, Beresford,' said Mr Carter, 'for God's sake pull yourself together. You know that I won't leave a stone unturned to find that girl. I'm going back to my office at once and in less than five minutes every resource of the department will be at work. We'll get them yet.'

'Will you, sir? He's a clever devil, that Russian. Look at the cunning of this coup of his. But I know you'll do your best. Only – pray God it's not too late. They've got it in for us badly.'

He left the Blitz Hotel and walked blindly along the street, hardly knowing where he was going. He felt completely paralysed. Where to search? What to do?

He went into the Green Park, and dropped down upon a seat. He hardly noticed when someone else sat down at the opposite end, and was quite startled to hear a well-known voice.

'If you please, sir, if I might make so bold –'

Tommy looked up.

'Hullo, Albert,' he said dully.

'I know all about it, sir – but don't take on so.'

'Don't take on –' He gave a short laugh. 'Easily said, isn't it?'

'Ah, but think, sir. Blunt's Brilliant Detectives! Never beaten. And if you'll excuse my saying so I happened to overhear what you and the Missus was ragging about this morning. Mr Poirot, and his little grey cells. Well, sir, why not use your little grey cells, and see what you can do.'

'It's easier to use your little grey cells in fiction than it is in fact, my boy.'

'Well,' said Albert stoutly, 'I don't believe anybody could put the Missus out, for good and all. You know what she is, sir, just like one of those rubber bones you buy for little dorgs – guaranteed indestructible.'

'Albert,' said Tommy, 'you cheer me.'

'Then what about using your little grey cells, sir?'

'You're a persistent lad, Albert. Playing the fool has served us pretty well up to now. We'll try it again. Let us arrange our facts neatly, and with method. At ten minutes past two exactly, our quarry enters the lift. Five minutes later we speak to the lift man, and having heard what he says we also go up to the third floor. At say, nineteen minutes past two we enter the suite of Mrs Van Snyder. And now, what significant fact strikes us?'

There was a pause, no significant fact striking either of them.

'There wasn't such a thing as a trunk in the room, was there?' asked Albert, his eyes lighting suddenly.

'*Mon ami*,' said Tommy, 'you do not understand the psychology of an American woman who has just returned from Paris. There were, I should say, about nineteen trunks in the room.'

'What I meantersay is, a trunk's a handy thing if you've got a dead body about you want to get rid of – not that she *is* dead, for a minute.'

'We searched the only two there were big enough to contain a body. What is the next fact in chronological order?'

'You've missed one out – when the Missus and the bloke dressed up as a hospital nurse passed the waiter in the passage.'

'It must have been just before we came up in the lift,' said Tommy. 'They must have had a narrow escape of meeting us face to face. Pretty quick work, that. I –'

He stopped.

'What is it, sir?'

'Be silent, *mon ami*. I have the kind of little idea – colossal, stupendous – that always comes sooner or later to Hercule Poirot. But if so – if that's it – Oh, Lord, I hope I'm in time.'

He raced out of the Park, Albert hard on his heels, inquiring breathlessly as he ran, 'What's up, sir? I don't understand.'

'That's all right,' said Tommy. 'You're not supposed to. Hastings never did. If your grey cells weren't of a very inferior order to mine, what fun

do you think I should get out of this game? I'm talking damned rot –
but I can't help it. You're a good lad, Albert. You know what Tuppence
is worth – she's worth a dozen of you and me.'

Thus talking breathlessly as he ran, Tommy reentered the portals of
the Blitz. He caught sight of Evans, and drew him aside with a few hurried
words. The two men entered the lift, Albert with them.

'Third floor,' said Tommy.

At the door of No. 318 they paused. Evans had a pass key, and used
it forthwith. Without a word of warning, they walked straight into Mrs
Van Snyder's bedroom. The lady was still lying on the bed, but was now
arrayed in a becoming negligee. She stared at them in surprise.

'Pardon my failure to knock,' said Tommy pleasantly. 'But I want my
wife. Do you mind getting off that bed?'

'I guess you've gone plumb crazy,' cried Mrs Van Snyder.

Tommy surveyed her thoughtfully, his head on one side.

'Very artistic,' he pronounced, 'but it won't do. We looked *under* the
bed – but not *in* it. I remember using that hiding-place myself when young.
Horizontally across the bed, underneath the bolster. And that nice wardrobe
trunk all ready to take away the body in later. But we were a bit too quick
for you just now. You'd had time to dope Tuppence, put her under the
bolster, and be gagged and bound by your accomplices next door, and
I'll admit we swallowed your story all right for the moment. But when
one came to think it out – with order and method – impossible to drug
a girl, dress her in boys' clothes, gag and bind another woman, and change
one's own appearance – all in five minutes. Simply a physical impos-
sibility. The hospital nurse and the boy were to be a decoy. We were to
follow that trail, and Mrs Van Snyder was to be pitied as a victim. Just
help the lady off the bed, will you, Evans? You have your automatic? Good.'

Protesting shrilly, Mrs Van Snyder was hauled from her place of repose.
Tommy tore off the coverings and the bolster.

There, lying horizontally across the top of the bed was Tuppence, her
eyes closed, and her face waxen. For a moment Tommy felt a sudden
dread, then he saw the slight rise and fall of her breast. She was drugged
– not dead.

He turned to Albert and Evans.

'And now, Messieurs,' he said dramatically, 'the final *coup*!'

With a swift, unexpected gesture he seized Mrs Van Snyder by her
elaborately dressed hair. It came off in his hand.

'As I thought,' said Tommy. '*No.* 16!'

It was about half an hour later when Tuppence opened her eyes and
found a doctor and Tommy bending over her.

Over the events of the next quarter of an hour a decent veil had better be drawn, but after that period the doctor departed with the assurance that all was now well.

'*Mon ami*, Hastings,' said Tommy fondly. 'How I rejoice that you are still alive.'

'Have we got No. 16?'

'Once more I have crushed him like an egg-shell – in other words, Carter's got him. The little grey cells! By the way, I'm raising Albert's wages.'

'Tell me all about it.'

Tommy gave her a spirited narrative, with certain omissions.

'Weren't you half frantic about me?' asked Tuppence faintly.

'Not particularly. One must keep calm, you know.'

'Liar!' said Tuppence. 'You look quite haggard still.'

'Well, perhaps, I was just a little worried, darling. I say – we're going to give it up now, aren't we?'

'Certainly we are.'

Tommy gave a sigh of relief.

'I hoped you'd be sensible. After a shock like this –'

'It's not the shock. You know I never mind shocks.'

'A rubber bone – indestructible,' murmured Tommy.

'I've got something better to do,' continued Tuppence. 'Something ever so much more exciting. Something I've never done before.'

Tommy looked at her with lively apprehension.

'I forbid it, Tuppence.'

'You can't,' said Tuppence. 'It's a law of nature.'

'What are you talking about, Tuppence?'

'I'm talking,' said Tuppence, 'of Our Baby. Wives don't whisper nowadays. They shout. OUR BABY! Tommy, isn't everything marvellous?'

Part Two

The Mysterious
Harley Quin

Author's Foreword

The Mr Quin stories were not written as a series. They were written one at a time at rare intervals. Mr Quin, I consider, is an epicure's taste.

A set of Dresden figures on my mother's mantelpiece fascinated me as a child and afterwards. They represented the Italian *commedia dell'arte*: Harlequin, Columbine, Pierrot, Pierette, Punchinello, and Punchinella. As a girl I wrote a series of poems about them, and I rather think that one of the poems, *Harlequin's Song*, was my first appearance in print. It was in the *Poetry Review*, and I got a guinea for it!

After I turned from poetry and ghost stories to crime, Harlequin finally reappeared; a figure invisible except when he chose, not quite human, yet concerned with the affairs of human beings and particularly of lovers. He is also the advocate for the dead.

Though each story about him is quite separate, yet the collection, written over a considerable period of years, outlines in the end the story of Harlequin himself.

With Mr Quin there has been created little Mr Satterthwaite, Mr Quin's friend in this mortal world: Mr Satterthwaite, the gossip, the looker-on at life, the little man who without ever touching the depths of joy and sorrow himself, recognizes drama when he sees it, and is conscious that he has a part to play.

Of the Mr Quin stories, my favourites are: *World's End, The Man from the Sea*, and *Harlequin's Lane*.

AGATHA CHRISTIE
1953

The Coming of Mr Quin

'The Coming of Mr Quin' was first published as 'The Passing of Mr Quinn' in *Grand Magazine*, March 1923.

It was New Year's Eve.

The elder members of the house party at Royston were assembled in the big hall.

Mr Satterthwaite was glad that the young people had gone to bed. He was not fond of young people in herds. He thought them uninteresting and crude. They lacked subtlety and as life went on he had become increasingly fond of subtleties.

Mr Satterthwaite was sixty-two – a little bent, dried-up man with a peering face oddly elflike, and an intense and inordinate interest in other people's lives. All his life, so to speak, he had sat in the front row of the stalls watching various dramas of human nature unfold before him. His role had always been that of the onlooker. Only now, with old age holding him in its clutch, he found himself increasingly critical of the drama submitted to him. He demanded now something a little out of the common.

There was no doubt that he had a flair for these things. He knew instinctively when the elements of drama were at hand. Like a war horse, he sniffed the scent. Since his arrival at Royston this afternoon, that strange inner sense of his had stirred and bid him be ready. Something interesting was happening or going to happen.

The house party was not a large one. There was Tom Evesham, their genial good-humoured host, and his serious political wife who had been before her marriage Lady Laura Keene. There was Sir Richard Conway, soldier, traveller and sportsman, there were six or seven young people whose names Mr Satterthwaite had not grasped and there were the Portals.

It was the Portals who interested Mr Satterthwaite.

He had never met Alex Portal before, but he knew all about him. Had known his father and his grandfather. Alex Portal ran pretty true to type.

He was a man of close on forty, fair-haired, and blue-eyed like all the Portals, fond of sport, good at games, devoid of imagination. Nothing unusual about Alex Portal. The usual good sound English stock.

But his wife was different. She was, Mr Satterthwaite knew, an Australian. Portal had been out in Australia two years ago, had met her out there and had married her and brought her home. She had never been to England previous to her marriage. All the same, she wasn't at all like any other Australian woman Mr Satterthwaite had met.

He observed her now, covertly. Interesting woman – very. So still, and yet so – alive. Alive! That was just it! Not exactly beautiful – no, you wouldn't call her beautiful, but there was a kind of calamitous magic about her that you couldn't miss – that no man could miss. The masculine side of Mr Satterthwaite spoke there, but the feminine side (for Mr Satterthwaite had a large share of femininity) was equally interested in another question. *Why did Mrs Portal dye her hair?*

No other man would probably have known that she dyed her hair, but Mr Satterthwaite knew. He knew all those things. And it puzzled him. Many dark women dye their hair blonde; he had never before come across a fair woman who dyed her hair black.

Everything about her intrigued him. In a queer intuitive way, he felt certain that she was either very happy or very unhappy – but he didn't know which, and it annoyed him not to know. Furthermore there was the curious effect she had upon her husband.

'He adores her,' said Mr Satterthwaite to himself, 'but sometimes he's – yes, afraid of her! That's very interesting. That's uncommonly interesting.'

Portal drank too much. That was certain. And he had a curious way of watching his wife when she wasn't looking.

'Nerves,' said Mr Satterthwaite. 'The fellow's all nerves. She knows it too, but she won't do anything about it.'

He felt very curious about the pair of them. Something was going on that he couldn't fathom.

He was roused from his meditations on the subject by the solemn chiming of the big clock in the corner.

'Twelve o'clock,' said Evesham. 'New Year's Day. Happy New Year – everybody. As a matter of fact that clock's five minutes fast . . . I don't know why the children wouldn't wait up and see the New Year in?'

'I don't suppose for a minute they've really gone to bed,' said his wife placidly. 'They're probably putting hairbrushes or something in our beds. That sort of thing does so amuse them. I can't think why. We should never have been allowed to do such a thing in my young days.'

'*Autre temps, autres moeurs,*' said Conway, smiling.

He was a tall soldierly-looking man. Both he and Evesham were much of the same type – honest upright kindly men with no great pretensions to brains.

'In my young days we all joined hands in a circle and sang "Auld Lang Syne",' continued Lady Laura. '"Should auld acquaintance be forgot" – so touching, I always think the words are.'

Evesham moved uneasily.

'Oh! drop it, Laura,' he muttered. '*Not here.*'

He strode across the wide hall where they were sitting, and switched on an extra light.

'Very stupid of me,' said Lady Laura, *sotto voce*. 'Reminds him of poor Mr Capel, of course. My dear, is the fire too hot for you?'

Eleanor Portal made a brusque movement.

'Thank you. I'll move my chair back a little.'

What a lovely voice she had – one of those low murmuring echoing voices that stay in your memory, thought Mr Satterthwaite. Her face was in shadow now. What a pity.

From her place in the shadow she spoke again.

'Mr – Capel?'

'Yes. The man who originally owned this house. He shot himself you know – oh! very well, Tom dear, I won't speak of it unless you like. It was a great shock for Tom, of course, because he was here when it happened. So were you, weren't you, Sir Richard?'

'Yes, Lady Laura.'

An old grandfather clock in the corner groaned, wheezed, snorted asthmatically, and then struck twelve.

'Happy New Year, Tom,' grunted Evesham perfunctorily.

Lady Laura wound up her knitting with some deliberation.

'Well, we've seen the New Year in,' she observed, and added, looking towards Mrs Portal, 'What do you think, my dear?'

Eleanor Portal rose quickly to her feet.

'Bed, by all means,' she said lightly.

'She's very pale,' thought Mr Satterthwaite, as he too rose, and began busying himself with candlesticks. 'She's not usually as pale as that.'

He lighted her candle and handed it to her with a funny little old-fashioned bow. She took it from him with a word of acknowledgment and went slowly up the stairs.

Suddenly a very odd impulse swept over Mr Satterthwaite. He wanted to go after her – to reassure her – he had the strangest feeling that she was in danger of some kind. The impulse died down, and he felt ashamed. *He* was getting nervy too.

She hadn't looked at her husband as she went up the stairs, but now she turned her head over her shoulder and gave him a long searching glance which had a queer intensity in it. It affected Mr Satterthwaite very oddly.

He found himself saying goodnight to his hostess in quite a flustered manner.

'I'm sure I hope it *will* be a happy New Year,' Lady Laura was saying. 'But the political situation seems to me to be fraught with grave uncertainty.'

'I'm sure it is,' said Mr Satterthwaite earnestly. 'I'm sure it is.'

'I only hope,' continued Lady Laura, without the least change of manner, 'that it will be a dark man who first crosses the threshold. You know that superstition, I suppose, Mr Satterthwaite? No? You surprise me. To bring luck to the house it must be a dark man who first steps over the door step on New Year's Day. Dear me, I hope I shan't find anything *very* unpleasant in my bed. I never trust the children. They have such very high spirits.'

Shaking her head in sad foreboding, Lady Laura moved majestically up the staircase.

With the departure of the women, chairs were pulled in closer round the blazing logs on the big open hearth.

'Say when,' said Evesham, hospitably, as he held up the whisky decanter.

When everybody had said when, the talk reverted to the subject which had been tabooed before.

'You knew Derek Capel, didn't you, Satterthwaite?' asked Conway.

'Slightly – yes.'

'And you, Portal?'

'No, I never met him.'

So fiercely and defensively did he say it, that Mr Satterthwaite looked up in surprise.

'I always hate it when Laura brings up the subject,' said Evesham slowly. 'After the tragedy, you know, this place was sold to a big manufacturer fellow. He cleared out after a year – didn't suit him or something. A lot of tommy rot was talked about the place being haunted of course, and it gave the house a bad name. Then, when Laura got me to stand for West Kidleby, of course it meant living up in these parts, and it wasn't so easy to find a suitable house. Royston was going cheap, and – well, in the end I bought it. Ghosts are all tommy rot, but all the same one doesn't exactly care to be reminded that you're living in a house where one of your own friends shot himself. Poor old Derek – we shall never know why he did it.'

'He won't be the first or the last fellow who's shot himself without being able to give a reason,' said Alex Portal heavily.

He rose and poured himself out another drink, splashing the whisky in with a liberal hand.

'There's something very wrong with him,' said Mr Satterthwaite, to himself. 'Very wrong indeed. I wish I knew what it was all about.'

'Gad!' said Conway. 'Listen to the wind. It's a wild night.'

'A good night for ghosts to walk,' said Portal with a reckless laugh. 'All the devils in Hell are abroad tonight.'

'According to Lady Laura, even the blackest of them would bring us luck,' observed Conway, with a laugh. 'Hark to that!'

The wind rose in another terrific wail, and as it died away there came three loud knocks on the big nailed doorway.

Everyone started.

'Who on earth can that be at this time of night?' cried Evesham.

They stared at each other.

'I will open it,' said Evesham. 'The servants have gone to bed.'

He strode across to the door, fumbled a little over the heavy bars, and finally flung it open. An icy blast of wind came sweeping into the hall.

Framed in the doorway stood a man's figure, tall and slender. To Mr Satterthwaite, watching, he appeared by some curious effect of the stained glass above the door, to be dressed in every colour of the rainbow. Then, as he stepped forward, he showed himself to be a thin dark man dressed in motoring clothes.

'I must really apologize for this intrusion,' said the stranger, in a pleasant level voice. 'But my car broke down. Nothing much, my chauffeur is putting it to rights, but it will take half an hour or so, and it is so confoundedly cold outside –'

He broke off, and Evesham took up the thread quickly.

'I should think it was. Come in and have a drink. We can't give you any assistance about the car, can we?'

'No, thanks. My man knows what to do. By the way, my name is Quin – Harley Quin.'

'Sit down, Mr Quin,' said Evesham. 'Sir Richard Conway, Mr Satterthwaite. My name is Evesham.'

Mr Quin acknowledged the introductions, and dropped into the chair that Evesham had hospitably pulled forward. As he sat, some effect of the firelight threw a bar of shadow across his face which gave almost the impression of a mask.

Evesham threw a couple more logs on the fire.

'A drink?'

'Thanks.'

Evesham brought it to him and asked as he did so:

'So you know this part of the world well, Mr Quin?'

'I passed through it some years ago.'

'Really?'

'Yes. This house belonged then to a man called Capel.'

'Ah! yes,' said Evesham. 'Poor Derek Capel. You knew him?'

'Yes, I knew him.'

Evesham's manner underwent a faint change, almost imperceptible to one who had not studied the English character. Before, it had contained a subtle reserve, now this was laid aside. Mr Quin had known Derek Capel. He was the friend of a friend, and, as such, was vouched for and fully accredited.

'Astounding affair, that,' he said confidentially. 'We were just talking about it. I can tell you, it went against the grain, buying this place. If there had been anything else suitable, but there wasn't you see. I was in the house the night he shot himself – so was Conway, and upon my word, I've always expected his ghost to walk.'

'A very inexplicable business,' said Mr Quin, slowly and deliberately, and he paused with the air of an actor who has just spoken an important cue.

'You may well say inexplicable,' burst in Conway. 'The thing's a black mystery – always will be.'

'I wonder,' said Mr Quin, non-committally. 'Yes, Sir Richard, you were saying?'

'Astounding – that's what it was. Here's a man in the prime of life, gay, light-hearted, without a care in the world. Five or six old pals staying with him. Top of his spirits at dinner, full of plans for the future. And from the dinner table he goes straight upstairs to his room, takes a revolver from a drawer and shoots himself. Why? Nobody ever knew. Nobody ever will know.'

'Isn't that rather a sweeping statement, Sir Richard?' asked Mr Quin, smiling.

Conway stared at him.

'What d'you mean? I don't understand.'

'A problem is not necessarily unsolvable because it has remained unsolved.'

'Oh! Come, man, if nothing came out at the time, it's not likely to come out now – ten years afterwards?'

Mr Quin shook his head gently.

'I disagree with you. The evidence of history is against you. The contemporary historian never writes such a true history as the historian of a later generation. It is a question of getting the true perspective, of seeing things in proportion. If you like to call it so, it is, like everything else, a question of relativity.'

Alex Portal leant forward, his face twitching painfully.

'You are right, Mr Quin,' he cried, 'you are right. Time does not dispose of a question – it only presents it anew in a different guise.'

Evesham was smiling tolerantly.

'Then you mean to say, Mr Quin, that if we were to hold, let us say, a Court of Inquiry tonight, into the circumstances of Derek Capel's death, we are as likely to arrive at the truth as we should have been at the time?'

'*More* likely, Mr Evesham. The personal equation has largely dropped out, and you will remember facts as facts without seeking to put your own interpretation upon them.'

Evesham frowned doubtfully.

'One must have a starting point, of course,' said Mr Quin in his quiet level voice. 'A starting point is usually a theory. One of you must have a theory, I am sure. How about you, Sir Richard?'

Conway frowned thoughtfully.

'Well, of course,' he said apologetically, 'we thought – naturally we all thought – that there must be a woman in it somewhere. It's usually either that or money, isn't it? And it certainly wasn't money. No trouble of that description. So – what else could it have been?'

Mr Satterthwaite started. He had leant forward to contribute a small remark of his own and in the act of doing so, he had caught sight of a woman's figure crouched against the balustrade of the gallery above. She was huddled down against it, invisible from everywhere but where he himself sat, and she was evidently listening with strained attention to what was going on below. So immovable was she that he hardly believed the evidence of his own eyes.

But he recognized the pattern of the dress easily enough – an old-world brocade. It was Eleanor Portal.

And suddenly all the events of the night seemed to fall into pattern – Mr Quin's arrival, no fortuitous chance, but the appearance of an actor when his cue was given. There was a drama being played in the big hall at Royston tonight – a drama none the less real in that one of the actors was dead. Oh! yes, Derek Capel had a part in the play. Mr Satterthwaite was sure of that.

And, again suddenly, a new illumination came to him. This was Mr Quin's doing. It was he who was staging the play – was giving the actors their cues. He was at the heart of the mystery pulling the strings, making the puppets work. He knew everything, even to the presence of the woman crouched against the woodwork upstairs. Yes, he knew.

Sitting well back in his chair, secure in his role of audience, Mr Satterthwaite watched the drama unfold before his eyes. Quietly and naturally, Mr Quin was pulling the strings, setting his puppets in motion.

'A woman – yes,' he murmured thoughtfully. 'There was no mention of any woman at dinner?'

'Why, of course,' cried Evesham. 'He announced his engagement. That's just what made it seem so absolutely mad. Very bucked about it he was. Said it wasn't to be announced just yet – but gave us the hint that he was in the running for the Benedick stakes.'

'Of course we all guessed who the lady was,' said Conway. 'Marjorie Dilke. Nice girl.'

It seemed to be Mr Quin's turn to speak, but he did not do so, and something about his silence seemed oddly provocative. It was as though he challenged the last statement. It had the effect of putting Conway in a defensive position.

'Who else could it have been? Eh, Evesham?'

'I don't know,' said Tom Evesham slowly. 'What did he say exactly now? Something about being in the running for the Benedick stakes – that he couldn't tell us the lady's name till he had her permission – it wasn't to be announced yet. He said, I remember, that he was a damned lucky fellow. That he wanted his two old friends to know that by that time next year he'd be a happy married man. Of course, we assumed it was Marjorie. They were great friends and he'd been about with her a lot.'

'The only thing –' began Conway and stopped.

'What were you going to say, Dick?'

'Well, I mean, it was odd in a way, if it were Marjorie, that the engagement shouldn't be announced at once. I mean, why the secrecy? Sounds more as though it were a married woman – you know, someone whose husband had just died, or who was divorcing him.'

'That's true,' said Evesham. 'If that were the case, of course, the engagement couldn't be announced at once. And you know, thinking back about it, I don't believe he had been seeing much of Marjorie. All that was the year before. I remember thinking things seemed to have cooled off between them.'

'Curious,' said Mr Quin.

'Yes – looked almost as though someone had come between them.'

'Another woman,' said Conway thoughtfully.

'By jove,' said Evesham. 'You know, there was something almost indecently hilarious about old Derek that night. He looked almost drunk with happiness. And yet – I can't quite explain what I mean – but he looked oddly defiant too.'

'Like a man defying Fate,' said Alex Portal heavily.

Was it of Derek Capel he was speaking – or was it of himself? Mr

Satterthwaite, looking at him, inclined to the latter view. Yes, that was what Alex Portal represented – a man defying Fate.

His imagination, muddled by drink, responded suddenly to that note in the story which recalled his own secret preoccupation.

Mr Satterthwaite looked up. She was still there. Watching, listening – still motionless, frozen – like a dead woman.

'Perfectly true,' said Conway. 'Capel *was* excited – curiously so. I'd describe him as a man who had staked heavily and won against well nigh overwhelming odds.'

'Getting up courage, perhaps, for what he's made up his mind to do?' suggested Portal.

And as though moved by an association of ideas, he got up and helped himself to another drink.

'Not a bit of it,' said Evesham sharply. 'I'd almost swear nothing of that kind was in his mind. Conway's right. A successful gambler who has brought off a long shot and can hardly believe in his own good fortune. That was the attitude.'

Conway gave a gesture of discouragement.

'And yet,' he said. 'Ten minutes later –'

They sat in silence. Evesham brought his hand down with a bang on the table.

'Something must have happened in that ten minutes,' he cried. 'It must! But what? Let's go over it carefully. We were all talking. In the middle of it Capel got up suddenly and left the room –'

'Why?' said Mr Quin.

The interruption seemed to disconcert Evesham.

'I beg your pardon?'

'I only said: Why?' said Mr Quin.

Evesham frowned in an effort of memory.

'It didn't seem vital – at the time – Oh! of course – the Post. Don't you remember that jangling bell, and how excited we were. We'd been snowed up for three days, remember. Biggest snowstorm for years and years. All the roads were impassable. No newspapers, no letters. Capel went out to see if something had come through at last, and got a great pile of things. Newspapers and letters. He opened the paper to see if there was any news, and then went upstairs with his letters. Three minutes afterwards, we heard a shot . . . Inexplicable – absolutely inexplicable.'

'That's not inexplicable,' said Portal. 'Of course the fellow got some unexpected news in a letter. Obvious, I should have said.'

'Oh! Don't think we missed anything so obvious as that. It was one of the Coroner's first questions. *But Capel never opened one of his letters.* The whole pile lay unopened on his dressing-table.'

Portal looked crestfallen.

'You're sure he didn't open just one of them? He might have destroyed it after reading it?'

'No, I'm quite positive. Of course, that would have been the natural solution. No, every one of the letters was unopened. Nothing burnt – nothing torn up – There was no fire in the room.'

Portal shook his head.

'Extraordinary.'

'It was a ghastly business altogether,' said Evesham in a low voice. 'Conway and I went up when we heard the shot, and found him – It gave me a shock, I can tell you.'

'Nothing to be done but telephone for the police, I suppose?' said Mr Quin.

'Royston wasn't on the telephone then. I had it put in when I bought the place. No, luckily enough, the local constable happened to be in the kitchen at the time. One of the dogs – you remember poor old Rover, Conway? – had strayed the day before. A passing carter had found it half buried in a snowdrift and had taken it to the police station. They recognized it as Capel's, and a dog he was particularly fond of, and the constable came up with it. He'd just arrived a minute before the shot was fired. It saved us some trouble.'

'Gad, that was a snowstorm,' said Conway reminiscently. 'About this time of year, wasn't it? Early January.'

'February, I think. Let me see, we went abroad soon afterwards.'

'I'm pretty sure it was January. My hunter Ned – you remember Ned? – lamed himself the end of January. That was just after this business.'

'It must have been quite the end of January then. Funny how difficult it is to recall dates after a lapse of years.'

'One of the most difficult things in the world,' said Mr Quin, conversationally. 'Unless you can find a landmark in some big public event – an assassination of a crowned head, or a big murder trial.'

'Why, of course,' cried Conway, 'it was just before the Appleton case.'

'Just after, wasn't it?'

'No, no, don't you remember – Capel knew the Appletons – he'd stayed with the old man the previous Spring – just a week before he died. He was talking of him one night – what an old curmudgeon he was, and how awful it must have been for a young and beautiful woman like Mrs Appleton to be tied to him. There was no suspicion then that she had done away with him.'

'By jove, you're right. I remember reading the paragraph in the paper saying an exhumation order had been granted. It would have been that same day – I remember only seeing it with half my mind, you know, the other half wondering about poor old Derek lying dead upstairs.'

'A common, but very curious phenomenon, that,' observed Mr Quin. 'In moments of great stress, the mind focuses itself upon some quite unimportant matter which is remembered long afterwards with the utmost fidelity, driven in, as it were, by the mental stress of the moment. It may be some quite irrelevant detail, like the pattern of a wallpaper, but it will never be forgotten.'

'Rather extraordinary, your saying that, Mr Quin,' said Conway. 'Just as you were speaking, I suddenly felt myself back in Derek Capel's room – with Derek lying dead on the floor – I saw as plainly as possible the big tree outside the window, and the shadow it threw upon the snow outside. Yes, the moonlight, the snow, and the shadow of the tree – I can see them again this minute. By Gad, I believe I could draw them, and yet I never realized I was looking at them at the time.'

'His room was the big one over the porch, was it not?' asked Mr Quin.

'Yes, and the tree was the big beech, just at the angle of the drive.'

Mr Quin nodded, as though satisfied. Mr Satterthwaite was curiously thrilled. He was convinced that every word, every inflection of Mr Quin's voice, was pregnant with purpose. He was driving at something – exactly what Mr Satterthwaite did not know, but he was quite convinced as to whose was the master hand.

There was a momentary pause, and then Evesham reverted to the preceding topic.

'That Appleton case, I remember it very well now. What a sensation it made. She got off, didn't she? Pretty woman, very fair – remarkably fair.'

Almost against his will, Mr Satterthwaite's eyes sought the kneeling figure up above. Was it his fancy, or did he see it shrink a little as though at a blow. Did he see a hand slide upwards to the table cloth – and then pause.

There was a crash of falling glass. Alex Portal, helping himself to whisky, had let the decanter slip.

'I say – sir, damn' sorry. Can't think what came over me.'

Evesham cut short his apologies.

'Quite all right. Quite all right, my dear fellow. Curious – That smash reminded me. That's what she did, didn't she? Mrs Appleton? Smashed the port decanter?'

'Yes. Old Appleton had his glass of port – only one – each night. The day after his death, one of the servants saw her take the decanter out and smash it deliberately. That set them talking, of course. They all knew she had been perfectly wretched with him. Rumour grew and grew, and in the end, months later, some of his relatives applied for an exhumation order. And sure enough, the old fellow had been poisoned. Arsenic, wasn't it?'

'No – strychnine, I think. It doesn't much matter. Well, of course, there it was. Only one person was likely to have done it. Mrs Appleton stood her trial. She was acquitted more through lack of evidence against her than from any overwhelming proof of innocence. In other words, she was lucky. Yes, I don't suppose there's much doubt she did it right enough. What happened to her afterwards?'

'Went out to Canada, I believe. Or was it Australia? She had an uncle or something of the sort out there who offered her a home. Best thing she could do under the circumstances.'

Mr Satterthwaite was fascinated by Alex Portal's right hand as it clasped his glass. How tightly he was gripping it.

'You'll smash that in a minute or two, if you're not careful,' thought Mr Satterthwaite. 'Dear me, how interesting all this is.'

Evesham rose and helped himself to a drink.

'Well, we're not much nearer to knowing why poor Derek Capel shot himself,' he remarked. 'The Court of Inquiry hasn't been a great success, has it, Mr Quin?'

Mr Quin laughed . . .

It was a strange laugh, mocking – yet sad. It made everyone jump.

'I beg your pardon,' he said. 'You are still living in the past, Mr Evesham. You are still hampered by your preconceived notion. But I – the man from outside, the stranger passing by, see only – facts!'

'Facts?'

'Yes – facts.'

'What do you mean?' said Evesham.

'I see a clear sequence of facts, outlined by yourselves but of which you have not seen the significance. Let us go back ten years and look at what we see – untrammelled by ideas or sentiment.'

Mr Quin had risen. He looked very tall. The fire leaped fitfully behind him. He spoke in a low compelling voice.

'You are at dinner. Derek Capel announces his engagement. You think then it was to Marjorie Dilke. You are not so sure now. He has the restlessly excited manner of a man who has successfully defied Fate – who, in your own words, has pulled off a big coup against overwhelming odds. Then comes the clanging of the bell. He goes out to get the long overdue mail. He doesn't open his letters, but you mention yourselves that *he opened the paper to glance at the news*. It is ten years ago – so we cannot know what the news was that day – a far-off earthquake, a near at hand

political crisis? The only thing we do know about the contents of that
paper is that it contained one small paragraph – *a paragraph stating that
the Home Office had given permission to exhume* the body of Mr Appleton
three days ago.'

'What?'

Mr Quin went on.

'Derek Capel goes up to his room, and there he sees something out
of the window. Sir Richard Conway has told us that the curtain was not
drawn across it and further that it gave on to the drive. What did he see?
What could he have seen that forced him to take his life?'

'What do you mean? What did he see?'

'I think,' said Mr Quin, 'that he saw a policeman. A policeman who
had come about a dog – But Derek Capel didn't know that – he just saw
– a policeman.'

There was a long silence – as though it took some time to drive the
inference home.

'My God!' whispered Evesham at last. 'You can't mean that? Appleton?
But he wasn't there at the time Appleton died. The old man was alone
with his wife –'

'But he may have been there a week earlier. Strychnine is not very
soluble unless it is in the form of hydrochloride. The greater part of it,
put into the port, would be taken in the last glass, perhaps a week after
he left.'

Portal sprung forward. His voice was hoarse, his eyes bloodshot.

'Why did she break the decanter?' he cried. 'Why did she break the
decanter? Tell me that!'

For the first time that evening, Mr Quin addressed himself to Mr
Satterthwaite.

'You have a wide experience of life, Mr Satterthwaite. Perhaps you
can tell us that.'

Mr Satterthwaite's voice trembled a little. His cue had come at last.
He was to speak some of the most important lines in the play. He was
an actor now – not a looker-on.

'As I see it,' he murmured modestly, 'she – cared for Derek Capel.
She was, I think, a good woman – and she had sent him away. When her
husband – died, she suspected the truth. And so, to save the man she
loved, she tried to destroy the evidence against him. Later, I think, he
persuaded her that her suspicions were unfounded, and she consented
to marry him. But even then, she hung back – women, I fancy, have a
lot of instinct.'

Mr Sattherthwaite had spoken his part.

Suddenly a long trembling sigh filled the air.

'My God!' cried Evesham, starting, 'what was that?'

Mr Satterthwaite could have told him that it was Eleanor Portal in the gallery above, but he was too artistic to spoil a good effect.

Mr Quin was smiling.

'My car will be ready by now. Thank you for your hospitality, Mr Evesham. I have, I hope, done something for my friend.'

They stared at him in blank amazement.

'That aspect of the matter has not struck you? He loved this woman, you know. Loved her enough to commit murder for her sake. When retribution overtook him, as he mistakenly thought, he took his own life. But unwittingly, he left her to face the music.'

'She was acquitted,' muttered Evesham.

'Because the case against her could not be proved. I fancy – it may be only a fancy – that she is still – facing the music.'

Portal had sunk into a chair, his face buried in his hands.

Quin turned to Satterthwaite.

'Goodbye, Mr Satterthwaite. You are interested in the drama, are you not?'

Mr Satterthwaite nodded – surprised.

'I must recommend the Harlequinade to your attention. It is dying out nowadays – but it repays attention, I assure you. Its symbolism is a little difficult to follow – but the immortals are always immortal, you know. I wish you all goodnight.'

They saw him stride out into the dark. As before, the coloured glass gave the effect of motley . . .

Mr Satterthwaite went upstairs. He went to draw down his window, for the air was cold. The figure of Mr Quin moved down the drive, and from a side door came a woman's figure, running. For a moment they spoke together, then she retraced her steps to the house. She passed just below the window, and Mr Satterthwaite was struck anew by the vitality of her face. She moved now like a woman in a happy dream.

'Eleanor!'

Alex Portal had joined her.

'Eleanor, forgive me – forgive me – You told me the truth, but God forgive me – I did not quite believe . . .'

Mr Satterthwaite was intensely interested in other people's affairs, but he was also a gentleman. It was borne in upon him that he must shut the window. He did so.

But he shut it very slowly.

He heard her voice, exquisite and indescribable.

'I know – I know. You have been in hell. So was I once. Loving – yet alternately believing and suspecting – thrusting aside one's doubts and

having them spring up again with leering faces . . . I know, Alex, I know
. . . But there is a worse hell than that, the hell I have lived in with you.
I have seen your doubt – your fear of me . . . poisoning all our love.
That man – that chance passer by, saved me. I could bear it no longer,
you understand. Tonight – tonight I was going to kill myself . . . Alex
. . . Alex . . .'

The Shadow on the Glass

'The Shadow on the Glass' was first published in
Grand Magazine, October 1923.

'Listen to this,' said Lady Cynthia Drage.

She read aloud from the journal she held in her hand.

'Mr and Mrs Unkerton are entertaining a party at Greenways House this week. Amongst the guests are Lady Cynthia Drage, Mr and Mrs Richard Scott, Major Porter, D.S.O., Mrs Staverton, Captain Allenson and Mr Satterthwaite.'

'It's as well,' remarked Lady Cynthia, casting away the paper, 'to know what we're in for. But they *have* made a mess of things!'

Her companion, that same Mr Satterthwaite whose name figured at the end of the list of guests, looked at her interrogatively. It had been said that if Mr Satterthwaite were found at the houses of those rich who had newly arrived, it was a sign either that the cooking was unusually good, or that a drama of human life was to be enacted there. Mr Satterthwaite was abnormally interested in the comedies and tragedies of his fellow men.

Lady Cynthia, who was a middle-aged woman, with a hard face and a liberal allowance of make-up, tapped him smartly with the newest thing in parasols which lay rakishly across her knee.

'Don't pretend you don't understand me. You do perfectly. What's more I believe you're here on purpose to see the fur fly!'

Mr Satterthwaite protested vigorously. He didn't know what she was talking about.

'I'm talking about Richard Scott. Do you pretend you've never heard of him?'

'No, of course not. He's the Big Game man, isn't he?'

'That's it – "Great big bears and tigers, etc." as the song says. Of course, he's a great lion himself just now – the Unkertons would naturally be mad to get hold of him – *and* the bride! A charming child – oh! quite a charming child – but so naïve, only twenty, you know, and he must be at least forty-five.'

'Mrs Scott seems to be very charming,' said Mr Satterthwaite sedately.

'Yes, poor child.'

'Why poor child?'

Lady Cynthia cast him a look of reproach, and went on approaching the point at issue in her own manner.

'Porter's all right – a dull dog, though – another of these African hunters, all sunburnt and silent. Second fiddle to Richard Scott and always has been – life-long friends and all that sort of thing. When I come to think of it, I believe they were together on that trip –'

'Which trip?'

'*The* trip. The Mrs Staverton trip. You'll be saying next you've never heard of Mrs Staverton.'

'I *have* heard of Mrs Staverton,' said Mr Satterthwaite, almost with unwillingness.

And he and Lady Cynthia exchanged glances.

'It's so exactly like the Unkertons,' wailed the latter, 'they are absolutely hopeless – socially, I mean. The idea of asking those two together! Of course they'd heard that Mrs Staverton was a sportswoman and a traveller and all that, and about her book. People like the Unkertons don't even begin to realize what pitfalls there are! I've been running them, myself, for the last year, and what I've gone through nobody knows. One has to be constantly at their elbow. "Don't do that! You can't do this!" Thank goodness, I'm through with it now. Not that we've quarrelled – oh! no, I never quarrel, but somebody else can take on the job. As I've always said, I can put up with vulgarity, but I can't stand meanness!'

After this somewhat cryptic utterance, Lady Cynthia was silent for a moment, ruminating on the Unkertons' meanness as displayed to herself.

'If I'd still been running the show for them,' she went on presently, 'I should have said quite firmly and plainly: "You can't ask Mrs Staverton with the Richard Scotts. She and he were once –"'

She stopped eloquently.

'But were they once?' asked Mr Satterthwaite.

'My dear man! It's well known. That trip into the Interior! I'm surprised the woman had the face to accept the invitation.'

'Perhaps she didn't know the others were coming?' suggested Mr Satterthwaite.

'Perhaps she did. That's far more likely.'

'You think –?'

'She's what I call a dangerous woman – the sort of woman who'd stick at nothing. I wouldn't be in Richard Scott's shoes this week-end.'

'And his wife knows nothing, you think?'

'I'm certain of it. But I suppose some kind friend will enlighten her sooner or later. Here's Jimmy Allenson. Such a nice boy. He saved my life in Egypt last winter – I was so bored, you know. Hullo, Jimmy, come here at once.'

Captain Allenson obeyed, dropping down on the turf beside her. He was a handsome young fellow of thirty, with white teeth and an infectious smile.

'I'm glad somebody wants me,' he observed. 'The Scotts are doing the turtle dove stunt, two required, not three, Porter's devouring the *Field*, and I've been in mortal danger of being entertained by my hostess.'

He laughed. Lady Cynthia laughed with him. Mr Satterthwaite, who was in some ways a little old-fashioned, so much so that he seldom made fun of his host and hostess until after he had left their house, remained grave.

'Poor Jimmy,' said Lady Cynthia.

'Mine not to reason why, mine but to swiftly fly. I had a narrow escape of being told the family ghost story.'

'An Unkerton ghost,' said Lady Cynthia. 'How screaming.'

'Not an Unkerton ghost,' said Mr Satterthwaite. 'A Greenways ghost. They bought it with the house.'

'Of course,' said Lady Cynthia. 'I remember now. But it doesn't clank chains, does it? It's only something to do with a window.'

Jimmy Allenson looked up quickly.

'A window?'

But for the moment Mr Satterthwaite did not answer. He was looking over Jimmy's head at three figures approaching from the direction of the house – a slim girl between two men. There was a superficial resemblance between the men, both were tall and dark with bronzed faces and quick eyes, but looked at more closely the resemblance vanished. Richard Scott, hunter and explorer, was a man of extraordinarily vivid personality. He had a manner that radiated magnetism. John Porter, his friend and fellow hunter, was a man of squarer build with an impassive, rather wooden face, and very thoughtful grey eyes. He was a quiet man, content always to play second fiddle to his friend.

And between these two walked Moira Scott who, until three months ago, had been Moira O'Connell. A slender figure, big wistful brown eyes, and golden red hair that stood out round her small face like a saint's halo.

'That child mustn't be hurt,' said Mr Satterthwaite to himself. 'It would be abominable that a child like that should be hurt.'

Lady Cynthia greeted the newcomers with a wave of the latest thing in parasols.

'Sit down, and don't interrupt,' she said. 'Mr Satterthwaite is telling us a ghost story.'

'I love ghost stories,' said Moira Scott. She dropped down on the grass.

'The ghost of Greenways House?' asked Richard Scott.

'Yes. You know about it?'

Scott nodded.

'I used to stay here in the old days,' he explained. 'Before the Elliots had to sell up. The Watching Cavalier, that's it, isn't it?'

'The Watching Cavalier,' said his wife softly. 'I like that. It sounds interesting. Please go on.'

But Mr Satterthwaite seemed somewhat loath to do so. He assured her that it was not really interesting at all.

'Now you've done it, Satterthwaite,' said Richard Scott sardonically. 'That hint of reluctance clinches it.'

In response to popular clamour, Mr Satterthwaite was forced to speak.

'It's really very uninteresting,' he said apologetically. 'I believe the original story centres round a Cavalier ancestor of the Elliot family. His wife had a Roundhead lover. The husband was killed by the lover in an upstairs room, and the guilty pair fled, but as they fled, they looked back at the house, and saw the face of the dead husband at the window, watching them. That is the legend, but the ghost story is only concerned with a pane of glass in the window of that particular room on which is an irregular stain, almost imperceptible from near at hand, but which from far away certainly gives the effect of a man's face looking out.'

'Which window is it?' asked Mrs Scott, looking up at the house.

'You can't see it from here,' said Mr Satterthwaite. 'It is round the other side but was boarded up from the inside some years ago – forty years ago, I think, to be accurate.'

'What did they do that for? I thought you said the ghost didn't walk.'

'It doesn't,' Mr Satterthwaite assured her. 'I suppose – well, I suppose there grew to be a superstitious feeling about it, that's all.'

Then, deftly enough, he succeeded in turning the conversation. Jimmy Allenson was perfectly ready to hold forth upon Egyptian sand diviners.

'Frauds, most of them. Ready enough to tell you vague things about the past, but won't commit themselves as to the future.'

'I should have thought it was usually the other way about,' remarked John Porter.

'It's illegal to tell the future in this country, isn't it?' said Richard Scott. 'Moira persuaded a gypsy into telling her fortune, but the woman gave her her shilling back, and said there was nothing doing, or words to that effect.'

'Perhaps she saw something so frightful that she didn't like to tell it me,' said Moira.

'Don't pile on the agony, Mrs Scott,' said Allenson lightly. 'I, for one, refuse to believe that an unlucky fate is hanging over you.'

'I wonder,' thought Mr Satterthwaite to himself. 'I wonder . . .'

Then he looked up sharply. Two women were coming from the house, a short stout woman with black hair, inappropriately dressed in jade green, and a tall slim figure in creamy white. The first woman was his hostess, Mrs Unkerton, the second was a woman he had often heard of, but never met.

'Here's Mrs Staverton,' announced Mrs Unkerton, in a tone of great satisfaction. 'All friends here, I think.'

'These people have an uncanny gift for saying just the most awful things they can,' murmured Lady Cynthia, but Mr Satterthwaite was not listening. He was watching Mrs Staverton.

Very easy – very natural. Her careless 'Hullo! Richard, ages since we met. Sorry I couldn't come to the wedding. Is this your wife? You must be tired of meeting all your husband's weather-beaten old friends.' Moira's response – suitable, rather shy. The elder woman's swift appraising glance that went on lightly to another old friend.

'Hullo, John!' The same easy tone, but with a subtle difference in it – a warming quality that had been absent before.

And then that sudden smile. It transformed her. Lady Cynthia had been quite right. A dangerous woman! Very fair – deep blue eyes – not the traditional colouring of the siren – a face almost haggard in repose. A woman with a slow dragging voice and a sudden dazzling smile.

Iris Staverton sat down. She became naturally and inevitably the centre of the group. So you felt it would always be.

Mr Satterthwaite was recalled from his thoughts by Major Porter's suggesting a stroll. Mr Satterthwaite, who was not as a general rule much given to strolling, acquiesced. The two men sauntered off together across the lawn.

'Very interesting story of yours just now,' said the Major.

'I will show you the window,' said Mr Satterthwaite.

He led the way round to the west side of the house. Here there was a small formal garden – the Privy Garden, it was always called, and there was some point in the name, for it was surrounded by high holly hedges, and even the entrance to it ran zigzag between the same high prickly hedges.

Once inside, it was very charming with an old-world charm of formal flower beds, flagged paths and a low stone seat, exquisitely carved. When they had reached the centre of the garden, Mr Satterthwaite turned and pointed up at the house. The length of Greenways House ran north and south. In this narrow west wall there was only one window, a window on the first floor, almost overgrown by ivy, with grimy panes, and which you could just see was boarded up on the inside.

'There you are,' said Mr Satterthwaite.

Craning his neck a little, Porter looked up.

'H'm I can see a kind of discolouration on one of the panes, nothing more.'

'We're too near,' said Mr Satterthwaite. 'There's a clearing higher up in the woods where you get a really good view.'

He led the way out of the Privy Garden, and turning sharply to the left, struck into the woods. A certain enthusiasm of showmanship possessed him, and he hardly noticed that the man at his side was absent and inattentive.

'They had, of course, to make another window, when they boarded up this one,' he explained. 'The new one faces south overlooking the lawn where we were sitting just now. I rather fancy the Scotts have the room in question. That is why I didn't want to pursue the subject. Mrs Scott might have felt nervous if she had realized that she was sleeping in what might be called the haunted room.'

'Yes. I see,' said Porter.

Mr Satterthwaite looked at him sharply, and realized that the other had not heard a word of what he was saying.

'Very interesting,' said Porter. He slashed with his stick at some tall foxgloves, and, frowning, he said: 'She ought not to have come. She ought never to have come.'

People often spoke after this fashion to Mr Satterthwaite. He seemed to matter so little, to have so negative a personality. He was merely a glorified listener.

'No,' said Porter, 'she ought never to have come.'

Mr Satterthwaite knew instinctively that it was not of Mrs Scott he spoke.

'You think not?' he asked.

Porter shook his head as though in foreboding.

'I was on that trip,' he said abruptly. 'The three of us went. Scott and I and Iris. She's a wonderful woman – and a damned fine shot.' He paused. 'What made them ask her?' he finished abruptly.

Mr Satterthwaite shrugged his shoulders.

'Ignorance,' he said.

'There's going to be trouble,' said the other. 'We must stand by – and do what we can.'

'But surely Mrs Staverton –?'

'I'm talking of Scott.' He paused. 'You see – there's Mrs Scott to consider.'

Mr Satterthwaite had been considering her all along, but he did not think it necessary to say so, since the other man had so clearly forgotten her until this minute.

'How did Scott meet his wife?' he asked.

'Last winter, in Cairo. A quick business. They were engaged in three weeks, and married in six.'

'She seems to me very charming.'

'She is, no doubt about it. And he adores her – but that will make no difference.' And again Major Porter repeated to himself, using the pronoun that meant to him one person only: 'Hang it all, she shouldn't have come . . .'

Just then they stepped out upon a high grassy knoll at some little distance from the house. With again something of the pride of the showman, Mr Satterthwaite stretched out his arm.

'Look,' he said.

It was fast growing dusk. The window could still be plainly descried, and apparently pressed against one of the panes was a man's face surmounted by a plumed Cavalier's hat.

'Very curious,' said Porter. 'Really very curious. What will happen when that pane of glass gets smashed some day?'

Mr Satterthwaite smiled.

'That is one of the most interesting parts of the story. That pane of glass has been replaced to my certain knowledge at least eleven times, perhaps oftener. The last time was twelve years ago when the then owner of the house determined to destroy the myth. But it's always the same. *The stain reappears* – not all at once, the discolouration spreads gradually. It takes a month or two as a rule.'

For the first time, Porter showed signs of real interest. He gave a sudden quick shiver.

'Damned odd, these things. No accounting for them. What's the real reason of having the room boarded up inside?'

'Well, an idea got about that the room was – unlucky. The Eveshams were in it just before the divorce. Then Stanley and his wife were staying here, and had that room when he ran off with his chorus girl.'

Porter raised his eyebrows.

'I see. Danger, not to life, but to morals.'

'And now,' thought Mr Satterthwaite to himself, 'the Scotts have it . . . I wonder . . .'

They retraced their steps in silence to the house. Walking almost noise-lessly on the soft turf, each absorbed in his own thoughts, they became unwittingly eavesdroppers.

They were rounding the corner of the holly hedge when they heard

Iris Staverton's voice raised fierce and clear from the depths of the Privy Garden.

'You shall be sorry – sorry – for this!'

Scott's voice answered low and uncertain, so that the words could not be distinguished, and then the woman's voice rose again, speaking words that they were to remember later.

'Jealousy – it drives one to the Devil – it *is* the Devil! It can drive one to black murder. Be careful, Richard, for God's sake, be careful!'

And then on that she had come out of the Privy Garden ahead of them, and on round the corner of the house without seeing them, walking swiftly, almost running, like a woman hag-ridden and pursued.

Mr Satterthwaite thought again of Lady Cynthia's words. A dangerous woman. For the first time, he had a premonition of tragedy, coming swift and inexorable, not to be gainsaid.

Yet that evening he felt ashamed of his fears. Everything seemed normal and pleasant. Mrs Staverton, with her easy insouciance, showed no sign of strain. Moira Scott was her charming, unaffected self. The two women appeared to be getting on very well. Richard Scott himself seemed to be in boisterous spirits.

The most worried looking person was stout Mrs Unkerton. She confided at length in Mr Satterthwaite.

'Think it silly or not, as you like, there's something giving me the creeps. And I'll tell you frankly, I've sent for the glazier unbeknown to Ned.'

'The glazier?'

'To put a new pane of glass in that window. It's all very well. Ned's proud of it – says it gives the house a tone. I don't like it. I tell you flat. We'll have a nice plain modern pane of glass, with no nasty stories attached to it.'

'You forget,' said Mr Satterthwaite, 'or perhaps you don't know. The stain comes back.'

'That's as it may be,' said Mrs Unkerton. 'All I can say is if it does, it's against nature!'

Mr Satterthwaite raised his eyebrows, but did not reply.

'And what if it does?' pursued Mrs Unkerton defiantly. 'We're not so bankrupt, Ned and I, that we can't afford a new pane of glass every month – or every week if need be for the matter of that.'

Mr Satterthwaite did not meet the challenge. He had seen too many things crumple and fall before the power of money to believe that even a Cavalier ghost could put up a successful fight. Nevertheless, he was interested by Mrs Unkerton's manifest uneasiness. Even she was not exempt from the tension in the atmosphere – only she attributed it to an attenuated ghost story, not to the clash of personalities amongst her guests.

Mr Sattherwaite was fated to hear yet another scrap of conversation which threw light upon the situation. He was going up the wide stair-case to bed, John Porter and Mrs Staverton were sitting together in an alcove of the big hall. She was speaking with a faint irritation in her golden voice.

'I hadn't the least idea the Scotts were going to be here. I daresay, if I had known, I shouldn't have come, but I can assure you, my dear John, that now I am here, I'm not going to run away –'

Mr Satterthwaite passed on up the staircase out of earshot. He thought to himself: 'I wonder now – How much of that is true? Did she know? I wonder – what's going to come of it?'

He shook his head.

In the clear light of the morning he felt that he had perhaps been a little melodramatic in his imaginings of the evening before. A moment of strain – yes, certainly – inevitable under the circumstances – but nothing more. People adjusted themselves. His fancy that some great catastrophe was pending was nerves – pure nerves – or possibly liver. Yes, that was it, liver. He was due at Carlsbad in another fortnight.

On his own account he proposed a little stroll that evening just as it was growing dusk. He suggested to Major Porter that they should go up to the clearing and see if Mrs Unkerton had been as good as her word, and had a new pane of glass put in. To himself, he said: 'Exercise, that's what I need. Exercise.'

The two men walked slowly through the woods. Porter, as usual, was taciturn.

'I can't help feeling,' said Mr Satterthwaite loquaciously, 'that we were a little foolish in our imaginings yesterday. Expecting – er – trouble, you know. After all, people have to behave themselves – swallow their feelings and that sort of thing.'

'Perhaps,' said Porter. After a minute or two he added: 'Civilized people.'

'You mean –?'

'People who've lived outside civilization a good deal sometimes go back. Revert. Whatever you call it.'

They emerged on to the grassy knoll. Mr Satterthwaite was breathing rather fast. He never enjoyed going up hill.

He looked towards the window. The face was still there, more life-like than ever.

'Our hostess has repented, I see.'

Porter threw it only a cursory glance.

'Unkerton cut up rough, I expect,' he said indifferently. 'He's the sort of man who is willing to be proud of another family's ghost, and who isn't going to run the risk of having it driven away when he's paid spot cash for it.'

He was silent a minute or two, staring, not at the house, but at the thick undergrowth by which they were surrounded.

'Has it ever struck you,' he said, 'that civilization's damned dangerous?'

'Dangerous?' Such a revolutionary remark shocked Mr Satterthwaite to the core.

'Yes. There are no safety valves, you see.'

He turned abruptly, and they descended the path by which they had come.

'I really am quite at a loss to understand you,' said Mr Satterthwaite, pattering along with nimble steps to keep up with the other's strides. 'Reasonable people –'

Porter laughed. A short disconcerting laugh. Then he looked at the correct little gentleman by his side.

'You think it's all bunkum on my part, Mr Satterthwaite? But there are people, you know, who can tell you when a storm's coming. They feel it beforehand in the air. And other people can foretell trouble. There's trouble coming now, Mr Satterthwaite, big trouble. It may come any minute. It may –'

He stopped dead, clutching Mr Satterthwaite's arm. And in that tense minute of silence it came – the sound of two shots and following them a cry – a cry in a woman's voice.

'My god!' cried Porter, 'it's come.'

He raced down the path, Mr Satterthwaite panting behind him. In a minute they came out on to the lawn, close by the hedge of the Privy Garden. At the same time, Richard Scott and Mr Unkerton came round the opposite corner of the house. They halted, facing each other, to left and right of the entrance to the Privy Garden.

'It – it came from in there,' said Unkerton, pointing with a flabby hand.

'We must see,' said Porter. He led the way into the enclosure. As he rounded the last bend of the holly hedge, he stopped dead. Mr Satterthwaite peered over his shoulder. A loud cry burst from Richard Scott.

There were three people in the Privy Garden. Two of them lay on the grass near the stone seat, a man and a woman. The third was Mrs Staverton. She was standing quite close to them by the holly hedge, gazing with horror-stricken eyes, and holding something in her right hand.

'Iris,' cried Porter. 'Iris. For God's sake! What's that you've got in your hand?'

She looked down at it then – with a kind of wonder, an unbelievable indifference.

'It's a pistol,' she said wonderingly. And then – after what seemed an interminable time, but was in reality only a few seconds, 'I – picked it up.'

Mr Satterthwaite had gone forward to where Unkerton and Scott were kneeling on the turf.

'A doctor,' the latter was murmuring. 'We must have a doctor.'

But it was too late for any doctor. Jimmy Allenson who had complained that the sand diviners hedged about the future, and Moira Scott to whom the gypsy had returned a shilling, lay there in the last great stillness.

It was Richard Scott who completed a brief examination. The iron nerve of the man showed in this crisis. After the first cry of agony, he was himself again.

He laid his wife gently down again.

'Shot from behind,' he said briefly. 'The bullet has passed right through her.'

Then he handled Jimmy Allenson. The wound here was in the breast and the bullet was lodged in the body.

John Porter came towards them.

'Nothing should be touched,' he said sternly. 'The police must see it all exactly as it is now.'

'The police,' said Richard Scott. His eyes lit up with a sudden flame as he looked at the woman standing by the holly hedge. He made a step in that direction, but at the same time John Porter also moved, so as to bar his way. For a moment it seemed as though there was a duel of eyes between the two friends.

Porter very quietly shook his head.

'No, Richard,' he said. 'It looks like it – but you're wrong.'

Richard Scott spoke with difficulty, moistening his dry lips.

'Then why – has she got that in her hand?'

And again Iris Staverton said in the same lifeless tone: 'I – picked it up.'

'The police,' said Unkerton rising. 'We must send for the police – at once. You will telephone perhaps, Scott? Someone should stay here – yes, I am sure someone should stay here.'

In his quiet gentlemanly manner, Mr Satterthwaite offered to do so. His host accepted the offer with manifest relief.

'The ladies,' he explained. 'I must break the news to the ladies, Lady Cynthia and my dear wife.'

Mr Satterthwaite stayed in the Privy Garden looking down on the body of that which had once been Moira Scott.

'Poor child,' he said to himself. 'Poor child . . .'

He quoted to himself the tag about the evil men do living after them. For was not Richard Scott in a way responsible for his innocent wife's death? They would hang Iris Staverton, he supposed, not that he liked to think of it, but was not it at least a part of the blame he laid at the man's door? The evil that men do –

And the girl, the innocent girl, had paid.

He looked down at her with a very deep pity. Her small face, so white and wistful, a half smile on the lips still. The ruffled golden hair, the delicate ear. There was a spot of blood on the lobe of it. With an inner feeling of being something of a detective, Mr Satterthwaite deduced an ear-ring, torn away in her fall. He craned his neck forward. Yes, he was right, there was a small pearl drop hanging from the other ear.

Poor child, poor child.

'And now, sir,' said Inspector Winkfield.

They were in the library. The Inspector, a shrewd-looking forceful man of forty odd, was concluding his investigations. He had questioned most of the guests, and had by now pretty well made up his mind on the case. He was listening to what Major Porter and Mr Satterthwaite had to say. Mr Unkerton sat heavily in a chair, staring with protruding eyes at the opposite wall.

'As I understand it, gentlemen,' said the Inspector, 'you'd been for a walk. You were returning to the house by a path that winds round the left side of what they call the Privy Garden. Is that correct?'

'Quite correct, Inspector.'

'You heard two shots, and a woman's scream?'

'Yes.'

'You then ran as fast as you could, emerged from the woods and made your way to the entrance of the Privy Garden. If anybody had left that garden, they could only do so by one entrance. The holly bushes are impassable. If anyone had run out of the garden and turned to the right, he would have been met by Mr Unkerton and Mr Scott. If he had turned to the left, he could not have done so without being seen by you. Is that right?'

'That is so,' said Major Porter. His face was very white.

'That seems to settle it,' said the Inspector. 'Mr and Mrs Unkerton and Lady Cynthia Drage were sitting on the lawn, Mr Scott was in the Billiard Room which opens on to that lawn. At ten minutes past six, Mrs Staverton came out of the house, spoke a word or two to those sitting there, and went round the corner of the house towards the Privy Garden. Two minutes later the shots were heard. Mr Scott rushed out of the house and together with Mr Unkerton ran to the Privy Garden. At the same time you and Mr – er – Satterthwaite arrived from the opposite direction. Mrs Staverton was in the Privy Garden with a pistol in her hand from which two shots had been fired. As I see it, she shot the lady first from behind as she was sitting on the bench. Then Captain Allenson sprang up and went for her, and she shot him in the chest as he came towards her. I understand that there had been a – er – previous attachment between her and Mr Richard Scott –'

'That's a damned lie,' said Porter.

His voice rang out hoarse and defiant. The Inspector said nothing, merely shook his head.

'What is her own story?' asked Mr Satterthwaite.

'She says that she went into the Privy Garden to be quiet for a little. Just before she rounded the last hedge, she heard the shots. She came round the corner, saw the pistol lying at her feet, and picked it up. No one passed her, and she saw no one in the garden but the two victims.' The Inspector gave an eloquent pause. 'That's what she says – and although I cautioned her, she insisted on making a statement.'

'If she said that,' said Major Porter, and his face was still deadly white, 'she was speaking the truth. I know Iris Staverton.'

'Well, sir,' said the Inspector, 'there'll be plenty of time to go into all that later. In the meantime, I've got my duty to do.'

With an abrupt movement, Porter turned to Mr Satterthwaite.

'You! Can't you help? Can't *you* do something?'

Mr Satterthwaite could not help feeling immensely flattered. He had been appealed to, he, most insignificant of men, and by a man like John Porter.

He was just about to flutter out a regretful reply, when the butler, Thompson, entered, with a card upon a salver which he took to his master with an apologetic cough. Mr Unkerton was still sitting huddled up in a chair, taking no part in the proceedings.

'I told the gentleman you would probably not be able to see him, sir,' said Thompson. 'But he insisted that he had an appointment and that it was most urgent.'

Unkerton took the card.

'Mr Harley Quin,' he read. 'I remember, he was to see me about a picture. I did make an appointment, but as things are –'

But Mr Satterthwaite had started forward.

'Mr Harley Quin, did you say?' he cried. 'How extraordinary, how very extraordinary. Major Porter, you asked me if I could help you. I think I can. This Mr Quin is a friend – or I should say, an acquaintance of mine. He is a most remarkable man.'

'One of these amateur solvers of crime, I suppose,' remarked the Inspector disparagingly.

'No,' said Mr Satterthwaite. 'He is not that kind of man at all. But he has a power – an almost uncanny power – of showing you what you have seen with your own eyes, of making clear to you what you have heard with your own ears. Let us, at any rate, give him an outline of the case, and hear what he has to say.'

Mr Unkerton glanced at the Inspector, who merely snorted and looked at the ceiling. Then the former gave a short nod to Thompson, who left the room and returned ushering in a tall, slim stranger.

'Mr Unkerton?' The stranger shook him by the hand. 'I am sorry to intrude upon you at such a time. We must leave our little picture chat until another time. Ah! my friend, Mr Satterthwaite. Still as fond of the drama as ever?'

A faint smile played for a minute round the stranger's lips as he said these last words.

'Mr Quin,' said Mr Satterthwaite impressively, 'we have a drama here, we are in the midst of one, I should like, and my friend, Major Porter, would like, to have your opinion of it.'

Mr Quin sat down. The red-shaded lamp threw a broad band of coloured light over the checked pattern of his overcoat, and left his face in shadow almost as though he wore a mask.

Succinctly, Mr Satterthwaite recited the main points of the tragedy. Then he paused, breathlessly awaiting the words of the oracle.

But Mr Quin merely shook his head.

'A sad story,' he said. 'A very sad and shocking tragedy. The lack of motive makes it very intriguing.'

Unkerton stared at him.

'You don't understand,' he said. 'Mrs Staverton was heard to threaten Richard Scott. She was bitterly jealous of his wife. Jealousy –'

'I agree,' said Mr Quin. 'Jealousy or Demoniac Possession. It's all the same. But you misunderstand me. I was not referring to the murder of Mrs Scott, but to that of Captain Allenson.'

'You're right,' cried Porter, springing forward. 'There's a flaw there. If Iris had ever contemplated shooting Mrs Scott, she'd have got her alone somewhere. No, we're on the wrong tack. And I think I see another solution. Only those three people went into the Privy Garden. That is indisputable and I don't intend to dispute it. But I reconstruct the tragedy differently. Supposing Jimmy Allenson shoots first Mrs Scott and then himself. That's possible, isn't it? He flings the pistol from him as he falls – Mrs Staverton finds it lying on the ground and picks it up just as she said. How's that?'

The Inspector shook his head.

'Won't wash, Major Porter. If Captain Allenson had fired that shot close to his body, the cloth would have been singed.'

'He might have held the pistol at arm's length.'

'Why should he? No sense in it. Besides, there's no motive.'

'Might have gone off his head suddenly,' muttered Porter, but without any great conviction. He fell to silence again, suddenly rousing himself to say defiantly: 'Well, Mr Quin?'

The latter shook his head.

'I'm not a magician. I'm not even a criminologist. But I will tell you one thing – I believe in the value of impressions. In any time of crisis, there is always one moment that stands out from all the others, one picture that remains when all else has faded. Mr Satterthwaite is, I think, likely to have been the most unprejudiced observer of those present. Will you cast your mind back, Mr Satterthwaite, and tell us the moment that made the strongest impression on you? Was it when you heard the shots? Was it when you first saw the dead bodies? Was it when you first observed the pistol in Mrs Staverton's hand? Clear your mind of any preconceived standard of values, and tell us.'

Mr Satterthwaite fixed his eyes on Mr Quin's face, rather as a schoolboy might repeat a lesson of which he was not sure.

'No,' he said slowly. 'It was not any of those. The moment that I shall always remember was when I stood alone by the bodies – afterwards – looking down on Mrs Scott. She was lying on her side. Her hair was ruffled. There was a spot of blood on her little ear.'

And instantly, as he said it, he felt that he had said a terrific, a significant thing.

'Blood on her ear? Yes, I remember,' said Unkerton slowly.

'Her ear-ring must have been torn out when she fell,' explained Mr Satterthwaite.

But it sounded a little improbable as he said it.

'She was lying on her left side,' said Porter. 'I suppose it was that ear?'

'No,' said Mr Satterthwaite quickly. 'It was her right ear.'

The Inspector coughed.

'I found this in the grass,' he vouchsafed. He held up a loop of gold wire.

'But my God, man,' cried Porter. 'The thing can't have been wrenched to pieces by a mere fall. It's more as though it had been shot away by a bullet.'

'So it was,' cried Mr Satterthwaite. 'It was a bullet. It must have been.'

'There were only two shots,' said the Inspector. 'A shot can't have grazed her ear and shot her in the back as well. And if one shot carried away the ear-ring, and the second shot killed her, it can't have killed Captain Allenson as well – not unless he was standing close in front of her – very close – facing her as it might be. Oh! no, not even then, unless, that is –'

'Unless she was in his arms, you were going to say,' said Mr Quin, with a queer little smile. 'Well, why not?'

Everyone stared at each other. The idea was so vitally strange to them – Allenson and Mrs Scott – Mr Unkerton voiced the same feeling.

'But they hardly knew each other,' he said.

'I don't know,' said Mr Satterthwaite thoughtfully. 'They might have known each other better than we thought. Lady Cynthia said he saved her from being bored in Egypt last winter, and you' – he turned to Porter – 'you told me that Richard Scott met his wife in Cairo last winter. They might have known each other very well indeed out there . . .'

'They didn't seem to be together much,' said Unkerton.

'No – they rather avoided each other. It was almost unnatural, now I come to think of it –'

They all looked at Mr Quin, as if a little startled at the conclusions at which they had arrived so unexpectedly.

Mr Quin rose to his feet.

'You see,' he said, 'what Mr Satterthwaite's impression has done for us.' He turned to Unkerton. 'It is your turn now.'

'Eh? I don't understand you.'

'You were very thoughtful when I came into this room. I should like to know exactly what thought it was that obsessed you. Never mind if it has nothing to do with the tragedy. Never mind if it seems to you – superstitious –' Mr Unkerton started, ever so slightly. 'Tell us.'

'I don't mind telling you,' said Unkerton. 'Though it's nothing to do with the business, and you'll probably laugh at me into the bargain. I was wishing that my Missus had left well alone and not replaced that pane of glass in the haunted window. I feel as though doing that has maybe brought a curse upon us.'

He was unable to understand why the two men opposite him stared so.

'But she hasn't replaced it yet,' said Mr Satterthwaite at last.

'Yes, she has. Man came first thing this morning.'

'My God!' said Porter, 'I begin to understand. That room, it's panelled, I supposed, not papered?'

'Yes, but what does that –?'

But Porter had swung out of the room. The others followed him. He went straight upstairs to the Scotts' bedroom. It was a charming room, panelled in cream with two windows facing south. Porter felt with his hands along the panels on the western wall.

'There's a spring somewhere – must be. Ah!' There was a click, and a section of the panelling rolled back. It disclosed the grimy panes of the haunted window. One pane of glass was clean and new. Porter stooped quickly and picked up something. He held it out on the palm of his hand. It was a fragment of ostrich feather. Then he looked at Mr Quin. Mr Quin nodded.

He went across to the hat cupboard in the bedroom. There were several hats in it – the dead woman's hats. He took out one with a large brim and curling feathers – an elaborate Ascot hat.

Mr Quin began speaking in a gentle, reflective voice.

'Let us suppose,' said Mr Quin, 'a man who is by nature intensely jealous. A man who has stayed here in bygone years and knows the secret of the spring in the panelling. To amuse himself he opens it one day, and looks out over the Privy Garden. There, secure as they think from being overlooked, he sees his wife and another man. There can be no possible doubt in his mind as to the relations between them. He is mad with rage. What shall he do? An idea comes to him. He goes to the cupboard and puts on the hat with the brim and feathers. It is growing dusk, and he remembers the story of the stain on the glass. Anyone looking up at the window will see as they think the Watching Cavalier. Thus secure he watches them, and at the moment they are clasped in each other's arms, he shoots. He is a good shot – a wonderful shot. As they fall, he fires once more – that shot carries away the ear-ring. He flings the pistol out of the window into the Privy Garden, rushes downstairs and out through the billiard room.'

Porter took a step towards him.

'But he let her be accused!' he cried. 'He stood by and let her be accused. Why? Why?'

'I think I know why,' said Mr Quin. 'I should guess – it's only guess-work on my part, mind – that Richard Scott was once madly in love with Iris Staverton – so madly that even meeting her years afterwards stirred up the embers of jealousy again. I should say that Iris Staverton once fancied that she might love him, that she went on a hunting trip with him and another – and that she came back in love with the better man.'

'The better man,' muttered Porter, dazed. 'You mean –?'

'Yes,' said Mr Quin, with a faint smile. 'I mean you.' He paused a minute, and then said: 'If I were you – I should go to her now.'

'I will,' said Porter.

He turned and left the room.

At the 'Bells and Motley'

'At the "Bells and Motley"' was first published as 'A Man of Magic' in *Grand Magazine*, November 1925.

Mr Satterthwaite was annoyed. Altogether it had been an unfortunate day. They had started late, there had been two punctures already, finally they had taken the wrong turning and lost themselves amidst the wilds of Salisbury Plain. Now it was close on eight o'clock, they were still a matter of forty miles from Marswick Manor whither they were bound, and a third puncture had supervened to render matters still more trying.

Mr Satterthwaite, looking like some small bird whose plumage had been ruffled, walked up and down in front of the village garage whilst his chauffeur conversed in hoarse undertones with the local expert.

'Half an hour at *least*,' said that worthy pronouncing judgment.

'And lucky at that,' supplemented Masters, the chauffeur. 'More like three quarters if you ask me.'

'What is this – place, anyway?' demanded Mr Satterthwaite fretfully. Being a little gentleman considerate of the feelings of others, he substituted the word 'place' for 'God-forsaken hole' which had first risen to his lips.

'Kirtlington Mallet.'

Mr Satterthwaite was not much wiser, and yet a faint familiarity seemed to linger round the name. He looked round him disparagingly. Kirtlington Mallet seemed to consist of one straggling street, the garage and the post office on one side of it balanced by three indeterminate shops on the other side. Farther down the road, however, Mr Satterthwaite perceived something that creaked and swung in the wind, and his spirits rose ever so slightly.

'There's an Inn here, I see,' he remarked.

'"Bells and Motley",' said the garage man. 'That's it – yonder.'

'If I might make a suggestion, sir,' said Masters, 'why not try it? They would be able to give you some sort of a meal, no doubt – not, of course, what you are accustomed to.' He paused apologetically, for Mr Satterthwaite was accustomed to the best cooking of continental chefs, and had in his own service a *cordon bleu* to whom he paid a fabulous salary.

'We shan't be able to take the road again for another three quarters of an hour, sir. I'm sure of that. And it's already past eight o'clock. You could ring up Sir George Foster, sir, from the Inn, and acquaint him with the cause of our delay.'

'You seem to think you can arrange everything, Masters,' said Mr Satterthwaite snappily.

Masters, who did think so, maintained a respectful silence.

Mr Satterthwaite, in spite of his earnest wish to discountenance any suggestion that might possibly be made to him – he was in that mood – nevertheless looked down the road towards the creaking Inn sign with faint inward approval. He was a man of birdlike appetite, an epicure, but even such men can be hungry.

'The "Bells and Motley",' he said thoughtfully. 'That's an odd name for an Inn. I don't know that I ever heard it before.'

'There's odd folks come to it by all account,' said the local man.

He was bending over the wheel, and his voice came muffled and indistinct.

'Odd folks?' queried Mr Satterthwaite. 'Now what do you mean by that?'

The other hardly seemed to know what he meant.

'Folks that come and go. That kind,' he said vaguely.

Mr Satterthwaite reflected that people who come to an Inn are almost of necessity those who 'come and go'. The definition seemed to him to lack precision. But nevertheless his curiosity was stimulated. Somehow or other he had got to put in three quarters of an hour. The 'Bells and Motley' would be as good as anywhere else.

With his usual small mincing steps he walked away down the road. From afar there came a rumble of thunder. The mechanic looked up and spoke to Masters.

'There's a storm coming over. Thought I could feel it in the air.'

'Crikey,' said Masters. 'And forty miles to go.'

'Ah!' said the other. 'There's no need to be hurrying over this job. You'll not be wanting to take the road till the storm's passed over. That little boss of yours doesn't look as though he'd relish being out in thunder and lightning.'

'Hope they'll do him well at that place,' muttered the chauffeur. 'I'll be pushing along there for a bite myself presently.'

'Billy Jones is all right,' said the garage man. 'Keeps a good table.'

Mr William Jones, a big burly man of fifty and landlord of the 'Bells and Motley', was at this minute beaming ingratiatingly down on little Mr Satterthwaite.

'Can do you a nice steak, sir – *and* fried potatoes, and as good a cheese as any gentleman could wish for. This way, sir, in the coffee-room. We're not very full at present, the last of the fishing gentlemen just gone. A little later we'll be full again for the hunting. Only one gentleman here at present, name of Quin –'

Mr Satterthwaite stopped dead.

'Quin?' he said excitedly. 'Did you say Quin?'

'That's the name, sir. Friend of yours perhaps?'

'Yes, indeed. Oh! yes, most certainly.' Twittering with excitement, Mr Satterthwaite hardly realized that the world might contain more than one man of that name. He had no doubts at all. In an odd way, the information fitted in with what the man at the garage had said. 'Folks that come and go . . .' a very apt description of Mr Quin. And the name of the Inn, too, seemed a peculiarly fitting and appropriate one.

'Dear me, dear me,' said Mr Satterthwaite. 'What a *very* odd thing. That we should meet like this! Mr Harley Quin, is it not?'

'That's right, sir. This is the coffee-room, sir. Ah! here is the gentleman.'

Tall, dark, smiling, the familiar figure of Mr Quin rose from the table at which he was sitting, and the well-remembered voice spoke.

'Ah! Mr Satterthwaite, we meet again. An unexpected meeting!'

Mr Satterthwaite was shaking him warmly by the hand.

'Delighted. Delighted, I'm sure. A lucky breakdown for me. My car, you know. And you are staying here? For long?'

'One night only.'

'Then I am indeed fortunate.'

Mr Satterthwaite sat down opposite his friend with a little sigh of satisfaction, and regarded the dark, smiling face opposite him with a pleasurable expectancy.

The other man shook his head gently.

'I assure you,' he said, 'that I have not a bowl of goldfish or a rabbit to produce from my sleeve.'

'Too bad,' cried Mr Satterthwaite, a little taken aback. 'Yes, I must confess – I do rather adopt that attitude towards you. A man of magic. Ha, ha. That is how I regard you. A man of magic.'

'And yet,' said Mr Quin, 'it is you who do the conjuring tricks, not I.'

'Ah!' said Mr Satterthwaite eagerly. 'But I cannot do them without you. I lack – shall we say – inspiration?'

Mr Quin smilingly shook his head.

'That is too big a word. I speak the cue, that is all.'

The landlord came in at that minute with bread and a slab of yellow butter. As he set the things on the table there was a vivid flash of lightning, and a clap of thunder almost overhead.

'A wild night, gentlemen.'

'On such a night –' began Mr Satterthwaite, and stopped.

'Funny now,' said the landlord, unconscious of the question, 'if those weren't just the words I was going to use myself. It was just such a night as this when Captain Harwell brought his bride home, the very day before he disappeared for ever.'

'Ah!' cried Mr Satterthwaite suddenly. 'Of course!'

He had got the clue. He knew now why the name Kirtlington Mallet was familiar. Three months before he had read every detail of the astonishing disappearance of Captain Richard Harwell. Like other newspaper readers all over Great Britain he had puzzled over the details of the disappearance, and, also like every other Briton, had evolved his own theories.

'Of course,' he repeated. 'It was at Kirtlington Mallet it happened.'

'It was at this house he stayed for the hunting last winter,' said the landlord. 'Oh! I knew him well. A main handsome young gentleman and not one that you'd think had a care on his mind. He was done away with – that's my belief. Many's the time I've seen them come riding home together – he and Miss Le Couteau, and all the village saying there'd be a match come of it – and sure enough, so it did. A very beautiful young lady, and well thought of, for all she was a Canadian and a stranger. Ah! there's some dark mystery there. We'll never know the rights of it. It broke her heart, it did, sure enough. You've heard as she's sold the place up and gone abroad, couldn't bear to go on here with everyone staring and pointing after her – through no fault of her own, poor young dear! A black mystery, that's what it is.'

He shook his head, then suddenly recollecting his duties, hurried from the room.

'A black mystery,' said Mr Quin softly.

His voice was provocative in Mr Satterthwaite's ears.

'Are you pretending that we can solve the mystery where Scotland Yard failed?' he asked sharply.

The other made a characteristic gesture.

'Why not? Time has passed. Three months. That makes a difference.'

'That is a curious idea of yours,' said Mr Satterthwaite slowly. 'That one sees things better afterwards than at the time.'

'The longer the time that has elapsed, the more things fall into proportion. One sees them in their true relationship to one another.'

There was a silence which lasted for some minutes.

'I am not sure,' said Mr Satterthwaite, in a hesitating voice, 'that I remember the facts clearly by now.'

'I think you do,' said Mr Quin quietly.

It was all the encouragement Mr Satterthwaite needed. His general role in life was that of listener and looker-on. Only in the company of Mr Quin was the position reversed. There Mr Quin was the appreciative listener, and Mr Satterthwaite took the centre of the stage.

'It was just over a year ago,' he said, 'that Ashley Grange passed into the possession of Miss Eleanor Le Couteau. It is a beautiful old house, but it had been neglected and allowed to remain empty for many years. It could not have found a better chatelaine. Miss Le Couteau was a French Canadian, her forebears were *émigrés* from the French Revolution, and had handed down to her a collection of almost priceless French relics and antiques. She was a buyer and a collector also, with a very fine and discriminating taste. So much so, that when she decided to sell Ashley Grange and everything it contained after the tragedy, Mr Cyrus G. Bradburn, the American millionaire, made no bones about paying the fancy price of sixty thousand pounds for the Grange as it stood.'

Mr Satterthwaite paused.

'I mention these things,' he said apologetically, 'not because they are relevant to the story – strictly speaking, they are not – but to convey an atmosphere, the atmosphere of young Mrs Harwell.'

Mr Quin nodded.

'Atmosphere is always valuable,' he said gravely.

'So we get a picture of this girl,' continued the other. 'Just twenty-three, dark, beautiful, accomplished, nothing crude and unfinished about her. And rich – we must not forget that. She was an orphan. A Mrs St Clair, a lady of unimpeachable breeding and social standing, lived with her as duenna. But Eleanor Le Couteau had complete control of her own fortune. And fortune-hunters are never hard to seek. At least a dozen impecunious young men were to be found dangling round her on all occasions, in the hunting field, in the ballroom, wherever she went. Young Lord Leccan, the most eligible *parti* in the country, is reported to have asked her to marry him, but she remained heart free. That is, until the coming of Captain Richard Harwell.

'Captain Harwell had put up at the local Inn for the hunting. He was a dashing rider to hounds. A handsome, laughing daredevil of a fellow. You remember the old saying, Mr Quin? "Happy the wooing that's not long doing." The adage was carried out at least in part. At the end of two months, Richard Harwell and Eleanor Le Couteau were engaged.

'The marriage followed three months afterwards. The happy pair went abroad for a two weeks' honeymoon, and then returned to take up their residence at Ashley Grange. The landlord has just told us that it was on a night of storm such as this that they returned to their home. An omen, I wonder? Who can tell? Be that as it may, the following morning very early – about half-past seven, Captain Harwell was seen walking in the garden by one of the gardeners, John Mathias. He was bareheaded, and was whistling. We have a picture there, a picture of light-heartedness, of careless happiness. And yet from that minute, as far as we know, no one ever set eyes on Captain Richard Harwell again.'

Mr Satterthwaite paused, pleasantly conscious of a dramatic moment. The admiring glance of Mr Quin gave him the tribute he needed, and he went on.

'The disappearance was remarkable – unaccountable. It was not till the following day that the distracted wife called in the police. As you know, they have not succeeded in solving the mystery.'

'There have, I suppose, been theories?' asked Mr Quin.

'Oh! theories, I grant you. Theory No. 1, that Captain Harwell had been murdered, done away with. But if so, where was the body? It could hardly have been spirited away. And besides, what motive was there? As far as was known, Captain Harwell had not an enemy in the world.'

He paused abruptly, as though uncertain. Mr Quin leaned forward.

'You are thinking,' he said softly, 'of young Stephen Grant.'

'I am,' admitted Mr Satterthwaite. 'Stephen Grant, if I remember rightly, had been in charge of Captain Harwell's horses, and had been discharged by his master for some trifling offence. On the morning after the home-coming, very early, Stephen Grant was seen in the vicinity of Ashley Grange, and could give no good account of his presence there. He was detained by the police as being concerned in the disappearance of Captain Harwell, but nothing could be proved against him, and he was eventually discharged. It is true that he might be supposed to bear a grudge against Captain Harwell for his summary dismissal, but the motive was undeniably of the flimsiest. I suppose the police felt they must do something. You see, as I said just now, Captain Harwell had not an enemy in the world.'

'As far as was known,' said Mr Quin reflectively.

Mr Satterthwaite nodded appreciatively.

'We are coming to that. What, after all, *was* known of Captain Harwell? When the police came to look into his antecedents they were confronted with a singular paucity of material. Who was Richard Harwell? Where did he come from? He had appeared, literally out of the blue as it seemed. He was a magnificent rider, and apparently well off. Nobody in Kirtlington Mallet had bothered to inquire further. Miss Le Couteau had had no parents or guardians to make inquiries into the prospects and standing of her fiancé. She was her own mistress. The police theory at this point was clear enough. A rich girl and an impudent impostor. The old story!

'But it was not quite that. True, Miss Le Couteau had no parents or guardians, but she had an excellent firm of solicitors in London who acted for her. Their evidence made the mystery deeper. Eleanor Le Couteau had wished to settle a sum outright upon her prospective husband, but he had refused. He himself was well off, he declared. It was proved conclusively that Harwell never had a penny of his wife's money. Her fortune was absolutely intact.

'He was, therefore, no common swindler, but was his object a refinement of the art? Did he propose blackmail at some future date if Eleanor Harwell should wish to marry some other man? I will admit that something of that kind seemed to me the most likely solution. It had always seemed so to me – until tonight.'

Mr Quin leaned forward, prompting him.

'Tonight?'

'Tonight. I am not satisfied with that. How did he manage to disappear so suddenly and completely – at that hour in the morning, with every labourer bestirring himself and tramping to work? Bareheaded, too.'

'There is no doubt about the latter point – since the gardener saw him?'

'Yes – the gardener – John Mathias. Was there anything there, I wonder?'

'The police would not overlook him,' said Mr Quin.

'They questioned him closely. He never wavered in his statement. His wife bore him out. He left his cottage at seven to attend to the greenhouses, he returned at twenty minutes to eight. The servants in the house heard the front door slam at about a quarter after seven. That fixes the time when Captain Harwell left the house. Ah! yes, I know what you are thinking.'

'Do you, I wonder?' said Mr Quin.

'I fancy so. Time enough for Mathias to have made away with his master. But why, man, why? And if so, where did he hide the body?'

The landlord came in bearing a tray.

'Sorry to have kept you so long, gentlemen.'

He set upon the table a mammoth steak and beside it a dish filled to overflowing with crisp brown potatoes. The odour from the dishes was pleasant to Mr Satterthwaite's nostrils. He felt gracious.

'This looks excellent,' he said. 'Most excellent. We have been discussing the disappearance of Captain Harwell. What became of the gardener, Mathias?'

'Took a place in Essex, I believe. Didn't care to stay hereabouts. There were some as looked askance at him, you understand. Not that I ever believe he had anything to do with it.'

Mr Satterthwaite helped himself to steak. Mr Quin followed suit. The landlord seemed disposed to linger and chat. Mr Satterthwaite had no objection, on the contrary.

'This Mathias now,' he said. 'What kind of a man was he?'

'Middle-aged chap, must have been a powerful fellow once but bent and crippled with rheumatism. He had that mortal bad, was laid up many a time with it, unable to do any work. For my part, I think it was sheer kindness on Miss Eleanor's part to keep him on. He'd outgrown his usefulness as a gardener, though his wife managed to make herself useful up at the house. Been a cook she had, and always willing to lend a hand.'

'What sort of a woman was she?' asked Mr Satterthwaite, quickly.

The landlord's answer disappointed him.

'A plain body. Middle-aged, and dour like in manner. Deaf, too. Not that I ever knew much of them. They'd only been here a month, you understand, when the thing happened. They say he'd been a rare good gardener in his time, though. Wonderful testimonials Miss Eleanor had with him.'

'Was she interested in gardening?' asked Mr Quin, softly.

'No, sir, I couldn't say that she was, not like some of the ladies round here who pay good money to gardeners and spend the whole of their time grubbing about on their knees as well. Foolishness I call it. You see, Miss Le Couteau wasn't here very much except in the winter for hunting. The rest of the time she was up in London and away in those foreign seaside places where they say the French ladies don't so much as put a toe into the water for fear of spoiling their costumes, or so I've heard.'

Mr Satterthwaite smiled.

'There was no – er – woman of any kind mixed up with Captain Harwell?' he asked.

Though his first theory was disposed of, he nevertheless clung to his idea.

Mr William Jones shook his head.

'Nothing of that sort. Never a whisper of it. No, it's a dark mystery, that's what it is.'

'And your theory? What do you yourself think?' persisted Mr Satterthwaite.

'What do I think?'

'Yes.'

'Don't know what to think. It's my belief as how he was done in, but who by I can't say. I'll fetch you gentlemen the cheese.'

He stumped from the room bearing empty dishes. The storm, which had been quietening down, suddenly broke out with redoubled vigour. A flash of forked lightning and a great clap of thunder close upon each other made little Mr Satterthwaite jump, and before the last echoes of the thunder had died away, a girl came into the room carrying the advertised cheese.

She was tall and dark, and handsome in a sullen fashion of her own. Her likeness to the landlord of the 'Bells and Motley' was apparent enough to proclaim her his daughter.

'Good evening, Mary,' said Mr Quin. 'A stormy night.'

She nodded.

'I hate these stormy nights,' she muttered.

'You are afraid of thunder, perhaps?' said Mr Satterthwaite kindly.

'Afraid of thunder? Not me! There's little that I'm afraid of. No, but the storm sets them off. Talking, talking, the same thing over and over again, like a lot of parrots. Father begins it. "It reminds me, this does, of the night poor Captain Harwell . . ." And so on, and so on.' She turned on Mr Quin. 'You've heard how he goes on. What's the sense of it? Can't anyone let past things be?'

'A thing is only past when it is done with,' said Mr Quin.

'Isn't this done with? Suppose he wanted to disappear? These fine gentlemen do sometimes.'

'You think he disappeared of his own free will?'

'Why not? It would make better sense than to suppose a kind-hearted creature like Stephen Grant murdered him. What should he murder him for, I should like to know? Stephen had had a drop too much one day and spoke to him saucy like, and got the sack for it. But what of it? He got another place just as good. Is that a reason to murder a man in cold blood?'

'But surely,' said Mr Satterthwaite, 'the police were quite satisfied of his innocence?'

'The police! What do the police matter? When Stephen comes into the bar of an evening, every man looks at him queer like. They don't really believe he murdered Harwell, but they're not sure, and so they look at him sideways and edge away. Nice life for a man, to see people shrink away from you, as though you were something different from the rest of folks. Why won't Father hear of our getting married, Stephen and I? "You can take your pigs to a better market, my girl. I've nothing against Stephen, but – well, we don't know, do we?"'

She stopped, her breast heaving with the violence of her resentment.

'It's cruel, cruel, that's what it is,' she burst out. 'Stephen, that wouldn't hurt a fly! And all through life there'll be people who'll think he did. It's turning him queer and bitter like. I don't wonder, I'm sure. And the more he's like that, the more people think there must have been something in it.'

Again she stopped. Her eyes were fixed on Mr Quin's face, as though something in it was drawing this outburst from her.

'Can nothing be done?' said Mr Satterthwaite.

He was genuinely distressed. The thing was, he saw, inevitable. The very vagueness and unsatisfactoriness of the evidence against Stephen Grant made it the more difficult for him to disprove the accusation.

The girl whirled round on him.

'Nothing but the truth can help him,' she cried. 'If Captain Harwell were to be found, if he was to come back. If the true rights of it were only known –'

She broke off with something very like a sob, and hurried quickly from the room.

'A fine-looking girl,' said Mr Satterthwaite. 'A sad case altogether. I wish – I very much wish that something could be done about it.'

His kind heart was troubled.

'We are doing what we can,' said Mr Quin. 'There is still nearly half an hour before your car can be ready.'

Mr Satterthwaite stared at him.

'You think we can come at the truth just by – talking it over like this?'

'You have seen much of life,' said Mr Quin gravely. 'More than most people.'

'Life has passed me by,' said Mr Satterthwaite bitterly.

'But in so doing has sharpened your vision. Where others are blind you can see.'

'It is true,' said Mr Satterthwaite. 'I am a great observer.'

He plumed himself complacently. The moment of bitterness was passed.

'I look at it like this,' he said after a minute or two. 'To get at the cause for a thing, we must study the effect.'

'Very good,' said Mr Quin approvingly.

'The effect in this case is that Miss Le Couteau – Mrs Harwell, I mean, is a wife and yet not a wife. She is not free – she cannot marry again. And look at it as we will, we see Richard Harwell as a sinister figure, a man from nowhere with a mysterious past.'

'I agree,' said Mr Quin. 'You see what all are bound to see, what cannot be missed, Captain Harwell in the limelight, a suspicious figure.'

Mr Satterthwaite looked at him doubtfully. The words seemed somehow to suggest a faintly different picture to his mind.

'We have studied the effect,' he said. 'Or call it the *result*. We can now pass –'

Mr Quin interrupted him.

'You have not touched on the result on the strictly material side.'

'You are right,' said Mr Satterthwaite, after a moment or two for consideration. 'One should do the thing thoroughly. Let us say then that the result of the tragedy is that Mrs Harwell is a wife and not a wife, unable to marry again, that Mr Cyrus Bradburn has been able to buy Ashley Grange and its contents for – sixty thousand pounds, was it? – and that somebody in Essex has been able to secure John Mathias as a gardener! For all that we do not suspect "somebody in Essex" or Mr Cyrus Bradburn of having engineered the disappearance of Captain Harwell.'

'You are sarcastic,' said Mr Quin.

Mr Satterthwaite looked sharply at him.

'But surely you agree –?'

'Oh! I agree,' said Mr Quin. 'The idea is absurd. What next?'

'Let us imagine ourselves back on the fatal day. The disappearance has taken place, let us say, this very morning.'

'No, no,' said Mr Quin, smiling. 'Since, in our imagination, at least, we have power over time, let us turn it the other way. Let us say the disappearance of Captain Harwell took place a hundred years ago. That we, in the year two thousand twenty-five are looking back.'

'You are a strange man,' said Mr Satterthwaite slowly. 'You believe in the past, not the present. Why?'

'You used, not long ago, the word atmosphere. There is no atmosphere in the present.'

'That is true, perhaps,' said Mr Satterthwaite thoughtfully. 'Yes, it is true. The present is apt to be – parochial.'

'A good word,' said Mr Quin.

Mr Satterthwaite gave a funny little bow.

'You are too kind,' he said.

'Let us take – not this present year, that would be too difficult, but say – last year,' continued the other. 'Sum it up for me, you who have the gift of the neat phrase.'

Mr Satterthwaite thought for a minute. He was jealous of his reputation.

'A hundred years ago we have the age of powder and patches,' he said. 'Shall we say that 1924 was the age of Crossword Puzzles and Cat Burglars?'

'Very good,' approved Mr Quin. 'You mean that nationally, not internationally, I presume?'

'As to Crossword Puzzles, I must confess that I do not know,' said Mr Satterthwaite. 'But the Cat Burglar had a great innings on the Continent. You remember that series of famous thefts from French chateaux? It is surmised that one man alone could not have done it. The most miraculous feats were performed to gain admission. There was a theory that a troupe of acrobats were concerned – the Clondinis. I once saw their performance – truly masterly. A mother, son and daughter. They vanished from the stage in a rather mysterious fashion. But we are wandering from our subject.'

'Not very far,' said Mr Quin. 'Only across the Channel.'

'Where the French ladies will not wet their toes, according to our worthy host,' said Mr Satterthwaite, laughing.

There was a pause. It seemed somehow significant.

'Why did he disappear?' cried Mr Satterthwaite. 'Why? Why? It is incredible, a kind of conjuring trick.'

'Yes,' said Mr Quin. 'A conjuring trick. That describes it exactly. Atmosphere again, you see. And wherein does the essence of a conjuring trick lie?'

'The quickness of the hand deceives the eye,' quoted Mr Satterthwaite glibly.

'That is everything, is it not? To deceive the eye? Sometimes by the quickness of the hand, sometimes – by other means. There are many devices, the pistol shot, the waving of a red handkerchief, something that seems important, but in reality is not. The eye is diverted from the real business, it is caught by the spectacular action that means nothing – nothing at all.'

Mr Satterthwaite leant forward, his eyes shining.

'There is something in that. It is an idea.'

He went on softly. 'The pistol shot. What was the pistol shot in the conjuring trick we were discussing? What is the spectacular moment that holds the imagination?'

He drew in his breath sharply.

'The disappearance,' breathed Mr Satterthwaite. 'Take that away, and it leaves nothing.'

'Nothing? Suppose things took the same course without that dramatic gesture?'

'You mean – supposing Miss Le Couteau were still to sell Ashley Grange and leave – for no reason?'

'Well.'

'Well, why not? It would have aroused talk, I suppose, there would have been a lot of interest displayed in the value of the contents in – Ah! wait!'

He was silent a minute, then burst out.

'You are right, there is too much limelight, the limelight on Captain Harwell. And because of that, *she* has been in shadow. *Miss Le Couteau!* Everyone asking. "Who was Captain Harwell? Where did he come from?" But because she is the injured party, no one makes inquiries about her.

Was she really a French Canadian? Were those wonderful heirlooms really handed down to her? You were right when you said just now that we had not wandered far from our subject – *only across the Channel*. Those so-called heirlooms were stolen from the French châteaux, most of them valuable *objects d'art*, and in consequence difficult to dispose of. She buys the house – for a mere song, probably. Settles down there and pays a good sum to an irreproachable English woman to chaperone her. Then *he* comes. The plot is laid beforehand. The marriage, the disappearance and the nine days' wonder! What more natural than that a broken-hearted woman should want to sell everything that reminds her of her past happiness. The American is a connoisseur, the things are genuine and beautiful, some of them beyond price. He makes an offer, she accepts it. She leaves the neighbourhood, a sad and tragic figure. The great *coup* has come off. The eye of the public has been deceived by the quickness of the hand and the spectacular nature of the trick.'

Mr Satterthwaite paused, flushed with triumph.

'But for you, I should never have seen it,' he said with sudden humility. 'You have a most curious effect upon me. One says things so often without even seeing what they really mean. You have the knack of showing one. But it is still not quite clear to me. It must have been most difficult for Harwell to disappear as he did. After all, the police all over England were looking for him.'

'It would have been simplest to remain hidden at the Grange,' mused Mr Satterthwaite. 'If it could be managed.'

'He was, I think, very near the Grange,' said Mr Quin.

His look of significance was not lost on Mr Satterthwaite.

'Mathias' cottage?' he exclaimed. 'But the police must have searched it?'

'Repeatedly, I should imagine,' said Mr Quin.

'Mathias,' said Mr Satterthwaite, frowning.

'And Mrs Mathias,' said Mr Quin.

Mr Satterthwaite stared hard at him.

'If that gang was really the Clondinis,' he said dreamily, 'there were three of them in it. The two young ones were Harwell and Eleanor Le Couteau. The mother now, was she Mrs Mathias? But in that case . . .'

'*Mathias* suffered from rheumatism, did he not?' said Mr Quin innocently.

'Oh!' cried Mr Satterthwaite. 'I have it. But could it be done? I believe it could. Listen. Mathias was there a month. During that time, Harwell and Eleanor were away for a fortnight on a honeymoon. For the fortnight before the wedding, they were supposedly in town. A clever man could have doubled the parts of Harwell and Mathias. When Harwell was at

Kirtlington Mallet, Mathias was conveniently laid up with rheumatism, with Mrs Mathias to sustain the fiction. Her part was very necessary. Without her, someone might have suspected the truth. As you say, Harwell was hidden in Mathias' cottage. He *was* Mathias. When at last the plans matured, and Ashley Grange was sold, he and his wife gave out they were taking a place in Essex. Exit John Mathias and his wife – for ever.'

There was a knock at the coffee-room door, and Masters entered. 'The car is at the door, sir,' he said.

Mr Satterthwaite rose. So did Mr Quin, who went across to the window, pulling the curtains. A beam of moonlight streamed into the room.

'The storm is over,' he said.

Mr Satterthwaite was pulling on his gloves.

'The Commissioner is dining with me next week,' he said importantly. 'I shall put my theory – ah! – before him.'

'It will be easily proved or disproved,' said Mr Quin. 'A comparison of the objects at Ashley Grange with a list supplied by the French police –!'

'Just so,' said Mr Satterthwaite. 'Rather hard luck on Mr Bradburn, but – well –'

'He can, I believe, stand the loss,' said Mr Quin.

Mr Satterthwaite held out his hand.

'Goodbye,' he said. 'I cannot tell you how much I have appreciated this unexpected meeting. You are leaving here tomorrow, I think you said?'

'Possibly tonight. My business here is done . . . I come and go, you know.'

Mr Satterthwaite remembered hearing those same words earlier in the evening. Rather curious.

He went out to the car and the waiting Masters. From the open door into the bar the landlord's voice floated out, rich and complacent.

'A dark mystery,' he was saying. 'A dark mystery, that's what it is.'

But he did not use the word 'dark'. The word he used suggested quite a different colour. Mr William Jones was a man of discrimination who suited his adjectives to his company. The company in the bar liked their adjectives full flavoured.

Mr Satterthwaite reclined luxuriously in the comfortable limousine. His breast was swelled with triumph. He saw the girl Mary come out on the steps and stand under the creaking Inn sign.

'She little knows,' said Mr Satterthwaite to himself. 'She little knows what *I* am going to do!'

The sign of the 'Bells and Motley' swayed gently in the wind.

The Sign in the Sky

'The Sign in the Sky' was first published in the USA in
The Police Magazine, June 1925, and then as 'A Sign in the Sky'
in *Grand Magazine*, July 1925.

The Judge was finishing his charge to the jury.

'Now, gentlemen, I have almost finished what I want to say to you. There is evidence for you to consider as to whether this case is plainly made out against this man so that you may say he is guilty of the murder of Vivien Barnaby. You have had the evidence of the servants as to the time the shot was fired. They have one and all agreed upon it. You have had the evidence of the letter written to the defendant by Vivien Barnaby on the morning of that same day, Friday, September 13th – a letter which the defence has not attempted to deny. You have had evidence that the prisoner first denied having been at Deering Hill, and later, after evidence had been given by the police, admitted he had. You will draw your own conclusions from that denial. This is not a case of direct evidence. You will have to come to your own conclusions on the subject of motive – of means, of opportunity. The contention of the defence is that some person unknown entered the music room after the defendant had left it, and shot Vivien Barnaby with the gun which, by strange forgetfulness, the defendant had left behind him. You have heard the defendant's story of the reason it took him half an hour to get home. If you disbelieve the defendant's story and are satisfied, beyond any reasonable doubt, that the defendant did, upon Friday, September 13th, discharge his gun at close quarters to Vivien Barnaby's head with intent to kill her, then, gentlemen, your verdict must be Guilty. If, on the other hand, you have any reasonable doubt, it is your duty to acquit the prisoner. I will now ask you to retire to your room and consider and let me know when you have arrived at a conclusion.'

The jury were absent a little under half an hour. They returned the verdict that to everyone had seemed a foregone conclusion, the verdict of 'Guilty'.

Mr Satterthwaite left the court after hearing the verdict, with a thoughtful frown on his face.

A mere murder trial as such did not attract him. He was of too fastidious a temperament to find interest in the sordid details of the average crime. But the Wylde case had been different. Young Martin Wylde was what is termed a gentleman – and the victim, Sir George Barnaby's young wife, had been personally known to the elderly gentleman.

He was thinking of all this as he walked up Holborn, and then plunged into a tangle of mean streets leading in the direction of Soho. In one of these streets there was a small restaurant, known only to the few, of whom Mr Satterthwaite was one. It was not cheap – it was, on the contrary, exceedingly expensive, since it catered exclusively for the palate of the jaded *gourmet*. It was quiet – no strains of jazz were allowed to disturb the hushed atmosphere – it was rather dark, waiters appeared soft-footed out of the twilight, bearing silver dishes with the air of participating in some holy rite. The name of the restaurant was Arlecchino.

Still thoughtful, Mr Satterthwaite turned into the Arlecchino and made for his favourite table in a recess in the far corner. Owing to the twilight before mentioned, it was not until he was quite close to it that he saw it was already occupied by a tall dark man who sat with his face in shadow, and with a play of colour from a stained window turning his sober garb into a kind of riotous motley.

Mr Satterthwaite would have turned back, but just at that moment the stranger moved slightly and the other recognized him.

'God bless my soul,' said Mr Satterthwaite, who was given to old-fashioned expressions. 'Why, it's Mr Quin!'

Three times before he had met Mr Quin, and each time the meeting had resulted in something a little out of the ordinary. A strange person, this Mr Quin, with a knack of showing you the things you had known all along in a totally different light.

At once Mr Satterthwaite felt excited – pleasurably excited. His role was that of the looker-on, and he knew it, but sometimes when in the company of Mr Quin he had the illusion of being an actor – and the principal actor at that.

'This is very pleasant,' he said, beaming all over his dried-up little face. 'Very pleasant indeed. You've no objection to my joining you, I hope?'

'I shall be delighted,' said Mr Quin. 'As you see, I have not yet begun my meal.'

A deferential head waiter hovered up out of the shadows. Mr Satterthwaite, as befitted a man with a seasoned palate, gave his whole mind to the task of selection. In a few minutes, the head waiter, a slight smile of approbation on his lips, retired, and a young satellite began his ministrations. Mr Satterthwaite turned to Mr Quin.

'I have just come from the Old Bailey,' he began. 'A sad business, I thought.'

'He was found guilty?' said Mr Quin.

'Yes, the jury were out only half an hour.'

Mr Quin bowed his head.

'An inevitable result – on the evidence,' he said.

'And yet,' began Mr Satterthwaite – and stopped.

Mr Quin finished the sentence for him.

'And yet your sympathies were with the accused? Is that what you were going to say?'

'I suppose it was. Martin Wylde is a nice-looking young fellow – one can hardly believe it of him. All the same, there have been a good many nice-looking young fellows lately who have turned out to be murderers of a particularly cold-blooded and repellent type.'

'Too many,' said Mr Quin quietly.

'I beg your pardon?' said Mr Satterthwaite, slightly startled.

'Too many for Martin Wylde. There has been a tendency from the beginning to regard this as just one more of a series of the same type of crime – a man seeking to free himself from one woman in order to marry another.'

'Well,' said Mr Satterthwasite doubtfully. 'On the evidence –'

'Ah!' said Mr Quin quickly. 'I am afraid I have not followed all the evidence.'

Mr Satterthwaite's self-confidence came back to him with a rush. He felt a sudden sense of power. He was tempted to be consciously dramatic.

'Let me try and show it to you. I have met the Bamabys, you understand. I know the peculiar circumstances. With me, you will come behind the scenes – you will see the thing from inside.'

Mr Quin leant forward with his quick encouraging smile.

'If anyone can show me that, it will be Mr Satterthwaite,' he murmured.

Mr Satterthwaite gripped the table with both hands. He was uplifted, carried out of himself. For the moment, he was an artist pure and simple – an artist whose medium was words.

Swiftly, with a dozen broad strokes, he etched in the picture of life at Deering Hill. Sir George Barnaby, elderly, obese, purse-proud. A man perpetually fussing over the little things of life. A man who wound up his clocks every Friday afternoon, and who paid his own house-keeping books every Tuesday morning, and who always saw to the locking of his own front door every night. A careful man.

And from Sir George he went on to Lady Barnaby. Here his touch was gentler, but none the less sure. He had seen her but once, but his impression of her was definite and lasting. A vivid defiant creature – pitifully young. A trapped child, that was how he described her.

'She hated him, you understand? She had married him before she knew what she was doing. And now –'

She was desperate – that was how he put it. Turning this way and that. She had no money of her own, she was entirely dependent on this elderly husband. But all the same she was a creature at bay – still unsure of her own powers, with a beauty that was as yet more promise than actuality. And she was greedy. Mr Satterthwaite affirmed that definitely. Side by side with defiance there ran a greedy streak – a clasping and a clutching at life.

'I never met Martin Wylde,' continued Mr Satterthwaite. 'But I heard of him. He lived less than a mile away. Farming, that was his line. And she took an interest in farming – or pretended to. If you ask me, it was pretending. I think that she saw in him her only way of escape – and she grabbed at him, greedily, like a child might have done. Well, there could only be one end to that. We know what that end was, because the letters were read out in court. He kept her letters – she didn't keep his, but from the text of hers one can see that he was cooling off. He admits as much. There was the other girl. She also lived in the village of Deering Vale. Her father was the doctor there. You saw her in court, perhaps? No, I remember, you were not there, you said. I shall have to describe her to you. A fair girl – very fair. Gentle. Perhaps – yes, perhaps a tiny bit stupid. But very restful, you know. And loyal. Above all, loyal.'

He looked at Mr Quin for encouragement, and Mr Quin gave it him by a slow appreciative smile. Mr Satterthwaite went on.

'You heard that last letter read – you must have seen it, in the papers, I mean. The one written on the morning of Friday, September 13th. It was full of desperate reproaches and vague threats, and it ended by begging Martin Wylde to come to Deering Hill that same evening at six o'clock. *"I will leave the side door open for you, so that no one need know you have been here. I shall be in the music room."* It was sent by hand.'

Mr Satterthwaite paused for a minute or two.

'When he was first arrested, you remember, Martin Wylde denied that he had been to the house at all that evening. His statement was that he had taken his gun and gone out shooting in the woods. But when the police brought forward their evidence, that statement broke down. They had found his finger-prints, you remember, both on the wood of the side door and on one of the two cocktail glasses on the table in the music room. He admitted then that he had come to see Lady Barnaby, that they had had a stormy interview, but that it had ended in his having managed to soothe her down. He swore that he left his gun outside leaning against the wall near the door, and that he left Lady Barnaby alive and well, the time being then a minute or two after a quarter past six. He went straight home, he says. But evidence was called to show that he did not reach his farm until a quarter to seven, and as I have just mentioned, it is barely a mile away. It would not take half an hour to get there. He forgot all about his gun, he declares. Not a very likely statement – and yet –'

'And yet?' queried Mr Quin.

'Well,' said Mr Satterthwaite slowly, 'it's a possible one, isn't it? Counsel ridiculed the supposition, of course, but I think he was wrong. You see, I've known a good many young men, and these emotional scenes upset them very much – especially the dark, nervous type like Martin Wylde. Women now, can go through a scene like that and feel positively better for it afterwards, with all their wits about them. It acts like a safety valve for them, steadies their nerves down and all that. But I can see Martin Wylde going away with his head in a whirl, sick and miserable, and without a thought of the gun he had left leaning up against the wall.'

He was silent for some minutes before he went on.

'Not that it matters. For the next part is only too clear, unfortunately. It was exactly twenty minutes past six when the shot was heard. All the servants heard it, the cook, the kitchen-maid, the butler, the housemaid and Lady Barnaby's own maid. They came rushing to the music room. She was lying huddled over the arm of her chair. The gun had been discharged close to the back of her head, so that the shot hadn't a chance to scatter. At least two of them penetrated the brain.'

He paused again and Mr Quin asked casually:

'The servants gave evidence, I suppose?'

Mr Satterthwaite nodded.

'Yes. The butler got there a second or two before the others, but their evidence was practically a repetition of each other's.'

'So they *all* gave evidence,' said Mr Quin musingly. 'There were no exceptions?'

'Now I remember it,' said Mr Satterthwaite, 'the housemaid was only called at the inquest. She's gone to Canada since, I believe.'

'I see,' said Mr Quin.

There was a silence, and somehow the air of the little restaurant seemed to be charged with an uneasy feeling. Mr Satterthwaite felt suddenly as though he were on the defensive.

'Why shouldn't she?' he said abruptly.

'Why should she?' said Mr Quin with a very slight shrug of the shoulders.

Somehow, the question annoyed Mr Satterthwaite. He wanted to shy away from it – to get back on familiar ground.

'There couldn't be much doubt who fired the shot. As a matter of fact the servants seemed to have lost their heads a bit. There was no one in the house to take charge. It was some minutes before anyone thought of ringing up the police, and when they did so they found that the telephone was out of order.'

'Oh!' said Mr Quin. 'The telephone was out of order.'

'It was,' said Mr Satterthwaite – and was struck suddenly by the feeling that he had said something tremendously important. 'It might, of course, have been done on purpose,' he said slowly. 'But there seems no point in that. Death was practically instantaneous.'

Mr Quin said nothing, and Mr Satterthwaite felt that his explanation was unsatisfactory.

'There was absolutely no one to suspect but young Wylde,' he went on. 'By his own account, even, he was only out of the house three minutes before the shot was fired. And who else could have fired it? Sir George was at a bridge party a few houses away. He left there at half-past six and was met just outside the gate by a servant bringing him the news. The last rubber finished at half-past six exactly – no doubt about that. Then there was Sir George's secretary, Henry Thompson. He was in London that day, and actually at a business meeting at the moment the shot was fired. Finally, there is Sylvia Dale, who after all, had a perfectly good motive, impossible as it seems that she should have had anything to do with such a crime. She was at the station of Deering Vale seeing a friend off by the 6.28 train. That lets her out. Then the servants. What earthly motive could any one of them have? Besides they all arrived on the spot practically simultaneously. No, it must have been Martin Wylde.'

But he said it in a dissatisfied kind of voice.

They went on with their lunch. Mr Quin was not in a talkative mood, and Mr Satterthwaite had said all he had to say. But the silence was not a barren one. It was filled with the growing dissatisfaction of Mr Satterthwaite, heightened and fostered in some strange way by the mere acquiescence of the other man.

Mr Satterthwaite suddenly put down his knife and fork with a clatter.

'Supposing that that young man is really innocent,' he said. 'He's going to be hanged.'

He looked very startled and upset about it. And still Mr Quin said nothing.

'It's not as though –' began Mr Satterthwaite, and stopped. 'Why shouldn't the woman go to Canada?' he ended inconsequently.

Mr Quin shook his head.

'I don't even know what part of Canada she went to,' continued Mr Satterthwaite peevishly.

'Could you find out?' suggested the other.

'I suppose I could. The butler, now. He'd know. Or possibly Thompson, the secretary.'

He paused again. When he resumed speech, his voice sounded almost pleading.

'It's not as though it were anything to do with me?'

'That a young man is going to be hanged in a little over three weeks?'

'Well, yes – if you put it that way, I suppose. Yes, I see what you mean. Life and death. And that poor girl, too. It's not that I'm hard-headed – but, after all – what good will it do? Isn't the whole thing rather fantastic? Even if I found out where the woman's gone in Canada – why, it would probably mean that I should have to go out there myself.'

Mr Satterthwaite looked seriously upset.

'And I was thinking of going to the Riviera next week,' he said pathetically.

And his glance towards Mr Quin said as plainly as it could be said, 'Do let me off, won't you?'

'You have never been to Canada?'

'Never.'

'A very interesting country.'

Mr Satterthwaite looked at him undecidedly.

'You think I ought to go?'

Mr Quin leaned back in his chair and lighted a cigarette. Between puffs of smoke, he spoke deliberately.

'You are, I believe, a rich man, Mr Satterthwaite. Not a millionaire, but a man able to indulge a hobby without counting the expense. You have looked on at the dramas of other people. Have you never contemplated stepping in and playing a part? Have you never seen yourself for a minute as the arbiter of other people's destinies – standing in the centre of the stage with life and death in your hands?'

Mr Satterthwaite leant forward. The old eagerness surged over him.

'You mean – if I go on this wild-goose chase to Canada –?'

Mr Quin smiled.

'Oh! it was your suggestion, going to Canada, not mine,' he said lightly.

'You can't put me off like that,' said Mr Satterthwaite earnestly. 'Whenever I have come across you –' He stopped.

'Well?'

'There is something about you I do not understand. Perhaps I never shall. The last time I met you –'

'On Midsummer's Eve.'

Mr Satterthwaite was startled, as though the words held a clue that he did not quite understand.

'Was it Midsummer's Eve?' he asked confusedly.

'Yes. But let us not dwell on that. It is unimportant, is it not?'

'Since you say so,' said Mr Satterthwaite courteously. He felt that elusive clue slipping through his fingers. 'When I come back from Canada' – he paused a little awkwardly – 'I – I – should much like to see you again.'

'I am afraid I have no fixed address for the moment,' said Mr Quin regretfully. 'But I often come to this place. If you also frequent it, we shall no doubt meet before very long.'

They parted pleasantly.

Mr Satterthwaite was very excited. He hurried round to Cook's and inquired about boat sailings. Then he rang up Deering Hill. The voice of a butler, suave and deferential, answered him.

'My name is Satterthwaite. I am speaking for a – er – firm of solicitors. I wished to make a few inquiries about a young woman who was recently housemaid in your establishment.'

'Would that be Louisa, sir? Louisa Bullard?'

'That is the name,' said Mr Satterthwaite, very pleased to be told it.

'I regret she is not in this country, sir. She went to Canada six months ago.'

'Can you give me her present address?'

The butler was afraid he couldn't. It was a place in the mountains she had gone to – a Scotch name – ah! Banff, that was it. Some of the other young women in the house had been expecting to hear from her, but she had never written or given them any address.

Mr Satterthwaite thanked him and rang off. He was still undaunted. The adventurous spirit was strong in his breast. He would go to Banff. If this Louisa Bullard was there, he would track her down somehow or other.

To his own surprise, he enjoyed the trip greatly. It was many years since he had taken a long sea voyage. The Riviera, Le Touquet and Deauville, and Scotland had been his usual round. The feeling that he was setting off on an impossible mission added a secret zest to his journey. What an utter fool these fellow travellers of his would think him did they but know the object of his quest! But then – they were not acquainted with Mr Quin.

In Banff he found his objective easily attained. Louisa Bullard was employed in the large Hotel there. Twelve hours after his arrival he was standing face to face with her.

She was a woman of about thirty-five, anaemic looking, but with a strong frame. She had pale brown hair inclined to curl, and a pair of honest brown eyes. She was, he thought, slightly stupid, but very trustworthy.

She accepted quite readily his statement that he had been asked to collect a few further facts from her about the tragedy at Deering Hill.

'I saw in the paper that Mr Martin Wylde had been convicted, sir. Very sad, it is, too.'

She seemed, however, to have no doubt as to his guilt.

'A nice young gentleman gone wrong. But though I wouldn't speak ill of the dead, it was her ladyship what led him on. Wouldn't leave him alone, she wouldn't. Well, they've both got their punishment. There's a text used to hang on my wall when I was a child, "God is not mocked," and it's very true. I knew something was going to happen that very evening – and sure enough it did.'

'How was that?' said Mr Satterthwaite.

'I was in my room, sir, changing my dress, and I happened to glance out of the window. There was a train going along, and the white smoke of it rose up in the air, and if you'll believe me it formed itself into the sign of a gigantic hand. A great white hand against the crimson of the sky. The fingers were crooked like, as though they were reaching out for something. It fair gave me a turn. "Did you ever now?" I said to myself. "That's a sign of something coming" – and sure enough at that very minute I heard the shot. "It's come," I said to myself, and I rushed downstairs and joined Carrie and the others who were in the hall, and we went into the music room and there she was, shot through the head – and the blood and everything. Horrible! I spoke up, I did, and told Sir George how I'd seen the sign beforehand, but he didn't seem to think much of it. An unlucky day, that was, I'd felt it in my bones from early in the morning. Friday, and the 13th – what could you expect?'

She rambled on. Mr Satterthwaite was patient. Again and again he took her back to the crime, questioning her closely. In the end he was forced to confess defeat. Louisa Bullard had told all she knew, and her story was perfectly simple and straightforward.

Yet he did discover one fact of importance. The post in question had been suggested to her by Mr Thompson, Sir George's secretary. The wages attached were so large that she was tempted, and accepted the job, although it involved her leaving England very hurriedly. A Mr Denman had made all the arrangements this end and had also warned her not to write to her fellow-servants in England, as this might 'get her into trouble with the immigration authorities', which statement she had accepted in blind faith.

The amount of wages, casually mentioned by her, was indeed so large that Mr Satterthwaite was startled. After some hesitation he made up his mind to approach this Mr Denman.

He found very little difficulty in inducing Mr Denman to tell all he knew. The latter had come across Thompson in London and Thompson had done him a good turn. The secretary had written to him in September saying that for personal reasons Sir George was anxious to get this girl out of England. Could he find her a job? A sum of money had been sent to raise the wages to a high figure.

'Usual trouble, I guess,' said Mr Denman, leaning back nonchalantly in his chair. 'Seems a nice quiet girl, too.'

Mr Satterthwaite did not agree that this was the usual trouble. Louisa Bullard, he was sure, was not a cast-off fancy of Sir George Barnaby's. For some reason it had been vital to get her out of England. But why? And who was at the bottom of it? Sir George himself, working through Thompson? Or the latter working on his own initiative, and dragging in his employer's name?

Still pondering over these questions, Mr Satterthwaite made the return journey. He was cast down and despondent. His journey had done no good.

Smarting under a sense of failure, he made his way to the *Arlecchino* the day after his return. He hardly expected to be successful the first time, but to his satisfaction the familiar figure was sitting at the table in the recess, and the dark face of Mr Harley Quin smiled a welcome.

'Well,' said Mr Satterthwaite as he helped himself to a pat of butter, 'you sent me on a nice wild-goose chase.'

Mr Quin raised his eyebrows.

'I sent you?' he objected. 'It was your own idea entirely.'

'Whosever idea it was, it's not succeeded. Louisa Bullard has nothing to tell.'

Thereupon Mr Satterthwaite related the details of his conversation with the housemaid and then went on to his interview with Mr Denman. Mr Quin listened in silence.

'In one sense, I was justified,' continued Mr Satterthwaite. 'She was deliberately got out of the way. But why? I can't see it.'

'No?' said Mr Quin, and his voice was, as ever, provocative.

Mr Satterthwaite flushed.

'I daresay you think I might have questioned her more adroitly. I can assure you that I took her over the story again and again. It was not my fault that I did not get what we want.'

'Are you sure,' said Mr Quin, 'that you did not get what you want?'

Mr Satterthwaite looked up at him in astonishment, and met that sad, mocking gaze he knew so well.

The little man shook his head, slightly bewildered.

There was a silence, and then Mr Quin said, with a total change of manner:

'You gave me a wonderful picture the other day of the people in this business. In a few words you made them stand out as clearly as though they were etched. I wish you would do something of that kind for the place – you left that in shadow.'

Mr Satterthwaite was flattered.

'The place? Deering Hill? Well, it's a very ordinary sort of house nowadays. Red brick, you know, and bay windows. Quite hideous outside, but very comfortable inside. Not a very large house. About two acres of ground. They're all much the same, those houses round the links. Built for rich men to live in. The inside of the house is reminiscent of a hotel – the bedrooms are like hotel suites. Baths and hot and cold basins in all the bedrooms and a good many gilded electric-light fittings. All wonderfully comfortable, but not very country-like. You can tell that Deering Vale is only nineteen miles from London.'

Mr Quin listened attentively.

'The train service is bad, I have heard,' he remarked.

'Oh! I don't know about that,' said Mr Satterthwaite, warming to his subject. 'I was down there for a bit last summer. I found it quite convenient for town. Of course the trains only go every hour. Forty-eight minutes past the hour from Waterloo – up to 10.48.'

'And how long does it take to Deering Vale?'

'Just about three-quarters of an hour. Twenty-eight minutes past the hour at Deering Vale.'

'Of course,' said Mr Quin with a gesture of vexation. 'I should have remembered. Miss Dale saw someone off by the 6.28 that evening, didn't she?'

Mr Satterthwaite did not reply for a minute or two. His mind had gone back with a rush to his unsolved problem. Presently he said:

'I wish you would tell me what you meant just now when you asked me if I was sure I had not got what I wanted?'

It sounded rather complicated, put that way, but Mr Quin made no pretence of not understanding.

'I just wondered if you weren't being a little too exacting. After all, you found out that Louisa Bullard was deliberately got out of the country. That being so, there must be a reason. And the reason must lie in what she said to you.'

'Well,' said Mr Satterthwaite argumentatively. 'What did she say? If she'd given evidence at the trial, what could she have said?'

'She might have told what she saw,' said Mr Quin.

'What did she see?'

'A sign in the sky.'

Mr Satterthwaite stared at him.

'Are you thinking of *that* nonsense? That superstitious notion of its being the hand of God?'

'Perhaps,' said Mr Quin, 'for all you and I know it may have been the hand of God, you know.'

The other was clearly puzzled at the gravity of his manner.

'Nonsense,' he said. 'She said herself it was the smoke of the train.'

'An up train or a down train, I wonder?' murmured Mr Quin.

'Hardly an up train. They go at ten minutes to the hour. It must have been a down train – the 6.28 – no, that won't do. She said the shot came immediately afterwards, and we know the shot was fired at twenty minutes past six. The train couldn't have been ten minutes early.'

'Hardly, on that line,' agreed Mr Quin.

Mr Satterthwaite was staring ahead of him.

'Perhaps a goods train,' he murmured. 'But surely, if so –'

'There would have been no need to get her out of England. I agree,' said Mr Quin.

Mr Satterthwaite gazed at him, fascinated.

'The 6.28,' he said slowly. 'But if so, if the shot was fired then, why did everyone say it was earlier?'

'Obvious,' said Mr Quin. 'The clocks must have been wrong.'

'All of them?' said Mr Satterthwaite doubtfully. 'That's a pretty tall coincidence, you know.'

'I wasn't thinking of it as a coincidence,' said the other. 'I was thinking it was Friday.'

'Friday?' said Mr Satterthwaite.

'You did tell me, you know, that Sir George always wound the clocks on a Friday afternoon,' said Mr Quin apologetically.

'He put them back ten minutes,' said Mr Satterthwaite, almost in a whisper, so awed was he by the discoveries he was making. 'Then he went out to bridge. I think he must have opened the note from his wife to Martin Wylde that morning – yes, decidedly he opened it. He left his bridge party at 6.30, found Martin's gun standing by the side door, and went in and shot her from behind. Then he went out again, threw the gun into the bushes where it was found later, and was apparently just coming out of the neighbour's gate when someone came running to fetch him. But the telephone – what about the telephone? Ah! yes, I see. He disconnected it so that a summons could not be sent to the police that way – they might have noted the time it was received. And Wylde's story works out now. The real time he left was five and twenty minutes past six. Walking slowly, he would reach home about a quarter to seven. Yes, I see it all. Louisa was the only danger with her endless talk about her superstitious fancies. Someone might realize the significance of the train and then – goodbye to that excellent *alibi*.'

'Wonderful,' commented Mr Quin.

Mr Satterthwaite turned to him, flushed with success.

'The only thing is – how to proceed now?'

'I should suggest Sylvia Dale,' said Mr Quin.

Mr Satterthwaite looked doubtful.

'I mentioned to you,' he said, 'she seemed to me a little – er – stupid.'

'She has a father and brothers who will take the necessary steps.'

'That is true,' said Mr Satterthwaite, relieved.

A very short time afterwards he was sitting with the girl telling her the story. She listened attentively. She put no questions to him but when he had done she rose.

'I must have a taxi – at once.'

'My dear child, what are you going to do?'

'I am going to Sir George Barnaby.'

'Impossible. Absolutely the wrong procedure. Allow me to –'

He twittered on by her side. But he produced no impression. Sylvia Dale was intent on her own plans. She allowed him to go with her in the taxi, but to all his remonstrances she addressed a deaf ear. She left him in the taxi while she went into Sir George's city office.

It was half an hour later when she came out. She looked exhausted, her fair beauty drooping like a waterless flower. Mr Satterthwaite received her with concern.

'I've won,' she murmured, as she leant back with half-closed eyes.

'What?' He was startled. 'What did you do? What did you say?'

She sat up a little.

'I told him that Louisa Bullard had been to the police with her story. I told him that the police had made inquiries and that he had been seen going into his own grounds and out again a few minutes after half-past six. I told him that the game was up. He – he went to pieces. I told him that there was still time for him to get away, that the police weren't coming for another hour to arrest him. I told him that if he'd sign a confession that he'd killed Vivien I'd do nothing, but that if he didn't I'd scream and tell the whole building the truth. He was so panicky that he didn't know what he was doing. He signed the paper without realizing what he was doing.'

She thrust it into his hands.

'Take it – take it. You know what to do with it so that they'll set Martin free.'

'He actually signed it,' cried Mr Satterthwaite, amazed.

'He is a little stupid, you know,' said Sylvia Dale. 'So am I,' she added as an afterthought. 'That's why I know how stupid people behave. We get rattled, you know, and then we do the wrong thing and are sorry afterwards.'

She shivered and Mr Satterthwaite patted her hand.

'You need something to pull you together,' he said. 'Come, we are close to a very favourite resort of mine – the *Arlecchino*. Have you ever been there?'

She shook her head.

Mr Satterthwaite stopped the taxi and took the girl into the little restaurant. He made his way to the table in the recess, his heart beating hopefully. But the table was empty.

Sylvia Dale saw the disappointment in his face.

'What is it?' she asked.

'Nothing,' said Mr Satterthwaite. 'That is, I half expected to see a friend of mine here. It doesn't matter. Some day, I expect, I shall see him again . . .'

The Soul of the Croupier

'The Soul of the Croupier' was first published in the USA in *Flynn's Weekly*, 13 November 1926, and then as 'The Magic of Mr Quin No. 2: The Soul of the Croupier' in *Storyteller* magazine, January 1927.

Mr Satterthwaite was enjoying the sunshine on the terrace at Monte Carlo.

Every year regularly on the second Sunday in January, Mr Satterthwaite left England for the Riviera. He was far more punctual than any swallow. In the month of April he returned to England, May and June he spent in London, and had never been known to miss Ascot. He left town after the Eton and Harrow match, paying a few country house visits before repairing to Deauville or Le Touquet. Shooting parties occupied most of September and October, and he usually spent a couple of months in town to wind up the year. He knew everybody and it may safely be said that everybody knew him.

This morning he was frowning. The blue of the sea was admirable, the gardens were, as always, a delight, but the people disappointed him – he thought them an ill-dressed, shoddy crowd. Some, of course, were gamblers, doomed souls who could not keep away. Those Mr Satterthwaite tolerated. They were a necessary background. But he missed the usual leaven of the *élite* – his own people.

'It's the exchange,' said Mr Satterthwaite gloomily. 'All sorts of people come here now who could never have afforded it before. And then, of course, I'm getting old . . . All the young people – the people coming on – they go to these Swiss places.'

But there were others that he missed, the well-dressed Barons and Counts of foreign diplomacy, the Grand Dukes and the Royal Princes. The only Royal Prince he had seen so far was working a lift in one of the less well-known hotels. He missed, too, the beautiful and expensive ladies. There was still a few of them, but not nearly as many as there used to be.

Mr Satterthwaite was an earnest student of the drama called Life, but he liked his material to be highly coloured. He felt discouragement sweep over him. Values were changing – and he – was too old to change.

It was at that moment that he observed the Countess Czarnova coming towards him.

Mr Satterthwaite had seen the Countess at Monte Carlo for many seasons now. The first time he had seen her she had been in the company of a Grand Duke. On the next occasion she was with an Austrian Baron. In successive years her friends had been of Hebraic extraction, sallow men with hooked noses, wearing rather flamboyant jewellery. For the last year or two she was much seen with very young men, almost boys.

She was walking with a very young man now. Mr Satterthwaite happened to know him, and he was sorry. Franklin Rudge was a young American, a typical product of one of the Middle West States, eager to register impression, crude, but loveable, a curious mixture of native shrewdness and idealism. He was in Monte Carlo with a party of other young Americans of both sexes, all much of the same type. It was their first glimpse of the Old World and they were outspoken in criticism and in appreciation.

On the whole they disliked the English people in the hotel, and the English people disliked them. Mr Satterthwaite, who prided himself on being a cosmopolitan, rather liked them. Their directness and vigour appealed to him, though their occasional solecisms made him shudder.

It occurred to him that the Countess Czarnova was a most unsuitable friend for young Franklin Rudge.

He took off his hat politely as they came abreast of him, and the Countess gave him a charming bow and smile.

She was a very tall woman, superbly made. Her hair was black, so were her eyes, and her eyelashes and eyebrows were more superbly black than any Nature had ever fashioned.

Mr Satterthwaite, who knew far more of feminine secrets than it is good for any man to know, rendered immediate homage to the art with which she was made up. Her complexion appeared to be flawless, of a uniform creamy white.

The very faint bistre shadows under her eyes were most effective. Her mouth was neither crimson nor scarlet, but a subdued wine colour. She was dressed in a very daring creation of black and white and carried a parasol of the shade of pinky red which is most helpful to the complexion.

Franklin Rudge was looking happy and important.

'There goes a young fool,' said Mr Satterthwaite to himself. 'But I suppose it's no business of mine and anyway he wouldn't listen to me. Well, well, I've bought experience myself in my time.'

But he still felt rather worried, because there was a very attractive little American girl in the party, and he was sure that she would not like Franklin Rudge's friendship with the Countess at all.

He was just about to retrace his steps in the opposite direction when he caught sight of the girl in question coming up one of the paths towards him. She wore a well-cut tailor-made 'suit' with a white muslin shirt waist, she had on good, sensible walking shoes, and carried a guide-book. There are some Americans who pass through Paris and emerge clothed as the Queen of Sheba, but Elizabeth Martin was not one of them. She was 'doing Europe' in a stern, conscientious spirit. She had high ideas of culture and art and she was anxious to get as much as possible for her limited store of money.

It is doubtful if Mr Satterthwaite thought of her as either cultured or artistic. To him she merely appeared very young.

'Good morning, Mr Satterthwaite,' said Elizabeth. 'Have you seen Franklin – Mr Rudge – anywhere about?'

'I saw him just a few minutes ago.'

'With his friend the Countess, I suppose,' said the girl sharply.

'Er – with the Countess, yes,' admitted Mr Satterthwaite.

'That Countess of his doesn't cut any ice with me,' said the girl in a rather high, shrill voice. 'Franklin's just crazy about her. *Why* I can't think.'

'She's got a very charming manner, I believe,' said Mr Satterthwaite cautiously.

'Do you know her?'

'Slightly.'

'I'm right down worried about Franklin,' said Miss Martin. 'That boy's got a lot of sense as a rule. You'd never think he'd fall for this sort of siren stuff. And he won't hear a thing, he gets madder than a hornet if anyone tries to say a word to him. Tell me, anyway – is she a real Countess?'

'I shouldn't like to say,' said Mr Satterthwaite. 'She may be.'

'That's the real Ha Ha English manner,' said Elizabeth with signs of displeasure. 'All I can say is that in Sargon Springs – that's our home town, Mr Satterthwaite – that Countess would look a mighty queer bird.'

Mr Satterthwaite thought it possible. He forebore to point out that they were not in Sargon Springs but in the principality of Monaco, where the Countess happened to synchronize with her environment a great deal better than Miss Martin did.

He made no answer and Elizabeth went on towards the Casino. Mr Satterthwaite sat on a seat in the sun, and was presently joined by Franklin Rudge.

Rudge was full of enthusiasm.

'I'm enjoying myself,' he announced with naïve enthusiasm. 'Yes, *sir*!

This is what I call seeing life – rather a different kind of life from what we have in the States.'

The elder man turned a thoughtful face to him.

'Life is lived very much the same everywhere,' he said rather wearily. 'It wears different clothes – that's all.'

Franklin Rudge stared.

'I don't get you.'

'No,' said Mr Satterthwaite. 'That's because you've got a long way to travel yet. But I apologize. No elderly man should permit himself to get into the habit of preaching.'

'Oh! that's all right.' Rudge laughed, displaying the beautiful teeth of all his countrymen. 'I don't say, mind you, that I'm not disappointed in the Casino. I thought the gambling would be different – something much more feverish. It seems just rather dull and sordid to me.'

'Gambling is life and death to the gambler, but it has no great spectacular value,' said Mr Satterthwaite. 'It is more exciting to read about than to see.'

The young man nodded his agreement.

'You're by way of being rather a big bug socially, aren't you?' he asked with a diffident candour that made it impossible to take offence. 'I mean, you know all the Duchesses and Earls and Countesses and things.'

'A good many of them,' said Mr Satterthwaite. 'And also the Jews and the Portuguese and the Greeks and the Argentines.'

'Eh?' said Mr Rudge.

'I was just explaining,' said Mr Satterthwaite, 'that I move in English society.'

Franklin Rudge meditated for a moment or two.

'You know the Countess Czarnova, don't you?' he said at length.

'Slightly,' said Mr Satterthwaite, making the same answer he had made to Elizabeth.

'Now there's a woman whom it's been very interesting to meet. One's inclined to think that the aristocracy of Europe is played out and effete. That may be true of the men, but the women are different. Isn't it a pleasure to meet an exquisite creature like the Countess? Witty, charming, intelligent, generations of civilization behind her, an aristocrat to her finger-tips!'

'Is she?' asked Mr Satterthwaite.

'Well, isn't she? You know what her family are?'

'No,' said Mr Satterthwaite. 'I'm afraid I know very little about her.'

'She was a Radzynski,' explained Franklin Rudge. 'One of the oldest families in Hungary. She's had the most extraordinary life. You know that great rope of pearls she wears?'

Mr Satterthwaite nodded.

'That was given her by the King of Bosnia. She smuggled some secret papers out of the kingdom for him.'

'I heard,' said Mr Satterthwaite, 'that the pearls had been given her by the King of Bosnia.'

The fact was indeed a matter of common gossip, it being reported that the lady had been a *chère amie* of His Majesty's in days gone by.

'Now I'll tell you something more.'

Mr Satterthwaite listened, and the more he listened the more he admired the fertile imagination of the Countess Czarnova. No vulgar 'siren stuff' (as Elizabeth Martin had put it) for her. The young man was shrewd enough in that way, clean living and idealistic. No, the Countess moved austerely through a labyrinth of diplomatic intrigues. She had enemies, detractors – naturally! It was a glimpse, so the young American was made to feel, into the life of the old regime with the Countess as the central figure, aloof, aristocratic, the friend of counsellors and princes, a figure to inspire romantic devotion.

'And she's had any amount to contend against,' ended the young man warmly. 'It's an extraordinary thing but she's never found a woman who would be a real friend to her. Women have been against her all her life.'

'Probably,' said Mr Satterthwaite.

'Don't you call it a scandalous thing?' demanded Rudge hotly.

'N – no,' said Mr Satterthwaite thoughtfully. 'I don't know that I do. Women have got their own standards, you know. It's no good our mixing ourselves up in their affairs. They must run their own show.'

'I don't agree with you,' said Rudge earnestly. 'It's one of the worst things in the world today, the unkindness of woman to woman. You know Elizabeth Martin? Now she agrees with me in theory absolutely. We've often discussed it together. She's only a kid, but her ideas are all right. But the moment it comes to a practical test – why, she's as bad as any of them. Got a real down on the Countess without knowing a darned thing about her, and won't listen when I try to tell her things. It's all wrong, Mr Satterthwaite. I believe in democracy – and – what's that but brotherhood between men and sisterhood between women?'

He paused earnestly. Mr Satterthwaite tried to think of any circumstances in which a sisterly feeling might arise between the Countess and Elizabeth Martin and failed.

'Now the Countess, on the other hand,' went on Rudge, 'admires Elizabeth immensely, and thinks her charming in every way. Now what does that show?'

'It shows,' said Mr Satterthwaite dryly, 'that the Countess has lived a considerable time longer than Miss Martin has.'

Franklin Rudge went off unexpectedly at a tangent.

'Do you know how old she is? She told me. Rather sporting of her. I should have guessed her to be twenty-nine, but she told me of her own accord that she was thirty-five. She doesn't look it, does she?' Mr Satterthwaite, whose private estimate of the lady's age was between forty-five and forty-nine, merely raised his eyebrows.

'I should caution you against believing all you are told at Monte Carlo,' he murmured.

He had enough experience to know the futility of arguing with the lad. Franklin Rudge was at a pitch of white hot chivalry when he would have disbelieved any statement that was not backed with authoritative proof.

'Here is the Countess,' said the boy, rising.

She came up to them with the languid grace that so became her. Presently they all three sat down together. She was very charming to Mr Satterthwaite, but in rather an aloof manner. She deferred to him prettily, asking his opinion, and treating him as an authority on the Riviera.

The whole thing was cleverly managed. Very few minutes had elapsed before Franklin Rudge found himself gracefully but unmistakably dismissed, and the Countess and Mr Satterthwaite were left *tête-à-tête*.

She put down her parasol and began drawing patterns with it in the dust.

'You are interested in the nice American boy, Mr Satterthwaite, are you not?'

Her voice was low with a caressing note in it.

'He's a nice young fellow,' said Mr Satterthwaite, noncommittally.

'I find him sympathetic, yes,' said the Countess reflectively. 'I have told him much of my life.'

'Indeed,' said Mr Satterthwaite.

'Details such as I have told to few others,' she continued dreamily. 'I have had an extraordinary life, Mr Satterthwaite. Few would credit the amazing things that have happened to me.'

Mr Satterthwaite was shrewd enough to penetrate her meaning. After all, the stories that she had told to Franklin Rudge *might* be the truth. It was extremely unlikely, and in the last degree improbable, but it was *possible* . . . No one could definitely say: 'That is not so –'

He did not reply, and the Countess continued to look out dreamily across the bay.

And suddenly Mr Satterthwaite had a strange and new impression of her. He saw her no longer as a harpy, but as a desperate creature at bay, fighting tooth and nail. He stole a sideways glance at her. The parasol was down, he could see the little haggard lines at the corners of her eyes. In one temple a pulse was beating.

It flowed through him again and again – that increasing certitude. She was a creature desperate and driven. She would be merciless to him or to anyone who stood between her and Franklin Rudge. But he still felt he hadn't got the hang of the situation. Clearly she had plenty of money. She was always beautifully dressed, and her jewels were marvellous. There could be no real urgency of that kind. Was it love? Women of her age did, he well knew, fall in love with boys. It might be that. There was, he felt sure, something out of the common about the situation.

Her *tête-à-tête* with him was, he recognized, a throwing down of the gauntlet. She had singled him out as her chief enemy. He felt sure that she hoped to goad him into speaking slightingly of her to Franklin Rudge. Mr Satterthwaite smiled to himself. He was too old a bird for that. He knew when it was wise to hold one's tongue.

He watched her that night in the Cercle Privé, as she tried her fortunes at roulette.

Again and again she staked, only to see her stake swept away. She bore her losses well, with the stoical *sang froid* of the old *habitué*. She staked *en plein* once or twice, put the maximum on red, won a little on the middle dozen and then lost it again, finally she backed *manque* six times and lost every time. Then with a little graceful shrug of the shoulders she turned away.

She was looking unusually striking in a dress of gold tissue with an underlying note of green. The famous Bosnian pearls were looped round her neck and long pearl ear-rings hung from her ears.

Mr Satterthwaite heard two men near him appraise her.

'The Czarnova,' said one, 'she wears well, does she not? The Crown jewels of Bosnia look fine on her.'

The other, a small Jewish-looking man, stared curiously after her.

'So those are the pearls of Bosnia, are they?' he asked. '*En vérité.* That is odd.'

He chuckled softly to himself.

Mr Satterthwaite missed hearing more, for at the moment he turned his head and was overjoyed to recognize an old friend.

'My dear Mr Quin.' He shook him warmly by the hand. 'The last place I should ever have dreamed of seeing you.'

Mr Quin smiled, his dark attractive face lighting up.

'It should not surprise you,' he said. 'It is Carnival time. I am often here in Carnival time.'

'Really? Well, this is a great pleasure. Are you anxious to remain in the rooms? I find them rather warm.'

'It will be pleasanter outside,' agreed the other. 'We will walk in the gardens.'

The air outside was sharp, but not chill. Both men drew deep breaths.
'That is better,' said Mr Satterthwaite.

'Much better,' agreed Mr Quin. 'And we can talk freely. I am sure that there is much that you want to tell me.'

'There is indeed.'

Speaking eagerly, Mr Satterthwaite unfolded his perplexities. As usual he took pride in his power of conveying atmosphere. The Countess, young Franklin, uncompromising Elizabeth – he sketched them all in with a deft touch.

'You have changed since I first knew you,' said Mr Quin, smiling, when the recital was over.

'In what way?'

'You were content then to look on at the drama that life offered. Now – you want to take part – to act.'

'It is true,' confessed Mr Satterthwaite. 'But in this case I do not know what to do. It is all very perplexing. Perhaps –' He hesitated. 'Perhaps you will help me?'

'With pleasure,' said Mr Quin. 'We will see what we can do.'

Mr Satterthwaite had an odd sense of comfort and reliance.

The following day he introduced Franklin Rudge and Elizabeth Martin to his friend Mr Harley Quin. He was pleased to see that they got on together. The Countess was not mentioned, but at lunch time he heard news that aroused his attention.

'Mirabelle is arriving in Monte this evening,' he confided excitedly to Mr Quin.

'The Parisian stage favourite?'

'Yes. I daresay you know – it's common property – she is the King of Bosnia's latest craze. He has showered jewels on her, I believe. They say she is the most exacting and extravagant woman in Paris.'

'It should be interesting to see her and the Countess Czarnova meet tonight.'

'Exactly what I thought.'

Mirabelle was a tall, thin creature with a wonderful head of dyed fair hair. Her complexion was a pale mauve with orange lips. She was amazingly chic. She was dressed in something that looked like a glorified bird of paradise, and she wore chains of jewels hanging down her bare back. A heavy bracelet set with immense diamonds clasped her left ankle.

She created a sensation when she appeared in the Casino.

'Your friend the Countess will have a difficulty in outdoing this,' murmured Mr Quin in Mr Satterthwaite's ear.

The latter nodded. He was curious to see how the Countess comported herself.

She came late, and a low murmur ran round as she walked unconcernedly to one of the centre roulette tables.

She was dressed in white – a mere straight slip of marocain such as a débutante might have worn and her gleaming white neck and arms were unadorned. She wore not a single jewel.

'It is clever, that,' said Mr Satterthwaite with instant approval. 'She disdains rivalry and turns the tables on her adversary.'

He himself walked over and stood by the table. From time to time he amused himself by placing a stake. Sometimes he won, more often he lost.

There was a terrific run on the last dozen. The numbers 31 and 34 turned up again and again. Stakes flocked to the bottom of the cloth.

With a smile Mr Satterthwaite made his last stake for the evening, and placed the maximum on Number 5.

The Countess in her turn leant forward and placed the maximum on Number 6.

'*Faites vos jeux*,' called the croupier hoarsely. '*Rien ne va plus. Plus rien.*'

The ball span, humming merrily. Mr Satterthwaite thought to himself: '*This means something different to each of us. Agonies of hope and despair, boredom, idle amusement, life and death.*'

Click!

The croupier bent forward to see.

'*Numéro cinque, rouge, impair et manque.*'

Mr Satterthwaite had won!

The croupier, having raked in the other stakes, pushed forward Mr Satterthwaite's winnings. He put out his hand to take them. The Countess did the same. The croupier looked from one to the other of them.

'*A madame*,' he said brusquely.

The Countess picked up the money. Mr Satterthwaite drew back. He remained a gentleman. The Countess looked him full in the face and he returned her glance. One or two of the people round pointed out to the croupier that he had made a mistake, but the man shook his head impatiently. He had decided. That was the end. He raised his raucous cry:

'*Faites vos jeux, Messieurs et Mesdames.*'

Mr Satterthwaite rejoined Mr Quin. Beneath his impeccable demeanour, he was feeling extremely indignant. Mr Quin listened sympathetically.

'Too bad,' he said, 'but these things happen.'

'We are to meet your friend Franklin Rudge later. I am giving a little supper party.'

The three met at midnight, and Mr Quin explained his plan.

'It is what is called a "Hedges and Highways" party,' he explained. 'We choose our meeting place, then each one goes out and is bound in honour to invite the first person he meets.'

Franklin Rudge was amused by the idea.

'Say, what happens if they won't accept?'

'You must use your utmost powers of persuasion.'

'Good. And where's the meeting place?'

'A somewhat Bohemian café – where one can take strange guests. It is called Le Caveau.'

He explained its whereabouts, and the three parted. Mr Satterthwaite was so fortunate as to run straight into Elizabeth Martin and he claimed her joyfully. They reached Le Caveau and descended into a kind of cellar where they found a table spread for supper and lit by old-fashioned candles in candlesticks.

'We are the first,' said Mr Satterthwaite. 'Ah! here comes Franklin –'

He stopped abruptly. With Franklin was the Countess. It was an awkward moment. Elizabeth displayed less graciousness than she might have done. The Countess, as a woman of the world, retained the honours.

Last of all came Mr Quin. With him was a small, dark man, neatly dressed, whose face seemed familiar to Mr Satterthwaite. A moment later he recognized him. It was the croupier who earlier in the evening had made such a lamentable mistake.

'Let me introduce you to the company, M. Pierre Vaucher,' said Mr Quin.

The little man seemed confused. Mr Quin performed the necessary introductions easily and lightly. Supper was brought – an excellent supper. Wine came – very excellent wine. Some of the frigidity went out of the atmosphere. The Countess was very silent, so was Elizabeth. Franklin Rudge became talkative. He told various stories – not humorous stories, but serious ones. And quietly and assiduously Mr Quin passed round the wine.

'I'll tell you – and this is a true story – about a man who made good,' said Franklin Rudge impressively.

For one coming from a Prohibition country he had shown no lack of appreciation of champagne.

He told his story – perhaps at somewhat unnecessary length. It was, like many true stories, greatly inferior to fiction.

As he uttered the last word, Pierre Vaucher, opposite him, seemed to wake up. He also had done justice to the champagne. He leaned forward across the table.

'I, too, will tell you a story,' he said thickly. 'But mine is the story of a man who did not make good. It is the story of a man who went, not up, but down the hill. And, like yours, it is a true story.'

'Pray tell it to us, monsieur,' said Mr Satterthwaite courteously.

Pierre Vaucher leant back in his chair and looked at the ceiling.

'It is in Paris that the story begins. There was a man there, a working jeweller. He was young and light-hearted and industrious in his profession. They said there was a future before him. A good marriage was already arranged for him, the bride not too bad-looking, the dowry most satisfactory. And then, what do you think? One morning he sees a girl. Such a miserable little wisp of a girl, messieurs. Beautiful? Yes, perhaps, if she were not half starved. But anyway, for this young man, she has a magic that he cannot resist. She has been struggling to find work, she is virtuous – or at least that is what she tells him. I do not know if it is true.'

The Countess's voice came suddenly out of the semi-darkness.

'Why should it not be true? There are many like that.'

'Well, as I say, the young man believed her. And he married her – an act of folly! His family would have no more to say to him. He had outraged their feelings. He married – I will call her Jeanne – it was a good action. He told her so. He felt that she should be very grateful to him. He had sacrificed much for her sake.'

'A charming beginning for the poor girl,' observed the Countess sarcastically.

'He loved her, yes, but from the beginning she maddened him. She had moods – tantrums – she would be cold to him one day, passionate the next. At last he saw the truth. She had never loved him. She had married him so as to keep body and soul together. That truth hurt him, it hurt him horribly, but he tried his utmost to let nothing appear on the surface. And he still felt he deserved gratitude and obedience to his wishes. They quarrelled. She reproached him – Mon Dieu, what did she not reproach him with?

'You can see the next step, can you not? The thing that was bound to come. She left him. For two years he was alone, working in his little shop with no news of her. He had one friend – absinthe. The business did not prosper so well.

'And then one day he came into the shop to find her sitting there. She was beautifully dressed. She had rings on her hands. He stood considering her. His heart was beating – but beating! He was at a loss what to do. He would have liked to have beaten her, to have clasped her in his arms, to have thrown her down on the floor and trampled on her, to have thrown himself at her feet. He did none of those things. He took up his pincers and went on with his work. "Madame desires?" he asked formally.

'That upset her. She did not look for that, see you. "Pierre," she said, "I have come back." He laid aside his pincers and looked at her. "You

wish to be forgiven?" he said. "You want me to take you back? You are
sincerely repentant?" "Do you want me back?" she murmured. Oh! very
softly she said it.

'He knew she was laying a trap for him. He longed to seize her in his
arms, but he was too clever for that. He pretended indifference.

'"I am a Christian man," he said. "I try to do what the Church directs."
"Ah!" he thought, "I will humble her, humble her to her knees."

'But Jeanne, that is what I will call her, flung back her head and laughed.
Evil laughter it was. "I mock myself at you, little Pierre," she said. "Look
at these rich clothes, these rings and bracelets. I came to show myself to
you. I thought I would make you take me in your arms and when you
did so, then – *then* I would spit in your face and tell you how I hated
you!"

'And on that she went out of the shop. Can you believe, messieurs,
that a woman could be as evil as all that – to come back only to torment
me?'

'No,' said the Countess. 'I would not believe it, and any man who was
not a fool would not believe it either. But all men are blind fools.'

Pierre Vaucher took no notice of her. He went on.

'And so that young man of whom I tell you sank lower and lower. He
drank more absinthe. The little shop was sold over his head. He became
of the dregs, of the gutter. Then came the war. Ah! it was good, the war.
It took that man out of the gutter and taught him to be a brute beast no
longer. It drilled him – and sobered him. He endured cold and pain and
the fear of death – but he did not die and when the war ended, he was
a man again.

'It was then, messieurs, that he came South. His lungs had been affected
by the gas, they said he must find work in the South. I will not weary
you with all the things he did. Suffice it to say that he ended up as a
croupier, and there – there in the Casino one evening, he saw her again
– the woman who had ruined his life. She did not recognize him, but he
recognized her. She appeared to be rich and to lack for nothing – but
messieurs, the eyes of a croupier are sharp. There came an evening when
she placed her last stake in the world on the table. Ask me not how I
know – I do know – one feels these things. Others might not believe. She
still had rich clothes – why not pawn them, one would say? But to do
that – pah! your credit is gone at once. Her jewels? Ah no! Was I not a
jeweller in my time? Long ago the real jewels have gone. The pearls of
a King are sold one by one, are replaced with false. And meantime one
must eat and pay one's hotel bill. Yes, and the rich men – well, they have
seen one about for many years. Bah! they say – she is over fifty. A younger
chicken for my money.'

A long shuddering sigh came out of the windows where the Countess leant back.

'Yes. It was a great moment, that. Two nights I have watched her. Lose, lose, and lose again. And now the end. She put all on one number. Beside her, an English milord stakes the maximum also – on the next number. The ball rolls . . . The moment has come, she has lost . . .

'Her eyes meet mine. What do I do? I jeopardize my place in the Casino. I rob the English milord. "*A Madame*" I say, and pay over the money.'

'Ah!' There was a crash, as the Countess sprang to her feet and leant across the table, sweeping her glass on to the floor.

'Why?' she cried. 'That's what I want to know, *why* did you do it?'

There was a long pause, a pause that seemed interminable, and still those two facing each other across the table looked and looked . . . It was like a duel.

A mean little smile crept across Pierre Vaucher's face. He raised his hands.

'Madame,' he said, 'there is such a thing as pity . . .'

'Ah!'

She sank down again.

'I see.'

She was calm, smiling, herself again.

'An interesting story, M. Vaucher, is it not? Permit me to give you a light for your cigarette.'

She deftly rolled up a spill, and lighted it at the candle and held it towards him. He leaned forward till the flame caught the tip of the cigarette he held between his lips.

Then she rose unexpectedly to her feet.

'And now I must leave you all. Please – I need no one to escort me.'

Before one could realize it she was gone. Mr Satterthwaite would have hurried out after her, but he was arrested by a startled oath from the Frenchman.

'*A thousand thunders!*'

He was staring at the half-burned spill which the Countess had dropped on the table. He unrolled it.

'*Mon Dieu!*' he muttered. 'A fifty thousand franc bank note. You understand? Her winnings tonight. All that she had in the world. And she lighted my cigarette with it! Because she was too proud to accept – pity. Ah! proud, she was always proud as the Devil. She is unique – wonderful.'

He sprang up from his seat and darted out. Mr Satterthwaite and Mr Quin had also risen. The waiter approached Franklin Rudge.

'*La note, monsieur,*' he observed unemotionally.

Mr Quin rescued it from him quickly.

'I feel kind of lonesome, Elizabeth,' remarked Franklin Rudge. 'These foreigners – they beat the band! I don't understand them. What's it all mean, anyhow?'

He looked across at her.

'Gee, it's good to look at anything so hundred per cent American as you.' His voice took on the plaintive note of a small child. 'These foreigners are so *odd*.'

They thanked Mr Quin and went out into the night together. Mr Quin picked up his change and smiled across at Mr Satterthwaite, who was preening himself like a contented bird.

'Well,' said the latter. 'That's all gone off splendidly. Our pair of love birds will be all right now.'

'Which ones?' asked Mr Quin.

'Oh!' said Mr Satterthwaite, taken aback. 'Oh! yes, well, I suppose you are right, allowing for the Latin point of view and all that –'

He looked dubious.

Mr Quin smiled, and a stained glass panel behind him invested him for just a moment in a motley garment of coloured light.

The Man from the Sea

'The Man from the Sea' was first published in *Britannia & Eve*, October 1929.

Mr Satterthwaite was feeling old. That might not have been surprising since in the estimation of many people he *was* old. Careless youths said to their partners: 'Old Satterthwaite? Oh! he must be a hundred – or at any rate about eighty.' And even the kindest of girls said indulgently, 'Oh! Satterthwaite. Yes, he's quite old. He *must* be sixty.' Which was almost worse, since he was sixty-nine.

In his own view, however, he was not old. Sixty-nine was an interesting age – an age of infinite possibilities – an age when at last the experience of a lifetime was beginning to tell. But to feel old – that was different, a tired discouraged state of mind when one was inclined to ask oneself depressing questions. What was he after all? A little dried-up elderly man, with neither chick nor child, with no human belongings, only a valuable Art collection which seemed at the moment strangely unsatisfying. No one to care whether he lived or died . . .

At this point in his meditations Mr Satterthwaite pulled himself up short. What he was thinking was morbid and unprofitable. He knew well enough, who better, that the chances were that a wife would have hated him or alternatively that he would have hated her, that children would have been a constant source of worry and anxiety, and that demands upon his time and affection would have worried him considerably.

'To be safe and comfortable,' said Mr Satterthwaite firmly – that was the thing.

The last thought reminded him of a letter he had received that morning. He drew it from his pocket and re-read it, savouring its contents pleasurably. To begin with, it was from a Duchess, and Mr Satterthwaite liked hearing from Duchesses. It is true that the letter began by demanding a large subscription for charity and but for that would probably never have been written, but the terms in which it was couched were so agreeable that Mr Satterthwaite was able to gloss over the first fact.

> *So you've deserted the Riviera*, wrote the Duchess. *What is this island of yours like? Cheap? Cannotti put up his prices shamefully this year, and I shan't go to the Riviera again. I might try your island next year if you report favourably, though I should hate five days on a boat. Still anywhere you recommend is sure to be pretty comfortable – too much so. You'll get to be one of those people who do nothing but coddle themselves and think of their comfort. There's only one thing that will save you, Satterthwaite, and that is your inordinate interest in other people's affairs . . .*

As Mr Satterthwaite folded the letter, a vision came up vividly before him of the Duchess. Her meanness, her unexpected and alarming kindness, her caustic tongue, her indomitable spirit.

Spirit! Everyone needed spirit. He drew out another letter with a German stamp upon it – written by a young singer in whom he had interested himself. It was a grateful affectionate letter.

> *'How can I thank you, dear Mr Satterthwaite? It seems too wonderful to think that in a few days I shall be singing Isolde . . .'*

A pity that she had to make her *début* as Isolde. A charming, hardworking child, Olga, with a beautiful voice but no temperament. He hummed to himself. *'Nay order him! Pray understand it! I command it. I, Isolde.'* No, the child hadn't got it in her – the spirit – the indomitable will – all expressed in that final *'Ich Isoldé!'*

Well, at any rate he had done something for somebody. This island depressed him – why, oh! why had he deserted the Riviera which he knew so well and where he was so well known? Nobody here took any interest in him. Nobody seemed to realize that here was *the* Mr Satterthwaite – the friend of Duchesses and Countesses and singers and writers. No one in the island was of any social importance or of any artistic importance either. Most people had been there seven, fourteen, or twenty-one years running and valued themselves and were valued accordingly.

With a deep sigh Mr Satterthwaite proceeded down from the Hotel to the small straggling harbour below. His way lay between an avenue of bougainvillaea – a vivid mass of flaunting scarlet, that made him feel older and greyer than ever.

'I'm getting old,' he murmured. 'I'm getting old and tired.'

He was glad when he had passed the bougainvillaea and was walking down the white street with the blue sea at the end of it. A disreputable dog was standing in the middle of the road, yawning and stretching himself in the sun. Having prolonged his stretch to the utmost limits of ecstasy, he sat down and treated himself to a really good scratch. He then rose, shook himself, and looked round for any other good things that life might have to offer.

There was a dump of rubbish by the side of the road and to this he went sniffing in pleasurable anticipation. True enough, his nose had not deceived him! A smell of such rich putrescence that surpassed even his anticipations! He sniffed with growing appreciation, then suddenly abandoning himself, he lay on his back and rolled frenziedly on the delicious dump. Clearly the world this morning was a dog paradise!

Tiring at last, he regained his feet and strolled out once more into the middle of the road. And then, without the least warning, a ramshackle car careered wildly round the corner, caught him full square and passed on unheeding.

The dog rose to his feet, stood a minute regarding Mr Satterthwaite, a vague dumb reproach in his eyes, then fell over. Mr Satterthwaite went up to him and bent down. The dog was dead. He went on his way, wondering at the sadness and cruelty of life. What a queer dumb look of reproach had been in the dog's eyes. 'Oh! World,' they seemed to say. 'Oh! Wonderful World in which I have trusted. Why have you done this to me?'

Mr Satterthwaite went on, past the palm trees and the straggling white houses, past the black lava beach where the surf thundered and where once, long ago, a well-known English swimmer had been carried out to sea and drowned, past the rock pools were children and elderly ladies bobbed up and down and called it bathing, along the steep road that winds upwards to the top of the cliff. For there on the edge of the cliff was a house, appropriately named La Paz. A white house with faded green shutters tightly closed, a tangled beautiful garden, and a walk between cypress trees that led to a plateau on the edge of the cliff where you looked down – down – down – to the deep blue sea below.

It was to this spot that Mr Satterthwaite was bound. He had developed a great love for the garden of La Paz. He had never entered the villa. It seemed always to be empty. Manuel, the Spanish gardener, wished one good-morning with a flourish and gallantly presented ladies with a bouquet and gentlemen with a single flower as a buttonhole, his dark face wreathed in smiles.

Sometimes Mr Satterthwaite made up stories in his own mind about the owner of the villa. His favourite was a Spanish dancer, once world-famed for her beauty, who hid herself here so that the world should never know that she was no longer beautiful.

He pictured her coming out of the house at dusk and walking through the garden. Sometimes he was tempted to ask Manuel for the truth, but he resisted the temptation. He preferred his fancies.

After exchanging a few words with Manuel and graciously accepting an orange rosebud, Mr Satterthwaite passed on down the cypress walk to the sea. It was rather wonderful sitting there – on the edge of nothing – with that sheer drop below one. It made him think of Tristan and Isolde, of the beginning of the third act with Tristan and Kurwenal – that lonely waiting and of Isolde rushing up from the sea and Tristan dying in her arms. (No, little Olga would never make an Isolde. Isolde of Cornwall, that Royal hater and Royal lover . . .) He shivered. He felt old, chilly, alone . . . What had he had out of life? Nothing – nothing. Not as much as that dog in the street . . .

It was an unexpected sound that roused him from his reverie. Footsteps coming along the cypress walk were inaudible, the first he knew of somebody's presence was the English monosyllable 'Damn.'

He looked round to find a young man staring at him in obvious surprise and disappointment. Mr Satterthwaite recognized him at once as an arrival of the day before who had more or less intrigued him. Mr Satterthwaite called him a young man – because in comparison to most of the diehards in the Hotel he *was* a young man, but he would certainly never see forty again and was probably drawing appreciably near to his half century. Yet in spite of that, the term young man fitted him – Mr Satterthwaite was usually right about such things – there was an impression of immaturity about him. As there is a touch of puppyhood about many a full grown dog so it was with the stranger.

Mr Satterthwaite thought: 'This chap has really never grown up – not properly, that is.'

And yet there was nothing Peter Pannish about him. He was sleek – almost plump, he had the air of one who has always done himself exceedingly well in the material sense and denied himself no pleasure or satisfaction. He had brown eyes – rather round – fair hair turning grey – a little moustache and rather florid face.

The thing that puzzled Mr Satterthwaite was what had brought him to the island. He could imagine him shooting things, hunting things, playing polo or golf or tennis, making love to pretty women. But in the Island there was nothing to hunt or shoot, no games except Golf-Croquet, and the nearest approach to a pretty woman was represented by elderly Miss Baba Kindersley. There were, of course, artists, to whom the beauty of the scenery made appeal, but Mr Satterthwaite was quite certain that the young man was not an artist. He was clearly marked with the stamp of the Philistine.

While he was resolving these things in his mind, the other spoke, realizing somewhat belatedly that his single ejaculation so far might be open to criticism.

'I beg your pardon,' he said with some embarrassment. 'As a matter of fact, I was – well, startled. I didn't expect anyone to be here.'

He smiled disarmingly. He had a charming smile – friendly – appealing.

'It is rather a lonely spot,' agreed Mr Satterthwaite, as he moved politely a little further up the bench. The other accepted the mute invitation and sat down.

'I don't know about lonely,' he said. 'There always seems to be *someone* here.'

There was a tinge of latent resentment in his voice. Mr Satterthwaite wondered why. He read the other as a friendly soul. Why this insistence on solitude? A rendezvous, perhaps? No – not that. He looked again with carefully veiled scrutiny at his companion. Where had he seen that particular expression before quite lately? That look of dumb bewildered resentment.

'You've been up here before then?' said Mr Satterthwaite, more for the sake of saying something than for anything else.

'I was up here last night – after dinner.'

'Really? I thought the gates were always locked.'

There was a moment's pause and then, almost sullenly, the young man said:

'I climbed over the wall.'

Mr Satterthwaite looked at him with real attention now. He had a sleuthlike habit of mind and he was aware that his companion had only arrived on the preceding afternoon. He had had little time to discover the beauty of the villa by daylight and he had so far spoken to nobody. Yet after dark he had made straight for La Paz. Why? Almost involuntarily Mr Satterthwaite turned his head to look at the green-shuttered villa, but it was as ever serenely lifeless, close shuttered. No, the solution of the mystery was not there.

'And you actually found someone here then?'

The other nodded.

'Yes. Must have been from the other Hotel. He had on fancy dress.'

'Fancy dress?'

'Yes. A kind of Harlequin rig.'

'What?'

The query fairly burst from Mr Satterthwaite's lips. His companion turned to stare at him in surprise.

'They often do have fancy dress shows at the Hotels, I suppose?'

'Oh! quite,' said Mr Satterthwaite. 'Quite, quite, quite.'

He paused breathlessly, then added:

'You must excuse my excitement. Do you happen to know anything about catalysis?'

The young man stared at him.

'Never heard of it. What is it?'

Mr Satterthwaite quoted gravely: '*A chemical reaction depending for its success on the presence of a certain substance which itself remains unchanged.*'

'Oh,' said the young man uncertainly.

'I have a certain friend – his name is Mr Quin, and he can best be described in the terms of catalysis. His presence is a sign that things are going to happen, because when he is there strange revelations come to light, discoveries are made. And yet – he himself takes no part in the proceedings. I have a feeling that it was my friend you met here last night.'

'He's a very sudden sort of chap then. He gave me quite a shock. One minute he wasn't there and the next minute he was! Almost as though he came up out of the sea.'

Mr Satterthwaite looked along the little plateau and down the sheer drop below.

'That's nonsense, of course,' said the other. 'But it's the feeling he gave me. Of course, really, there isn't the foothold for a fly.' He looked over the edge. 'A straight clear drop. If you went over – well, that would be the end right enough.'

'An ideal spot for a murder, in fact,' said Mr Satterthwaite pleasantly.

The other stared at him, almost as though for the moment he did not follow. Then he said vaguely: 'Oh! yes – of course . . .'

He sat there, making little dabs at the ground with his stick and frowning. Suddenly Mr Satterthwaite got the resemblance he had been seeking. That dumb bewildered questioning. *So had the dog looked who was run over.* His eyes and this young man's eyes asked the same pathetic question with the same reproach. '*Oh! world that I have trusted – what have you done to me?*'

He saw other points of resemblance between the two, the same pleasure-loving easy-going existence, the same joyous abandon to the delights of life, the same absence of intellectual questioning. Enough for both to live in the moment – the world was a good place, a place of carnal delights – sun, sea, sky – a discreet garbage heap. And then – what? A car had hit the dog. What had hit the man?

The subject of these cogitations broke in at this point, speaking, however, more to himself than to Mr Satterthwaite.

'One wonders,' he said, 'what it's All For?'

Familiar words – words that usually brought a smile to Mr Satterthwaite's lips, with their unconscious betrayal of the innate egoism of humanity which insists on regarding every manifestation of life as directly designed for its delight or its torment. He did not answer and presently the stranger said with a slight, rather apologetic laugh:

'I've heard it said that every man should build a house, plant a tree and have a son.' He paused and then added: 'I believe I planted an acorn once . . .'

Mr Satterthwaite stirred slightly. His curiosity was aroused – that ever-present interest in the affairs of other people of which the Duchess had accused him was roused. It was not difficult. Mr Satterthwaite had a very feminine side to his nature, he was as good a listener as any woman, and he knew the right moment to put in a prompting word. Presently he was hearing the whole story.

Anthony Cosden, that was the stranger's name, and his life had been much as Mr Satterthwaite had imagined it. He was a bad hand at telling a story but his listener supplied the gaps easily enough. A very ordinary life – an average income, a little soldiering, a good deal of sport when-ever sport offered, plenty of friends, plenty of pleasant things to do, a sufficiency of women. The kind of life that practically inhibits thought of any description and substitutes sensation. To speak frankly, an animal's life. 'But there are worse things than that,' thought Mr Satterthwaite from the depths of his experience. 'Oh! many worse things than that . . .' This world had seemed a very good place to Anthony Cosden. He had grumbled because everyone always grumbled but it had never been a serious grumble. And then – *this*.

He came to it at last – rather vaguely and incoherently. Hadn't felt quite the thing – nothing much. Saw his doctor, and the doctor had persuaded him to go to a Harley Street man. And then – the incredible truth. They'd tried to hedge about it – spoke of great care – a quiet life, but they hadn't been able to disguise that that was all eyewash – letting him down lightly. It boiled down to this – six months. That's what they gave him. Six months.

He turned those bewildered brown eyes on Mr Satterthwaite. It was, of course, rather a shock to a fellow. One didn't – one didn't somehow, know what do *do*.

Mr Satterthwaite nodded gravely and understandingly.

It was a bit difficult to take in all at once, Anthony Cosden went on. How to put in the time. Rather a rotten business waiting about to get pipped. He didn't feel really ill – not yet. Though that might come later, so the specialist had said – in fact, it was bound to. It seemed such nonsense to be going to die when one didn't in the least want to. The best thing, he had thought, would be to carry on as usual. But somehow that hadn't worked.

Here Mr Satterthwaite interrupted him. Wasn't there, he hinted delicately, any woman?

But apparently there wasn't. There were women, of course, but not that kind. His crowd was a very cheery crowd. They didn't, so he implied, like corpses. He didn't wish to make a kind of walking funeral of himself. It would have been embarrassing for everybody. So he had come abroad.

'You came to see these islands? But why?' Mr Satterthwaite was hunting for something, something intangible but delicate that eluded him and yet which he was sure was there. 'You've been here before, perhaps?'

'Yes.' He admitted it almost unwillingly. 'Years ago when I was a youngster.'

And suddenly, almost unconsciously so it seemed, he shot a quick glance backward over his shoulder in the direction of the villa.

'I remembered this place,' he said, nodding at the sea. '*One step to eternity!*'

'And that is why you came up here last night,' finished Mr Satterthwaite calmly.

Anthony Cosden shot him a dismayed glance.

'Oh! I say – really –' he protested.

'Last night you found someone here. This afternoon you have found me. Your life has been saved – twice.'

'You may put it that way if you like – but damn it all, it's *my* life. I've a right to do what I like with it.'

'That is a cliché,' said Mr Satterthwaite wearily.

'Of course I see your point, said Anthony Cosden generously. 'Naturally you've got to say what you can. I'd try to dissuade a fellow myself, even though I knew deep down that he was right. And you know that I'm right. A clean quick end is better than a lingering one – causing trouble and expense and bother to all. In any case it's not as though I had anyone in the world belonging to me . . .'

'If you had –?' said Mr Satterthwaite sharply.

Cosden drew a deep breath.

'I don't know. Even then, I think, this way would be best. But anyway – I haven't . . .'

He stopped abruptly. Mr Satterthwaite eyed him curiously. Incurably romantic, he suggested again that there was, somewhere, some woman. But Cosden negatived it. He oughtn't, he said, to complain. He had had, on the whole, a very good life. It was a pity it was going to be over so soon, that was all. But at any rate he had had, he supposed, everything worth having. Except a son. He would have liked a son. He would like to know now that he had a son living after him. Still, he reiterated the fact, he had had a very good life –

It was at this point that Mr Satterthwaite lost patience. Nobody, he pointed out, who was still in the larval stage, could claim to know anything of life at all. Since the words *larval stage* clearly meant nothing at all to Cosden, he proceeded to make his meaning clearer.

'You have not begun to live yet. You are still at the beginning of life.'

Cosden laughed.

'Why, my hair's grey. I'm forty –'

Mr Satterthwaite interrupted him.

'That has nothing to do with it. Life is a compound of physical and mental experiences. I, for instance, am sixty-nine, and I am really sixty-nine. I have known, either at first or second hand, nearly all the experiences life has to offer. You are like a man who talks of a full year and has seen nothing but snow and ice! The flowers of Spring, the languorous days of Summer, the falling leaves of Autumn – he knows nothing of them – not even that there are such things. And you are going to turn your back on even this opportunity of knowing them.'

'You seem to forget,' said Anthony Cosden dryly, 'that, in any case, I have only six months.'

'Time, like everything else, is relative,' said Mr Satterthwaite. 'That six months might be the longest and most varied experience of your whole life.'

Cosden looked unconvinced.

'In my place,' he said, 'you would do the same.'

Mr Satterthwaite shook his head.

'No,' he said simply. 'In the first place, I doubt if I should have the courage. It needs courage and I am not at all a brave individual. And in the second place –'

'Well?'

'I always want to know what is going to happen tomorrow.'

Cosden rose suddenly with a laugh.

'Well, sir, you've been very good in letting me talk to you. I hardly know why – anyway, there it is. I've said a lot too much. Forget it.'

'And tomorrow, when an accident is reported, I am to leave it at that? To make no suggestion of suicide?'

'That's as you like. I'm glad you realize one thing – that you can't prevent me.'

'My dear young man,' said Mr Satterthwaite placidly, 'I can hardly attach myself to you like the proverbial limpet. Sooner or later you would give me the slip and accomplish your purpose. But you are frustrated at any rate for this afternoon. You would hardly like to go to your death leaving me under the possible imputation of having pushed you over.'

'That is true,' said Cosden. 'If you insist on remaining here –'

'I do,' said Mr Satterthwaite firmly.

Cosden laughed good-humouredly.

'Then the plan must be deferred for the moment. In which case I will go back to the hotel. See you later perhaps.'

Mr Satterthwaite was left looking at the sea.

'And now,' he said to himself softly, 'what next? There must be a next. I wonder . . .'

He got up. For a while he stood at the edge of the plateau looking down on the dancing water beneath. But he found no inspiration there, and turning slowly he walked back along the path between the cypresses and into the quiet garden. He looked at the shuttered, peaceful house and he wondered, as he had often wondered before, who had lived there and what had taken place within those placid walls. On a sudden impulse he walked up some crumbling stone steps and laid a hand on one of the faded green shutters.

To his surprise it swung back at his touch. He hesitated a moment, then pushed it boldly open. The next minute he stepped back with a little exclamation of dismay. A woman stood in the window facing him. She wore black and had a black lace mantilla draped over her head.

Mr Satterthwaite floundered wildly in Italian interspersed with German – the nearest he could get in the hurry of the moment to Spanish. He was desolated and ashamed, he explained haltingly. The Signora must forgive. He thereupon retreated hastily, the woman not having spoken one word.

He was halfway across the courtyard when she spoke – two sharp words like a pistol crack.

'Come back!'

It was a barked-out command such as might have been addressed to a dog, yet so absolute was the authority it conveyed, that Mr Satterthwaite had swung round hurriedly and trotted back to the window almost automatically before it occurred to him to feel any resentment. He obeyed like a dog. The woman was still standing motionless at the window. She looked him up and down appraising him with perfect calmness.

'You are English,' she said. 'I thought so.'

Mr Satterthwaite started off on a second apology.

'If I had known you were English,' he said, 'I could have expressed myself better just now. I offer my most sincere apologies for my rudeness in trying the shutter. I am afraid I can plead no excuse save curiosity. I had a great wish to see what the inside of this charming house was like.'

She laughed suddenly, a deep, rich laugh.

'If you really want to see it,' she said, 'you had better come in.'

She stood aside, and Mr Satterthwaite, feeling pleasurably excited, stepped into the room. It was dark, since the shutters of the other windows were closed, but he could see that it was scantily and rather shabbily furnished and that the dust lay thick everywhere.

'Not here,' she said. 'I do not use this room.'

She led the way and he followed her, out of the room across a passage and into a room the other side. Here the windows gave on the sea and the sun streamed in. The furniture, like that of the other room, was poor in quality, but there were some worn rugs that had been good in their time, a large screen of Spanish leather and bowls of fresh flowers.

'You will have tea with me,' said Mr Satterthwaite's hostess. She added reassuringly: 'It is perfectly good tea and will be made with boiling water.'

She went out of the door and called out something in Spanish, then she returned and sat down on a sofa opposite her guest. For the first time, Mr Satterthwaite was able to study her appearance.

The first effect she had upon him was to make him feel even more grey and shrivelled and elderly than usual by contrast with her own forceful personality. She was a tall woman, very sunburnt, dark and handsome though no longer young. When she was in the room the sun seemed to be shining twice as brightly as when she was out of it, and presently a curious feeling of warmth and aliveness began to steal over Mr Satterthwaite. It was as though he stretched out thin, shrivelled hands to a reassuring flame. He thought, 'She's so much vitality herself that she's got a lot left over for other people.'

He recalled the command in her voice when she had stopped him, and wished that his protégée, Olga, could be imbued with a little of that force. He thought: 'What an Isolde she'd make! And yet she probably hasn't got the ghost of a singing voice. Life is badly arranged.' He was, all the same, a little afraid of her. He did not like domineering women.

She had clearly been considering him as she sat with her chin in her hands, making no pretence about it. At last she nodded as though she had made up her mind.

'I am glad you came,' she said at last. 'I needed someone very badly to talk to this afternoon. And you are used to that, aren't you?'

'I don't quite understand.'

'I meant people tell you things. You knew what I meant! Why pretend?'

'Well – perhaps –'

She swept on, regardless of anything he had been going to say.

'One could say anything to you. That is because you are half a woman. You know what we feel – what we think – the queer, queer things we do.'

Her voice died away. Tea was brought by a large, smiling Spanish girl. It was good tea – China – Mr Satterthwaite sipped it appreciatively.

'You live here?' he inquired conversationally.

'Yes.'

'But not altogether. The house is usually shut up, is it not? At least so I have been told.'

'I am here a good deal, more than anyone knows. I only use these rooms.'

'You have had the house long?'

'It has belonged to me for twenty-two years – and I lived here for a year before that.'

Mr Satterthwaite said rather inanely (or so he felt): 'That is a very long time.'

'The year? Or the twenty-two years?'

His interest stirred, Mr Satterthwaite said gravely: 'That depends.'

She nodded.

'Yes, it depends. They are two separate periods. They have nothing to do with each other. Which is long? Which is short? Even now I cannot say.'

She was silent for a minute, brooding. Then she said with a little smile:

'It is such a long time since I have talked with anyone – such a long time! I do not apologize. You came to my shutter. You wished to look through my window. And that is what you are always doing, is it not? Pushing aside the shutter and looking through the window into the truth of people's lives. If they will let you. And often if they will not let you! It would be difficult to hide anything from you. You would guess – and guess right.'

Mr Satterthwaite had an odd impulse to be perfectly sincere.

'I am sixty-nine,' he said. 'Everything I know of life I know at second hand. Sometimes that is very bitter to me. And yet, because of it, I know a good deal.'

She nodded thoughtfully.

'I know. Life is very strange. I cannot imagine what it must be like to be that – always a looker-on.'

Her tone was wondering. Mr Satterthwaite smiled.

'No, you would not know. Your place is in the centre of the stage. You will always be the Prima Donna.'

'What a curious thing to say.'

'But I am right. Things have happened to you – will always happen to you. Sometimes, I think, there have been tragic things. Is that so?'

Her eyes narrowed. She looked across at him.

'If you are here long, somebody will tell you of the English swimmer who was drowned at the foot of this cliff. They will tell you how young and strong he was, how handsome, and they will tell you that his young wife looked down from the top of the cliff and saw him drowning.'

'Yes, I have already heard that story.'

'That man was my husband. This was his villa. He brought me out here with him when I was eighteen, and a year later he died – driven by the surf on the black rocks, cut and bruised and mutilated, battered to death.'

Mr Satterthwaite gave a shocked exclamation. She leant forward, her burning eyes focused on his face.

'You spoke of tragedy. Can you imagine a greater tragedy than that? For a young wife, only a year married, to stand helpless while the man she loved fought for his life – and lost it – horribly.'

'Terrible,' said Mr Satterthwaite. He spoke with real emotion. 'Terrible. I agree with you. Nothing in life could be so dreadful.'

Suddenly she laughed. Her head went back.

'You are wrong,' she said. 'There is something more terrible. And that is for a young wife to stand there and hope and long for her husband to drown . . .'

'But good God,' cried Mr Satterthwaite, 'you don't mean –?'

'Yes, I do. That's what it was really. I knelt there – knelt down on the cliff and prayed. The Spanish servants thought I was praying for his life to be saved. I wasn't. I was praying that I might wish him to be spared. I was saying one thing over and over again, "God, help me not to wish him dead. God, help me not to wish him dead." But it wasn't any good. All the time I hoped – hoped – and my hope came true.'

She was silent for a minute or two and then she said very gently in quite a different voice:

'That is a terrible thing, isn't it? It's the sort of thing one can't forget. I was terribly happy when I knew he was really dead and couldn't come back to torture me any more.'

'My child,' said Mr Satterthwaite, shocked.

'I know. I was too young to have that happen to me. Those things should happen to one when one is older – when one is more prepared for – for beastliness. Nobody knew, you know, what he was really like. I thought he was wonderful when I first met him and was so happy and proud when he asked me to marry him. But things went wrong almost at once. He was angry with me – nothing I could do pleased him – and yet I tried so hard. And then he began to like hurting me. And above all to terrify me. That's what he enjoyed most. He thought out all sorts of things . . . dreadful things. I won't tell you. I suppose, really, he must have been a little mad. I was alone here, in his power, and cruelty began to be his hobby.' Her eyes widened and darkened. 'The worst was my baby. I was going to have a baby. Because of some of the things he did to me – it was born dead. My little baby. I nearly died, too – but I didn't. I wish I had.'

Mr Satterthwaite made an inarticulate sound.

'And then I was delivered – in the way I've told you. Some girls who were staying at the hotel dared him. That's how it happened. All the Spaniards told him it was madness to risk the sea just there. But he was very vain – he wanted to show off. And I – I saw him drown – and was glad. God oughtn't to let such things happen.'

Mr Satterthwaite stretched out his little dry hand and took hers. She squeezed it hard as a child might have done. The maturity had fallen away from her face. He saw her without difficulty as she had been at nineteen.

'At first it seemed too good to be true. The house was mine and I could live in it. And no one could hurt me any more! I was an orphan, you know, I had no near relations, no one to care what became of me. That simplified things. I lived on here – in this villa – and it seemed like Heaven. Yes, like Heaven. I've never been so happy since, and never shall again. Just to wake up and know that everything was all right – no pain, no terror, no wondering what he was going to do to me next. Yes, it was Heaven.'

She paused a long time, and Mr Satterthwaite said at last:

'And then?'

'I suppose human beings aren't ever satisfied. At first, just being free was enough. But after a while I began to get – well, lonely, I suppose. I began to think about my baby that died. If only I had had my baby! I wanted it as a baby, and also as a plaything. I wanted dreadfully something or someone to play with. It sounds silly and childish, but there it was.'

'I understand,' said Mr Satterthwaite gravely.

'It's difficult to explain the next bit. It just – well, happened, you see. There was a young Englishman staying at the hotel. He strayed in the garden by mistake. I was wearing Spanish dress and he took me for a Spanish girl. I thought it would be rather fun to pretend I was one, so I played up. His Spanish was very bad but he could just manage a little. I told him the villa belonged to an English lady who was away. I said she had taught me a little English and I pretended to speak broken English. It was such fun – such fun – even now I can remember what fun it was. He began to make love to me. We agreed to pretend that the villa was our home, that we were just married and coming to live there. I suggested that we should try one of the shutters – the one you tried this evening. It was open and inside the room was dusty and uncared for. We crept in. It was exciting and wonderful. We pretended it was our own house.'

She broke off suddenly, looked appealingly at Mr Satterthwaite.

'It all seemed lovely – like a fairy tale. And the lovely thing about it, to me, was that it wasn't true. It wasn't real.'

Mr Satterthwaite nodded. He saw her, perhaps more clearly than she saw herself – that frightened, lonely child entranced with her make believe that was so safe because it wasn't real.

'He was, I suppose, a very ordinary young man. Out for adventure, but quite sweet about it. We went on pretending.'

She stopped, looked at Mr Satterthwaite and said again:

'You understand? We went on pretending . . .'

She went on again in a minute.

'He came up again the next morning to the villa. I saw him from my bedroom through the shutter. Of course he didn't dream I was inside. He still thought I was a little Spanish peasant girl. He stood there looking about him. He'd asked me to meet him. I'd said I would but I never meant to.

'He just stood there looking worried. I think he was worried about me. It was nice of him to be worried about me. He *was* nice . . .'

She paused again.

'The next day he left. I've never seen him again.

'My baby was born nine months later. I was wonderfully happy all the time. To be able to have a baby so peacefully, with no one to hurt you or make you miserable. I wished I'd remembered to ask my English boy his Christian name. I would have called the baby after him. It seemed unkind not to. It seemed rather unfair. He'd given me the thing I wanted most in the world, and he would never even know about it! But of course I told myself that he wouldn't look at it that way – that to know would probably only worry and annoy him. I had been just a passing amusement for him, that was all.'

'And the baby?' asked Mr Satterthwaite.

'He was splendid. I called him John. Splendid. I wish you could see him now. He's twenty. He's going to be a mining engineer. He's been the best and dearest son in the world to me. I told him his father had died before he was born.'

Mr Satterthwaite stared at her. A curious story. And somehow, a story that was not completely told. There was, he felt sure, something else.

'Twenty years is a long time,' he said thoughtfully. 'You've never contemplated marrying again?'

She shook her head. A slow, burning blush spread over her tanned cheeks.

'The child was enough for you – always?'

She looked at him. Her eyes were softer than he had yet seen them.

'Such queer things happen!' she murmured. 'Such queer things . . . You wouldn't believe them – no, I'm wrong, *you* might, perhaps. I didn't love John's father, not at the time. I don't think I even knew what love was. I assumed, as a matter of course, that the child would be like me. But he wasn't. He mightn't have been my child at all. He was like his father – he was like no one but his father. I learnt to know that man – through his child. Through the child, I learnt to love him. I love him now. I always shall love him. You may say that it's imagination, that I've built up an ideal, but it isn't so. I love the man, the real, human man. I'd know him if I saw him tomorrow – even though it's over twenty years since we met. Loving him has made me into a woman. I love him as a woman loves a man. For twenty years I've lived loving him. I shall die loving him.'

She stopped abruptly – then challenged her listener.

'Do you think I'm mad – to say these strange things?'

'Oh! my dear,' said Mr Satterthwaite. He took her hand again.

'You do understand?'

'I think I do. But there's something more, isn't there? Something that you haven't yet told me?'

Her brow clouded over.

'Yes, there's something. It was clever of you to guess. I knew at once you weren't the sort one can hide things from. But I don't want to tell you – and the reason I don't want to tell you is because it's best for you not to know.'

He looked at her. Her eyes met his bravely and defiantly.

He said to himself: 'This is the test. All the clues are in my hand. I ought to be able to know. If I reason rightly I shall know.'

There was a pause, then he said slowly:

'Something's gone wrong.' He saw her eyelids give the faintest quiver and knew himself to be on the right track.

'Something's gone wrong – suddenly – after all these years.' He felt himself groping – groping – in the dark recesses of her mind where she was trying to hide her secret from him.

'The boy – it's got to do with him. You wouldn't mind about anything else.'

He heard the very faint gasp she gave and knew he had probed correctly. A cruel business but necessary. It was her will against his. She had got a dominant, ruthless will, but he too had a will hidden beneath his meek manners. And he had behind him the Heaven-sent assurance of a man who is doing his proper job. He felt a passing contemptuous pity for men whose business it was to track down such crudities as crime. This detective business of the mind, this assembling of clues, this delving for the truth, this wild joy as one drew nearer to the goal . . . Her very passion to keep the truth from him helped her. He felt her stiffen defiantly as he drew nearer and nearer.

'It is better for me not to know, you say. Better for *me*? But you are not a very considerate woman. You would not shrink from putting a stranger to a little temporary inconvenience. It is more than that, then? If you tell me you make me an accomplice before the fact. That sounds like crime. Fantastic! I could not associate crime with you. Or only one sort of crime. A crime against yourself.'

Her lids drooped in spite of herself, veiled her eyes. He leaned forward and caught her wrist.

'It *is* that, then! You are thinking of taking your life.'

She gave a low cry.

'How did you know? How did you know?'

'But why? You are not tired of life. I never saw a woman less tired of it – more radiantly alive.'

She got up, went to the window, pushing back a strand of her dark hair as she did so.

'Since you have guessed so much I might as well tell you the truth. I should not have let you in this evening. I might have known that you would see too much. You are that kind of man. You were right about the cause. It's the boy. He knows nothing. But last time he was home, he spoke tragically of a friend of his, and I discovered something. If he finds out that he is illegitimate it will break his heart. He is proud – horribly proud! There is a girl. Oh! I won't go into details. But he is coming very soon – and he wants to know all about his father – he wants details. The girl's parents, naturally, want to know. When he discovers the truth, he will break with her, exile himself, ruin his life. Oh! I know the things you would say. He is young, foolish, wrong-headed to take it like that! All true, perhaps. But does it matter what people ought to be? They are what they are. *It will break his heart* . . . But if, before he comes, there has been an accident, everything will be swallowed up in grief for me. He will look through my papers, find nothing, and be annoyed that I told him so little. But he will not suspect the truth. It is the best way. One must pay for happiness, and I have had so much – oh! so much happiness. And in reality the price will be easy, too. A little courage – to take the leap – perhaps a moment or so of anguish.'

'But, my dear child –'

'Don't argue with me.' She flared round on him. 'I won't listen to conventional arguments. My life is my own. Up to now, it has been needed – for John. But he needs it no longer. He wants a mate – a companion – he will turn to her all the more willingly because I am no longer there. My life is useless, but my death will be of use. And I have the right to do what I like with my own life.'

'Are you sure?'

The sternness of his tone surprised her. She stammered slightly.

'If it is no good to anyone – and I am the best judge of that –'

He interrupted her again.

'Not necessarily.'

'What do you mean?'

'Listen. I will put a case to you. A man comes to a certain place – to commit suicide, shall we say? But by chance he finds another man there, so he fails in his purpose and goes away – to live. The second man has saved the first man's life, not by being necessary to him or prominent in his life, but just by the mere physical fact of having been in a certain place at a certain moment. You take your life today and perhaps, some five, six, seven years hence, someone will go to death or disaster simply for lack of your presence in a given spot or place. It may be a runaway horse coming down a street that swerved aside at sight of you and so fails to trample a child that is playing in the gutter. That child may live to grow up and be a great musician, or discover a cure for cancer. Or it may be less melodramatic than that. He may just grow up to ordinary everyday happiness . . .'

She stared at him.

'You are a strange man. These things you say – I have never thought of them . . .'

'You say your life is your own,' went on Mr Satterthwaite. 'But can you dare to ignore the chance that you are taking part in a gigantic drama under the orders of a divine Producer? Your cue may not come till the end of the play – it may be totally unimportant, a mere walking-on part, but upon it may hang the issues of the play if you do not give the cue to another player. The whole edifice may crumple. You as you, may not matter to anyone in the world, but you as a person in a particular place may matter unimaginably.'

She sat down, still staring.

'What do you want me to do?' she said simply.

It was Mr Satterthwaite's moment of triumph. He issued orders.

'I want you at least to promise me one thing – to do nothing rash for twenty-four hours.'

She was silent for a moment or two and then she said: 'I promise.'

'There is one other thing – a favour.'

'Yes?'

'Leave the shutter of the room I came in by unfastened, and keep vigil there tonight.'

She looked at him curiously, but nodded assent.

'And now,' said Mr Satterthwaite, slightly conscious of anticlimax, 'I really must be going. God bless you, my dear.'

He made a rather embarrassed exit. The stalwart Spanish girl met him in the passage and opened a side door for him, staring curiously at him the while.

It was just growing dark as he reached the hotel. There was a solitary figure sitting on the terrace. Mr Satterthwaite made straight for it. He was excited and his heart was beating quite fast. He felt that tremendous issues lay in his hands. One false move –

But he tried to conceal his agitation and to speak naturally and casually to Anthony Cosden.

'A warm evening,' he observed. 'I quite lost count of time sitting up there on the cliff.'

'Have you been up there all this time?'

Mr Satterthwaite nodded. The swing door into the hotel opened to let someone through, and a beam of light fell suddenly on the other's face, illuminating its look of dull suffering, of uncomprehending dumb endurance.

Mr Satterthwaite thought to himself: 'It's worse for him than it would be for me. Imagination, conjecture, speculation – they can do a lot for you. You can, as it were, ring the changes upon pain. The uncomprehending blind suffering of an animal – that's terrible . . .'

Cosden spoke suddenly in a harsh voice.

'I'm going for a stroll after dinner. You – you understand? The third time's lucky. For God's sake don't interfere. I know your interference will be well-meaning and all that – but take it from me, it's useless.'

Mr Satterthwaite drew himself up.

'I never interfere,' he said, thereby giving the lie to the whole purpose and object of his existence.

'I know what you think –' went on Cosden, but he was interrupted.

'You must excuse me, but there I beg to differ from you,' said Mr Satterthwaite. 'Nobody knows what another person is thinking. They may imagine they do, but they are nearly always wrong.'

'Well, perhaps that's so.' Cosden was doubtful, slightly taken aback.

'Thought is yours only,' said his companion. 'Nobody can alter or influence the use you mean to make of it. Let us talk of a less painful subject. That old villa, for instance. It has a curious charm, withdrawn, sheltered from the world, shielding heaven knows what mystery. It tempted me to do a doubtful action. I tried one of the shutters.'

'You did?' Cosden turned his head sharply. 'But it was fastened, of course?'

'No,' said Mr Satterthwaite. 'It was open.' He added gently: 'The third shutter from the end.'

'Why,' Cosden burst out, 'that was the one –'

He broke off suddenly, but Mr Satterthwaite had seen the light that had sprung up in his eyes. He rose – satisfied.

Some slight tinge of anxiety still remained with him. Using his favourite metaphor of a drama, he hoped that he had spoken his few lines correctly. For they were very important lines.

But thinking it over, his artistic judgment was satisfied. On his way up to the cliff, Cosden would try that shutter. It was not in human nature to resist. A memory of twenty odd years ago had brought him to this spot, the same memory would take him to the shutter. And afterwards?

'I shall know in the morning,' said Mr Satterthwaite, and proceeded to change methodically for his evening meal.

It was somewhere round ten o'clock that Mr Satterthwaite set foot once more in the garden of La Paz. Manuel bade him a smiling 'Good morning,' and handed him a single rosebud which Mr Satterthwaite put carefully into his buttonhole. Then he went on to the house. He stood there for some minutes looking up at the peaceful white walls, the trailing orange creeper, and the faded green shutters. So silent, so peaceful. Had the whole thing been a dream?

But at that moment one of the windows opened and the lady who occupied Mr Satterthwaite's thoughts came out. She came straight to him with a buoyant swaying walk, like someone carried on a great wave of exultation. Her eyes were shining, her colour high. She looked like a figure of joy on a frieze. There was no hesitation about her, no doubts or tremors. Straight to Mr Satterthwaite she came, put her hands on his shoulders and kissed him – not once but many times. Large, dark, red roses, very velvety – that is how he thought of it afterwards. Sunshine, summer, birds singing – that was the atmosphere into which he felt himself caught up. Warmth, joy and tremendous vigour.

'I'm so happy,' she said. 'You darling! How did you know? How *could* you know? You're like the good magician in the fairy tales.'

She paused, a sort of breathlessness of happiness upon her.

'We're going over today – to the Consul – to get married. When John comes, his father will be there. We'll tell him there was some misunderstanding in the past. Oh! he won't ask questions. Oh! I'm so happy – so happy – so happy.'

Happiness did indeed surge from her like a tide. It lapped round Mr Satterthwaite in a warm exhilarating flood.

'It's so wonderful to Anthony to find he has a son. I never dreamt he'd mind or care.' She looked confidently into Mr Satterthwaite's eyes. 'Isn't it strange how things come right and end all beautifully?'

He had his clearest vision of her yet. A child – still a child – with her love of make believe – her fairy tales that ended beautifully with two people 'living happily ever afterwards'.

He said gently:

'If you bring this man of yours happiness in these last months, you will indeed have done a very beautiful thing.'

Her eyes opened wide – surprised.

'Oh!' she said. 'You don't think I'd let him die, do you? After all these years – when he's come to me. I've known lots of people whom doctors have given up and who are alive today. Die? Of course he's not going to die!'

He looked at her – her strength, her beauty, her vitality – her indomitable courage and will. He, too, had known doctors to be mistaken . . . The personal factor – you never knew how much and how little it counted.

She said again, with scorn and amusement in her voice:

'You don't think I'd let him die, do you?'

'No,' said Mr Satterthwaite at last very gently. 'Somehow, my dear, I don't think you will . . .'

Then at last he walked down the cypress path to the bench over-looking the sea and found there the person he was expecting to see. Mr Quin rose and greeted him – the same as ever, dark, saturnine, smiling and sad.

'You expected me?' he asked.

And Mr Satterthwaite answered: 'Yes, I expected you.'

They sat together on the bench.

'I have an idea that you have been playing Providence once more, to judge by your expression,' said Mr Quin presently.

Mr Satterthwaite looked at him reproachfully.

'As if you didn't know all about it.'

'You always accuse me of omniscience,' said Mr Quin, smiling.

'If you know nothing, why were you here the night before last – waiting?' countered Mr Satterthwaite.

'Oh, that –?'

'Yes, that.'

'I had a – commission to perform.'

'For whom?'

'You have sometimes fancifully named me an advocate for the dead.'

'The dead?' said Mr Satterthwaite, a little puzzled. 'I don't under-stand.'

Mr Quin pointed a long, lean finger down at the blue depths below.

'A man was drowned down there twenty-two years ago.'

'I know – but I don't see –'

'Supposing that, after all, that man loved his young wife. Love can make devils of men as well as angels. She had a girlish adoration for him, but he could never touch the womanhood in her – and that drove him mad. He tortured her because he loved her. Such things happen. You know that as well as I do.'

'Yes,' admitted Mr Satterthwaite, 'I have seen such things – but rarely – very rarely . . .'

'And you have also seen, more commonly, that there is such a thing as remorse – the desire to make amends – at all costs to make amends.'

'Yes, but death came too soon . . .'

'Death!' There was contempt in Mr Quin's voice. 'You believe in a life after death, do you not? And who are you to say that the same wishes, the same desires, may not operate in that other life? If the desire is strong enough – a messenger may be found.'

His voice tailed away.

Mr Satterthwaite got up, trembling a little.

'I must get back to the hotel,' he said. 'If you are going that way.'

But Mr Quin shook his head.

'No,' he said. 'I shall go back the way I came.'

When Mr Satterthwaite looked back over his shoulder, he saw his friend walking towards the edge of the cliff.

The Voice in the Dark

'The Voice in the Dark' was first published in the USA in *Flynn's Weekly*, 4 December 1926, and then as 'The Magic of Mr Quin No. 4' in *Storyteller* magazine, March 1927.

'I am a little worried about Margery,' said Lady Stranleigh.

'My girl, you know,' she added.

She sighed pensively.

'It makes one feel terribly old to have a grown-up daughter.'

Mr Satterthwaite, who was the recipient of these confidences, rose to the occasion gallantly.

'No one could believe it possible,' he declared with a little bow.

'Flatterer,' said Lady Stranleigh, but she said it vaguely and it was clear that her mind was elsewhere.

Mr Satterthwaite looked at the slender white-clad figure in some admiration. The Cannes sunshine was searching, but Lady Stranleigh came through the test very well. At a distance the youthful effect was really extraordinary. One almost wondered if she were grown-up or not. Mr Satterthwaite, who knew everything, knew that it was perfectly possible for Lady Stranleigh to have grown-up grandchildren. She represented the extreme triumph of art over nature. Her figure was marvellous, her complexion was marvellous. She had enriched many beauty parlours and certainly the results were astounding.

Lady Stranleigh lit a cigarette, crossed her beautiful legs encased in the finest of nude silk stockings and murmured: 'Yes, I really am rather worried about Margery.'

'Dear me,' said Mr Satterthwaite, 'what is the trouble?'

Lady Stranleigh turned her beautiful blue eyes upon him

'You have never met her, have you? She is Charles' daughter,' she added helpfully.

If entries in 'Who's Who' were strictly truthful, the entries concerning

Lady Stranleigh might have ended as follows: *hobbies: getting married.* She had floated through life shedding husbands as she went. She had lost three by divorce and one by death.

'If she had been Rudolph's child I could have understood it,' mused Lady Stranleigh. 'You remember Rudolf? He was always temperamental. Six months after we married I had to apply for those queer things – what do they call them? Conjugal what nots, you know what I mean. Thank goodness it is all much simpler nowadays. I remember I had to write him the silliest kind of letter – my lawyer practically dictated it to me. Asking him to come back, you know, and that I would do all I could, etc., etc., but you never could count on Rudolf, he was so temperamental. He came rushing home at once, which was quite the wrong thing to do, and not at all what the lawyers meant.'

She sighed.

'About Margery?' suggested Mr Satterthwaite, tactfully leading her back to the subject under discussion.

'Of course. I was just going to tell you, wasn't I? Margery has been seeing things, or hearing them. Ghosts, you know, and all that. I should never have thought that Margery could be so imaginative. She is a dear good girl, always has been, but just a shade – dull.'

'Impossible,' murmured Mr Satterthwaite with a confused idea of being complimentary.

'In fact, very dull,' said Lady Stranleigh. 'Doesn't care for dancing, or cocktails or any of the things a young girl ought to care about. She much prefers staying at home to hunt instead of coming out here with me.'

'Dear, dear,' said Mr Satterthwaite, 'she wouldn't come out with you, you say?'

'Well, I didn't exactly press her. Daughters have a depressing effect upon one, I find.'

Mr Satterthwaite tried to think of Lady Stranleigh accompanied by a serious-minded daughter and failed.

'I can't help wondering if Margery is going off her head,' continued Margery's mother in a cheerful voice. 'Hearing voices is a very bad sign, so they tell me. It is not as though Abbot's Mede were haunted. The old building was burnt to the ground in 1836, and they put up a kind of early Victorian château which simply cannot be haunted. It is much too ugly and common-place.'

Mr Satterthwaite coughed. He was wondering why he was being told all this.

'I thought perhaps,' said Lady Stranleigh, smiling brilliantly upon him, 'that *you* might be able to help me.'

'I?'

'Yes. You are going back to England tomorrow, aren't you?'

'I am. Yes, that is so,' admitted Mr Satterthwaite cautiously.

'And you know all these psychical research people. Of course you do, you know everybody.'

Mr Satterthwaite smiled a little. It was one of his weaknesses to know everybody.

'So what can be simpler?' continued Lady Stranleigh. 'I never get on with that sort of person. You know – earnest men with beards and usually spectacles. They bore me terribly and I am quite at my worst with them.'

Mr Satterthwaite was rather taken aback. Lady Stranleigh continued to smile at him brilliantly.

'So that is all settled, isn't it?' she said brightly. 'You will go down to Abbot's Mede and see Margery, and make all the arrangements. I shall be terribly grateful to you. Of course if Margery is *really* going off her head, I will come home. Ah! here is Bimbo.'

Her smile from being brilliant became dazzling.

A young man in white tennis flannels was approaching them. He was about twenty-five years of age and extremely good-looking.

The young man said simply:

'I have been looking for you everywhere, Babs.'

'What has the tennis been like?'

'Septic.'

Lady Stranleigh rose. She turned her head over her shoulder and murmured in dulcet tones to Mr Satterthwaite: 'It is simply marvellous of you to help me. I shall never forget it.'

Mr Satterthwaite looked after the retreating couple.

'I wonder,' he mused to himself, 'If Bimbo is going to be No. 5.'

The conductor of the Train de Luxe was pointing out to Mr Satterthwaite where an accident on the line had occurred a few years previously. As he finished his spirited narrative, the other looked up and saw a well-known face smiling at him over the conductor's shoulder.

'My dear Mr Quin,' said Mr Satterthwaite.

His little withered face broke into smiles.

'What a coincidence! That we should both be returning to England on the same train. You are going there, I suppose.'

'Yes,' said Mr Quin. 'I have business there of rather an important nature. Are you taking the first service of dinner?'

'I always do so. Of course, it is an absurd time – half-past six, but one runs less risk with the cooking.'

Mr Quin nodded comprehendingly.

'I also,' he said. 'We might perhaps arrange to sit together.'

Half-past six found Mr Quin and Mr Satterthwaite established opposite each other at a small table in the dining-car. Mr Satterthwaite gave due attention to the wine list and then turned to his companion.

'I have not seen you since – ah, yes not since Corsica. You left very suddenly that day.'

Mr Quin shrugged his shoulders.

'Not more so than usual. I come and go, you know. I come and go.'

The words seemed to awake some echo of remembrance in Mr Satterthwaite's mind. A little shiver passed down his spine – not a disagreeable sensation, quite the contrary. He was conscious of a pleasurable sense of anticipation.

Mr Quin was holding up a bottle of red wine, examining the label on it. The bottle was between him and the light but for a minute or two a red glow enveloped his person.

Mr Satterthwaite felt again that sudden stir of excitement.

'I too have a kind of mission in England,' he remarked, smiling broadly at the remembrance. 'You know Lady Stranleigh perhaps?'

Mr Quin shook his head.

'It is an old title,' said Mr Satterthwaite, 'a very old title. One of the few that can descend in the female line. She is a Baroness in her own right. Rather a romantic history really.'

Mr Quin settled himself more comfortably in his chair. A waiter, flying down the swinging car, deposited cups of soup before them as if by a miracle. Mr Quin sipped it cautiously.

'You are about to give me one of those wonderful descriptive portraits of yours,' he murmured, 'that is so, is it not?'

Mr Satterthwaite beamed on him.

'She is really a marvellous woman,' he said. 'Sixty, you know – yes, I should say at least sixty. I knew them as girls, she and her sister. Beatrice, that was the name of the elder one. Beatrice and Barbara. I remember them as the Barron girls. Both good-looking and in those days very hard up. But that was a great many years ago – why, dear me, I was a young man myself then.' Mr Satterthwaite sighed. 'There were several lives then between them and the title. Old Lord Stranleigh was a first cousin once removed, I think. Lady Stranleigh's life has been quite a romantic affair. Three unexpected deaths – two of the old man's brothers and a nephew. Then there was the "Uralia". You remember the wreck of the "Uralia"? She went down off the coast of New Zealand. The Barron girls were on board. Beatrice was drowned. This one, Barbara, was amongst the few survivors. Six months later, old Stranleigh died and she succeeded to the title and came into a considerable fortune. Since then she has lived for one thing only – herself! She has always been the same, beautiful, unscrupulous, completely callous, interested solely in herself. She has had four husbands, and I have no doubt could get a fifth in a minute.'

He went on to describe the mission with which he had been entrusted by Lady Stranleigh.

'I thought of running down to Abbot's Mede to see the young lady,' he explained. 'I – I feel that something ought to be done about the matter. It is impossible to think of Lady Stranleigh as an ordinary mother.' He stopped, looking across the table at Mr Quin.

'I wish you would come with me,' he said wistfully. 'Would it not be possible?'

'I'm afraid not,' said Mr Quin. 'But let me see, Abbot's Mede is in Wiltshire, is it not?'

Mr Satterthwaite nodded.

'I thought as much. As it happens, I shall be staying not far from Abbot's Mede, at a place you and I both know.' He smiled. 'You remember that little inn, the "Bells and Motley"?'

'Of course,' cried Mr Satterthwaite; 'you will be there?'

Mr Quin nodded. 'For a week or ten days. Possibly longer. If you will come and look me up one day, I shall be delighted to see you.'

And somehow or other Mr Satterthwaite felt strangely comforted by the assurance.

'My dear Miss – er – Margery,' said Mr Satterthwaite, 'I assure you that I should not dream of laughing at you.'

Margery Gale frowned a little. They were sitting in the large comfortable hall of Abbot's Mede. Margery Gale was a big squarely built girl. She bore no resemblance to her mother, but took entirely after her father's side of the family, a line of hard-riding country squires. She looked fresh and wholesome and the picture of sanity. Nevertheless, Mr Satterthwaite was reflecting to himself that the Barrons as a family were all inclined to mental instability. Margery might have inherited her physical appearance from her father and at the same time have inherited some mental kink from her mother's side of the family.

'I wish,' said Margery, 'that I could get rid of that Casson woman. I don't believe in spiritualism, and I don't like it. She is one of these silly women that run a craze to death. She is always bothering me to have a medium down here.'

Mr Satterthwaite coughed, fidgeted a little in his chair and then said in a judicial manner:

'Let me be quite sure that I have all the facts. The first of the – er – phenomena occurred two months ago, I understand?'

'About that,' agreed the girl. 'Sometimes it was a whisper and some-times it was quite a clear voice but it always said much the same thing.'

'Which was?'

'*Give back what is not yours. Give back what you have stolen.* On each occasion I switched on the light, but the room was quite empty and there was no one there. In the end I got so nervous that I got Clayton, mother's maid, to sleep on the sofa in my room.'

'And the voice came just the same?'

'Yes – and this is what frightens me – Clayton did not hear it.'

Mr Satterthwaite reflected for a minute or two.

'Did it come loudly or softly that evening?'

'It was almost a whisper,' admitted Margery. 'If Clayton was sound asleep I suppose she would not really have heard it. She wanted me to see a doctor.' The girl laughed bitterly.

'But since last night even Clayton believes,' she continued.

'What happened last night?'

'I am just going to tell you. I have told no one as yet. I had been out hunting yesterday and we had had a long run. I was dead tired, and slept very heavily. I dreamt – a horrible dream – that I had fallen over some iron railings and that one of the spikes was entering slowly into my throat. I woke to find that it was true – there was some sharp point pressing into the side of my neck, and at the same time a voice was murmuring softly: "*You have stolen what is mine. This is death.*"

'I screamed,' continued Margery, 'and clutched at the air, but there was nothing there. Clayton heard me scream from the room next door where she was sleeping. She came rushing in, and she distinctly felt some-thing brushing past her in the darkness, but she says that whatever that something was, it was not anything human.'

Mr Satterthwaite stared at her. The girl was obviously very shaken and upset. He noticed on the left side of her throat a small square of sticking plaster. She caught the direction of his gaze and nodded.

'Yes,' she said, 'it was not imagination, you see.'

Mr Satterthwaite put a question almost apologetically, it sounded so melodramatic.

'You don't know of anyone – er – who has a grudge against you?' he asked.

'Of course not,' said Margery. 'What an idea!'

Mr Satterthwaite started on another line of attack.

'What visitors have you had during the last two months?'

'You don't mean just people for week-ends, I suppose? Marcia Keane has been with me all along. She is my best friend, and just as keen on horses as I am. Then my cousin Roley Vavasour has been here a good deal.'

Mr Satterthwaite nodded. He suggested that he should see Clayton, the maid.

'She has been with you a long time, I suppose?' he asked.

'Donkey's years,' said Margery. 'She was Mother's and Aunt Beatrice's maid when they were girls. That is why Mother has kept her on, I suppose, although she has got a French maid for herself. Clayton does sewing and pottering little odd jobs.'

She took him upstairs and presently Clayton came to them. She was a tall, thin, old woman, with grey hair neatly parted, and she looked the acme of respectability.

'No, sir,' she said in answer to Mr Satterthwaite's inquiries. 'I have never heard anything of the house being haunted. To tell you the truth, sir, I thought it was all Miss Margery's imagination until last night. But I actually felt something – brushing by me in the darkness. And I can tell you this, sir, *it was not anything human*. And then there is that wound in Miss Margery's neck. She didn't do that herself, poor lamb.'

But her words were suggestive to Mr Satterthwaite. Was it possible that Margery could have inflicted that wound herself? He had heard of strange cases where girls apparently just as sane and well-balanced as Margery had done the most amazing things.

'It will soon heal up,' said Clayton. 'It's not like this scar of mine.'

She pointed to a mark on her own forehead.

'That was done forty years ago, sir; I still bear the mark of it.'

'It was the time the "Uralia" went down,' put in Margery. 'Clayton was hit on the head by a spar, weren't you, Clayton?'

'Yes, Miss.'

'What do you think yourself, Clayton,' asked Mr Satterthwaite, 'what do you think was the meaning of this attack on Miss Margery?'

'I really should not like to say, sir.'

Mr Satterthwaite read this correctly as the reserve of the well-trained servant.

'What do you really think, Clayton?' he said persuasively.

'I think, sir, that something very wicked must have been done in this house, and that until that is wiped out there won't be any peace.'

The woman spoke gravely, and her faded blue eyes met his steadily.

Mr Satterthwaite went downstairs rather disappointed. Clayton evidently held the orthodox view, a deliberate 'haunting' as a consequence of some evil deed in the past. Mr Satterthwaite himself was not so easily satisfied. The phenomena had only taken place in the last two months. Had only taken place since Marcia Keane and Roley Vavasour had been there. He must find out something about these two. It was possible that the whole thing was a practical joke. But he shook his head, dissatisfied with that solution. The thing was more sinister than that. The post had just come in and Margery was opening and reading her letters. Suddenly she gave an exclamation.

'Mother is too absurd,' she said. 'Do read this.' She handed the letter to Mr Satterthwaite.

It was an epistle typical of Lady Stranleigh.

Darling Margery (she wrote),

I am so glad you have that nice little Mr Satterthwaite there. He is awfully clever and knows all the big-wig spook people. You must have them all down and investigate things thoroughly. I am sure you will have a perfectly marvellous time, and I only wish I could be there, but I have really been quite ill the last few days. The hotels are so careless about the food they give one. The doctor says it is some kind of food poisoning. I was really very ill.

Sweet of you to send me the chocolates, darling, but surely just a wee bit silly, wasn't it? I mean, there's such wonderful confectionery out here.

Bye-bye, darling, and have a lovely time laying the family ghosts. Bimbo says my tennis is coming on marvellously. Oceans of love.

Yours,
Barbara.

'Mother always wants me to call her Barbara,' said Margery. 'Simply silly, I think.'

Mr Satterthwaite smiled a little. He realized that the stolid conservatism of her daughter must on occasions be very trying to Lady Stranleigh. The contents of her letter struck him in a way in which obviously they did not strike Margery.

'Did you send your mother a box of chocolates?' he asked.

Margery shook her head. 'No, I didn't, it must have been someone else.'

Mr Satterthwaite looked grave. Two things struck him as of significance. Lady Stranleigh had received a gift of a box of chocolates and she was suffering from a severe attack of poisoning. Apparently she had not connected these two things. Was there a connection? He himself was inclined to think there was.

A tall dark girl lounged out of the morning-room and joined them.

She was introduced to Mr Satterthwaite as Marcia Keane. She smiled on the little man in an easy good-humoured fashion.

'Have you come down to hunt Margery's pet ghost?' she asked in a drawling voice. 'We all rot her about that ghost. Hello, here's Roley.'

A car had just drawn up at the front door. Out of it tumbled a tall young man with fair hair and an eager boyish manner.

'Hello, Margery,' he cried. 'Hello, Marcia! I have brought down re-inforcements.' He turned to the two women who were just entering the hall. Mr Satterthwaite recognized in the first one of the two the Mrs Casson of whom Margery had spoken just now.

'You must forgive me, Margery, dear,' she drawled, smiling broadly. 'Mr Vavasour told us that it would be quite all right. It was really his idea that I should bring down Mrs Lloyd with me.'

She indicated her companion with a slight gesture of the hand.

'This is Mrs Lloyd,' she said in a tone of triumph. 'Simply the most wonderful medium that ever existed.'

Mrs Lloyd uttered no modest protest, she bowed and remained with her hands crossed in front of her. She was a highly-coloured young woman of commonplace appearance. Her clothes were unfashionable but rather ornate. She wore a chain of moonstones and several rings.

Margery Gale, as Mr Satterthwaite could see, was not too pleased at this intrusion. She threw an angry look at Roley Vavasour, who seemed quite unconscious of the offence he had caused.

'Lunch is ready, I think,' said Margery.

'Good,' said Mrs Casson. 'We will hold a *séance* immediately after-wards. Have you got some fruit for Mrs Lloyd? She never eats a solid meal before a *séance*.'

They all went into the dining-room. The medium ate two bananas and an apple, and replied cautiously and briefly to the various polite remarks which Margery addressed to her from time to time. Just before they rose from the table, she flung back her head suddenly and sniffed the air.

'There is something very wrong in this house. I feel it.'

'Isn't she wonderful?' said Mrs Casson in a low delighted voice.

'Oh! undoubtedly,' said Mr Satterthwaite dryly.

The *séance* was held in the library. The hostess was, as Mr Satterthwaite could see, very unwilling, only the obvious delight of her guests in the proceedings reconciled her to the ordeal.

The arrangements were made with a good deal of care by Mrs Casson, who was evidently well up in those matters, the chairs were set round in a circle, the curtains were drawn, and presently the medium announced herself ready to begin.

'Six people,' she said, looking round the room. 'That is bad. We must have an uneven number, Seven is ideal. I get my best results out of a circle of seven.'

'One of the servants,' suggested Roley. He rose. 'I will rout out the butler.'

'Let's have Clayton,' said Margery.

Mr Satterthwaite saw a look of annoyance pass over Roley Vavasour's good-looking face.

'But why Clayton?' he demanded.

'You don't like Clayton,' said Margery slowly.

Roley shrugged his shoulders. 'Clayton doesn't like me,' he said whimsically. 'In fact she hates me like poison.' He waited a minute or two, but Margery did not give way. 'All right,' he said, 'have her down.'

The circle was formed.

There was a period of silence broken by the usual coughs and fidgetings. Presently a succession of raps were heard and then the voice of the medium's control, a Red Indian called Cherokee.

'Indian Brave says you Good evening ladies and gentlemen. Someone here very anxious speak. Someone here very anxious give message to young lady. I go now. The spirit say what she come to say.'

A pause and then a new voice, that of a woman, said softly:

'Is Margery here?'

Roley Vavasour took it upon himself to answer.

'Yes,' he said, 'she is. Who is that speaking?'

'I am Beatrice.'

'Beatrice? Who is Beatrice?'

To everyone's annoyance the voice of the Red Indian Cherokee was heard once more.

'I have message for all of you people. Life here very bright and beautiful. We all work very hard. Help those who have not yet passed over.'

Again a silence and then the woman's voice was heard once more.

'This is Beatrice speaking.'

'Beatrice who?'

'Beatrice Barron.'

Mr Sattherwaite leaned forward. He was very excited.

'Beatrice Barron who was drowned in the "Uralia"?'

'Yes, that is right. I remember the "Uralia". I have a message – for this house – *Give back what is not yours.*'

'I don't understand,' said Margery helplessly. 'I – oh, are you really Aunt Beatrice?'

'Yes, I am your aunt.'

'Of course she is,' said Mrs Casson reproachfully. 'How can you be so suspicious? The spirits don't like it.'

And suddenly Mr Satterthwaite thought of a very simple test. His voice quivered as he spoke.

'Do you remember Mr Bottacetti?' he asked.

Immediately there came a ripple of laughter.

'Poor old Boatsupsetty. Of course.'

Mr Sattherwaite was dumbfounded. The test had succeeded. It was an incident of over forty years ago which had happened when he and the Barron girls had found themselves at the same seaside resort. A young Italian acquaintance of theirs had gone out in a boat and capsized, and Beatrice Barron had jestingly named him Boatsupsetty. It seemed impossible that anyone in the room could know of this incident except himself.

The medium stirred and groaned.

'She is coming out,' said Mrs Casson. 'That is all we will get out of her today, I am afraid.'

The daylight shone once more on the room full of people, two of whom at least were badly scared.

Mr Satterthwaite saw by Margery's white face that she was deeply perturbed. When they had got rid of Mrs Casson and the medium, he sought a private interview with his hostess.

'I want to ask you one or two questions, Miss Margery. If you and your mother were to die who succeeds to the title and estates?'

'Roley Vavasour, I suppose. His mother was Mother's first cousin.'

Mr Satterthwaite nodded.

'He seems to have been here a lot this winter,' he said gently. 'You will forgive me asking – but is he – fond of you?'

'He asked me to marry him three weeks ago,' said Margery quietly. 'I said No.'

'Please forgive me, but are you engaged to anyone else?'

He saw the colour sweep over her face.

'I am,' she said emphatically. 'I am going to marry Noel Barton. Mother laughs and says it is absurd. She seems to think it is ridiculous to be engaged to a curate. Why, I should like to know! There are curates and curates! You should see Noel on a horse.'

'Oh, quite so,' said Mr Satterthwaite. 'Oh, undoubtedly.'

A footman entered with a telegram on a salver. Margery tore it open. 'Mother is arriving home tomorrow,' she said. 'Bother. I wish to goodness she would stay away.'

Mr Satterthwaite made no comment on this filial sentiment. Perhaps he thought it justified. 'In that case,' he murmured, 'I think I am returning to London.'

Mr Satterthwaite was not quite pleased with himself. He felt that he had left this particular problem in an unfinished state. True that, on Lady Stranleigh's return, his responsibility was ended, yet he felt assured that he had not heard the last of the Abbot's Mede mystery.

But the next development when it came was so serious in its character that it found him totally unprepared. He learnt of it in the pages of his morning paper. 'Baroness Dies in her Bath,' as the *Daily Megaphone* had it. The other papers were more restrained and delicate in their language, but the fact was the same. Lady Stranleigh had been found dead in her bath and her death was due to drowning. She had, it was assumed, lost consciousness, and whilst in that state her head had slipped below the water.

But Mr Satterthwaite was not satisfied with that explanation. Calling for his valet he made his toilet with less than his usual care, and ten minutes later his big Rolls-Royce was carrying him out of London as fast as it could travel.

But strangely enough it was not for Abbot's Mede he was bound, but for a small inn some fifteen miles distant which bore the rather unusual name of the 'Bells and Motley'. It was with great relief that he heard that Mr Harley Quin was still staying there. In another minute he was face to face with his friend.

Mr Satterthwaite clasped him by the hand and began to speak at once in an agitated manner.

'I am terribly upset. You must help me. Already I have a dreadful feeling that it may be too late – that that nice girl may be the next to go, for she is a nice girl, nice through and through.'

'If you will tell me,' said Mr Quin, smiling, 'what it is all about?'

Mr Satterthwaite looked at him reproachfully.

'You know. I am perfectly certain that you know. But I will tell you.'

He poured out the story of his stay at Abbot's Mede and, as always with Mr Quin, he found himself taking pleasure in his narrative. He was eloquent and subtle and meticulous as to detail.

'So you see,' he ended, 'there must be an explanation.'

He looked hopefully at Mr Quin as a dog looks at his master.

'But it is you who must solve the problem, not I,' said Mr Quin. 'I do not know these people. You do.'

'I knew the Barron girls forty years ago,' said Mr Satterthwaite with pride.

Mr Quin nodded and looked sympathetic, so much so that the other went on dreamily.

'That time at Brighton now, Bottacetti-Boatsupsetty, quite a silly joke but how we laughed. Dear, dear, I was young then. Did a lot of foolish things. I remember the maid they had with them. Alice, her name was, a little bit of a thing – very ingenuous. I kissed her in the passage of the hotel, I remember, and one of the girls nearly caught me doing it. Dear, dear, how long ago that all was.'

He shook his head again and sighed. Then he looked at Mr Quin.

'So you can't help me?' he said wistfully. 'On other occasions –'

'On other occasions you have proved successful owing entirely to your own efforts,' said Mr Quin gravely. 'I think it will be the same this time. If I were you, I should go to Abbot's Mede now.'

'Quite so, quite so,' said Mr Satterthwaite, 'as a matter of fact that is what I thought of doing. I can't persuade you to come with me?'

Mr Quin shook his head.

'No,' he said, 'my work here is done. I am leaving almost immediately.'

At Abbot's Mede, Mr Satterthwaite was taken at once to Margery Gale. She was sitting dry-eyed at a desk in the morning-room on which were strewn various papers. Something in her greeting touched him. She seemed so very pleased to see him.

'Roley and Maria have just left. Mr Satterthwaite, it is not as the doctors think. I am convinced, absolutely convinced, that Mother was pushed under the water and held there. She was murdered, and whoever murdered her wants to murder me too. I am sure of that. That is why –' she indicated the document in front of her.

'I have been making my will,' she explained. 'A lot of the money and some of the property does not go with the title, and there is my father's money as well. I am leaving everything I can to Noel. I know he will make a good use of it and I do not trust Roley, he has always been out for what he can get. Will you sign it as a witness?'

'My dear young lady,' said Mr Satterthwaite, 'you should sign a will in the presence of two witnesses and they should then sign themselves at the same time.'

Margery brushed aside this legal pronouncement.

'I don't see that it matters in the least,' she declared. 'Clayton saw me sign and then she signed her name. I was going to ring for the butler, but you will do instead.'

Mr Satterthwaite uttered no fresh protest, he unscrewed his fountain pen and then, as he was about to append his signature, he paused suddenly. The name, written just above his own, recalled a flow of memories. Alice Clayton.

Something seemed to be struggling very hard to get through to him. Alice Clayton, there was some significance about that. Something to do with Mr Quin was mixed up with it. Something he had said to Mr Quin only a very short time ago.

Ah, he had it now. Alice Clayton, that was her name. *The little bit of a thing.* People changed – yes, *but not like that.* And the Alice Clayton he knew had had brown eyes. The room seemed whirling round him. He felt for a chair and presently, as though from a great distance, he heard

Margery's voice speaking to him anxiously. 'Are you ill? Oh, what is it? I am sure you are ill.'

He was himself again. He took her hand.

'My dear, I see it all now. You must prepare yourself for a great shock. The woman upstairs whom you call Clayton is not Clayton at all. The real Alice Clayton was drowned on the "Uralia".'

Margery was staring at him. 'Who – who is she then?'

'I am not mistaken, I cannot be mistaken. The woman you call Clayton is your mother's sister, Beatrice Barron. You remember telling me that she was struck on the head by a spar? I should imagine that that blow destroyed her memory, and that being the case, your mother saw the chance –'

'Of pinching the title, you mean?' asked Margery bitterly. 'Yes, she would do that. It seems dreadful to say that now she is dead, but she was like that.'

'Beatrice was the elder sister,' said Mr Satterthwaite. 'By your uncle's death she would inherit everything and your mother would get nothing. Your mother claimed the wounded girl as her *maid*, not as her *sister*. The girl recovered from the blow and believed, of course, what was told her, that she was Alice Clayton, your mother's maid. I should imagine that just lately her memory had begun to return, but that the blow on the head, given all these years ago, has at last caused mischief on the brain.'

Margery was looking at him with eyes of horror.

'She killed Mother and she wanted to kill me,' she breathed.

'It seems so,' said Mr Satterthwaite. 'In her brain there was just one muddled idea – that her inheritance had been stolen and was being kept from her by you and your mother.'

'But – but Clayton is so old.'

Mr Satterthwaite was silent for a minute as a vision rose up before him – the faded old woman with grey hair, and the radiant golden-haired creature sitting in the sunshine at Cannes. Sisters! Could it really be so? He remembered the Barron girls and their likeness to each other. Just because two lives had developed on different tracks –

He shook his head sharply, obsessed by the wonder and pity of life . . .

He turned to Margery and said gently: 'We had better go upstairs and see her.'

They found Clayton sitting in the little workroom where she sewed. She did not turn her head as they came in for a reason that Mr Satterthwaite soon found out.

'Heart failure,' he murmured, as he touched the cold rigid shoulder. 'Perhaps it is best that way.'

The Face of Helen

'The Face of Helen' was first published as 'The Magic of Mr Quin No. 5' in *The Storyteller*, April 1927.

Mr Satterthwaite was at the Opera and sat alone in his big box on the first tier. Outside the door was a printed card bearing his name. An appreciator and a connoisseur of all the arts, Mr Satterthwaite was especially fond of good music, and was a regular subscriber to Covent Garden every year, reserving a box for Tuesdays and Fridays throughout the season.

But it was not often that he sat in it alone. He was a gregarious little gentleman, and he liked filling his box with the élite of the great world to which he belonged, and also with the aristocracy of the artistic world in which he was equally at home. He was alone tonight because a Countess had disappointed him. The Countess, besides being a beautiful and celebrated woman, was also a good mother. Her children had been attacked by that common and distressing disease, the mumps, and the Countess remained at home in tearful confabulation with exquisitely starched nurses. Her husband, who had supplied her with the aforementioned children and a title, but who was otherwise a complete nonentity, had seized at the chance to escape. Nothing bored him more than music.

So Mr Satterthwaite sat alone. *Cavalleria Rusticana* and *Pagliacci* were being given that night, and since the first had never appealed to him, he arrived just after the curtain went down, on Santuzza's death agony, in time to glance round the house with practised eyes, before everyone streamed out, bent on paying visits or fighting for coffee or lemonade. Mr Satterthwaite adjusted his opera glasses, looked round the house, marked down his prey and sallied forth with a well mapped out plan of campaign ahead of him. A plan, however, which he did not put into execution, for just outside his box he cannoned into a tall dark man, and recognized him with a pleasurable thrill of excitement.

'Mr Quin,' cried Mr Satterthwaite.

He seized his friend warmly by the hand, clutching him as though he feared any minute to see him vanish into thin air.

'You must share my box,' said Mr Satterthwaite determinedly. 'You are not with a party?'

'No, I am sitting by myself in the stalls,' responded Mr Quin with a smile.

'Then, that is settled,' said Mr Satterthwaite with a sigh of relief.

His manner was almost comic, had there been anyone to observe it.

'You are very kind,' said Mr Quin.

'Not at all. It is a pleasure. I didn't know you were fond of music?'

'There are reasons why I am attracted to – *Pagliacci.*'

'Ah! of course,' said Mr Satterthwaite, nodding sapiently, though, if put to it, he would have found it hard to explain just why he had used that expression. 'Of course, you would be.'

They went back to the box at the first summons of the bell, and leaning over the front of it, they watched the people returning to the stalls.

'That's a beautiful head,' observed Mr Satterthwaite suddenly.

He indicated with his glasses a spot immediately beneath them in the stalls circle. A girl sat there whose face they could not see – only the pure gold of her hair that fitted with the closeness of a cap till it merged into the white neck.

'A Greek head,' said Mr Satterthwaite reverently. 'Pure Greek.' He sighed happily. 'It's a remarkable thing when you come to think of it – how very few people have hair that *fits* them. It's more noticeable now that everyone is shingled.'

'You are so observant,' said Mr Quin.

'I see things,' admitted Mr Satterthwaite. 'I do see things. For instance, I picked out that head at once. We must have a look at her face sooner or later. But it won't match, I'm sure. That would be a chance in a thousand.'

Almost as the words left his lips, the lights flickered and went down, the sharp rap of the conductor's baton was heard, and the opera began. A new tenor, said to be a second Caruso, was singing that night. He had been referred to by the newspapers as a Jugo Slav, a Czech, an Albanian, a Magyar, and a Bulgarian, with a beautiful impartiality. He had given an extraordinary concert at the Albert Hall, a programme of the folk songs of his native hills, with a specially tuned orchestra. They were in strange half-tones and the would-be musical had pronounced them 'too marvellous'. Real musicians had reserved judgment, realizing that the ear had to be specially trained and attuned before any criticism was possible. It was quite a relief to some people to find this evening that Yoaschbim could sing in ordinary Italian with all the traditional sobs and quivers.

The curtain went down on the first act and applause burst out vociferously. Mr Satterthwaite turned to Mr Quin. He realized that the latter was waiting for him to pronounce judgment, and plumed himself a little. After all, he *knew*. As a critic he was well-nigh infallible.

Very slowly he nodded his head.

'It is the real thing,' he said.

'You think so?'

'As fine a voice as Caruso's. People will not recognize that it is so at first, for his technique is not yet perfect. There are ragged edges, a lack of certainty in the attack. But the voice is there – magnificent.'

'I went to his concert at the Albert Hall,' said Mr Quin.

'Did you? I could not go.'

'He made a wonderful hit with a Shepherd's Song.'

'I read about it,' said Mr Satterthwaite. 'The refrain ends each time with a high note – a kind of cry. A note midway between A and B flat. Very curious.'

Yoaschbim had taken three calls, bowing and smiling. The lights went up and the people began to file out. Mr Satterthwaite leant over to watch the girl with the golden head. She rose, adjusted her scarf, and turned.

Mr Satterthwaite caught his breath. There were, he knew, such faces in the world – faces that made history.

The girl moved to the gangway, her companion, a young man, beside her. And Mr Satterthwaite noticed how every man in the vicinity looked – and continued to look covertly.

'Beauty!' said Mr Satterthwaite to himself. 'There is such a thing. Not charm, nor attraction, nor magnetism, nor any of the things we talk about so glibly – just sheer beauty. The shape of a face, the line of an eyebrow, the curve of a jaw. He quoted softly under his breath: '*The face that launched a thousand ships.*' And for the first time he realized the meaning of those words.

He glanced across at Mr Quin, who was watching him in what seemed such perfect comprehension that Mr Satterthwaite felt there was no need for words.

'I've always wondered,' he said simply, 'what such women were really like.'

'You mean?'

'The Helens, the Cleopatras, the Mary Stuarts.'

Mr Quin nodded thoughtfully.

'If we go out,' he suggested, 'we may – see.'

They went out together, and their quest was successful. The pair they were in search of were seated on a lounge half-way up the staircase. For the first time, Mr Satterthwaite noted the girl's companion, a dark young man, not handsome, but with a suggestion of restless fire about him. A face full of strange angles; jutting cheek-bones, a forceful, slightly crooked jaw, deep-set eyes that were curiously light under the dark, overhanging brows.

'An interesting face,' said Mr Satterthwaite to himself. 'A real face. It means something.'

The young man was leaning forward talking earnestly. The girl was listening. Neither of them belonged to Mr Satterthwaite's world. He took them to be of the 'Arty' class. The girl wore a rather shapeless garment of cheap green silk. Her shoes were of soiled, white satin. The young man wore his evening clothes with an air of being uncomfortable in them.

The two men passed and re-passed several times. The fourth time they did so, the couple had been joined by a third – a fair young man with a suggestion of the clerk about him. With his coming a certain tension had set in. The newcomer was fidgetting with his tie and seemed ill at ease, the girl's beautiful face was turned gravely up towards him, and her companion was scowling furiously.

'The usual story,' said Mr Quin very softly, as they passed.

'Yes,' said Mr Satterthwaite with a sigh. 'It's inevitable, I suppose. The snarling of two dogs over a bone. It always has been, it always will be. And yet, one could wish for something different. Beauty –' he stopped. Beauty, to Mr Satterthwaite, meant something very wonderful. He found it difficult to speak of it. He looked at Mr Quin, who nodded his head gravely in understanding.

They went back to their seats for the second act.

At the close of the performance, Mr Satterthwaite turned eagerly to his friend.

'It is a wet night. My car is here. You must allow me to drive you – er – somewhere.'

The last word was Mr Satterthwaite's delicacy coming into play. 'To drive you home' would, he felt, have savoured of curiosity. Mr Quin had always been singularly reticent. It was extraordinary how little Mr Satterthwaite knew about him.

'But perhaps,' continued the little man, 'you have your own car waiting?'

'No,' said Mr Quin, 'I have no car waiting.'

'Then –'

But Mr Quin shook his head.

'You are most kind,' he said, 'but I prefer to go my own way. Besides,' he said with a rather curious smile, 'if anything should – happen, it will be for you to act. Goodnight, and thank you. Once again we have seen the drama together.'

He had gone so quickly that Mr Satterthwaite had no time to protest, but he was left with a faint uneasiness stirring in his mind. To what drama did Mr Quin refer? *Pagliacci* or another?'

Masters, Mr Satterthwaite's chauffeur, was in the habit of waiting in a side street. His master disliked the long delay while the cars drew up in turn before the Opera house. Now, as on previous occasions, he walked rapidly round the corner and along the street towards where he knew he should find Masters awaiting him. Just in front of him were a girl and a man, and even as he recognized them, another man joined them.

It all broke out in a minute. A man's voice, angrily uplifted. Another man's voice in injured protest. And then the scuffle. Blows, angry breathing, more blows, the form of a policeman appearing majestically from nowhere – and in another minute Mr Satterthwaite was beside the girl where she shrank back against the wall.

'Allow me,' he said. 'You must not stay here.'

He took her by the arm and marshalled her swiftly down the street. Once she looked back.

'Oughtn't I –?' she began uncertainly.

Mr Satterthwaite shook his head.

'It would be very unpleasant for you to be mixed up in it. You would probably be asked to go along to the police station with them. I am sure neither of your – friends would wish that.'

He stopped.

'This is my car. If you will allow me to do so, I shall have much pleasure in driving you home.'

The girl looked at him searchingly. The staid respectability of Mr Satterthwaite impressed her favourably. She bent her head.

'Thank you,' she said, and got into the car, the door of which Masters was holding open.

In reply to a question from Mr Satterthwaite, she gave an address in Chelsea, and he got in beside her.

The girl was upset and not in the mood for talking, and Mr Satterthwaite was too tactful to intrude upon her thoughts. Presently, however, she turned to him and spoke of her own accord.

'I wish,' she said pettishly, 'people wouldn't be so silly.'

'It is a nuisance,' agreed Mr Satterthwaite.

His matter-of-fact manner put her at her ease, and she went on as though feeling the need of confiding in someone.

'It wasn't as though – I mean, well, it was like this. Mr Eastney and I have been friends for a long time – ever since I came to London. He's taken no end of trouble about my voice, and got me some very good introductions, and he's been more kind to me than I can say. He's absolutely music mad. It was very good of him to take me tonight. I'm sure he can't really afford it. And then Mr Burns came up and spoke to us – quite nicely, I'm sure, and Phil (Mr Eastney) got sulky about it. I don't know why he should. It's a free country, I'm sure. And Mr Burns is always pleasant, and good-tempered. Then just as we were walking to the Tube, he came up and joined us, and he hadn't so much as said two words before Philip flew out at him like a madman. And – Oh! I don't like it.'

'Don't you?' asked Mr Satterthwaite very softly.

She blushed, but very little. There was none of the conscious siren about her. A certain measure of pleasurable excitement in being fought for there must be – that was only nature, but Mr Satterthwaite decided that a worried perplexity lay uppermost, and he had the clue to it in another moment when she observed inconsequently:

'I do hope he hasn't hurt him.'

'Now which is "him"?' thought Mr Satterthwaite, smiling to himself in the darkness.

He backed his own judgment and said:

'You hope Mr – er – Eastney hasn't hurt Mr Burns?'

She nodded.

'Yes, that's what I said. It seems so dreadful. I wish I knew.'

The car was drawing up.

'Are you on the telephone?' he asked.

'Yes.'

'If you like, I will find out exactly what has happened, and then telephone to you.'

The girl's face brightened.

'Oh, that would be very kind of you. Are you sure it's not too much bother?'

'Not in the least.'

She thanked him again and gave him her telephone number, adding with a touch of shyness: 'My name is Gillian West.'

As he was driven through the night, bound on his errand, a curious smile came to Mr Satterthwaite's lips.

He thought: 'So that is all it is . . . "*The shape of a face, the curve of a jaw!*"'

But he fulfilled his promise.

The following Sunday afternoon Mr Satterthwaite went to Kew Gardens to admire the rhododendrons. Very long ago (incredibly long ago, it seemed to Mr Satterthwaite) he had driven down to Kew Gardens with a certain

young lady to see the bluebells. Mr Satterthwaite had arranged very carefully beforehand in his own mind exactly what he was going to say, and
the precise words he would use in asking the young lady for her hand in
marriage. He was just conning them over in his mind, and responding
to her raptures about the bluebells a little absent-mindedly, when the
shock came. The young lady stopped exclaiming at the bluebells and
suddenly confided in Mr Satterthwaite (as a true friend) her love for
another. Mr Satterthwaite put away the little set speech he had prepared,
and hastily rummaged for sympathy and friendship in the bottom drawer
of his mind.

Such was Mr Satterthwaite's romance – a rather tepid early Victorian
one, but it had left him with a romantic attachment to Kew Gardens,
and he would often go there to see the bluebells, or, if he had been abroad
later than usual, the rhododendrons, and would sigh to himself, and feel
rather sentimental, and really enjoy himself very much indeed in an old-
fashioned, romantic way.

This particular afternoon he was strolling back past the tea houses
when he recognized a couple sitting at one of the small tables on the
grass. They were Gillian West and the fair young man, and at that same
moment they recognized him. He saw the girl flush and speak eagerly to
her companion. In another minute he was shaking hands with them both
in his correct, rather prim fashion, and had accepted the shy invitation
proffered him to have tea with them.

'I can't tell you, sir,' said Mr Burns, 'how grateful I am to you for
looking after Gillian the other night. She told me all about it.'

'Yes, indeed,' said the girl. 'It was ever so kind of you.'

Mr Satterthwaite felt pleased and interested in the pair. Their naïveté
and sincerity touched him. Also, it was to him a peep into a world with
which he was not well acquainted. These people were of a class unknown
to him.

In his little dried-up way, Mr Satterthwaite could be very sympathetic.
Very soon he was hearing all about his new friends. He noted that Mr
Burns had become Charlie, and he was not unprepared for the statement
that the two were engaged.

'As a matter of fact,' said Mr Burns with refreshing candour, 'it just
happened this afternoon, didn't it, Gil?'

Burns was a clerk in a shipping firm. He was making a fair salary, had
a little money of his own, and the two proposed to be married quite soon.

Mr Satterthwaite listened, and nodded, and congratulated.

'An ordinary young man,' he thought to himself, 'a very ordinary
young man. Nice, straightforward young chap, plenty to say for himself,
good opinion of himself without being conceited, nice-looking without

being unduly handsome. Nothing remarkable about him and will never set the Thames on fire. And the girl loves him . . .'

Aloud he said: 'And Mr Eastney –'

He purposely broke off, but he had said enough to produce an effect for which he was not unprepared. Charlie Burns's face darkened, and Gillian looked troubled. More than troubled, he thought. She looked afraid.

'I don't like it,' she said in a low voice. Her words were addressed to Mr Satterthwaite, as though she knew by instinct that he would understand a feeling incomprehensible to her lover. 'You see – he's done a lot for me. He's encouraged me to take up singing, and – and helped me with it. But I've known all the time that my voice wasn't really good – not first-class. Of course, I've had engagements –'

She stopped.

'You've had a bit of trouble too,' said Burns. 'A girl wants someone to look after her. Gillian's had a lot of unpleasantness, Mr Satterthwaite. Altogether she's had a lot of unpleasantness. She's a good-looker, as you can see, and – well, that often leads to trouble for a girl.'

Between them, Mr Satterthwaite became enlightened as to various happenings which were vaguely classed by Burns under the heading of 'unpleasantness'. A young man who had shot himself, the extraordinary conduct of a Bank Manager (who was a married man!), a violent stranger (who must have been balmy!), the wild behaviour of an elderly artist. A trail of violence and tragedy that Gillian West had left in her wake, recited in the commonplace tones of Charles Burns. 'And it's my opinion,' he ended, 'that this fellow Eastney is a bit cracked. Gillian would have had trouble with him if I hadn't turned up to look after her.'

His laugh sounded a little fatuous to Mr Satterthwaite, and no responsive smile came to the girl's face. She was looking earnestly at Mr Satterthwaite.

'Phil's all right,' she said slowly. 'He cares for me, I know, and I care for him like a friend – but – but not anything more. I don't know how he'll take the news about Charlie, I'm sure. He – I'm so afraid he'll be –'

She stopped, inarticulate in face of the dangers she vaguely sensed.

'If I can help you in any way,' said Mr Satterthwaite warmly, 'pray command me.'

He fancied Charlie Burns looked vaguely resentful, but Gillian said at once: 'Thank you.'

Mr Satterthwaite left his new friends after having promised to take tea with Gillian on the following Thursday.

When Thursday came, Mr Satterthwaite felt a little thrill of pleasurable anticipation. He thought: 'I'm an old man – but not too old to be thrilled by a face. A face . . .' Then he shook his head with a sense of foreboding.

Gillian was alone. Charlie Burns was to come in later. She looked much happier, Mr Satterthwaite thought, as though a load had been lifted from her mind. Indeed, she frankly admitted as much.

'I dreaded telling Phil about Charles. It was silly of me. I ought to have known Phil better. He was upset, of course, but no one could have been sweeter. Really sweet he was. Look what he sent me this morning – a wedding present. Isn't it magnificent?'

It was indeed rather magnificent for a young man in Philip Eastney's circumstances. A four-valve wireless set, of the latest type.

'We both love music so much, you see,' explained the girl. 'Phil said that when I was listening to a concert on this, I should always think of him a little. And I'm sure I shall. Because we have been such friends.'

'You must be proud of your friend,' said Mr Satterthwaite gently. 'He seems to have taken the blow like a true sportsman.'

Gillian nodded. He saw the quick tears come into her eyes.

'He asked me to do one thing for him. Tonight is the anniversary of the day we first met. He asked me if I would stay at home quietly this evening and listen to the wireless programme – not to go out with Charlie anywhere. I said, of course I would, and that I was very touched, and that I would think of him with a lot of gratitude and affection.'

Mr Satterthwaite nodded, but he was puzzled. He was seldom at fault in his delineation of character, and he would have judged Philip Eastney quite incapable of such a sentimental request. The young man must be of a more banal order than he supposed. Gillian evidently thought the idea quite in keeping with her rejected lover's character. Mr Satterthwaite was a little – just a little – disappointed. He was sentimental himself, and knew it, but he expected better things of the rest of the world. Besides sentiment belonged to his age. It had no part to play in the modern world.

He asked Gillian to sing and she complied. He told her her voice was charming, but he knew quite well in his own mind that it was distinctly second-class. Any success that could have come to her in the profession she had adopted would have been won by her face, not her voice.

He was not particularly anxious to see young Burns again, so presently he rose to go. It was at that moment that his attention was attracted by an ornament on the mantelpiece which stood out among the other rather gimcrack objects like a jewel on a dust heap.

It was a curving beaker of thin green glass, long-stemmed and graceful, and poised on the edge of it was what looked like a gigantic soap-bubble, a ball of iridescent glass. Gillian noticed his absorption.

'That's an extra wedding present from Phil. It's rather pretty, I think. He works in a sort of glass factory.'

'It is a beautiful thing,' said Mr Satterthwaite reverently. 'The glass blowers of Murano might have been proud of that.'

He went away with his interest in Philip Eastney strangely stimulated. An extraordinarily interesting young man. And yet the girl with the wonderful face preferred Charlie Burns. What a strange and inscrutable universe!

It had just occurred to Mr Satterthwaite that, owing to the remarkable beauty of Gillian West, his evening with Mr Quin had somehow missed fire. As a rule, every meeting with that mysterious individual had resulted in some strange and unforeseen happening. It was with the hope of perhaps running against the man of mystery that Mr Satterthwaite bent his steps towards the *Arlecchino* Restaurant where once, in the days gone by, he had met Mr Quin, and which Mr Quin had said he often frequented.

Mr Satterthwaite went from room to room at the *Arlecchino*, looking hopefully about him, but there was no sign of Mr Quin's dark, smiling face. There was, however, somebody else. Sitting at a small table alone was Philip Eastney.

The place was crowded and Mr Satterthwaite took his seat opposite the young man. He felt a sudden strange sense of exultation, as though he were caught up and made part of a shimmering pattern of events. He was in this thing – whatever it was. He knew now what Mr Quin had meant that evening at the Opera. There was a drama going on, and in it was a part, an important part, for Mr Satterthwaite. He must not fail to take his cue and speak his lines.

He sat down opposite Philip Eastney with the sense of accomplishing the inevitable. It was easy enough to get into conversation. Eastney seemed anxious to talk. Mr Satterthwaite was, as always, an encouraging and sympathetic listener. They talked of the war, of explosives, of poison gases. Eastney had a lot to say about these last, for during the greater part of the war he had been engaged in their manufacture. Mr Satterthwaite found him really interesting.

There was one gas, Eastney said, that had never been tried. The Armistice had come too soon. Great things had been hoped for it. One whiff of it was deadly. He warmed to animation as he spoke.

Having broken the ice, Mr Satterthwaite gently turned the conversation to music. Eastney's thin face lit up. He spoke with the passion and abandon of the real music lover. They discussed Yoaschbim, and the young man was enthusiastic. Both he and Mr Satterthwaite agreed that nothing on earth could surpass a really fine tenor voice. Eastney as a boy had heard Caruso and he had never forgotten it.

'Do you know that he could sing to a wine-glass and shatter it?' he demanded.

'I always thought that was a fable,' said Mr Satterthwaite smiling.

'No, it's gospel truth, I believe. The thing's quite possible. It's a question of resonance.'

He went off into technical details. His face was flushed and his eyes shone. The subject seemed to fascinate him, and Mr Satterthwaite noted that he seemed to have a thorough grasp of what he was talking about. The elder man realized that he was talking to an exceptional brain, a brain that might almost be described as that of a genius. Brilliant, erratic, undecided as yet as to the true channel to give it outlet, but undoubtedly genius.

And he thought of Charlie Burns and wondered at Gillian West.

It was with quite a start that he realized how late it was getting, and he called for his bill. Eastney looked slightly apologetic.

'I'm ashamed of myself – running on so,' he said. 'But it was a lucky chance sent you along here tonight. I – I needed someone to talk to this evening.'

He ended his speech with a curious little laugh. His eyes were still blazing with some subdued excitement. Yet there was something tragic about him.

'It has been quite a pleasure,' said Mr Satterthwaite. 'Our conversation has been most interesting and instructive to me.'

He then made his funny, courteous little bow and passed out of the restaurant. The night was a warm one and as he walked slowly down the street a very odd fancy came to him. He had the feeling that he was not alone – that someone was walking by his side. In vain he told himself that the idea was a delusion – it persisted. Someone was walking beside him down that dark, quiet street, someone whom he could not see. He wondered what it was that brought the figure of Mr Quin so clearly before his mind. He felt exactly as though Mr Quin were there walking beside him, and yet he had only to use his eyes to assure himself that it was not so, that he was alone.

But the thought of Mr Quin persisted, and with it came something else: a need, an urgency of some kind, an oppressive foreboding of calamity. There was something he must do – and do quickly. There was something very wrong, and it lay in his hands to put it right.

So strong was the feeling that Mr Satterthwaite forebore to fight against it. Instead, he shut his eyes and tried to bring that mental image of Mr Quin nearer. If he could only have asked Mr Quin – but even as the thought flashed through his mind he knew it was wrong. It was never any use asking Mr Quin anything. 'The threads are all in your hands' – that was the kind of thing Mr Quin would say.

The threads. Threads of what? He analysed his own feeling and impressions carefully. That presentiment of danger, now. Whom did it threaten?

At once a picture rose up before his eyes, the picture of Gillian West sitting alone listening to the wireless.

Mr Satterthwaite flung a penny to a passing newspaper boy, and snatched at a paper. He turned at once to the London Radio programme. Yoaschbim was broadcasting tonight, he noted with interest. He was singing 'Salve Dimora', from Faust and, afterwards, a selection of his folk songs. 'The Shepherd's Song', 'The Fish', 'The Little Deer', etc.

Mr Satterthwaite crumpled the paper together. The knowledge of what Gillian was listening to seemed to make the picture of her clearer. Sitting there alone . . .

An odd request, that, of Philip Eastney's. Not like the man, not like him at all. There was no sentimentality in Eastney. He was a man of violent feeling, a dangerous man, perhaps –

Again his thought brought up with a jerk. A dangerous man – that meant something. '*The threads are all in your hands.*' That meeting with Philip Eastney tonight – rather odd. A lucky chance, Eastney had said. Was it chance? Or was it part of that interwoven design of which Mr Satterthwaite had once or twice been conscious this evening?

He cast his mind back. There must be *something* in Eastney's conversation, some clue there. There must, or else why this strange feeling of urgency? What had he talked about? Singing, war work, Caruso.

Caruso – Mr Satterthwaite's thoughts went off at a tangent. Yoaschbim's voice was very nearly equal to that of Caruso. Gillian would be sitting listening to it now as it rang out true and powerful, echoing round the room, setting glasses ringing –

He caught his breath. Glasses ringing! Caruso, singing to a wine-glass and the wine-glass breaking. Yoachbim singing in the London studio and in a room over a mile away the crash and tinkle of glass – not a wine-glass, a thin, green, glass beaker. A crystal soap bubble falling, a soap bubble that perhaps was not empty . . .

It was at that moment that Mr Satterthwaite, as judged by passers-by, suddenly went mad. He tore open the newspaper once more, took a brief glance at the wireless announcements and then began to run for his life down the quiet street. At the end of it he found a crawling taxi, and jumping into it, he yelled an address to the driver and the information that it was life or death to get there quickly. The driver, judging him mentally afflicted but rich, did his utmost.

Mr Satterthwaite lay back, his head a jumble of fragmentary thoughts, forgotten bits of science learned at school, phrases used by Eastney that night. Resonance – natural periods – if the period of the force coincides with the natural period – there was something about a suspension bridge, soldiers marching over it and the swing of their stride being the same as the period of the bridge. Eastney had studied the subject. Eastney knew. And Eastney was a genius.

At 10.45 Yoaschbim was to broadcast. It was that now. Yes, but the Faust had to come first. It was the 'Shepherd's Song', with the great shout after the refrain that would – that would – do what?

His mind went whirling round again. Tones, overtones, half-tones. He didn't know much about these things – but Eastney knew. Pray heaven he would be in time!

The taxi stopped. Mr Satterthwaite flung himself out and raced up the stone stairs to a second floor like a young athlete. The door of the flat was ajar. He pushed it open and the great tenor voice welcomed him. The words of the 'Shepherd's Song' were familiar to him in a less unconventional setting.

> *'Shepherd, see they horse's flowing main –'*

He was in time then. He burst open the sitting-room door. Gillian was sitting there in a tall chair by the fireplace.

> *'Bayra Mischa's daughter is to wed today:*
> *To the wedding I must haste away.'*

She must have thought him mad. He clutched at her, crying out something incomprehensible, and half pulled, half dragged her out till they stood upon the stairway.

> *'To the wedding I must haste away –*
> *Ya-ha!'*

A wonderful high note, full-throated, powerful, hit full in the middle, a note any singer might be proud of. And with it another sound, the faint tinkle of broken glass.

A stray cat darted past them and in through the flat door. Gillian made a movement, but Mr Satterthwaite held her back, speaking incoherently.

'No, no – it's deadly: no smell, nothing to warn you. A mere whiff, and it's all over. Nobody knows quite how deadly it would be. It's unlike anything that's ever been tried before.'

He was repeating the things that Philip Eastney had told him over the table at dinner.

Gillian stared at him uncomprehendingly.

Philip Eastney drew out his watch and looked at it. It was just half-past eleven. For the past three-quarters of an hour he had been pacing up and down the Embankment. He looked out over the Thames and then turned – to look into the face of his dinner companion.

'That's odd,' he said, and laughed. 'We seem fated to run into each other tonight.'

'If you call it Fate,' said Mr Satterthwaite.

Philip Eastney looked at him more attentively and his own expression changed.

'Yes?' he said quietly.

Mr Satterthwaite went straight to the point.

'I have just come from Miss West's flat.'

'Yes?'

The same voice, with the same deadly quiet.

'We have – taken a dead cat out of it.'

There was silence, then Eastney said:

'Who are you?'

Mr Satterthwaite spoke for some time. He recited the whole history of events.

'So you see, I was in time,' he ended up. He paused and added quite gently:

'Have you anything – to say?'

He expected something, some outburst, some wild justification. But nothing came.

'No,' said Philip Eastney quietly, and turned on his heel and walked away,

Mr Satterthwaite looked after him till his figure was swallowed up in the gloom. In spite of himself, he had a strange fellow-feeling for Eastney, the feeling of an artist for another artist, of a sentimentalist for a real lover, of a plain man for a genius.

At last he roused himself with a start and began to walk in the same direction as Eastney. A fog was beginning to come up. Presently he met a policeman who looked at him suspiciously.

'Did you hear a kind of splash just now?' asked the policeman.

'No,' said Mr Satterthwaite.

The policeman was peering out over the river.

'Another of these suicides, I expect,' he grunted disconsolately. 'They will do it.'

'I suppose,' said Mr Satterthwaite, 'that they have their reasons.'

'Money, mostly,' said the policeman. 'Sometimes it's a woman,' he said, as he prepared to move away. 'It's not always their fault, but some women cause a lot of trouble.'

'Some women,' agreed Mr Satterthwaite softly.

When the policeman had gone on, he sat down on a seat with the fog coming up all around him, and thought about Helen of Troy, and wondered if she were a nice, ordinary woman, blessed or cursed with a wonderful face.

The Dead Harlequin

'The Dead Harlequin' was first published in *Grand Magazine,*
March 1929.

Mr Satterthwaite walked slowly up Bond Street enjoying the sunshine.
He was, as usual, carefully and beautifully dressed, and was bound for
the Harchester Galleries where there was an exhibition of the paintings
of one Frank Bristow, a new and hitherto unknown artist who showed
signs of suddenly becoming the rage. Mr Satterthwaite was a patron of
the arts.

As Mr Satterthwaite entered the Harchester Galleries, he was greeted
at once with a smile of pleased recognition.

'Good morning, Mr Satterthwaite, I thought we should see you before
long. You know Bristow's work? Fine – very fine indeed. Quite unique of
its kind.'

Mr Satterthwaite purchased a catalogue and stepped through the open
archway into the long room where the artist's works were displayed. They
were water colours, executed with such extraordinary technique and finish
that they resembled coloured etchings. Mr Satterthwaite walked slowly
round the walls scrutinizing and, on the whole, approving. He thought
that this young man deserved to arrive. Here was originality, vision, and
a most severe and exacting technique. There were crudities, of course.
That was only to be expected – but there was also something closely
allied to genius. Mr Satterthwaite paused before a little masterpiece repre-
senting Westminster Bridge with its crowd of buses, trams and hurrying
pedestrians. A tiny thing and wonderfully perfect. It was called, he noted,
The Ant Heap. He passed on and quite suddenly drew in his breath with
a gasp, his imagination held and riveted.

The picture was called The Dead Harlequin. The forefront of it represented a floor of inlaid squares of black and white marble. In the middle
of the floor lay Harlequin on his back with his arms outstretched, in his

motley of black and red. Behind him was a window and outside that window, gazing in at the figure on the floor, was what appeared to be the same man silhouetted against the red glow of the setting sun.

The picture excited Mr Satterthwaite for two reasons, the first was that he recognized, or thought that he recognized, the face of the man in the picture. It bore a distinct resemblance to a certain Mr Quin, an acquaintance whom Mr Satterthwaite had encountered once or twice under somewhat mystifying circumstances.

'Surely I can't be mistaken,' he murmured. 'If it *is* so – what does it mean?'

For it had been Mr Satterthwaite's experience that every appearance of Mr Quin had some distinct significance attaching to it.

There was, as already mentioned, a second reason for Mr Satterthwaite's interest. He recognized the scene of the picture.

'The Terrace Room at Charnley,' said Mr Satterthwaite. 'Curious – and very interesting.'

He looked with more attention at the picture, wondering what exactly had been in the artist's mind. One Harlequin dead on the floor, another Harlequin looking through the window – or was it the same Harlequin? He moved slowly along the walls gazing at other pictures with unseeing eyes, with his mind always busy on the same subject. He was excited. Life, which had seemed a little drab this morning, was drab no longer. He knew quite certainly that he was on the threshold of exciting and interesting events. He crossed to the table where sat Mr Cobb, a dignitary of the Harchester Galleries, whom he had known for many years.

'I have a fancy for buying no. 39,' he said, 'if it is not already sold.'

Mr Cobb consulted a ledger.

'The pick of the bunch,' he murmured, 'quite a little gem, isn't it? No, it is not sold.' He quoted a price. 'It is a good investment, Mr Satterthwaite. You will have to pay three times as much for it this time next year.'

'That is always said on these occasions,' said Mr Satterthwaite, smiling.

'Well, and haven't I been right?' demanded Mr Cobb. 'I don't believe if you were to sell your collection, Mr Satterthwaite, that a single picture would fetch less than you gave for it.'

'I will buy this picture,' said Mr Satterthwaite. 'I will give you a cheque now.'

'You won't regret it. We believe in Bristow.'

'He is a young man?'

'Twenty-seven or -eight, I should say.'

'I should like to meet him,' said Mr Satterthwaite. 'Perhaps he will come and dine with me one night?'

'I can give you his address. I am sure he would leap at the chance. Your name stands for a good deal in the artistic world.'

'You flatter me,' said Mr Satterthwaite, and was going on when Mr Cobb interrupted:

'Here he is now. I will introduce you to him right away.'

He rose from behind his table. Mr Satterthwaite accompanied him to where a big, clumsy young man was leaning against the wall surveying the world at large from behind the barricade of a ferocious scowl.

Mr Cobb made the necessary introductions and Mr Satterthwaite made a formal and gracious little speech.

'I have just had the pleasure of acquiring one of your pictures – The Dead Harlequin.'

'Oh! Well, you won't lose by it,' said Mr Bristow ungraciously. 'It's a bit of damned good work, although I say it.'

'I can see that,' said Mr Satterthwaite. 'Your work interests me very much, Mr Bristow. It is extraordinarily mature for so young a man. I wonder if you would give me the pleasure of dining with me one night? Are you engaged this evening?'

'As a matter of fact, I am not,' said Mr Bristow, still with no overdone appearance of graciousness.

'Then shall we say eight o'clock?' said Mr Satterthwaite. 'Here is my card with the address on it.'

'Oh, all right,' said Mr Bristow. 'Thanks,' he added as a somewhat obvious afterthought.

'A young man who has a poor opinion of himself and is afraid that the world should share it.'

Such was Mr Satterthwaite's summing up as he stepped out into the sunshine of Bond Street, and Mr Satterthwaite's judgment of his fellow men was seldom far astray.

Frank Bristow arrived about five minutes past eight to find his host and a third guest awaiting him. The other guest was introduced as a Colonel Monckton. They went in to dinner almost immediately. There was a fourth place laid at the oval mahogany table and Mr Satterthwaite uttered a word of explanation.

'I half expected my friend, Mr Quin, might drop in,' he said. 'I wonder if you have ever met him. Mr Harley Quin?'

'I never meet people,' growled Bristow.

Colonel Monckton stared at the artist with the detached interest he might have accorded to a new species of jelly fish. Mr Satterthwaite exerted himself to keep the ball of conversation rolling amicably.

'I took a special interest in that picture of yours because I thought I recognized the scene of it as being the Terrace Room at Charnley. Was

I right?' As the artist nodded, he went on. 'That is very interesting. I have stayed at Charnley several times myself in the past. Perhaps you know some of the family?'

'No, I don't!' said Bristow. 'That sort of family wouldn't care to know me. I went there in a charabanc.'

'Dear me,' said Colonel Monckton for the sake of saying something. 'In a charabanc! Dear me.'

Frank Bristow scowled at him.

'Why not?' he demanded ferociously.

Poor Colonel Monckton was taken aback. He looked reproachfully at Mr Satterthwaite as though to say:

'These primitive forms of life may be interesting to you as a naturalist, but why drag *me* in?'

'Oh, beastly things, charabancs!' he said. 'They jolt you so going over the bumps.'

'If you can't afford a Rolls Royce you have got to go in charabancs,' said Bristow fiercely.

Colonel Monckton stared at him. Mr Satterthwaite thought:

'Unless I can manage to put this young man at his ease we are going to have a very distressing evening.'

'Charnley aways fascinated me,' he said. 'I have been there only once since the tragedy. A grim house – and a ghostly one.'

'That's true,' said Bristow.

'There are actually two authentic ghosts,' said Monckton. 'They say that Charles I walks up and down the terrace with his head under his arm – I have forgotten why, I'm sure. Then there is the Weeping Lady with the Silver Ewer, who is always seen after one of the Charnleys dies.'

'Tosh,' said Bristow scornfully.

'They have certainly been a very ill-fated family,' said Mr Satterthwaite hurriedly. 'Four holders of the title have died a violent death and the late Lord Charnley committed suicide.'

'A ghastly business,' said Monckton gravely. 'I was there when it happened.'

'Let me see, that must be fourteen years ago,' said Mr Satterthwaite, 'the house has been shut up ever since.'

'I don't wonder at that,' said Monckton. 'It must have been a terrible shock for a young girl. They had been married a month, just home from their honeymoon. Big fancy dress ball to celebrate their home-coming. Just as the guests were starting to arrive Charnley locked himself into the Oak Parlour and shot himself. That sort of thing isn't done. I beg your pardon?'

He turned his head sharply to the left and looked across at Mr Satterthwaite with an apologetic laugh.

'I am beginning to get the jimjams, Satterthwaite. I thought for a moment there was someone sitting in that empty chair and that he said something to me.'

'Yes,' he went on after a minute or two, 'it was a pretty ghastly shock to Alix Charnley. She was one of the prettiest girls you could see anywhere and cram full of what people call the joy of living, and now they say she is like a ghost herself. Not that I have seen her for years. I believe she lives abroad most of the time.'

'And the boy?'

'The boy is at Eton. What he will do when he comes of age I don't know. I don't think, somehow, that he will reopen the old place.'

'It would make a good People's Pleasure Park,' said Bristow.

Colonel Monckton looked at him with cold abhorrence.

'No, no, you don't really mean that,' said Mr Satterthwaite. 'You wouldn't have painted that picture if you did. Tradition and atmosphere are intangible things. They take centuries to build up and if you destroyed them you couldn't rebuild them again in twenty-four hours.'

He rose. 'Let us go into the smoking-room. I have some photographs there of Charnley which I should like to show you.'

One of Mr Satterthwaite's hobbies was amateur photography. He was also the proud author of a book, 'Homes of My Friends'. The friends in question were all rather exalted and the book itself showed Mr Satterthwaite forth in rather a more snobbish light than was really fair to him.

'That is a photograph I took of the Terrace Room last year,' he said. He handed it to Bristow. 'You see it is taken at almost the same angle as is shown in your picture. That is rather a wonderful rug – it is a pity that photographs can't show colouring.'

'I remember it,' said Bristow, 'a marvellous bit of colour. It glowed like a flame. All the same it looked a bit incongruous there. The wrong size for that big room with its black and white squares. There is no rug anywhere else in the room. It spoils the whole effect – it was like a gigantic blood stain.'

'Perhaps that gave you your idea for your picture?' said Mr Satterthwaite.

'Perhaps it did,' said Bristow thoughtfully. 'On the face of it, one would naturally stage a tragedy in the little panelled room leading out of it.'

'The Oak Parlour,' said Monckton. 'Yes, that is the haunted room right enough. There is a Priests' hiding hole there – a movable panel by the fireplace. Tradition has it that Charles I was concealed there once. There were two deaths from duelling in that room. And it was there, as I say, that Reggie Charnley shot himself.'

He took the photograph from Bristow's hand.

'Why, that is the Bokhara rug,' he said, 'worth a couple of thousand pounds, I believe. When I was there it was in the Oak Parlour – the right place for it. It looks silly on that great expanse of marble flags.'

Mr Satterthwaite was looking at the empty chair which he had drawn up beside his. Then he said thoughtfully: 'I wonder when it was moved?'

'It must have been recently. Why, I remember having a conversation about it on the very day of the tragedy. Charnley was saying it really ought to be kept under glass.'

Mr Satterthwaite shook his head. 'The house was shut up immediately after the tragedy and everything was left exactly as it was.'

Bristow broke in with a question. He had laid aside his aggressive manner.

'Why did Lord Charnley shoot himself?' he asked.

Colonel Monckton shifted uncomfortably in his chair.

'No one ever knew,' he said vaguely.

'I suppose,' said Mr Satterthwaite slowly, 'that it *was* suicide.'

The Colonel looked at him in blank astonishment.

'Suicide,' he said, 'why, of course it was suicide. My dear fellow, I was there in the house myself.'

Mr Satterthwaite looked towards the empty chair at his side and, smiling to himself as though at some hidden joke the others could not see, he said quietly:

'Sometimes one sees things more clearly years afterwards than one could possibly at the time.'

'Nonsense,' spluttered Monckton, 'arrant nonsense! How can you possibly see things better when they are vague in your memory instead of clear and sharp?'

But Mr Satterthwaite was reinforced from an unexpected quarter.

'I know what you mean,' said the artist. 'I should say that possibly you were right. It is a question of proportion, isn't it? And more than proportion probably. Relativity and all that sort of thing.'

'If you ask me,' said the Colonel, 'all this Einstein business is a lot of dashed nonsense. So are spiritualists and the spook of one's grandmother!' He glared round fiercely.

'Of course it was suicide,' he went on. 'Didn't I practically see the thing happen with my own eyes?'

'Tell us about it,' said Mr Satterthwaite, 'so that we shall see it with our eyes also.'

With a somewhat mollified grunt the Colonel settled himself more comfortably in his chair.

'The whole thing was extraordinarily unexpected,' he began. 'Charnley had been his usual normal self. There was a big party staying in the house for this ball. No one could ever have guessed he would go and shoot himself just as the guests began arriving.'

'It would have been better taste if he had waited until they had gone,' said Mr Satterthwaite.

'Of course it would. Damned bad taste – to do a thing like that.'

'Uncharacteristic,' said Mr Satterthwaite.

'Yes,' admitted Monckton, 'it wasn't like Charnley.'

'And yet it *was* suicide?'

'Of course it was suicide. Why, there were three or four of us there at the top of the stairs. Myself, the Ostrander girl, Algie Darcy – oh, and one or two others. Charnley passed along the hall below and went into the Oak Parlour. The Ostrander girl said there was a ghastly look on his face and his eyes were staring – but, of course, that is nonsense – she couldn't even see his face from where we were – but he did walk in a hunched way, as if he had the weight of the world on his shoulders. One of the girls called to him – she was somebody's governess, I think, whom Lady Charnley had included in the party out of kindness. She was looking for him with a message. She called out "Lord Charnley, Lady Charnley wants to know –" He paid no attention and went into the Oak Parlour and slammed the door and we heard the key turn in the lock. Then, one minute after, *we heard the shot.*

'We rushed down to the hall. There is another door from the Oak Parlour leading into the Terrace Room. We tried that but it was locked, too. In the end we had to break the door down. Charnley was lying on the floor – dead – with a pistol close beside his right hand. Now, what could that have been but suicide? Accident? Don't tell me. There is only one other possibility – murder – and you can't have murder without a murderer. You admit that, I suppose.'

'The murderer might have escaped,' suggested Mr Satterthwaite.

'That is impossible. If you have a bit of paper and a pencil I will draw you a plan of the place. There are two doors into the Oak Parlour, one into the hall and one into the Terrace Room. Both these doors were locked in the inside *and the keys were in the locks.*'

'The window?'

'Shut, and the shutters fastened across it.'

There was a pause.

'So that is that,' said Colonel Monckton triumphantly.

'It certainly seems to be,' said Mr Satterthwaite sadly.

'Mind you,' said the Colonel, 'although I was laughing just now at the spiritualists, I don't mind admitting that there was a deuced rummy atmosphere about the place – about that room in particular. There are several bullet holes in the panels of the walls, the results of the duels that took place in that room, and there is a queer stain on the floor, that always comes back though they have replaced the wood several times. I suppose there will be another blood stain on the floor now – poor Charnley's blood.'

'Was there much blood?' asked Mr Satterthwaite.

'Very little – curiously little – so the doctor said.'

'Where did he shoot himself, through the head?'

'No, through the heart.'

'That is not the easy way to do it,' said Bristow. 'Frightfully difficult to know where one's heart is. I should never do it that way myself.'

Mr Satterthwaite shook his head. He was vaguely dissatisfied. He had hoped to get at something – he hardly knew what. Colonel Monckton went on.

'It is a spooky place, Charnley. Of course, *I* didn't see anything.'

'You didn't see the Weeping Lady with the Silver Ewer?'

'No, I did not, sir,' said the Colonel emphatically. 'But I expect every servant in the place swore they did.'

'Superstition was the curse of the Middle Ages,' said Bristow. 'There are still traces of it here and there, but thank goodness, we are getting free from it.'

'Superstition,' mused Mr Satterthwaite, his eyes turned again to the empty chair. 'Sometimes, don't you think – it might be useful?'

Bristow stared at him.

'Useful, that's a queer word.'

'Well, I hope you are convinced now, Satterthwaite,' said the Colonel.

'Oh, quite,' said Mr Satterthwaite. 'On the face of it, it seems odd – so purposeless for a newly-married man, young, rich, happy, celebrating his home-coming – curious – but I agree there is no getting away from the facts.' He repeated softly, 'The facts,' and frowned.

'I suppose the interesting thing is a thing we none of us will ever know,' said Monckton, 'the story behind it all. Of course there were rumours – all sorts of rumours. You know the kind of things people say.'

'But no one *knew* anything,' said Mr Satterthwaite thoughtfully.

'It's not a best seller mystery, is it?' remarked Bristow. 'No one gained by the man's death.'

'No one except an unborn child,' said Mr Satterthwaite.

Monckton gave a sharp chuckle. 'Rather a blow to poor Hugo Charnley,' he observed. 'As soon as it was known that there was going to be a child he had the graceful task of sitting tight and waiting to see if it would be a girl or boy. Rather an anxious wait for his creditors, too. In the end a boy it was and a disappointment for the lot of them.'

'Was the widow very disconsolate?' asked Bristow.

'Poor child,' said Monckton, 'I shall never forget her. She didn't cry or break down or anything. She was like something – frozen. As I say, she shut up the house shortly afterwards and, as far as I know, it has never been reopened since.'

'So we are left in the dark as to motive,' said Bristow with a slight laugh. 'Another man or another woman, it must have been one or the other, eh?'

'It seems like it,' said Mr Satterthwaite.

'And the betting is strongly on another woman,' continued Bristow, 'since the fair widow has not married again. I hate women,' he added dispassionately.

Mr Satterthwaite smiled a little and Frank Bristow saw the smile and pounced upon it.

'You may smile,' he said, 'but I do. They upset everything. They interfere. They get between you and your work. They – I only once met a woman who was – well, interesting.'

'I thought there would be one,' said Mr Satterthwaite.

'Not in the way you mean. I – I just met her casually. As a matter of fact – it was in a train. After all,' he added defiantly, 'why shouldn't one meet people in trains?'

'Certainly, certainly,' said Mr Satterthwaite soothingly, 'a train is as good a place as anywhere else.'

'It was coming down from the North. We had the carriage to ourselves. I don't know why, but we began to talk. I don't know her name and I don't suppose I shall ever meet her again. I don't know that I want to. It might be – a pity.' He paused, struggling to express himself. 'She wasn't quite real, you know. Shadowy. Like one of the people who come out of the hills in Gaelic fairy tales.'

Mr Satterthwaite nodded gently. His imagination pictured the scene easily enough. The very positive and realistic Bristow and a figure that was silvery and ghostly – shadowy, as Bristow had said.

'I suppose if something very terrible had happened, so terrible as to be almost unbearable, one might get like that. One might. run away from reality into a half world of one's own and then, of course, after a time, one wouldn't be able to get back.'

'Was that what had happened to her?' asked Mr Satterthwaite curiously.

'I don't know,' said Bristow. 'She didn't tell me anything, I am only guessing. One has to guess if one is going to get anywhere.'

'Yes,' said Mr Satterthwaite slowly. 'One has to guess.'

He looked up as the door opened. He looked up quickly and expectantly but the butler's words disappointed him.

'A lady, sir, has called to see you on very urgent business. Miss Aspasia Glen.'

Mr Satterthwaite rose in some astonishment. He knew the name of Aspasia Glen. Who in London did not? First advertised as the Woman with the Scarf, she had given a series of matinées single-handed that had taken London by storm. With the aid of her scarf she had impersonated rapidly various characters. In turn the scarf had been the coif of a nun, the shawl of a mill-worker, the head-dress of a peasant and a hundred other things, and in each impersonation Aspasia Glen had been totally and utterly different. As an artist, Mr Satterthwaite paid full reverence to her. As it happened, he had never made her acquaintance. A call upon him at this unusual hour intrigued him greatly. With a few words of apology to the others he left the room and crossed the hall to the drawing-room.

Miss Glen was sitting in the very centre of a large settee upholstered in gold brocade. So poised she dominated the room. Mr Satterthwaite perceived at once that she meant to dominate the situation. Curiously enough, his first feeling was one of repulsion. He had been a sincere admirer of Aspasia Glen's art. Her personality, as conveyed to him over the footlights, had been appealing and sympathetic. Her effects there had been wistful and suggestive rather than commanding. But now, face to face with the woman herself, he received a totally different impression. There was something hard – bold – forceful about her. She was tall and dark, possibly about thirty-five years of age. She was undoubtedly very good-looking and she clearly relied upon the fact.

'You must forgive this unconventional call, Mr Satterthwaite,' she said. Her voice was full and rich and seductive.

'I won't say that I have wanted to know you for a long time, but I *am* glad of the excuse. As for coming tonight' – she laughed – 'well, when I want a thing, I simply can't wait. When I want a thing, I simply *must* have it.'

'Any excuse that has brought me such a charming lady guest must be welcomed by me,' said Mr Satterthwaite in an old-fashioned gallant manner.

'How nice you are to me,' said Aspasia Glen.

'My dear lady,' said Mr Satterthwaite, 'may I thank you here and now for the pleasure you have so often given me – in my seat in the stalls.'

She smiled delightfully at him.

'I am coming straight to the point. I was at the Harchester Galleries today. I saw a picture there I simply couldn't live without. I wanted to buy it and I couldn't because you had already bought it. So' – she paused – 'I do want it so,' she went on. 'Dear Mr Satterthwaite, I simply *must* have it. I brought my cheque book.' She looked at him hopefully. 'Everyone tells me you are so frightfully kind. People are kind to me, you know. It is very bad for me – but there it is.'

So these were Aspasia Glen's methods. Mr Satterthwaite was inwardly coldly critical of this ultra-femininity and of this spoilt child pose. It ought to appeal to him, he supposed, but it didn't. Aspasia Glen had made a mistake. She had judged him as an elderly dilettante, easily flattered by a pretty woman. But Mr Satterthwaite behind his gallant manner had a shrewd and critical mind. He saw people pretty well as they were, not as they wished to appear to him. He saw before him, not a charming woman pleading for a whim, but a ruthless egoist determined to get her own way for some reason which was obscure to him. And he knew quite certainly that Aspasia Glen was not going to get her own way. He was not going to give up the picture of the Dead Harlequin to her. He sought rapidly in his mind for the best way of circumventing her without overt rudeness.

'I am sure,' he said, 'that everyone gives you your own way as often as they can and is only too delighted to do so.'

'Then you are really going to let me have the picture?'

Mr Satterthwaite shook his head slowly and regretfully.

'I am afraid that is impossible. You see' – he paused – 'I bought that picture for a lady. It is a present.'

'Oh! but surely –'

The telephone on the table rang sharply. With a murmured word of excuse Mr Satterthwaite took up the receiver. A voice spoke to him, a small, cold voice that sounded very far away.

'Can I speak to Mr Satterthwaite, please?'

'It is Mr Satterthwaite speaking.'

'I am Lady Charnley, Alix Charnley. I daresay you don't remember me Mr Satterthwaite, it is a great many years since we met.'

'My dear Alix. Of course, I remember you.'

'There is something I wanted to ask you. I was at the Harchester Galleries at an exhibition of pictures today, there was one called The Dead Harlequin, perhaps you recognized it – it was the Terrace Room at Charnley. I – I want to have that picture. It was sold to you.' She paused. 'Mr Satterthwaite, for reasons of my own I want that picture. Will you resell it to me?'

Mr Satterthwaite thought to himself: 'Why, this is a miracle.' As he spoke into the receiver he was thankful that Aspasia Glen could only hear one side of the conversation. 'If you will accept my gift, dear lady, it will make me very happy.' He heard a sharp exclamation behind him and hurried on. 'I bought it for you. I did indeed. But listen, my dear Alix, I want to ask you to do me a great favour, if you will.'

'Of course. Mr Satterthwaite, I am so *very* grateful.'

He went on. 'I want you to come round now to my house, at once.'

There was a slight pause and then she answered quietly:

'I will come at once.'

Mr Satterthwaite put down the receiver and turned to Miss Glen. She said quickly and angrily:

'That was the picture you were talking about?'

'Yes,' said Mr Satterthwaite, 'the lady to whom I am presenting it is coming round to this house in a few minutes.'

Suddenly Aspasia Glen's face broke once more into smiles. 'You will give me a chance of persuading her to turn the picture over to me?'

'I will give you a chance of persuading her.'

Inwardly he was strangely excited. He was in the midst of a drama that was shaping itself to some foredoomed end. He, the looker-on, was playing a star part. He turned to Miss Glen.

'Will you come into the other room with me? I should like you to meet some friends of mine.'

He held the door open for her and, crossing the hall, opened the door of the smoking-room.

'Miss Glen,' he said, 'let me introduce you to an old friend of mine, Colonel Monckton. Mr Bristow, the painter of the picture you admire so much.' Then he started as a third figure rose from the chair which he had left empty beside his own.

'I think you expected me this evening,' said Mr Quin. 'During your absence I introduced myself to your friends. I am so glad I was able to drop in.'

'My dear friend,' said Mr Satterthwaite, 'I – I have been carrying on as well as I am able, but –' He stopped before the slightly sardonic glance of Mr Quin's dark eyes. 'Let me introduce you. Mr Harley Quin, Miss Aspasia Glen.'

Was it fancy – or did she shrink back slightly. A curious expression flitted over her face. Suddenly Bristow broke in boisterously. 'I have got it.'

'Got what?'

'Got hold of what was puzzling me. There is a likeness, there is a distinct likeness.' He was staring curiously at Mr Quin. 'You see it?' – he turned to Mr Satterthwaite – 'don't you see a distinct likeness to the Harlequin of my picture – the man looking in through the window?'

It was no fancy this time. He distinctly heard Miss Glen draw in her breath sharply and even saw that she stepped back one pace.

'I told you that I was expecting someone,' said Mr Satterthwaite. He spoke with an air of triumph. 'I must tell you that my friend, Mr Quin, is a most extraordinary person. He can unravel mysteries. He can make you see things.'

'Are you a medium, sir?' demanded Colonel Monckton, eyeing Mr Quin doubtfully.

The latter smiled and slowly shook his head.

'Mr Satterthwaite exaggerates,' he said quietly. 'Once or twice when I have been with him he has done some extraordinarily good deductive work. Why he puts the credit down to me I can't say. His modesty, I suppose.'

'No, no,' said Mr Satterthwaite excitedly. 'It isn't. You make me see things – things that I ought to have seen all along – that I actually have seen – but without knowing that I saw them.'

'It sounds to me deuced complicated,' said Colonel Monckton.

'Not really,' said Mr Quin. 'The trouble is that we are not content just to see things – we will tack the wrong interpretation on to the things we see.'

Aspasia Glen turned to Frank Bristow.

'I want to know,' she said nervously, 'what put the idea of painting that picture into your head?'

Bristow shrugged his shoulders. 'I don't quite know,' he confessed. 'Something about the place – about Charnley, I mean, took hold of my imagination. The big empty room. The terrace outside, the idea of ghosts and things, I suppose. I have just been hearing the tale of the last Lord Charnley, who shot himself. Supposing you are dead, and your spirit lives on? It must be odd, you know. You might stand outside on the terrace looking in at the window at your own dead body, and you would see everything.'

'What do you mean?' said Aspasia Glen. '*See* everything?'

'Well, you would see what happened. You would see –'

The door opened and the butler announced Lady Charnley.

Mr Satterthwaite went to meet her. He had not seen her for nearly thirteen years. He remembered her as she once was, an eager, glowing girl. And now he saw – a Frozen Lady. Very fair, very pale, with an air of drifting rather than walking, a snowflake driven at random by an icy breeze. Something unreal about her. So cold, so far away.

'It was very good of you to come,' said Mr Satterthwaite.

He led her forward. She made a half gesture of recognition towards Miss Glen and then paused as the other made no response.

'I am so sorry,' she murmured, 'but surely I have met you somewhere, haven't I?'

'Over the footlights, perhaps,' said Mr Satterthwaite. 'This is Miss Aspasia Glen, Lady Charnley.'

'I am very pleased to meet you, Lady Charnley,' said Aspasia Glen.

Her voice had suddenly a slight trans-Atlantic tinge to it. Mr Satterthwaite was reminded of one of her various stage impersonations.

'Colonel Monckton you know,' continued Mr Satterthwaite, 'and this is Mr Bristow.'

He saw a sudden faint tinge of colour in her cheeks.

'Mr Bristow and I have met too,' she said, and smiled a little. 'In a train.'

'And Mr Harley Quin.'

He watched her closely, but this time there was no flicker of recognition. He set a chair for her, and then, seating himself, he cleared his throat and spoke a little nervously. 'I – this is rather an unusual little gathering. It centres round this picture. I – I think that if we liked we could – clear things up.'

'You are not going to hold a *séance*, Satterthwaite?' asked Colonel Monckton. 'You are very odd this evening.'

'No,' said Mr Satterthwaite, 'not exactly a *séance*. But my friend, Mr Quin, believes, and I agree, that one can, by looking back over the past, see things as they were and not as they appeared to be.'

'The past?' said Lady Charnley.

'I am speaking of your husband's suicide, Alix. I know it hurts you –'

'No,' said Alix Charnley, 'it doesn't hurt me. Nothing hurts me now.'

Mr Satterthwaite thought of Frank Bristow's words. '*She was not quite real you know. Shadowy. Like one of the people who come out of hills in Gaelic fairy tales.*'

'Shadowy,' he had called her. That described her exactly. A shadow, a reflection of something else. Where then was the real Alix, and his mind answered quickly: '*In the past. Divided from us by fourteen years of time.*'

'My dear,' he said, 'you frighten me. You are like the Weeping Lady with the Silver Ewer.'

Crash! The coffee cup on the table by Aspasia's elbow fell shattered to the floor. Mr Satterthwaite waved aside her apologies. He thought: 'We are getting nearer, we are getting nearer every minute – but nearer to what?'

'Let us take our minds back to that night fourteen years ago,' he said. 'Lord Charnley killed himself. For what reason? No one knows.'

Lady Charnley stirred slightly in her chair.

'Lady Charnley knows,' said Frank Bristow abruptly.

'Nonsense,' said Colonel Monckton, then stopped, frowning at her curiously.

She was looking across at the artist. It was as though he drew the words out of her. She spoke, nodding her head slowly, and her voice was like a snowflake, cold and soft.

'Yes, you are quite right. I *know*. That is why as long as I live I can never go back to Charnley. That is why when my boy Dick wants me to open the place up and live there again I tell him it can't be done.'

'Will you tell us the reason, Lady Charnley?' said Mr Quin.

She looked at him. Then, as though hypnotised, she spoke as quietly and naturally as a child.

'I will tell you if you like. Nothing seems to matter very much now. I found a letter among his papers and I destroyed it.'

'What letter?' said Mr Quin.

'The letter from the girl – from that poor child. She was the Merriams' nursery governess. He had – he had made love to her – yes, while he was engaged to me just before we were married. And she – she was going to have a child too. She wrote saying so, and that she was going to tell me about it. So, you see, he shot himself.'

She looked round at them wearily and dreamily like a child who has repeated a lesson it knows too well.

Colonel Monckton blew his nose.

'My God,' he said, 'so that was it. Well, that explains things with a vengeance.'

'Does it?' said Mr Satterthwaite, 'it doesn't explain one thing. *It doesn't explain why Mr Bristow painted that picture.*'

'What do you mean?'

Mr Satterthwaite looked across at Mr Quin as though for encouragement, and apparently got it, for he proceeded:

'Yes, I know I sound mad to all of you, but that picture is the focus of the whole thing. We are all here tonight because of that picture. That picture *had* to be painted – that is what I mean.'

'You mean the uncanny influence of the Oak Parlour?' began Colonel Monckton.

'No,' said Mr Satterthwaite. '*Not* the Oak Parlour. The Terrace Room. That is it! The spirit of the dead man standing outside the window and looking in and seeing his own dead body on the floor.'

'Which he couldn't have done,' said the Colonel, 'because the body was in the Oak Parlour.'

'Supposing it wasn't,' said Mr Satterthwaite, 'supposing it was exactly where Mr Bristow saw it, saw it imaginatively, I mean on the black and white flags in front of the window.'

'You are talking nonsense,' said Colonel Monckton, 'if it was there we shouldn't have found it in the Oak Parlour.'

'Not unless someone carried it there,' said Mr Satterthwaite.

'And in that case how could we have seen Charnley going in at the door of the Oak Parlour?' inquired Colonel Monckton.

'Well, you didn't see his face, did you?' asked Mr Satterthwaite. 'What I mean is, you saw a man going into the Oak Parlour in fancy dress, I suppose.'

'Brocade things and a wig,' said Monckton.

'Just so, and you thought it was Lord Charnley because the girl called out to him as Lord Charnley.'

'And because when we broke in a few minutes later there was only Lord Charnley there dead. You can't get away from that, Satterthwaite.'

'No,' said Mr Satterthwaite, discouraged. 'No – unless there was a hiding-place of some kind.'

'Weren't you saying something about there being a Priests' hole in that room?' put in Frank Bristow.

'Oh!' cried Mr Satterthwaite. 'Supposing –?' He waved a hand for silence and sheltered his forehead with his other hand and then spoke slowly and hesitatingly.

'I have got an idea – it may be just an idea, but I think it hangs together. Supposing someone shot Lord Charnley. Shot him in the Terrace Room. Then he – and another person – dragged the body into the Oak Parlour. They laid it down there with the pistol by its right hand. Now we go on to the next step. It must seem absolutely certain that Lord Charnley has committed suicide. I think that could be done very easily. The man in his brocade and wig passes along the hall by the Oak Parlour door and someone, to make sure of things, calls out to him as Lord Charnley from the top of the stairs. He goes in and locks both doors and fires a shot into the woodwork. There were bullet holes already in that room if you remember, one more wouldn't be noticed. He then hides quietly in the secret chamber. The doors are broken open and people rush in. It seems certain that Lord Charnley has committed suicide. No other hypothesis is even entertained.'

'Well, I think that is balderdash,' said Colonel Monckton. 'You forget that Charnley had a motive right enough for suicide.'

'A letter found afterwards,' said Mr Satterthwaite. 'A lying cruel letter written by a very clever and unscrupulous little actress who meant one day to be Lady Charnley herself.'

'You mean?'

'I mean the girl in league with Hugo Charnley,' said Mr Satterthwaite. 'You know, Monckton, everyone knows, that that man was a blackguard. He thought that he was certain to come into the title.' He turned sharply to Lady Charnley. 'What was the name of the girl who wrote that letter?'

'Monica Ford,' said Lady Charnley.

'Was it Monica Ford, Monckton, who called out to Lord Charnley from the top of the stairs?'

'Yes, now you come to speak of it, I believe it was.'

'Oh, that's impossible,' said Lady Charnley. 'I – I went to her about it. She told me it was all true. I only saw her once afterwards, but surely she couldn't have been acting the whole time.'

Mr Satterthwaite looked across the room at Aspasia Glen.

'I think she could,' he said quietly. 'I think she had in her the makings of a very accomplished actress.'

'There is one thing you haven't got over,' said Frank Bristow, 'there would be blood on the floor of the Terrace Room. Bound to be. They couldn't clear that up in a hurry.'

'No,' admitted Mr Satterthwaite, 'but there is one thing they could do – a thing that would only take a second or two – they could throw over the blood-stains the Bokhara rug. Nobody ever saw the Bokhara rug in the Terrace Room before that night.'

'I believe you are right,' said Monckton, 'but all the same those blood-stains would have to be cleared up some time?'

'Yes,' said Mr Satterthwaite, 'in the middle of the night. A woman with a jug and basin could go down the stairs and clear up the blood-stains quite easily.'

'But supposing someone saw her?'

'It wouldn't matter,' said Mr Satterthwaite. 'I am speaking now of things as they *are*. I said a woman with a jug and basin. But if I had said a Weeping Lady with a Silver Ewer that is what they would have *appeared* to be.' He got up and went across to Aspasia Glen. 'That is what you did, wasn't it?' he said. 'They call you the "Woman with the Scarf" now, but it was that night you played your first part, the "Weeping Lady with the Silver Ewer". That is why you knocked the coffee cup off that table just now. You were afraid when you saw that picture. You thought someone knew.'

Lady Charnley stretched out a white accusing hand.

'Monica Ford,' she breathed. 'I recognize you now.'

Aspasia Glen sprang to her feet with a cry. She pushed little Mr Satterthwaite aside with a shove of the hand and stood shaking in front of Mr Quin.

'So I was right. Someone *did* know! Oh, I haven't been deceived by this tomfoolery. This pretence of working things out.' She pointed at Mr Quin. '*You* were there. *You* were there outside the window looking in. You saw what we did, Hugo and I. I *knew* there was someone looking in, I felt it all the time. And yet when I looked up, there was nobody there. I knew someone was watching us. I thought once I caught a glimpse of a face at the window. It has frightened me all these years. Why did you break silence now? That is what I want to know?'

'Perhaps so that the dead may rest in peace,' said Mr Quin.

Suddenly Aspasia Glen made a rush for the door and stood there flinging a few defiant words over her shoulder.

'Do what you like. God knows there are witnesses enough to what I have been saying. I don't care, I don't care. I loved Hugo and I helped him with the ghastly business and he chucked me afterwards. He died last year. You can set the police on my tracks if you like, but as that little dried-up fellow there said, I am a pretty good actress. They will find it hard to find me.' She crashed the door behind her, and a moment later they heard the slam of the front door, also.

'Reggie,' cried Lady Charnley, 'Reggie.' The tears were streaming down her face. 'Oh, my dear, my dear, I can go back to Charnley now. I can live there with Dickie. I can tell him what his father was, the finest, the most splendid man in all the world.'

'We must consult very seriously as to what must be done in the matter,' said Colonel Monckton. 'Alix, my dear, if you will let me take you home I shall be glad to have a few words with you on the subject.'

Lady Charnley rose. She came across to Mr Satterthwaite, and laying both hands on his shoulders, she kissed him very gently.

'It is so wonderful to be alive again after being so long dead,' she said. 'It was like being dead, you know. Thank you, dear Mr Satterthwaite.' She went out of the room with Colonel Monckton. Mr Satterthwaite gazed after them. A grunt from Frank Bristow whom he had forgotten made him turn sharply round.

'She is a lovely creature,' said Bristow moodily. 'But she's not nearly so interesting as she was,' he said gloomily.

'There speaks the artist,' said Mr Satterthwaite.

'Well, she isn't,' said Mr Bristow. 'I suppose I should only get the cold shoulder if I ever went butting in at Charnley. I don't want to go where I am not wanted.'

'My dear young man,' said Mr Satterthwaite, 'if you will think a little less of the impression you are making on other people, you will, I think, be wiser and happier. You would also do well to disabuse your mind of some very old-fashioned notions, one of which is that birth has any significance at all in our modern conditions. You are one of those large proportioned young men whom women always consider good-looking, and you have possibly, if not certainly, genius. Just say that over to yourself ten times before you go to bed every night and in three months' time go and call on Lady Charnley at Charnley. That is my advice to you, and I am an old man with considerable experience of the world.'

A very charming smile suddenly spread over the artist's face.

'You have been thunderingly good to me,' he said suddenly. He seized

Mr Sattherthwaite's hand and wrung it in a powerful grip. 'I am no end grateful. I must be off now. Thanks very much for one of the most extraordinary evenings I have ever spent.'

He looked round as though to say goodbye to someone else and then started.

'I say, sir, your friend has gone. I never saw him go. He is rather a queer bird, isn't he?'

'He goes and comes very suddenly,' said Mr Satterthwaite. 'That is one of his characteristics. One doesn't always see him come and go.'

'Like Harlequin,' said Frank Bristow, 'he is invisible,' and laughed heartily at his own joke.

The Bird with the Broken Wing

'The Bird with the Broken Wing' was published in *The Mysterious Mr Quin* by Collins, April 1930. No prior magazine publication has been located.

Mr Satterthwaite looked out of the window. It was raining steadily. He shivered. Very few country houses, he reflected, were really properly heated. It cheered him to think that in a few hours' time he would be speeding towards London. Once one had passed sixty years of age, London was really much the best place.

He was feeling a little old and pathetic. Most of the members of the house party were so young. Four of them had just gone off into the library to do table turning. They had invited him to accompany them, but he had declined. He failed to derive any amusement from the monotonous counting of the letters of the alphabet and the usual meaningless jumble of letters that resulted.

Yes, London was the best place for him. He was glad that he had declined Madge Keeley's invitation when she had rung up to invite him over to Laidell half an hour ago. An adorable young person, certainly, but London was best.

Mr Satterthwaite shivered again and remembered that the fire in the library was usually a good one. He opened the door and adventured cautiously into the darkened room.

'If I'm not in the way –'

'Was that N or M? We shall have to count again. No, of course not, Mr Satterthwaite. Do you know, the most exciting things have been happening. The spirit says her name is Ada Spiers, and John here is going to marry someone called Gladys Bun almost immediately.'

Mr Satterthwaite sat down in a big easy chair in front of the fire. His eyelids drooped over his eyes and he dozed. From time to time he returned to consciousness, hearing fragments of speech.

'It can't be P A B Z L – not unless he's a Russian. John, you're shoving. I *saw* you. I believe it's a new spirit come.'

Another interval of dozing. Then a name jerked him wide awake.

'Q-U-I-N. Is that right?' 'Yes, it's rapped once for "Yes." Quin. Have you a message for someone here? Yes. For me? For John? For Sarah? For Evelyn? No – but there's no one else. Oh! it's for Mr Satterthwaite, perhaps? It says "Yes." Mr Satterthwaite, it's a message for you.'

'What does it say?'

Mr Satterthwaite was broad awake now, sitting taut and erect in his chair, his eyes shining.

The table rocked and one of the girls counted.

'LAI – it can't be – that doesn't make sense. No word begins LAI.'

'Go on,' said Mr Satterthwaite, and the command in his voice was so sharp that he was obeyed without question.

'LAIDEL? and another L – Oh! that seems to be all.'

'Go on.'

'Tell us some more, please.'

A pause.

'There doesn't seem to be any more. The table's gone quite dead. How silly.'

'No,' said Mr Satterthwaite thoughtfully. 'I don't think it's silly.'

He rose and left the room. He went straight to the telephone. Presently he was through.

'Can I speak to Miss Keeley? Is that you, Madge, my dear? I want to change my mind, if I may, and accept your kind invitation. It is not so urgent as I thought that I should get back to town. Yes – yes – I will arrive in time for dinner.'

He hung up the receiver, a strange flush on his withered cheeks. Mr Quin – the mysterious Mr Harley Quin. Mr Satterthwaite counted over on his fingers the times he had been brought into contact with that man of mystery. Where Mr Quin was concerned – things happened! What had happened or was going to happen – at Laidell?

Whatever it was, there was work for him, Mr Satterthwaite, to do. In some way or other, he would have an active part to play. He was sure of that.

Laidell was a large house. Its owner, David Keeley, was one of those quiet men with indeterminate personalities who seem to count as part of the furniture. Their inconspicuousness has nothing to do with brain power – David Keeley was a most brilliant mathematician, and had written a book totally incomprehensible to ninety-nine hundreds of humanity. But like so many men of brilliant intellect, he radiated no bodily vigour or magnetism. It was a standing joke that David Keeley was a real 'invisible man'. Footmen passed him by with the vegetables, and guests forgot to say how do you do or goodbye.

His daughter Madge was very different. A fine upstanding young woman, bursting with energy and life. Thorough, healthy and normal, and extremely pretty.

It was she who received Mr Satterthwaite when he arrived.

'How nice of you to come – after all.'

'Very delightful of you to let me change my mind. Madge, my dear, you're looking very well.'

'Oh! I'm always well.'

'Yes, I know. But it's more than that. You look – well, blooming is the word I have in mind. Has anything happened my dear? Anything – well – special?'

She laughed – blushed a little.

'It's too bad, Mr Satterthwaite. You always guess things.'

He took her hand.

'So it's that, is it? Mr Right has come along?'

It was an old-fashioned term, but Madge did not object to it. She rather liked Mr Satterthwaite's old-fashioned ways.

'I suppose so – yes. But nobody's supposed to know. It's a secret. But I don't really mind your knowing, Mr Satterthwaite. You're always so nice and sympathetic.'

Mr Satterthwaite thoroughly enjoyed romance at second hand. He was sentimental and Victorian.

'I mustn't ask who the lucky man is? Well, then all I can say is that I hope he is worthy of the honour you are conferring on him.'

Rather a duck, old Mr Satterthwaite, thought Madge.

'Oh! we shall get on awfully well together, I think,' she said. 'You see, we like doing the same things, and that's so awfully important, isn't it? We've really got a lot in common – and we know all about each other and all that. It's really been coming on for a long time. That gives one such a nice safe feeling, doesn't it?'

'Undoubtedly,' said Mr Satterthwaite. 'But in my experience one can never really know all about anyone else. That is part of the interest and charm of life.'

'Oh! I'll risk it,' said Madge, laughing, and they went up to dress for dinner.

Mr Satterthwaite was late. He had not brought a valet, and having his things unpacked for him by a stranger always flurried him a little. He came down to find everyone assembled, and in the modern style Madge merely said: 'Oh! here's Mr Satterthwaite. I'm starving. Let's go in.'

She led the way with a tall grey-haired woman – a woman of striking personality. She had a very clear rather incisive voice, and her face was clear cut and rather beautiful.

'How d'you do, Satterthwaite,' said Mr Keeley.

Mr Satterthwaite jumped.

'How do you do,' he said. 'I'm afraid I didn't see you.'

'Nobody does,' said Mr Keeley sadly.

They went in. The table was a low oval of mahogany. Mr Satterthwaite was placed between his young hostess and a short dark girl – a very hearty girl with a loud voice and a ringing determined laugh that expressed more the determination to be cheerful at all costs than any real mirth. Her name seemed to be Doris, and she was the type of young woman Mr Satterthwaite most disliked. She had, he considered, no artistic justification for existence.

On Madge's other side was a man of about thirty, whose likeness to the grey-haired woman proclaimed them mother and son.

Next to him –

Mr Satterthwaite caught his breath.

He didn't know what it was exactly. It was not beauty. It was something else – something much more elusive and intangible than beauty.

She was listening to Mr Keeley's rather ponderous dinner-table conversation, her head bent a little sideways. She was there, it seemed to Mr Satterthwaite – and yet she was not there! She was somehow a great deal less substantial than anyone else seated round the oval table. Something in the droop of her body sideways was beautiful – was more than beautiful. She looked up – her eyes met Mr Satterthwaite's for a moment across the table – and the word he wanted leapt to his mind.

Enchantment – that was it. She had the quality of enchantment. She might have been one of those creatures who are only half-human – one of the Hidden People from the Hollow Hills. She made everyone else look rather too real . . .

But at the same time, in a queer way, she stirred his pity. It was as though semi-humanity handicapped her. He sought for a phrase and found it.

'A bird with a broken wing,' said Mr Satterthwaite.

Satisfied, he turned his mind back to the subject of Girl Guides and hoped that the girl Doris had not noticed his abstraction. When she turned to the man on the other side of her – a man Mr Satterthwaite had hardly noticed, he himself turned to Madge.

'Who is the lady sitting next to your father?' he asked in a low voice.

'Mrs Graham? Oh, no! you mean Mabelle. Don't you know her? Mabelle Annesley. She was a Clydesley – one of the illfated Clydesleys.'

He started. The ill-fated Clydesleys. He remembered. A brother had shot himself, a sister had been drowned, another had perished in an earth-quake. A queer doomed family. This girl must be the youngest of them.

His thoughts were recalled suddenly. Madge's hand touched his under the table. Everyone else was talking. She gave a faint inclination of her head to her left.

'That's him,' she murmured ungrammatically.

Mr Satterthwaite nodded quickly in comprehension. So this young Graham was the man of Madge's choice. Well, she could hardly have done better as far as appearances went – and Mr Satterthwaite was a shrewd observer. A pleasant, likeable, rather matter-of-fact young fellow. They'd make a nice pair – no nonsense about either of them – good healthy sociable young folk.

Laidell was run on old-fashioned lines. The ladies left the dining-room first. Mr Satterthwaite moved up to Graham and began to talk to him. His estimate of the young man was confirmed, yet there was something that struck him as being not quite true to type. Roger Graham was distrait, his mind seemed far away, his hand shook as he replaced the glass on the table.

'He's got something on his mind,' thought Mr Satterthwaite acutely. 'Not nearly as important as he thinks it is, I dare say. All the same, I wonder what it is.'

Mr Satterthwaite was in the habit of swallowing a couple of digestive pastilles after meals. Having neglected to bring them down with him, he went up to his room to fetch them.

On his way down to the drawing-room, he passed along the long corridor on the ground floor. About half-way along it was a room known as the terrace room. As Mr Satterthwaite looked through the open doorway in passing, he stopped short.

Moonlight was streaming into the room. The latticed panes gave it a queer rhythmic pattern. A figure was sitting on the low window sill, drooping a little sideways and softly twanging the string of a ukelele – not in a jazz rhythm, but in a far older rhythm, the beat of fairy horses riding on fairy hills.

Mr Satterthwaite stood fascinated. She wore a dress of dull dark blue chiffon, ruched and pleated so that it looked like the feathers of a bird. She bent over the instrument crooning to it.

He came into the room – slowly, step by step. He was close to her when she looked up and saw him. She didn't start, he noticed, or seem surprised.

'I hope I'm not intruding,' he began.

'Please – sit down.'

He sat near her on a polished oak chair. She hummed softly under her breath.

'There's a lot of magic about tonight,' she said. 'Don't you think so?'

'Yes, there was a lot of magic about.'

'They wanted me to fetch my uke,' she explained. 'And as I passed here, I thought it would be so lovely to be alone here – in the dark and the moon.'

'Then I –' Mr Satterthwaite half rose, but she stopped him.

'Don't go. You – you fit in, somehow. It's queer, but you do.'

He sat down again.

'It's been a queer sort of evening,' she said. 'I was out in the woods late this afternoon, and I met a man – such a strange sort of man – tall and dark, like a lost soul. The sun was setting, and the light of it through the trees made him look like a kind of Harlequin.'

'Ah!' Mr Satterthwaite leant forward – his interest quickened.

'I wanted to speak to him – he – he looked so like somebody I know. But I lost him in the trees.'

'I think I know him,' said Mr Satterthwaite.

'Do you? He is – interesting, isn't he?'

'Yes, he is interesting.'

There was a pause. Mr Satterthwaite was perplexed. There was something, he felt, that he ought to do – and he didn't know what it was. But surely – surely, it had to do with this girl. He said rather clumsily:

'Sometimes – when one is unhappy – one wants to get away –'

'Yes. That's true.' She broke off suddenly. 'Oh! I see what you mean. But you're wrong. It's just the other way round. I wanted to be alone because I'm happy.'

'Happy?'

'Terribly happy.'

She spoke quite quietly, but Mr Satterthwaite had a sudden sense of shock. What this strange girl meant by being happy wasn't the same as Madge Keeley would have meant by the same words. Happiness, for Mabelle Annesley, meant some kind of intense and vivid ecstasy . . . something that was not only human, but more than human. He shrank back a little.

'I – didn't know,' he said clumsily.

'Of course you couldn't. And it's not – the actual thing – I'm not happy yet – but I'm going to be.' She leaned forward. 'Do you know what it's like to stand in a wood – a big wood with dark shadows and trees very close all round you – a wood you might never get out of – and then, suddenly – just in front of you, you see the country of your dreams – shining and beautiful – you've only got to step out from the trees and the darkness and you've found it . . .'

'So many things look beautiful,' said Mr Satterthwaite, 'before we've reached them. Some of the ugliest things in the world look the most beautiful . . .'

There was a step on the floor. Mr Satterthwaite turned his head. A fair man with a stupid, rather wooden face, stood there. He was the man Mr Satterthwaite had hardly noticed at the dinner-table.

'They're waiting for you, Mabelle,' he said.

She got up, the expression had gone out of her face, her voice was flat and calm.

'I'm coming, Gerard,' she said. 'I've been talking to Mr Satterthwaite.'

She went out of the room, Mr Satterthwaite following. He turned his head over his shoulder as he went and caught the expression on her husband's face. A hungry, despairing look.

'Enchantment,' thought Mr Satterthwaite. 'He feels it right enough. Poor fellow – poor fellow.'

The drawing-room was well lighted. Madge and Doris Coles were vociferous in reproaches.

'Mabelle, you little beast – you've been ages.'

She sat on a low stool, tuned the ukelele and sang. They all joined in.

'Is it possible,' thought Mr Satterthwaite, 'that so many idiotic songs could have been written about My Baby.'

But he had to admit that the syncopated wailing tunes were stirring. Though, of course, they weren't a patch on the old-fashioned waltz.

The air got very smoky. The syncopated rhythm went on.

'No conversation,' thought Mr Satterthwaite. 'No good music. No *peace*.' He wished the world had not become definitely so noisy.

Suddenly Mabelle Annesley broke off, smiled across the room at him, and began to sing a song of Grieg's.

'My swan – my fair one . . .'

It was a favourite of Mr Satterthwaite's. He liked the note of ingenuous surprise at the end.

'Wert only a swan then? A swan then?'

After that, the party broke up. Madge offered drinks whilst her father picked up the discarded ukelele and began twanging it absent-mindedly. The party exchanged goodnights, drifted nearer and nearer to the door. Everyone talked at once. Gerard Annesley slipped away unostentatiously, leaving the others.

Outside the drawing-room door, Mr Satterthwaite bade Mrs Graham a ceremonious goodnight. There were two staircases, one close at hand, the other at the end of a long corridor. It was by the latter that Mr Satterthwaite reached his room. Mrs Graham and her son passed by the stairs near at hand whence the quiet Gerard Annesley had already preceded them.

'You'd better get your ukelele, Mabelle,' said Madge. 'You'll forget it in the morning if you don't. You've got to make such an early start.'

'Come on, Mr Satterthwaite,' said Doris Coles, seizing him boisterously by one arm. 'Early to bed – etcetera.'

Madge took him by the other arm and all three ran down the corridor to peals of Doris's laughter. They paused at the end to wait for David Keeley, who was following at a much more sedate pace, turning out electric lights as he came. The four of them went upstairs together.

Mr Satterthwaite was just preparing to descend to the diningroom for breakfast on the following morning, when there was a light tap on the door and Madge Keeley entered. Her face was dead white, and she was shivering all over.

'Oh, Mr Satterthwaite.'

'My dear child, what's happened?' He took her hand.

'Mabelle – Mabelle Annesley . . .'

'Yes?'

What had happened? What? Something terrible – he knew that. Madge could hardly get the words out.

'She – she hanged herself last night . . . On the back of her door. Oh! it's too horrible.' She broke down – sobbing.

Hanged herself. Impossible. Incomprehensible!

He said a few soothing old-fashioned words to Madge, and hurried downstairs. He found David Keeley looking perplexed and incompetent.

'I've telephoned to the police, Satterthwaite. Apparently that's got to be done. So the doctor said. He's just finished examining the – the – good lord, it's a beastly business. She must have been desperately unhappy – to do it that way – Queer that song last night. Swan song, eh? She looked rather like a swan – a black swan.'

'Yes.'

'Swan Song,' repeated Keeley. 'Shows it was in her mind, eh?'

'It would seem so – yes, certainly it would seem so.'

He hesitated, then asked if he might see – if, that is . . .

His host comprehended the stammering request.

'If you want to – I'd forgotten you have a *penchant* for human tragedies.'

He led the way up the broad staircase. Mr Satterthwaite followed him. At the head of the stairs was the room occupied by Roger Graham and opposite it, on the other side of the passage, his mother's room. The latter door was ajar and a faint wisp of smoke floated through it.

A momentary surprise invaded Mr Satterthwaite's mind. He had not judged Mrs Graham to be a woman who smoked so early in the day. Indeed, he had had the idea that she did not smoke at all.

They went along the passage to the end door but one. David Keeley entered the room and Mr Satterthwaite followed him.

The room was not a very large one and showed signs of a man's occupation. A door in the wall led into a second room. A bit of cut rope still dangled from a hook high up on the door. On the bed . . .

Mr Satterthwaite stood for a minute looking down on the heap of huddled chiffon. He noticed that it was ruched and pleated like the plumage of a bird. At the face, after one glance, he did not look again.

He glanced from the door with its dangling rope to the communicating door through which they had come.

'Was that open?'

'Yes. At least the maid says so.'

'Annesley slept in there? Did he hear anything?'

'He says – nothing.'

'Almost incredible,' murmured Mr Satterthwaite. He looked back at the form on the bed.

'Where is he?'

'Annesley? He's downstairs with the doctor.'

They went downstairs to find an Inspector of police had arrived. Mr Satterthwaite was agreeably surprised to recognize in him an old acquaintance, Inspector Winkfield. The Inspector went upstairs with the doctor, and a few minutes later a request came that all members of the house party should assemble in the drawing-room.

The blinds had been drawn, and the whole room had a funereal aspect. Doris Coles looked frightened and subdued. Every now and then she dabbed her eyes with a handkerchief. Madge was resolute and alert, her feelings fully under control by now. Mrs Graham was composed, as always, her face grave and impassive. The tragedy seemed to have affected her son more keenly than anyone. He looked a positive wreck this morning. David Keeley, as usual, had subsided into the background.

The bereaved husband sat alone, a little apart from the others. There was a queer dazed looked about him, as though he could hardly realize what had taken place.

Mr Satterthwaite, outwardly composed, was inwardly seething with the importance of a duty shortly to be performed.

Inspector Winkfield, followed by Dr Morris, came in and shut the door behind him. He cleared his throat and spoke.

'This is a very sad occurrence – very sad, I'm sure. It's necessary, under the circumstances, that I should ask everybody a few questions. You'll not object, I'm sure. I'll begin with Mr Annesley. You'll forgive my asking, sir, but had your good lady ever threatened to take her life?'

Mr Satterthwaite opened his lips impulsively, then closed them again. There was plenty of time. Better not speak too soon.

'I – no, I don't think so.'

His voice was so hesitating, so peculiar, that everyone shot a covert glance at him.

'You're not sure, sir?'

'Yes – I'm – quite sure. She didn't.'

'Ah! Were you aware that she was unhappy in any way?'

'No. I – no, I wasn't.'

'She said nothing to you. About feeling depressed, for instance?'

'I – no, nothing.'

Whatever the Inspector thought, he said nothing. Instead he proceeded to his next point.

'Will you describe to me briefly the events of last night?'

'We – all went up to bed. I fell asleep immediately and heard nothing. The housemaid's scream aroused me this morning. I rushed into the adjoining room and found my wife – and found her –'

His voice broke. The Inspector nodded.

'Yes, yes, that's quite enough. We needn't go into that. When did you last see your wife the night before?'

'I – downstairs.'

'Downstairs?'

'Yes, we all left the drawing-room together. I went straight up leaving the others talking in the hall.'

'And you didn't see your wife again? Didn't she say goodnight when she came up to bed?'

'I was asleep when she came up.'

'But she only followed you a few minutes later. That's right, isn't it, sir?' He looked at David Keeley, who nodded.

'She hadn't come up half an hour later.'

Annesley spoke stubbornly. The Inspector's eyes strayed gently to Mrs Graham.

'She didn't stay in your room talking, Madam?'

Did Mr Satterthwaite fancy it, or was there a slight pause before Mrs Graham said with her customary quiet decision of manner:

'No, I went straight into my room and closed the door. I heard nothing.'

'And you say, sir' – the Inspector had shifted his attention back to

Annesley – 'that you slept and heard nothing. The communicating door was open, was it not?'

'I – I believe so. But my wife would have entered her room by the other door from the corridor.'

'Even so, sir, there would have been certain sounds – a choking noise, a drumming of heels on the door –'

'No.'

It was Mr Satterthwaite who spoke, impetuously, unable to stop himself. Every eye turned towards him in surprise. He himself became nervous, stammered, and turned pink.

'I – I beg your pardon, Inspector. But I must speak. You are on the wrong track – the wrong track altogether. Mrs Annesley did not kill herself – I am sure of it. She was murdered.'

There was a dead silence, then Inspector Winkfield said quietly:

'What leads you to say that, sir?'

'I – it is a feeling. A very strong feeling.'

'But I think, sir, there must be more than that to it. There must be some particular reason.'

Well, of course there *was* a particular reason. There was the mysterious message from Mr Quin. But you couldn't tell a police inspector that. Mr Satterthwaite cast about desperately, and found nothing.

'Last night – when we were talking together, she said she was very happy. Very happy – just that. That wasn't like a woman thinking of committing suicide.'

He was triumphant. He added:

'She went back to the drawing-room to fetch her ukelele, so that she wouldn't forget it in the morning. That didn't look like suicide either.'

'No,' admitted the Inspector. 'No, perhaps it didn't.' He turned to David Keeley. 'Did she take the ukelele upstairs with her?'

The mathematician tried to remember.

'I think – yes, she did. She went upstairs carrying it in her hand. I remember seeing it just as she turned the corner of the staircase before I turned off the light down here.'

'Oh!' cried Madge. 'But it's here now.'

She pointed dramatically to where the ukelele lay on a table.

'That's curious,' said the Inspector. He stepped swiftly across and rang the bell.

A brief order sent the butler in search of the housemaid whose business it was to do the rooms in the morning. She came, and was quite positive in her answer. The ukelele had been there first thing that morning when she had dusted.

Inspector Winkfield dismissed her and then said curtly:

'I would like to speak to Mr Satterthwaite in private, please. Everyone may go. But no one is to leave the house.'

Mr Satterthwaite twittered into speech as soon as the door had closed behind the others.

'I – I am sure, Inspector, that you have the case excellently in hand. Excellently. I just felt that – having, as I say, a very strong feeling –'

The Inspector arrested further speech with an upraised hand.

'You're quite right, Mr Satterthwaite. The lady was murdered.'

'You knew it?' Mr Satterthwaite was chagrined.

'There were certain things that puzzled Dr Morris.' He looked across at the doctor, who had remained, and the doctor assented to his statement with a nod of the head. 'We made a thorough examination. The rope that was round her neck wasn't the rope that she was strangled with – it was something much thinner that did the job, something more like a wire. It had cut right into the flesh. The mark of the rope was superimposed on it. She was strangled and then hung up on the door afterwards to make it look like suicide.'

'But who –?'

'Yes,' said the Inspector. 'Who? That's the question. What about the husband sleeping next door, who never said goodnight to his wife and who heard nothing? I should say we hadn't far to look. Must find out what terms they were on That's where you can be useful to us, Mr Satterthwaite. You've the *ongtray* here, and you can get the hang of things in a way we can't. Find out what relations there were between the two.'

'I hardly like –' began Mr Satterthwaite, stiffening.

'It won't be the first murder mystery you've helped us with. I remember the case of Mrs Strangeways. You've got a *flair* for that sort of thing, sir. An absolute *flair.*'

Yes, it was true – he *had a flair.* He said quietly:

'I will do my best, Inspector.'

Had Gerard Annesley killed his wife? Had he? Mr Satterthwaite recalled that look of misery last night. He loved her – and he was suffering. Suffering will drive a man to strange deeds.

But there was something else – some other factor. Mabelle had spoken of herself as coming out of a wood – she was looking forward to happiness – not a quiet rational happiness – but a happiness that was irrational – a wild ecstasy . . .

If Gerard Annesley had spoken the truth, Mabelle had not come to her room till at least half an hour later than he had done. Yet David Keeley had seen her going up those stairs. There were two other rooms occupied in that wing. There was Mrs Graham's, and there was her son's.

Her son's. But he and Madge . . .

Surely Madge would have guessed . . . But Madge wasn't the guessing kind. All the same, no smoke without fire – Smoke!

Ah! he remembered. *A wisp of smoke curling out through Mrs Graham's bedroom door.*

He acted on impulse. Straight up the stairs and into her room. It was empty. He closed the door behind him and locked it.

He went across to the grate. A heap of charred fragments. Very gingerly he raked them over with his finger. His luck was in. In the very centre were some unburnt fragments – fragments of letters . . .

Very disjointed fragments, but they told him something of value.

'Life can be wonderful, Roger darling. I never knew . . . all my life has been a dream till I met you, Roger . . .'

'. . . Gerard knows, I think . . . I am sorry but what can I do? Nothing is real to me but you, Roger . . . We shall be together, soon.'

'What are you going to tell him at Laidell, Roger? You write strangely – but I am not afraid . . .'

Very carefully, Mr Satterthwaite put the fragments into an envelope from the writing-table. He went to the door, unlocked it and opened it to find himself face to face with Mrs Graham.

It was an awkward moment, and Mr Satterthwaite was momentarily out of countenance. He did what was, perhaps, the best thing, attacked the situation with simplicity.

'I have been searching your room, Mrs Graham. I have found something – a packet of letters imperfectly burnt.'

A wave of alarm passed over her face. It was gone in a flash, but it had been there.

'Letters from Mrs Annesley to your son.'

She hesitated for a minute, then said quietly: 'That is so. I thought they would be better burnt.'

'For what reason?'

'My son is engaged to be married. These letters – if they had been brought into publicity through the poor girl's suicide – might have caused much pain and trouble.'

'Your son could burn his own letters.'

She had no answer ready for that. Mr Satterthwaite pursued his advantage.

'You found these letters in his room, brought them into your room and burnt them. Why? You were afraid, Mrs Graham.'

'I am not in the habit of being afraid, Mr Satterthwaite.'

'No – but this was a desperate case.'

'Desperate?'

'Your son might have been in danger of arrest – for murder.'

'Murder!'

He saw her face go white. He went on quickly:

'You heard Mrs Annesley go into your son's room last night. He had told her of his engagement? No, I see he hadn't. He told her then. They quarrelled, and he –'

'That's a lie!'

They had been so absorbed in their duel of words that they had not heard approaching footsteps. Roger Graham had come up behind them unperceived by either.

'It's all right, Mother. Don't – worry. Come into my room, Mr Satterthwaite.'

Mr Sattherwaite followed him into his room. Mrs Graham had turned away and did not attempt to follow them. Roger Graham shut the door.

'Listen, Mr Satterthwaite, you think I killed Mabelle. You think I strangled her – here – and took her along and hung her up on that door – later – when everyone was asleep?'

Mr Satterthwaite stared at him. Then he said surprisingly:

'No, I do not think so.'

'Thank God for that. I couldn't have killed Mabelle. I – I loved her. Or didn't I? I don't know. It's a tangle that I can't explain. I'm fond of Madge – I always have been. And she's such a good sort. We suit each other. But Mabelle was different. It was – I can't explain it – a sort of enchantment. I was, I think – afraid of her.'

Mr Satterthwaite nodded.

'It was madness – a kind of bewildering ecstasy . . . But it was impossible. It wouldn't have worked. That sort of thing – doesn't last. I know what it means now to have a spell cast over you.'

'Yes, it must have been like that,' said Mr Satterthwaite thoughtfully.

'I – I wanted to get out of it all. I was going to tell Mabelle – last night.'

'But you didn't?'

'No, I didn't,' said Graham slowly. 'I swear to you, Mr Satterthwaite, that I never saw her after I said goodnight downstairs.'

'I believe you,' said Mr Satterthwaite.

He got up. It was not Roger Graham who had killed Mabelle Annesley. He could have fled from her, but he could not have killed her. He had been afraid of her, afraid of that wild intangible fairy-like quality of hers. He had known enchantment – and turned his back on it. He had gone for the safe sensible thing that he had known 'would work' and had relinquished the intangible dream that might lead him he knew not where.

He was a sensible young man, and, as such, uninteresting to Mr Satterthwaite, who was an artist and a connoisseur in life.

He left Roger Graham in his room and went downstairs. The drawing-room was empty. Mabelle's ukelele lay on a stool by the window. He took it up and twanged it absent-mindedly. He knew nothing of the instrument, but his ear told him that it was abominably out of tune. He turned a key experimentally.

Doris Coles came into the room. She looked at him reproachfully.

'Poor Mabelle's uke,' she said.

Her clear condemnation made Mr Satterthwaite feel obstinate.

'Tune it for me,' he said, and added: 'If you can.'

'Of course I can,' said Doris, wounded at the suggestion of incompetence in any direction.

She took it from him, twanged a string, turned a key briskly – and the string snapped.

'Well, I never. Oh! I see – but how extraordinary! It's the wrong string – a size too big. It's an A string. How stupid to put that on. Of course it snaps when you try to tune it up. How stupid people are.'

'Yes,' said Mr Satterthwaite. 'They are – even when they try to be clever . . .'

His tone was so odd that she stared at him. He took the ukelele from her and removed the broken string He went out of the room holding it in his hand. In the library he found David Keeley.

'Here,' he said.

He held out the string. Keeley took it.

'What's this?'

'A broken ukelele string.' He paused and then went on: '*What did you do with the other one?*'

'The other one?'

'*The one you strangled her with.* Your were very clever, weren't you? It was done very quickly – just in that moment we were all laughing and talking in the hall.

'Mabelle came back into this room for her ukelele. You had taken the string off as you fiddled with it just before. You caught her round the throat with it and strangled her. Then you came out and locked the door and joined us. Later, in the dead of night, you came down and – and disposed of the body by hanging it on the door of her room. And you put another string on the ukelele – *but it was the wrong string*, that's why you were stupid.'

There was a pause.

338   Detectives and Young Adventurers: The Complete Short Stories

'But why did you do it?' said Mr Satterthwaite. 'In God's name, *why*?'

Mr Keeley laughed, a funny giggling little laugh that made Mr Satterthwaite feel rather sick.

'It was so very simple,' he said. 'That's why! And then – nobody ever noticed me. Nobody ever noticed what I was doing. I thought – I thought I'd have the laugh of them . . .'

And again he gave that furtive little giggle and looked at Mr Satterthwaite with mad eyes.

Mr Satterthwaite was glad that at that moment Inspector Winkfield came into the room.

It was twenty-four hours later, on his way to London, that Mr Satterthwaite awoke from a doze to find a tall dark man sitting opposite to him in the railway carriage. He was not altogether surprised.

'My dear Mr Quin!'

'Yes – I am here.'

Mr Satterthwaite said slowly: 'I can hardly face you. I am ashamed – I failed.'

'Are you sure of that?'

'I did not save her.'

'But you discovered the truth?'

'Yes – that is true. One or other of those young men might have been accused – might even have been found guilty. So, at any rate, I saved a man's life. But, she – she – that strange enchanting creature . . .' His voice broke off.

Mr Quin looked at him.

'Is death the greatest evil that can happen to anyone?'

'I – well – perhaps – No . . .'

Mr Satterthwaite remembered . . . Madge and Roger Graham . . . Mabelle's face in the moonlight – its serene unearthly happiness . . .

'No,' he admitted. 'No – perhaps death is not the greatest evil . . .'

He remembered the ruffled blue chiffon of her dress that had seemed to him like the plumage of a bird . . . A bird with a broken wing . . .

When he looked up, he found himself alone. Mr Quin was no longer there.

But he had left something behind.

On the seat was a roughly carved bird fashioned out of some dim blue stone. It had, possibly, no great artistic merit. But it had something else.

It had the vague quality of enchantment.

So said Mr Satterthwaite – and Mr Satterthwaite was a connoisseur.

The World's End

'The World's End' was first published in the USA as 'World's End' in
Flynn's Weekly, 20 November 1926, and then as 'The Magic of Mr
Quin No.3: The World's End' in Storyteller magazine, February 1927.

Mr Satterthwaite had come to Corsica because of the Duchess. It was
out of his beat. On the Riviera he was sure of his comforts, and to be
comfortable meant a lot to Mr Satterthwaite. But though he liked his
comfort, he also liked a Duchess. In his way, a harmless, gentlemanly,
old-fashioned way, Mr Satterthwaite was a snob. He liked the best people.
And the Duchess of Leith was a very authentic Duchess. There were no
Chicago pork butchers in her ancestry. She was the daughter of a Duke
as well as the wife of one.

For the rest, she was rather a shabby-looking old lady, a good deal
given to black bead trimmings on her clothes. She had quantities of
diamonds in old-fashioned settings, and she wore them as her mother
before her had worn them: pinned all over her indiscriminately. Someone
had suggested once that the Duchess stood in the middle of the room
whilst her maid flung brooches at her haphazard. She subscribed generously to charities, and looked well after her tenants and dependents, but
was extremely mean over small sums. She cadged lifts from her friends,
and did her shopping in bargain basements.

The Duchess was seized with a whim for Corsica. Cannes bored her
and she had a bitter argument with the hotel proprietor over the price
of her rooms.

'And you shall go with me, Satterthwaite,' she said firmly. 'We needn't
be afraid of scandal at our time of life.'

Mr Satterthwaite was delicately flattered. No one had ever mentioned
scandal in connection with him before. He was far too insignificant.
Scandal – and a Duchess – delicious!

'Picturesque you know,' said the Duchess. 'Brigands – all that sort of thing. And extremely cheap, so I've heard. Manuel was positively impudent this morning. These hotel proprietors need putting in their place. They can't expect to get the best people if they go on like this. I told him so plainly.'

'I believe,' said Mr Satterthwaite, 'that one can fly over quite comfortably. From Antibes.'

'They probably charge you a pretty penny for it,' said the Duchess sharply. 'Find out, will you?'

'Certainly, Duchess.'

Mr Satterthwaite was still in a flutter of gratification despite the fact that his role was clearly to be that of a glorified courier.

When she learned the price of a passage by Avion, the Duchess turned it down promptly.

'They needn't think I'm going to pay a ridiculous sum like that to go in one of their nasty dangerous things.'

So they went by boat, and Mr Satterthwaite endured ten hours of acute discomfort. To begin with, as the boat sailed at seven, he took it for granted that there would be dinner on board. But there was no dinner. The boat was small and the sea was rough. Mr Satterthwaite was decanted at Ajaccio in the early hours of the morning more dead than alive.

The Duchess, on the contrary, was perfectly fresh. She never minded discomfort if she could feel she was saving money. She waxed enthusiastic over the scene on the quay, with the palm trees and the rising sun. The whole population seemed to have turned out to watch the arrival of the boat, and the launching of the gangway was attended with excited cries and directions.

'*On dirait*,' said a stout Frenchman who stood beside them, '*que jamais avant on n'a fait cette manoeuvre là!*'

'That maid of mine has been sick all night,' said the Duchess. 'The girl's a perfect fool.'

Mr Satterthwaite smiled in a pallid fashion.

'A waste of good food, I call it,' continued the Duchess robustly.

'Did she get any food?' asked Mr Satterthwaite enviously.

'I happened to bring some biscuits and a stick of chocolate on board with me,' said the Duchess. 'When I found there was no dinner to be got, I gave the lot to her. The lower classes always make such a fuss about going without their meals.'

With a cry of triumph the launching of the gangway was accomplished. A Musical Comedy chorus of brigands rushed aboard and wrested hand-luggage from the passengers by main force.

'Come on, Satterthwaite,' said the Duchess. 'I want a hot bath and some coffee.'

So did Mr Satterthwaite. He was not wholly successful, however. They

were received at the hotel by a bowing manager and were shown to their
rooms. The Duchess's had a bathroom attached. Mr Satterthwaite,
however, was directed to a bath that appeared to be situated in somebody
else's bedroom. To expect the water to be hot at that hour in the morning
was, perhaps, unreasonable. Later he drank intensely black coffee, served
in a pot without a lid. The shutters and the window of his room had
been flung open, and the crisp morning air came in fragrantly. A day of
dazzling blue and green.

The waiter waved his hand with a flourish to call attention to the view.

'*Ajaccio*,' he said solemnly. '*Le plus beau port du monde!*'

And he departed abruptly.

Looking out over the deep blue of the bay, with the snowy mountains
beyond, Mr Satterthwaite was almost inclined to agree with him. He
finished his coffee, and lying down on the bed, fell fast asleep.

At *déjeuner* the Duchess was in great spirits.

'This is just what will be good for you, Satterthwaite,' she said. 'Get
you out of all those dusty little old-maidish ways of yours.' She swept a
lorgnette round the room. 'Upon my word, there's Naomi Carlton Smith.'

She indicated a girl sitting by herself at a table in the window. A round-
shouldered girl, who slouched as she sat. Her dress appeared to be made
of some kind of brown sacking. She had black hair, untidily bobbed.

'An artist?' asked Mr Satterthwaite.

He was always good at placing people.

'Quite right,' said the Duchess. 'Calls herself one anyway. I knew she
was mooching around in some queer quarter of the globe. Poor as a church
mouse, proud as Lucifer, and a bee in her bonnet like all the Carlton Smiths.
Her mother was my first cousin.'

'She's one of the Knowlton lot then?'

The Duchess nodded.

'Been her own worst enemy,' she volunteered. 'Clever girl too. Mixed
herself up with a most undesirable young man. One of that Chelsea crowd.
Wrote plays or poems or something unhealthy. Nobody took 'em, of course.
Then he stole somebody's jewels and got caught out. I forget what they
gave him. Five years, I think. But you must remember? It was last winter.'

'Last winter I was in Egypt,' explained Mr Satterthwaite. 'I had 'flu very
badly the end of January, and the doctors insisted on Egypt afterwards. I
missed a lot.'

His voice rang with a note of real regret.

'That girl seems to me to be moping,' said the Duchess, raising her
lorgnette once more. 'I can't allow that.'

On her way out, she stopped by Miss Carlton Smith's table and tapped
the girl on the shoulder.

'Well, Naomi, you don't seem to remember me?'

Naomi rose rather unwillingly to her feet.

'Yes, I do, Duchess. I saw you come in. I thought it was quite likely you mightn't recognize me.'

She drawled the words lazily, with a complete indifference of manner.

'When you've finished your lunch, come and talk to me on the terrace,' ordered the Duchess.

'Very well.'

Naomi yawned.

'Shocking manners,' said the Duchess, to Mr Satterthwaite, as she resumed her progress. 'All the Carlton Smiths have.'

They had their coffee outside in the sunshine. They had been there about six minutes when Naomi Carlton Smith lounged out from the hotel and joined them. She let herself fall slackly on to a chair with her legs stretched out ungracefully in front of her.

An odd face, with its jutting chin and deep-set grey eyes. A clever, unhappy face – a face that only just missed being beautiful.

'Well, Naomi,' said the Duchess briskly. 'And what are you doing with yourself?'

'Oh, I dunno. Just marking time.'

'Been painting?'

'A bit.'

'Show me your things.'

Naomi grinned. She was not cowed by the autocrat. She was amused. She went into the hotel and came out again with a portfolio.

'You won't like 'em, Duchess,' she said warningly. 'Say what you like. You won't hurt my feelings.'

Mr Satterthwaite moved his chair a little nearer. He was interested. In another minute he was more interested still. The Duchess was frankly unsympathetic.

'I can't even see which way the things ought to be,' she complained. 'Good gracious, child, there was never a sky that colour – or a sea either.'

'That's the way I see 'em,' said Naomi placidly.

'Ugh!' said the Duchess, inspecting another. 'This gives me the creeps.'

'It's meant to,' said Naomi. 'You're paying me a compliment without knowing it.'

It was a queer vorticist study of a prickly pear – just recognizable as such. Grey-green with slodges of violent colour where the fruit glittered like jewels. A swirling mass of evil, fleshy – festering. Mr Satterthwaite shuddered and turned his head aside.

He found Naomi looking at him and nodding her head in comprehension.

'I know,' she said. 'But it *is* beastly.'

The Duchess cleared her throat.

'It seems quite easy to be an artist nowadays,' she observed wither-ingly. 'There's no attempt to copy things. You just shovel on some paint – I don't know what with, not a brush, I'm sure –'

'Palette knife,' interposed Naomi, smiling broadly once more.

'A good deal at a time,' continued the Duchess. 'In lumps. And there you are! Everyone says: "How clever." Well, I've no patience with that sort of thing. Give me –'

'A nice picture of a dog or a horse, by Edwin Landseer.'

'And why not?' demanded the Duchess. 'What's wrong with Landseer?'

'Nothing,' said Naomi. 'He's all right. And you're all right. The tops of things are always nice and shiny and smooth. I respect you, Duchess, you've got force. You've met life fair and square and you've come out on top. But the people who are underneath see the under side of things. And that's interesting in a way.'

The Duchess stared at her.

'I haven't the faintest idea what you're talking about,' she declared.

Mr Satterthwaite was still examining the sketches. He realized, as the Duchess could not, the perfection of technique behind them. He was startled and delighted. He looked up at the girl.

'Will you sell me one of these, Miss Carlton Smith?' he asked.

'You can have any one you like for five guineas,' said the girl indiffer-ently.

Mr Satterthwaite hesitated a minute or two and then he selected a study of prickly pear and aloe. In the foreground was a vivid blur of yellow mimosa, the scarlet of the aloe flower danced in and out of the picture, and inexorable, mathematically underlying the whole, was the oblong pattern of the prickly pear and the sword motif of the aloe.

He made a little bow to the girl.

'I am very happy to have secured this, and I think I have made a bargain. Some day, Miss Carlton Smith, I shall be able to sell this sketch at a very good profit – if I want to!'

The girl leant forward to see which one he had taken. He saw a new look come into her eyes. For the first time she was really aware of his existence, and there was respect in the quick glance she gave him.

'You have chosen the best,' she said. 'I – I am glad.'

'Well, I suppose you know what you're doing,' said the Duchess. 'And I daresay you're right. I've heard that you are quite a connoisseur. But you can't tell me that all this new stuff is art, because it isn't. Still, we needn't go into that. Now I'm only going to be here a few days and I want to see something of the island. You've got a car, I suppose, Naomi?'

344 Detectives and Young Adventurers: The Complete Short Stories

The girl nodded.

'Excellent,' said the Duchess. 'We'll make a trip somewhere tomorrow.'

'It's only a two-seater.'

'Nonsense, there's a dickey, I suppose, that will do for Mr Satterthwaite?'

A shuddering sigh went through Mr Satterthwaite. He had observed the Corsican roads that morning. Naomi was regarding him thoughtfully.

'I'm afraid my car would be no good to you,' she said. 'It's a terribly battered old bus. I bought it second-hand for a mere song. It will just get me up the hills – with coaxing. But I can't take passengers. There's quite a good garage, though, in the town. You can hire a car there.'

'Hire a car?' said the Duchess, scandalized. 'What an idea. Who's that nice-looking man, rather yellow, who drove up in a four-seater just before lunch?'

'I expect you mean Mr Tomlinson. He's a retired Indian judge.'

'That accounts for the yellowness,' said the Duchess. 'I was afraid it might be jaundice. He seems quite a decent sort of man. I shall talk to him.'

That evening, on coming down to dinner, Mr Satterthwaite found the Duchess resplendent in black velvet and diamonds, talking earnestly to the owner of the four-seater car. She beckoned authoritatively.

'Come here, Mr Satterthwaite, Mr Tomlinson is telling me the most interesting things, and what do you think? – he is actually going to take us on an expedition tomorrow in his car.'

Mr Satterthwaite regarded her with admiration.

'We must go in to dinner,' said the Duchess. 'Do come and sit at our table, Mr Tomlinson, and then you can go on with what you were telling me.'

'Quite a decent sort of man,' the Duchess pronounced later.

'With quite a decent sort of car,' retorted Mr Satterthwaite.

'Naughty,' said the Duchess, and gave him a resounding blow on the knuckles with the dingy black fan she always carried. Mr Satterthwaite winced with pain.

'Naomi is coming too,' said the Duchess. 'In her car. That girl wants taking out of herself. She's very selfish. Not exactly self-centred, but totally indifferent to everyone and everything. Don't you agree?'

'I don't think that's possible,' said Mr Satterthwaite, slowly. 'I mean, everyone's interest must go *somewhere*. There are, of course, the people who revolve round themselves – but I agree with you, she's not one of that kind. She's totally uninterested in herself. And yet she's got a strong character – there must be *something*. I thought at first it was her art – but it isn't. I've never met anyone so detached from life. That's dangerous.'

'Dangerous? What do you mean?'

'Well, you see – it must mean an obsession of some kind, and obsessions are always dangerous.'

'Satterthwaite,' said the Duchess, 'don't be a fool. And listen to me. About tomorrow –'

Mr Satterthwaite listened. It was very much his role in life.

They started early the following morning, taking their lunch with them. Naomi, who had been six months in the island, was to be the pioneer. Mr Satterthwaite went over to her as she sat waiting to start.

'You are sure that – I can't come with you?' he said wistfully.

She shook her head.

'You'll be much more comfortable in the back of the other car. Nicely padded seats and all that. This is a regular old rattle trap. You'd leap in the air going over the bumps.'

'And then, of course, the hills.'

Naomi laughed.

'Oh, I only said that to rescue you from the dickey. The Duchess could perfectly well afford to have hired a car. She's the meanest woman in England. All the same, the old thing is rather a sport, and I can't help liking her.'

'Then I could come with you after all?' said Mr Satterthwaite eagerly.

She looked at him curiously.

'Why are you so anxious to come with me?'

'Can you ask?' Mr Satterthwaite made his funny old-fashioned bow.

She smiled, but shook her head.

'That isn't the reason,' she said thoughtfully. 'It's odd . . . But you can't come with me – not today.'

'Another day, perhaps,' suggested Mr Satterthwaite politely.

'Oh, another day!' she laughed suddenly, a very queer laugh, Mr Satterthwaite thought. 'Another day! Well, we'll see.'

They started. They drove through the town, and then round the long curve of the bay, winding inland to cross a river and then back to the coast with its hundreds of little sandy coves. And then they began to climb. In and out, round nerve-shattering curves, upwards, ever upwards on the tortuous winding road. The blue bay was far below them, and on the other side of it Ajaccio sparkled in the sun, white, like a fairy city.

In and out, in and out, with a precipice first one side of them, then the other. Mr Satterthwaite felt slightly giddy, he also felt slightly sick. The road was not very wide. And still they climbed.

It was cold now. The wind came to them straight off the snow peaks. Mr Satterthwaite turned up his coat collar and buttoned it tightly under his chin.

It was very cold. Across the water, Ajaccio was still bathed in sunlight, but up here thick grey clouds came drifting across the face of the sun. Mr Satterthwaite ceased to admire the view. He yearned for a steam-heated hotel and a comfortable armchair.

Ahead of them Naomi's little two-seater drove steadily forward. Up, still up. They were on top of the world now. On either side of them were lower hills, hills sloping down to valleys. They looked straight across to the snow peaks. And the wind came tearing over them, sharp, like a knife. Suddenly Naomi's car stopped, and she looked back.

'We've arrived,' she said. 'At the World's End. And I don't think it's an awfully good day for it.'

They all got out. They had arrived in a tiny village, with half a dozen stone cottages. An imposing name was printed in letters a foot high.

'Coti Chiaveeri.'

Naomi shrugged her shoulders.

'That's its official name, but I prefer to call it the World's End.'

She walked on a few steps, and Mr Satterthwaite joined her. They were beyond the houses now. The road stopped. As Naomi had said, this was the end, the back of beyond, the beginning of nowhere. Behind them the white ribbon of the road, in front of them – nothing. Only far, far below, the sea . . .

Mr Satterthwaite drew a deep breath.

'It's an extraordinary place. One feels that anything might happen here, that one might meet – anyone –'

He stopped, for just in front of them a man was sitting on a boulder, his face turned to the sea. They had not seen him till this moment, and his appearance had the suddenness of a conjuring trick. He might have sprung from the surrounding landscape.

'I wonder –' began Mr Satterthwaite.

But at that minute the stranger turned, and Mr Satterthwaite saw his face.

'Why, Mr Quin! How extraordinary. Miss Carlton Smith, I want to introduce my friend Mr Quin to you. He's the most unusual fellow. You are, you know. You always turn up in the nick of time –'

He stopped, with the feeling that he had said something awkwardly significant, and yet for the life of him he could not think what it was.

Naomi had shaken hands with Mr Quin in her usual abrupt style.

'We're here for a picnic,' she said. 'And it seems to me we shall be pretty well frozen to the bone.'

Mr Satterthwaite shivered.

'Perhaps,' he said uncertainly, 'we shall find a sheltered spot?'

'Which this isn't,' agreed Naomi. 'Still, it's worth seeing, isn't it?'

'Yes, indeed.' Mr Satterthwaite turned to Mr Quin. 'Miss Carlton Smith calls this place the World's End. Rather a good name, eh?'

Mr Quin nodded his head slowly several times.

'Yes – a very suggestive name. I suppose one only comes once in one's life to a place like that – a place where one can't go on any longer.'

'What do you mean?' asked Naomi sharply.

He turned to her.

'Well, usually, there's a choice, isn't there? To the right or to the left. Forward or back. Here – there's the road behind you and in front of you – nothing.'

Naomi stared at him. Suddenly she shivered and began to retrace her steps towards the others. The two men fell in beside her. Mr Quin continued to talk, but his tone was now easily conversational.

'Is the small car yours, Miss Carlton Smith?'

'Yes.'

'You drive yourself? One needs, I think, a good deal of nerve to do that round here. The turns are rather appalling. A moment of inattention, a brake that failed to hold, and – over the edge – down – down – down. It would be – very easily done.'

They had now joined the others. Mr Satterthwaite introduced his friend. He felt a tug at his arm. It was Naomi. She drew him apart from the others.

'Who is he?' she demanded fiercely.

Mr Satterthwaite gazed at her in astonishment.

'Well, I hardly know. I mean, I have known him for some years now – we have run across each other from time to time, but in the sense of knowing actually –'

He stopped. These were futilities that he was uttering, and the girl by his side was not listening. She was standing with her head bent down, her hands clenched by her sides.

'He knows things,' she said. 'He knows things . . . How does he know?'

Mr Satterthwaite had no answer. He could only look at her dumbly, unable to comprehend the storm that shook her.

'I'm afraid,' she muttered.

'Afraid of Mr Quin?'

'I'm afraid of his eyes. He sees things . . .'

Something cold and wet fell on Mr Satterthwaite's cheek. He looked up.

'Why, it's snowing,' he exclaimed, in great surprise.

'A nice day to have chosen for a picnic,' said Naomi.

She had regained control of herself with an effort.

What was to be done? A babel of suggestions broke out. The snow came down thick and fast. Mr Quin made a suggestion and everyone welcomed it. There was a little stone Cassecroute at the end of the row of houses. There was a stampede towards it.

'You have your provisions,' said Mr Quin, 'and they will probably be able to make you some coffee.'

It was a tiny place, rather dark, for the one little window did little towards lighting it, but from one end came a grateful glow of warmth. An old Corsican woman was just throwing a handful of branches on the fire. It blazed up, and by its light the newcomers realized that others were before them.

Three people were sitting at the end of a bare wooden table. There was something unreal about the scene to Mr Satterthwaite's eye, there was something even more unreal about the people.

The woman who sat at the end of the table looked like a duchess – that is, she looked more like a popular conception of a duchess. She was the ideal stage *grande dame*. Her aristocratic head was held high, her exquisitely dressed hair was of a snowy white. She was dressed in grey – soft draperies that fell about her in artistic folds. One long white hand supported her chin, the other was holding a roll spread with *pâté de foie gras*. On her right was a man with a very white face, very black hair, and horn-rimmed spectacles. He was marvellously and beautifully dressed. At the moment his head was thrown back, and his left arm was thrown out as though he were about to declaim something.

On the left of the white-haired lady was a jolly-looking little man with a bald head. After the first glance, nobody looked at him.

There was just a moment of uncertainty, and then the Duchess (the authentic Duchess) took charge.

'Isn't this storm too dreadful?' she said pleasantly, coming forward, and smiling a purposeful and efficient smile that she had found very useful when serving on Welfare and other committees. 'I suppose you've been caught in it just like we have? But Corsica is a marvellous place. I only arrived this morning.'

The man with the black hair got up, and the Duchess with a gracious smile slipped into his seat.

The white-haired lady spoke.

'We have been here a week,' she said.

Mr Satterthwaite started. Could anyone who had once heard that voice ever forget it? It echoed round the stone room, charged with emotion – with exquisite melancholy. It seemed to him that she had said something wonderful, memorable, full of meaning. She had spoken from her heart.

He spoke in a hurried aside to Mr Tomlinson.

'The man in spectacles is Mr Vyse – the producer, you know.'

The retired Indian judge was looking at Mr Vyse with a good deal of dislike.

'What does he produce?' he asked. 'Children?'

'Oh, dear me, no,' said Mr Satterthwaite, shocked by the mere mention of anything so crude in connection with Mr Vyse. 'Plays.'

'I think,' said Naomi, 'I'll go out again. It's too hot in here.'

Her voice, strong and harsh, made Mr Satterthwaite jump. She made almost blindly, as it seemed, for the door, brushing Mr Tomlinson aside. But in the doorway itself she came face to face with Mr Quin, and he barred her way.

'Go back and sit down,' he said.

His voice was authoritative. To Mr Satterthwaite's surprise the girl hesitated a minute and then obeyed. She sat down at the foot of the table as far from the others as possible.

Mr Satterthwaite bustled forward and button-holed the producer.

'You may not remember me,' he began, 'my name is Satterthwaite.'

'Of course!' A long bony hand shot out and enveloped the other's in a painful grip. 'My dear man. Fancy meeting you here. You know Miss Nunn, of course?'

Mr Satterthwaite jumped. No wonder that voice had been familiar. Thousands, all over England, had thrilled to those wonderful emotion-laden tones. Rosina Nunn! England's greatest emotional actress. Mr Satterthwaite too had lain under her spell. No one like her for interpreting a part – for bringing out the finer shades of meaning. He had thought of her always as an intellectual actress, one who comprehended and got inside the soul of her part.

He might be excused for not recognizing her. Rosina Nunn was volatile in her tastes. For twenty-five years of her life she had been a blonde. After a tour in the States she had returned with the locks of the raven, and she had taken up tragedy in earnest. This 'French Marquise' effect was her latest whim.

'Oh, by the way, Mr Judd – Miss Nunn's husband,' said Vyse, carelessly introducing the man with the bald head.

Rosina Nunn had had several husbands, Mr Satterthwaite knew. Mr Judd was evidently the latest.

Mr Judd was busily unwrapping packages from a hamper at his side. He addressed his wife.

'Some more *pâté*, dearest? That last wasn't as thick as you like it.'

Rosina Nunn surrendered her roll to him, as she murmured simply:

'Henry thinks of the most enchanting meals. I always leave the commissariat to him.'

'Feed the brute,' said Mr Judd, and laughed. He patted his wife on the shoulder.

'Treats her just as though she were a dog,' murmured the melancholy voice of Mr Vyse in Mr Satterthwaite's ear. 'Cuts up her food for her. Odd creatures, women.'

Mr Satterthwaite and Mr Quin between them unpacked lunch. Hard-boiled eggs, cold ham and Gruyère cheese were distributed round the table. The Duchess and Miss Nunn appeared to be deep in murmured confidences. Fragments came along in the actress's deep contralto.

'The bread must be lightly toasted, you understand? Then just a *very* thin layer of marmalade. Rolled up and put in the oven for one minute – not more. Simply delicious.'

'That woman lives for food,' murmured Mr Vyse. 'Simply lives for it. She can't think of anything else. I remember in Riders to the Sea – you know "and it's the fine quiet time I'll be having." I could *not* get the effect I wanted. At last I told her to think of peppermint creams – she's very fond of peppermint creams. I got the effect at once – a sort of far-away look that went to your very soul.'

Mr Satterthwaite was silent. He was remembering.

Mr Tomlinson opposite cleared his throat preparatory to entering into conversation.

'You produce plays, I hear, eh? I'm fond of a good play myself. Jim the Penman, now, that was a play.'

'My God,' said Mr Vyse, and shivered down all the long length of him.

'A tiny clove of garlic,' said Miss Nunn to the Duchess. 'You tell your cook. It's wonderful.'

She sighed happily and turned to her husband.

'Henry,' she said plaintively, 'I've never even *seen* the caviare.'

'You're as near as nothing to sitting on it,' returned Mr Judd cheerfully. 'You put it behind you on the chair.'

Rosina Nunn retrieved it hurriedly, and beamed round the table.

'Henry is too wonderful. I'm so terribly absent-minded. I never know where I've put anything.'

'Like the day you packed your pearls in your sponge bag,' said Henry jocosely. 'And then left it behind at the hotel. My word, I did a bit of wiring and phoning that day.'

'They were insured,' said Miss Nunn dreamily. 'Not like my opal.'

A spasm of exquisite heartrending grief flitted across her face.

Several times, when in the company of Mr Quin, Mr Satterthwaite had had the feeling of taking part in a play. The illusion was with him very strongly now. This was a dream. Everyone had his part. The words 'my opal' were his own cue. He leant forward.

'Your opal, Miss Nunn?'

'Have you got the butter, Henry? Thank you. Yes, my opal. It was stolen, you know. And I never got it back.'

'Do tell us,' said Mr Satterthwaite.

'Well – I was born in October – so it was lucky for me to wear opals, and because of that I wanted a real beauty. I waited a long time for it. They said it was one of the most perfect ones known. Not very large – about the size of a two-shilling piece – but oh! the colour and the fire.'

She sighed. Mr Satterthwaite observed that the Duchess was fidgeting and seemed uncomfortable, but nothing could stop Miss Nunn now. She went on, and the exquisite inflections of her voice made the story sound like some mournful Saga of old.

'It was stolen by a young man called Alec Gerard. He wrote plays.'

'Very good plays,' put in Mr Vyse professionally. 'Why, I once kept one of his plays for six months.'

'Did you produce it?' asked Mr Tomlinson.

'Oh, *no*,' said Mr Vyse, shocked at the idea. 'But do you know, at one time I actually thought of doing so?'

'It had a wonderful part in it for me,' said Miss Nunn. 'Rachel's Children, it was called – though there wasn't anyone called Rachel in the play. He came to talk to me about it – at the theatre. I liked him. He was a nice-looking – and very shy, poor boy. I remember' – a beautiful far-away look stole over her face – 'he bought me some peppermint creams. The opal was lying on the dressing-table. He'd been out in Australia, and he knew something about opals. He took it over to the light to look at it. I suppose he must have slipped it into his pocket then. I missed it as soon as he'd gone. There *was* a to-do. You remember?'

She turned to Mr Vyse.

'Oh, I remember,' said Mr Vyse with a groan.

'They found the empty case in his rooms,' continued the actress. 'He'd been terribly hard up, but the very next day he was able to pay large sums into his bank. He pretended to account for it by saying that a friend of his had put some money on a horse for him, but he couldn't produce the friend. He said he must have put the case in his pocket by mistake. I think that was a terribly weak thing to say, don't you? He might have thought of something better than that . . . I had to go and give evidence. There were pictures of me in all the papers. My press agent said it was very good publicity – but I'd much rather have had my opal back.'

She shook her head sadly.

'Have some preserved pineapple?' said Mr Judd.

Miss Nunn brightened up.

'Where is it?'

'I gave it to you just now.'

Miss Nunn looked behind her and in front of her, eyed her grey silk pochette, and then slowly drew up a large purple silk bag that was reposing on the ground beside her. She began to turn the contents out slowly on the table, much to Mr Satterthwaite's interest.

There was a powder puff, a lip-stick, a small jewel case, a skein of wool, another powder puff, two handkerchiefs, a box of chocolate creams, an enamelled paper knife, a mirror, a little dark brown wooden box, five letters, a walnut, a small square of mauve crêpe de chine, a piece of ribbon and the end of a *croissant*. Last of all came the preserved pineapple.

'*Eureka*,' murmured Mr Satterthwaite softly.

'I beg your pardon?'

'Nothing,' said Mr Satterthwaite hastily. 'What a charming paper knife.'

'Yes, isn't it? Somebody gave it to me. I can't remember who.'

'That's an Indian box,' remarked Mr Tomlinson. 'Ingenious little things, aren't they?'

'Somebody gave me that too,' said Miss Nunn. 'I've had it a long time. It used always to stand on my dressing-table at the theatre. I don't think it's very pretty, though, do you?'

The box was of plain dark brown wood. It pushed open from the side. On the top of it were two plain flaps of wood that could be turned round and round.

'Not pretty, perhaps,' said Mr Tomlinson with a chuckle. 'But I'll bet you've never seen one like it.'

Mr Satterthwaite leaned forward. He had an excited feeling.

'Why did you say it was ingenious?' he demanded.

'Well, isn't it?'

The judge appealed to Miss Nunn. She looked at him blankly.

'I suppose I mustn't show them the trick of it – eh?' Miss Nunn still looked blank.

'What trick?' asked Mr Judd.

'God bless my soul, don't you know?'

He looked round the inquiring faces.

'Fancy that now. May I take the box a minute? Thank you.'

He pushed it open.

'Now then, can anyone give me something to put in it – not too big. Here's a small piece of Gruyère cheese. That will do capitally. I place it inside, shut the box.'

He fumbled for a minute or two with his hands.

'Now see –'

He opened the box again. It was empty.

'Well, I never,' said Mr Judd. 'How do you do it?'

'It's quite simple. Turn the box upside down, and move the left hand flap half-way round, then shut the right hand flap. Now to bring our piece of cheese back again we must reverse that. The right hand flap half-way round, and the left one closed, still keeping the box upside down. And now – Hey Presto!'

The box slid open. A gasp went round the table. The cheese was there – but so was something else. A round thing that blinked forth every colour of the rainbow.

'*My opal!*'

It was a clarion note. Rosina Nunn stood upright, her hands clasped to her breast.

'My opal! How did it get there?'

Henry Judd cleared his throat.

'I – er – I rather think, Rosy, my girl, you must have put it there yourself.'

Someone got up from the table and blundered out into the air. It was Naomi Carlton Smith. Mr Quin followed her.

'But when? Do you mean –?'

Mr Satterthwaite watched her while the truth dawned on her. It took over two minutes before she got it.

'You mean last year – at the theatre.'

'You know,' said Henry apologetically. 'You *do* fiddle with things, Rosy. Look at you with the caviare today.'

Miss Nunn was painfully following out her mental processes.

'I just slipped it in without thinking, and then I suppose I turned the box about and did the thing by accident, but then – but then –' At last it came. 'But then Alec Gerard didn't steal it after all. Oh!' – a full-throated cry, poignant, moving – 'How dreadful!'

'Well,' said Mr Vyse, 'that can be put right now.'

'Yes, but he's been in prison a year.' And then she startled them. She turned sharp on the Duchess. 'Who is that girl – that girl who has just gone out?'

'Miss Carlton Smith,' said the Duchess, 'was engaged to Mr Gerard. She – took the thing very hard.'

Mr Satterthwaite stole softly away. The snow had stopped, Naomi was sitting on the stone wall. She had a sketch book in her hand, some coloured crayons were scattered around. Mr Quin was standing beside her.

She held out the sketch book to Mr Satterthwaite. It was a very rough affair – but it had genius. A kaleidoscopic whirl of snowflakes with a figure in the centre.

'Very good,' said Mr Satterthwaite.

Mr Quin looked up at the sky.

'The storm is over,' he said. 'The roads will be slippery, but I do not think there will be any accident – now.'

'There will be no accident,' said Naomi. Her voice was charged with some meaning that Mr Satterthwaite did not understand. She turned and smiled at him – a sudden dazzling smile. 'Mr Satterthwaite can drive back with me if he likes.'

He knew then to what length desperation had driven her.

'Well,' said Mr Quin, 'I must bid you goodbye.'

He moved away.

'Where is he going?' said Mr Satterthwaite, staring after him.

'Back where he came from, I suppose,' said Naomi in an odd voice.

'But – but there isn't anything there,' said Mr Satterthwaite, for Mr Quin was making for that spot on the edge of the cliff where they had first seen him. 'You know you said yourself it was the World's End.'

He handed back the sketch book.

'It's very good,' he said. 'A very good likeness. But why – er – why did you put him in Fancy Dress?'

Her eyes met his for a brief second.

'I see him like that,' said Naomi Carlton Smith.

Harlequin's Lane

'Harlequin's Lane' was first published as 'The Magic of Mr Quin No. 6' in *Storyteller*, May 1927.

Mr Satterthwaite was never quite sure what took him to stay with the Denmans. They were not of his kind – that is to say, they belonged neither to the great world, nor to the more interesting artistic circles. They were Philistines, and dull Philistines at that. Mr Satterthwaite had met them first at Biarritz, had accepted an invitation to stay with them, had come, had been bored, and yet strangely enough had come again and yet again.

Why? He was asking himself that question on this twenty-first of June, as he sped out of London in his Rolls Royce.

John Denman was a man of forty, a solid well-established figure respected in the business world. His friends were not Mr Satterthwaite's friends, his ideas even less so. He was a man clever in his own line but devoid of imagination outside it.

Why am I doing this thing? Mr Satterthwaite asked himself once more – and the only answer that came seemed to him so vague and so inherently preposterous that he almost put it aside. For the only reason that presented itself was the fact that one of the rooms in the house (a comfortable well-appointed house), stirred his curiosity. That room was Mrs Denman's own sitting-room.

It was hardly an expression of her personality because, so far as Mr Satterthwaite could judge, she had no personality. He had never met a woman so completely expressionless. She was, he knew, a Russian by birth. John Denman had been in Russia at the outbreak of the European war, he had fought with the Russian troops, had narrowly escaped with his life on the outbreak of the Revolution, and had brought this Russian girl with him, a penniless refugee. In face of strong disapproval from his parents he had married her.

Mrs Denman's room was in no way remarkable. It was well and solidly furnished with good Hepplewhite furniture – a trifle more masculine than feminine in atmosphere. But in it there was one incongruous item: a Chinese lacquer screen – a thing of creamy yellow and pale rose. Any museum might have been glad to own it. It was a collector's piece, rare and beautiful.

It was out of place against that solid English background. It should have been the key-note of the room with everything arranged to harmonize subtly with it. And yet Mr Satterthwaite could not accuse the Denmans of lack of taste. Everything else in the house was in perfectly blended accord.

He shook his head. The thing – trivial though it was – puzzled him. Because of it, so he verily believed, he had come again and again to the house. It was, perhaps, a woman's fantasy – but that solution did not satisfy him as he thought of Mrs Denman – a quiet hard-featured woman, speaking English so correctly that no one would ever have guessed her a foreigner.

The car drew up at his destination and he got out, his mind still dwelling on the problem of the Chinese screen. The name of the Denman's house was 'Ashmead', and it occupied some five acres of Melton Heath, which is thirty miles from London, stands five hundred feet above sea level and is, for the most part, inhabited by those who have ample incomes.

The butler received Mr Satterthwaite suavely. Mr and Mrs Denman were both out – at a rehearsal – they hoped Mr Satterthwaite would make himself at home until they returned.

Mr Satterthwaite nodded and proceeded to carry out these injunctions by stepping into the garden. After a cursory examination of the flower beds, he strolled down a shady walk and presently came to a door in the wall. It was unlocked and he passed through it and came out into a narrow lane.

Mr Satterthwaite looked to left and right. A very charming lane, shady and green, with high hedges – a rural lane that twisted and turned in good old-fashioned style. He remembered the stamped address: ASHMEAD, HARLEQUIN'S LANE – remembered too, a local name for it that Mrs Denman had once told him.

'Harlequin's Lane,' he murmured to himself softly. 'I wonder –'

He turned a corner.

Not at the time, but afterwards, he wondered why this time he felt no surprise at meeting that elusive friend of his: Mr Harley Quin. The two men clasped hands.

'So *you're* down here,' said Mr Satterthwaite.

'Yes,' said Mr Quin. 'I'm staying in the same house as you are.'

'Staying there?'

'Yes. Does it surprise you?'

'No,' said Mr Satterthwaite slowly. 'Only – well, you never stay anywhere for long, do you?'

'Only as long as is necessary,' said Mr Quin gravely.

'I see,' said Mr Satterthwaite.

They walked on in silence for some minutes.

'This lane,' began Mr Satterthwaite, and stopped.

'Belongs to me,' said Mr Quin.

'I thought it did,' said Mr Satterthwaite. 'Somehow, I thought it must. There's the other name for it, too, the local name. They call it the "Lovers' Lane". You know that?'

Mr Quin nodded.

'But surely,' he said gently, 'there is a "Lovers' Lane" in every village?'

'I suppose so,' said Mr Satterthwaite, and he sighed a little.

He felt suddenly rather old and out of things, a little dried-up wizened old fogey of a man. Each side of him were the hedges, very green and alive.

'Where does this lane end, I wonder?' he asked suddenly.

'It ends – *here*,' said Mr Quin.

They came round the last bend. The lane ended in a piece of waste ground, and almost at their feet a great pit opened. In it were tin cans gleaming in the sun, and other cans that were too red with rust to gleam, old boots, fragments of newspapers, a hundred and one odds and ends that were no longer of account to anybody.

'A rubbish heap,' exclaimed Mr Satterthwaite, and breathed deeply and indignantly.

'Sometimes there are very wonderful things on a rubbish heap,' said Mr Quin.

'I know, I know,' cried Mr Satterthwaite, and quoted with just a trace of self-consciousness: '*Bring me the two most beautiful things in the city, said God.* You know how it goes, eh?'

Mr Quin nodded.

Mr Satterthwaite looked up at the ruins of a small cottage perched on the brink of the wall of the cliff.

'Hardly a pretty view for a house,' he remarked.

'I fancy this wasn't a rubbish heap in those days,' said Mr Quin. 'I believe the Denmans lived there when they were first married. They moved into the big house when the old people died. The cottage was pulled down when they began to quarry the rock here – but nothing much was done, as you can see.'

They turned and began retracing their steps.

'I suppose,' said Mr Satterthwaite, smiling, 'that many couples come wandering down this lane on these warm summer evenings.'

'Probably.'

'Lovers,' said Mr Satterthwaite. He repeated the word thoughtfully and quite without the normal embarrassment of the Englishman. Mr Quin had that effect upon him. 'Lovers . . . You have done a lot for lovers, Mr Quin.'

The other bowed his head without replying.

'You have saved them from sorrow – from worse than sorrow, from death. You have been an advocate for the dead themselves.'

'You are speaking of yourself – of what *you* have done – not of me.'

'It is the same thing,' said Mr Satterthwaite. 'You know it is,' he urged, as the other did not speak. 'You have acted – through me. For some reason or other you do not act directly – yourself.'

'Sometimes I do,' said Mr Quin.

His voice held a new note. In spite of himself Mr Satterthwaite shivered a little. The afternoon, he thought, must be growing chilly. And yet the sun seemed as bright as ever.

At that moment a girl turned the corner ahead of them and came into sight. She was a very pretty girl, fair-haired and blue-eyed, wearing a pink cotton frock. Mr Satterthwaite recognized her as Molly Stanwell, whom he had met down here before.

She waved a hand to welcome him.

'John and Anna have just gone back,' she cried. 'They thought you must have come, but they simply had to be at the rehearsal.'

'Rehearsal of what?' inquired Mr Satterthwaite.

'This masquerade thing – I don't quite know what you'll call it. There is singing and dancing and all sorts of things in it. Mr Manly, do you remember him down here? He had quite a good tenor voice, is to be Pierrot, and I am Pierrette. Two professionals are coming down for the dancing – Harlequin and Columbine, you know. And then there is a big chorus of girls. Lady Roscheimer is so keen on training village girls to sing. She's really getting the thing up for that. The music is rather lovely – but very modern – next to no tune anywhere. Claude Wickam. Perhaps you know him?'

Mr Satterthwaite nodded, for, as has been mentioned before, it was his *métier* to know everybody. He knew all about that aspiring genius Claude Wickam, and about Lady Roscheimer who was a fat Jewess with a *penchant* for young men of the artistic persuasion. And he knew all about Sir Leopold Roscheimer who liked his wife to be happy and, most rare among husbands, did not mind her being happy in her own way.

They found Claude Wickam at tea with the Denmans, cramming his mouth indiscriminately with anything handy, talking rapidly, and waving long white hands that had a double-jointed appearance. His short-sighted eyes peered through large hornrimmed spectacles.

John Denman, upright, slightly florid, with the faintest possible tendency to sleekness, listened with an air of bored attention. On the appearance of Mr Satterthwaite, the musician transferred his remarks to him. Anna Denman sat behind the tea things, quiet and expressionless as usual.

Mr Satterthwaite stole a covert glance at her. Tall, gaunt, very thin, with the skin tightly stretched over high cheek bones, black hair parted in the middle, a skin that was weather-beaten. An out of door woman who cared nothing for the use of cosmetics. A Dutch Doll of a woman, wooden, lifeless – and yet . . .

He thought: 'There *should* be meaning behind that face, and yet there isn't. That's what's all wrong. Yes, all wrong.' And to Claude Wickam he said: 'I beg your pardon? You were saying?'

Claude Wickam, who liked the sound of his own voice, began all over again. 'Russia,' he said, 'that was the only country in the world worth being interested in. They experimented. With lives, if you like, but still they experimented. Magnificent!' He crammed a sandwich into his mouth with one hand, and added a bite of the chocolate éclair he was waving about in the other. 'Take,' he said (with his mouth full), 'the Russian Ballet.' Remembering his hostess, he turned to her. What did *she* think of the Russian Ballet?

The question was obviously only a prelude to the important point – what Claude Wickam thought of the Russian Ballet, but her answer was unexpected and threw him completely out of his stride.

'I have never seen it.'

'What?' He gazed at her open-mouthed. 'But – surely –'

Her voice went on, level and emotionless.

'Before my marriage, I was a dancer. So now –'

'A busman's holiday,' said her husband.

'Dancing.' She shrugged her shoulders. 'I know all the tricks of it. It does not interest me.'

'Oh!'

It took but a moment for Claude to recover his aplomb. His voice went on.

'Talking of lives,' said Mr Satterthwaite, 'and experimenting in them. The Russian nation made one costly experiment.'

Claude Wickam swung round on him.

'I know what you are going to say,' he cried. 'Kharsanova! The immortal, the only Kharsanova! You saw her dance?'

'Three times,' said Mr Satterthwaite. 'Twice in Paris, once in London. I shall – not forget it.'

He spoke in an almost reverent voice.

'I saw her, too,' said Claude Wickam. 'I was ten years old. An uncle took me. God! I shall never forget it.'

He threw a piece of bun fiercely into a flower bed.

'There is a statuette of her in a Museum in Berlin,' said Mr Satterthwaite. 'It is marvellous. That impression of fragility – as though you could break her with a flip of the thumb nail. I have seen her as Columbine, in the Swan, as the dying Nymph.' He paused, shaking his head. 'There was genius. It will be long years before such another is born. She was young too. Destroyed ignorantly and wantonly in the first days of the Revolution.'

'Fools! Madmen! Apes!' said Claude Wickam. He choked with a mouthful of tea.

'I studied with Kharsanova,' said Mrs Denman. 'I remember her well.'

'She was wonderful?' said Mr Satterthwaite.

'Yes,' said Mrs Denman quietly. 'She was wonderful.'

Claude Wickam departed and John Denman drew a deep sigh of relief at which his wife laughed.

Mr Satterthwaite nodded. 'I know what you think. But in spite of everything, the music that that boy writes *is* music.'

'I suppose it is,' said Denman.

'Oh, undoubtedly. How long it will be – well, that is different.'

John Denman looked at him curiously.

'You mean?'

'I mean that success has come early. And that is dangerous. Always dangerous.' He looked across at Mr Quin. 'You agree with me?'

'You are always right,' said Mr Quin.

'We will come upstairs to my room,' said Mrs Denman. 'It is pleasant there.'

She led the way, and they followed her. Mr Satterthwaite drew a deep breath as he caught sight of the Chinese screen. He looked up to find Mrs Denman watching him.

'You are the man who is always right,' she said, nodding her head slowly at him. 'What do you make of my screen?'

He felt that in some way the words were a challenge to him, and he answered almost haltingly, stumbling over the words a little.

'Why, it's – it's beautiful. More, it's unique.'

'You're right.' Denman had come up behind him. 'We bought it early in our married life. Got it for about a tenth of its value, but even then – well, it crippled us for over a year. You remember, Anna?'

'Yes,' said Mrs Denman, 'I remember.'

'In fact, we'd no business to buy it at all – not then. Now, of course, it's different. There was some very good lacquer going at Christie's the other day. Just what we need to make this room perfect. All Chinese together. Clear out the other stuff. Would you believe it, Satterthwaite, my wife wouldn't hear of it?'

'I like this room as it is,' said Mrs Denman.

There was a curious look on her face. Again Mr Satterthwaite felt challenged and defeated. He looked round him, and for the first time he noticed the absence of all personal touch. There were no photographs, no flowers, no knick-knacks. It was not like a woman's room at all. Save for that one incongruous factor of the Chinese screen, it might have been a sample room shown at some big furnishing house.

He found her smiling at him.

'Listen,' she said. She bent forward, and for a moment she seemed less English, more definitely foreign. 'I speak to you for you will understand. We bought that screen with more than money – with love. For love of it, because it was beautiful and unique, we went without other things, things we needed and missed. These other Chinese pieces my husband speaks of, those we should buy with money only, we should not pay away anything of ourselves.'

Her husband laughed.

'Oh, have it your own way,' he said, but with a trace of irritation in his voice. 'But it's all wrong against this English background. This other stuff, it's good enough of its kind, genuine solid, no fake about it – but mediocre. Good plain late Hepplewhite.'

She nodded.

'Good, solid, genuine English,' she murmured softly.

Mr Satterthwaite stared at her. He caught a meaning behind these words. The English room – the flaming beauty of the Chinese screen . . . No, it was gone again.

'I met Miss Stanwell in the lane,' he said conversationally. 'She tells me she is going to be Pierrette in this show tonight.'

'Yes,' said Denman. 'And she's awfully good, too.'

'She has clumsy feet,' said Anna.

'Nonsense,' said her husband. 'All women are alike, Satterthwaite. Can't bear to hear another woman praised. Molly is a very good-looking girl, and so of course every woman has to have their knife into her.'

'I spoke of dancing,' said Anna Denman. She sounded faintly surprised. 'She is very pretty, yes, but her feet move clumsily. You cannot tell me anything else because I know about dancing.'

Mr Satterthwaite intervened tactfully.

'You have two professional dancers coming down, I understand?'

'Yes. For the ballet proper. Prince Oranoff is bringing them down in his car.'

'Sergius Oranoff?'

The question came from Anna Denman. Her husband turned and looked at her.

'You know him?'

'I used to know him – in Russia.'

Mr Satterthwaite thought that John Denman looked disturbed.

'Will he know you?'

'Yes. He will know me.'

She laughed – a low, almost triumphant laugh. There was nothing of the Dutch Doll about her face now. She nodded reassuringly at her husband.

'Sergius. So he is bringing down the two dancers. He was always interested in dancing.'

'I remember.'

John Denman spoke abruptly, then turned and left the room. Mr Quin followed him. Anna Denman crossed to the telephone and asked for a number. She arrested Mr Satterthwaite with a gesture as he was about to follow the example of the other two men.

'Can I speak to Lady Roscheimer. Oh! it is you. This is Anna Denman speaking. Has Prince Oranoff arrived yet? What? *What?* Oh, my dear! But how ghastly.'

She listened for a few moments longer, then replaced the receiver. She turned to Mr Satterthwaite.

'There has been an accident. There would be with Sergius Ivanovitch driving. Oh, he has not altered in all these years. The girl was not badly hurt, but bruised and shaken, too much to dance tonight. The man's arm is broken. Sergius Ivanovitch himself is unhurt. The devil looks after his own, perhaps.'

'And what about tonight's performance?'

'Exactly, my friend. Something must be done about it.'

She sat thinking. Presently she looked at him.

'I am a bad hostess, Mr Satterthwaite. I do not entertain you.'

'I assure you that it is not necessary. There's one thing though, Mrs Denman, that I would very much like to know.'

'Yes?'

'How did you come across Mr Quin?'

'He is often down here,' she said slowly. 'I think he owns land in this part of the world.'

'He does, he does. He told me so this afternoon,' said Mr Satterthwaite.

'He is –' She paused. Her eyes met Mr Satterthwaite's. 'I think you know what he is better than I do,' she finished.

'I?'

'Is it not so?'

He was troubled. His neat little soul found her disturbing. He felt that she wished to force him further than he was prepared to go, that she wanted him to put into words that which he was not prepared to admit to himself.

'*You* know!' she said. 'I think you know most things, Mr Satterthwaite.'

Here was incense, yet for once it failed to intoxicate him. He shook his head in unwonted humility.

'What can anyone know?' he asked. 'So little – so very little.'

She nodded in assent. Presently she spoke again, in a queer brooding voice, without looking at him.

'Supposing I were to tell you something – you would not laugh? No, I do not think you would laugh. Supposing, then, that to carry on one's' – she paused – 'one's trade, one's profession, one were to make use of a fantasy – one were to pretend to oneself something that did not exist – that one were to imagine a certain person . . . It is a pretence, you understand, a make believe – nothing more. But one day –'

'Yes?' said Mr Satterthwaite.

He was keenly interested.

'The fantasy came true! The thing one imagined – the impossible thing, the thing that could not be – was real! Is that madness? Tell me, Mr Satterthwaite. Is that madness – or do you believe it too?'

'I –' Queer how he could not get the words out. How they seemed to stick somewhere at the back of his throat.

'Folly,' said Anna Denman. 'Folly.'

She swept out of the room and left Mr Satterthwaite with his confession of faith unspoken.

He came down to dinner to find Mrs Denman entertaining a guest, a tall dark man approaching middle age.

'Prince Oranoff – Mr Satterthwaite.'

The two men bowed. Mr Satterthwaite had the feeling that some conversation had been broken off on his entry which would not be resumed. But there was no sense of strain. The Russian conversed easily and naturally on those objects which were nearest to Mr Satterthwaite's heart. He was a man of very fine artistic taste, and they soon found that they had many friends in common. John Denman joined them, and the talk became localized. Oranoff expressed regret for the accident.

'It was not my fault. I like to drive fast – yes, but I am a good driver. It was Fate – chance' – he shrugged his shoulders – 'the masters of all of us.'

'There speaks the Russian in you, Sergius Ivanovitch,' said Mrs Denman.

'And finds an echo in you, Anna Mikalovna,' he threw back quickly.

Mr Satterthwaite looked from one to the other of the three of them. John Denman, fair, aloof, English, and the other two, dark, thin, strangely alike. Something rose in his mind – what was it? Ah! he had it now. The first Act of the Walküre. Siegmund and Sieglinde – so alike – and the alien Hunding. Conjectures began to stir in his brain. Was this the meaning of the presence of Mr Quin? One thing he believed in firmly – wherever Mr Quin showed himself – there lay drama. Was this it here – the old hackneyed three-cornered tragedy?

He was vaguely disappointed. He had hoped for better things.

'What has been arranged, Anna?' asked Denman. 'The thing will have to be put off, I suppose. I heard you ringing the Roscheimers up.'

She shook her head.

'No – there is no need to put it off.'

'But you can't do it without the ballet?'

'You certainly couldn't have a Harlequinade without Harlequin and Columbine,' agreed Anna Denman drily. 'I'm going to be Columbine, John.'

'You?' He was astonished – disturbed, Mr Satterthwaite thought.

She nodded composedly.

'You need not be afraid, John. I shall not disgrace you. You forget – it was my profession once.'

Mr Satterthwaite thought: 'What an extraordinary thing a voice is. The things it says – and the things it leaves unsaid and means! I wish I knew . . .'

'Well,' said John Denman grudgingly, 'that solves one half of the problem. What about the other? Where will you find Harlequin?'

'I *have* found him – there!'

She gestured towards the open doorway where Mr Quin had just appeared. He smiled back at her.

'Good lord, Quin,' said John Denman. 'Do you know anything of this game? I should never have imagined it.'

'Mr Quin is vouched for by an expert,' said his wife. 'Mr Satterthwaite will answer for him.'

She smiled at Mr Satterthwaite, and the little man found himself murmuring:

'Oh, yes – I answer for Mr Quin.'

Denman turned his attention elsewhere.

'You know there's to be a fancy dress dance business afterwards. Great nuisance. We'll have to rig you up, Satterthwaite.'

Mr Satterthwaite shook his head very decidedly.

'My years will excuse me.' A brilliant idea struck him. A table napkin under his arm. 'There I am, an elderly waiter who has seen better days.'

He laughed.

'An interesting profession,' said Mr Quin. 'One sees so much.'

'I've got to put on some fool pierrot thing,' said Denman gloomily. 'It's cool anyway, that's one thing. What about you?' He looked at Oranoff.

'I have a Harlequin costume,' said the Russian. His eyes wandered for a minute to his hostess's face.

Mr Satterthwaite wondered if he was mistaken in fancying that there was just a moment of constraint.

'There might have been three of us,' said Denman, with a laugh. 'I've got an old Harlequin costume my wife made me when we were first married for some show or other.' He paused, looking down on his broad shirt front. 'I don't suppose I could get into it now.'

'No,' said his wife. 'You couldn't get into it now.'

And again her voice said something more than mere words.

She glanced up at the clock.

'If Molly doesn't turn up soon, we won't wait for her.'

But at that moment the girl was announced. She was already wearing her Pierrette dress of white and green, and very charming she looked in it, so Mr Satterthwaite reflected.

She was full of excitement and enthusiasm over the forthcoming performance.

'I'm getting awfully nervous, though,' she announced, as they drank coffee after dinner. 'I know my voice will wobble, and I shall forget the words.'

'Your voice is very charming,' said Anna. 'I should not worry about it if I were you.'

'Oh, but I do. The other I don't mind about – the dancing, I mean. That's sure to go all right. I mean, you can't go very far wrong with your feet, can you?'

She appealed to Anna, but the older woman did not respond. Instead she said:

'Sing something now to Mr Satterthwaite. You will find that he will reassure you.'

Molly went over to the piano. Her voice rang out, fresh and tuneful, in an old Irish ballad.

> 'Shiela, dark Shiela, what is it that you're seeing?
> What is it that you're seeing, that you're seeing in the fire?'
> 'I see a lad that loves me – and I see a lad that leaves me,
> And a third lad, a Shadow Lad – and he's the lad that grieves me.'

The song went on. At the end, Mr Satterthwaite nodded vigorous approval.

'Mrs Denman is right. Your voice is charming. Not, perhaps, very fully trained, but delightfully natural, and with that unstudied quality of youth in it.'

'That's right,' agreed John Denman. 'You go ahead, Molly, and don't be downed by stage fright. We'd better be getting over to the Roscheimers now.'

The party separated to don cloaks. It was a glorious night and they proposed to walk over, the house being only a few hundred yards down the road.

Mr Satterthwaite found himself by his friend.

'It's an odd thing,' he said, 'but that song made me think of you. *A third lad – a Shadow Lad –* there's mystery there, and wherever there's mystery I – well, think of you.'

'Am I so mysterious?' smiled Mr Quin.

Mr Satterthwaite nodded vigorously.

'Yes, indeed. Do you know, until tonight, I had no idea that you were a professional dancer.'

'Really?' said Mr Quin.

'Listen,' said Mr Satterthwaite. He hummed the love motif from the Walküre. 'That is what has been ringing in my head all through dinner as I looked at those two.'

'Which two?'

'Prince Oranoff and Mrs Denman. Don't you see the difference in her tonight? It's as though – as though a shutter had suddenly been opened and you see the glow within.'

'Yes,' said Mr Quin. 'Perhaps so.'

'The same old drama,' said Mr Satterthwaite. 'I am right, am I not? Those two belong together. They are of the same world, think the same thoughts, dream the same dreams . . . One sees how it has come about. Ten years ago Denman must have been very good-looking, young, dashing, a figure of romance. And he saved her life. All quite natural. But now – what is he, after all? A good fellow – prosperous, successful – but – well, mediocre. Good honest English stuff – very much like that Hepplewhite furniture upstairs. As English – and as ordinary – as that pretty English girl with her fresh untrained voice. Oh, you may smile, Mr Quin, but you cannot deny what I am saying.'

'I deny nothing. In what you see you are always right. And yet –'

'Yet what?'

Mr Quin leaned forward. His dark melancholy eyes searched for those of Mr Satterthwaite.

'Have you learned so little of life?' he breathed.

He left Mr Satterthwaite vaguely disquieted, such a prey to meditation that he found the others had started without him owing to his delay in selecting a scarf for his neck. He went out by the garden, and through the same door as in the afternoon. The lane was bathed in moonlight, and even as he stood in the doorway he saw a couple enlaced in each other's arms.

For a moment he thought –

And then he saw. *John Denman and Molly Stanwell.* Denman's voice came to him, hoarse and anguished.

'I can't live without you. What are we to do?'

Mr Satterthwaite turned to go back the way he had come, but a hand stayed him. Someone else stood in the doorway beside him, someone else whose eyes had also seen.

Mr Satterthwaite had only to catch one glimpse of her face to know how wildly astray all his conclusions had been.

Her anguished hand held him there until those other two had passed up the lane and disappeared from sight. He heard himself speaking to her, saying foolish little things meant to be comforting, and ludicrously inadequate to the agony he had divined. She only spoke once.

'Please,' she said, 'don't leave me.'

He found that oddly touching. He was, then, of use to someone. And he went on saying those things that meant nothing at all, but which were, somehow, better than silence. They went that way to the Roscheimers. Now and then her hand tightened on his shoulder, and he understood that she was glad of his company. She only took it away when they finally came to their destination. She stood very erect, her head held high.

'Now,' she said, 'I shall dance! Do not be afraid for me, my friend. I shall dance.'

She left him abruptly. He was seized upon by Lady Roscheimer, much bediamonded and very full of lamentations. By her he was passed on to Claude Wickam.

'Ruined! Completely ruined. The sort of thing that always happens to me. All these country bumpkins think they can dance. I was never even consulted –' His voice went on – went on interminably. He had found a sympathetic listener, a man who *knew*. He gave himself up to an orgy of self-pity. It only ended when the first strains of music began.

Mr Satterthwaite came out of his dreams. He was alert, once more the critic. Wickam was an unutterable ass, but he could write music – delicate gossamer stuff, intangible as a fairy web – yet with nothing of the pretty pretty about it.

The scenery was good. Lady Roscheimer never spared expense when aiding her protégés. A glade of Arcady with lighting effects that gave it the proper atmosphere of unreality.

Two figures dancing as they had danced through time immemorial. A slender Harlequin flashing spangles in the moonlight with magic wand and masked face . . . A white Columbine pirouetting like some immortal dream . . .

Mr Satterthwaite sat up. He had lived through this before. Yes, surely . . .

Now his body was far away from Lady Roscheimer's drawingroom. It was in a Berlin Museum at a statuette of an immortal Columbine.

Harlequin and Columbine danced on. The wide world was theirs to dance in . . .

Moonlight – and a human figure. Pierrot wandering through the wood, singing to the moon. Pierrot who has seen Columbine and knows no rest. The Immortal two vanish, but Columbine looks back. She has heard the song of a human heart.

Pierrot wandering on through the wood . . . darkness . . . his voice dies away in the distance . . .

The village green – dancing of village girls – pierrots and pierrettes. Molly as Pierrette. No dancer – Anna Denman was right there – but a fresh tuneful voice as she sings her song 'Pierrette dancing on the Green'.

A good tune – Mr Satterthwaite nodded approval. Wickham wasn't above writing a tune when there was a need for it. The majority of the village girls made him shudder, but he realized that Lady Roscheimer was determinedly philanthropical.

They press Pierrot to join the dance. He refuses. With white face he wanders on – the eternal lover seeking his ideal. Evening falls. Harlequin and Columbine, invisible, dance in and out of the unconscious throng. The place is deserted, only Pierrot, weary, falls asleep on a grassy bank. Harlequin and Columbine dance round him. He wakes and sees Columbine. He woos her in vain, pleads, beseeches . . .

She stands uncertain. Harlequin beckons to her to begone. But she sees him no longer. She is listening to Pierrot, to his song of love outpoured once more. She falls into his arms, and the curtain comes down.

The second Act is Pierrot's cottage. Columbine sits on her hearth. She is pale, weary. She listens – for what? Pierrot sings to her – woos her back to thoughts of him once more. The evening darkens. Thunder is heard . . . Columbine puts aside her spinning wheel. She is eager, stirred . . . She listens no longer to Pierrot. It is her own music that is in the air, the music of Harlequin and Columbine . . . She is awake. She remembers.

A crash of thunder! Harlequin stands in the doorway. Pierrot cannot see him, but Columbine springs up with a glad laugh. Children come running, but she pushes them aside. With another crash of thunder the walls fall, and Columbine dances out into the wild night with Harlequin.

Darkness, and through it the tune that Pierrette has sung. Light comes slowly. The cottage once more. Pierrot and Pierrette grown old and grey sit in front of the fire in two armchairs. The music is happy, but subdued. Pierrette nods in her chair. Through the window comes a shaft of moonlight, and with it the motif of Pierrot's long-forgotten song. He stirs in his chair.

Faint music – fairy music . . . Harlequin and Columbine outside. The door swings open and Columbine dances in. She leans over the sleeping Pierrot, kisses him on the lips . . .

Crash! A peal of thunder. She is outside again. In the centre of the stage is the lighted window and through it are seen the two figures of Harlequin and Columbine dancing slowly away, growing fainter and fainter . . .

A log falls. Pierrette jumps up angrily, rushes across to the window and pulls the blind. So it ends, on a sudden discord . . .

Mr Satterthwaite sat very still among the applause and vociferations. At last he got up and made his way outside. He came upon Molly Stanwell, flushed and eager, receiving compliments. He saw John Denman, pushing and elbowing his way through the throng, his eyes alight with a new flame. Molly came towards him, but, almost unconsciously, he put her aside. It was not her he was seeking.

'My wife? Where is she?'

'I think she went out in the garden.'

It was, however, Mr Satterthwaite who found her, sitting on a stone seat under a cypress tree. When he came up to her, he did an odd thing. He knelt down and raised her hand to his lips.

'Ah!' she said. 'You think I danced well?'

'You danced – as you always danced, Madame Kharsanova.'

She drew in her breath sharply.

'So – you have guessed.'

'There is only one Kharsanova. No one could see you dance and forget. But why – why?'

'What else is possible?'

'You mean?'

She had spoken very simply. She was just as simple now. 'Oh! but you understand. You are of the world. A great dancer – she can have lovers, yes – but a husband, that is different. And he – he did not want the other. He wanted me to belong to him as – as Kharsanova could never have belonged.'

'I see,' said Mr Satterthwaite. 'I see. So you gave it up?'

She nodded.

'You must have loved him very much,' said Mr Satterthwaite gently.

'To make such a sacrifice?' She laughed.

'Not quite that. To make it so light-heartedly.'

'Ah, yes – perhaps – you are right.'

'And now?' asked Mr Satterthwaite.

Her face grew grave.

'Now?' She paused, then raised her voice and spoke into the shadows. 'Is that you, Sergius Ivanovitch?'

Prince Oranoff came out into the moonlight. He took her hand and smiled at Mr Satterthwaite without self-consciousness.

'Ten years ago I mourned the death of Anna Kharsanova,' he said simply. 'She was to me as my other self. Today I have found her again. We shall part no more.'

'At the end of the lane in ten minutes,' said Anna. 'I shall not fail you.'

Oranoff nodded and went off again. The dancer turned to Mr Satterthwaite. A smile played about her lips.

'Well – you are not satisfied, my friend?'

'Do you know,' said Mr Satterthwaite abruptly, 'that your husband is looking for you?'

He saw the tremor that passed over her face, but her voice was steady enough.

'Yes,' she said gravely. 'That may well be.'

'I saw his eyes. They –' he stopped abruptly.

She was still calm.

'Yes, perhaps. For an hour. An hour's magic, born of past memories, of music, of moonlight – That is all.'

'Then there is nothing that I can say?' He felt old, dispirited.

'For ten years I have lived with the man I love,' said Anna Kharsanova. 'Now I am going to the man who for ten years has loved me.'

Mr Satterthwaite said nothing. He had no arguments left. Besides it really seemed the simplest solution. Only – only, somehow, it was not the solution he wanted. He felt her hand on his shoulder.

'I know, my friend, I know. But there is no third way. Always one looks for one thing – the lover, the perfect, the eternal lover . . . It is the music of Harlequin one hears. No lover ever satisfies one, for all lovers are mortal. And Harlequin is only a myth, an invisible presence . . . unless –'

'Yes,' said Mr Satterthwaite. 'Yes?'

'Unless – his name is – Death!'

Mr Satterthwaite shivered. She moved away from him, was swallowed up in the shadows . . .

He never knew quite how long he sat on there, but suddenly he started up with the feeling that he had been wasting valuable time. He hurried away, impelled in a certain direction almost in spite of himself.

As he came out into the lane he had a strange feeling of unreality. Magic – magic and moonlight! And two figures coming towards him . . .

Oranoff in his Harlequin dress. So he thought at first. Then, as they passed him, he knew his mistake. That lithe swaying figure belonged to one person only – Mr Quin . . .

They went on down the lane – their feet light as though they were treading on air. Mr Quin turned his head and looked back, and Mr Satterthwaite had a shock, for it was not the face of Mr Quin as he had ever seen it before. It was the face of a stranger – no, not quite a stranger. Ah! he had it now, it was the face of John Denman as it might have looked before life went too well with him. Eager, adventurous, the face at once of a boy and a lover . . .

Her laugh floated down to him, clear and happy . . . He looked after them and saw in the distance the lights of a little cottage. He gazed after them like a man in a dream.

He was rudely awakened by a hand that fell on his shoulder and he was jerked round to face Sergius Oranoff. The man looked white and distracted.

'Where is she? Where is she? She promised – and she has not come.'

'Madam has just gone up the lane – alone.'

It was Mrs Denman's maid who spoke from the shadow of the door behind them. She had been waiting with her mistress's wraps.

'I was standing here and saw her pass,' she added.

Mr Satterthwaite threw one harsh word at her.

'Alone? Alone, did you say?'

The maid's eyes widened in surprise.

'Yes, sir. Didn't you see her off?'

Mr Satterthwaite clutched at Oranoff.

'Quickly,' he muttered. 'I'm – I'm afraid.'

They hurried down the lane together, the Russian talking in quick disjointed sentences.

'She is a wonderful creature. Ah! how she danced tonight. And that friend of yours. Who is he? Ah! but he is wonderful – unique. In the old days, when she danced the Columbine of Rimsky Korsakoff, she never found the perfect Harlequin. Mordoff, Kassnine – none of them were quite perfect. She had her own little fancy. She told me of it once. Always she danced with a dream Harlequin – a man who was not really there. It was Harlequin himself, she said, who came to dance with her. It was that fancy of hers that made her Columbine so wonderful.'

Mr Satterthwaite nodded. There was only one thought in his head.

'Hurry,' he said. 'We must be in time. Oh! we must be in time.'

They came round the last corner – came to the deep pit and to something lying in it that had not been there before, the body of a woman lying in a wonderful pose, arms flung wide and head thrown back. A dead face and body that were triumphant and beautiful in the moonlight.

Words came back to Mr Satterthwaite dimly – Mr Quin's words: '*wonderful things on a rubbish heap*' . . . He understood them now.

Oranoff was murmuring broken phrases. The tears were streaming down his face.

'I loved her. Always I loved her.' He used almost the same words that had occurred to Mr Satterthwaite earlier in the day. 'We were of the same world, she and I. We had the same thoughts, the same dreams. I would have loved her always . . .'

'How do you know?'

The Russian stared at him – at the fretful peevishness of the tone.

'How do you know?' went on Mr Satterthwaite. 'It is what all lovers think – what all lovers say . . . There is only one lover –'

He turned and almost ran into Mr Quin. In an agitated manner, Mr Satterthwaite caught him by the arm and drew him aside.

'It was *you*,' he said. 'It was *you* who were with her just now?'

Mr Quin waited a minute and then said gently:

'You can put it that way, if you like.'

'And the maid didn't see you?'

'The maid didn't see me.'

'But *I* did. Why was that?'

'Perhaps, as a result of the price you have paid, you see things that other people – do not.'

Mr Satterthwaite looked at him uncomprehendingly for a minute or two. Then he began suddenly to quiver all over like an aspen leaf.

'What is this place?' he whispered. 'What is this place?'

'I told you earlier today. It is *My* lane.'

'A Lovers' Lane,' murmured Mr Satterthwaite. 'And people pass along it.'

'Most people, sooner or later.'

'And at the end of it – what do they find?'

Mr Quin smiled. His voice was very gentle. He pointed at the ruined cottage above them.

'The house of their dreams – or a rubbish heap – who shall say?'

Mr Satterthwaite looked up at him suddenly. A wild rebellion surged over him. He felt cheated, defrauded.

'But *I* –' His voice shook. '*I* have never passed down your lane . . .'

'And do you regret?'

Mr Satterthwaite quailed. Mr Quin seemed to have loomed to enormous proportions . . . Mr Satterthwaite had a vista of something at once menacing and terrifying . . . Joy, Sorrow, Despair.

And his comfortable little soul shrank back appalled.

'Do you regret?' Mr Quin repeated his question. There was something terrible about him.

'No,' Mr Satterthwaite stammered. 'N-no.'

And then suddenly he rallied.

'But I see things,' he cried. 'I may have been only a looker-on at Life – but I see things that other people do not. You said so yourself, Mr Quin . . .'

But Mr Quin had vanished.

The Love Detectives

'The Love Detectives' was first published in the USA as
'At the Crossroads' in *Flynn's Weekly*, 30 Oct 1926, and then as
'The Magic of Mr Quin No. 1: At the Cross Roads' in *Storyteller*,
December 1926.

Little Mr Satterthwaite looked thoughtfully across at his host. The friendship between these two men was an odd one. The colonel was a simple country gentleman whose passion in life was sport. The few weeks that he spent perforce in London, he spent unwillingly. Mr Satterthwaite, on the other hand, was a town bird. He was an authority on French cooking, on ladies' dress, and on all the latest scandals. His passion was observing human nature, and he was an expert in his own special line – that of an onlooker at life.

It would seem, therefore, that he and Colonel Melrose would have little in common, for the colonel had no interest in his neighbours' affairs and a horror of any kind of emotion. The two men were friends mainly because their fathers before them had been friends. Also they knew the same people and had reactionary views about *nouveaux riches*.

It was about half past seven. The two men were sitting in the colonel's comfortable study, and Melrose was describing a run of the previous winter with a keen hunting man's enthusiasm. Mr Satterthwaite, whose knowledge of horses consisted chiefly of the time-honoured Sunday morning visit to the stables which still obtains in old-fashioned country houses, listened with his invariable politeness.

The sharp ringing of the telephone interrupted Melrose. He crossed to the table and took up the receiver.

'Hello, yes – Colonel Melrose speaking. What's that?' His whole demeanour altered – became stiff and official. It was the magistrate speaking now, not the sportsman.

He listened for some moments, then said laconically, 'Right, Curtis.

I'll be over at once.' He replaced the receiver and turned to his guest. 'Sir James Dwighton has been found in his library – murdered.'

'What?'

Mr Satterthwaite was startled – thrilled.

'I must go over to Alderway at once. Care to come with me?'

Mr Satterthwaite remembered that the colonel was chief constable of the county.

'If I shan't be in the way –' He hesitated.

'Not at all. That was Inspector Curtis telephoning. Good, honest fellow, but no brains. I'd be glad if you would come with me, Satterthwaite. I've got an idea this is going to turn out a nasty business.'

'Have they got the fellow who did it?'

'No,' replied Melrose shortly.

Mr Satterthwaite's trained ear detected a nuance of reserve behind the curt negative. He began to go over in his mind all that he knew of the Dwightons.

A pompous old fellow, the late Sir James, brusque in his manner. A man that might easily make enemies. Veering on sixty, with grizzled hair and a florid face. Reputed to be tight-fisted in the extreme.

His mind went on to Lady Dwighton. Her image floated before him, young, auburn-haired, slender. He remembered various rumours, hints, odd bits of gossip. So that was it – that was why Melrose looked so glum. Then he pulled himself up – his imagination was running away with him.

Five minutes later Mr Satterthwaite took his place beside his host in the latter's little two seater, and they drove off together into the night.

The colonel was a taciturn man. They had gone quite a mile and a half before he spoke. Then he jerked out abruptly. 'You know 'em, I suppose?'

'The Dwightons? I know all about them, of course.' Who was there Mr Satterthwaite didn't know all about? 'I've met him once, I think, and her rather oftener.'

'Pretty woman,' said Melrose.

'Beautiful!' declared Mr Satterthwaite.

'Think so?'

'A pure Renaissance type,' declared Mr Satterthwaite, warming up to his theme. 'She acted in those theatricals – the charity matinee, you know, last spring. I was very much struck. Nothing modern about her – a pure survival. One can imagine her in the doge's palace, or as Lucrezia Borgia.'

The colonel let the car swerve slightly, and Mr Satterthwaite came to an abrupt stop. He wondered what fatality had brought the name of Lucrezia Borgia to his tongue. Under the circumstances –

'Dwighton was not poisoned, was he?' he asked abruptly.

Melrose looked at him sideways, somewhat curiously. 'Why do you ask that, I wonder?' he said.

'Oh, I – I don't know.' Mr Satterthwaite was flustered. 'I – It just occurred to me.'

'Well, he wasn't,' said Melrose gloomily. 'If you want to know, he was crashed on the head.'

'With a blunt instrument,' murmured Mr Satterthwaite, nodding his head sagely.

'Don't talk like a damned detective story, Satterthwaite. He was hit on the head with a bronze figure.'

'Oh,' said Satterthwaite, and relapsed into silence.

'Know anything of a chap called Paul Delangua?' asked Melrose after a minute or two.

'Yes. Good-looking young fellow.'

'I daresay women would call him so,' growled the colonel.

'You don't like him?'

'No, I don't.'

'I should have thought you would have. He rides very well.'

'Like a foreigner at the horse show. Full of monkey tricks.'

Mr Satterthwaite suppressed a smile. Poor old Melrose was so very British in his outlook. Agreeably conscious himself of a cosmopolitan point of view, Mr Satterthwaite was able to deplore the insular attitude toward life.

'Has he been down in this part of the world?' he asked.

'He's been staying at Alderway with the Dwightons. The rumour goes that Sir James kicked him out a week ago.'

'Why?'

'Found him making love to his wife, I suppose. What the hell –'

There was a violent swerve, and a jarring impact.

'Most dangerous crossroads in England,' said Melrose. 'All the same, the other fellow should have sounded his horn. We're on the main road. I fancy we've damaged him rather more than he has damaged us.'

He sprang out. A figure alighted from the other car and joined him. Fragments of speech reached Satterthwaite.

'Entirely my fault, I'm afraid,' the stranger was saying. 'But I do not know this part of the country very well, and there's absolutely no sign of any kind to show you're coming onto the main road.'

The colonel, mollified, rejoined suitably. The two men bent together over the stranger's car, which a chauffeur was already examining. The conversation became highly technical.

'A matter of half an hour, I'm afraid,' said the stranger. 'But don't let me detain you. I'm glad your car escaped injury as well as it did.'

'As a matter of fact –' the colonel was beginning, but he was interrupted.

Mr Satterthwaite, seething with excitement, hopped out of the car with a birdlike action, and seized the stranger warmly by the hand.

'It *is!* I thought I recognized the voice,' he declared excitedly. 'What an extraordinary thing. What a very extraordinary thing.'

'Eh?' said Colonel Melrose.

'Mr Harley Quin. Melrose, I'm sure you've heard me speak many times of Mr Quin?'

Colonel Melrose did not seem to remember the fact, but he assisted politely at the scene while Mr Satterthwaite was chirruping gaily on. 'I haven't seen you – let me see –'

'Since the night at the Bells and Motley,' said the other quietly.

'The Bells and Motley, eh?' said the colonel.

'An inn,' explained Mr Satterthwaite.

'What an odd name for an inn.'

'Only an old one,' said Mr Quin. 'There was a time, remember, when bells and motley were more common in England than they are nowadays.'

'I suppose so, yes, no doubt you are right,' said Melrose vaguely. He blinked. By a curious effect of light – the headlights of one car and the red tail-light of the other – Mr Quin seemed for a moment to be dressed in motley himself. But it was only the light.

'We can't leave you here stranded on the road,' continued Mr Satterthwaite. 'You must come along with us. There's plenty of room for three, isn't there, Melrose?'

'Oh rather.' But the colonel's voice was a little doubtful. 'The only thing is,' he remarked, 'the job we're on. Eh, Satterthwaite?'

Mr Satterthwaite stood stock-still. Ideas leaped and flashed over him. He positively shook with excitement.

'No,' he cried. 'No, I should have known better! There is no chance where you are concerned, Mr Quin. It was not an accident that we all met tonight at the crossroads.'

Colonel Melrose stared at his friend in astonishment. Mr Satterthwaite took him by the arm.

'You remember what I told you – about our friend Derek Capel? The motive for his suicide, which no one could guess? It was Mr Quin who solved that problem – and there have been others since. He shows you things that are there all the time, but which you haven't seen. He's marvellous.'

'My dear Satterthwaite, you are making me blush,' said Mr Quin, smiling. 'As far as I can remember, these discoveries were all made by you, not by me.'

'They were made because you were there,' said Mr Satterthwaite with intense conviction.

'Well,' said Colonel Melrose, clearing his throat uncomfortably. 'We mustn't waste any more time. Let's get on.'

He climbed into the driver's seat. He was not too well pleased at having the stranger foisted upon him through Mr Satterthwaite's enthusiasm, but he had no valid objection to offer, and he was anxious to get on to Alderway as fast as possible.

Mr Satterthwaite urged Mr Quin in next, and himself took the outside seat. The car was a roomy one and took three without undue squeezing.

'So you are interested in crime, Mr Quin?' said the colonel, doing his best to be genial.

'No, not exactly in crime.'

'What, then?'

Mr Quin smiled. 'Let us ask Mr Satterthwaite. He is a very shrewd observer.'

'I think,' said Satterthwaite slowly, 'I may be wrong, but I think – that Mr Quin is interested in – lovers.'

He blushed as he said the last word, which is one no Englishman can pronounce without self-consciousness. Mr Satterthwaite brought it out apologetically, and with an effect of inverted commas.

'By gad!' said the colonel, startled and silenced.

He reflected inwardly that this seemed to be a very rum friend of Satterthwaite's. He glanced at him sideways. The fellow looked all right – quite a normal young chap. Rather dark, but not at all foreign-looking.

'And now,' said Satterthwaite importantly, 'I must tell you all about the case.'

He talked for some ten minutes. Sitting there in the darkness, rushing through the night, he had an intoxicating feeling of power. What did it matter if he were only a looker-on at life? He had words at his command, he was master of them, he could string them to a pattern – a strange Renaissance pattern composed of the beauty of Laura Dwighton, with her white arms and red hair – and the shadowy dark figure of Paul Delangua, whom women found handsome.

Set that against the background of Alderway – Alderway that had stood since the days of Henry VII and, some said, before that. Alderway that was English to the core, with its clipped yew and its old beak barn and the fishpond, where monks had kept their carp for Fridays.

In a few deft strokes he had etched in Sir James, a Dwighton who was a true descendant of the old De Wittons, who long ago had wrung money out of the land and locked it fast in coffers, so that whoever else had fallen on evil days, the masters of Alderway had never become impoverished.

At last Mr Satterthwaite ceased. He was sure, had been sure all along, of the sympathy of his audience. He waited now the word of praise which was his due. It came.

'You are an artist, Mr Satterthwaite.'

'I – I do my best.' The little man was suddenly humble.

They had turned in at the lodge gates some minutes ago. Now the car drew up in front of the doorway, and a police constable came hurriedly down the steps to meet them.

'Good evening, sir. Inspector Curtis is in the library.'

'Right.'

Melrose ran up the steps followed by the other two. As the three of them passed across the wide hall, an elderly butler peered from a doorway apprehensively. Melrose nodded to him.

'Evening, Miles. This is a sad business.'

'It is indeed,' the other quavered. 'I can hardly believe it, sir; indeed I can't. To think that anyone should strike down the master.'

'Yes, yes,' said Melrose, cutting him short. 'I'll have a talk with you presently.'

He strode on to the library. There a big, soldierly-looking inspector greeted him with respect.

'Nasty business, sir. I have not disturbed things. No fingerprints on the weapon. Whoever did it knew his business.'

Mr Satterthwaite looked at the bowed figure sitting at the big writing table, and looked hurriedly away again. The man had been struck down from behind, a smashing blow that had crashed in the skull. The sight was not a pretty one.

The weapon lay on the floor – a bronze figure about two feet high, the base of it stained and wet. Mr Satterthwaite bent over it curiously.

'A Venus,' he said softly. 'So he was struck down by Venus.'

He found food for poetic meditation in the thought.

'The windows,' said the inspector, 'were all closed and bolted on the inside.'

He paused significantly.

'Making an inside job of it,' said the chief constable reluctantly. 'Well – well, we'll see.'

The murdered man was dressed in golf clothes, and a bag of golf clubs had been flung untidily across a big leather couch.

'Just come in from the links,' explained the inspector, following the chief constable's glance. 'At five-fifteen, that was. Had tea brought here by the butler. Later he rang for his valet to bring him down a pair of soft slippers. As far as we can tell, the valet was the last person to see him alive.'

Melrose nodded, and turned his attention once more to the writing table.

A good many of the ornaments had been overturned and broken. Prominent among these was a big dark enamel clock, which lay on its side in the very centre of the table.

The inspector cleared his throat.

'That's what you might call a piece of luck, sir,' he said. 'As you see, it's stopped. *At half past six*. That gives us the time of the crime. Very convenient.'

The colonel was staring at the clock.

'As you say,' he remarked. 'Very convenient.' He paused a minute, and then added, 'Too damned convenient! I don't like it, Inspector.'

He looked around at the other two. His eye sought Mr Quin's with a look of appeal in it.

'Damn it all,' he said. 'It's too neat. You know what I mean. Things don't happen like that.'

'You mean,' murmured Mr Quin, 'that clocks don't fall like that?'

Melrose stared at him for a moment, then back at the clock, which had that pathetic and innocent look familiar to objects which have been suddenly bereft of their dignity. Very carefully Colonel Melrose replaced it on its legs again. He struck the table a violent blow. The clock rocked, but it did not fall. Melrose repeated the action, and very slowly, with a kind of unwillingness, the clock fell over on its back.

'What time was the crime discovered?' demanded Melrose sharply.

'Just about seven o'clock, sir.'

'Who discovered it?'

'The butler.'

'Fetch him in,' said the chief constable. 'I'll see him now. Where is Lady Dwighton, by the way?'

'Lying down, sir. Her maid says that she's prostrated and can't see anyone.'

Melrose nodded, and Inspector Curtis went in search of the butler. Mr Quin was looking thoughtfully into the fireplace. Mr Satterthwaite followed his example. He blinked at the smouldering logs for a minute or two, and then something bright lying in the grate caught his eye. He stooped and picked up a little sliver of curved glass.

'You wanted me, sir?'

It was the butler's voice, still quavering and uncertain. Mr Satterthwaite slipped the fragment of glass into his waistcoat pocket and turned round.

The old man was standing in the doorway.

'Sit down,' said the chief constable kindly. 'You're shaking all over. It's been a shock to you, I expect.'

'It has indeed, sir.'

'Well, I shan't keep you long. Your master came in just after five, I believe?'

'Yes, sir. He ordered tea to be brought to him here. Afterward, when I came to take it away, he asked for Jennings to be sent to him – that's his valet, sir.'

'What time was that?'

'About ten minutes past six, sir.'

'Yes – well?'

'I sent word to Jennings, sir. And it wasn't till I came in here to shut the windows and draw the curtains at seven o'clock that I saw –'

Melrose cut him short. 'Yes, yes, you needn't go into all that. You didn't touch the body, or disturb anything, did you?'

'Oh! No indeed, sir! I went as fast as I could go to the telephone to ring up the police.'

'And then?'

'I told Jane – her ladyship's maid, sir – to break the news to her ladyship.'

'You haven't seen your mistress at all this evening?'

Colonel Melrose put the question casually enough, but Mr Satterthwaite's keen ears caught anxiety behind the words.

'Not to speak to, sir. Her ladyship has remained in her own apartments since the tragedy.'

'Did you see her before?'

The question came sharply, and everyone in the room noted the hesitation before the butler replied.

'I – I just caught a glimpse of her, sir, descending the staircase.'

'Did she come in here?'

Mr Satterthwaite held his breath.

'I – I think so, sir.'

'What time was that?'

You might have heard a pin drop. Did the old man know, Mr Satterthwaite wondered, what hung on his answer?

'It was just upon half past six, sir.'

Colonel Melrose drew a deep breath. 'That will do, thank you. Just send Jennings, the valet, to me, will you?'

Jennings answered the summons with promptitude. A narrow-faced man with a catlike tread. Something sly and secretive about him.

A man, thought Mr Satterthwaite, who would easily murder his master if he could be sure of not being found out.

He listened eagerly to the man's answers to Colonel Melrose's questions. But his story seemed straightforward enough. He had brought his master down some soft hide slippers and removed the brogues.

'What did you do after that, Jennings?'

'I went back to the stewards' room, sir.'

'At what time did you leave your master?'

'It must have been just after a quarter past six, sir.'

'Where were you at half past six, Jennings?'

'In the stewards' room, sir.'

Colonel Melrose dismissed the man with a nod. He looked across at Curtis inquiringly.

'Quite correct, sir, I checked that up. He was in the stewards' room from about six-twenty until seven o'clock.'

'Then that lets him out,' said the chief constable a trifle regretfully. 'Besides, there's no motive.'

They looked at each other.

There was a tap at the door.

'Come in,' said the colonel.

A scared-looking lady's maid appeared.

'If you please, her ladyship has heard that Colonel Melrose is here and she would like to see him.'

'Certainly,' said Melrose. 'I'll come at once. Will you show me the way?'

But a hand pushed the girl aside. A very different figure now stood in the doorway. Laura Dwighton looked like a visitor from another world.

She was dressed in a clinging medieval tea gown of dull blue brocade. Her auburn hair was parted in the middle and brought down over her ears. Conscious of the fact she had a style of her own, Lady Dwighton had never had her hair cut. It was drawn back into a simple knot on the nape of her neck. Her arms were bare.

One of them was outstretched to steady herself against the frame of the doorway, the other hung down by her side, clasping a book. *She looks*, Mr Satterthwaite thought, *like a Madonna from an early Italian canvas*.

She stood there, swaying slightly from side to side. Colonel Melrose sprang toward her.

'I've come to tell you – to tell you –'

Her voice was low and rich. Mr Satterthwaite was so entranced with the dramatic value of the scene that he had forgotten its reality.

'Please, Lady Dwighton –' Melrose had an arm round her, supporting her. He took her across the hall into a small anteroom, its walls hung with faded silk. Quin and Satterthwaite followed. She sank down on the low settee, her head resting back on a rust-coloured cushion, her eyelids closed. The three men watched her. Suddenly she opened her eyes and sat up. She spoke very quietly.

'*I killed him*,' she said. 'That's what I came to tell you. *I killed him!*'

There was a moment's agonized silence. Mr Satterthwaite's heart missed a beat.

'Lady Dwighton,' said Melrose. 'You've had a great shock – you're unstrung. I don't think you quite know what you're saying.'

Would she draw back now – while there was yet time?

'I know perfectly what I'm saying. It was I who shot him.'

Two of the men in the room gasped, the other made no sound. Laura Dwighton leaned still farther forward.

'Don't you understand? I came down and shot him. I admit it.'

The book she had been holding in her hand clattered to the floor. There was a paper cutter in it, a thing shaped like a dagger with a jewelled hilt. Mr Satterthwaite picked it up mechanically and placed it on the table. As he did so he thought, *That's a dangerous toy. You could kill a man with that.*

'Well –' Laura Dwighton's voice was impatient. '– what are you going to do about it? Arrest me? Take me away?'

Colonel Melrose found his voice with difficulty.

'What you have told me is very serious, Lady Dwighton. I must ask you to go to your room till I have – er – made arrangements.'

She nodded and rose to her feet. She was quite composed now, grave and cold.

As she turned toward the door, Mr Quin spoke. 'What did you do with the revolver, Lady Dwighton?'

A flicker of uncertainty passed across her face. 'I – I dropped it there on the floor. No, I think I threw it out of the window – oh! I can't remember now. What does it matter? I hardly knew what I was doing. It doesn't matter, does it?'

'No,' said Mr Quin. 'I hardly think it matters.'

She looked at him in perplexity with a shade of something that might have been alarm. Then she flung back her head and went imperiously out of the room. Mr Satterthwaite hastened after her. She might, he felt, collapse at any minute. But she was already halfway up the staircase, displaying no sign of her earlier weakness. The scared-looking maid was standing at the foot of the stairway, and Mr Satterthwaite spoke to her authoritatively.

'Look after your mistress,' he said.

'Yes, sir.' The girl prepared to ascend after the blue-robed figure. 'Oh, please, sir, they don't suspect him, do they?'

'Suspect whom?'

'Jennings, sir. Oh! Indeed, sir, he wouldn't hurt a fly.'

'Jennings? No, of course not. Go and look after your mistress.'

'Yes, sir.'

The girl ran quickly up the staircase. Mr Satterthwaite returned to the room he had just vacated.

Colonel Melrose was saying heavily, 'Well, I'm jiggered. There's more in this than meets the eye. It – it's like those dashed silly things heroines do in many novels.'

'It's unreal,' agreed Mr Satterthwaite. 'It's like something on the stage.'

Mr Quin nodded. 'Yes, you admire the drama, do you not? You are a man who appreciates good acting when you see it.'

Mr Satterthwaite looked hard at him.

In the silence that followed a far-off sound came to their ears.

'Sounds like a shot,' said Colonel Melrose. 'One of the keepers, I daresay. That's probably what she heard. Perhaps she went down to see. She wouldn't go close or examine the body. She'd leap at once to the conclusion –'

'Mr Delangua, sir.' It was the old butler who spoke, standing apologetically in the doorway.

'Eh?' said Melrose. 'What's that?'

'Mr Delangua is here, sir, and would like to speak to you if he may.'

Colonel Melrose leaned back in his chair. 'Show him in,' he said grimly.

A moment later Paul Delangua stood in the doorway. As Colonel Melrose had hinted, there was something un-English about him – the easy grace of his movements, the dark, handsome face, the eyes set a little too near together. There hung about him the air of the Renaissance. He and Laura Dwighton suggested the same atmosphere.

'Good evening, gentlemen,' said Delangua. He made a little theatrical bow.

'I don't know what your business may be, Mr Delangua,' said Colonel Melrose sharply, 'but if it is nothing to do with the matter at hand –'

Delangua interrupted him with a laugh. 'On the contrary,' he said, 'it has everything to do with it.'

'What do you mean?'

'I mean,' said Delangua quietly, 'that I have come to give myself up for the murder of Sir James Dwighton.'

'You know what you are saying?' said Melrose gravely.

'Perfectly.'

The young man's eyes were riveted to the table.

'I don't understand –'

'Why I give myself up? Call it remorse – call it anything you please. I stabbed him, right enough – you may be quite sure of that.' He nodded toward the table. 'You've got the weapon there, I see. A very handy little tool. Lady Dwighton unfortunately left it lying around in a book, and I happened to snatch it up.'

'One minute,' said Colonel Melrose. 'Am I to understand that you admit stabbing Sir James with this?' He held the dagger aloft.

'Quite right. I stole in through the window, you know. He had his back to me. It was quite easy. I left the same way.'

'Through the window?'

'Through the window, of course.'

'And what time was this?'

Delangua hesitated. 'Let me see – I was talking to the keeper fellow – that was at a quarter past six. I heard the church tower chime. It must have been – well, say somewhere about half past.'

A grim smile came to the colonel's lips.

'Quite right, young man,' he said. 'Half past six was the time. Perhaps you've heard that already? But this is altogether a most peculiar murder!'

'Why?'

'So many people confess to it,' said Colonel Melrose.

They heard the sharp intake of the other's breath.

'Who else has confessed to it?' he asked in a voice that he vainly strove to render steady.

'Lady Dwighton.'

Delangua threw back his head and laughed in rather a forced manner. 'Lady Dwighton is apt to be hysterical,' he said lightly. 'I shouldn't pay any attention to what she says if I were you.'

'I don't think I shall,' said Melrose. 'But there's another odd thing about this murder.'

'What's that?'

'Well,' said Melrose, 'Lady Dwighton has confessed to having shot Sir James, and you have confessed to having stabbed him. But luckily for both of you, he wasn't shot or stabbed, you see. His skull was smashed in.'

'My God!' cried Delangua. 'But a woman couldn't possibly do that –'

He stopped, biting his lip. Melrose nodded with the ghost of a smile.

'Often read of it,' he volunteered. 'Never seen it happen.'

'What?'

'Couple of young idiots each accusing themselves because they thought the other had done it,' said Melrose. 'Now we've got to begin at the beginning.'

'The valet,' cried Mr Satterthwaite. 'That girl just now – I wasn't paying any attention at the time.' He paused, striving for coherence. 'She was afraid of our suspecting him. There must be some motive that he had and which we don't know, but she does.'

Colonel Melrose frowned, then he rang the bell. When it was answered, he said, 'Please ask Lady Dwighton if she will be good enough to come down again.'

They waited in silence until she came. At sight of Delangua she started and stretched out a hand to save herself from falling. Colonel Melrose came quickly to the rescue.

'It's quite all right, Lady Dwighton. Please don't be alarmed.'

'I don't understand. What is Mr Delangua doing here?'

Delangua came over to her, 'Laura – Laura – why did you do it?'

'Do it?'

'I know. It was for me – because you thought that – After all, it was natural, I suppose. But, oh! You angel!'

Colonel Melrose cleared his throat. He was a man who disliked emotion and had a horror of anything approaching a 'scene'.

'If you'll allow me to say so, Lady Dwighton, both you and Mr Delangua have had a lucky escape. He had just arrived in his turn to "confess" to the murder – oh, it's quite all right, he didn't do it! But what we want to know is the truth. No more shillyshallying. The butler says you went into the library at half past six – is that so?'

Laura looked at Delangua. He nodded.

'The truth, Laura,' he said. 'That is what we want now.'

She breathed a deep sigh. 'I will tell you.'

She sank down on a chair that Mr Satterthwaite had hurriedly pushed forward.

'I did come down. I opened the library door and I saw –'

She stopped and swallowed. Mr Satterthwaite leaned forward and patted her hand encouragingly.

'Yes,' he said. 'Yes. You saw?'

'My husband was lying across the writing table. I saw his head – the blood – oh!'

She put her hands to her face. The chief constable leaned forward.

'Excuse me, Lady Dwighton. You thought Mr Delangua had shot him?'

She nodded. 'Forgive me, Paul,' she pleaded. 'But you said – you said –'

'That I'd shoot him like a dog,' said Delangua grimly. 'I remember. That was the day I discovered he'd been ill-treating you.'

The chief constable kept sternly to the matter in hand.

'Then I am to understand, Lady Dwighton, that you went upstairs again and – er – said nothing. We needn't go into your reason. You didn't touch the body or go near the writing table?'

She shuddered.

'No, no. I ran straight out of the room.'

'I see, I see. And what time was this exactly? Do you know?'

'It was just half past six when I got back to my bedroom.'

'Then at – say five-and-twenty past six, Sir James was already dead.'

The chief constable looked at the others. 'That clock – it was faked, eh? We suspected that all along. Nothing easier than to move the hands to whatever time you wished, but they made a mistake to lay it down on its side like that. Well, that seems to narrow it down to the butler or the valet, and I can't believe it's the butler. Tell me, Lady Dwighton, did this man Jennings have any grudge against your husband?'

Laura lifted her face from her hands. 'Not exactly a grudge, but – well, James told me only this morning that he'd dismissed him. He'd found him pilfering.'

'Ah! Now we're getting at it. Jennings would have been dismissed without a character. A serious matter for him.'

'You said something about a clock,' said Laura Dwighton. 'There's just a chance – if you want to fix the time – James would have been sure to have his little golf watch on him. Mightn't that have been smashed, too, when he fell forward?'

'It's an idea,' said the colonel slowly. 'But I'm afraid – Curtis!'

The inspector nodded in quick comprehension and left the room. He returned a minute later. On the palm of his hand was a silver watch marked like a golf ball, the kind that are sold for golfers to carry loose in a pocket with balls.

'Here it is, sir,' he said, 'but I doubt if it will be any good. They're tough, these watches.'

The colonel took it from him and held it to his ear.

'It seems to have stopped, anyway,' he observed.

He pressed with his thumb, and the lid of the watch flew open. Inside the glass was cracked across.

'Ah!' he said exultantly.

The hand pointed to exactly a quarter past six.

'A very good glass of port, Colonel Melrose,' said Mr Quin.

It was half past nine, and the three men had just finished a belated dinner at Colonel Melrose's house. Mr Satterthwaite was particularly jubilant.

'I was quite right,' he chuckled. 'You can't deny it, Mr Quin. You turned up tonight to save two absurd young people who were both bent on putting their heads into a noose.'

'Did I?' said Mr Quin. 'Surely not. I did nothing at all.'

'As it turned out, it was not necessary,' agreed Mr Satterthwaite. 'But it might have been. It was touch and go, you know. I shall never forget the moment when Lady Dwighton said, "I killed him." I've never seen anything on the stage half as dramatic.'

'I'm inclined to agree with you,' said Mr Quin.

'Wouldn't have believed such a thing could happen outside a novel,' declared the colonel, for perhaps the twentieth time that night.

'Does it?' asked Mr Quin.

The colonel stared at him, 'Damn it, it happened tonight.'

'Mind you,' interposed Mr Satterthwaite, leaning back and sipping his port, 'Lady Dwighton was magnificent, quite magnificent, but she made one mistake. She shouldn't have leaped to the conclusion that her husband had been shot. In the same way Delangua was a fool to assume that he had been stabbed just because the dagger happened to be lying on the table in front of us. It was a mere coincidence that Lady Dwighton should have brought it down with her.'

'Was it?' asked Mr Quin.

'Now if they'd only confined themselves to saying that they'd killed Sir James, without particularizing how –' went on Mr Satterthwaite – 'what would have been the result?'

'They might have been believed,' said Mr Quin with an odd smile.

'The whole thing was exactly like a novel,' said the colonel.

'That's where they got the idea from, I daresay,' said Mr Quin.

'Possibly,' agreed Mr Satterthwaite. 'Things one has read do come back to one in the oddest way.' He looked across at Mr Quin. 'Of course,' he said, 'the clock really looked suspicious from the first. One ought never to forget how easy it is to put the hands of a clock or watch forward or back.'

Mr Quin nodded and repeated the words. 'Forward,' he said, and paused. 'Or back.'

There was something encouraging in his voice. His bright, dark eyes were fixed on Mr Satterthwaite.

'The hands of the clock were put forward,' said Mr Satterthwaite. 'We know that.'

'Were they?' asked Mr Quin.

Mr Satterthwaite stared at him. 'Do you mean,' he said slowly, 'that it was the watch which was put back? But that doesn't make sense. It's impossible.'

'Not impossible,' murmured Mr Quin.

'Well – absurd. To whose advantage could that be?'

'Only, I suppose, to someone who had an *alibi* for that time.'

'By gad!' cried the colonel. 'That's the time young Delangua said he was talking to the keeper.'

'He told us that very particularly,' said Mr Satterthwaite.

They looked at each other. They had an uneasy feeling as of solid ground failing beneath their feet. Facts went spinning round, turning new and unexpected faces. And in the centre of the kaleidoscope was the dark, smiling face of Mr Quin.

'But in that case –' began Melrose '– in that case –'

Mr Satterthwaite, nimble-witted, finished his sentence for him. 'It's all the other way round. A plant just the same – but a plant against the valet. Oh, but it can't be! It's impossible. Why each of them accused themselves of the crime.'

'Yes,' said Mr Quin. 'Up till then you suspected them, didn't you?' His voice went on, placid and dreamy. 'Just like something out of a book, you said, colonel. They got the idea there. It's what the innocent hero and heroine do. Of course it made you think them innocent – there was the force of tradition behind them. Mr Satterthwaite has been saying all along it was like something on the stage. You were both right. It wasn't real. You've been saying so all along without knowing what you were saying. They'd have told a much better story than that if they'd wanted to be believed.'

The two men looked at him helplessly.

'It would be clever,' said Mr Satterthwaite slowly. 'It would be diabolically clever. And I've thought of something else. The butler said he went in at seven to shut the windows – so he must have expected them to be open.'

'That's the way Delangua came in,' said Mr Quin. 'He killed Sir James with one blow, and he and she together did what they had to do –'

He looked at Mr Satterthwaite, encouraging him to reconstruct the scene. He did so, hesitatingly.

'They smashed the clock and put it on its side. Yes. They altered the watch and smashed it. Then he went out of the window, and she fastened it after him. But there's one thing I don't see. Why bother with the watch at all? Why not simply put back the hands of the clock?'

'The clock was always a little obvious,' said Mr Quin.

'Anyone might have seen through a rather transparent device like that.'

'But surely the watch was too far-fetched. Why, it was pure chance that we ever thought of the watch.'

'Oh, no,' said Mr Quin. 'It was the lady's suggestion, remember.'

Mr Satterthwaite stared at him, fascinated.

'And yet, you know,' said Mr Quin dreamily, 'the one person who wouldn't be likely to overlook the watch would be the valet. Valets know better than anyone what their masters carry in their pockets. If he altered the clock, the valet would have altered the watch, too. They don't understand human nature, those two. They are not like Mr Satterthwaite.'

Mr Satterthwaite shook his head.

'I was all wrong,' he murmured humbly. 'I thought that you had come to save them.'

'So I did,' said Mr Quin. 'Oh! Not those two – the others. Perhaps you didn't notice the lady's maid? She wasn't wearing blue brocade, or acting a dramatic part. But she's really a very pretty girl, and I think she loves that man Jennings very much. I think that between you you'll be able to save her man from getting hanged.'

'We've no proof of any kind,' said Colonel Melrose heavily.

Mr Quin smiled. 'Mr Satterthwaite has.'

'I?' Mr Satterthwaite was astonished.

Mr Quin went on. 'You've got a proof that that watch wasn't smashed in Sir James's pocket. You can't smash a watch like that without opening the case. Just try it and see. Someone took the watch out and opened it, set back the hands, smashed the glass, and then shut it and put it back. They never noticed that a fragment of glass was missing.'

'Oh!' cried Mr Satterthwaite. His hand flew to his waistcoat pocket. He drew out a fragment of curved glass.

It was his moment.

'With this,' said Mr Satterthwaite importantly, 'I shall save a man from death.'

The Harlequin Tea Set

'The Harlequin Tea Set' was first published in *Winter's Crimes* by Macmillan in 1971. It was the last of Agatha Christie's short stories to be published, 48 years after 'The Affair at the Victory Ball' first appeared in *The Sketch* in 1923.

Mr Satterthwaite clucked twice in vexation. Whether right in his assumption or not, he was more and more convinced that cars nowadays broke down far more frequently than they used to do. The only cars he trusted were old friends who had survived the test of time. They had their little idiosyncrasies, but you knew about those, provided for them, fulfilled their wants before the demand became too acute. But new cars! Full of new gadgets, different kinds of windows, an instrument panel newly and differently arranged, handsome in its glistening wood but being unfamiliar, your groping hand hovered uneasily over fog lights, windscreen wipers, the choke, etcetera. All these things with knobs in a place you didn't expect them. And when your gleaming new purchase failed in performance, your local garage uttered the intensely irritating words: 'Teething troubles. Splendid car, sir, these roadsters Super Superbos. All the latest accessories. But bound to have their teething troubles, you know. Ha, ha.' Just as though a car was a baby.

But Mr Satterthwaite, being now of an advanced age, was strongly of the opinion that a new car ought to be fully adult. Tested, inspected, and its teething troubles already dealt with before it came into its purchaser's possession.

Mr Satterthwaite was on his way to pay a weekend visit to friends in the country. His new car had already, on the way from London, given certain symptoms of discomfort, and was now drawn up in a garage waiting for the diagnosis, and how long it would take before he could resume progress towards his destination. His chauffeur was in consultation with a mechanic. Mr Satterthwaite sat, striving for patience. He had assured his hosts, on the telephone the night before, that he would be arriving in good time for tea. He would reach Doverton Kingsbourne, he assured them, well before four o'clock.

He clucked again in irritation and tried to turn his thoughts to something pleasant. It was no good sitting here in a state of acute irritation, frequently consulting his wristwatch, clucking once more and giving, he had to realize, a very good imitation of a hen pleased with its prowess in laying an egg.

Yes. Something pleasant. Yes, now hadn't there been something – something he had noticed as they were driving along. Not very long ago. Something that he had seen through the window which had pleased and excited him. But before he had had time to think about it, the car's misbehaviour had become more pronounced and a rapid visit to the nearest service station had been inevitable.

What was it that he had seen? On the left – no, on the right. Yes, on the right as they drove slowly through the village street. Next door to a post office. Yes, he was quite sure of that. Next door to a post office because the sight of the post office had given him the idea of telephoning to the Addisons to break the news that he might be slightly late in his arrival. The post office. A village post office. And next to it – yes, definitely, next to it, next door or if not next door the door after. Something that had stirred old memories, and he had wanted – just what was it that he had wanted? Oh dear, it would come to him presently. It was mixed up with a colour. Several colours. Yes, a colour or colours. Or a word. Some definite word that had stirred memories, thoughts, pleasures gone by, excitement, recalling something that had been vivid and alive. Something in which he himself had not only seen but observed. No, he had done more. He had taken part. Taken part in what, and why, and where? All sorts of places. The answer came quickly at the last thought. All sorts of places.

On an island? In Corsica? At Monte Carlo watching the croupier spinning his roulette wheel? A house in the country? All sorts of places. And he had been there, and someone else. Yes, someone else. It all tied up with that. He was getting there at last. If he could just . . . He was interrupted at that moment by the chauffeur coming to the window with the garage mechanic in tow behind him.

'Won't be long now, sir,' the chauffeur assured Mr Satterthwaite cheerfully. 'Matter of ten minutes or so. Not more.'

'Nothing seriously wrong,' said the mechanic, in a low, hoarse, country voice. 'Teething troubles, as you might say.'

Mr Satterthwaite did not cluck this time. He gnashed his own teeth. A phrase he had often read in books and which in old age he seemed to

have got into the habit of doing himself, due, perhaps, to the slight loose-
ness of his upper plate. Really, teething trouble! Toothache. Teeth gnashing.
False teeth. One's whole life centred, he thought, about teeth.

'Doverton Kingsbourne's only a few miles away,' said the chauffeur,
'and they've a taxi here. You could go on in that, sir, and I'd bring the
car along later as soon as it's fixed up.'

'No!' said Mr Satterthwaite.

He said the word explosively and both the chauffeur and the mechanic
looked startled. Mr Satterthwaite's eyes were sparkling. His voice was
clear and decisive. Memory had come to him.

'I propose,' he said, 'to walk along the road we have just come by.
When the car is ready, you will pick me up there. The Harlequin Cafe,
I think it is called.'

'It's not very much of a place, sir,' the mechanic advised.

'That is where I shall be,' said Mr Satterthwaite, speaking with a kind
of regal autocracy.

He walked off briskly. The two men stared after him.

'Don't know what's got into him,' said the chauffeur. 'Never seen him
like that before.'

The village of Kingsbourne Ducis did not live up to the old world
grandeur of its name. It was a smallish village consisting of one street. A
few houses. Shops that were dotted rather unevenly, sometimes betraying
the fact that they were houses which had been turned into shops or that
they were shops which now existed as houses without any industrial
intentions.

It was not particularly old world or beautiful. It was just simple and
rather unobtrusive. Perhaps that was why, thought Mr Satterthwaite, that
a dash of brilliant colour had caught his eye. Ah, here he was at the post
office. The post office was a simply functioning post office with a pillar
box outside, a display of some newspapers and some postcards, and
surely, next to it, yes there was the sign up above. The Harlequin Cafe.
A sudden qualm struck Mr Satterthwaite. Really, he was getting too old.
He had fancies. Why should that one word stir his heart? *The Harlequin
Cafe.*

The mechanic at the service station had been quite right. It did not
look like a place in which one would really be tempted to have a meal.
A snack perhaps. A morning coffee. Then why? But he suddenly realized
why. Because the cafe, or perhaps one could better put it as the house
that sheltered the cafe, was in two portions. One side of it had small
tables with chairs round them arranged ready for patrons who came here
to eat. But the other side was a shop. A shop that sold china. It was not
an antique shop. It had no little shelves of glass vases or mugs. It was a

shop that sold modern goods, and the show window that gave on the
street was at the present moment housing every shade of the rainbow. A
tea set of largish cups and saucers, each one of a different colour. Blue,
red, yellow, green, pink, purple. Really, Mr Satterthwaite thought, a
wonderful show of colour. No wonder it had struck his eye as the car
had passed slowly beside the pavement, looking ahead for any sign of
a garage or a service station. It was labelled with a large card as 'A
Harlequin Tea Set'.

It was the word 'harlequin' of course which had remained fixed in Mr
Satterthwaite's mind, although just far enough back in his mind so that
it had been difficult to recall it. The gay colours. The harlequin colours.
And he had thought, wondered, had the absurd but exciting idea that in
some way here was a call to him. To him specially. Here, perhaps, eating
a meal or purchasing cups and saucers might be his own old friend, Mr
Harley Quin. How many years was it since he had last seen Mr Quin?
A large number of years. Was it the day he had seen Mr Quin walking
away from him down a country lane, Lovers' Lane they had called it?
He had always expected to see Mr Quin again, once a year at least.
Possibly twice a year. But no. That had not happened.

And so today he had had the wonderful and surprising idea that here,
in the village of Kingsbourne Ducis, he might once again find Mr Harley
Quin.

'Absurd of me,' said Mr Satterthwaite, 'quite absurd of me. Really, the
ideas one has as one gets old!'

He had missed Mr Quin. Missed something that had been one of the
most exciting things in the late years of his life. Someone who might turn
up anywhere and who, if he did turn up, was always an announcement that
something was going to happen. Something that was going to happen
to him. No, that was not quite right. Not *to* him, but through him.
That was the exciting part. Just from the words that Mr Quin might
utter. Words. Things he might show him, ideas would come to Mr
Satterthwaite. He would see things, he would imagine things, he would
find out things. He would deal with something that needed to be dealt
with. And opposite him would sit Mr Quin, perhaps smiling approval.
Something that Mr Quin said would start the flow of ideas, the active
person would be he himself. He – Mr Satterthwaite. The man with so
many old friends. A man among whose friends had been duchesses,
an occasional bishop, people that counted. Especially, he had to admit,
people who had counted in the social world. Because, after all, Mr
Satterthwaite had always been a snob. He had liked duchesses, he had
liked knowing old families, families who had represented the landed
gentry of England for several generations. And he had had, too, an

interest in young people not necessarily socially important. Young people who were in trouble, who were in love, who were unhappy, who needed help. Because of Mr Quin, Mr Satterthwaite was enabled to give help.

And now, like an idiot, he was looking into an unprepossessing village cafe and a shop for modern china and tea sets and casseroles no doubt.

'All the same,' said Mr Satterthwaite to himself, 'I must go in. Now I've been foolish enough to walk back here, I must go in just – well, just in case. They'll be longer, I expect, doing the car than they say. It will be more than ten minutes. Just in case there was anything interesting inside.'

He looked once more at the window full of china. He appreciated suddenly that it was good china. Well made. A good modern product. He looked back into the past, remembering. The Duchess of Leith, he remembered. What a wonderful old lady she had been. How kind she had been to her maid on the occasion of a very rough sea voyage to the island of Corsica. She had ministered to her with the kindliness of a ministering angel and only on the next day had she resumed her autocratic, bullying manner which the domestics of those days had seemed able to stand quite easily without any sign of rebellion.

Maria. Yes, that's what the Duchess's name had been. Dear old Maria Leith. Ah well. She had died some years ago. But she had had a harlequin breakfast set, he remembered. Yes. Big round cups in different colours. Black. Yellow, red and a particularly pernicious shade of puce. Puce, he thought, must have been a favourite colour of hers. She had had a Rockingham tea set, he remembered, in which the predominating colour had been puce decorated with gold.

'Ah,' sighed Mr Satterthwaite, 'those were the days. Well, I suppose I'd better go in. Perhaps order a cup of coffee or something. It will be very full of milk, I expect, and possibly already sweetened. But still, one has to pass the time.'

He went in. The cafe side was practically empty. It was early, Mr Satterthwaite supposed, for people to want cups of tea. And anyway, very few people did want cups of tea nowadays. Except, that is, occasionally elderly people in their own homes. There was a young couple in the far window and two women gossiping at a table against the back wall.

'I said to her,' one of them was saying, 'I said you can't do that sort of thing. No, it's not the sort of thing that I'll put up with, and I said the same to Henry and he agreed with me.'

It shot through Mr Satterthwaite's mind that Henry must have rather a hard life and that no doubt he had found it always wise to agree, whatever the proposition put up to him might be. A most unattractive woman with a most unattractive friend. He turned his attention to the other side of the building, murmuring, 'May I just look round?'

There was quite a pleasant woman in charge and she said 'Oh yes, sir. We've got a good stock at present.'

Mr Satterthwaite looked at the coloured cups, picked up one or two of them, examined the milk jug, picked up a china zebra and considered it, examined some ashtrays of a fairly pleasing pattern. He heard chairs being pushed back and turning his head, noted that the two middle-aged women still discussing former grievances had paid their bill and were now leaving the shop. As they went out of the door, a tall man in a dark suit came in. He sat down at the table which they had just vacated. His back was to Mr Satterthwaite, who thought that he had an attractive back. Lean, strong, well-muscled but rather dark and sinister-looking because there was very little light in the shop. Mr Satterthwaite looked back again at the ashtrays. 'I might buy an ashtray so as not to cause a disappointment to the shop owner,' he thought. As he did so, the sun came out suddenly.

He had not realized that the shop had looked dim because of the lack of sunshine. The sun must have been under a cloud for some time. It had clouded over, he remembered, at about the time they had got to the service station. But now there was this sudden burst of sunlight. It caught up the colours of the china and through a coloured glass window of somewhat ecclesiastical pattern which must, Mr Satterthwaite thought, have been left over in the original Victorian house. The sun came through the window and lit up the dingy cafe. In some curious way it lit up the back of the man who had just sat down there. Instead of a dark black silhouette, there was now a festoon of colours. Red and blue and yellow. And suddenly Mr Satterthwaite realized that he was looking at exactly what he had hoped to find. His intuition had not played him false. He knew who it was who had just come in and sat down there. He knew so well that he had no need to wait until he could look at the face. He turned his back on the china, went back into the cafe, round the corner of the round table and sat down opposite the man who had just come in.

'Mr Quin,' said Mr Satterthwaite. 'I knew somehow it was going to be you.'

Mr Quin smiled.

'You always know so many things,' he said.

'It's a long time since I've seen you,' said Mr Satterthwaite.

'Does time matter?' said Mr Quin.

'Perhaps not. You may be right. Perhaps not.'

'May I offer you some refreshment?'

'Is there any refreshment to be had?' said Mr Satterthwaite doubtfully. 'I suppose you must have come in for that purpose.'

'One is never quite sure of one's purpose, is one?' said Mr Quin.

'I am so pleased to see you again,' said Mr Satterthwaite. 'I'd almost forgotten, you know. I mean forgotten the way you talk, the things you say. The things you make me think of, the things you make me do.'

'I – make you do? You are so wrong. You have always known yourself just what you wanted to do and why you want to do them and why you know so well that they have to be done.'

'I only feel that when you are here.'

'Oh no,' said Mr Quin lightly. 'I have nothing to do with it. I am just – as I've often told you – I am just passing by. That is all.'

'Today you are passing by through Kingsbourne Ducis.'

'And you are not passing by. You are going to a definite place. Am I right?'

'I'm going to see a very old friend. A friend I have not seen for a good many years. He's old now. Somewhat crippled. He has had one stroke. He has recovered from it quite well, but one never knows.'

'Does he live by himself?'

'Not now, I am glad to say. His family have come back from abroad, what is left of his family that is. They have been living with him now for some months. I am glad to be able to come and see them again all together. Those, that's to say, that I have seen before, and those that I have not seen.'

'You mean children?'

'Children and grandchildren.' Mr Satterthwaite sighed. Just for a moment he was sad that he had had no children and no grandchildren and no great-grandchildren himself. He did not usually regret it at all.

'They have some special Turkish coffee here,' said Mr Quin. 'Really good of its kind. Everything else is, as you have guessed, rather unpalatable. But one can always have a cup of Turkish coffee, can one not? Let us have one because I suppose you will soon have to get on with your pilgrimage, or whatever it is.'

In the doorway came a small black dog. He came and sat down by the table and looked up at Mr Quin.

'Your dog?' said Mr Satterthwaite.

'Yes. Let me introduce you to Hermes.' He stroked the black dog's head. 'Coffee,' he said. 'Tell Ali.'

The black dog walked from the table through a door at the back of the shop. They heard him give a short, incisive bark. Presently he reappeared and with him came a young man with a very dark complexion, wearing an emerald green pullover.

'Coffee, Ali,' said Mr Quin. 'Two coffees.'

'Turkish coffee. That's right, isn't it, sir?' He smiled and disappeared.

The dog sat down again.

'Tell me,' said Mr Satterthwaite, 'tell me where you've been and what you have been doing and why I have not seen you for so long.'

'I have just told you that time really means nothing. It is clear in my mind and I think it is clear in yours the occasion when we last met.'

'A very tragic occasion,' said Mr Satterthwaite. 'I do not really like to think of it.'

'Because of death? But death is not always a tragedy. I have told you that before.'

'No,' said Mr Satterthwaite, 'perhaps that death – the one we are both thinking of – was not a tragedy. But all the same . . .'

'But all the same it is life that really matters. You are quite right, of course,' said Mr Quin. 'Quite right. It is life that matters. We do not want someone young, someone who is happy, or could be happy, to die. Neither of us want that, do we. That is the reason why we must always save a life when the command comes.'

'Have you got a command for me?'

'Me – command for you?' Harley Quin's long, sad face brightened into its peculiarly charming smile. 'I have no commands for *you*, Mr Satterthwaite. I have never had commands. You yourself know things, see things, know what to do, do them. It has nothing to do with me.'

'Oh yes, it has,' said Mr Satterthwaite. 'You're not going to change my mind on that point. But tell me. Where have you been during what it is too short to call time?'

'Well, I have been here and there. In different countries, different climates, different adventures. But mostly, as usual, just passing by. I think it is more for you to tell me not only what you have been doing but what you are going to do now. More about where you are going. Who you are going to meet. Your friends, what they are like.'

'Of course I will tell you. I should enjoy telling you because I have been wondering, thinking you know about these friends I am going to. When you have not seen a family for a long time, when you have not been closely connected with them for many years, it is always a nervous moment when you are going to resume old friendships and old ties.'

'You are so right,' said Mr Quin.

The Turkish coffee was brought in little cups of oriental pattern. Ali placed them with a smile and departed. Mr Satterthwaite sipped approvingly.

'As sweet as love, as black as night and as hot as hell. That is the old Arab phrase, isn't it?'

Harley smiled over his shoulder and nodded.

'Yes,' said Mr Satterthwaite, 'I must tell you where I am going though what I am doing hardly, matters. I am going to renew old friendships, to make acquaintance with the younger generation. Tom Addison, as I have said, is a very old friend of mine. We did many things together in our young days. Then, as often happens, life parted us. He was in the Diplomatic Service, went abroad for several foreign posts in turn. Sometimes I went and stayed with him, sometimes I saw him when he was home in England. One of his early posts was in Spain. He married a Spanish girl, a very beautiful, dark girl called Pilar. He loved her very much.'

'They had children?'

'Two daughters. A fair-haired baby like her father, called Lily, and a second daughter, Maria, who took after her Spanish mother. I was Lily's godfather. Naturally, I did not see either of the children very often. Two or three times a year either I gave a party for Lily or went to see her at her school. She was a sweet and lovely person. Very devoted to her father and he was very devoted to her. But in between these meetings, these revivals of friendship, we went through some difficult times. You will know about it as well as I do. I and my contemporaries had difficulties in meeting through the war years. Lily married a pilot in the Air Force. A fighter pilot. Until the other day I had even forgotten his name. Simon Gilliatt. Squadron Leader Gilliatt.'

'He was killed in the war?'

'No, no. No. He came through safely. After the war he resigned from the Air Force and he and Lily went out to Kenya as so many did. They settled there and they lived very happily. They had a son, a little boy called Roland. Later when he was at school in England I saw him once or twice. The last time, I think, was when he was twelve years old. A nice boy. He had red hair like his father. I've not seen him since so I am looking forward to seeing him today. He is twenty-three – twenty-four now. Time goes on so.'

'Is he married?'

'No. Well, not yet.'

'Ah. Prospects of marriage?'

'Well, I wondered from something Tom Addison said in his letter. There is a girl cousin. The younger daughter Maria married the local doctor. I never knew her very well. It was rather sad. She died in childbirth. Her little girl was called Inez, a family name chosen by her Spanish grandmother. As it happens I have only seen Inez once since she grew up. A dark, Spanish type very much like her grandmother. But I am boring you with all this.'

'No. I want to hear it. It is very interesting to me.'

'I wonder why,' said Mr Satterthwaite.

He looked at Mr Quin with that slight air of suspicion which sometimes came to him.

'You want to know all about this family. Why?'

'So that I can picture it, perhaps, in my mind.'

'Well, this house I am going to, Doverton Kingsbourne it is called. It is quite a beautiful old house. Not so spectacular as to invite tourists or to be open to visitors on special days. Just a quiet country house to live in by an Englishman who has served his country and comes back to enjoy a mellow life when the age of retirement comes. Tom was always fond of country life. He enjoyed fishing. He was a good shot and we had very happy days together in his family home of his boyhood. I spent many of my own holidays as a boy at Doverton Kingsbourne. And all through my life I have had that image in my mind. No place like Doverton Kingsbourne. No other house to touch it. Every time I drove near it I would make a detour perhaps and just pass to see the view through a gap in the trees of the long lane that runs in front of the house, glimpses of the river where we used to fish, and of the house itself. And I would remember all the things that Tom and I did together. He has been a man of action. A man who has done things. And I – I have just been an old bachelor.'

'You have been more than that,' said Mr Quin. 'You have been a man who made friends, who had many friends and who has served his friends well.'

'Well, if I can think that. Perhaps you are being too kind.'

'Not at all. You are very good company besides. The stories you can tell, the things you've seen, the places you have visited. The curious things that have happened in your life. You could write a whole book on them,' said Mr Quin.

'I should make you the main character in it if I did.'

'No, you would not,' said Mr Quin. 'I am the one who passes by. That is all. But go on. Tell me more.'

'Well, this is just a family chronicle that I'm telling you. As I say, there were long periods, years of time when I did not see any of them. But they have been always my old friends. I saw Tom and Pilar until the time when Pilar died – she died rather young, unfortunately – Lily, my godchild, Inez, the quiet doctor's daughter who lives in the village with her father . . .'

'How old is the daughter?'

'Inez is nineteen or twenty, I think. I shall be glad to make friends with her.'

'So it is on the whole a happy chronicle?'

'Not entirely. Lily, my godchild – the one who went to Kenya with her husband – was killed there in an automobile accident. She was killed outright, leaving behind her a baby of barely a year old, little Roland.

Simon, her husband, was quite broken-hearted. They were an unusually happy couple. However, the best thing happened to him that could happen, I suppose. He married again, a young widow who was the widow of a Squadron Leader, a friend of his and who also had been left with a baby the same age. Little Timothy and little Roland had only two or three months in age between them. Simon's marriage, I believe, has been quite happy though I've not seen them, of course, because they continued to live in Kenya. The boys were brought up like brothers. They went to the same school in England and spent their holidays usually in Kenya. I have not seen them, of course, for many years. Well, you know what has happened in Kenya. Some people have managed to stay on. Some people, friends of mine, have gone to Western Australia and have settled again happily there with their families. Some have come home to this country.

'Simon Gilliatt and his wife and their two children left Kenya. It was not the same to them and so they came home and accepted the invitation that has always been given them and renewed every year by old Tom Addison. They have come, his son-in-law, his son-in-law's second wife and the two children, now grown up boys, or rather, young men. They have come to live as a family there and they are happy. Tom's other grandchild, Inez Horton, as I told you, lives in the village with her father, the doctor, and she spends a good deal of her time, I gather, at Doverton Kingsbourne with Tom Addison who is very devoted to his grand-daughter. They sound all very happy together there. He has urged me several times to come there and see. Meet them all again. And so I accepted the invitation. Just for a weekend. It will be sad in some ways to see dear old Tom again, somewhat crippled, with perhaps not a very long expectation of life but still cheerful and gay, as far as I can make out. And to see also the old house again. Doverton Kingsbourne. Tied up with all my boyish memories. When one has not lived a very eventful life, when nothing has happened to one personally, and that is true of me, the things that remain with you are the friends, the houses and the things you did as a child and a boy and a young man. There is only one thing that worries me.'

'You should not be worried. What is it that worries you?'

'That I might be – disappointed. The house one remembers, one has dreams of, when one might come to see it again it would not be as you remembered it or dreamt it. A new wing would have been added, the garden would have been altered, all sorts of things can have happened to it. It is a very long time, really, since I have been there.'

'I think your memories will go with you,' said Mr Quin. 'I am glad you are going there.'

'I have an idea,' said Mr Satterthwaite. 'Come with me. Come with me on this visit. You need not fear that you'll not be welcome. Dear Tom

Addison is the most hospitable fellow in the world. Any friend of mine would immediately be a friend of his. Come with me. You must. I insist.'

Making an impulsive gesture, Mr Satterthwaite nearly knocked his coffee cup off the table. He caught it just in time.

At that moment the shop door was pushed open, ringing its old-fashioned bell as it did so. A middle-aged woman came in. She was slightly out of breath and looked somewhat hot. She was good-looking still with a head of auburn hair only just touched here and there with grey. She had that clear ivory-coloured skin that so often goes with reddish hair and blue eyes, and she had kept her figure well. The newcomer swept a quick glance round the cafe and turned immediately into the china shop.

'Oh!' she exclaimed, 'you've still got some of the Harlequin cups.'

'Yes, Mrs Gilliatt, we had a new stock arrived in yesterday.'

'Oh, I'm so pleased. I really have been very worried. I rushed down here. I took one of the boys' motor bikes. They'd gone off somewhere and I couldn't find either of them. But I really had to do something. There was an unfortunate accident this morning with some of the cups and we've got people arriving for tea and a party this afternoon. So if you can give me a blue and a green and perhaps I'd better have another red one as well in case. That's the worst of these different coloured cups, isn't it?'

'Well, I know they do say as it's a disadvantage and you can't always replace the particular colour you want.'

Mr Satterthwaite's head had gone over his shoulder now and he was looking with some interest at what was going on. Mrs Gilliatt, the shop woman had said. But of course. He realized it now. This must be – he rose from his seat, half hesitating, and then took a step or two into the shop.

'Excuse me,' he said, 'but are you – are you Mrs Gilliatt from Doverton Kingsbourne?'

'Oh yes. I am Beryl Gilliatt. Do you – I mean . . . ?'

She looked at him, wrinkling her brows a little. An attractive woman, Mr Satterthwaite thought. Rather a hard face, perhaps, but competent. So this was Simon Gilliatt's second wife. She hadn't got the beauty of Lily, but she seemed an attractive woman, pleasant and efficient. Suddenly a smile came to Mrs Gilliatt's face.

'I do believe . . . yes, of course. My father-in-law, Tom, has got a photo-graph of you and you must be the guest we are expecting this afternoon. You must be Mr Satterthwaite.'

'Exactly,' said Mr Satterthwaite. 'That is who I am. But I shall have to apologize very much for being so much later in arriving than I said. But unfortunately my car has had a breakdown. It's in the garage now being attended to.'

'Oh, how miserable for you. But what a shame. But it's not tea time yet. Don't worry. We've put it off anyway. As you probably heard, I ran down to replace a few cups which unfortunately got swept off a table this morning. Whenever one has anyone to lunch or tea or dinner, something like that always happens.'

'There you are, Mrs Gilliatt,' said the woman in the shop. 'I'll wrap them up in here. Shall I put them in a box for you?'

'No, if you'll just put some paper around them and put them in this shopping bag of mine, they'll be quite all right that way.'

'If you are returning to Doverton Kingsbourne,' said Mr Satterthwaite, 'I could give you a lift in my car. It will be arriving from the garage any moment now.'

'That's very kind of you. I wish really I could accept. But I've simply got to take the motorbike back. The boys will be miserable without it. They're going somewhere this evening.'

'Let me introduce you,' said Mr Satterthwaite. He turned towards Mr Quin, who had risen to his feet and was now standing quite near. 'This is an old friend of mine, Mr Harley Quin, whom I have just happened to run across here. I've been trying to persuade him to come along to Doverton Kingsbourne. Would it be possible, do you think, for Tom to put up yet another guest for tonight?'

'Oh, I'm sure it would be quite all right,' said Beryl Gilliatt. 'I'm sure he'd be delighted to see another friend of yours. Perhaps it's a friend of his as well.'

'No,' said Mr Quin, 'I've never met Mr Addison though I've often heard my friend, Mr Satterthwaite, speak of him.'

'Well then, do let Mr Satterthwaite bring you. We should be delighted.'

'I am very sorry,' said Mr Quin. 'Unfortunately, I have another engagement. Indeed –' he looked at his watch '– I must start for it immediately. I am late already, which is what comes of meeting old friends.'

'Here you are, Mrs Gilliatt,' said the saleswoman. 'It'll be quite all right, I think, in your bag.'

Beryl Gilliatt put the parcel carefully into the bag she was carrying, then said to Mr Satterthwaite:

'Well, see you presently. Tea isn't until quarter past five, so don't worry. I'm so pleased to meet you at last, having heard so much about you always both from Simon and from my father-in-law.'

She said a hurried goodbye to Mr Quin and went out of the shop.

'Bit of a hurry she's in, isn't she?' said the shop woman, 'but she's always like that. Gets through a lot in a day, I'd say.'

The sound of the bicycle outside was heard as it revved up.

'Quite a character, isn't she?' said Mr Satterthwaite.

'It would seem so,' said Mr Quin.

'And I really can't persuade you?'

'I'm only passing by,' said Mr Quin.

'And when shall I see you again? I wonder now.'

'Oh, it will not be very long,' said Mr Quin. 'I think you will recognize me when you do see me.'

'Have you nothing more – nothing more to tell me? Nothing more to explain?'

'To explain what?'

'To explain why I have met you here.'

'You are a man of considerable knowledge,' said Mr Quin. 'One word might mean something to you. I think it would and it might come in useful.'

'What word?'

'Daltonism,' said Mr Quin. He smiled.

'I don't think –' Mr Satterthwaite frowned for a moment. 'Yes. Yes, I do know only just for the moment I can't remember . . .'

'Goodbye for the present,' said Mr Quin. 'Here is your car.'

At that moment the car was indeed pulling up by the post office door. Mr Satterthwaite went out to it. He was anxious not to waste more time and keep his hosts waiting longer than need be. But he was sad all the same at saying goodbye to his friend.

'There is nothing I can do for you?' he said, and his tone was almost wistful.

'Nothing you can do for *me*.'

'For someone else?'

'I think so. Very likely.'

'I hope I know what you mean.'

'I have the utmost faith in you,' said Mr Quin. 'You always know things. You are very quick to observe and to know the meaning of things. You have not changed, I assure you.'

His hand rested for a moment on Mr Satterthwaite's shoulder, then he walked out and proceeded briskly down the village street in the opposite direction to Doverton Kingsbourne. Mr Satterthwaite got into his car.

'I hope we shan't have any more trouble,' he said.

His chauffeur reassured him.

'It's no distance from here, sir. Three or four miles at most, and she's running beautifully now.'

He ran the car a little way along the street and turned where the road widened so as to return the way he had just come. He said again,

'Only three or four miles.'

Mr Satterthwaite said again, 'Daltonism.' It still didn't mean anything to him, but yet he felt it should. It was a word he'd heard used before.

'Doverton Kingsbourne,' said Mr Satterthwaite to himself. He said it very softly under his breath. The two words still meant to him what they had always meant. A place of joyous reunion, a place where he couldn't get there too quickly. A place where he was going to enjoy himself, even though so many of those whom he had known would not be there any longer. But Tom would be there. His old friend, Tom, and he thought again of the grass and the lake and the river and the things they had done together as boys.

Tea was set out upon the lawn. Steps led out from the French windows in the drawing room and down to where a big copper beech at one side and a cedar of Lebanon on the other made the setting for the afternoon scene. There were two painted and carved white tables and various garden chairs. Upright ones with coloured cushions and lounging ones where you could lean back and stretch your feet out and sleep, if you wished to do so. Some of them had hoods over them to guard you from the sun.

It was a beautiful early evening and the green of the grass was a soft deep colour. The golden light came through the copper beech and the cedar showed the lines of its beauty against a soft pinkish-golden sky.

Tom Addison was waiting for his guest in a long basket chair, his feet up, Mr Satterthwaite noted with some amusement what he remembered from many other occasions of meeting his host, he had comfortable bedroom slippers suited to his slightly swollen gouty feet, and the shoes were odd ones. One red and one green. Good old Tom, thought Mr Satterthwaite, he hasn't changed. Just the same. And he thought, 'What an idiot I am. Of course I know what that word meant. Why didn't I think of it at once?'

'Thought you were never going to turn up, you old devil,' said Tom Addison.

He was still a handsome old man, a broad face with deep-set twinkling grey eyes, shoulders that were still square and gave him a look of power. Every line in his face seemed a line of good humour and of affectionate welcome. 'He never changes,' thought Mr Satterthwaite.

'Can't get up to greet you,' said Tom Addison. 'Takes two strong men and a stick to get me on my feet. Now, do you know our little crowd, or don't you? You know Simon, of course.'

'Of course I do. It's a good few years since I've seen you, but you haven't changed much.'

Squadron Leader Simon Gilliatt was a lean, handsome man with a mop of red hair.

'Sorry you never came to see us when we were in Kenya,' he said.

'You'd have enjoyed yourself. Lots of things we could have shown you. Ah well, one can't see what the future may bring. I thought I'd lay my bones in that country.'

'We've got a very nice churchyard here,' said Tom Addison. 'Nobody's ruined our church yet by restoring it and we haven't very much new building round about so there's plenty of room in the churchyard still. We haven't had one of these terrible additions of a new intake of graves.'

'What a gloomy conversation you're having,' said Beryl Gilliatt, smiling. 'These are our boys,' she said, 'but you know them already, don't you, Mr Satterthwaite?'

'I don't think I'd have known them now,' said Mr Satterthwaite.

Indeed, the last time he had seen the two boys was on a day when he had taken them out from their prep school. Although there was no relationship between them – they had had different fathers and mothers – yet the boys could have been, and often were, taken for brothers. They were about the same height and they both had red hair. Roland, presumably, having inherited it from his father and Timothy from his auburn-haired mother. There seemed also to be a kind of comradeship between them. Yet really, Mr Satterthwaite thought, they were very different. The difference was clearer now when they were, he supposed, between twenty-two and twenty-five years old. He could see no resemblance in Roland to his grandfather. Nor apart from his red hair did he look like his father.

Mr Satterthwaite had wondered sometimes whether the boy would look like Lily, his dead mother. But there again he could see little resemblance. If anything, Timothy looked more as a son of Lily's might have looked. The fair skin and the high forehead and a delicacy of bone structure. At his elbow, a soft deep voice said,

'I'm Inez. I don't expect you remember me. It was quite a long time ago when I saw you.'

A beautiful girl, Mr Satterthwaite thought at once. A dark type. He cast his mind back a long way to the days when he had come to be best man at Tom Addison's wedding to Pilar. She showed her Spanish blood, he thought, the carriage of her head and the dark aristocratic beauty. Her father, Dr Horton, was standing just behind her. He looked much older than when Mr Satterthwaite had seen him last. A nice man and kindly. A good general practitioner, unambitious but reliable and devoted, Mr Satterthwaite thought, to his daughter. He was obviously immensely proud of her.

Mr Satterthwaite felt an enormous happiness creeping over him. All these people, he thought, although some of them strange to him, it seemed like friends he had already known. The dark beautiful girl, the two red-haired boys, Beryl Gilliatt, fussing over the tea tray, arranging cups and saucers, beckoning to a maid from the house to bring out cakes and plates of sandwiches. A splendid tea. There were chairs that pulled up to the tables so that you could sit comfortably eating all you wanted to eat. The boys settled themselves, inviting Mr Satterthwaite to sit between them.

He was pleased at that. He had already planned in his own mind that it was the boys he wanted to talk to first, to see how much they recalled to him Tom Addison in the old days, and he thought, 'Lily. How I wish Lily could be here now'. Here he was, thought Mr Satterthwaite, here he was back in his boyhood. Here where he had come and been welcomed by Tom's father and mother, an aunt or so, too, there had been and a great-uncle and cousins. And now, well, there were not so many in this family, but it *was* a family. Tom in his bedroom slippers, one red, one green, old but still merry and happy. Happy in those who were spread round him. And here was Doverton just, or almost just, as it had been. Not quite so well kept up, perhaps, but the lawn was in good condition. And down there he could see the gleam of the river through the trees and the trees, too. More trees than there had been. And the house needing, perhaps, another coat of paint but not too badly. After all, Tom Addison was a rich man. Well provided for, owning a large quantity of land. A man with simple tastes who spent enough to keep his place up but was not a spendthrift in other ways. He seldom travelled or went abroad nowadays, but he entertained. Not big parties, just friends. Friends who came to stay, friends who usually had some connection going back into the past. A friendly house.

He turned a little in his chair, drawing it away from the table and turning it sideways so that he could see better the view down to the river. Down there was the mill, of course, and beyond the other side there were fields. And in one of the fields, it amused him to see a kind of scarecrow, a dark figure on which birds were settling on the straw. Just for a moment he thought it looked like Mr Harley Quin. Perhaps, thought Mr Satterthwaite, it *is* my friend Mr Quin. It was an absurd idea and yet if someone had piled up the scarecrow and tried to make it look like Mr Quin, it could have had the sort of slender elegance that was foreign to most scarecrows one saw.

'Are you looking at our scarecrow?' said Timothy. 'We've got a name for him, you know. We call him Mister Harley Barley.'

'Do you indeed' said Mr Satterthwaite. 'Dear me, I find that very interesting.'

'Why do you find it interesting?' said Roly, with some curiosity.

'Well, because it rather resembles someone that I know, whose name happens to be Harley. His first name, that is.'

The boys began singing, '*Harley Barley, stands on guard, Harley Barley takes things hard. Guards the ricks and guards the hay, Keeps the trespassers away.*'

'Cucumber sandwich, Mr Satterthwaite?' said Beryl Gilliatt, 'or do you prefer a home-made pâté one?'

Mr Satterthwaite accepted the home-made pâté. She deposited by his side a puce cup, the same colour as he had admired in the shop. How gay it looked, all that tea set on the table. Yellow, red, blue, green and all the rest of it. He wondered if each one had their favourite colour. Timothy, he noticed, had a red cup, Roland had a yellow one. Beside Timothy's cup was an object Mr Satterthwaite could not at first identify. Then he saw it was a meerschaum pipe. It was years since Mr Satterthwaite had thought of or seen a meerschaum pipe. Roland, noticing what he was looking at, said, 'Tim brought that back from Germany when he went. He's killing himself with cancer smoking his pipe all the time.'

'Don't you smoke, Roland?'

'No. I'm not one for smoking. I don't smoke cigarettes and I don't smoke pot either.'

Inez came to the table and sat down the other side of him. Both the young men pressed food upon her. They started a laughing conversation together.

Mr Satterthwaite felt very happy among these young people. Not that they took very much notice of him apart from their natural politeness. But he liked hearing them. He liked, too, making up his judgement about them. He thought, he was almost sure, that both the young men were in love with Inez. Well, it was not surprising. Propinquity brings these things about. They had come to live here with their grandfather. A beautiful girl, Roland's first cousin, was living almost next door. Mr Satterthwaite turned his head. He could just see the house through the trees where it poked up from the road just beyond the front gate. That was the same house that Dr Horton had lived in last time he came here, seven or eight years ago.

He looked at Inez. He wondered which of the two young men she preferred or whether her affections were already engaged elsewhere. There was no reason why she should fall in love with one of these two attractive young specimens of the male race.

Having eaten as much as he wanted, it was not very much, Mr Satterthwaite drew his chair back altering its angle a little so that he could look all round him.

Mrs Gilliatt was still busy. Very much the housewife, he thought, making perhaps rather more of a fuss than she need of domesticity. Continually offering people cakes, taking their cups away and replenishing them, handing things round. Somehow, he thought, it would be more pleasant and more informal if she let people help themselves. He wished she was not so busy a hostess.

He looked up to the place where Tom Addison lay stretched out in his chair. Tom Addison was also watching Beryl Gilliatt. Mr Satterthwaite thought to himself: 'He doesn't like her. No. Tom doesn't like her. Well, perhaps that's to be expected.' After all, Beryl had taken the place of his own daughter, of Simon Gilliatt's first wife, Lily. 'My beautiful Lily,' thought Mr Satterthwaite again, and wondered why for some reason he felt that although he could not see anyone like her, yet Lily in some strange way was here. She was here at this tea party.

'I suppose one begins to imagine these things as one gets old,' said Mr Satterthwaite. 'After all, why shouldn't Lily be here to see her son.'

He looked affectionately at Timothy and then suddenly realized that he was not looking at Lily's son. Roland was Lily's son. Timothy was Beryl's son.

'I believe Lily knows I'm here. I believe she'd like to speak to me,' said Mr Satterthwaite. 'Oh dear, oh dear, I mustn't start imagining foolish things.'

For some reason he looked again at the scarecrow. It didn't look like a scarecrow now. It looked like Mr Harley Quin. Some tricks of the light, of the sunset, were providing it with colour, and there was a black dog like Hermes chasing the birds.

'Colour,' said Mr Satterthwaite, and looked again at the table and the tea set and the people having tea. 'Why am I here?' said Mr Satterthwaite to himself. 'Why am I here and what ought I to be doing? There's a reason . . .'

Now he knew, he felt, there was something, some crisis, something affecting – affecting all these people or only some of them? Beryl Gilliatt, Mrs Gilliatt. She was nervous about something. On edge. Tom? Nothing wrong with Tom. He wasn't affected. A lucky man to own this beauty, to own Doverton and to have a grandson so that when he died all this would come to Roland. All this would be Roland's. Was Tom hoping that Roland would marry Inez? Or would he have a fear of first cousins marrying? Though throughout history, Mr Satterthwaite thought, brothers had married sisters with no ill result. 'Nothing must happen,' said Mr Satterthwaite, 'nothing must happen. I must prevent it.'

Really, his thoughts were the thoughts of a madman. A peaceful scene. A tea set. The varying colours of the Harlequin cups. He looked at the white meerschaum pipe lying against the red of the cup. Beryl Gilliatt said something to Timothy. Timothy nodded, got up and went off towards the house. Beryl removed some empty plates from the table, adjusted a chair or two, murmured something to Roland, who went across and offered a frosted cake to Dr Horton.

Mr Satterthwaite watched her. He had to watch her. The sweep of her sleeve as she passed the table. He saw a red cup get pushed off the table. It broke on the iron feet of a chair. He heard her little exclamation as she picked up the bits. She went to the tea tray, came back and placed on the table a pale blue cup and saucer. She replaced the meerschaum pipe, putting it close against it. She brought the teapot and poured tea, then she moved away.

The table was untenanted now. Inez also had got up and left it. Gone to speak to her grandfather. 'I don't understand,' said Mr Satterthwaite to himself. 'Something's going to happen. What's going to happen?'

A table with different coloured cups round, and – yes, Timothy, his red hair glowing in the sun. Red hair glowing with that same tint, that attractive sideways wave that Simon Gilliatt's hair had always had. Timothy, coming back, standing a moment, looking at the table with a slightly puzzled eye, then going to where the meerschaum pipe rested against the pale blue cup.

Inez came back then. She laughed suddenly and she said, 'Timothy, you're drinking your tea out of the wrong cup. The blue cup's mine. Yours is the red one.'

And Timothy said, 'Don't be silly, Inez, I know my own cup. It's got sugar in it and you won't like it. Nonsense. This is my cup. The meerschaum's up against it.'

It came to Mr Satterthwaite then. A shock. Was he mad? Was he imagining things? Was any of this real?

He got up. He walked quickly towards the table, and as Timothy raised the blue cup to his lips, he shouted.

'Don't drink that!' he called. 'Don't drink it, I say.'

Timothy turned a surprised face. Mr Satterthwaite turned his head. Dr Horton, rather startled, got up from his seat and was coming near.

'What's the matter, Satterthwaite?'

'That cup. There's something wrong about it,' said Mr Satterthwaite. 'Don't let the boy drink from it.'

Horton stared at it. 'My dear fellow –'

'I know what I'm saying. The red cup was his,' said Mr Satterthwaite, 'and the red cup's broken. It's been replaced with a blue one. He doesn't know the red from blue, does he?'

Dr Horton looked puzzled. 'D'you mean – d'you mean – like Tom?'

'Tom Addison. He's colour blind. You know that, don't you?'

'Oh yes, of course. We all know that. That's why he's got odd shoes on today. He never knew red from green.'

'This boy is the same.'

'But – but surely not. Anyway, there's never been any sign of it in – in Roland.'

'There might be, though, mightn't there?' said Mr Satterthwaite. 'I'm right in thinking – Daltonism. That's what they call it, don't they?'

'It was a name they used to call it by, yes.'

'It's not inherited by a female, but it passes through the female. Lily wasn't colour blind, but Lily's son might easily be colour blind.'

'But my dear Satterthwaite, Timothy isn't Lily's son. Roly is Lily's son. I know they're rather alike. Same age, same coloured hair and things, but – well, perhaps you don't remember.'

'No,' said Mr Satterthwaite, 'I shouldn't have remembered. But I know now. I can see the resemblance too. Roland's Beryl's son. They were both babies, weren't they, when Simon re-married. It is very easy for a woman looking after two babies, especially if both of them were going to have red hair. Timothy's Lily's son and Roland is Beryl's son. Beryl's and Christopher Eden's. There is no reason why he should be colour blind. I know it, I tell you. I know it!'

He saw Dr Horton's eyes go from one to the other. Timothy, not catching what they said but standing holding the blue cup and looking puzzled.

'I saw her buy it,' said Mr Satterthwaite. 'Listen to me, man. You must listen to me. You've known me for some years. You know that I don't make mistakes if I say a thing positively.'

'Quite true. I've never known you make a mistake.'

'Take that cup away from him,' said Mr Satterthwaite. 'Take it back to your surgery or take it to an analytic chemist and find out what's in it. I saw that woman buy that cup. She bought it in the village shop. She knew then that she was going to break a red cup, replace it by a blue and that Timothy would never know that the colours were different.'

'I think you're mad, Satterthwaite. But all the same I'm going to do what you say.'

He advanced on the table, stretched out a hand to the blue cup.

'Do you mind letting me have a look at that?' said Dr Horton.

'Of course,' said Timothy. He looked slightly surprised.

'I think there's a flaw in the china, here, you know. Rather interesting.'

Beryl came across the lawn. She came quickly and sharply.

'What are you doing? What's the matter? What is happening?'

'Nothing's the matter,' said Dr Horton, cheerfully. 'I just want to show the boys a little experiment I'm going to make with a cup of tea.'

He was looking at her very closely and he saw the expression of fear, of terror. Mr Satterthwaite saw the entire change of countenance.

'Would you like to come with me, Satterthwaite? Just a little experiment, you know. A matter of testing porcelain and different qualities in it nowadays. A very interesting discovery was made lately.'

Chatting, he walked along the grass. Mr Satterthwaite followed him and the two young men, chatting to each other, followed him.

'What's the Doc up to now, Roly?' said Timothy.

'I don't know,' said Roland. 'He seems to have got some very extraordinary ideas. Oh well, we shall hear about it later, I expect. Let's go and get our bikes.'

Beryl Gilliatt turned abruptly. She retraced her steps rapidly up the lawn towards the house. Tom Addison called to her:

'Anything the matter, Beryl?'

'Something I'd forgotten,' said Beryl Gilliatt. 'That's all.'

Tom Addison looked inquiringly towards Simon Gilliatt.

'Anything wrong with your wife?' he said.

'Beryl? Oh no, not that I know of. I expect it's some little thing or other that she's forgotten. Nothing I can do for you, Beryl?' he called.

'No. No, I'll be back later.' She turned her head half sideways, looking at the old man lying back in the chair. She spoke suddenly and vehemently. 'You silly old fool. You've got the wrong shoes on again today. They don't match. Do you know you've got one shoe that's red and one shoe that's green?'

'Ah, done it again, have I?' said Tom Addison. 'They look exactly the same colour to me, you know. It's odd, isn't it, but there it is.'

She went past him, her steps quickening.

Presently Mr Satterthwaite and Dr Horton reached the gate that led out into the roadway. They heard a motor bicycle speeding along.

'She's gone,' said Dr Horton. 'She's run for it. We ought to have stopped her, I suppose. Do you think she'll come back?'

'No,' said Mr Satterthwaite, 'I don't think she'll come back. Perhaps,' he said thoughtfully, 'it's best left that way.'

'You mean?'

'It's an old house,' said Mr Satterthwaite. 'And old family. A good family. A lot of good people in it. One doesn't want trouble, scandal, everything brought upon it. Best to let her go, I think.'

'Tom Addison never liked her,' said Dr Horton. 'Never. He was always polite and kind but he didn't like her.'

'And there's the boy to think of,' said Mr Satterthwaite.

'The boy. You mean?'

'The other boy. Roland. This way he needn't know about what his mother was trying to do.'

'Why did she do it? Why on earth did she do it?'

'You've no doubt now that she did,' said Mr Satterthwaite.

'No. I've no doubt now. I saw her face, Satterthwaite, when she looked at me. I knew then that what you'd said was truth. But why?'

'Greed, I suppose,' said Mr Satterthwaite. 'She hadn't any money of her own, I believe. Her husband, Christopher Eden, was a nice chap by all accounts but he hadn't anything in the way of means. But Tom Addison's grandchild has got big money coming to him. A lot of money. Property all around here has appreciated enormously. I've no doubt that Tom Addison will leave the bulk of what he has to his grandson. She wanted it for her own son and through her own son, of course, for herself. She is a greedy woman.'

Mr Satterthwaite turned his head back suddenly.

'Something's on fire over there,' he said.

'Good lord, so it is. Oh, it's the scarecrow down in the field. Some young chap or other's set fire to it, I suppose. But there's nothing to worry about. There are no ricks or anything anywhere near. It'll just burn itself out.'

'Yes,' said Mr Satterthwaite. 'Well, you go on, Doctor. You don't need me to help you in your tests.'

'I've no doubt of what I shall find. I don't mean the exact substance, but I have come to your belief that this blue cup holds death.'

Mr Satterthwaite had turned back through the gate. He was going now down in the direction where the scarecrow was burning. Behind it was the sunset. A remarkable sunset that evening. Its colours illuminated the air round it, illuminated the burning scarecrow.

'So that's the way you've chosen to go,' said Mr Satterthwaite.

He looked slightly startled then, for in the neighbourhood of the flames he saw the tall, slight figure of a woman. A woman dressed in some pale mother-of-pearl colouring. She was walking in the direction of Mr Satterthwaite. He stopped dead, watching.

'Lily,' he said. 'Lily.'

He saw her quite plainly now. It was Lily walking towards him. Too far away for him to see her face but he knew very well who it was. Just for a moment or two he wondered whether anyone else would see her or whether the sight was only for him. He said, not very loud, only in a whisper,

'It's all right, Lily, your son is safe.'

She stopped then. She raised one hand to her lips. He didn't see her smile, but he knew she was smiling. She kissed her hand and waved it to him and then she turned. She walked back towards where the scarecrow was disintegrating into a mass of ashes.

'She's going away again,' said Mr Satterthwaite to himself. 'She's going away with him. They're walking away together. They belong to the same world, of course. They only come – those sort of people – they only come when it's a case of love or death or both.'

He wouldn't see Lily again, he supposed, but he wondered how soon he would meet Mr Quin again. He turned then and went back across the lawn towards the tea table and the Harlequin tea set, and beyond that, to his old friend Tom Addison. Beryl wouldn't come back. He was sure of it. Doverton Kingsbourne was safe again.

Across the lawn came the small black dog in flying leaps. It came to Mr Satterthwaite, panting a little and wagging its tail. Through its collar was twisted a scrap of paper. Mr Satterthwaite stooped and detached it – smoothing it out – on it in coloured letters was written a message:

CONGRATULATIONS! TO OUR NEXT MEETING
H.Q.

'Thank you, Hermes,' said Mr Satterthwaite, and watched the black dog flying across the meadow to rejoin the two figures that he himself knew were there but could no longer see.

Part Three

Parker Pyne,
Investigator

Author's Foreword

One day, having lunch at a Corner House, I was enraptured by a conversation on statistics going on at a table behind me. I turned my head and caught a vague glimpse of a bald head, glasses, and a beaming smile – I caught sight, that is, of Mr Parker Pyne. I had never thought about statistics before (and indeed seldom think about them now!) but the enthusiasm with which they were being discussed awakened my interest. I was just considering a new series of short stories and then and there I decided on the general treatment and scope, and in due course enjoyed writing them.

My own favourites are *The Case of the Discontented Husband* and *The Case of the Rich Woman*, the theme for the latter being suggested to me by having been addressed by a strange woman ten years before when I was looking into a shop window. She said with the utmost venom: 'I'd like to know what I can do with all the money I've got. I'm too seasick for a yacht – I've got a couple of cars and three fur coats – and too much rich food fair turns my stomach.'

Startled, I suggested 'Hospitals?'

She snorted 'Hospitals? I don't mean *charity*. I want to get my money's worth', and departed wrathfully.

That, of course, was now twenty-five years ago. Today all such problems would be solved for her by the income tax inspector, and she would probably be more wrathful still!

AGATHA CHRISTIE
1953

1

The Case of the
Middle-Aged Wife

'The Case of the Middle-Aged Wife' was first published as
'The Woman Concerned' in *Woman's Pictorial*, 8 October 1932.

Four grunts, an indignant voice asking why nobody could leave a hat alone, a slammed door, and Mr Packington had departed to catch the eight forty-five to the city. Mrs Packington sat on at the breakfast table. Her face was flushed, her lips were pursed, and the only reason she was not crying was that at the last minute anger had taken the place of grief. 'I won't stand it,' said Mrs Packington. 'I won't stand it!' She remained for some moments brooding, and then murmured: 'The minx. Nasty sly little cat! How George can be such a fool!'

Anger faded; grief came back. Tears came into Mrs Packington's eyes and rolled slowly down her middle-aged cheeks. 'It's all very well to say I won't stand it, but what can I do?'

Suddenly she felt alone, helpless, utterly forlorn. Slowly she took up the morning paper and read, not for the first time, an advertisement on the front page.

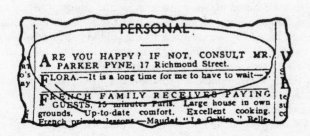

PERSONAL.

ARE YOU HAPPY? IF NOT, CONSULT MR. PARKER PYNE, 17 Richmond Street.

FLORA.—It is a long time for me to have to wait—.

FRENCH FAMILY RECEIVES PAYING GUESTS, 15 minutes Paris. Large house in own grounds. Up-to-date comfort. Excellent cooking. French private lessons.—Maudet "La Colline," Belle.

'Absurd!' said Mrs Packington. 'Utterly absurd.' Then: 'After all, I might just see . . .'

Which explains why at eleven o'clock Mrs Packington, a little nervous, was being shown into Mr Parker Pyne's private office.

As has been said, Mrs Packington was nervous, but somehow or other, the mere sight of Mr Parker Pyne brought a feeling of reassurance. He was large, not to say fat; he had a bald head of noble proportions, strong glasses, and little twinkling eyes.

'Pray sit down,' said Mr Parker Pyne. 'You have come in answer to my advertisement?' he added helpfully.

'Yes,' said Mrs Packington, and stopped there.

'And you are not happy,' said Mr Parker Pyne in a cheerful, matter-of-fact voice. 'Very few people are. You would really be surprised if you knew how few people are happy.'

'Indeed?' said Mrs Packington, not feeling, however, that it mattered whether other people were unhappy or not.

'Not interesting to you, I know,' said Mr Parker Pyne, 'but very interesting to me. You see, for thirty-five years of my life I have been engaged in the compiling of statistics in a government office. Now I have retired, and it has occurred to me to use the experience I have gained in a novel fashion. It is all so simple. Unhappiness can be classified under five main heads – no more, I assure you. Once you know the cause of a malady, the remedy should not be impossible.

'I stand in the place of the doctor. The doctor first diagnoses the patient's disorder, then he proceeds to recommend a course of treatment. There are cases where no treatment can be of avail. If that is so, I say frankly that I can do nothing. But I assure you, Mrs Packington, that if I undertake a case, the cure is practically guaranteed.'

Could it be so? Was this nonsense, or could it, perhaps be true? Mrs Packington gazed at him hopefully.

'Shall we diagnose your case?' said Mr Parker Pyne, smiling. He leaned back in his chair and brought the tips of his fingers together. 'The trouble concerns your husband. You have had, on the whole, a happy married life. You husband has, I think, prospered. I think there is a young lady concerned in the case – perhaps a young lady in your husband's office.'

'A typist,' said Mrs Packington. 'A nasty made-up little minx, all lipstick and silk stockings and curls.' The words rushed from her.

Mr Parker Pyne nodded in a soothing manner. 'There is no real harm in it – that is your husband's phrase, I have no doubt.'

'His very words.'

'Why, therefore, should he not enjoy a pure friendship with this young lady, and be able to bring a little brightness, a little pleasure, into her dull existence? Poor child, she has so little fun. Those, I imagine, are his sentiments.'

Mrs Packington nodded with vigour. 'Humbug – all humbug! He takes her on the river – I'm fond of going on the river myself, but five or six years ago he said it interfered with his golf. But he can give up golf for *her*. I like the theatre – George has always said he's too tired to go out at night. Now he takes her out to dance – *dance*! And comes back at three in the morning. I – I –'

'And doubtless he deplores the fact that women are so jealous, so unreasonably jealous when there is absolutely no cause for jealousy?'

Again Mrs Packington nodded. 'That's it.' She asked sharply: 'How do you know all this?'

'Statistics,' Mr Parker Pyne said simply.

'I'm so miserable,' said Mrs Packington. 'I've always been a good wife to George. I worked my fingers to the bone in our early days. I helped him to get on. I've never looked at any other man. His things are always mended, he gets good meals, and the house is well and economically run. And now that we've got on in the world and could enjoy ourselves and go about a bit and do all the things I've looked forward to doing some day – well, this!' She swallowed hard.

Mr Parker Pyne nodded gravely. 'I assure you I understand your case perfectly.'

'And – can you do anything?' She asked it almost in a whisper.

'Certainly, my dear lady. There is a cure. Oh yes, there is a cure.'

'What is it?' She waited, round-eyed and expectant.

Mr Parker Pyne spoke quietly and firmly. 'You will place yourself in my hands, and the fee will be two hundred guineas.'

'Two hundred guineas!'

'Exactly. You can afford to pay such a fee, Mrs Packington. You would pay that sum for an operation. Happiness is just as important as bodily health.'

'I pay you afterwards, I suppose?'

'On the contrary,' said Mr Parker Pyne. 'You pay me in advance.'

Mrs Packington rose. 'I'm afraid I don't see my way –'

'To buying a pig in a poke?' said Mr Parker Pyne cheerfully. 'Well, perhaps you're right. It's a lot of money to risk. You've got to trust me, you see. You've got to pay the money and take a chance. Those are my terms.'

'Two hundred guineas!'

'Exactly. Two hundred guineas. It's a lot of money. Good-morning, Mrs Packington. Let me know if you change your mind.' He shook hands with her, smiling in an unperturbed fashion.

When she had gone he pressed a buzzer on his desk. A forbidding-looking young woman with spectacles answered it.

'A file, please, Miss Lemon. And you might tell Claude that I am likely to want him shortly.'

'A new client?'

'A new client. At the moment she has jibbed, but she will come back. Probably this afternoon about four. Enter her.'

'Schedule A?'

'Schedule A, of course. Interesting how everyone thinks his own case unique. Well, well, warn Claude. Not too exotic, tell him. No scent and he'd better get his hair cut short.'

It was a quarter-past four when Mrs Packington once more entered Mr Parker Pyne's office. She drew out a cheque book, made out a cheque and passed it to him. A receipt was given.

'And now?' Mrs Packington looked at him hopefully.

'And now,' said Mr Parker Pyne, smiling, 'you will return home. By the first post tomorrow you will receive certain instructions which I shall be glad if you will carry out.'

Mrs Packington went home in a state of pleasant anticipation. Mr Packington came home in a defensive mood, ready to argue his position if the scene at the breakfast table was reopened. He was relieved, however, to find that his wife did not seem to be in a combative mood. She was unusually thoughtful.

George listened to the radio and wondered whether that dear child Nancy would allow him to give her a fur coat. She was very proud, he knew. He didn't want to offend her. Still, she had complained of the cold. That tweed coat of hers was a cheap affair; it didn't keep the cold out. He could put it so that she wouldn't mind, perhaps . . .

They must have another evening out soon. It was a pleasure to take a girl like that to a smart restaurant. He could see several young fellows were envying him. She was uncommonly pretty. And she liked him. To her, as she had told him, he didn't seem a bit old.

He looked up and caught his wife's eye. He felt suddenly guilty, which annoyed him. What a narrowminded, suspicious woman Maria was! She grudged him any little bit of happiness.

He switched off the radio and went to bed.

Mrs Packington received two unexpected letters the following morning. One was a printed form confirming an appointment at a noted beauty specialist's. The second was an appointment with a dressmaker. The third was from Mr Parker Pyne, requesting the pleasure of her company at lunch at the Ritz that day.

Mr Packington mentioned that he might not be home to dinner that evening as he had to see a man on business. Mrs Packington merely nodded absently, and Mr Packington left the house congratulating himself on having escaped the storm.

The beauty specialist was impressive. Such neglect! Madame, but *why?* This should have been taken in hand years ago. However, it was not too late.

Things were done to her face; it was pressed and kneaded and steamed. It had mud applied to it. It had creams applied to it. It was dusted with powder. There were various finishing touches.

At last she was given a mirror. 'I believe I *do* look younger,' she thought to herself.

The dressmaking seance was equally exciting. She emerged feeling smart, modish, up-to-date.

At half-past one, Mrs Packington kept her appointment at the Ritz. Mr Parker Pyne, faultlessly dressed and carrying with him his atmosphere of soothing reassurance, was waiting for her.

'Charming,' he said, an experienced eye sweeping her from head to foot. 'I have ventured to order you a White Lady.'

Mrs Packington, who had not contracted the cocktail habit, made no demur. As she sipped the exciting fluid gingerly, she listened to her benevolent instructor.

'Your husband, Mrs Packington,' said Mr Parker Pyne, 'must be made to Sit Up. You understand – to Sit Up. To assist in that, I am going to introduce to you a young friend of mine. You will lunch with him today.'

At that moment a young man came along, looking from side to side. He espied Mr Parker Pyne and came gracefully towards them.

'Mr Claude Luttrell, Mrs Packington.'

Mr Claude Luttrell was perhaps just short of thirty. He was graceful, debonair, perfectly dressed, extremely handsome.

'Delighted to meet you,' he murmured.

Three minutes later Mrs Packington was facing her new mentor at a small table for two.

She was shy at first, but Mr Luttrell soon put her at her ease. He knew Paris well and had spent a good deal of time on the Riviera. He asked Mrs Packington if she were fond of dancing. Mrs Packington said she was, but that she seldom got any dancing nowadays as Mr Packington didn't care to go out in the evenings.

'But he couldn't be so unkind as to keep *you* at home,' said Claude Luttrell, smiling and displaying a dazzling row of teeth. 'Women will not tolerate male jealousy in these days.'

Mrs Packington nearly said that jealousy didn't enter into the question. But the words remained unspoken. After all, it was an agreeable idea.

Claude Luttrell spoke airily of night clubs. It was settled that on the following evening Mrs Packington and Mr Luttrell should patronize the popular Lesser Archangel.

Mrs Packington was a little nervous about announcing this fact to her husband. George, she felt, would think it extraordinary and possibly ridiculous. But she was saved all trouble on this score. She had been too nervous to make her announcement at breakfast, and at two o'clock a telephone message came to the effect that Mr Packington would be dining in town.

The evening was a great success. Mrs Packington had been a good dancer as a girl and under Claude Luttrell's skilled guidance she soon picked up modern steps. He congratulated her on her gown and also on the arrangement of her hair. (An appointment had been made for her that morning with a fashionable hairdresser.) On bidding her farewell, he kissed her hand in a most thrilling manner. Mrs Packington had not enjoyed an evening so much for years.

A bewildering ten days ensued. Mrs Packington lunched, teaed, tangoed, dined, danced and supped. She heard all about Claude Luttrell's sad childhood. She heard the sad circumstances in which his father lost all his money. She heard of his tragic romance and his embittered feelings towards women generally.

On the eleventh day they were dancing at the Red Admiral. Mrs Packington saw her spouse before he saw her. George was with the young lady from his office. Both couples were dancing.

'Hallo, George,' said Mrs Packington lightly, as their orbits brought them together.

It was with considerable amusement that she saw her husband's face grow first red, then purple with astonishment. With the astonishment was blended an expression of guilt detected.

Mrs Packington felt amusedly mistress of the situation. Poor old George! Seated once more at her table, she watched them. How stout he was, how bald, how terribly he bounced on his feet! He danced in the style of twenty years ago. Poor George, how terribly he wanted to be young! And that poor girl he was dancing with had to pretend to like it. She looked bored enough now, her face over his shoulder where he couldn't see it.

How much more enviable, thought Mrs Packington contentedly, was her own situation. She glanced at the perfect Claude, now tactfully silent. How well he understood her. He never jarred – as husbands so inevitably did jar after a lapse of years.

She looked at him again. Their eyes met. He smiled; his beautiful dark eyes, so melancholy, so romantic, looked tenderly into hers.

'Shall we dance again?' he murmured.

They danced again. It was heaven!

She was conscious of George's apologetic gaze following them. It had been the idea, she remembered, to make George jealous. What a long time ago that was! She really didn't want George to be jealous now. It might upset him. Why should he be upset, poor thing? Everyone was so happy . . .

Mr Packington had been home an hour when Mrs Packington got in. He looked bewildered and unsure of himself.

'Humph,' he remarked. 'So you're back.'

Mrs Packington cast off an evening wrap which had cost her forty guineas that very morning. 'Yes,' she said, smiling. 'I'm back.'

George coughed. 'Er – rather odd meeting you.'

'Wasn't it?' said Mrs Packington.

'I – well, I thought it would be a kindness to take that girl somewhere. She's been having a lot of trouble at home. I thought – well, kindness, you know.'

Mrs Packington nodded. Poor old George – bouncing on his feet and getting so hot and being so pleased with himself.

'Who's that chap you were with? I don't know him, do I?'

'Luttrell, his name is. Claude Luttrell.'

'How did you come across him?'

'Oh, someone introduced me,' said Mrs Packington vaguely.

'Rather a queer thing for you to go out dancing – at your time of life. Musn't make a fool of yourself, my dear.'

Mrs Packington smiled. She was feeling much too kindly to the universe in general to make the obvious reply. 'A change is always nice,' she said amiably.

'You've got to be careful, you know. A lot of these lounge-lizard fellows going about. Middle-aged women sometimes make awful fools of them-selves. I'm just warning you, my dear. I don't like to see you doing anything unsuitable.'

'I find the exercise very beneficial,' said Mrs Packington.

'Um – yes.'

'I expect you do, too,' said Mrs Packington kindly.

'The great thing is to be happy, isn't it? I remember your saying so one morning at breakfast, about ten days ago.'

Her husband looked at her sharply, but her expression was devoid of sarcasm. She yawned.

'I must go to bed. By the way, George, I've been dreadfully extrava-gant lately. Some terrible bills will be coming in. You don't mind, do you?'

'Bills?' said Mr Packington.

'Yes. For clothes. And massage. And hair treatment. Wickedly extrava-gant I've been – but I know you don't mind.'

She passed up the stairs. Mr Packington remained with his mouth open. Maria had been amazingly nice about this evening's business; she hadn't seemed to care at all. But it was a pity she had suddenly taken to spending Money. Maria – that model of economy!

Women! George Packington shook his head. The scrapes that girl's brothers had been getting into lately. Well, he'd been glad to help. All the same – and dash it all, things weren't going too well in the city.

Sighing, Mr Packington in his turn slowly climbed the stairs.

Sometimes words that fail to make their effect at the time are remembered later. Not till the following morning did certain words uttered by Mr Packington really penetrate his wife's consciousness.

Lounge lizards; middle-aged women; awful fools of themselves.

Mrs Packington was courageous at heart. She sat down and faced facts. A gigolo. She had read all about gigolos in the papers. Had read, too, of the follies of middle-aged women.

Was Claude a gigolo? She supposed he was. But then, gigolos were paid for and Claude always paid for her. Yes, but it was Mr Parker Pyne who paid, not Claude – or, rather, it was really her own two hundred guineas.

Was she a middle-aged fool? Did Claude Luttrell laugh at her behind her back? Her face flushed at the thought.

Well, what of it? Claude was a gigolo. She was a middle-aged fool. She supposed she should have given him something. A gold cigarette case. That sort of thing.

A queer impulse drove her out there and then to Asprey's. The cigarette case was chosen and paid for. She was to meet Claude at Claridge's for lunch.

As they were sipping coffee she produced it from her bag. 'A little present,' she murmured.

He looked up, frowned. 'For me?'

'Yes. I – I hope you like it.'

His hand closed over it and he slid it violently across the table. 'Why did you give me that? I won't take it. Take it back. Take it back, I say.' He was angry. His dark eyes flashed.

She murmured, 'I'm sorry,' and put it away in her bag again.

There was constraint between them that day.

The following morning he rang her up. 'I must see you. Can I come to your house this afternoon?'

She told him to come at three o'clock.

He arrived very white, very tense. They greeted each other. The constraint was more evident.

Suddenly he sprang up and stood facing her. 'What do you think I am? That is what I've come to ask you. We've been friends, haven't we? Yes, friends. But all the same, you think I'm – well, a gigolo. A creature who lives on women. A lounge lizard. You do, don't you?'

'No, no.'

He swept aside her protest. His face had gone very white. 'You *do* think that! Well, it's true. That's what I've come to say. It's true! I had my orders to take you about, to amuse you, to make love to you, to make you forget your husband. That was my job. A despicable one, eh?'

'Why are you telling me this?' she asked.

'Because I'm through with it. I can't carry on with it. Not with *you*. You're different. You're the kind of woman I could believe in, trust, adore. You think I'm just saying this; that it's part of the game.' He came closer to her. 'I'm going to prove to you it isn't. I'm going away – because of you. I'm going to make myself into a man instead of the loathsome creature I am because of you.'

He took her suddenly in his arms. His lips closed on hers. Then he released her and stood away.

'Goodbye. I've been a rotter – always. But I swear it will be different now. Do you remember once saying you liked to read the advertisements in the Agony column? On this day every year you'll find there a message from me saying that I remember and am making good. You'll know, then, all you've meant to me. One thing more. I've taken nothing from you. I want you to take something from me.' He drew a plain gold seal ring from his finger. 'This was my mother's. I'd like you to have it. Now goodbye.'

George Packington came home early. He found his wife gazing into the fire with a faraway look. She spoke kindly but absently to him.

'Look here, Maria,' he jerked out suddenly. 'About that girl?'

'Yes, dear?'

'I – I never meant to upset you, you know. About her. Nothing in it.'

'I know. I was foolish. See as much as you like of her if it makes you happy.'

These words, surely, should have cheered George Packington. Strangely enough, they annoyed him. How could you enjoy taking a girl about when your wife fairly urged you on? Dash it all, it wasn't decent! All that feeling of being a gay dog, of being a strong man playing with fire, fizzled out and died an ignominious death. George Packington felt suddenly tired and a great deal poorer in pocket. The girl was a shrewd little piece.

'We might go away together somewhere for a bit if you like, Maria?' he suggested timidly.

'Oh, never mind about me. I'm quite happy.'

'But I'd like to take you away. We might go to the Riviera.'

Mrs Packington smiled at him from a distance.

Poor old George. She was fond of him. He was such a pathetic old dear. There was no secret splendour in his life as there was in hers. She smiled more tenderly still.

'That would be lovely, my dear,' she said.

Mr Parker Pyne was speaking to Miss Lemon. 'Entertainment account?'

'One hundred and two pounds, fourteen and sixpence,' said Miss Lemon.

The door was pushed open and Claude Luttrell entered. He looked moody.

'Morning, Claude,' said Mr Parker Pyne. 'Everything go off satisfactorily?'

'I suppose so.'

'The ring? What name did you put in it, by the way?'

'Matilda,' said Claude gloomily. '1899.'

'Excellent. What wording for the advertisement?'

'"Making good. Still remember. Claude."'

'Make a note of that, please, Miss Lemon. The Agony column. November third for – let me see, expenses a hundred and two pounds, fourteen and six. Yes, for ten years, I think. That leaves us a profit of ninety-two pounds, two and fourpence. Adequate. Quite adequate.'

Miss Lemon departed.

'Look here,' Claude burst out. 'I don't like this. It's a rotten game.'

'My dear boy!'

'A rotten game. That was a decent woman – a good sort. Telling her all those lies, filling her up with this sob-stuff, dash it all, it makes me sick!'

Mr Parker Pyne adjusted his glasses and looked at Claude with a kind of scientific interest. 'Dear me!' he said drily. 'I do not seem to remember that your conscience ever troubled you during your somewhat – ahem! – notorious career. Your affairs on the Riviera were particularly brazen, and your exploitation of Mrs Hattie West, the Californian Cucumber King's wife, was especially notable for the callous mercenary instinct you displayed.'

'Well, I'm beginning to feel different,' grumbled Claude. 'It isn't – nice, this game.'

Mr Parker Pyne spoke in the voice of a headmaster admonishing a favourite pupil. 'You have, my dear Claude, performed a meritorious action. You have given an unhappy woman what every woman needs – a romance. A woman tears a passion to pieces and gets no good from it, but a romance can be laid up in lavender and looked at all through the long years to come. I know human nature, my boy, and I tell you that a woman can feed on such an incident for years.' He coughed. 'We have discharged our commission to Mrs Packington very satisfactorily.'

'Well,' muttered Claude, 'I don't like it.' He left the room.

Mr Parker Pyne took a new file from a drawer. He wrote:

'Interesting vestiges of a conscience noticeable in hardened Lounge Lizard. Note: Study developments.'

The Case of the
Discontented Soldier

'The Case of the Discontented Soldier' was first published in the
USA as 'The Soldier Who Wanted Danger' in *Cosmopolitan*,
August 1932, then as 'Adventure – By Request' in
Woman's Pictorial, 15 October 1932.

Major Wilbraham hesitated outside the door of Mr Parker Pyne's office
to read, not for the first time, the advertisement from the morning paper
which had brought him there. It was simple enough:

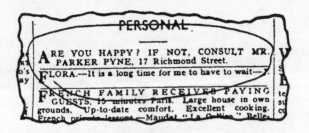

The major took a deep breath and abruptly plunged through the swing
door leading to the outer office. A plain young woman looked up from
her typewriter and glanced at him inquiringly.

'Mr Parker Pyne?' said Major Wilbraham, blushing.

'Come this way, please.'

He followed her into an inner office – into the presence of the bland
Mr Parker Pyne.

'Good-morning,' said Mr Pyne. 'Sit down, won't you? And now tell
me what I can do for you?'

'My name is Wilbraham –' began the other.

'Major? Colonel?' said Mr Pyne.

'Major.'

'Ah! And recently returned from abroad? India? East Africa?'

'East Africa.'

'A fine country, I believe. Well, so you are home again – and you don't like it. Is that the trouble?'

'You're absolutely right. Though how you knew –'

Mr Parker Pyne waved an impressive hand. 'It is my business to know. You see, for thirty-five years of my life I have been engaged in the compiling of statistics in a government office. Now I have retired and it has occurred to me to use the experience I have gained in a novel fashion. It is all so simple. Unhappiness can be classified under five main heads – no more I assure you. Once you know the cause of a malady, the remedy should not be impossible.

'I stand in the place of the doctor. The doctor first diagnoses the patient's disorder, then he recommends a course of treatment. There are cases where no treatment can be of any avail. If that is so, I say quite frankly that I can do nothing about it. But if I undertake a case, the cure is practically guaranteed.

'I can assure you. Major Wilbraham, that ninety-six per cent of retired empire builders – as I call them – are unhappy. They exchange an active life, a life full of responsibility, a life of possible danger, for – what? Straitened means, a dismal climate and a general feeling of being a fish out of water.'

'All you've said is true,' said the major. 'It's the boredom I object to. The boredom and the endless tittle-tattle about petty village matters. But what can I do about it? I've got a little money besides my pension. I've a nice cottage near Cobham. I can't afford to hunt or schoot or fish. I'm not married. My neighbours are all pleasant folk, but they've no ideas beyond this island.'

'The long and short of the matter is that you find life tame,' said Mr Parker Pyne.

'Damned tame.'

'You would like excitement, possibly danger?' asked Mr Pyne.

The soldier shrugged. 'There's no such thing in this tinpot country.'

'I beg your pardon,' said Mr Pyne seriously. 'There you are wrong. There is plenty of danger, plenty of excitement, here in London if you know where to go for it. You have seen only the surface of our English life, calm, pleasant. But there is another side. If you wish it, I can show you that other side.'

Major Wilbraham regarded him thoughtfully. There was something reassuring about Mr Pyne. He was large, not to say fat; he had a bald head of noble proportions, strong glasses and little twinkling eyes. And he had an aura – an aura of dependability.

'I should warn you, however,' continued Mr Pyne, 'that there is an element of risk.'

The soldier's eye brightened. 'That's all right,' he said. Then, abruptly: 'And – your fees?'

'My fee,' said Mr Pyne, 'is fifty pounds, payable in advance. If in a month's time you are still in the same state of boredom, I will refund your money.'

Wilbraham considered. 'Fair enough,' he said at last. 'I agree. I'll give you a cheque now.'

The transaction was completed. Mr Parker Pyne pressed a buzzer on his desk.

'It is now one o'clock,' he said. 'I am going to ask you to take a young lady out to lunch.' The door opened. 'Ah, Madeleine, my dear, let me introduce Major Wilbraham, who is going to take you out to lunch.'

Wilbraham blinked slightly, which was hardly to be wondered at. The girl who entered the room was dark, languorous, with wonderful eyes and long black lashes, a perfect complexion and a voluptuous scarlet mouth. Her exquisite clothes set off the swaying grace of her figure. From head to foot she was perfect.

'Er – delighted,' said Major Wilbraham.

'Miss de Sara,' said Mr Parker Pyne.

'How very kind of you,' murmured Madeleine de Sara.

'I have your address here,' announced Mr Parker Pyne. 'Tomorrow morning you will receive my further instructions.'

Major Wilbraham and the lovely Madeleine departed.

It was three o'clock when Madeleine returned.

Mr Parker Pyne looked up. 'Well?' he demanded.

Madeleine shook her head. 'Scared of me,' she said. 'Thinks I'm a vamp.'

'I thought as much,' said Mr Parker Pyne. 'You carried out my instructions?'

'Yes. We discussed the occupants of the other tables freely. The type he likes is fair-haired, blue-eyed, slightly anaemic, not too tall.'

'That should be easy,' said Mr Pyne. 'Get me Schedule B and let me see what we have in stock at present.' He ran his finger down a list, finally stopping at a name. 'Freda Clegg. Yes, I think Freda Clegg will do excellently. I had better see Mrs Oliver about it.'

★   ★   ★

The next day Major Wilbraham received a note, which read:

> *On Monday morning next at eleven o'clock go to Eaglemont, Friars*
> *Lane, Hampstead, and ask for Mr Jones. You will represent yourself*
> *as coming from the Guava Shipping Company.*

Obediently on the following Monday (which happened to be Bank
Holiday), Major Wilbraham set out for Eaglemont, Friars Lane. He set
out, I say, but he never got there. For before he got there, something
happened.

All the world and his wife seemed to be on their way to Hampstead.
Major Wilbraham got entangled in crowds, suffocated in the tube and
found it hard to discover the whereabouts of Friars Lane.

Friars Lane was a cul-de-sac, a neglected road full of ruts, with houses
on either side standing back from the road. They were largish houses
which had seen better days and had been allowed to fall into disrepair.

Wilbraham walked along peering at the half-erased names on the
gate-posts, when suddenly he heard something that made him stiffen to
attention. It was a kind of gurgling, half-choked cry.

It came again and this time it was faintly recognizable as the word
'Help!' It came from inside the wall of the house he was passing.

Without a moment's hesitation, Major Wilbraham pushed open the
rickety gate and sprinted noiselessly up the weed-covered drive. There in
the shrubbery was a girl struggling in the grasp of two enormous Negroes.
She was putting up a brave fight, twisting and turning and kicking. One
Negro held his hand over her mouth in spite of her furious efforts to get
her head free.

Intent on their struggle with the girl, neither of the blacks had noticed
Wilbraham's approach. The first they knew of it was when a violent punch
on the jaw sent the man who was covering the girl's mouth reeling backwards. Taken by surprise, the other man relinquished his hold of the girl
and turned. Wilbraham was ready for him. Once again his fist shot out,
and the Negro reeled backwards and fell. Wilbraham turned on the other
man, who was closing in behind him.

But the two men had had enough. The second one rolled over, sat up;
then, rising, he made a dash for the gate. His companion followed suit.
Wilbraham started after them, but changed his mind and turned towards
the girl, who was leaning against a tree, panting.

'Oh, thank you!' she gasped. 'It was terrible.'

Major Wilbraham saw for the first time who it was he had rescued so
opportunely. She was a girl of about twenty-one or two, fair-haired and
blue-eyed, pretty in a rather colourless way.

'If you hadn't come!' she gasped.

'There, there,' said Wilbraham soothingly. 'It's all right now. I think, though, that we'd better get away from here. It's possible those fellows might come back.'

A faint smile came to the girl's lips. 'I don't think they will – not after the way you hit them. Oh, it was splendid of you!'

Major Wilbraham blushed under the warmth of her glance of admiration. 'Nothin' at all,' he said indistinctly. 'All in day's work. Lady being annoyed. Look here, if you take my arm, can you walk? It's been a nasty shock, I know.'

'I'm all right now,' said the girl. However, she took the proffered arm. She was still rather shaky. She glanced behind her at the house as they emerged through the gate. 'I can't understand it,' she murmured. 'That's clearly an empty house.'

'It's empty, right enough,' agreed the major, looking up at the shuttered windows and general air of decay.

'And yet it *is* Whitefriars.' She pointed to a half-obliterated name on the gate. 'And Whitefriars was the place I was to go.'

'Don't worry about anything now,' said Wilbraham. 'In a minute or two we'll be able to get a taxi. Then we'll drive somewhere and have a cup of coffee.'

At the end of the lane they came out into a more frequented street, and by good fortune a taxi had just set down a fare at one of the houses. Wilbraham hailed it, gave an address to the driver and they got in.

'Don't try to talk,' he admonished his companion. 'Just lie back. You've had a nasty experience.'

She smiled at him gratefully.

'By the way – er – my name is Wilbraham.'

'Mine is Clegg – Freda Clegg.'

Ten minutes later, Freda was sipping hot coffee and looking gratefully across a small table at her rescuer.

'It seems like a dream,' she said. 'A bad dream.' She shuddered. 'And only a short while ago I was wishing for something to happen – anything! Oh, I don't like adventures.'

'Tell me how it happened.'

'Well, to tell you properly I shall have to talk a lot about myself, I'm afraid.'

'An excellent subject,' said Wilbraham, with a bow.

'I am an orphan. My father – he was a sea captain – died when I was eight. My mother died three years ago. I work in the city. I am with the Vacuum Gas Company – a clerk. One evening last week I found a gentleman waiting to see me when I returned to my lodgings. He was a lawyer, a Mr Reid from Melbourne.

'He was very polite and asked me several questions about my family. He explained that he had known my father many years ago. In fact, he had transacted some legal business for him. Then he told me the object of his visit. "Miss Clegg," he said, "I have reason to suppose that you might benefit as the result of a financial transaction entered into by your father several years before he died." I was very much surprised, of course.

'"It is unlikely that you would ever have heard anything of the matter," he explained. "John Clegg never took the affair seriously, I fancy. However, it has materialized unexpectedly, but I am afraid any claim you might put in would depend on your ownership of certain papers. These papers would be part of your father's estate, and of course it is possible that they have been destroyed as worthless. Have you kept any of your father's papers?"

'I explained that my mother had kept various things of my father's in an old sea chest. I had looked through it cursorily, but had discovered nothing of interest.

'"You would hardly be likely to recognize the importance of these documents, perhaps," he said, smiling.

'Well, I went to the chest, took out the few papers it contained and brought them to him. He looked at them, but said it was impossible to say off-hand what might or might not be connected with the matter in question. He would take them away with him and would communicate with me if anything turned up.

'By the last post on Saturday I received a letter from him in which he suggested that I come to his house to discuss the matter. He gave me the address: Whitefriars, Friars Lane, Hampstead. I was to be there at a quarter to eleven this morning.

'I was a little late finding the place. I hurried through the gate and up towards the house, when suddenly those two dreadful men sprang at me from the bushes. I hadn't time to cry out. One man put his hand over my mouth. I wrenched my head free and screamed for help. Luckily you heard me. If it hadn't been for you –' She stopped. Her looks were more eloquent than further words.

'Very glad I happened to be on the spot. By Gad, I'd like to get hold of those two brutes. You'd never seen them before, I suppose?'

She shook her head. 'What do you think it means?'

'Difficult to say. But one thing seems pretty sure. There's something someone wants among your father's papers. This man Reid told you a cock-and-bull story so as to get the opportunity of looking through them. Evidently what he wanted wasn't there.'

'Oh!' said Freda. 'I wonder. When I got home on Saturday I thought my things had been tampered with. To tell you the truth, I suspected my landlady of having pried about in my room out of curiosity. But now –'

'Depend upon it, that's it. Someone gained admission to your room and searched it, without finding what he was after. He suspected that you knew the value of this paper, whatever it was, and that you carried it about on your person. So he planned this ambush. If you had it with you, it would have been taken from you. If not, you would have been held prisoner while he tried to make you tell where it was hidden.'

'But what can it possibly *be*?' cried Freda.

'I don't know. But it must be something pretty good for him to go to this length.'

'It doesn't seem possible.'

'Oh, I don't know. Your father was a sailor. He went to out-of-the-way places. He might have come across something the value of which he never knew.'

'Do you really think so?' A pink flush of excitement showed in the girl's pale cheeks.

'I do indeed. The question is, what shall we do next? You don't want to go to the police, I suppose?'

'Oh, no, please.'

'I'm glad you say that. I don't see what good the police could do, and it would only mean unpleasantness for you. Now I suggest that you allow me to give you lunch somewhere and that I then accompany you back to your lodgings, so as to be sure you reach them safely. And then, we might have a look for the paper. Because, you know, it must be somewhere.'

'Father may have destroyed it himself.'

'He may, of course, but the other side evidently doesn't think so, and that looks hopeful for us.'

'What do you think it can be? Hidden treasure?'

'By jove, it might be!' exclaimed Major Wilbraham, all the boy in him rising joyfully to the suggestion. 'But now, Miss Clegg, lunch!'

They had a pleasant meal together. Wilbraham told Freda all about his life in East Africa. He described elephant hunts, and the girl was thrilled. When they had finished, he insisted on taking her home in a taxi.

Her lodgings were near Notting Hill Gate. On arriving there, Freda had a brief conversation with her landlady. She returned to Wilbraham and took him up to the second floor, where she had a tiny bedroom and sitting-room.

'It's exactly as we thought,' she said. 'A man came on Saturday morning to see about laying a new electric cable; he told her there was a fault in the wiring in my room. He was there some time.'

'Show me this chest of your father's,' said Wilbraham.

Freda showed him a brass-bound box. 'You see,' she said, raising the lid, 'it's empty.'

The soldier nodded thoughtfully. 'And there are no papers anywhere else?'

'I'm sure there aren't. Mother kept everything in here.'

Wilbraham examined the inside of the chest. Suddenly he uttered an exclamation. 'Here's a slit in the lining.' Carefully he inserted his hand, feeling about. A slight crackle rewarded him. 'Something's slipped down behind.'

In another minute he had drawn out his find. A piece of dirty paper folded several times. He smoothed it out on the table; Freda was looking over his shoulder. She uttered an exclamation of disappointment.

'It's just a lot of queer marks.'

'Why, the thing's in Swahili. *Swahili*, of all things!' cried Major Wilbraham. 'East African native dialect, you know.'

'How extraordinary!' said Freda. 'Can you read it, then?'

'Rather. But what an amazing thing.' He took the paper to the window.

'Is it anything?' asked Freda tremulously. Wilbraham read the thing through twice, and then came back to the girl. 'Well,' he said, with a chuckle, 'here's your hidden treasure, all right.'

'Hidden treasure? Not *really*? You mean Spanish gold – a sunken galleon – that sort of thing?'

'Not quite so romantic as that, perhaps. But it comes to the same thing. This paper gives the hiding-place of a cache of ivory.'

'Ivory?' said the girl, astonished.

'Yes. Elephants, you know. There's a law about the number you're allowed to shoot. Some hunter got away with breaking that law on a grand scale. They were on his trail and he cached the stuff. There's a thundering lot of it – and this gives fairly clear directions how to find it. Look here, we'll have to go after this, you and I.'

'You mean there's really a lot of money in it?'

'Quite a nice little fortune for you.'

'But how did that paper come to be among my father's things?'

Wilbraham shrugged. 'Maybe the Johnny was dying or something. He may have written the thing down in Swahili for protection and given it to your father, who possibly had befriended him in some way. Your father, not being able to read it, attached no importance to it. That's only a guess on my part, but I dare say it's not far wrong.'

Freda gave a sigh. 'How frightfully exciting!'

'The thing is – what to do with the precious document,' said Wilbraham. 'I don't like leaving it here. They might come and have another look. I suppose you wouldn't entrust it to me?'

'Of course I would. But – mightn't it be dangerous for you?' she faltered.

'I'm a tough nut,' said Wilbraham grimly. 'You needn't worry about me.' He folded up the paper and put it in his pocket-book. 'May I come to see you tomorrow evening?' he asked. 'I'll have worked out a plan by then, and I'll look up the places on my map. What time do you get back from the city?'

'I get back about half-past six.'

'Capital. We'll have a powwow and then perhaps you'll let me take you out to dinner. We ought to celebrate. So long, then. Tomorrow at half-past six.'

Major Wilbraham arrived punctually on the following day. He rang the bell and enquired for Miss Clegg. A maid-servant had answered the door.

'Miss Clegg? She's out.'

'Oh!' Wilbraham did not like to suggest that he come in and wait. 'I'll call back presently,' he said.

He hung about in the street opposite, expecting every minute to see Freda tripping towards him. The minutes passed. Quarter to seven. Seven. Quarter-past seven. Still no Freda. A feeling of uneasiness swept over him. He went back to the house and rang the bell again.

'Look here,' he said, 'I had an appointment with Miss Clegg at half-past six. Are you sure she isn't in or hasn't – er – left any message?'

'Are you Major Wilbraham?' asked the servant.

'Yes.'

'Then there's a note for you. It come by hand.'

Dear Major Wilbraham, – Something rather strange has happened. I won't write more now, but will you meet me at Whitefriars? Go there as soon as you get this.
Yours sincerely,
Freda Clegg

Wilbraham drew his brows together as he thought rapidly. His hand drew a letter absent-mindedly from his pocket. It was to his tailor. 'I wonder,' he said to the maid-servant, 'if you could let me have a stamp.'

'I expect Mrs Parkins could oblige you.'

She returned in a moment with the stamp. It was paid for with a shilling. In another minute Wilbraham was walking towards the tube station, dropping the envelope in a box as he passed.

Freda's letter had made him most uneasy. What could have taken the girl, alone, to the scene of yesterday's sinister encounter?

He shook his head. Of all the foolish things to do! Had Reid appeared? Had he somehow or other prevailed upon the girl to trust him? What had taken her to Hampstead?

He looked at his watch. Nearly half-past seven. She would have counted on his starting at half-past six. An hour late. Too much. If only she had had the sense to give him some hint.

The letter puzzled him. Somehow its independent tone was not characteristic of Freda Clegg.

It was ten minutes to eight when he reached Friars Lane. It was getting dark. He looked sharply about him; there was no one in sight. Gently he pushed the rickety gate so that it swung noiselessly on its hinges. The drive was deserted. The house was dark. He went up the path cautiously, keeping a look out from side to side. He did not intend to be caught by surprise.

Suddenly he stopped. Just for a minute a chink of light had shone through one of the shutters. The house was not empty. There was someone inside.

Softly Wilbraham slipped into the bushes and worked his way round to the back of the house. At last he found what he was looking for. One of the windows on the ground floor was unfastened. It was the window of a kind of scullery. He raised the sash, flashed a torch (he had bought it at a shop on the way over) around the deserted interior and climbed in.

Carefully he opened the scullery door. There was no sound. He flashed the torch once more. A kitchen – empty. Outside the kitchen were half a dozen steps and a door evidently leading to the front part of the house.

He pushed open the door and listened. Nothing. He slipped through. He was now in the front hall. Still there was no sound. There was a door to the right and a door to the left. He chose the right-hand door, listened for a time, then turned the handle. It gave. Inch by inch he opened the door and stepped inside.

Again he flashed the torch. The room was unfurnished and bare.

Just at that moment he heard a sound behind him, whirled round – too late. Something came down on his head and he pitched forward into unconsciousness . . .

How much time elapsed before he regained consciousness Wilbraham had no idea. He returned painfully to life, his head aching. He tried to move and found it impossible. He was bound with ropes.

His wits came back to him suddenly. He remembered now. He had been hit on the head.

A faint light from a gas jet high up on the wall showed him that he was in a small cellar. He looked around and his heart gave a leap. A few feet away lay Freda, bound like himself. Her eyes were closed, but even as he watched her anxiously, she sighed and they opened. Her bewildered gaze fell on him and joyous recognition leaped into them.

'You, too!' she said. 'What has happened?'

'I've let you down badly,' said Wilbraham. 'Tumbled headlong into the trap. Tell me, did you send me a note asking me to meet you here?'

The girl's eyes opened in astonishment. '*I*? But you sent *me* one.'

'Oh, I sent you one, did I?'

'Yes. I got it at the office. It asked me to meet you here instead of at home.'

'Same method for both of us,' he groaned, and he explained the situation.

'I see,' said Freda. 'Then the idea was –?'

'To get the paper. We must have been followed yesterday. That's how they got on to me.'

'And – have they got it?' asked Freda.

'Unfortunately, I can't feel and see,' said the soldier, regarding his bound hands ruefully.

And then they both started. For a voice spoke, a voice that seemed to come from the empty air.

'Yes, thank you,' it said. 'I've got it, all right. No mistake about that.'

The unseen voice made them both shiver.

'Mr Reid,' murmured Freda.

'Mr Reid is one of my names, my dear young lady,' said the voice. 'But only one of them. I have a great many. Now, I am sorry to say that you two have interfered with my plans – a thing I never allow. Your discovery of this house is a serious matter. You have not told the police about it yet, but you might do so in the future.

'I very much fear that I cannot trust you in the matter. You might promise – but promises are seldom kept. And, you see, this house is very useful to me. It is, you might say, my clearing house. The house from which there is no return. From here you pass on – elsewhere. You, I am sorry to say, are so passing on. Regrettable – but necessary.'

The voice paused for a brief second, then resumed: 'No bloodshed. I abhor bloodshed. My method is much simpler. And really not too painful, so I understand. Well, I must be getting along. Good-evening to you both.'

'Look here!' It was Wilbraham who spoke. 'Do what you like to me, but this young lady has done nothing – nothing. It can't hurt you to let her go.'

But there was no answer.

At that moment there came a cry from Freda. 'The water – the water!'

Wilbraham twisted himself painfully and followed the direction of her eyes. From a hole up near the ceiling a steady trickle of water was pouring in.

Freda gave a hysterical cry. 'They're going to drown us!'

The perspiration broke out on Wilbraham's brow. 'We're not done yet,' he said. 'We'll shout for help. Surely somebody will hear us. Now, both together.'

They yelled and shouted at the tops of their voices. Not until they were hoarse did they stop.

'No use, I'm afraid,' said Wilbraham sadly. 'We're too far underground and I expect the doors are muffled. After all, if we could be heard, I've no doubt that brute would have gagged us.'

'Oh,' cried Freda. 'And it's all my fault. I got you into this.'

'Don't worry about that, little girl. It's you I'm thinking about. I've been in tight corners before now and got out of them. Don't you lose heart. I'll get you out of this. We've plenty of time. At the rate that water's flowing in, it will be hours before the worst happens.'

'How wonderful you are!' said Freda. 'I've never met anybody like you – except in books.'

'Nonsense – just common sense. Now, I've got to loosen those infernal ropes.'

At the end of a quarter of an hour, by dint of straining and twisting, Wilbraham had the satisfaction of feeling that his bonds were appreciably loosened. He managed to bend his head down and his wrists up till he was able to attack the knots with his teeth.

Once his hands were free, the rest was only a matter of time. Cramped, stiff, but free, he bent over the girl. A minute later she was also free.

So far the water was only up to their ankles.

'And now,' said the soldier, 'to get out of here.'

The door of the cellar was up a few stairs. Major Wilbraham examined it.

'No difficulty here,' he said. 'Flimsy stuff. It will soon give at the hinges.' He set his shoulders to it and heaved.

There was a cracking of wood – a crash, and the door burst from its hinges.

Outside was a flight of stairs. At the top was another door – a very different affair – of solid wood, barred with iron.

'A bit more difficult, this,' said Wilbraham. 'Hallo, here's a piece of luck. It's unlocked.'

He pushed it open, peered round it, then beckoned the girl to come on. They emerged into a passage behind the kitchen. In another moment they were standing under the stars in Friars Lane.

'Oh!' Freda gave a little sob. 'Oh, how dreadful it's been!'

'My poor darling.' He caught her in his arms. 'You've been so wonderfully brave. Freda – darling angel – could you ever – I mean, would you – I love you, Freda. Will you marry me?'

After a suitable interval, highly satisfactory to both parties, Major Wilbraham said, with a chuckle:

'And what's more, we've still got the secret of the ivory cache.'

'But they took it from you!'

The major chuckled again. 'That's just what they didn't do! You see, I wrote out a proof copy, and before joining you here tonight, I put the real thing in a letter I was sending to my tailor and posted it. They've got the spoof copy – and I wish them joy of it! Do you know what we'll do, sweetheart! We'll go to East Africa for our honeymoon and hunt out the cache.'

Mr Parker Pyne left his office and climbed two flights of stairs. Here in a room at the top of the house sat Mrs Oliver, the sensational novelist, now a member of Mr Pyne's staff.

Mr Parker Pyne tapped at the door and entered. Mrs Oliver sat at a table on which were a typewriter, several notebooks, a general confusion of loose manuscripts and a large bag of apples.

'A very good story, Mrs Oliver,' said Mr Parker Pyne genially.

'It went off well?' said Mrs Oliver. 'I'm glad.'

'That water-in-the-cellar business,' said Mr Parker Pyne. 'You don't think, on a future occasion, that something more original – perhaps?' He made the suggestion with proper diffidence.

Mrs Oliver shook her head and took an apple from her bag. 'I think not, Mr Pyne. You see, people are used to reading about such things. Water rising in a cellar, poison gas, et cetera. Knowing about it beforehand gives it an extra thrill when it happens to oneself. The public is conservative, Mr Pyne; it likes the old well-worn gadgets.'

'Well, you should know,' admitted Mr Parker Pyne, mindful of the authoress's forty-six successful works of fiction, all best sellers in England and America, and freely translated into French, German, Italian, Hungarian, Finnish, Japanese and Abyssinian. 'How about expenses?'

Mrs Oliver drew a paper towards her. 'Very moderate, on the whole. The two darkies, Percy and Jerry, wanted very little. Young Lorrimer, the actor, was willing to enact the part of Mr Reid for five guineas. The cellar speech was a phonograph record, of course.'

'Whitefriars has been extremely useful to me,' said Mr Pyne. 'I bought it for a song and it has already been the scene of eleven exciting dramas.'

'Oh, I forgot,' said Mrs Oliver. 'Johnny's wages. Five shillings.'
'Johnny?'
'Yes. The boy who poured the water from the watering cans through the hole in the wall.'
'Ah yes. By the way, Mrs Oliver, how did you happen to know Swahili?'
'I didn't.'
'I see. The British Museum perhaps?'
'No. Delfridge's Information Bureau.'
'How marvellous are the resources of modern commerce!' he murmured.
'The only thing that worries me,' said Mrs Oliver, 'is that those two young people won't find any cache when they get there.'
'One cannot have everything in this world,' said Mr Parker Pyne. 'They will have had a honeymoon.'

Mrs Wilbraham was sitting in a deck-chair. Her husband was writing a letter. 'What's the date, Freda?'
'The sixteenth.'
'The sixteenth. By jove!'
'What is it, dear?'
'Nothing. I just remembered a chap named Jones.'
However happily married, there are some things one never tells.
'Dash it all,' thought Major Wilbraham. 'I ought to have called at that place and got my money back.' And then, being a fair-minded man, he looked at the other side of the question. 'After all, it was I who broke the bargain. I suppose if I'd gone to see Jones something would have happened. And, anyway, as it turns out, if I hadn't been going to see Jones, I should never have heard Freda cry for help, and we might never have met. So, indirectly, perhaps they have a right to the fifty pounds!'
Mrs Wilbraham was also following out a train of thought. 'What a silly little fool I was to believe in that advertisement and pay those people three guineas. Of course, they never did anything for it and nothing ever happened. If I'd only known what was coming – first Mr Reid, and then the queer, romantic way that Charlie came into my life. And to think that but for pure chance *I might never have met him!*'
She turned and smiled adoringly at her husband.

The Case of the Distressed Lady

'The Case of the Distressed Lady' was first published in the USA as
'The Pretty Girl Who Wanted a Ring' in *Cosmopolitan*, August 1932,
then as 'Faked!' in *Woman's Pictorial*, 22 October 1932.

The buzzer on Mr Parker Pyne's desk purred discreetly. 'Yes?' said the
great man.

'A young lady wishes to see you,' announced his secretary. 'She has
no appointment.'

'You may send her in, Miss Lemon.' A moment later he was shaking
hands with his visitor. 'Good-morning,' he said. 'Do sit down.'

The girl sat down and looked at Mr Parker Pyne. She was a pretty
girl and quite young. Her hair was dark and wavy with a row of curls at
the nape of the neck. She was beautifully turned out from the white
knitted cap on her head to the cobweb stockings and dainty shoes. Clearly
she was nervous.

'You are Mr Parker Pyne?' she asked.

'I am.'

'The one who – advertises?'

'The one who advertises.'

'You say that if people aren't – aren't happy – to – to come to you.'

'Yes.'

She took the plunge. 'Well, I'm frightfully unhappy. So I thought I'd
come along and just – and just see.'

Mr Parker Pyne waited. He felt there was more to come.

'I – I'm in frightful trouble.' She clenched her hands nervously.

'So I see,' said Mr Parker Pyne. 'Do you think you could tell me about
it?'

That, it seemed, was what the girl was by no means sure of. She stared at Mr Parker Pyne with a desperate intentness. Suddenly she spoke with a rush.

'Yes, I will tell you. I've made up my mind now. I've been nearly crazy with worry. I didn't know what to do or whom to go to. And then I saw your advertisement. I thought it was probably just a ramp, but it stayed in my mind. It sounded so comforting, somehow. And then I thought – well, it would do no harm to come and *see*. I could always make an excuse and get away again if I didn't – well, it didn't –'

'Quite so; quite so,' said Mr Pyne.

'You see,' said the girl, 'it means, well, *trusting* somebody.'

'And you feel you can trust me?' he said, smiling.

'It's odd,' said the girl with unconsciousness rudeness, 'but I do. Without knowing anything about you! I'm *sure* I can trust you.'

'I can assure you,' said Mr Pyne, 'that your trust will not be misplaced.'

'Then,' said the girl, 'I'll tell you about it. My name is Daphne St John.'

'Yes, Miss St John.'

'Mrs I'm – I'm married.'

'Pshaw!' muttered Mr Pyne, annoyed with himself as he noted the platinum circlet on the third finger of her left hand. 'Stupid of me.'

'If I weren't married,' said the girl, 'I shouldn't mind so much. I mean, it wouldn't matter so much. It's the thought of Gerald – well, here – here's what all the trouble's about!'

She dived into her bag, took something out and flung it down on the desk where, gleaming and flashing, it rolled over to Mr Parker Pyne.

It was a platinum ring with a large solitaire diamond.

Mr Pyne picked it up, took it to the window, tested it on the pane, applied a jeweller's lens to his eye and examined it closely.

'An exceedingly fine diamond,' he remarked, coming back to the table; 'worth, I should say, about two thousand pounds at least.'

'Yes. And it's stolen! I stole it! And I don't know what to do.'

'Dear me!' said Mr Parker Pyne. 'This is very interesting.'

His client broke down and sobbed into an inadequate handkerchief.

'Now, now,' said Mr Pyne. 'Everything's going to be all right.'

The girl dried her eyes and sniffed. 'Is it?' she said. 'Oh, *is* it?'

'Of course it is. Now, just tell me the whole story.'

'Well, it began by my being hard up. You see, I'm frightfully extravagant. And Gerald gets so annoyed about it. Gerald's my husband. He's a lot older than I am, and he's got very – well, very austere ideas. He thinks running into debt is dreadful. So I didn't tell him. And I went over to Le Touquet with some friends and I thought perhaps I might be lucky at chemmy and get straight again. I did win at first. And then I lost, and then I thought I must go on. And I went on. And – and –'

'Yes, yes,' said Mr Parker Pyne. 'You need not go into details. You were in a worse plight than ever. That is right, is it not?'

Daphne St John nodded. 'And by then, you see, I simply couldn't tell Gerald. Because he hates gambling. Oh, I was in an awful mess. Well, we went down to stay with the Dortheimers near Cobham. He's frightfully rich, of course. His wife, Naomi, was at school with me. She's pretty and a dear. While we were there, the setting of this ring got loose. On the morning we were leaving, she asked me to take it up to town and drop it at her jeweller's in Bond Street.' She paused.

'And now we come to the difficult part,' said Mr Pyne helpfully. 'Go on, Mrs St John.'

'You won't ever tell, will you?' demanded the girl pleadingly.

'My clients' confidences are sacred. And anyway, Mrs St John, you have told me so much already that I could probably finish the story for myself.'

'That's true. All right. But I hate saying it – it sounds so awful. I went to Bond Street. There's another shop there – Viro's. They – copy jewellery. Suddenly I lost my head. I took the ring in and said I wanted an exact copy; I said I was going abroad and didn't want to take real jewellery with me. They seemed to think it quite natural.

'Well, I got the paste replica – it was so good you couldn't have told it from the original – and I sent it off by registered post to Lady Dortheimer. I had a box with the jeweller's name on it, so that was all right, and I made a professional-looking parcel. And then I – I – pawned the real one.' She hid her face in her hands. 'How could I? How *could* I? I was a low, mean, common thief.'

Mr Parker Pyne coughed. 'I do not think you have quite finished,' he said.

'No, I haven't. This, you understand, was about six weeks ago. I paid off all my debts and got square again, but, of course, I was miserable all the time. And then an old cousin of mine died and I came into some money. The first thing I did was to redeem the wretched ring. Well, that's all right; here it is. But, something terribly difficult has happened.'

'Yes?'

'We've had a quarrel with the Dortheimers. It's over some shares that Sir Reuben persuaded Gerald to buy. He was terribly let in over them and he told Sir Reuben what he thought of him – and oh, it's all dreadful! And now, you see, I can't get the ring back.'

'Couldn't you send it to Lady Dortheimer anonymously?'

'That gives the whole thing away. She'll examine her own ring, find it's a fake and guess at once what I've done.'

'You say she's a friend of yours. What about telling her the whole truth – throwing yourself on her mercy?'

Mrs St John shook her head. 'We're not such friends as that. Where money or jewellery is concerned, Naomi's as hard as nails. Perhaps she couldn't prosecute me if I gave the ring back, but she could tell everyone what I've done and I'd be ruined. Gerald would know and he would never forgive me. Oh, how awful everything is!' She began to cry again. 'I've thought and I've thought, and I can't see *what* to do! Oh, Mr Pyne, can't you do anything?'

'Several things,' said Mr Parker Pyne.

'You can? Really?'

'Certainly. I suggested the simplest way because in my long experience I have always found it the best. It avoids unlooked-for complications. Still, I see the force of your objections. At present no one knows of this unfortunate occurrence but yourself?'

'And you,' said Mrs St John.

'Oh, I do not count. Well, then, your secret is safe at present. All that is needed is to exchange the rings in some unsuspicious manner.'

'That's it,' the girl said eagerly.

'That should not be difficult. We must take a little time to consider the best method –'

She interrupted him. 'But there is no time! That's what's driving me nearly crazy. She's going to have the ring reset.'

'How do you know?'

'Just by chance. I was lunching with a woman the other day and I admired a ring she had on – a big emerald. She said it was the newest thing – and that Naomi Dortheimer was going to have her diamond reset that way.'

'Which means that we shall have to act quickly,' said Mr Pyne thoughtfully. 'It means gaining admission to the house – and if possible not in any menial capacity. Servants have little chance of handling valuable rings. Have you any ideas yourself, Mrs St John?'

'Well, Naomi is giving a big party on Wednesday. And this friend of mine mentioned that she had been looking for some exhibition dancers. I don't know if anything has been settled –'

'I think it can be managed,' said Mr Parker Pyne. 'If the matter is already settled it will be more expensive, that is all. One thing more, do you happen to know where the main light switch is situated?'

'As it happens I *do* know that, because a fuse blew out late one night when the servants had all gone to bed. It's a box at the back of the hall – inside a little cupboard.'

At Mr Parker Pyne's request she drew him a sketch.

'And now,' said Mr Parker Pyne, 'everything is going to be all right, so don't worry, Mrs St John. What about the ring? Shall I take it now, or would you rather keep it till Wednesday?'

'Well, perhaps I'd better keep it.'

'Now, no more worry, mind you,' Mr Parker Pyne admonished her.

'And your – fee?' she asked timidly.

'That can stand over for the moment. I will let you know on Wednesday what expenses have been necessary. The fee will be nominal, I assure you.'

He conducted her to the door, then rang the buzzer on his desk.

'Send Claude and Madeleine here.'

Claude Luttrell was one of the handsomest specimens of lounge lizard to be found in England. Madeleine de Sara was the most seductive of vamps.

Mr Parker Pyne surveyed them with approval. 'My children,' he said, 'I have a job for you. You are going to be internationally famous exhibition dancers. Now, attend to this carefully, Claude, and mind you get it right . . .'

Lady Dortheimer was fully satisfied with the arrangements for her ball. She surveyed the floral decorations and approved, gave a few last orders to the butler, and remarked to her husband that so far nothing had gone wrong!

It was a slight disappointment that Michael and Juanita, the dancers from the Red Admiral, had been unable to fulfil their contract at the last moment, owing to Juanita's spraining her ankle, but instead, two new dancers were being sent (so ran the story over the telephone) who had created a furore in Paris.

The dancers duly arrived and Lady Dortheimer approved. The evening went splendidly. Jules and Sanchia did their turn, and most sensational it was. A wild Spanish Revolution dance. Then a dance called the Degenerate's Dream. Then an exquisite exhibition of modern dancing.

The 'cabaret' over, normal dancing was resumed. The handsome Jules requested a dance with Lady Dortheimer. They floated away. Never had Lady Dortheimer had such a perfect partner.

Sir Reuben was searching for the seductive Sanchia – in vain. She was not in the ballroom.

She was, as a matter of fact, out in the deserted hall near a small box, with her eyes fixed on the jewelled watch which she wore round her wrist.

'You are not English – you cannot be English – to dance as you do,' murmured Jules into Lady Dortheimer's ear. 'You are the sprite, the spirit of the wind. *Droushcka petrovka navarouchi.*'

'What is that language?'

'Russian,' said Jules mendaciously. 'I say something to you in Russian that I dare not say in English.'

Lady Dortheimer closed her eyes. Jules pressed her closer to him.

Suddenly the lights went out. In the darkness Jules bent and kissed the hand that lay on his shoulder. As she made to draw it away, he caught it, raised it to his lips again. Somehow a ring slipped from her finger into his hand.

To Lady Dortheimer it seemed only a second before the lights went on again. Jules was smiling at her.

'Your ring,' he said. 'It slipped off. You permit?' He replaced it on her finger. His eyes said a number of things while he was doing it.

Sir Reuben was talking about the main switch. 'Some idiot. Practical joke, I suppose.'

Lady Dortheimer was not interested. Those few minutes of darkness had been very pleasant.

Mr Parker Pyne arrived at his office on Thursday morning to find Mrs St John already awaiting him.

'Show her in,' said Mr Pyne.

'Well?' She was all eagerness.

'You look pale,' he said accusingly.

She shook her head. 'I couldn't sleep last night. I was wondering –'

'Now, here is the little bill for expenses. Train fares, costumes, and fifty pounds to Michael and Juanita. Sixty-five pounds, seventeen shillings.'

'Yes, yes! But about last night – was it all right? Did it happen?'

Mr Parker Pyne looked at her in surprise. 'My dear young lady, naturally it is all right. I took it for granted that you understood that.'

'What a relief! I was afraid –'

Mr Parker Pyne shook his head reproachfully. 'Failure is a word not tolerated in this establishment. If I do not think I can succeed I refuse to undertake a case. If I do take a case, its success is practically a foregone conclusion.'

'She's really got her ring back and suspects nothing?'

'Nothing whatever. The operation was most delicately conducted.'

Daphne St John sighed. 'You don't know the load off my mind. What were you saying about expenses?'

'Sixty-five pounds, seventeen shillings.'

Mrs St John opened her bag and counted out the money. Mr Parker Pyne thanked her and wrote out a receipt.

'But your fee?' murmured Daphne. 'This is only for expenses.'

'In this case there is no fee.'

'Oh, Mr Pyne! I couldn't, *really!*'

'My dear young lady, I insist. I will not touch a penny. It would be against my principles. Here is your receipt. And now –'

With the smile of a happy conjuror bringing off a successful trick, he drew a small box from his pocket and pushed it across the table. Daphne opened it. Inside, to all appearances, lay the identical diamond ring.

'Brute!' said Mrs St John, making a face at it. 'How I hate you! I've a good mind to throw you out of the window.'

'I shouldn't do that,' said Mr Pyne. 'It might surprise people.'

'You're quite sure it isn't the real one?' said Daphne.

'No, no! The one you showed me the other day is safely on Lady Dortheimer's finger.'

'Then, that's all right.' Daphne rose with a happy laugh.

'Curious you asked me that,' said Mr Parker Pyne. 'Of course Claude, poor fellow, hasn't many brains. He might easily have got muddled. So, to make sure, I had an expert look at this thing this morning.'

'Mrs St John sat down again rather suddenly. 'Oh! And he said?'

'That it was an extraordinarily good imitation,' said Mr Parker Pyne, beaming. 'First-class work. So that sets your mind at rest, doesn't it?'

Mrs St John started to say something, then stopped. She was staring at Mr Parker Pyne.

The latter resumed his seat behind the desk and looked at her benevolently. 'The cat who pulled the chestnuts out of the fire,' he said dreamily. 'Not a pleasant role. Not a role I should care to have any of my staff undertake. Excuse me. Did you say anything?'

'I – no, nothing.'

'Good. I want to tell you a little story, Mrs St John. It concerns a young lady. A fair-haired young lady, I think. She is not married. Her name is not St John. Her Christian name is not Daphne. On the contrary, her name is Ernestine Richards, and until recently she was secretary to Lady Dortheimer.

'Well, one day the setting of Lady Dortheimer's diamond ring became loose and Miss Richards brought it up to town to have it fixed. Quite like your story here, is it not? The same idea occurred to Miss Richards that occurred to you. She had the ring copied. But she was a far-sighted young lady. She saw a day coming when Lady Dortheimer would discover the substitution. When that happened, she would remember who had taken the ring to town and Miss Richards would be instantly suspected.

'So what happened? First, I fancy, Miss Richards invested in a La Merveilleuse transformation – Number Seven side parting, I think' – his eyes rested innocently on his client's wavy locks – 'shade dark brown. Then she called on me. She showed me the ring, allowed me to satisfy myself that it was genuine, thereby disarming suspicion on my part. That done, and a plan of substitution arranged, the young lady took the ring to the jeweller, who, in due course, returned it to Lady Dortheimer.

'Yesterday evening the other ring, the false ring, was hurriedly handed over at the last minute at Waterloo Station. Quite rightly, Miss Richards did not not consider that Mr Luttrell was likely to be an authority on diamonds. But just to satisfy myself that everything was above board I arranged for a friend of mine, a diamond merchant, to be on the train. He looked at the ring and pronounced at once, 'This is not a real diamond; it is an excellent paste replica.'

'You see the point, of course, Mrs St John? When Lady Dortheimer discovered her loss, what would she remember? The charming young dancer who slipped the ring off her finger when the lights went out! She would make enquiries and find out that the dancers originally engaged were bribed not to come. If matters were traced back to my office, my story of a Mrs St John would seem feeble in the extreme. Lady Dortheimer never knew a Mrs St John. The story would sound a flimsy fabrication.

'Now you see, don't you, that I could not allow that? And so my friend Claude replaced on Lady Dortheimer's finger *the same ring that he took off*.' Mr Parker Pyne's smile was less benevolent now.

'You see why I could not take a fee? I guarantee to give happiness. Clearly I have not made *you* happy. I will say just one thing more. You are young; possibly this is your first attempt at anything of the kind. Now I, on the contrary, am comparatively advanced in years, and I have had a long experience in the compilation of statistics. From that experience I can assure you that in eighty-seven per cent of cases dishonesty does not pay. Eighty-seven per cent. Think of it!'

With a brusque movement the pseudo Mrs St John rose. 'You oily old brute!' she said. 'Leading me on! Making me pay expenses! And all the time –' She choked, and rushed towards the door.

'Your ring,' said Mr Parker Pyne, holding it out to her.

She snatched it from him, looked at it and flung it out of the open window.

A door banged and she was gone.

Mr Parker Pyne was looking out of the window with some interest. 'As I thought,' he said. 'Considerable surprise has been created. The gentleman selling Dismal Desmonds does not know what to make of it.'

The Case of the
Discontented Husband

'The Case of the Discontented Husband' was first published in
the USA as 'The Husband Who Wanted To Keep His Wife' in
Cosmopolitan, August 1932, and then as 'His Lady's Affair'
in *Woman's Pictorial*, 29 October 1932.

Undoubtedly one of Mr Parker Pyne's greatest assets was his sympathetic manner. It was a manner that invited confidence. He was well acquainted with the kind of paralysis that descended on clients as soon as they got inside his office. It was Mr Pyne's task to pave the way for the necessary disclosures.

On this particular morning he sat facing a new client, a Mr Reginald Wade. Mr Wade, he deduced at once, was the inarticulate type. The type that finds it hard to put into words anything connected with the emotions.

He was a tall, broadly-built man with mild, pleasant blue eyes and a well-tanned complexion. He sat pulling absent-mindedly at a little moustache while he looked at Mr Parker Pyne with all the pathos of a dumb animal.

'Saw your advertisement, you know,' he jerked. 'Thought I might as well come along. Rum sort of show, but you never know, what?'

Mr Parker Pyne interpreted these cryptic remarks correctly. 'When things go badly, one is willing to take a chance,' he suggested.

'That's it. That's it, exactly. I'm willing to take a chance – any chance. Things are in a bad way with me, Mr Pyne. I don't know what to do about it. Difficult, you know; damned difficult.'

'That,' said Mr Pyne, 'is where I come in. I *do* know what to do! I am a specialist in every kind of human trouble.'

'Oh, I say – bit of a tall order, that!'

'Not really. Human troubles are easily classified into a few main heads.

There is ill health. There is boredom. There are wives who are in trouble over their husbands. There are husbands' – he paused – 'who are in trouble over their wives.'

'Matter of fact, you've hit it. You've hit it absolutely.'

'Tell me about it,' said Mr Pyne.

'There's nothing much to tell. My wife wants me to give her a divorce so that she can marry another chap.'

'Very common indeed in these days. Now you, I gather, don't see eye to eye with her in this business?'

'I'm fond of her,' said Mr Wade simply. 'You see – well, I'm fond of her.'

A simple and somewhat tame statement, but if Mr Wade had said, 'I adore her. I worship the ground she walks on. I would cut myself into little pieces for her,' he could not have been more explicit to Mr Parker Pyne.

'All the same, you know,' went on Mr Wade, 'what can I do? I mean, a fellow's so helpless. If she prefers this other fellow – well, one's got to play the game; stand aside and all that.'

'The proposal is that she should divorce you?'

'Of course. I couldn't let her be dragged through the divorce court.'

Mr Pyne looked at him thoughtfully. 'But you come to me? Why?'

The other laughed in a shamefaced manner. 'I don't know. You see, I'm not a clever chap. I can't think of things. I thought you might – well, suggest something. I've got six months, you see. She agreed to that. If at the end of six months she is still of the same mind – well, then, I get out. I thought you might give me a hint or two. At present everything I do annoys her.'

'You see, Mr Pyne, what it comes to is this: I'm not a clever chap! I like knocking balls about. I like a round of golf and a good set of tennis. I'm no good at music and art and such things. My wife's clever. She likes pictures and the opera and concerts, and naturally she gets bored with me. This other fellow – nasty, long-haired chap – he knows all about these things. He can talk about them. I can't. In a way, I can understand a clever, beautiful woman getting fed up with an ass like me.'

Mr Parker Pyne groaned. 'You have been married – how long? . . . Nine years? And I suppose you have adopted that attitude from the start. Wrong, my dear sir; disastrously wrong! Never adopt an apologetic attitude with a woman. She will take you at your own valuation – and you deserve it. You should have gloried in your athletic prowess. You should have spoken of art and music as "all that nonsense my wife likes". You should have condoled with her on not being able to play games better. The humble spirit, my dear sir, is a wash-out in matrimony! No woman can be expected to stand up against it. No wonder your wife has been unable to last the course.'

Mr Wade was looking at him in bewilderment. 'Well,' he said, 'what do you think I ought to do?'

'That certainly is the question. Whatever you should have done nine years ago, it is too late now. New tactics must be adopted. Have you ever had any affairs with other women?'

'Certainly not.'

'I should have said, perhaps, any light flirtations?'

'I never bothered about women much.'

'A mistake. You must start now.'

Mr Wade looked alarmed. 'Oh, look here, I couldn't really. I mean –'

'You will be put to no trouble in the matter. One of my staff will be supplied for the purpose. She will tell you what is required of you, and any attentions you pay her she will, of course, understand to be merely a matter of business.'

Mr Wade looked relieved. 'That's better. But do you really think – I mean, it seems to me that Iris will be keener to get rid of me than ever.'

'You do not understand human nature, Mr Wade. Still less do you understand feminine human nature. At the present moment you are, from a feminine point of view, merely a waste product. Nobody wants you. What use has a woman for something that no one wants? None whatever. But take another angle. Suppose your wife discovers that you are looking forward to regaining your freedom as much as she is?'

'Then she ought to be pleased.'

'She ought to be, perhaps, but she will not be! Moreover, she will see that you have attracted a fascinating young woman – a young woman who could pick and choose. Immediately your stock goes up. Your wife knows that all her friends will say it was you who tired of her and wished to marry a more attractive woman. That will annoy her.'

'You think so?'

'I am sure of it. You will no longer be "poor dear old Reggie". You will be "that sly dog Reggie". All the difference in the world! Without relinquishing the other man, she will doubtless try to win you back. You will not be won. You will be sensible and repeat to her all her arguments. "Much better to part." "Temperamentally unsuited." You realize that while what she said was true – that you had never understood her – it is also true that *she* had never understood *you*. But we need not go into this now; you will be given full instructions when the time comes.'

Mr Wade seemed doubtful still. 'You really think that this plan of yours will do the trick?' he asked dubiously.

'I will not say I am absolutely sure of it,' said Mr Parker Pyne cautiously.

'There is a bare possibility that your wife may be so overwhelmingly in love with this other man that nothing you could say or do will affect her, but I consider that unlikely. She has probably been driven into this affair through boredom – boredom with the atmosphere of uncritical devotion and absolute fidelity with which you have most unwisely surrounded her. If you follow my instructions, the chances are, I should say, ninety-seven per cent in your favour.'

'Good enough,' said Mr Wade. 'I'll do it. By the way – er – how much?'

'My fee is two hundred guineas, payable in advance.'

Mr Wade drew out a cheque book.

The grounds of Lorrimer Court were lovely in the afternoon sunshine. Iris Wade, lying on a long chair, made a delicious spot of colour. She was dressed in delicate shades of mauve and by skilful make-up managed to look much younger than her thirty-five years.

She was talking to her friend Mrs Massington, whom she always found sympathetic. Both ladies were afflicted with athletic husbands who talked stocks and shares and golf alternately.

'And so one learns to live and let live,' finished Iris.

'You're wonderful, darling,' said Mrs Massington, and added too quickly: 'Tell me, who *is* this girl?'

Iris raised a weary shoulder. 'Don't ask me! Reggie found her. She's Reggie's little friend! So amusing. You know he never looks at girls as a rule. He came to me and hemmed and hawed, and finally said he wanted to ask this Miss de Sara down for the weekend. Of course I laughed – I couldn't help it. *Reggie* you know! Well, here she is.'

'Where did he meet her?'

'I don't know. He was very vague about it all.'

'Perhaps he's known her some time.'

'Oh, I don't think so,' said Mrs Wade. 'Of course,' she went on, 'I'm delighted – simply delighted. I mean, it makes it so much easier for me, as things are. Because I *have* been unhappy about Reggie; he's such a dear old thing. That's what I kept saying to Sinclair – that it would hurt Reggie so. But he insisted that Reggie would soon get over it; it looks as if he were right. Two days ago Reggie seemed heartbroken – and now he wants this girl down! As I say, I'm *amused*. I like to see Reggie enjoying himself. I fancy the poor fellow actually thought I might be jealous. Such an absurd idea! "Of course," I said, "have your friend down." Poor Reggie – as though a girl like that could ever care about him. She's just amusing herself.'

'She's extremely attractive,' said Mrs Massington. 'Almost dangerously so, if you know what I mean. The sort of girl who cares only for men. I don't feel, somehow, she can be a really nice girl.'

'Probably not,' said Mrs Wade.

'She has marvellous clothes,' said Mrs Massington.

'Almost too exotic don't you think?'

'But very expensive.'

'Opulent. She's too opulent looking.'

'Here they come,' said Mrs Massington.

Madeleine de Sara and Reggie Wade were walking across the lawn. They were laughing and talking together and seemed very happy. Madeleine flung herself into a chair, tore off the beret she was wearing and ran her hands through her exquisitely dark curls.

She was undeniably beautiful.

'We've had such a marvellous afternoon!' she cried. 'I'm terribly hot. I must be looking too dreadful.'

Reggie Wade started nervously at the sound of his cue. 'You look – you look –' He gave a little laugh. 'I won't say it,' he finished.

Madeleine's eyes met his. It was a glance of complete understanding on her part. Mrs Massington noted it alertly.

'You should play golf,' said Madeleine to her hostess. 'You miss such a lot. Why don't you take it up? I have a friend who did and became quite good, and she was a lot older than you.'

'I don't care for that sort of thing,' said Iris coldly.

'Are you bad at games? How rotten for you! It makes one feel so out of things. But really, Mrs Wade, coaching nowadays is so good that almost anyone can play fairly well. I improved my tennis no end last summer. Of course I'm hopeless at golf.'

'Nonsense!' said Reggie. 'You only need coaching. Look how you were getting those brassie shots this afternoon.'

'Because you showed me how. You're a wonderful teacher. Lots of people simply can't teach. But you've got the gift. It must be wonderful to be you – you can do everything.'

'Nonsense. I'm no good – no use whatever.' Reggie was confused.

'You must be very proud of him,' said Madeleine, turning to Mrs Wade. 'How have you managed to keep him all these years? You must have been very clever. Or have you hidden him away?'

Her hostess made no reply. She picked up her book with a hand that trembled.

Reggie murmured something about changing, and went off.

'I do think it's so sweet of you to have me here,' said Madeleine to her hostess. 'Some women are so suspicious of their husbands' friends. I do think jealousy is absurd, don't you?'

'I do indeed. I should never dream of being jealous of Reggie.'

'That's wonderful of you! Because anyone can see that he's a man who's frightfully attractive to women. It was a shock to me when I heard he was married. Why do all the attractive men get snapped up so young?'

'I'm glad you find Reggie so attractive,' said Mrs Wade.

'Well, he is, isn't he? So good-looking, and so frightfully good at games. And that pretended indifference of his to women. That spurs us on of course.'

'I suppose you have lots of men friends,' said Mrs Wade.

'Oh, yes. I like men better than women. Women are never really nice to me. I can't think why.'

'Perhaps you are too nice to their husbands,' said Mrs Massington with a tinkly laugh.

'Well, one's sorry for people sometimes. So many nice men are tied to such dull wives. You know, "arty" women and highbrow women. Naturally, the men want someone young and bright to talk to. I think that the modern ideas of marriage and divorce are so sensible. Start again while one is still young with someone who shares one's tastes and ideas. It's better for everybody in the end. I mean, the highbrow wives probably pick up some long-haired creature of their own type who satisfies them. I think cutting your losses and starting again is a wise plan, don't you, Mrs Wade?'

'Certainly.'

A certain frostiness in the atmosphere seemed to penetrate Madeleine's consciousness. She murmured something about changing for tea and left them.

'Detestable creatures these modern girls are,' said Mrs Wade. 'Not an idea in their heads.'

'She's got one idea in hers, Iris,' said Mrs Massington. 'That girl's in love with Reggie.'

'Nonsense!'

'She is. I saw the way she looked at him just now. She doesn't care a pin whether he's married or not. She means to have him. Disgusting, I call it.'

Mrs Wade was silent a moment, then she laughed uncertainly. 'After all,' she said, 'what does it matter?'

Presently Mrs Wade, too, went upstairs. Her husband was in his dressing-room changing. He was singing.

'Enjoyed yourself, dear?' said Mrs Wade.

'Oh, er – rather, yes.'

'I'm glad. I want you to be happy.'

'Yes, rather.'

Acting a part was not Reggie Wade's strong point, but as it happened, the acute embarrassment occasioned by his fancying he was doing so did just as well. He avoided his wife's eye and jumped when she spoke to him. He felt ashamed; hated the farce of it all. Nothing could have produced a better effect. He was the picture of conscious guilt.

'How long have you known her?' asked Mrs Wade suddenly.

'Er – who?'

'Miss de Sara, of course.'

'Well, I don't quite know. I mean – oh, some time.'

'Really? You never mentioned her.'

'Didn't I? I suppose I forgot.'

'Forgot indeed!' said Mrs Wade. She departed with a whisk of mauve draperies.

After tea Mr Wade showed Miss de Sara the rose garden. They walked across the lawn conscious of two pairs of eyes raking their backs.

'Look here.' Safe out of sight in the rose garden Mr Wade unburdened himself. 'Look here, I think we'll have to give this up. My wife looked at me just now as though she hated me.'

'Don't worry,' said Madeleine. 'It's quite all right.'

'Do you think so? I mean, I don't want to put her against me. She said several nasty things at tea.'

'It's all right,' said Madeleine. 'You're doing splendidly.'

'Do you really think so?'

'Yes.' In a lower voice she went on: 'Your wife is walking round the corner of the terrace. She wants to see what we're doing. You'd better kiss me.'

'Oh!' said Mr Wade nervously. 'Must I? I mean –'

'Kiss me!' said Madeleine fiercely.

Mr Wade kissed her. Any lack of élan in the performance was remedied by Madeleine. She flung her arms around him. Mr Wade staggered.

'Oh!' he said.

'Did you hate it very much?' said Madeleine.

'No, of course not,' said Mr Wade gallantly. 'It – it just took me by surprise.' He added wistfully: 'Have we been in the rose garden long enough, do you think?'

'I think so,' said Madeleine. 'We've put in a bit of good work here.'

They returned to the lawn. Mrs Massington informed them that Mrs Wade had gone to lie down.

Later, Mr Wade joined Madeleine with a perturbed face.

'She's in an awful state – hysterics.'

'Good.'

'She saw me kissing you.'

'Well, we meant her to.'

'I know, but I couldn't say that, could I? I didn't know what to say. I said it had just – just – well, happened.'

'Excellent.'

'She said you were scheming to marry me and that you were no better than you should be. That upset me – it seemed such awfully rough luck on you. I mean, when you're just doing a job. I said that I had the utmost respect for you and that what she said wasn't true at all, and I'm afraid I got angry when she went on about it.'

'Magnificent!'

'And then she told me to go away. She doesn't ever want to speak to me again. She talked of packing up and leaving.' His face was dismayed.

Madeleine smiled. 'I'll tell you the answer to that one. Tell her that you'll be the one to go; that you'll pack up and clear out to town.'

'But I don't want to!'

'That's all right. You won't have to. Your wife would hate to think of you amusing yourself in London.'

The following morning Reggie Wade had a fresh bulletin to impart.

'She says she's been thinking that it isn't fair for her to go away when she agreed to stay six months. But she says that as I have my friends down here she doesn't see why she shouldn't have hers. She is asking Sinclair Jordan.'

'Is he *the* one?'

'Yes, and I'm damned if I'll have him in my house!'

'You must,' said Madeleine. 'Don't worry, I'll attend to him. Say that on thinking things over you have no objection and that you know she won't mind you asking me to stay on, too.'

'Oh dear!' sighed Mr Wade.

'Now don't lose heart,' said Madeleine. 'Everything is going splendidly. Another fortnight – and all your troubles will be over.'

'A fortnight? Do you really think so?' demanded Mr Wade.

'Think so? I'm sure of it,' said Madeleine.

A week later Madeleine de Sara entered Mr Parker Pyne's office and sank wearily into a chair.

'Enter the Queen of the Vamps,' said Mr Parker Pyne, smiling.

'Vamps!' said Madeleine. She gave a hollow laugh. 'I've never had such uphill work being a vamp. That man is obsessed by his wife! It's a disease.'

Mr Parker Pyne smiled. 'Yes, indeed. Well, in one way it made our task easier. It is not every man, my dear Madeleine, whom I would expose to your fascination so lightheartedly.'

The girl laughed. 'If you knew the difficulty I had to make him even kiss me as though he liked it!'

'A novel experience for you, my dear. Well, is your task accomplished?'

'Yes, I think all is well. We had a tremendous scene last night. Let me see, my last report was three days ago?'

'Yes.'

'Well, as I told you, I only had to look at that miserable worm, Sinclair Jordan, once. He was all over me – especially as he thought from my clothes that I had money. Mrs Wade was furious, of course. Here were both her men dancing attendance on me. I soon showed where my preference lay. I made fun of Sinclair Jordan, to his face and to her. I laughed at his clothes, and at the length of his hair. I pointed out that he had knock knees.'

'Excellent technique,' said Mr Parker Pyne appreciatively.

'Everything boiled up last night. Mrs Wade came out in the open. She accused me of breaking up her home. Reggie Wade mentioned the little matter of Sinclair Jordan. She said that that was only the result of her unhappiness and loneliness. She had noticed her husband's abstraction for some time, but had no idea as to the cause of it. She said they had always been ideally happy, that she adored him and he knew it, and that she wanted him and only him.

'I said it was too late for that. Mr Wade followed his instructions splendidly. He said he didn't give a damn! He was going to marry me! Mrs Wade could have her Sinclair as soon as she pleased. There was no reason why the divorce proceedings shouldn't be started at once; waiting six months was absurd.

'Within a few days, he said, she should have the necessary evidence and could instruct her solicitors. He said he couldn't live without me. Then Mrs Wade clutched her chest and talked about her weak heart and had to be given brandy. He didn't weaken. He went up to town this morning, and I've no doubt she's gone after him by this time.'

'So that's all right,' said Mr Pyne cheerfully. 'A very satisfactory case.'

The door flew open. In the doorway stood Reggie Wade.

'Is she here?' he demanded, advancing into the room. 'Where is she?' He caught sight of Madeleine. 'Darling!' he cried. He seized both her hands. 'Darling, darling. You knew, didn't you, that it was real last night – that I meant every word I said to Iris? I don't know why I was blind so long. But I've known for the last three days.'

'Known what?' said Madeleine faintly.

'That I adored you. That there was no woman in the world for me but you. Iris can bring her divorce and when it's gone through you'll marry me, won't you? Say you will, Madeleine, I adore you.'

He caught the paralysed Madeleine in his arms just as the door flew open again, this time to admit a thin woman dressed in untidy green.

'I thought so,' said the newcomer. 'I followed you! I knew you'd go to her!'

'I can assure you –' began Mr Parker Pyne, recovering from the stupefaction that had descended upon him.

The intruder took no notice of him. She swept on: 'Oh, Reggie, you can't want to break my heart! Only come back! I'll not say a word about this. I'll learn golf. I won't have any friends you don't care about. After all these years, when we've been so happy together –'

'I've never been happy till now,' said Mr Wade, still gazing at Madeleine. 'Dash it all, Iris, you wanted to marry that ass Jordan. Why don't you go and do it?'

Mrs Wade gave a wail. 'I hate him! I hate the very sight of him.' She turned to Madeleine. 'You wicked woman! You horrible vampire – stealing my husband from me.'

'I don't want your husband,' said Madeleine distractedly.

'Madeleine!' Mr Wade was gazing at her in agony.

'Please go away,' said Madeleine.

'But look here, I'm not pretending. I mean it.'

'Oh, go away!' cried Madeleine hysterically. 'Go *away*!'

Reggie moved reluctantly towards the door. 'I shall come back,' he warned her. 'You've not seen the last of me.' He went out, banging the door.

'Girls like you ought to be flogged and branded!' cried Mrs Wade. 'Reggie was an angel to me always till you came along. Now he's so changed I don't know him.' With a sob, she hurried out after her husband.

Madeleine and Mr Parker Pyne looked at each other.

'I can't help it,' said Madeleine helplessly. 'He's a very nice man – a dear – but I don't want to marry him. I'd no idea of all this. If you knew the difficulty I had making him kiss me!'

'Ahem!' said Mr Parker Pyne. 'I regret to admit it, but it was an error of judgement on my part.' He shook his head sadly, and drawing Mr Wade's file towards him, wrote across it:

FAILURE – *owing to natural causes.*
N.B. – *They should have been foreseen.*

The Case of the City Clerk

'The Case of the City Clerk' was first published in the USA as 'The Clerk Who Wanted Excitement' in *Cosmopolitan*, August 1932, and then as 'The £10 Adventure' in *Strand Magazine*, November 1932.

Mr Parker Pyne leaned back thoughtfully in his swivel chair and surveyed his visitor. He saw a small sturdily built man of forty-five with wistful, puzzled, timid eyes that looked at him with a kind of anxious hopefulness.

'I saw your advertisement in the paper,' said that little man nervously.

'You are in trouble, Mr Roberts?'

'No, not in trouble exactly.'

'You are unhappy?'

'I shouldn't like to say that either. I've a great deal to be thankful for.'

'We all have,' said Mr Parker Pyne. 'But when we have to remind ourselves of the fact it is a bad sign.'

'I know,' said the little man eagerly. 'That's just it! You've hit the nail on the head, sir.'

'Supposing you tell me all about yourself,' suggested Mr Parker Pyne.

'There's not much to tell, sir. As I say, I've a great deal to be thankful for. I have a job; I've managed to save a little money; the children are strong and healthy.'

'So you want – what?'

'I – I don't know.' He flushed. 'I expect that sounds foolish to you, sir.'

'Not at all,' said Mr Parker Pyne.

By skilled questioning he elicited further confidences. He heard of Mr Roberts' employment in a well-known firm and of his slow but steady rise. He heard of his marriage; of the struggle to present a decent appearance, to educate the children and have them 'looking nice'; of the plotting and planning and skimping and saving to put aside a few pounds each year. He heard, in fact, the saga of a life of ceaseless effort to survive.

'And – well, you see how it is,' confessed Mr Roberts. 'The wife's away. Staying with her mother with the two children. Little change for them and a rest for her. No room for me and we can't afford to go elsewhere. And being alone and reading the paper, I saw your advertisement and it set me thinking. I'm forty-eight. I just wondered . . . Things going on everywhere,' he ended, with all his wistful suburban soul in his eyes.

'You want,' said Mr Pyne, 'to live gloriously for ten minutes?'

'Well, I shouldn't put it like that. But perhaps you're right. Just to get out of the rut. I'd go back to it thankful afterwards – if only I had something to think about.' He looked at the other man anxiously. 'I suppose there's nothing possible, sir? I'm afraid – I'm afraid I couldn't afford to pay much.'

'How much could you afford?'

'I could manage five pounds, sir.' He waited, breathless.

'Five pounds,' said Mr Parker Pyne. 'I fancy – I just fancy we might be able to manage something for five pounds. Do you object to danger?' he added sharply.

A tinge of colour came into Mr Roberts' sallow face. 'Danger did you say, sir? Oh, no, not at all. I – I've never done anything dangerous.'

Mr Parker Pyne smiled. 'Come to see me again tomorrow and I'll tell you what I can do for you.'

The Bon Voyageur is a little-known hostelry. It is a restaurant frequented by a few habitués. They dislike newcomers.

To the Bon Voyageur came Mr Pyne and was greeted with respectful recognition. 'Mr Bonnington here?' he asked.

'Yes, sir. He's at his usual table.'

'Good. I'll join him.'

Mr Bonnington was a gentleman of military appearance with a somewhat bovine face. He greeted his friend with pleasure.

'Hallo, Parker. Hardly ever see you nowadays. Didn't know you came here.'

'I do now and then. Especially when I want to lay my hand on an old friend.'

'Meaning me?'

'Meaning you. As a matter of fact, Lucas, I've been thinking over what we were talking about the other day.'

'The Peterfield business? Seen the latest in the papers? No, you can't have. It won't be in till this evening.'

'What is the latest?'

'They murdered Peterfield last night,' said Mr Bonnington, placidly eating salad.

'Good heavens!' cried Mr Pyne.

'Oh, I'm not surprised,' said Mr Bonnington. 'Pigheaded old man, Peterfield. Wouldn't listen to us. Insisted on keeping the plans in his own hands.'

'Did they get them?'

'No; it seems some woman came round and gave the professor a recipe for boiling a ham. The old ass, absent-minded as usual, put the recipe for the ham in his safe and the plans in the kitchen.'

'Fortunate.'

'Almost providential. But I still don't know who's going to take 'em to Geneva. Maitland's in the hospital. Carslake's in Berlin. I can't leave. It means young Hooper.' He looked at his friend.

'You're still of the same opinion?' asked Mr Parker Pyne.

'Absolutely. He's been got at! I know it. I haven't a shadow of proof, but I tell you, Parker, I know when a chap's crooked! And I want those plans to get to Geneva. The League needs 'em. For the first time an invention isn't going to be sold to a nation. It's going to be handed over voluntarily to the League.

'It's the finest peace gesture that's ever been attempted, and it's got to be put through. And Hooper's crooked. You'll see, he'll be drugged on the train! If he goes in a plane it'll come down at some convenient spot! But confound it all, I can't pass him over. Discipline! You've got to have discipline! That's why I spoke to you the other day.'

'You asked me whether I knew of anyone.'

'Yes. Thought you might in your line of business. Some fire eater spoiling for a row. Whoever *I* send stands a good chance of being done in. Your man would probably not be suspected at all. But he's got to have nerve.'

'I think I know of someone who would do,' said Mr Parker Pyne.

'Thank God there are still chaps who will take a risk. Well, it's agreed then?'

'It's agreed,' said Mr Parker Pyne.

Mr Parker Pyne was summing up instructions. 'Now, that's quite clear? You will travel in a first-class sleeper to Geneva. You leave London at ten forty-five, via Folkestone and Boulogne, and you get into your first-class sleeper at Boulogne. You arrive at Geneva at eight the following morning. Here is the address at which you will report. Please memorize it and I will destroy it. Afterwards go to this hotel and await further instructions. Here is sufficient money in French and Swiss notes and currency. You understand?'

'Yes, sir.' Roberts' eyes were shining with excitement. 'Excuse me, sir, but am I allowed to – er – know anything of what it is I am carrying?'

Mr Parker Pyne smiled beneficently. 'You are carrying a cryptogram which reveals the secret hiding-place of the crown jewels of Russia,' he said solemnly. 'You can understand, naturally, that Bolshevist agents will be alert to intercept you. If it is necessary for you to talk about yourself, I should recommend that you say you have come into money and are enjoying a little holiday abroad.'

Mr Roberts sipped a cup of coffee and looked out over the Lake of Geneva. He was happy but at the same time he was disappointed.

He was happy because, for the first time in his life, he was in a foreign country. Moreover, he was staying in the kind of hotel he would never stay in again, and not for one moment had he had to worry about money! He had a room with private bathroom, delicious meals and attentive service. All these things Mr Roberts had enjoyed very much indeed.

He was disappointed because so far nothing that could be described as adventure had come his way. No disguised Bolshevists or mysterious Russians had crossed his path. A pleasant chat on the train with a French commercial traveller who spoke excellent English was the only human intercourse that had come his way. He had secreted the papers in his sponge bag as he had been told to do and had delivered them according to instructions. There had been no dangers to overcome, no hair's breadth escapes. Mr Roberts was disappointed.

It was at that moment that a tall, bearded man murmured '*Pardon*,' and sat down on the other side of the little table. 'You will excuse me,' he said, 'but I think you know a friend of mine. "P.P." are the initials.'

Mr Roberts was pleasantly thrilled. Here, at last, was a mysterious Russian. 'Qu-quite right.'

'Then I think we understand each other,' said the stranger.

Mr Roberts looked at him searchingly. This was far more like the real thing. The stranger was a man of about fifty, of distinguished though foreign appearance. He wore an eye-glass, and a small coloured ribbon in his button-hole.

'You have accomplished your mission in the most satisfactory manner,' said the stranger. 'Are you prepared to undertake a further one?'

'Certainly. Oh, yes.'

'Good. You will book a sleeper on the Geneva-Paris train for tomorrow night. You will ask for Berth Number Nine.'

'Supposing it is not free?'

'It will be free. That will have been seen to.'

'Berth Number Nine,' repeated Roberts. 'Yes, I've got that.'

'During the course of your journey someone will say to you, "Pardon, Monsieur, but I think you were recently at Grasse?" To that you will reply

"Yes, last month." The person will then say, "Are you interested in scent?" And you will reply, "Yes, I am a manufacturer of synthetic Oil of Jasmine." After that you will place yourself entirely at the disposal of the person who has spoken to you. By the way, are you armed?'

'No,' said Mr Roberts in a flutter. 'No; I never thought – that is –'

'That can soon be remedied,' said the bearded man. He glanced around. No one was near them. Something hard and shining was pressed into Mr Roberts' hand. 'A small weapon but efficacious,' said the stranger, smiling.

Mr Roberts, who had never fired a revolver in his life, slipped it gingerly into a pocket. He had an uneasy feeling that it might go off at any minute.

They went over the passwords again. Then Roberts' new friend rose.

'I wish you good luck,' he said. 'May you come through safely. You are a brave man, Mr Roberts.'

'Am I?' thought Roberts, when the other had departed. 'I'm sure I don't want to get killed. That would never do.'

A pleasant thrill shot down his spine, slightly adulterated by a thrill that was not quite so pleasant.

He went to his room and examined the weapon. He was still uncertain about its mechanism and hoped he would not be called upon to use it.

He went out to book his seat.

The train left Geneva at nine-thirty. Roberts got to the station in good time. The sleeping-car conductor took his ticket and his passport, and stood aside while an underling swung Roberts' suitcase on to the rack. There was other luggage there: a pigskin case and a Gladstone bag.

'Number Nine is the lower berth,' said the conductor.

As Roberts turned to leave the carriage he ran into a big man who was entering. They drew apart with apologies – Roberts' in English and the stranger's in French. He was a big burly man, with a closely shaven head and thick eye-glasses through which his eyes seemed to peer suspiciously.

'An ugly customer,' said the little man to himself.

He sensed something vaguely sinister about his travelling companion. Was it to keep a watch on this man that he had been told to ask for Berth Number Nine? He fancied it might be.

He went out again into the corridor. There was still ten minutes before the train was due to start and he thought he would walk up and down the platform. Half-way along the passage he stood back to allow a lady to pass him. She was just entering the train and the conductor preceded her, ticket in hand. As she passed Roberts she dropped her handbag. The Englishman picked it up and handed it to her.

'Thank you, Monsieur.' She spoke in English but her voice was foreign, a rich low voice very seductive in quality. As she was about to pass on, she hesitated and murmured: 'Pardon, Monsieur, but I think you were recently at Grasse?'

Roberts' heart leaped with excitement. He was to place himself at the disposal of this lovely creature – for she *was* lovely, of that there was no doubt. She wore a travelling coat of fur, a chic hat. There were pearls round her neck. She was dark and her lips were scarlet.

Roberts made the required answer. 'Yes, last month.'

'You are interested in scent?'

'Yes, I am a manufacturer of synthetic Oil of Jasmine.'

She bent her head and passed on, leaving a mere whisper behind her. 'In the corridor as soon as the train starts.'

The next ten minutes seemed an age to Roberts. At last the train started. He walked slowly along the corridor. The lady in the fur coat was struggling with a window. He hurried to her assistance.

'Thank you, Monsieur. Just a little air before they insist on closing everything.' And then in a soft, low, rapid voice: 'After the frontier, when our fellow traveller is asleep – not before – go into the washing place and through it into the compartment on the other side. You understand?'

'Yes.' He let down the window and said in a louder voice: 'Is that better, Madame?'

'Thank you very much.'

He retired to his compartment. His travelling companion was already stretched out in the upper berth. His preparations for the night had obviously been simple. The removal of boots and a coat, in fact.

Roberts debated his own costume. Clearly, if he were going into a lady's compartment he could not undress.

He found a pair of slippers, substituting them for his boots, and then lay down, switching out the light. A few minutes later, the man above began to snore.

Just after ten o'clock they reached the frontier. The door was thrown open; a perfunctory question was asked. Had Messieurs anything to declare? The door was closed again. Presently the train drew out of Bellegarde.

The man in the upper berth was snoring again. Roberts allowed twenty minutes to elapse, then he slipped to his feet and opened the door of the lavatory compartment. Once inside, he bolted the door behind him and eyed the door on the farther side. It was not bolted. He hesitated. Should he knock?

Perhaps it would be absurd to knock. But he didn't quite like entering without knocking. He compromised, opened the door gently about an inch and waited. He even ventured on a small cough.

The response was prompt. The door was pulled open, he was seized by the arm, pulled through into the farther compartment, and the girl closed and bolted the door behind him.

Roberts caught his breath. Never had he imagined anything so lovely. She was wearing a long foamy garment of cream chiffon and lace. She leaned against the door into the corridor, panting. Roberts had often read of beautiful hunted creatures at bay. Now for the first time, he saw one – a thrilling sight.

'Thank God!' murmured the girl.

She was quite young, Roberts noted, and her loveliness was such that she seemed to him like a being from another world. Here was romance at last – and he was in it!

She spoke in a low, hurried voice. Her English was good but the inflection was wholly foreign. 'I am so glad you have come,' she said. 'I have been horribly frightened. Vassilievitch is on the train. You understand what that means?'

Roberts did not understand in the least what it meant, but he nodded.

'I thought I had given them the slip. I might have known better. What are we to do? Vassilievitch is in the next carriage to me. Whatever happens, he must not get the jewels.'

'He's not going to murder you and he's not going to get the jewels,' said Robert with determination.

'Then what am I to do with them?'

Roberts looked past her to the door. 'The door's bolted,' he said.

The girl laughed. 'What are locked doors to Vassilievitch?'

Roberts felt more and more as though he were in the middle of one of his favourite novels. 'There's only one thing to be done. Give them to me.'

She looked at him doubtfully. 'They are worth a quarter of a million.'

Roberts flushed. 'You can trust me.'

The girl hesitated a moment longer, then: 'Yes, I will trust you,' she said. She made a swift movement. The next minute she was holding out to him a rolled-up pair of stockings – stockings of cobweb silk. 'Take them, my friend,' she said to the astonished Roberts.

He took them and at once he understood. Instead of being light as air, the stockings were unexpectedly heavy.

'Take them to your compartment,' she said. 'You can give them to me in the morning – if – if I am still here.'

Roberts coughed. 'Look here,' he said. 'About you.' He paused. 'I – I must keep guard over you.' Then he flushed in an agony of propriety. 'Not in here, I mean. I'll stay in there.' He nodded towards the lavatory compartment.

'If you like to stay here –' She glanced at the upper unoccupied berth.
Roberts flushed to the roots of his hair. 'No, no,' he protested. 'I shall
be all right in there. If you need me, call out.'

'Thank you, my friend,' said the girl softly.

She slipped into the lower berth, drew up the covers and smiled at
him gratefully. He retreated into the washroom.

Suddenly – it must have been a couple of hours later – he thought he
heard something. He listened – nothing. Perhaps he had been mistaken.
And yet it certainly seemed to him that he had heard a faint sound from
the next carriage. Supposing – just supposing . . .

He opened the door softly. The compartment was as he had left it,
with the tiny blue light in the ceiling. He stood there with his eyes straining
through the dimness till they got accustomed to it. The girl was not there!

He switched the light full on. The compartment was empty. Suddenly
he sniffed. Just a whiff but he recognized it – the sweet, sickly odour of
chloroform!

He stepped from the compartment (unlocked now, he noted) out into
the corridor and looked up and down it. Empty! His eyes fastened on
the door next to the girl's. She had said that Vassilievitch was in the next
compartment. Gingerly Roberts tried the handle. The door was bolted
on the inside.

What should he do? Demand admittance? But the man would refuse
– and after all, the girl might not be there! And if she were, would she
thank him for making a public business of the matter? He had gathered
that secrecy was essential in the game they were playing.

A perturbed little man wandered slowly along the corridor. He paused
at the end compartment. The door was open, and the conductor lay there
sleeping. And above him, on a hook, *hung his brown uniform coat and
peaked cap.*

In a flash Roberts had decided on his course of action. In another minute
he had donned the coat and cap, and was hurrying back along the corridor.
He stopped at the door next to that of the girl, summoned all his resolu-
tion and knocked peremptorily.

When the summons was not answered, he knocked again.

'Monsieur,' he said in his best accent.

The door opened a little way and a head peered out – the head of a
foreigner, clean-shaven except for a black moustache. It was an angry,
malevolent face.

'*Qu'est-ce-qu'il y a?*' he snapped.

'*Votre passeport, monsieur.*' Roberts stepped back and beckoned.

The other hesitated, then stepped out into the corridor. Roberts had counted on his doing that. If he had the girl inside, he naturally would not want the conductor to come in. Like a flash, Roberts acted. With all his force he shoved the foreigner aside – the man was unprepared and the swaying of the train helped – bolted into the carriage himself, shut the door and locked it.

Lying across the end of the berth was the girl, a gag across her mouth and her wrists tied together. He freed her quickly and she fell against him with a sigh.

'I feel so weak and ill,' she murmured. 'It was chloroform, I think. Did he – did he get them?'

'No.' Roberts tapped his pocket. 'What are we going to do now?' he asked.

The girl sat up. Her wits were returning. She took in his costume.

'How clever of you. Fancy thinking of that! He said that he would kill me if I did not tell him where the jewels were. I have been so afraid – and then you came.' Suddenly she laughed. 'But we have outwitted him! He will not dare to do anything. He cannot even try to get back into his own compartment.

'We must stay here till morning. Probably he will leave the train at Dijon; we are due to stop there in about half an hour. He will telegraph to Paris and they will pick up our trail there. In the meantime, you had better throw that coat and cap out of the window. They might get you into trouble.'

Roberts obeyed.

'We must not sleep,' the girl decided. 'We must stay on guard till morning.'

It was a strange, exciting vigil. At six o'clock in the morning, Roberts opened the door carefully and looked out. No one was about. The girl slipped quickly into her own compartment. Roberts followed her in. The place had clearly been ransacked. He regained his own carriage through the washroom. His fellow-traveller was still snoring.

They reached Paris at seven o'clock. The conductor was declaiming at the loss of his coat and cap. He had not yet discovered the loss of a passenger.

Then began a most entertaining chase. The girl and Roberts took taxi after taxi across Paris. They entered hotels and restaurants by one door and left them by another. At last the girl gave a sign.

'I feel sure we are not followed now,' she said. 'We have shaken them off.'

They breakfasted and drove to Le Bourget. Three hours later they were at Croydon. Roberts had never flown before.

At Croydon a tall gentleman with a far-off resemblance to Mr Roberts' mentor at Geneva was waiting for them. He greeted the girl with especial respect.

'The car is here, madam,' he said.

'This gentleman will accompany us, Paul,' said the girl. And to Roberts: 'Count Paul Stepanyi.'

The car was a vast limousine. They drove for about an hour, then they entered the grounds of a country house and pulled up at the door of an imposing mansion. Mr Roberts was taken to a room furnished as a study. There he handed over the precious pair of stockings. He was left alone for a while. Presently Count Stepanyi returned.

'Mr Roberts,' he said, 'our thanks and gratitude are due to you. You have proved yourself a brave and resourceful man.' He held out a red morocco case. 'Permit me to confer upon you the Order of St Stanislaus – tenth class with laurels.'

As in a dream Roberts opened the case and looked at the jewelled order. The old gentleman was still speaking.

'The Grand Duchess Olga would like to thank you herself before you depart.'

He was led to a big drawing-room. There, very beautiful in a flowing robe, stood his travelling companion.

She made an imperious gesture of the hand, and the other man left them.

'I owe you my life, Mr Roberts,' said the grand duchess.

She held out her hand. Roberts kissed it. She leaned suddenly towards him.

'You are a brave man,' she said.

His lips met hers; a waft of rich Oriental perfume surrounded him.

For a moment he held that slender, beautiful form in his arms . . .

He was still in a dream when somebody said to him: 'The car will take you anywhere you wish.'

An hour later, the car came back for the Grand Duchess Olga. She got into it and so did the white-haired man. He had removed his beard for coolness. The car set down the Grand Duchess Olga at a house in Streatham. She entered it and an elderly woman looked up from a tea table.

'Ah, Maggie, dear, so there you are.'

In the Geneva-Paris express this girl was the Grand Duchess Olga; in Mr Parker Pyne's office she was Madeleine de Sara, and in the house at Streatham she was Maggie Sayers, fourth daughter of an honest, hard-working family.

How are the mighty fallen!

★   ★   ★

Mr Parker Pyne was lunching with his friend. 'Congratulations,' said the latter, 'your man carried the thing through without a hitch. The Tormali gang must be wild to think the plans of that gun have gone to the League. Did you tell your man what he was carrying?'

'No. I thought it better to – er – embroider.'

'Very discreet of you.'

'It wasn't exactly discretion. I wanted him to enjoy himself. I fancied he might find a gun a little tame. I wanted him to have some adventures.'

'Tame?' said Mr Bonnington, staring at him. 'Why, that lot would murder him as soon as look at him.'

'Yes,' said Mr Parker Pyne mildly. 'But I didn't want him to be murdered.'

'Do you make a lot of money in your business, Parker?' asked Mr Bonnington.

'Sometimes I lose it,' said Mr Parker Pyne. 'That is, if it is a deserving case.'

Three angry gentlemen were abusing one another in Paris.

'That confounded Hooper!' said one. 'He let us down.'

'The plans were not taken by anyone from the office,' said the second. 'But they went Wednesday, I am assured of that. And so I say *you* bungled it.'

'I didn't,' said the third sulkily; 'there was no Englishman on the train except a little clerk. He'd never heard of Peterfield or of the gun. I know. I tested him. Peterfield and the gun meant nothing to him.' He laughed. 'He had a Bolshevist complex of some kind.'

Mr Roberts was sitting in front of a gas fire. On his knee was a letter from Mr Parker Pyne. It enclosed a cheque for fifty pounds 'from certain people who are delighted with the way a certain commission was executed.'

On the arm of his chair was a library book. Mr Roberts opened it at random. 'She crouched against the door like a beautiful, hunted creature at bay.'

Well, he knew all about that.

He read another sentence: 'He sniffed the air. The faint, sickly odour of chloroform came to his nostrils.'

That he knew all about too.

'He caught her in his arms and felt the responsive quiver of her scarlet lips.'

Mr Roberts gave a sigh. It wasn't a dream. It had all happened. The journey out had been dull enough, but the journey home! He had enjoyed it. But he was glad to be home again. He felt vaguely that life could not be lived indefinitely at such a pace. Even the Grand Duchess Olga – even that last kiss – partook already of the unreal quality of a dream.

Mary and the children would be home tomorrow. Mr Roberts smiled happily.

She would say: 'We've had such a nice holiday. I hated thinking of you all alone here, poor old boy.' And he'd say: 'That's all right, old girl. I had to go to Geneva for the firm on business – delicate bit of negotiations – and look what they've sent me.' And he'd show her the cheque for fifty pounds.

He thought of the Order of St Stanislaus, tenth class with laurels. He'd hidden it, but supposing Mary found it! It would take a bit of explaining . . .

Ah, that was it – he'd tell her he'd picked it up abroad. A curio.

He opened his book again and read happily. No longer was there a wistful expression on his face.

He, too, was of that glorious company to whom Things Happened.

The Case of the Rich Woman

'The Case of the Rich Woman' was the first Parker Pyne story, published in the USA as 'The Rich Woman Who Wanted Only To Be Happy' in *Cosmopolitan*, August 1932.

The name of Mrs Abner Rymer was brought to Mr Parker Pyne. He knew the name and he raised his eyebrows.

Presently his client was shown into the room.

Mrs Rymer was a tall woman, big-boned. Her figure was ungainly and the velvet dress and the heavy fur coat she wore did not disguise the fact. The knuckles of her large hands were pronounced. Her face was big and broad and highly coloured. Her black hair was fashionably dressed, and there were many tips of curled ostrich in her hat.

She plumped herself down on a chair with a nod. 'Good-morning,' she said. Her voice had a rough accent. 'If you're any good at all you'll tell me how to spend my money!'

'Most original,' murmured Mr Parker Pyne. 'Few ask me that in these days. So you really find it difficult, Mrs Rymer?'

'Yes, I do,' said the lady bluntly. 'I've got three fur coats, a lot of Paris dresses and such like. I've got a car and a house in Park Lane. I've had a yacht but I don't like the sea. I've got a lot of those high-class servants that look down their nose at you. I've travelled a bit and seen foreign parts. And I'm blessed if I can think of anything more to buy or do.' She looked hopefully at Mr Pyne.

'There are hospitals,' he said.

'What? Give it away, you mean? No, that I won't do! That money was worked for, let me tell you, worked for hard. If you think I'm going to hand it out like so much dirt – well, you're mistaken. I want to spend it; spend it and get some good out of it. Now, if you've got any ideas that are worthwhile in that line, you can depend on a good fee.'

'Your proposition interests me,' said Mr Pyne. 'You do not mention a country house.'

'I forgot it, but I've got one. Bores me to death.'

'You must tell me more about yourself. Your problem is not easy to solve.'

'I'll tell you and willing. I'm not ashamed of what I've come from. Worked in a farmhouse, I did, when I was a girl. Hard work it was too. Then I took up with Abner – he was a workman in the mills near by. He courted me for eight years, and then we got married.'

'And you were happy?' asked Mr Pyne.

'I was. He was a good man to me, Abner. We had a hard struggle of it, though; he was out of a job twice, and children coming along. Four we had, three boys and a girl. And none of them lived to grow up. I dare say it would have been different if they had.' Her face softened; looked suddenly younger.

'His chest was weak – Abner's was. They wouldn't take him for the war. He did well at home. He was made foreman. He was a clever fellow, Abner. He worked out a process. They treated him fair, I will say; gave him a good sum for it. He used that money for another idea of his. That brought in money hand over fist. It's still coming in.

'Mind you, it was rare fun at first. Having a house and a tip-top bathroom and servants of one's own. No more cooking and scrubbing and washing to do. Just sit back on your silk cushions in the drawing-room and ring the bell for tea – like any countess might! Grand fun it was, and we enjoyed it. And then we came up to London. I went to swell dressmakers for my clothes. We went to Paris and the Riviera. Rare fun it was.'

'And then,' said Mr Parker Pyne.

'We got used to it, I suppose,' said Mrs Rymer. 'After a bit it didn't seem so much fun. Why, there were days when we didn't even fancy our meals properly – us, with any dish we fancied to choose from! As for baths – well, in the end, one bath a day's enough for anyone. And Abner's health began to worry him. Paid good money to doctors, we did, but they couldn't do anything. They tried this and they tried that. But it was no use. He died.' She paused. 'He was a young man, only forty-three.'

Mr Pyne nodded sympathetically.

'That was five years ago. Money's still rolling in. It seems wasteful not to be able to do anything with it. But as I tell you, I can't think of anything else to buy that I haven't got already.'

'In other words,' said Mr Pyne, 'your life is dull. You are not enjoying it.'

'I'm sick of it,' said Mrs Rymer gloomily. 'I've no friends. The new lot only want subscriptions, and they laugh at me behind my back. The

474   Detectives and Young Adventurers: The Complete Short Stories

old lot won't have anything to do with me. My rolling up in a car makes them shy. Can you do anything or suggest anything?'

'It is possible that I can,' said Mr Pyne slowly. 'It will be difficult, but I believe there is a chance of success. I think it's possible I can give you back what you have lost – your interest in life.'

'How?' demanded Mrs Rymer curtly.

'That,' said Mr Parker Pyne, 'is my professional secret. I never disclose my methods beforehand. The question is, will you take a chance? I do not guarantee success, but I do think there is a reasonable possibility of it.

'I shall have to adopt unusual methods, and therefore it will be expensive. My charges will be one thousand pounds, payable in advance.'

'You can open your mouth all right, can't you?' said Mrs Rymer appreciatively. 'Well, I'll risk it. I'm used to paying top price. Only, when I pay for a thing, I take good care that I get it.'

'You shall get it,' said Mr Parker Pyne. 'Never fear.'

'I'll send you the cheque this evening,' said Mrs Rymer, rising. 'I'm sure I don't know why I should trust you. Fools and their money are soon parted, they say. I dare say I'm a fool. You've got nerve, to advertise in all the papers that you can make people happy!'

'Those advertisements cost me money,' said Mr Pyne. 'If I could not make my words good, that money would be wasted. I *know* what causes unhappiness, and consequently I have a clear idea of how to produce an opposite condition.'

Mrs Rymer shook her head doubtfully and departed, leaving a cloud of expensive mixed essences behind her.

The handsome Claude Luttrell strolled into the office. 'Something in my line?'

Mr Pyne shook his head. 'Nothing so simple,' he said. 'No, this is a difficult case. We must, I fear, take a few risks. We must attempt the unusual.'

'Mrs Oliver?'

Mr Pyne smiled at the mention of the world-famous novelist. 'Mrs Oliver,' he said, 'is really the most conventional of all of us. I have in mind a bold and audacious coup. By the way, you might ring up Dr Antrobus.'

'Antrobus?'

'Yes. His services will be needed.'

A week later Mrs Rymer once more entered Mr Parker Pyne's office. He rose to receive her.

'This delay, I assure you, has been necessary,' he said. 'Many things had to be arranged, and I had to secure the services of an unusual man who had to come half-across Europe.'

'Oh!' She said it suspiciously. It was constantly present in her mind that she had paid out a cheque for a thousand pounds and the cheque had been cashed.

Mr Parker Pyne touched a buzzer. A young girl, dark, Oriental looking, but dressed in white nurse's kit, answered it.

'Is everything ready, Nurse de Sara?'

'Yes. Doctor Constantine is waiting.'

'What are you going to do?' asked Mrs Rymer with a touch of uneasiness.

'Introduce you to some Eastern magic, dear lady,' said Mr Parker Pyne.

'Mrs Rymer followed the nurse up to the next floor. Here she was ushered into a room that bore no relation to the rest of the house. Oriental embroideries covered the walls. There were divans with soft cushions and beautiful rugs on the floor. A man was bending over a coffee-pot. He straightened as they entered.

'Doctor Constantine,' said the nurse.

The doctor was dressed in European clothes, but his face was swarthy and his eyes were dark and oblique with a peculiarly piercing power in their glance.

'So this is my patient?' he said in a low, vibrant voice.

'I'm not a patient,' said Mrs Rymer.

'Your body is not sick,' said the doctor, 'but your soul is weary. We of the East know how to cure that disease. Sit down and drink a cup of coffee.'

Mrs Rymer sat down and accepted a tiny cup of the fragrant brew. As she sipped it the doctor talked.

'Here in the West, they treat only the body. A mistake. The body is only the instrument. A tune is played upon it. It may be a sad, weary tune. It may be a gay tune full of delight. The last is what we shall give you. You have money. You shall spend it and enjoy. Life shall be worth living again. It is easy – easy – so easy . . .'

A feeling of languor crept over Mrs Rymer. The figures of the doctor and the nurse grew hazy. She felt blissfully happy and very sleepy. The doctor's figure grew bigger. The whole world was growing bigger.

The doctor was looking into her eyes. 'Sleep,' he was saying. 'Sleep. Your eyelids are closing. Soon you will sleep. You will sleep. You will sleep . . .'

Mrs Rymer's eyelids closed. She floated with a wonderful great big world . . .

★   ★   ★

When her eyes opened it seemed to her that a long time had passed. She remembered several things vaguely – strange, impossible dreams; then a feeling of waking; then further dreams. She remembered something about a car and the dark, beautiful girl in a nurse's uniform bending over her.

Anyway, she was properly awake now, and in her own bed.

At least, was it her own bed? It felt different. It lacked the delicious softness of her own bed. It was vaguely reminiscent of days almost forgotten. She moved, and it creaked. Mrs Rymer's bed in Park Lane never creaked.

She looked round. Decidedly, this was not Park Lane. Was it a hospital? No, she decided, not a hospital. Nor was it a hotel. It was a bare room, the walls an uncertain shade of lilac. There was a deal wash-stand with a jug and basin upon it. There was a deal chest of drawers and a tin trunk. There were unfamiliar clothes hanging on pegs. There was the bed covered with a much-mended quilt and there was herself in it.

'Where *am* I?' said Mrs Rymer.

The door opened and a plump little woman bustled in. She had red cheeks and a good-humoured air. Her sleeves were rolled up and she wore an apron.

'There!' she exclaimed. 'She's awake. Come in, doctor.'

Mrs Rymer opened her mouth to say several things – but they remained unsaid, for the man who followed the plump woman into the room was not in the least like the elegant, swarthy Doctor Constantine. He was a bent old man who peered through thick glasses.

'That's better,' he said, advancing to the bed and taking up Mrs Rymer's wrist. 'You'll soon be better now, my dear.'

'What's been the matter with me?' demanded Mrs Rymer.

'You had a kind of seizure,' said the doctor. 'You've been unconscious for a day or two. Nothing to worry about.'

'Gave us a fright you did, Hannah,' said the plump woman. 'You've been raving too, saying the oddest things.'

'Yes, yes, Mrs Gardner,' said the doctor repressively. 'But we musn't excite the patient. You'll soon be up and about again, my dear.'

'But don't you worry about the work, Hannah.' said Mrs Gardner. 'Mrs Roberts has been in to give me a hand and we've got on fine. Just lie still and get well, my dear.'

'Why do you call me Hannah?' said Mrs Rymer.

'Well, it's your name,' said Mrs Gardner, bewildered.

'No, it isn't. My name is Amelia. Amelia Rymer. Mrs Abner Rymer.'

The doctor and Mrs Gardner exchanged glances.

'Well, just you lie still,' said Mrs Gardner.

'Yes, yes; no worry,' said the doctor.

They withdrew. Mrs Rymer lay puzzling. Why did they call her Hannah, and why had they exchanged that glance of amused incredulity when she had given them her name? Where was she and what had happened?

She slipped out of bed. She felt a little uncertain on her legs, but she walked slowly to the small dormer window and looked out – on a farmyard! Completely mystified, she went back to bed. What was she doing in a farmhouse that she had never seen before?

Mrs Gardner re-entered the room with a bowl of soup on a tray.

Mrs Rymer began her questions. 'What am I doing in this house?' she demanded. 'Who brought me here?'

'Nobody brought you, my dear. It's your home. Leastways, you've lived here for the last five years – and me not suspecting once that you were liable to fits.'

'*Lived* here! *Five* years?'

'That's right. Why, Hannah, you don't mean that you still don't remember?'

'I've never lived here! I've never seen you before.'

'You see, you've had this illness and you've forgotten.'

'I've never lived here.'

'But you have, my dear.' Suddenly Mrs Gardner darted across to the chest of drawers and brought to Mrs Rymer a faded photograph in a frame.

It represented a group of four persons: a bearded man, a plump woman (Mrs Gardner), a tall, lank man with a pleasantly sheepish grin, and somebody in a print dress and apron – herself!

Stupefied, Mrs Rymer gazed at the photograph. Mrs Gardner put the soup down beside her and quietly left the room.

Mrs Rymer sipped the soup mechanically. It was good soup, strong and hot. All the time her brain was in a whirl. Who was mad? Mrs Gardner or herself? One of them must be! But there was the doctor too.

'I'm Amelia Rymer,' she said firmly to herself. 'I know I'm Amelia Rymer and nobody's going to tell me different.'

She had finished the soup. She put the bowl back on the tray. A folded newspaper caught her eye and she picked it up and looked at the date on it, October 19. What day had she gone to Mr Parker Pyne's office? Either the fifteenth or the sixteenth. Then she must have been ill for three days.

'That rascally doctor!' said Mrs Rymer wrathfully.

All the same, she was a shade relieved. She had heard of cases where people had forgotten who they were for years at a time. She had been afraid some such thing had happened to her.

She began turning the pages of the paper, scanning the columns idly, when suddenly a paragraph caught her eye.

Mrs Abner Rymer, widow of Abner Rymer, the 'button shank' king, was removed yesterday to a private home for mental cases. For the past two days she has persisted in declaring she was not herself, but a servant girl named Hannah Moorhouse.

'Hannah Moorhouse! So that's it,' said Mrs Rymer. 'She's me and I'm her. Kind of double, I suppose. Well, we can soon put *that* right! If that oily hypocrite of a Parker Pyne is up to some game or other –'

But at this minute her eye was caught by the name Constantine staring at her from the printed page. This time it was a headline.

DR CONSTANTINE'S CLAIM

At a farewell lecture given last night on the eve of his departure for Japan, Dr Claudius Constantine advanced some startling theories. He declared that it was possible to prove the existence of the soul by transferring a soul from one body to another. In the course of his experiments in the East he had, he claimed, successfully effected a double transfer – the soul of a hypnotized body A being transferred to a hypnotized body B and the soul of body B to the soul of body A. On recovering from the hypnotic sleep, A declared herself to be B, and B thought herself to be A. For the experiment to succeed, it was necessary to find two people with a great bodily resemblance. It was an undoubted fact that two people resembling each other were *en rapport*. This was very noticeable in the case of twins, but two strangers, varying widely in social position, but with a marked similarity of feature, were found to exhibit the same harmony of structure.

Mrs Rymer cast the paper from her. 'The scoundrel! The black scoundrel!'

She saw the whole thing now! It was a dastardly plot to get hold of her money. This Hannah Moorhouse was Mr Pyne's tool – possibly an innocent one. He and that devil Constantine had brought off this fantastic coup.

But she'd expose him! She'd show him up! She'd have the law on him! She'd tell everyone –

Abruptly Mrs Rymer came to a stop in the tide of her indignation. She remembered the first paragraph. Hannah Moorhouse had not been a docile tool. She had protested; had declared her individuality. And what had happened?

'Clapped into a lunatic asylum, poor girl,' said Mrs Rymer.

A chill ran down her spine.

A lunatic asylum. They got you in there and they never let you get out. The more you said you were sane, the less they'd believe you. There you were and there you stayed. No, Mrs Rymer wasn't going to run the risk of that.

The door opened and Mrs Gardner came in.

'Ah, you've drunk your soup, my dear. That's good. You'll soon be better now.'

'When was I taken ill?' demanded Mrs Rymer.

'Let me see. It was three days ago – on Wednesday.

That was the fifteenth. You were took bad about four o'clock.'

'Ah!' The ejaculation was fraught with meaning. It had been just about four o'clock when Mrs Rymer had entered the presence of Doctor Constantine.

'You slipped down in your chair,' said Mrs Gardner. "Oh!" you says. "Oh!" just like that. And then: 'I'm falling asleep,' you says in a dreamy voice. "I'm falling asleep." And fall asleep you did, and we put you to bed and sent for the doctor, and here you've been ever since.'

'I suppose,' Mrs Rymer ventured, 'there isn't any way you could know who I am – apart from my face, I mean.'

'Well, that's a queer thing to say,' said Mrs Gardner. 'What is there to go by better than a person's face, I'd like to know? There's your birth-mark, though, if that satisfies you better.'

'A birthmark?' said Mrs Rymer, brightening. She had no such thing.

'Strawberry mark just under the right elbow,' said Mrs Gardner. 'Look for yourself, my dear.'

'This will prove it,' said Mrs Rymer to herself. She knew that she had no strawberry mark under the right elbow. She turned back the sleeve of her nightdress. The strawberry mark was there.

Mrs Rymer burst into tears.

Four days later Mrs Rymer rose from her bed. She had thought out several plans of action and rejected them.

She might show the paragraph in the paper to Mrs Gardner and explain. Would they believe her? Mrs Rymer was sure they would not.

She might go to the police. Would they believe her? Again she thought not.

She might go to Mr Pyne's office. That idea undoubtedly pleased her best. For one thing, she would like to tell that oily scoundrel what she thought of him. She was debarred from putting this plan into operation by a vital obstacle. She was at present in Cornwall (so she had learned), and she had no money for the journey to London. Two and fourpence in a worn purse seemed to represent her financial position.

And so, after four days, Mrs Rymer made a sporting decision. For the present she would accept things! She was Hannah Moorhouse. Very well, she would be Hannah Moorhouse. For the present she would accept that role, and later, when she had saved sufficient money, she would go to London and beard the swindler in his den.

And having thus decided, Mrs Rymer accepted her role with perfect good temper, even with a kind of sardonic amusement. History was repeating itself indeed. This life reminded her of her girlhood. How long ago that seemed!

The work was a bit hard after her years of soft living, but after the first week she found herself slipping into the ways of the farm.

Mrs Gardner was a good-tempered, kindly woman. Her husband, a big, taciturn man, was kindly also. The lank, shambling man of the photograph had gone; another farmhand came in his stead, a good-humoured giant of forty-five, slow of speech and thought, but with a shy twinkle in his blue eyes.

The weeks went by. At last the day came when Mrs Rymer had enough money to pay her fare to London. But she did not go. She put it off. Time enough, she thought. She wasn't easy in her mind about asylums yet. That scoundrel, Parker Pyne, was clever. He'd get a doctor to say she was mad and she'd be clapped away out of sight with no one knowing anything about it.

'Besides,' said Mrs Rymer to herself, 'a bit of a change does one good.'

She rose early and worked hard. Joe Welsh, the new farmhand, was ill that winter, and she and Mrs Gardner nursed him. The big man was pathetically dependent on them.

Spring came – lambing time; there were wild flowers in the hedges, a treacherous softness in the air. Joe Welsh gave Hannah a hand with her work. Hannah did Joe's mending.

Sometimes, on Sundays, they went for a walk together. Joe was a widower. His wife had died four years before. Since her death he had, he frankly confessed it, taken a drop too much.

He didn't go much to the Crown nowadays. He bought himself some new clothes. Mr and Mrs Gardner laughed.

Hannah made fun of Joe. She teased him about his clumsiness. Joe didn't mind. He looked bashful but happy.

After spring came summer – a good summer that year. Everyone worked hard.

Harvest was over. The leaves were red and golden on the trees.

It was October eighth when Hannah looked up one day from a cabbage she was cutting and saw Mr Parker Pyne leaning over the fence.

'You!' said Hannah, alias Mrs Rymer. 'You . . .'

It was some time before she got it all out, and when she had said her say, she was out of breath.

Mr Parker Pyne smiled blandly. 'I quite agree with you,' he said.

'A cheat and a liar, that's what you are!' said Mrs Rymer, repeating herself. 'You with your Constantines and your hypnotizing, and that poor girl Hannah Moorhouse shut up with – loonies.'

'No,' said Mr Parker Pyne, 'there you misjudge me. Hannah Moorhouse is not in a lunatic asylum, because Hannah Moorhouse never existed.'

'Indeed?' said Mrs Rymer. 'And what about the photograph of her that I saw with my own eyes?'

'Faked,' said Mr Pyne. 'Quite a simple thing to manage.'

'And the piece in the paper about her?'

'The whole paper was faked so as to include two items in a natural manner which would carry conviction. As it did.'

'That rogue, Doctor Constantine!'

'An assumed name – assumed by a friend of mine with a talent for acting.'

Mrs Rymer snorted. 'Ho! And I wasn't hypnotized either, I suppose?'

'As a matter of fact, you were not. You drank in your coffee a preparation of Indian hemp. After that, other drugs were administered and you were brought down here by car and allowed to recover consciousness.'

'Then Mrs Gardner has been in it all the time?' said Mrs Rymer.

Mr Parker Pyne nodded.

'Bribed by you, I suppose! Or filled up with a lot of lies!'

'Mrs Gardner trusts me,' said Mr Pyne. 'I once saved her only son from penal servitude.'

Something in his manner silenced Mrs Rymer on that tack. 'What about the birthmark!' she demanded.

Mr Pyne smiled. 'It is already fading. In another six months it will have disappeared altogether.'

'And what's the meaning of all this tomfoolery? Making a fool of me, sticking me down here as a servant – me with all that good money in the bank. But I suppose I needn't ask. You've been helping yourself to it, my fine fellow. That's the meaning of all this.'

'It is true,' said Mr Parker Pyne, 'that I did obtain from you, while you were under the influence of drugs, a power of attorney and that during your – er – absence, I have assumed control of your financial affairs, but I can assure you, my dear madam, that apart from that original thousand pounds, no money of yours has found its way into my pocket.

As a matter of fact, by judicious investments your financial position is actually improved.' He beamed at her.

'Then why –?' began Mrs Rymer.

'I am going to ask you a question, Mrs Rymer,' said Mr Parker Pyne. 'You are an honest woman. You will answer me honestly, I know. I am going to ask you if you are happy.'

'Happy! That's a pretty question! Steal a woman's money and ask her if she's happy. I like your impudence!'

'You are still angry,' he said. 'Most natural. But leave my misdeeds out of it for the moment. Mrs Rymer, when you came to my office a year ago today, you were an unhappy woman. Will you tell me that you are unhappy now? If so, I apologize, and you are at liberty to take what steps you please against me. Moreover, I will refund the thousand pounds you paid me. Come, Mrs Rymer, are you an unhappy woman now?'

Mrs Rymer looked at Mr Parker Pyne, but she dropped her eyes when she spoke at last.

'No,' she said. 'I'm not unhappy.' A tone of wonder crept into her voice. 'You've got me there. I admit it. I've not been as happy as I am now since Abner died. I – I'm going to marry a man who works here – Joe Welsh. Our banns are going up next Sunday; that, is they *were* going up next Sunday.'

'But now, of course, everything is different.'

Mrs Rymer's face flamed. She took a step forward.

'What do you mean, different? Do you think that if I had all the money in the world it would make me a lady? I don't want to be a lady, thank you; a helpless good-for-nothing lot they are. Joe's good enough for me and I'm good enough for him. We suit each other and we're going to be happy. As you for, Mr Nosey Parker, you take yourself off and don't interfere with what doesn't concern you!'

Mr Parker Pyne took a paper from his pocket and handed it to her. 'The power of attorney,' he said. 'Shall I tear it up? You will assume control of your own fortune now, I take it.'

A strange expression came over Mrs Rymer's face. She thrust back the paper.

'Take it. I've said hard things to you – and some of them you deserved. You're a downy fellow, but all the same I trust you. Seven hundred pounds I'll have in the bank here – that'll buy us a farm we've got our eye on. The rest of it – well, let the hospitals have it.'

'You cannot mean to hand over your entire fortune to hospitals?'

'That's just what I do mean. Joe's a dear, good fellow, but he's weak. Give him money and you'd ruin him. I've got him off the drink now, and

I'll keep him off it. Thank God, I know my own mind. I'm not going to let money come between me and happiness.'

'You are a remarkable woman,' said Mr Pyne slowly. 'Only one woman in a thousand would act as you are doing.'

'Then only one woman in a thousand's got sense,' said Mrs Rymer.

'I take my hat off to you,' said Mr Parker Pyne, and there was an unusual note in his voice. He raised his hat with solemnity and moved away.

'And Joe's never to know, mind!' Mrs Rymer called after him.

She stood there with the dying sun behind her, a great blue-green cabbage in her hands, her head thrown back and her shoulders squared. A grand figure of a peasant woman, outlined against the setting sun . . .

Have You Got Everything You Want?

'Have You Got Everything You Want?' was first published in the USA in *Cosmopolitan*, April 1933, and then as 'On The Orient Express' in *Nash's Pall Mall*, June 1933.

'*Par ici, Madame.*'

A tall woman in a mink coat followed her heavily encumbered porter along the platform of the Gare de Lyon.

She wore a dark-brown knitted hat pulled down over one eye and ear. The other side revealed a charming tip-tilted profile and little golden curls clustering over a shell-like ear. Typically an American, she was altogether a very charming-looking creature and more than one man turned to look at her as she walked past the high carriages of the waiting train.

Large plates were stuck in holders on the sides of the carriages.

PARIS–ATHENES. PARIS–BUCHAREST. PARIS–STAMBOUL.

At the last named the porter came to an abrupt halt. He undid the strap which held the suitcases together and they slipped heavily to the ground. '*Voici, Madame.*'

The *wagon-lit* conductor was standing beside the steps. He came forward, remarking, '*Bonsoir, Madame,*' with an *empressement* perhaps due to the richness and perfection of the mink coat.

The woman handed him her sleeping-car ticket of flimsy paper.

'Number Six,' he said. 'This way.'

He sprang nimbly into the train, the woman following him. As she hurried down the corridor after him, she nearly collided with a portly gentleman who was emerging from the compartment next to hers. She had a momentary glimpse of a large bland face with benevolent eyes.

'*Voici, Madame.*'

The conductor displayed the compartment. He threw up the window and signalled to the porter. The lesser employee took in the baggage and put it up on the racks. The woman sat down.

Beside her on the seat she had placed a small scarlet case and her handbag. The carriage was hot, but it did not seem to occur to her to take off her coat. She stared out of the window with unseeing eyes. People were hurrying up and down the platform. There were sellers of newspapers, of pillows, of chocolate, of fruit, of mineral waters. They held up their wares to her, but her eyes looked blankly through them. The Gare de Lyon had faded from her sight. On her face were sadness and anxiety.

'If Madame will give me her passport?'

The words made no impression on her. The conductor, standing in the doorway, repeated them. Elsie Jeffries roused herself with a start.

'I beg your pardon?'

'Your passport, Madame.'

She opened her bag, took out the passport and gave it to him.

'That will be all right, Madame, I will attend to everything.' A slight significant pause. 'I shall be going with Madame as far as Stamboul.'

Elsie drew out a fifty-franc note and handed it to him. He accepted it in a business-like manner, and inquired when she would like her bed made up and whether she was taking dinner.

These matters settled, he withdrew and almost immediately the restaurant man came rushing down the corridor ringing his little bell frantically, and bawling out, '*Premier service. Premier service.*'

Elsie rose, divested herself of the heavy fur coat, took a brief glance at herself in the little mirror, and picking up her handbag and jewel case stepped out into the corridor. She had gone only a few steps when the restaurant man came rushing along on his return journey. To avoid him, Elsie stepped back for a moment into the doorway of the adjoining compartment, which was now empty. As the man passed and she prepared to continue her journey to the dining car, her glance fell idly on the label of a suitcase which was lying on the seat.

It was a stout pigskin case, somewhat worn. On the label were the words: 'J. Parker Pyne, passenger to Stamboul.' The suitcase itself bore the initials 'P.P.'

A startled expression came over the girl's face. She hesitated a moment in the corridor, then going back to her own compartment she picked up a copy of *The Times* which she had laid down on the table with some magazines and books.

She ran her eye down the advertisement columns on the front page, but what she was looking for was not there. A slight frown on her face, she made her way to the restaurant car.

The attendant allotted her a seat at a small table already tenanted by one person – the man with whom she had nearly collided in the corridor. In fact, the owner of the pigskin suitcase.

Elsie looked at him without appearing to do so. He seemed very bland, very benevolent, and in some way impossible to explain, delightfully reassuring. He behaved in reserved British fashion, and it was not until the fruit was on the table that he spoke.

'They keep these places terribly hot,' he said.

'I know,' said Elsie. 'I wish one could have the window open.'

He gave a rueful smile. 'Impossible! Every person present except ourselves would protest.'

She gave an answering smile. Neither said any more.

Coffee was brought and the usual indecipherable bill. Having laid some notes upon it, Elsie suddenly took her courage in both hands.

'Excuse me,' she murmured. 'I saw your name upon your suitcase – Parker Pyne. Are you – are you, by any chance –?'

She hesitated and he came quickly to her rescue.

'I believe I am. That is' – he quoted from the advertisement which Elsie had noticed more than once in *The Times*, and for which she had searched vainly just now: '"Are you happy? If not, consult Mr Parker Pyne." Yes, I'm that one, all right.'

'I see,' said Elsie. 'How – how extraordinary!'

He shook his head. 'Not really. Extraordinary from your point of view, but not from mine.' He smiled reassuringly, then leaned forward. Most of the other diners had left the car. 'So you are unhappy?' he said.

'I –' began Elsie, and stopped.

'You would not have said "How extraordinary" otherwise,' he pointed out.

Elsie was silent for a minute. She felt strangely soothed by the mere presence of Mr Parker Pyne. 'Ye – es,' she admitted at last. 'I am – unhappy. At least, I am worried.'

He nodded sympathetically.

'You see,' she continued, 'a very curious thing has happened – and I don't know the least what to make of it.'

'Suppose you tell me about it,' suggested Mr Pyne.

Elsie thought of the advertisement. She and Edward had often commented on it and laughed. She had never thought that she . . . perhaps she had better not . . . if Mr Parker Pyne were a charlatan . . . but he looked – nice!

Elsie made her decision. Anything to get this worry off her mind.

'I'll tell you. I'm going to Constantinople to join my husband. He does a lot of Oriental business, and this year he found it necessary to go there. He went a fortnight ago. He was to get things ready for me to join him. I've been very excited at the thought of it. You see, I've never been abroad before. We've been in England six months.'

'You and your husband are both American?'

'Yes.'

'And you have not, perhaps, been married very long?'

'We've been married a year and a half.'

'Happily?'

'Oh, yes! Edward's a perfect angel.' She hesitated. 'Not, perhaps, very much go to him. Just a little – well, I'd call it straightlaced. Lot of puritan ancestry and all that. But he's a *dear*,' she added hastily.

Mr Parker Pyne looked at her thoughtfully for a moment or two, then he said, 'Go on.'

'It was about a week after Edward had started. I was writing a letter in his study, and I noticed that the blotting paper was all new and clean, except for a few lines of writing across it. I'd just been reading a detective story with a clue in the blotter and so, just for fun, I held it up to a mirror. It really *was* just fun, Mr Pyne – I mean, he's such a mild lamb one wouldn't dream of anything of that kind.'

'Yes, yes; I quite understand.'

'The thing was quite easy to read. First there was the word "wife" then "Simplon Express", and lower down, "just before Venice would be the best time",' She stopped.

'Curious,' said Mr Pyne. 'Distinctly curious. It was your husband's handwriting?'

'Oh, yes. But I've cudgelled my brains and I cannot see under what circumstances he would write a letter with just those words in it.'

'"Just before Venice would be the best time",' repeated Mr Parker Pyne. 'Distinctly curious.'

Mrs Jeffries was leaning forward looking at him with a flattering hopefulness. 'What shall I do?' she asked simply.

'I am afraid,' said Mr Parker Pyne, 'that we shall have to wait until before Venice.' He took up a folder from the table. 'Here is the schedule time of our train. It arrives at Venice at two twenty-seven tomorrow afternoon.'

They looked at each other.

'Leave it to me,' said Parker Pyne.

It was five minutes past two. The Simplon Express was eleven minutes late. It had passed Mestre about a quarter of an hour before.

Mr Parker Pyne was sitting with Mrs Jeffries in her compartment. So far the journey had been pleasant and uneventful. But now the moment had arrived when, if anything was going to happen, it presumably would happen. Mr Parker Pyne and Elsie faced each other. Her heart was beating fast, and her eyes sought him in a kind of anguished appeal for reassurance.

'Keep perfectly calm,' he said. 'You are quite safe. I am here.'

Suddenly a scream broke out from the corridor.

'Oh, look – look! The train is on fire!'

With a bound Elsie and Mr Parker Pyne were in the corridor. An agitated woman with a Slav countenance was pointing a dramatic finger. Out of one of the front compartments smoke was pouring in a cloud. Mr Parker Pyne and Elsie ran along the corridor. Others joined them. The compartment in question was full of smoke. The first comers drew back, coughing. The conductor appeared.

'The compartment is empty!' he cried. 'Do not alarm yourselves, *messieurs et dames. Le feu*, it will be controlled.'

A dozen excited questions and answers broke out. The train was running over the bridge that joins Venice to the mainland.

Suddenly Mr Parker Pyne turned, forced his way through the little pack of people behind him and hurried down the corridor to Elsie's compartment. The lady with the Slav face was seated in it, drawing deep breaths from the open window.

'Excuse me, Madame,' said Parker Pyne. 'But this is not your compartment.'

'I know. I know,' said the Slav lady. '*Pardon*. It is the shock, the emotion – my heart.' She sank back on the seat and indicated the open window. She drew in her breath in great gasps.

Mr Parker Pyne stood in the doorway. His voice was fatherly and reassuring. 'You must not be afraid,' he said. 'I do not think for a moment the fire is serious.'

'Not? Ah, what a mercy! I feel restored.' She half-rose. 'I will return to my compartment.'

'Not just yet.' Mr Parker Pyne's hand pressed her gently back. 'I will ask you to wait a moment, Madame.'

'Monsieur, this is an outrage!'

'Madame, you will remain.'

His voice rang out coldly. The woman sat still looking at him. Elsie joined them.

'It seems it was a smoke bomb,' she said breathlessly. 'Some ridiculous practical joke. The conductor is furious. He is asking everybody –' She broke off, staring at the second occupant of the carriage.

'Mrs Jeffries,' said Mr Parker Pyne, 'what do you carry in your little scarlet case?'

'My jewellery.'

'Perhaps you would be so kind as to look and see that everything is there.'

There was immediately a torrent of words from the Slav lady. She broke into French, the better to do justice to her feelings.

In the meantime Elsie had picked up the jewel case. 'Oh!' she cried. 'It's unlocked.'

'*Et je porterai plainte à la Compagnie des Wagons-Lits,*' finished the Slav lady.

'They're gone!' cried Elsie. 'Everything! My diamond bracelet. And the necklace Pop gave me. And the emerald and ruby rings. And some lovely diamond brooches. Thank goodness I was wearing my pearls. Oh, Mr Pyne, what shall we do?'

'If you will fetch the conductor,' said Mr Parker Pyne, 'I will see that this woman does not leave this compartment till he comes.'

'*Scélérat! Monstre!*' shrieked the Slav lady. She went on to further insults. The train drew in to Venice.

The events of the next half-hour may be briefly summarized. Mr Parker Pyne dealt with several different officials in several different languages – and suffered defeat. The suspected lady consented to be searched – and emerged without a stain on her character. The jewels were not on her.

Between Venice and Trieste Mr Parker Pyne and Elsie discussed the case.

'When was the last time you actually saw your jewels?'

'This morning. I put away some sapphire earrings I was wearing yesterday and took out a pair of plain pearl ones.'

'And all the jewellery was there intact?'

'Well, I didn't go through it all, naturally. But it looked the same as usual. A ring or something like that might have been missing, but no more.'

Mr Parker Pyne nodded. 'Now, when the conductor made up the compartment this morning?'

'I had the case with me – in the restaurant car. I always take it with me. I've never left it except when I ran out just now.'

'Therefore,' said Mr Parker Pyne, 'that injured innocent, Madame Subayska, or whatever she calls herself, *must* have been the thief. But what the devil did she do with the things? She was only in here a minute and a half – just time to open the case with a duplicate key and take out the stuff – yes, but what next?'

'Could she have handed them to anyone else?'

'Hardly. I had turned back and was forcing my way along the corridor. If anyone had come out of this compartment I should have seen them.'

'Perhaps she threw them out of the window to someone.'

'An excellent suggestion; only, as it happens, we were passing over the sea at that moment. We were on the bridge.'

'Then she must have hidden them actually in the carriage.'

'Let's hunt for them.'

With true transatlantic energy Elsie began to look about. Mr Parker Pyne participated in the search in a somewhat absent fashion. Reproached for not trying, he excused himself.

'I'm thinking that I must send a rather important telegram at Trieste,' he explained.

Elsie received the explanation coldly. Mr Parker Pyne had fallen heavily in her estimation.

'I'm afraid you're annoyed with me, Mrs Jeffries,' he said meekly.

'Well, you've not been very successful,' she retorted.

'But, my dear lady, you must remember I am not a detective. Theft and crime are not in my line at all. The human heart is my province.'

'Well, I was a bit unhappy when I got on this train,' said Elsie, 'but nothing to what I am now! I could just cry buckets. My lovely, lovely bracelet – and the emerald ring Edward gave me when we were engaged.'

'But surely you are insured against theft?' Mr Parker Pyne interpolated.

'Am I? I don't know. Yes, I suppose I am. But it's the *sentiment* of the thing, Mr Pyne.'

The train slackened speed. Mr Parker Pyne peered out of the window. 'Trieste,' he said. 'I must send my telegram.'

'Edward!' Elsie's face lighted up as she saw her husband hurrying to meet her on the platform at Stamboul. For the moment even the loss of her jewellery faded from her mind. She forgot the curious words she had found on the blotter. She forgot everything except that it was a fortnight since she had seen her husband last, and that in spite of being sober and straightlaced he was really a most attractive person.

They were just leaving the station when Elsie felt a friendly tap on the shoulder and turned to see Mr Parker Pyne. His bland face was beaming good-naturedly.

'Mrs Jeffries,' he said, 'will you come to see me at the Hotel Tokatlian in half an hour? I think I may have some good news for you.'

Elsie looked uncertainly at Edward. Then she made the introduction. 'This – er – is my husband – Mr Parker Pyne.'

'As I believe your wife wired you, her jewels have been stolen,' said

Mr Parker Pyne. 'I have been doing what I can to help her recover them. I think I may have news for her in about half an hour.'

Elsie looked enquiringly at Edward. He replied promptly: 'You'd better go, dear. The Tokatlian, you said, Mr Pyne? Right; I'll see she makes it.'

It was just a half an hour later that Elsie was shown into Mr Parker Pyne's private sitting room. He rose to receive her.

'You've been disappointed in me, Mrs Jeffries,' he said. 'Now, don't deny it. Well, I don't pretend to be a magician but I do what I can. Take a look inside here.'

He passed along the table a small stout cardboard box. Elsie opened it. Rings, brooches, bracelets, necklace – they were all there.

'Mr Pyne, how marvellous! How – how too wonderful!'

Mr Parker Pyne smiled modestly. 'I am glad not to have failed you, my dear young lady.'

'Oh, Mr Pyne, you make me feel just mean! Ever since Trieste I've been horrid to you. And now – this. But how did you get hold of them? When? Where?'

Mr Parker Pyne shook his head thoughtfully. 'It's a long story,' he said. 'You may hear it one day. In fact, you may hear it quite soon.'

'Why can't I hear it now?'

'There are reasons,' said Mr Parker Pyne.

And Elsie had to depart with her curiosity unsatisfied.

When she had gone, Mr Parker Pyne took up his hat and stick and went out into the streets of Pera. He walked along smiling to himself, coming at last to a little café, deserted at the moment, which overlooked the Golden Horn. On the other side, the mosques of Stamboul showed slender minarets against the afternoon sky. It was very beautiful. Mr Pyne sat down and ordered two coffees. They came thick and sweet. He had just begun to sip his when a man slipped into the seat opposite. It was Edward Jeffries.

'I have ordered some coffee for you,' said Mr Parker Pyne, indicating the little cup.

Edward pushed the coffee aside. He leaned forward across the table. 'How did you know?' he asked.

Mr Parker Pyne sipped his coffee dreamily. 'Your wife will have told you about her discovery on the blotter? No? Oh, but she will tell you; it has slipped her mind for the moment.'

He mentioned Elsie's discovery.

'Very well; that linked up perfectly with the curious incident that happened just before Venice. For some reason or other you were engineering the theft of your wife's jewels. But why the phrase "just before Venice would be the best time"? There seemed nonsense in that. Why did you not leave it to your – agent – to choose her own time and place?

'And then, suddenly, I saw the point. *Your wife's jewels were stolen before you yourself left London and were replaced by paste duplicates.* But that solution did not satisfy you. You were a high-minded, conscientious young man. You have a horror of some servant or other innocent person being suspected. A theft must actually occur – at a place and in a manner which will leave no suspicion attached to anybody of your acquaintance or household.

'Your accomplice is provided with a key to the jewel box and a smoke bomb. At the correct moment she gives the alarm, darts into your wife's compartment, unlocks the jewel case and flings the paste duplicates into the sea. She may be suspected and searched, but nothing can be proved against her, since the jewels are not in her possession.

'And now the significance of the place chosen becomes apparent. If the jewels had merely been thrown out by the side of the line, they might have been found. Hence the importance of the one moment when the train is passing over the sea.

'In the meantime, you make your arrangements for selling the jewellery here. You have only to hand over the stones when the robbery has actually taken place. My wire, however, reached you in time. You obeyed my instructions and deposited the box of jewellery at the Tokatlian to await my arrival, knowing that otherwise I should keep my threat of placing the matter in the hands of the police. You also obeyed my instructions in joining me here.'

Edward Jeffries looked at Mr Parker Pyne appealingly. He was a good-looking young man, tall and fair, with a round chin and very round eyes. 'How can I make you understand?' he said hopelessly. 'To you I must seem just a common thief.'

'Not at all,' said Mr Parker Pyne. 'On the contrary, I should say you are almost painfully honest. I am accustomed to the classification of types. You, my dear sir, fall naturally into the category of victims. Now, tell me the whole story.'

'I can tell you in one word – blackmail.'

'Yes?'

'You've seen my wife: you realize what a pure, innocent creature she is – without knowledge or thought of evil.'

'Yes, yes.'

'She has the most marvellously pure ideals. If she were to find out about – about anything I had done, she would leave me.'

'I wonder. But that is not the point. What *have* you done, my young friend? I presume there is some affair with a woman?'

Edward Jeffries nodded.

'Since your marriage – or before?'

'Before – oh, before.'

'Well, well, what happened?'

'Nothing, nothing at all. This is just the cruel part of it. It was at a hotel in the West Indies. There was a very attractive woman – a Mrs Rossiter – staying there. Her husband was a violent man; he had the most savage fits of temper. One night he threatened her with a revolver. She escaped from him and came to my room. She was half-crazy with terror. She – she asked me to let her stay there till morning. I – what else could I do?'

Mr Parker Pyne gazed at the young man, and the young man gazed back with conscious rectitude. Mr Parker Pyne sighed. 'In other words, to put it plainly, you were had for a mug, Mr Jeffries.'

'Really –'

'Yes, yes. A very old trick – but it often comes off successfully with quixotic young men. I suppose, when your approaching marriage was announced, the screw was turned?'

'Yes. I received a letter. If I did not send a certain sum of money, everything would be disclosed to my prospective father-in-law. How I had – had alienated this young woman's affection from her husband; how she had been seen coming to my room. The husband would bring a suit for divorce. Really, Mr Pyne, the whole thing made me out the most utter blackguard.'

He wiped his brow in a harassed manner.

'Yes, yes, I know. And so you paid. And from time to time the screw has been put on again.'

'Yes. This was the last straw. Our business has been badly hit by the slump. I simply could not lay my hands on any ready money. I hit upon this plan.' He picked up his cup of cold coffee, looked at it absently, and drank it. 'What am I to do now?' he demanded pathetically. 'What *am* I to do, Mr Pyne?'

'You will be guided by me,' said Parker Pyne firmly. 'I will deal with your tormentors. As to your wife, you will go straight back to her and tell her the truth – or at least a portion of it. The only point where you will deviate from the truth is concerning the actual facts in the West Indies. You must conceal from her the fact that you were – well, had for a mug, as I said before.'

'But –'

'My dear Mr Jeffries, you do not understand women. If a woman has to choose between a mug and a Don Juan, she will choose Don Juan every time. Your wife, Mr Jeffries, is a charming, innocent, high-minded girl, and the only way she is going to get any kick out of her life with you is to believe that she has reformed a rake.'

Edward Jeffries was staring at him, open-mouthed.

'I mean what I say,' said Mr Parker Pyne. 'At the present moment your wife is in love with you, but I see signs that she may not remain so if you continue to present to her a picture of such goodness and rectitude that it is almost synonymous with dullness.'

'Go to her, my boy,' said Mr Parker Pyne kindly. 'Confess everything – that is, as many things as you can think of. Then explain that from the moment you met her you gave up all this life. You even stole so that it might not come to her ears. She will forgive you enthusiastically.'

'But when there's nothing really to forgive –'

'What is truth?' said Mr Parker Pyne. 'In my experience it is usually the thing that upsets the apple cart! It is a fundamental axiom of married life that you *must* lie to a woman. She likes it! Go and be forgiven, my boy. And live happily ever afterwards. I dare say your wife will keep a wary eye on you in future whenever a pretty woman comes along – some men would mind that, but I don't think you will.'

'I never want to look at any other woman but Elsie,' said Mr Jeffries simply.

'Splendid, my boy,' said Mr Parker Pyne. 'But I shouldn't let her know that if I were you. No woman likes to feel she's taken on too soft a job.'

Edward Jeffries rose. 'You really think –?'

'I *know*,' said Mr Parker Pyne, with force.

The Gate of Baghdad

'The Gate of Baghdad' was first published as
'At the Gate of Baghdad' in *Nash's Pall Mall*, June 1933.

'Four great gates has the city of Damascus . . .'

Mr Parker Pyne repeated Flecker's lines softly to himself.

'Postern of Fate, the Desert Gate, Disaster's Cavern, Fort of Fear,
The Portal of Baghdad am I, the Doorway of Diarbekir.'

He was standing in the streets of Damascus and drawn up outside the
Oriental Hotel he saw one of the huge six-wheeled Pullmans that was to
transport him and eleven other people across the desert to Baghdad on
the morrow.

'Pass not beneath, O Caravan, or pass not singing. Have you heard
That silence where the birds are dead yet something pipeth like a bird?
Pass out beneath, O Caravan, Doom's Caravan, Death's Caravan!'

Something of a contrast now. Formerly the Gate of Baghdad *had* been
the gate of Death. Four hundred miles of desert to traverse by caravan.
Long weary months of travel. Now the ubiquitous petrol-fed monsters
did the journey in thirty-six hours.

'What were you saying, Mr Parker Pyne?'

It was the eager voice of Miss Netta Pryce, youngest and most charming
of the tourist race. Though encumbered by a stern aunt with the suspicion
of a beard and a thirst for Biblical knowledge, Netta managed to enjoy
herself in many frivolous ways of which the elder Miss Pryce might
possibly have not approved.

Mr Parker Pyne repeated Flecker's lines to her.

'How thrilling,' said Netta.

Three men in Air Force uniform were standing near and one of them, an admirer of Netta's, struck in.

'There are still thrills to be got out of the journey,' he said. 'Even nowadays the convoy is occasionally shot up by bandits. Then there's losing yourself – that happens sometimes. And we are sent out to find you. One fellow was lost for five days in the desert. Luckily he had plenty of water with him. Then there are the bumps. Some bumps! One man was killed. It's the truth I'm telling you! He was asleep and his head struck the top of the car and it killed him.'

'In the six-wheeler, Mr O'Rourke?' demanded the elder Miss Pryce.

'No – not in the six-wheeler,' admitted the young man.

'But we must do some sight-seeing,' cried Netta.

Her aunt drew out a guide book.

Netta edged away.

'I know she'll want me to go to some place where St Paul was lowered out of a window,' she whispered. 'And I do so want to see the bazaars.'

O'Rourke responded promptly.

'Come with me. We'll start down the Street called Straight –'

They drifted off.

Mr Parker Pyne turned to a quiet man standing beside him, Hensley by name. He belonged to the public works department of Baghdad.

'Damascus is a little disappointing when one sees it for the first time,' he said apologetically. 'A little civilized. Trams and modern houses and shops.'

Hensley nodded. He was a man of few words.

'Not got – back of beyond – when you think you have,' he jerked out.

Another man drifted up, a fair young man wearing an old Etonian tie. He had an amiable but slightly vacant face which at the moment looked worried. He and Hensley were in the same department.

'Hello, Smethurst,' said his friend. 'Lost anything?'

Captain Smethurst shook his head. He was a young man of somewhat slow intellect.

'Just looking round,' he said vaguely. Then he seemed to rouse himself. 'Ought to have a beano tonight. What?'

The two friends went off together. Mr Parker Pyne bought a local paper printed in French.

He did not find it very interesting. The local news meant nothing to him and nothing of importance seemed to be going on elsewhere. He found a few paragraphs headed *Londres*.

The first referred to financial matters. The second dealt with the supposed destination of Mr Samuel Long, the defaulting financier. His defalcations now amounted to the sum of three millions and it was rumoured that he had reached South America.

'Not too bad for a man just turned thirty,' said Mr Parker Pyne to himself.

'I beg your pardon?'

Parker Pyne turned to confront an Italian General who had been on the same boat with him from Brindisi to Beirut.

Mr Parker Pyne explained his remark. The Italian General nodded his head several times.

'He is a great criminal, that man. Even in Italy we have suffered. He inspired confidence all over the world. He is a man of breeding, too, they say.'

'Well, he went to Eton and Oxford,' said Mr Parker Pyne cautiously.

'Will he be caught, do you think?'

'Depends on how much of a start he got. He may be still in England. He may be – anywhere.'

'Here with us?' the General laughed.

'Possibly.' Mr Parker Pyne remained serious. 'For all you know, General, *I* may be he.'

The General gave him a startled glance. Then his olive-brown face relaxed into a smile of comprehension.

'Oh! That is very good – very good indeed. But you –'

His eyes strayed downwards from Mr Parker Pyne's face.

Mr Parker Pyne interpreted the glance correctly.

'You mustn't judge by appearances,' he said. 'A little additional – er – *embonpoint* – is easily managed and has a remarkably ageing effect.'

He added dreamily:

'Then there is hair dye, of course, and face stain, and even a change of nationality.'

General Poli withdrew doubtfully. He never knew how far the English were serious.

Mr Parker Pyne amused himself that evening by going to a cinema. Afterwards he was directed to a 'Nightly Palace of Gaieties'. It appeared to him to be neither a palace nor gay. Various ladies danced with a distinct lack of *verve*. The applause was languid.

Suddenly Mr Parker Pyne caught sight of Smethurst. The young man was sitting at a table alone. His face was flushed and it occurred to Mr Parker Pyne that he had already drunk more than was good for him. He went across and joined the young man.

'Disgraceful, the way these girls treat you,' said Captain Smethurst gloomily. 'Bought her two drinks – three drinks – lots of drinks. Then she goes off laughing with some dago. Call it a disgrace.'

Mr Parker Pyne sympathized. He suggested coffee.

'Got some *araq* coming,' said Smethurst. 'Jolly good stuff. You try it.'

Mr Parker Pyne knew something of the properties of araq. He employed tact. Smethurst, however, shook his head.

'I'm in a bit of a mess,' he said. 'Got to cheer myself up. Don't know what you'd do in my place. Don't like to go back on a pal, what? I mean to say – and yet – what's a fellow to do?'

He studied Mr Parker Pyne as though noticing him for the first time.

'Who are you?' he demanded with the curtness born of his potations. 'What do you do?'

'The confidence trick,' said Mr Parker Pyne gently.

Smethurst gazed at him in lively concern.

'What – you too?'

Mr Parker Pyne drew from his wallet a cutting. He laid it on the table in front of Smethurst.

'*Are you unhappy?*' (So it ran.) *If so, consult Mr Parker Pyne.*'

Smethurst focused on it after some difficulty.

'Well, I'm damned,' he ejaculated. 'You meantersay – people come and tell you things?'

'They confide in me – yes.'

'Pack of idiotic women, I suppose.'

'A good many women,' admitted Mr Parker Pyne. 'But men also. What about you, my young friend? You wanted advice just now?'

'Shut your damned head,' said Captain Smethurst. 'No business of anybody's – anybody's 'cept mine. Where's that goddamed *araq*?'

Mr Parker Pyne shook his head sadly.

He gave up Captain Smethurst as a bad job.

The convoy for Baghdad started at seven o'clock in the morning. There was a party of twelve. Mr Parker Pyne and General Poli, Miss Pryce and her niece, three Air Force officers, Smethurst and Hensley and an Armenian mother and son by name Pentemian.

The journey started uneventfully. The fruit trees of Damascus were soon left behind. The sky was cloudy and the young driver looked at it doubtfully once or twice. He exchanged remarks with Hensley.

'Been raining a good bit the other side of Rutbah. Hope we shan't stick.'

They made a halt at midday and square cardboard boxes of lunch were handed round. The two drivers brewed tea which was served in cardboard cups. They drove on again across the flat interminable plain.

Mr Parker Pyne thought of the slow caravans and the weeks of journeying . . .

Just at sunset they came to the desert fort of Rutbah.

The great gates were unbarred and the six-wheeler drove in through them into the inner courtyard of the fort.

'This feels exciting,' said Netta.

After a wash she was eager for a short walk. Flight-Lieutenant O'Rourke and Mr Parker Pyne offered themselves as escorts. As they started the manager came up to them and begged them not to go far away as it might be difficult to find their way back after dark.

'We'll only go a short way,' O'Rourke promised.

Walking was not, indeed, very interesting owing to the sameness of the surroundings.

Once Mr Parker Pyne bent and picked something up.

'What is it?' asked Netta curiously.

He held it out to her.

'A prehistoric flint, Miss Pryce – a borer.'

'Did they – kill each other with them?'

'No – it had a more peaceful use. But I expect they could have killed with it if they'd wanted to. It's the *wish* to kill that counts – the mere instrument doesn't matter. *Something* can always be found.'

It was getting dark, and they ran back to the fort.

After a dinner of many courses of the tinned variety they sat and smoked. At twelve o'clock the six-wheeler was to proceed.

The driver looked anxious.

'Some bad patches near here,' he said. 'We may stick.' They all climbed into the big car and settled themselves. Miss Pryce was annoyed not to be able to get at one of her suitcases.

'I should like my bedroom slippers,' she said.

'More likely to need your gum boots,' said Smethurst. 'If I know the look of things we'll be stuck in a sea of mud.'

'I haven't even got a change of stockings,' said Netta.

'That's all right. You'll stay put. Only the stronger sex has to get out and heave.'

'Always carry spare socks,' said Hensley, patting his overcoat pocket. 'Never know.'

The lights were turned out. The big car started out into the night.

The going was not too good. They were not jolted as they would have been in a touring car, but nevertheless they got a bad bump now and then.

Mr Parker Pyne had one of the front seats. Across the aisle was the Armenian lady shrouded in wraps and shawls. Her son was behind her.

Behind Mr Parker Pyne were the two Miss Pryces. The General, Smethurst, Hensley and the R.A.F. men were at the back.

The car rushed on through the night. Mr Parker Pyne found it hard to sleep. His position was cramped. The Armenian lady's feet stuck out and encroached on his preserve. She, at any rate, was comfortable.

Everyone else seemed to be asleep. Mr Parker Pyne felt drowsiness stealing over him, when a sudden jolt threw him towards the roof of the car. He heard a drowsy protest from the back of the six-wheeler. 'Steady. Want to break our necks?'

Then the drowsiness returned. A few minutes later, his neck sagging uncomfortably, Mr Parker Pyne slept . . .

He was awakened suddenly. The six-wheeler had stopped. Some of the men were getting out. Hensley spoke briefly.

'We're stuck.'

Anxious to see all there was to see, Mr Parker Pyne stepped gingerly out in the mud. It was not raining now. Indeed there was a moon and by its light the drivers could be seen frantically at work with jacks and stones, striving to raise the wheels. Most of the men were helping. From the windows of the six-wheeler the three women looked out. Miss Pryce and Netta with interest, the Armenian lady with ill-concealed disgust.

At a command from the driver, the male passengers obediently heaved.

'Where's that Armenian fellow?' demanded O'Rourke. 'Keeping his toes warmed and comfortable like a cat? Let's have him out too.'

'Captain Smethurst too,' observed General Poli. 'He is not with us.'

'The blighter's asleep still. Look at him.'

True enough, Smethurst still sat in his armchair, his head sagging forward and his whole body slumped down.

'I'll rouse him,' said O'Rourke.

He sprang in through the door. A minute later he reappeared. His voice had changed.

'I say. I think he's ill – or something. Where's the doctor?'

Squadron Leader Loftus, the Air Force doctor, a quiet-looking man with greying hair, detached himself from the group at the wheel.

'What's the matter with him?' he asked.

'I – don't know.'

The doctor entered the car. O'Rourke and Parker Pyne followed him. He bent over the sagging figure. One look and touch was enough.

'He's dead,' he said quietly.

'Dead? But how?' Questions shot out. 'Oh! How dreadful!' from Netta. Loftus turned round in an irritated manner.

'Must have hit his head against the top,' he said. 'We went over one bad bump.'

'Surely that wouldn't kill him? Isn't there anything else?'

'I can't tell you unless I examine him properly,' snapped Loftus. He looked around him with a harassed air. The women were pressing closer. The men outside were beginning to crowd in.

Mr Parker Pyne spoke to the driver. He was a strong athletic young man. He lifted each female passenger in turn, carrying her across the mud and setting her down on dry land. Madame Pentemian and Netta he managed easily, but he staggered under the weight of the hefty Miss Pryce.

The interior of the six-wheeler was left clear for the doctor to make his examination.

The men went back to their efforts to jack up the car. Presently the sun rose over the horizon. It was a glorious day. The mud was drying rapidly, but the car was still stuck. Three jacks had been broken and so far no efforts had been of any avail. The driver started preparing break-fast – opening tins of sausages and boiling tea.

A little way apart Squadron Leader Loftus was giving his verdict.

'There's no mark or wound on him. As I said, he must have hit his head against the top.'

'You're satisfied he died naturally?' asked Mr Parker Pyne.

There was something in his voice that made the doctor look at him quickly.

'There's only one other possibility.'

'Yes.'

'Well, that someone hit him on the back of the head with something in the nature of a sandbag.' His voice sounded apologetic.

'That's not very likely,' said Williamson, the other Air Force officer. He was a cherubic-looking youth. 'I mean, nobody could do that without our seeing.'

'If we were asleep,' suggested the doctor.

'Fellow couldn't be sure of that,' pointed out the other.

'Getting up and all that would have roused someone or other.'

'The only way,' said General Poli, 'would be for anyone sitting behind him. He could choose his moment and need not even rise from his seat.'

'Who was sitting behind Captain Smethurst?' asked the doctor.

O'Rourke replied readily.

'Hensley, sir – so that's no good. Hensley was Smethurst's best pal.'

There was a silence. Then Mr Parker Pyne's voice rose with quiet certainty.

'I think,' he said, 'that Flight Lieutenant Williamson has something to tell us.'

'I, sir? I – well –'

'Out with it, Williamson,' said O'Rourke.

'It's nothing, really – nothing at all.'

'Out with it.'

'It's only a scrap of conversation I overheard – at Rutbah – in the courtyard. I'd got back into the six-wheeler to look for my cigarette case. I was hunting about. Two fellows were just outside talking. One of them was Smethurst. He was saying –'

He paused.

'Come on, man, out with it.'

'Something about not wanting to let a pal down. He sounded very distressed. Then he said: "I'll hold my tongue till Baghdad – but not a minute afterwards. You'll have to get out quickly".'

'And the other man?'

'I don't know sir. I swear I don't. It was dark and he only said a word or two and that I couldn't catch.'

'Who amongst you knows Smethurst well?'

'I don't think the words – a pal – could refer to anyone but Hensley,' said O'Rourke slowly. 'I knew Smethurst, but very slightly. Williamson is new out – so is Squadron Leader Loftus. I don't think either of them have ever met him before.'

Both men agreed.

'You, General?'

'I never saw the young man until we crossed the Lebanon in the same car from Beirut.'

'And that Armenian rat?'

'He couldn't be a pal,' said O'Rourke with decision. 'And no Armenian would have the nerve to kill anyone.'

'I have, perhaps, a small additional piece of evidence,' said Mr Parker Pyne.

He repeated the conversation he had had with Smethurst in the café at Damascus.

'He made use of the phrase – "don't like to go back on a pal," said O'Rourke thoughtfully. 'And he was worried.'

'Has no one else anything to add?' asked Mr Parker Pyne.

The doctor coughed.

'It may have nothing to do with –' he began.

He was encouraged.

'It was just that I heard Smethurst say to Hensley, "You can't deny that there is a leakage in your department".'

'When was this?'

'Just before starting from Damascus yesterday morning. I thought they were just talking shop. I didn't imagine –' He stopped.

'My friends, this is interesting,' said the General. 'Piece by piece you assemble the evidence.'

'You said a sandbag, doctor,' said Mr Parker Pyne. 'Could a man manufacture such a weapon?'

'Plenty of sand,' said the doctor drily. He took some up in his hand as he spoke.

'If you put some in a sock,' began O'Rourke and hesitated.

Everyone remembered the two short sentences spoken by Hensley the night before.

'*Always carry spare socks. Never know.*'

There was a silence. Then Mr Parker Pyne said quietly, 'Squadron Leader Loftus. I believe Mr Hensley's spare socks are in the pocket of his overcoat which is now in the car.'

Their eyes went for one minute to where a moody figure was pacing to and fro on the horizon. Hensley had held aloof since the discovery of the dead man. His wish for solitude had been respected since it was known that he and the dead man had been friends.

'Will you get them and bring them here?'

The doctor hesitated.

'I don't like –' he muttered. He looked again at that pacing figure. 'Seems a bit low down –'

'You must get them, please,' said Mr Parker Pyne.

'The circumstances are unusual. We are marooned here. And we have got to know the truth. If you will fetch those socks I fancy we shall be a step nearer.'

Loftus turned away obediently.

Mr Parker Pyne drew General Poli a little aside.

'General, I think it was you who sat across the aisle from Captain Smethurst.'

'That is so.'

'Did anyone get up and pass down the car?'

'Only the English lady, Miss Pryce. She went to the wash place at the back.'

'Did she stumble at all?'

'She lurched with the movement of the car, naturally.'

'She was the only person you saw moving about?'

'Yes.'

The General looked at him curiously and said, 'Who are you, I wonder? You take command, yet you are not a soldier.'

'I have seen a good deal of life,' said Mr Parker Pyne.

'You have travelled, eh?'

'No,' said Mr Parker Pyne. 'I have sat in an office.'

Loftus returned carrying the socks. Mr Parker Pyne took them from him and examined them. *To the inside of one of them wet sand still adhered.*

Mr Parker Pyne drew a deep breath.

'Now I know,' he said.

All their eyes went to the pacing figure on the horizon.

'I should like to look at the body if I may,' said Mr Parker Pyne.

He went with the doctor to where Smethurst's body had been laid down covered with a tarpaulin.

The doctor removed the cover.

'There's nothing to see,' he said.

But Mr Parker Pyne's eyes were fixed on the dead man's tie.

'So Smethurst was an old Etonian,' he said.

Loftus looked surprised.

Then Mr Parker Pyne surprised him still further.

'What do you know of young Williamson?' he asked.

'Nothing at all. I only met him at Beirut. I'd come from Egypt. But why? Surely –?'

'Well, it's on his evidence we're going to hang a man, isn't it?' said Mr Parker Pyne cheerfully. 'One's got to be careful.'

He still seemed to be interested in the dead man's tie and collar. He unfastened the studs and removed the collar. Then he uttered an exclamation.

'See that?'

On the back of the collar was a small round bloodstain.

He peered closer down at the uncovered neck.

'This man wasn't killed by a blow on the head, doctor,' he said briskly. 'He was stabbed – at the base of the skull. You can just see the tiny puncture.'

'And I missed it!'

'You'd got your preconceived notion,' said Mr Parker Pyne apologetically. 'A blow on the head. It's easy enough to miss this. You can hardly see the wound. A quick stab with a small sharp instrument and death would be instantaneous. The victim wouldn't even cry out.'

'Do you mean a stiletto? You think the General –?'

'Italians and stilettos go together in the popular fancy – Hallo, here comes a car!'

A touring car appeared over the horizon.

'Good,' said O'Rourke as he came up to join them. 'The ladies can go on in that.'

'What about our murderer?' asked Mr Parker Pyne.

'You mean Hensley –?'

'No, I don't mean Hensley,' said Mr Parker Pyne. 'I happen to know that Hensley's innocent.'

'You – but why?'

'Well, you see, he had sand in his sock.'

O'Rourke stared.

'I know my boy,' said Mr Parker Pyne gently, 'it doesn't sound like sense, but it is. Smethurst wasn't hit on the head, you see, he was stabbed.'

He paused a minute and then went on.

'Just cast your mind back to the conversation I told you about – the conversation we had in the café. You picked out what was, to you, the significant phrase. But it was another phrase that struck me. When I said to him that I did the Confidence Trick he said, "*What, you too?*" Doesn't that strike you as rather curious? I don't know that you'd describe a series of peculations from a Department as a "Confidence Trick". Confidence Trick is more descriptive of someone like the absconding Mr Samuel Long, for instance.'

The doctor started. O'Rourke said: 'Yes – perhaps . . .'

'I said in jest that perhaps the absconding Mr Long was one of our party. Suppose that this is the truth.'

'What – but it's impossible!'

'Not at all. What do you know of people besides their passports and the accounts they give of themselves. Am I really Mr Parker Pyne? Is General Poli really an Italian General? And what of the masculine Miss Pryce senior who needs a shave most distinctly.'

'But he – but Smethurst – didn't know Long?'

'Smethurst is an old Etonian. Long also, was at Eton. Smethurst may have known him although he didn't tell you so. He may have recognized him amongst us. And if so, what is he to do? He has a simple mind, and he worries over the matter. He decides at last to say nothing until Baghdad is reached. But after that he will hold his tongue no longer.'

'You think one of *us* is Long,' said O'Rourke, still dazed.

He drew a deep breath.

'It must be the Italian fellow – it *must* . . . or what about the Armenian?'

'To make up as a foreigner and to get a foreign passport is really much more difficult than to remain English,' said Mr Parker Pyne.

'Miss Pryce?' said O'Rourke incredulously.

'No,' said Mr Parker Pyne. '*This* is our man!'

He laid what seemed an almost friendly hand on the shoulder of the man beside him. But there was nothing friendly in his voice, and the fingers were vice-like in their grip.

'Squadron Leader Loftus or Mr Samuel Long, it doesn't matter what you call him!'

'But that's impossible – impossible,' spluttered O'Rourke. 'Loftus has been in the service for years.'

'But you've never met him before, have you? He was a stranger to all of you. It isn't the *real* Loftus naturally.'

The quiet man found his voice.

'Clever of you to guess. How did you, by the way?'

'Your ridiculous statement that Smethurst had been killed by bumping his head. O'Rourke put that idea into your head when we were standing talking in Damascus yesterday. You thought – how simple! You were the only doctor with us – whatever you said would be accepted. You'd got Loftus's kit. You'd got his instruments. It was easy to select a neat little tool for your purpose. You lean over to speak to him and as you are speaking you drive the little weapon home. You talk a minute or two longer. It is dark in the car. Who will suspect?

'Then comes the discovery of the body. You give your verdict. But it does not go as easily as you thought. Doubts are raised. You fall back on a second line of defence. Williamson repeats the conversation he has over-heard Smethurst having with you. It is taken to refer to Hensley and you add a damaging little invention of your own about a leakage in Hensley's department. And then I make a final test. I mention the sand and the socks. You are holding a handful of sand. I send you to find the socks so *that we may know the truth*. But by that I did not mean what you thought I meant. *I had already examined Hensley's socks*. There was no sand in either of them. You put it there.'

Mr Samuel Long lit a cigarette. 'I give it up,' he said. 'My luck's turned. Well, I had a good run while it lasted. They were getting hot on my trail when I reached Egypt. I came across Loftus. He was going to join up in Baghdad – and he knew none of them there. It was too good a chance to be missed. I bought him. It cost me twenty thousand pounds. What was that to me? Then, by cursed ill luck, I run into Smethurst – an ass if there ever was one! He was my fag at Eton. He had a bit of hero worship for me in those days. He didn't like the idea of giving me away. I did my best and at last he promised to say nothing till we reached Baghdad. What chance should I have then? None at all. There was only one way – to eliminate him. But I can assure you I am not a murderer by nature. My talents lie in quite another direction.'

His face changed – contracted. He swayed and pitched forward.

O'Rourke bent over him.

'Probably prussic acid – in the cigarette,' said Mr Parker Pyne. 'The gambler has lost his last throw.'

He looked around him – at the wide desert. The sun beat down on him. Only yesterday they had left Damascus – by the Gate of Baghdad.

'Pass not beneath, O Caravan, or pass not singing. Have you heard
That silence where the birds are dead yet something pipeth like a bird?'

The House at Shiraz

'The House at Shiraz' was first published in the USA in
Cosmopolitan, April 1933, and then as 'In the House at Shiraz'
in *Nash's Pall Mall*, June 1933.

It was six in the morning when Mr Parker Pyne left for Persia after a stop in Baghdad.

The passenger space in the little monoplane was limited, and the small width of the seats was not such as to accommodate the bulk of Mr Parker Pyne with anything like comfort. There were two fellow travellers – a large, florid man whom Mr Parker Pyne judged to be of a talkative habit and a thin woman with pursed-up lips and a determined air.

'At any rate,' thought Mr Parker Pyne, 'they don't look as though they would want to consult me professionally.'

Nor did they. The little woman was an American missionary, full of hard work and happiness, and the florid man was employed by an oil company. They had given their fellow traveller a résumé of their lives before the plane started.

'I am merely a tourist, I am afraid,' Mr Parker Pyne had said deprecatingly. 'I am going to Teheran and Ispahan and Shiraz.'

And the sheer music of the names enchanted him so much as he said them that he repeated them. Teheran. Ispahan. Shiraz.

Mr Parker Pyne looked out at the country below him. It was flat desert. He felt the mystery of these vast, unpopulated regions.

At Kermanshah the machine came down for passport examinations and customs. A bag of Mr Parker Pyne's was opened. A certain small cardboard box was scrutinized with some excitement. Questions were asked. Since Mr Parker Pyne did not speak or understand Persian, the matter was difficult.

The pilot of the machine strolled up. He was a fair-haired young

German, a fine-looking man, with deep-blue eyes and a weatherbeaten face. 'Please?' he inquired pleasantly.

Mr Parker Pyne, who had been indulging in some excellent realistic pantomime without, it seemed, much success, turned to him with relief. 'It's bug powder,' he said. 'Do you think you could explain it to them?'

The pilot looked puzzled. 'Please?'

Mr Parker Pyne repeated his plea in German. The pilot grinned and translated the sentence into Persian. The grave and sad officials were pleased; their sorrowful faces relaxed; they smiled. One even laughed. They found the idea humorous.

The three passengers took their places in the machine again and the flight continued. They swooped down at Hamadan to drop the mails, but the plane did not stop. Mr Parker Pyne peered down, trying to see if he could distinguish the rock of Behistun, that romantic spot where Darius describes the extent of his empire and conquests in three different languages – Babylonian, Median and Persian.

It was one o'clock when they arrived at Teheran. There were more police formalities. The German pilot had come up and was standing by smiling as Mr Parker Pyne finished answering a long interrogation which he had not understood.

'What have I said?' he asked of the German.

'That your father's Christian name is Tourist, that your profession is Charles, that the maiden name of your mother is Baghdad, and that you have come from Harriet.'

'Does it matter?'

'Not the least in the world. Just answer something; that is all they need.'

Mr Parker Pyne was disappointed in Teheran. He found it distressingly modern. He said as much the following evening when he happened to run into Herr Schlagal, the pilot, just as he was entering his hotel. On an impulse he asked the other man to dine, and the German accepted.

The Georgian waiter hovered over them and issued his orders. The food arrived.

When they had reached the stage of *la torte*, a somewhat sticky confection of chocolate, the German said:

'So you go to Shiraz?'

'Yes. I shall fly there. Then I shall come back from Shiraz to Ispahan and Teheran by road. Is it you who will fly me to Shiraz tomorrow?'

'*Ach*, no. I return to Baghdad.'

'You have been long here?'

'Three years. It has only been established three years, our service. So far, we have never had an accident – *unberufen!*' He touched the table.

Thick cups of sweet coffee were brought. The two men smoked.

'My first passengers were two ladies,' said the German reminiscently. 'Two English ladies.'

'Yes?' said Mr Parker Pyne.

'The one she was a young lady very well born, the daughter of one of your ministers, the – how does one say it? – the Lady Esther Carr. She was handsome, very handsome, but mad.'

'Mad?'

'Completely mad. She lives there at Shiraz in a big native house. She wears Eastern dress. She will see no Europeans. Is that a life for a well born lady to live?'

'There have been others,' said Mr Parker Pyne. 'There was Lady Hester Stanhope –'

'This one is mad,' said the other abruptly. 'You could see it in her eyes. Just so have I seen the eyes of my submarine commander in the war. He is now in an asylum.'

Mr Parker Pyne was thoughtful. He remembered Lord Micheldever, Lady Esther Carr's father, well. He had worked under him when the latter was Home Secretary – a big blond man with laughing blue eyes. He had seen Lady Micheldever once – a noted Irish beauty with her black hair and violet-blue eyes. They were both handsome, normal people, but for all that there *was* insanity in the Carr family. It cropped up every now and then, after missing a generation. It was odd, he thought, that Herr Schlagal should stress the point.

'And the other lady,' he asked idly.

'The other lady – is dead.'

Something in his voice made Mr Parker Pyne look up sharply.

'I have a heart,' said Herr Schlagal. 'I feel. She was, to me, most beautiful, that lady. You know how it is, these things come over you all of a sudden. She was a flower – a flower.' He sighed deeply. 'I went to see them once – at the house at Shiraz. The Lady Esther, she asked me to come. My little one, my flower, she was afraid of something, I could see it. When next I came back from Baghdad, I hear that she is dead. Dead!'

He paused and then said thoughtfully: 'It might be that the other one killed her. She was mad, I tell you.'

He sighed, and Mr Parker Pyne ordered two Benedictines.

'The curaçao, it is good,' said the Georgian waiter, and brought them two curaçaos.

Just after noon the following day, Mr Parker Pyne had his first view of Shiraz. They had flown over mountain ranges with narrow, desolate valleys between, and all arid, parched, dry wilderness. Then suddenly Shiraz came into view – an emerald-green jewel in the heart of the wilderness.

Mr Parker Pyne enjoyed Shiraz as he had not enjoyed Teheran. The primitive character of the hotel did not appal him, nor the equally primitive character of the streets.

He found himself in the midst of a Persian holiday. The Nan Ruz festival had begun on the previous evening – the fifteen-day period in which the Persians celebrate their New Years. He wandered through the empty bazaars and passed out into the great open stretch of common on the north side of the city. All Shiraz was celebrating.

One day he walked just outside the town. He had been to the tomb of Hafiz the poet, and it was on returning that he saw, and was fascinated by, a house. A house all tiled in blue and rose and yellow, set in a green garden with water and orange trees and roses. It was, he felt, the house of a dream.

That night he was dining with the English consul and he asked about the house.

'Fascinating place, isn't it? It was built by a former wealthy governor of Luristan, who had made a good thing out of his official position. An English-woman's got it now. You must have heard of her. Lady Esther Carr. Mad as a hatter. Gone completely native. Won't have anything to do with anything or anyone British.'

'Is she young?'

'Too young to play the fool in this way. She's about thirty.'

'There was another Englishwoman with her, wasn't there? A woman who died?'

'Yes; that was about three years ago. Happened the day after I took up my post here, as a matter of fact. Barham, my predecessor, died suddenly, you know.'

'How did she die?' asked Mr Parker Pyne bluntly.

'Fell from that courtyard or balcony place on the first floor. She was Lady Esther's maid or companion, I forget which. Anyway, she was carrying the breakfast tray and stepped back over the edge. Very sad; nothing to be done; cracked her skull on the stone below.'

'What was her name?'

'King, I think; or was it Willis? No, that's the missionary woman. Rather a nice-looking girl.'

'Was Lady Esther upset?'

'Yes – no. I don't know. She was very. queer; I couldn't make her out. She's a very – well, imperious creature. You can see she is somebody, if you know what I mean; she rather scared me with her commanding ways and her dark, flashing eyes.'

He laughed half-apologetically, then looked curiously at his companion. Mr Parker Pyne was apparently staring into space. The match he had

just struck to light his cigarette was burning away unheeded in his hand.
It burned down to his fingers and he dropped it with an ejaculation of
pain. Then he saw the consul's astonished expression and smiled.

'I beg your pardon,' he said.

'Wool gathering, weren't you?'

'Three bags full,' said Mr Parker Pyne enigmatically.

They talked of other matters.

That evening, by the light of a small oil lamp, Mr Parker Pyne wrote
a letter. He hesitated a good deal over its composition. Yet in the end it
was very simple:

> *Mr Parker Pyne presents his compliments to Lady Esther Carr and
> begs to state that he is staying at the Hotel Fars for the next three
> days should she wish to consult him.*

He enclosed a cutting – the famous advertisement

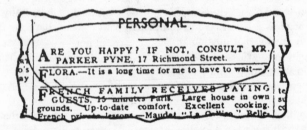

'That ought to do the trick,' said Mr Parker Pyne as he got gingerly into
his rather uncomfortable bed. 'Let me see, nearly three years; yes, it ought
to do it.'

On the following day about four o'clock the answer came. It was
brought by a Persian servant who knew no English.

Lady Esther Carr will be glad if Mr Parker Pyne will call upon her at
nine o'clock this evening.

Mr Parker Pyne smiled.

It was the same servant who received him that evening. He was taken
through the dark garden and up an outside staircase that led round to
the back of the house. From there a door was opened and he passed
through into the central court or balcony, which was open to the night.
A big divan was placed against the wall and on it reclined a striking
figure.

Lady Esther was attired in Eastern robes, and it might have been
suspected that one reason for her preference lay in the fact that they

suited her rich, Oriental style of beauty. Imperious, the consul called her, and indeed imperious she looked. Her chin was held high and her brows were arrogant.

'You are Mr Parker Pyne? Sit down there.'

Her hand pointed to a heap of cushions. On the third finger there flashed a big emerald carved with the arms of her family. It was an heirloom and must be worth a small fortune, Mr Parker Pyne reflected.

He lowered himself obediently, though with a little difficulty. For a man of his figure it is not easy to sit on the ground gracefully.

A servant appeared with coffee. Mr Parker Pyne took his cup and sipped appreciatively.

His hostess had acquired the Oriental habit of infinite leisure. She did not rush into conversation. She, too, sipped her coffee with half-closed eyes. At last she spoke.

'So you help unhappy people,' she said. 'At least, that is what your advertisement claims.'

'Yes.'

'Why did you send it to me? Is it your way of – doing business on your travels?'

There was something decidedly offensive in her voice, but Mr Parker Pyne ignored it. He answered simply, 'No. My idea in travelling is to have a complete holiday from business.'

'Then why send it to me?'

'Because I had reason to believe that you – are unhappy.'

There was a moment's silence. He was very curious. How would she take that? She gave herself a minute to decide that point. Then she laughed.

'I suppose you thought that anyone who leaves the world, who lives as I do, cut off from my race, from my country, must do so because she is unhappy! Sorrow, disappointment – you think something like that drove me into exile? Oh, well, how should you understand? There – in England – I was a fish out of water. Here I am myself. I am an Oriental at heart. I love this seclusion. I dare say you can't understand that. To you, I must seem' – she hesitated a moment – 'mad.'

'You're not mad,' said Mr Parker Pyne.

There was a good deal of quiet assurance in his voice. She looked at him curiously.

'But they've been saying I am, I suppose. Fools! It takes all kinds to make a world. I'm perfectly happy.'

'And yet you told me to come here,' said Mr Parker Pyne.

'I will admit I was curious to see you.' She hesitated. 'Besides, I never want to go back there – to England – but all the same, sometimes I like to hear what is going on in –'

'In the world you have left?'

She acknowledged the sentence with a nod.

Mr Parker Pyne began to talk. His voice, mellow and reassuring, began quietly, then rose ever so little as he emphasized this point and that.

He talked of London, of society gossip, of famous men and women, of new restaurants and new night clubs, of race meetings and shooting parties and country-house scandals. He talked of clothes, of fashions from Paris, of little shops in unfashionable streets where marvellous bargains could be had.

He described theatres and cinemas, he gave film news, he described the building of new garden suburbs, he talked of bulbs and gardening, and he came last to a homely description of London in the evening, with the trams and buses and the hurrying crowds going homeward after the day's work and of the little homes awaiting them, and of the whole strange intimate pattern of English family life.

It was a very remarkable performance, displaying as it did wide and unusual knowledge and a clever marshalling of the facts. Lady Esther's head had drooped; the arrogance of her poise had been abandoned. For some time her tears had been quietly falling, and now that he had finished, she abandoned all pretence and wept openly.

Mr Parker Pyne said nothing. He sat there watching her. His face had the quiet, satisfied expression of one who has conducted an experiment and obtained the desired result.

She raised her head at last. 'Well,' she said bitterly, 'are you satisfied?'

'I think so – now.'

'How shall I bear it; how shall I bear it? Never to leave here; never to see – anyone again!' The cry came as though wrung out of her. She caught herself up, flushing. 'Well?' she demanded fiercely. 'Aren't you going to make the obvious remark? Aren't you going to say, "If you want to go home so much, why not do so?"'

'No.' Mr Parker Pyne shook his head. 'It's not nearly as easy as that for you.'

For the first time a little look of fear crept into her eyes.

'Do you know why I can't go?'

'I think so.'

'Wrong.' She shook her head. 'The reason I can't go is a reason you'd never guess.'

'I don't guess,' said Mr Parker Pyne. 'I observe – and I classify.'

She shook her head. 'You don't know anything at all.'

'I shall have to convince you, I see,' said Mr Parker Pyne pleasantly. 'When you came out here, Lady Esther, you flew, I believe, by the new German Air Service from Baghdad?'

'Yes?'

'You were flown by a young pilot, Herr Schlagal, who afterwards came here to see you.'

'Yes.'

A different 'yes' in some indescribable way – a softer 'yes'.

'And you had a friend, or companion who – died.' A voice like steel now – cold, offensive.

'My companion.'

'Her name was –?'

'Muriel King.'

'Were you fond of her?'

'What do you mean, fond?' She paused, checked herself. 'She was useful to me.'

She said it haughtily and Mr Parker Pyne was reminded of the consul's saying: 'You can see she is somebody, if you know what I mean.'

'Were you sorry when she died?'

'I – naturally! Really, Mr Pyne, is it necessary to go into all this?' She spoke angrily, and went on without waiting for an answer: 'It has been very good of you to come. But I am a little tired. If you will tell me what I owe you –?'

But Mr Parker Pyne did not move. He showed no signs of taking offence. He went quietly on with his questions. 'Since she died, Herr Schlagal has not been to see you. Suppose he were to come, would you receive him?'

'Certainly not.'

'You refuse absolutely?'

'Absolutely. Herr Schlagal will not be admitted.'

'Yes,' said Mr Parker Pyne thoughtfully. 'You could not say anything else.'

The defensive armour of her arrogance broke down a little. She said uncertainly: 'I – I don't know what you mean.'

'Did you know, Lady Esther, that young Schlagal fell in love with Muriel King? He is a sentimental young man. He still treasures her memory.'

'Does he?' Her voice was almost a whisper.

'What was she like?'

'What do you mean, what was she like? How do I know?'

'You must have looked at her sometimes,' said Mr Parker Pyne mildly.

'Oh, that! She was quite a nice-looking young woman.'

'About your own age?'

'Just about.' There was a pause, and then she said:

'Why do you think that – that Schlagal cared for her?'

'Because he told me so. Yes, yes, in the most unmistakable terms. As I say, he is a sentimental young man. He was glad to confide in me. He was very upset at her dying the way she did.'

Lady Esther sprang to her feet. 'Do you believe I murdered her?'

Mr Parker Pyne did not spring to his feet. He was not a springing kind of man.

'No, my dear child,' he said. 'I do *not* believe that you murdered her, and that being so, I think the sooner you stop this play-acting and go home, the better.'

'What do you mean, play-acting?'

'The truth is, you lost your nerve. Yes, you did. You lost your nerve badly. You thought you'd be accused of murdering your employer.'

The girl made a sudden movement.

Mr Parker Pyne went on. 'You are not Lady Esther Carr. I knew that before I came here, but I've tested you to make sure.' His smile broke out, bland and benevolent.

'When I said my little piece just now, I was watching you, and every time you reacted as *Muriel King*, not as Esther Carr. The cheap shops, the cinemas, the new garden suburbs, going home by bus and tram – you reacted to all those. Country-house gossip, new night clubs, the chatter of Mayfair, race meetings – none of these meant anything to you.'

His voice became even more persuasive and fatherly. 'Sit down and tell me about it. You didn't murder Lady Esther, but you thought you might be accused of doing so. Just tell me how it all came about.'

She took a long breath; then she sank down once more on the divan and began to speak. Her words came hurriedly, in little bursts.

'I must begin – at the beginning. I – I was afraid of her. She was mad – not quite mad – just a little. She brought me out here with her. Like a fool I was delighted; I thought it was so romantic. Little fool. That's what I was, a little fool. There was some business about a chauffeur. She was man-mad – absolutely man-mad. He wouldn't have anything to do with her, and it got out; her friends got to know about it and laughed. And she broke loose from her family and came out here.

'It was all a pose to save her face – solitude in the desert – all that sort of thing. She would have kept it up for a bit, and then gone back. But she got queerer and queerer. And then there was the pilot. She – took a fancy to him. He came here to see me, and she thought – oh well, you can understand. But he must have made it clear to her . . .'

'And then she suddenly turned on me. She was awful, frightening. She said I should never go home again. She said I was in her power. She said I was a slave. Just that – a slave. She had the power of life and death over me.'

Mr Parker Pyne nodded. He saw the situation unfolding. Lady Esther slowly going over the edge of sanity, as others of her family had gone before her, and the frightened girl, ignorant and untravelled, believing everything that was said to her.

'But one day something in me seemed to snap. I stood up to her. I told her that if it came to it I was stronger than she was. I told her I'd throw her down on to the stones below. She was frightened, really frightened. I suppose she'd just thought me a worm. I took a step toward her – I don't know what she thought I meant to do. She moved backwards; she – she stepped back off the edge!' Muriel King buried her face in her hands.

'And then?' Mr Parker Pyne prompted gently.

'I lost my head. I thought they'd say I'd pushed her over. I thought nobody would listen to me. I thought I should be thrown into some awful prison out here.' Her lips worked. Mr Parker Pyne saw clearly enough the unreasoning fear that had possessed her. 'And then it came to me – if it were I! I knew that there would be a new British consul who'd never seen either of us. The other one had died.

'I thought I could manage the servants. To them we were two mad Englishwomen. When one was dead, the other carried on. I gave them good presents of money and told them to send for the British consul. He came and I received him as Lady Esther. I had her ring on my finger. He was very nice and arranged everything. Nobody seemed to have the least suspicion.'

Mr Parker Pyne nodded thoughtfully. Lady Esther Carr might be mad as a hatter, but she was still Lady Esther Carr.

'And then afterwards,' continued Muriel, 'I wished I hadn't. I saw that I'd been quite mad myself. I was condemned to stay on here playing a part. I didn't see how I could ever get away. If I confessed the truth now, it would look more than ever as though I'd murdered her. Oh, Mr Pyne, what shall I do? What shall I do?'

'Do?' Mr Parker Pyne rose to his feet as briskly as his figure allowed. 'My dear child, you will come with me now to the British consul, who is a very amiable and kindly man. There will be certain unpleasant formalities to go through. I don't promise you that it will be all plain sailing, but you won't be hanged for murder. By the way, why was the breakfast tray found with the body?'

'I threw it over. I – I thought it would look more like me to have a tray there. Was it silly of me?'

'It was rather a clever touch,' said Mr Parker Pyne. 'In fact, it was the one point which made me wonder if you might, perhaps, have done away with Lady Esther – that is, until I saw you. When I saw you, I knew that whatever else you might do in your life, you would never kill anyone.'

'Because I haven't the nerve, you mean?'

'Your reflexes wouldn't work that way,' said Mr Parker Pyne, smiling. 'Now, shall we go? There's an unpleasant job to be faced, but I'll see you through it, and then – home to Streatham Hill – it is Streatham Hill, isn't it? Yes, I thought so. I saw your face contract when I mentioned one particular bus number. Are you coming, my dear?'

Muriel King hung back. 'They'll never believe me,' she said nervously. 'Her family and all. They wouldn't believe she could act the way she did.'

'Leave it to me,' said Mr Parker Pyne. 'I know something of the family history, you see. Come, child, don't go on playing the coward. Remember, there's a young man sighing his heart out. We had better arrange that it is in his plane you fly to Baghdad.'

The girl smiled and blushed. 'I'm ready,' she said simply. Then, as she moved towards the door, she turned back. 'You said you knew I was not Lady Esther Carr before you saw me. How could you possibly tell that?'

'Statistics,' said Mr Parker Pyne.

'Statistics?'

'Yes. Both Lord and Lady Micheldever had blue eyes. When the consul mentioned that their daughter had flashing *dark* eyes I knew there was something wrong. Brown-eyed people may produce a blue-eyed child, but not the other way about. A scientific fact, I assure you.'

'I think you're wonderful!' said Muriel King.

The Pearl of Price

'The Pearl of Price' was first published as 'The Pearl' in
Nash's Pall Mall, July 1933.

The party had had a long and tiring day. They had started from Amman
early in the morning with a temperature of ninety-eight in the shade, and
had come at last just as it was growing dark into the camp situated in
the heart of that city of fantastic and preposterous red rock which is
Petra.

There were seven of them, Mr Caleb P. Blundell, that stout and prosperous American magnate. His dark and good-looking, if somewhat
taciturn, secretary, Jim Hurst. Sir Donald Marvel, M.P., a tired-looking
English politician. Doctor Carver, a world-renowned elderly archaeologist. A gallant Frenchman, Colonel Dubosc, on leave from Syria. A Mr
Parker Pyne, not perhaps so plainly labelled with his profession, but
breathing an atmosphere of British solidity. And lastly, there was Miss
Carol Blundell – pretty, spoiled, and extremely sure of herself as the only
woman among half a dozen men.

They dined in the big tent, having selected their tents or caves for
sleeping in. They talked of politics in the Near East – the Englishman
cautiously, the Frenchman discreetly, the American somewhat fatuously,
and the archaeologist and Mr Parker Pyne not at all. Both of them, it
seemed, preferred the rôle of listeners. So also did Jim Hurst.

Then they talked of the city they had come to visit.

'It's just too romantic for words,' said Carol. 'To think of those – what
do you call 'em – Nabataeans living here all that while ago, almost before
time began!'

'Hardly that,' said Mr Parker Pyne mildly. 'Eh, Doctor Carver?'

'Oh, that's an affair of a mere two thousand years back, and if racket-
eers are romantic, then I suppose the Nabataeans are too. They were a
pack of wealthy blackguards, I should say, who compelled travellers to

use their own caravan routes, and saw to it that all other routes were unsafe. Petra was the storehouse of their racketeering profits.'

'You think they were just robbers?' asked Carol. 'Just common thieves?'

'Thieves is a less romantic word, Miss Blundell. A thief suggests a pretty pilferer. A robber suggests a larger canvas.'

'What about a modern financier?' suggested Mr Parker Pyne with a twinkle.

'That's one for you, Pop!' said Carol.

'A man who makes money benefits mankind,' said Mr Blundell sententiously.

'Mankind,' murmured Mr Parker Pyne, 'is so ungrateful.'

'What is honesty?' demanded the Frenchman. 'It is a *nuance*, a convention. In different countries it means different things. An Arab is not ashamed of stealing. He is not ashamed of lying. With him it is from *whom* he steals or to *whom* he lies that matters.'

'That is the point of view – yes,' agreed Carver.

'Which shows the superiority of the West over the East,' said Blundell. 'When these poor creatures get education –'

Sir Donald entered languidly into the conversation. 'Education is rather rot, you know. Teaches fellows a lot of useless things. And what I mean is, nothing alters what you are.'

'You mean?'

'Well, what I mean to say is, for instance, once a thief, always a thief.'

There was a dead silence for a moment. Then Carol began talking feverishly about mosquitoes, and her father backed her up.

Sir Donald, a little puzzled, murmured to his neighbour, Mr Parker Pyne: 'Seems I dropped a brick, what?'

'Curious,' said Mr Parker Pyne.

Whatever momentary embarrassment had been caused, one person had quite failed to notice it. The archaeologist had sat silent, his eyes dreamy and abstracted. When a pause came, he spoke suddenly and abruptly.

'You know,' he said, 'I agree with that – at any rate, from the opposite point of view. A man's fundamentally honest, or he isn't. You can't get away from it.'

'You don't believe that sudden temptation, for instance, will turn an honest man into a criminal?' asked Mr Parker Pyne.

'Impossible!' said Carver.

Mr Parker Pyne shook his head gently. 'I wouldn't say impossible. You see, there are so many factors to take into account. There's the breaking point, for instance.'

'What do you call the breaking point?' asked young Hurst, speaking for the first time. He had a deep, rather attractive voice.

'The brain is adjusted to carry so much weight. The thing that precipitates the crisis – that turns an honest man into a dishonest one – may be a mere trifle. That is why most crimes are absurd. The cause, nine times out of ten, is that trifle of overweight – the straw that breaks the camel's back.'

'It is the psychology you talk there, my friend,' said the Frenchman.

'If a criminal were a psychologist, what a criminal he could be!' said Mr Parker Pyne. His voice dwelt lovingly on the idea. 'When you think that of ten people you meet, at least nine of them can be induced to act in any way you please by applying the right stimulus.'

'Oh, explain that!' cried Carol.

'There's the bullyable man. Shout loud enough at him – and he obeys. There's the contradictory man. Bully him the opposite way from the way in which you want him to go. Then there's the suggestible person, the commonest type of all. Those are the people who have *seen* a motor, because they have heard a motor horn; who *see* a postman because they hear the rattle of the letter-box; who *see* a knife in a wound because they are *told* a man has been stabbed; or who will have *heard* the pistol if they are told a man has been shot.'

'I guess no one could put that sort of stuff over on me,' said Carol incredulously.

'You're too smart for that, honey,' said her father.

'It is very true what you say,' said the Frenchman reflectively. 'The preconceived idea, it deceives the senses.'

Carol yawned. 'I'm going to my cave. I'm tired to death. Abbas Effendi said we had to start early tomorrow. He's going to take us up to the place of sacrifice – whatever that is.'

'It is where they sacrifice young and beautiful girls,' said Sir Donald.

'Mercy, I hope not! Well, goodnight, all. Oh, I've dropped my earring.'

Colonel Dubosc picked it up from where it had rolled across the table and returned it to her.

'Are they real?' asked Sir Donald abruptly. Discourteous for the moment, he was staring at the two large solitaire pearls in her ears.

'They're real all right,' said Carol.

'Cost me eighty thousand dollars,' said her father with relish. 'And she screws them in so loosely that they fall off and roll about the table. Want to ruin me, girl?'

'I'd say it wouldn't ruin you even if you had to buy me a new pair,' said Carol fondly.

'I guess it wouldn't,' her father acquiesced. 'I could buy you three pairs of earrings without noticing it in my bank balance.' He looked proudly around.

'How nice for you!' said Sir Donald.

'Well, gentlemen, I think I'll turn in now,' said Blundell. 'Good-night.' Young Hurst went with him.

The other four smiled at one another, as though in sympathy over some thought.

'Well,' drawled Sir Donald, 'it's nice to know he wouldn't miss the money. Purse-proud hog!' he added viciously.

'They have too much money, these Americans,' said Dubosc.

'It is difficult,' said Mr Parker Pyne gently, 'for a rich man to be appreciated by the poor.'

Dubosc laughed. 'Envy and malice?' he suggested. 'You are right, Monsieur. We all wish to be rich; to buy the pearl earrings several times over. Except, perhaps, Monsieur here.'

He bowed to Doctor Carver who, as seemed usual with him, was once more far away. He was fiddling with a little object in his hand.

'Eh?' he roused himself. 'No, I must admit I don't covet large pearls. Money is always useful, of course.' His tone put it where it belonged. 'But look at this,' he said. 'Here is something a hundred times more interesting than pearls.'

'What is it?'

'It's a cylinder seal of black haematite and it's got a presentation scene engraved on it – a god introducing a suppliant to a more enthroned god. The suppliant is carrying a kid by way of an offering, and the august god on the throne has the flies kept off him by a flunkey who wields a palm-branch fly whisk. That neat inscription mentions the man as a servant of Hammurabi, so that it must have been made just four thousand years ago.'

He took a lump of Plasticine from his pocket and smeared some on the table, then he oiled it with a little vaseline and pressed the seal upon it, rolling it out. Then, with a penknife, he detached a square of the Plasticine and levered it gently up from the table.

'You see?' he said.

The scene he had described was unrolled before them in the Plasticine, clear and sharply defined.

For a moment the spell of the past was laid upon them all. Then, from outside, the voice of Mr Blundell was raised unmusically.

'Say, you niggers! Change my baggage out of this darned cave and into a tent! The no-see-ums are biting good and hard. I shan't get a wink of sleep.'

'No-see-ums?' Sir Donald queried.

'Probably sand flies,' said Doctor Carver.

'I like no-see-ums,' said Mr Parker Pyne. 'It's a much more suggestive name.'

The party started early the following morning, getting under way after various exclamations at the colour and marking of the rocks. The 'rose-red' city was indeed a freak invented by Nature in her most extravagant and colourful mood. The party proceeded slowly, since Doctor Carver walked with his eyes bent on the ground, occasionally pausing to pick up small objects.

'You can always tell an archaeologist – so,' said Colonel Dubosc, smiling. 'He regards never the sky, nor the hills, nor the beauties of nature. He walks with head bent, searching.'

'Yes, but what for?' said Carol. 'What are the things you are picking up, Doctor Carver?'

With a slight smile the archaeologist held out a couple of muddy fragments of pottery.

'That rubbish!' cried Carol scornfully.

'Pottery is more interesting than gold,' said Doctor Carver. Carol looked disbelieving.

They came to a sharp bend and passed two or three rockcut tombs. The ascent was somewhat trying. The Bedouin guards went ahead, swinging up the precipitous slopes unconcernedly, without a downward glance at the sheer drop on one side of them.

Carol looked rather pale. One guard leaned down from above and extended a hand. Hurst sprang up in front of her and held out his stick like a rail on the precipitous side. She thanked him with a glance, and a minute later stood safely on a broad path of rock. The others followed slowly. The sun was now high and the heat was beginning to be felt.

At last they reached a broad plateau almost at the top. An easy climb led to the summit of a big square block of rock. Blundell signified to the guide that the party would go up alone. The Bedouins disposed themselves comfortably against the rocks and began to smoke. A few short minutes and the others had reached the summit.

It was a curious, bare place. The view was marvellous, embracing the valley on every side. They stood on a plain rectangular floor, with rock basins cut in the side and a kind of sacrificial altar.

'A heavenly place for sacrifices,' said Carol with enthusiasm. 'But my, they must have had a time getting the victims up here!'

'There was originally a kind of zigzag rock road,' explained Doctor Carver. 'We shall see traces of it as we go down the other way.'

They were some time longer commenting and talking. Then there was a tiny chink, and Doctor Carver said: 'I believe you dropped your earring again, Miss Blundell.'

Carol clapped a hand to her ear. 'Why, so I have.'

Dubosc and Hurst began searching about.

'It must be just here,' said the Frenchman. 'It can't have rolled away, because there is nowhere for it to roll to. The place is like a square box.'

'It can't have rolled into a crack?' queried Carol.

'There's not a crack anywhere,' said Mr Parker Pyne. 'You can see for yourself. The place is perfectly smooth. Ah, you have found something, Colonel?'

'Only a little pebble,' said Dubosc, smiling and throwing it away.

Gradually a different spirit – a spirit of tension – came over the search. They were not said aloud, but the words 'eighty thousand dollars' were present in everybody's mind.

'You are sure you had it, Carol?' snapped her father. 'I mean, perhaps you dropped it on the way up.'

'I had it just as we stepped on to the plateau here,' said Carol. 'I know, because Doctor Carver pointed out to me that it was loose and he screwed it up for me. That's so, isn't it, Doctor?'

Doctor Carver assented. It was Sir Donald who voiced the thoughts in everybody's mind.

'This is a rather unpleasant business, Mr Blundell,' he said. 'You were telling us last night what the value of these earrings is. One of them alone is worth a small fortune. If this earring is not found, and it does not look as though it will be found, every one of us will be under a certain suspicion.'

'And for one, I ask to be searched,' broke in Colonel Dubosc. 'I do not ask, I demand it as a right!'

'You search me too,' said Hurst. His voice sounded harsh.

'What does everyone else feel?' asked Sir Donald, looking around.

'Certainly,' said Mr Parker Pyne.

'An excellent idea,' said Doctor Carver.

'I'll be in on this too, gentlemen,' said Mr Blundell. 'I've got my reasons, though I don't want to stress them.'

'Just as you like, of course, Mr Blundell,' said Sir Donald courteously.

'Carol, my dear, will you go down and wait with the guides?'

Without a word the girl left them. Her face was set and grim. There was a despairing look upon it that caught the attention of one member of the party, at least. He wondered just what it meant.

The search proceeded. It was drastic and thorough – and completely unsatisfactory. One thing was certain. No one was carrying the earring on his person. It was a subdued little troop that negotiated the descent and listened half-heartedly to the guide's descriptions and information.

Mr Parker Pyne had just finished dressing for lunch when a figure appeared at the door of his tent.

'Mr Pyne, may I come in?'

'Certainly, my dear young lady, certainly.'

Carol came in and sat down on the bed. Her face had the same grim look upon it that he had noticed earlier in the day.

'You pretend to straighten out things for people when they are unhappy, don't you?' she demanded.

'I am on holiday, Miss Blundell. I am not taking any cases.'

'Well, you're going to take this one,' said the girl calmly. 'Look here, Mr Pyne, I'm just as wretched as anyone could well be.'

'What is troubling you?' he asked. 'Is it the business of the earring?'

'That's just it. You've said enough. Jim Hurst didn't take it, Mr Pyne. I know he didn't.'

'I don't quite follow you, Miss Blundell. Why should anyone assume he had?'

'Because of his record. Jim Hurst was once a thief, Mr Pyne. He was caught in our house. I – I was sorry for him. He looked so young and desperate –'

'And so good-looking,' thought Mr Parker Pyne.

'I persuaded Pop to give him a chance to make good. My father will do anything for me. Well, he gave Jim his chance and Jim has made good. Father's come to rely on him and to trust him with all his business secrets. And in the end he'll come around altogether, or would have if this hadn't happened.'

'When you say "come around" –?'

'I mean that I want to marry Jim and he wants to marry me.'

'And Sir Donald?'

'Sir Donald is Father's idea. He's not mine. Do you think I want to marry a stuffed fish like Sir Donald?'

Without expressing any views as to this description of the young Englishman, Mr Parker Pyne asked: 'And Sir Donald himself?'

'I dare say he thinks I'd be good for his impoverished acres,' said Carol scornfully.

Mr Parker Pyne considered the situation. 'I should like to ask you about two things,' he said. 'Last night the remark was made "once a thief, always a thief".'

The girl nodded.

'I see now the reason for the embarrassment that remark seemed to cause.'

'Yes, it was awkward for Jim – and for me and Pop too. I was so afraid Jim's face would show something that I just trotted out the first remarks I could think of.'

Mr Parker Pyne nodded thoughtfully. Then he asked: 'Just why did your father insist on being searched today?'

'You didn't get that? I did. Pop had it in his mind that I might think the whole business was a frame-up against Jim. You see, he's crazy for me to marry the Englishman. Well, he wanted to show me that he hadn't done the dirty on Jim.'

'Dear me,' said Mr Parker Pyne, 'this is all very illuminating. In a general sense, I mean. It hardly helps us in our particular inquiry.'

'You're not going to hand in your checks?'

'No, no.' He was silent a moment, then he said: 'What is it exactly you want me to do, Miss Carol?'

'Prove it wasn't Jim who took that pearl.'

'And suppose – excuse me – that it was?'

'If you think so, you're wrong – dead wrong.'

'Yes, but have you really considered the case carefully? Don't you think the pearl might prove a sudden temptation to Mr Hurst. The sale of it would bring in a large sum of money – a foundation on which to speculate, shall we say? – which will make him independent, so that he can marry you with or without your father's consent.'

'Jim didn't do it,' said the girl simply.

This time Mr Parker Pyne accepted her statement. 'Well, I'll do my best.'

She nodded abruptly and left the tent. Mr Parker Pyne in his turn sat down on the bed. He gave himself up to thought. Suddenly, he chuckled.

'I'm growing slow-witted,' he said aloud. At lunch he was very cheerful.

The afternoon passed peacefully. Most people slept. When Mr Parker Pyne came into the big tent at a quarter-past four only Doctor Carver was there. He was examining some fragments of pottery.

'Ah!' said Mr Parker Pyne, drawing up a chair to the table. 'Just the man I want to see. Can you let me have that bit of Plasticine you carry about?'

The doctor felt in his pockets and produced a stick of Plasticine, which he offered to Mr Parker Pyne.

'No,' said Mr Parker Pyne, waving it away, 'that's not the one I want. I want that lump you had last night. To be frank, it's not the Plasticine I want. It's the contents of it.'

There was a pause, and then Doctor Carver said quietly, 'I don't think I quite understand you.'

'I think you do,' said Mr Parker Pyne. 'I want Miss Blundell's pearl earring.'

There was a minute's dead silence. Then Carver slipped his hand into his pocket and took out a shapeless lump of Plasticine.

'Clever of you,' he said. His face was expressionless.

'I wish you'd tell me about it,' said Mr Parker Pyne. His fingers were busy. With a grunt, he extracted a somewhat smeared pearl earring. 'Just curiosity, I know,' he added apologetically. 'But I should like to hear about it.'

'I'll tell you,' said Carver, 'if you'll tell me just how you happened to pitch upon me. You didn't see anything, did you?'

Mr Parker Pyne shook his head. 'I just thought about it,' he said.

'It was really sheer accident, to start with,' said Carver. 'I was behind you all this morning and I came across it lying in front of me – it must have fallen from the girl's ear a moment before. She hadn't noticed it. Nobody had. I picked it up and put it into my pocket, meaning to return it to her as soon as I caught her up. But I forgot.

'And then, half-way up that climb, I began to think. The jewel meant nothing to that fool of a girl – her father would buy her another without noticing the cost. And it would mean a lot to me. The sale of that pearl would equip an expedition.' His impassive face suddenly twitched and came to life. 'Do you know the difficulty there is nowadays in raising subscriptions for digging? No, you don't. The sale of that pearl would make everything easy. There's a site I want to dig – up in Baluchistan. There's a whole chapter of the past there waiting to be discovered . . .

'What you said last night came into my mind – about a suggestible witness. I thought the girl was that type. As we reached the summit I told her her earring was loose. I pretended to tighten it. What I really did was to press the point of a small pencil into her ear. A few minutes later I dropped a little pebble. She was quite ready to swear then that the earring had been in her ear and had just dropped off. In the meantime I pressed the pearl into a lump of Plasticine in my pocket. That's my story. Not a very edifying one. Now for your turn.'

'There isn't much of my story,' said Mr Parker Pyne. 'You were the only man who'd picked up things from the ground – that's what made me think of you. And finding that little pebble was significant. It suggested the trick you'd played. And then –'

'Go on,' said Carver.

'Well, you see, you'd talked about honesty a little too vehemently last night. Protesting overmuch – well, you know what Shakespeare says. It looked, somehow, as though you were trying to convince *yourself*. And you were a little too scornful about money.'

The face of the man in front of him looked lined and weary. 'Well, that's that,' he said. 'It's all up with me now. You'll give the girl back her geegaw, I suppose? Odd thing, the barbaric instinct for ornamentation. You find it going back as far as Palaeolithic times. One of the first instincts of the female sex.'

'I think you misjudge Miss Carol,' said Mr Parker Pyne. 'She has brains – and what is more, a heart. I think she will keep this business to herself.'

'Father won't, though,' said the archaeologist.

'I think he will. You see "Pop" has his own reasons for keeping quiet. There's no forty-thousand-dollar touch about this earring. A mere fiver would cover its value.'

'You mean –?'

'Yes. The girl doesn't know. She thinks they are genuine, all right. I had my suspicions last night. Mr Blundell talked a little too much about all the money he had. When things go wrong and you're caught in the slump – well, the best thing to do is to put a good face on it and bluff. Mr Blundell was bluffing.'

Suddenly Doctor Carver grinned. It was an engaging small-boy grin, strange to see on the face of an elderly man.

'Then we're all poor devils together,' he said.

'Exactly,' said Mr Parker Pyne and quoted, '"A fellow feeling makes us wondrous kind."'

Death on the Nile

'Death on the Nile' was first published in the USA in *Cosmopolitan*,
April 1933, and then in *Nash's Pall Mall*, July 1933.

Lady Grayle was nervous. From the moment of coming on board the
S.S. *Fayoum* she complained of everything. She did not like her cabin. She
could bear the morning sun, but not the afternoon sun. Pamela Grayle, her
niece, obligingly gave up her cabin on the other side. Lady Grayle accepted
it grudgingly.

She snapped at Miss MacNaughton, her nurse, for having given her
the wrong scarf and for having packed her little pillow instead of leaving
it out. She snapped at her husband, Sir George, for having just bought
her the wrong string of beads. It was lapis she wanted, not carnelian.
George was a fool!

Sir George said anxiously, 'Sorry, me dear, sorry. I'll go back and
change 'em. Plenty of time.'

She did not snap at Basil West, her husband's private secretary,
because nobody ever snapped at Basil. His smile disarmed you before
you began.

But the worst of it fell assuredly to the dragoman – an imposing and
richly dressed personage whom nothing could disturb.

When Lady Grayle caught sight of a stranger in a basket chair and
realized that he was a fellow passenger, the vials of her wrath were poured
out like water.

'They told me distinctly at the office that we were the only passengers!
It was the end of the season and there was no one else going!'

'That right lady,' said Mohammed calmly. 'Just you and party and one
gentleman, that's all.'

'But I was told that there would be only ourselves.'

'That quite right, lady.'

'It's not all right! It was a lie! What is that man doing here?'

'He come later, lady. After you take tickets. He only decide to come this morning.'

'It's an absolute swindle!'

'That's all right, lady; him very quiet gentleman, very nice, very quiet.'

'You're a fool! You know nothing about it. Miss MacNaughton, where are you? Oh, there you are. I've repeatedly asked you to stay near me. I might feel faint. Help me to my cabin and give me an aspirin, and don't let Mohammed come near me. He keeps on saying "That's right, lady," till I feel I could scream.'

Miss McNaughton proffered an arm without a word.

She was a tall woman of about thirty-five, handsome in a quiet, dark way. She settled Lady Grayle in the cabin, propped her up with cushions, administered an aspirin and listened to the thin flow of complaint.

Lady Grayle was forty-eight. She had suffered since she was sixteen from the complaint of having too much money. She had married that impoverished baronet, Sir George Grayle, ten years before.

She was a big woman, not bad-looking as regarded features, but her face was fretful and lined, and the lavish make-up she applied only accentuated the blemishes of time and temper. Her hair had been in turn platinum-blonde and henna-red, and was looking tired in consequence. She was overdressed and wore too much jewellery.

'Tell Sir George,' she finished, while the silent Miss MacNaughton waited with an expressionless face – 'tell Sir George that he *must* get that man off the boat! I *must* have privacy. All I've gone through lately –' She shut her eyes.

'Yes, Lady Grayle,' said Miss MacNaughton, and left the cabin.

The offending last-minute passenger was still sitting in the deck-chair. He had his back to Luxor and was staring out across the Nile to where the distant hills showed golden above a line of dark green.

Miss MacNaughton gave him a swift, appraising glance as she passed.

She found Sir George in the lounge. He was holding a string of beads in his hand and looking at it doubtfully.

'Tell me, Miss MacNaughton, do you think these will be all right?'

Miss MacNaughton gave a swift glance at the lapis.

'Very nice indeed,' she said.

'You think Lady Grayle will be pleased – eh?'

'Oh no, I shouldn't say that, Sir George. You see, nothing *would* please her. That's the real truth of it. By the way, she sent me with a message to you. She wants you to get rid of this extra passenger.'

Sir George's jaw dropped. 'How can I? What could I say to the fellow?'

'Of course you can't.' Elsie MacNaughton's voice was brisk and kindly. 'Just say there was nothing to be done.'

She added encouragingly, 'It will be all right.'

'You think it will, eh?' His face was ludicrously pathetic.

Elsie MacNaughton's voice was still kinder as she said: 'You really must not take these things to heart, Sir George. It's just health, you know. Don't take it seriously.'

'You think she's really bad, nurse?'

A shadow crossed the nurse's face. There was something odd in her voice as she answered: 'Yes, I – I don't quite like her condition. But please don't worry, Sir George. You mustn't. You really mustn't.' She gave him a friendly smile and went out.

Pamela came in, very languid and cool in her white.

'Hallo, Nunks.'

'Hallo, Pam, my dear.'

'What have you got there? Oh, nice!'

'Well, I'm so glad you think so. Do you think your aunt will think so, too?'

'She's incapable of liking anything. I can't think why you married the woman, Nunks.'

Sir George was silent. A confused panorama of unsuccessful racing, pressing creditors and a handsome if domineering woman rose before his mental vision.

'Poor old dear,' said Pamela. 'I suppose you had to do it. But she does give us both rather hell, doesn't she?'

'Since she's been ill –' began Sir George.

Pamela interrupted him.

'She's not ill! Not really. She can always do anything she wants to. Why, while you were up at Assouan she was as merry as a – a cricket. I bet you Miss MacNaughton knows she's a fraud.'

'I don't know what we'd do without Miss MacNaughton,' said Sir George with a sigh.

'She's an efficient creature,' admitted Pamela. 'I don't exactly dote on her as you do, though, Nunks. Oh, you do! Don't contradict. You think she's wonderful. So she is, in a way. But she's a dark horse. I never know what she's thinking. Still, she manages the old cat quite well.'

'Look here, Pam, you mustn't speak of your aunt like that. Dash it all, she's very good to you.'

'Yes, she pays all our bills, doesn't she? It's a hell of a life, though.'

Sir George passed on to a less painful subject. 'What are we to do about this fellow who's coming on the trip? Your aunt wants the boat to herself.'

'Well, she can't have it,' said Pamela coolly. 'The man's quite present-able. His name's Parker Pyne. I should think he was a civil servant out of the Records Department – if there is such a thing. Funny thing is, I seem to have heard the name somewhere. Basil!' The secretary had just entered. 'Where have I seen the name Parker Pyne?'

'Front page of *The Times* Agony column,' replied the young man promptly. '"Are you happy? If not, consult Mr Parker Pyne."'

'Never! How frightfully amusing! Let's tell him all our troubles all the way to Cairo.'

'I haven't any,' said Basil West simply. 'We're going to glide down the golden Nile, and see temples' – he looked quickly at Sir George, who had picked up a paper – 'together.'

The last word was only just breathed, but Pamela caught it. Her eyes met his.

'You're right, Basil,' she said lightly. 'It's good to be alive.'

Sir George got up and went out. Pamela's face clouded over.

'What's the matter, my sweet?'

'My detested aunt by marriage –'

'Don't worry,' said Basil quickly. 'What does it matter what she gets into her head? Don't contradict her. You see,' he laughed, 'it's good camouflage.'

The benevolent figure of Mr Parker Pyne entered the lounge. Behind him came the picturesque figure of Mohammed, prepared to say his piece.

'Lady, gentlemans, we start now. In a few minutes we pass temples of Karnak right-hand side. I tell you story now about little boy who went to buy a roasted lamb for his father . . .'

Mr Parker Pyne mopped his forehead. He had just returned from a visit to the Temple of Dendera. Riding on a donkey was, he felt, an exercise ill suited to his figure. He was proceeding to remove his collar when a note propped up on the dressing table caught his attention. He opened it. It ran as follows:

> *Dear Sir, – I should be obliged if you should not visit the Temple of Abydos, but would remain on the boat, as I wish to consult you.*
> *Yours truly,*
> *Ariadne Grayle*

A smile creased Mr Parker Pyne's large, bland face. He reached for a sheet of paper and unscrewed his fountain pen.

> *Dear Lady Grayle (he wrote), I am sorry to disappoint you, but I am at present on holiday and am not doing any professional business.*

He signed his name and dispatched the letter by a steward. As he completed his change of toilet, another note was brought to him.

> *Dear Mr Parker Pyne, – I appreciate the fact that you are on holiday, but I am prepared to pay a fee of a hundred pounds for a consultation.*
> *Yours truly,*
> *Ariadne Grayle*

Mr Parker Pyne's eyebrows rose. He tapped his teeth thoughtfully with his fountain pen. He wanted to see Abydos, but a hundred pounds was a hundred pounds. And Egypt had been even more wickedly expensive than he had imagined.

> *Dear Lady Grayle (he wrote), – I shall not visit the Temple of Abydos.*
> *Yours faithfully,*
> *J. Parker Pyne*

Mr Parker Pyne's refusal to leave the boat was a source of great grief to Mohammed.

'Very nice temple. All my gentlemans like see that temple. I get you carriage. I get you chair and sailors carry you.'

Mr Parker Pyne refused all these tempting offers.

The others set off.

Mr Parker Pyne waited on deck. Presently the door of Lady Grayle's cabin opened and the lady herself trailed out on deck.

'Such a hot afternoon,' she observed graciously. 'I see you have stayed behind, Mr Pyne. Very wise of you. Shall we have some tea together in the lounge?'

Mr Parker Pyne rose promptly and followed her. It cannot be denied that he was curious.

It seemed as though Lady Grayle felt some difficulty in coming to the point. She fluttered from this subject to that. But finally she spoke in an altered voice.

'Mr Pyne, what I am about to tell you is in the strictest confidence! You do understand that, don't you?'

'Naturally.'

She paused, took a deep breath. Mr Parker Pyne waited.

'I want to know whether or not my husband is poisoning me.'

Whatever Mr Parker Pyne had expected, it was not this. He showed his astonishment plainly. 'That is a very serious accusation to make, Lady Grayle.'

'Well, I'm not a fool and I wasn't born yesterday. I've had my suspicions for some time. Whenever George goes away I get better. My food doesn't disagree with me and I feel a different woman. There must be some reason for that.'

'What you say is very serious, Lady Grayle. You must remember I am not a detective. I am, if you like to put it that way, a heart specialist –'

She interrupted him. 'Eh – and don't you think it worries me, all this? It's not a policeman I want – I can look after myself, thank you – it's certainty I want. I've got to *know*. I'm not a wicked woman, Mr Pyne. I act fairly by those who act fairly by me. A bargain's a bargain. I've kept my side of it. I've paid my husband's debts and I've not stinted him in money.'

Mr Parker Pyne had a fleeting pang of pity for Sir George. 'And as for the girl she's had clothes and parties and this, that and the other. Common gratitude is all I ask.'

'Gratitude is not a thing that can be produced to order, Lady Grayle.'

'Nonsense!' said Lady Grayle. She went on: 'Well, there it is! Find out the truth for me! Once I *know* –'

He looked at her curiously. 'Once you know, what then, Lady Grayle?'

'That's my business.' Her lips closed sharply.

Mr Parker Pyne hesitated a minute, then he said: 'You will excuse me, Lady Grayle, but I have the impression that you are not being entirely frank with me.'

'That's absurd. I've told you exactly what I want you to find out.'

'Yes, but not the reason *why*?'

Their eyes met. Hers fell first.

'I should think the reason was self-evident,' she said.

'No, because I am in doubt upon one point.'

'What is that?'

'Do you want your suspicions proved right or wrong?'

'Really, Mr Pyne!' The lady rose to her feet, quivering with indignation.

Mr Parker Pyne nodded his head gently. 'Yes, yes,' he said. 'But that doesn't answer my question, you know.'

'Oh!' Words seemed to fail her. She swept out of the room.

Left alone, Mr Parker Pyne became very thoughtful. He was so deep in his own thoughts that he started perceptibly when someone came in and sat down opposite him. It was Miss MacNaughton.

'Surely you're all back very soon,' said Mr Parker Pyne.

'The others aren't back. I said I had a headache and came back alone.' She hesitated. 'Where is Lady Grayle?'

'I should imagine lying down in her cabin.'

'Oh, then that's all right. I don't want her to know I've come back.'

'You didn't come on her account then?'

Miss MacNaughton shook her head. 'No, I came back to see you.'

Mr Parker Pyne was surprised. He would have said off-hand that Miss MacNaughton was eminently capable of looking after troubles herself without seeking outside advice. It seemed that he was wrong.

'I've watched you since we all came on board. I think you're a person of wide experience and good judgement. And I want advice very badly.'

'And yet – excuse me, Miss MacNaughton – but you're not the type that usually seeks advice. I should say that you were a person who was quite content to rely on her own judgement.'

'Normally, yes. But I am in a very peculiar position.'

She hesitated a moment. 'I do not usually talk about my cases. But in this instance I think it is necessary. Mr Pyne, when I left England with Lady Grayle, she was a straightforward case. In plain language, there was nothing the matter with her. That's not quite true, perhaps. Too much leisure and too much money do produce a definite pathological condition. Having a few floors to scrub every day and five or six children to look after would have made Lady Grayle a perfectly healthy and a much happier woman.'

Mr Parker Pyne nodded.

'As a hospital nurse, one sees a lot of these nervous cases. Lady Grayle *enjoyed* her bad health. It was my part not to minimize her sufferings, to be as tactful as I could – and to enjoy the trip myself as much as possible.'

'Very sensible,' said Mr Parker Pyne.

'But Mr Pyne, things are not as they were. The suffering that Lady Grayle complains of now is real and not imagined.'

'You mean?'

'I have come to suspect that Lady Grayle is being poisoned.'

'Since when have you suspected this?'

'For the past three weeks.'

'Do you suspect – any particular person?'

Her eyes dropped. For the first time her voice lacked sincerity. 'No.'

'I put it to you, Miss MacNaughton, that you do suspect one particular person, and that that person is Sir George Grayle.'

'Oh, no, no, I can't believe it of him! He is so pathetic, so child-like. He couldn't be a cold-blooded poisoner.' Her voice had an anguished note in it.

'And yet you have noticed that whenever Sir George is absent his wife is better and that her periods of illness correspond with his return.'

She did not answer.

'What poison do you suspect? Arsenic?'

'Something of that kind. Arsenic or antimony.'

'And what steps have you taken?'

'I have done my utmost to supervise what Lady Grayle eats and drinks.'

Mr Parker Pyne nodded. 'Do you think Lady Grayle has any suspicion herself?' he asked casually.

'Oh, no, I'm sure she hasn't.'

'There you are wrong,' said Mr Parker Pyne. 'Lady Grayle *does* suspect.'

Miss MacNaughton showed her astonishment.

'Lady Grayle is more capable of keeping a secret than you imagine,' said Mr Parker Pyne. 'She is a woman who knows how to keep her own counsel very well.'

'That surprises me very much,' said Miss MacNaughton slowly.

'I should like to ask you one more question, Miss MacNaughton. Do you think Lady Grayle likes you?'

'I've never thought about it.'

They were interrupted. Mohammed came in, his face beaming, his robes flowing behind him.

'Lady, she hear you come back; she ask for you. She say why you not come to her?'

Elsie MacNaughton rose hurriedly. Mr Parker Pyne rose also.

'Would a consultation early tomorrow morning suit you?' he asked.

'Yes, that would be the best time. Lady Grayle sleeps late. In the meantime, I shall be very careful.'

'I think Lady Grayle will be careful too.'

Miss MacNaughton disappeared.

Mr Parker Pyne did not see Lady Grayle till just before dinner. She was sitting smoking a cigarette and burning what seemed to be a letter. She took no notice at all of him, by which he gathered that she was still offended.

After dinner he played bridge with Sir George, Pamela and Basil. Everyone seemed a little distrait, and the bridge game broke up early.

It was some hours later when Mr Parker Pyne was roused. It was Mohammed who came to him.

'Old lady, she very ill. Nurse, she very frightened. I try to get doctor.'

Mr Parker Pyne hurried on some clothes. He arrived at the doorway of Lady Grayle's cabin at the same time as Basil West. Sir George and Pamela were inside. Elsie MacNaughton was working desperately over her patient. As Mr Parker Pyne arrived, a final convulsion seized the poor lady. Her arched body writhed and stiffened. Then she fell back on her pillows.

Mr Parker Pyne drew Pamela gently outside.

'How awful!' the girl was half-sobbing. 'How awful! Is she, is she –?'

'Dead? Yes, I am afraid it is all over.'

He put her into Basil's keeping. Sir George came out of the cabin, looking dazed.

'I never thought she was really ill,' he was muttering. 'Never thought it for a moment.'

Mr Parker Pyne pushed past him and entered the cabin.

Elsie MacNaughton's face was white and drawn. 'They have sent for a doctor?' she asked.

'Yes.' Then he said: 'Strychnine?'

'Yes. Those convulsions are unmistakable. Oh, I can't believe it!' She sank into a chair, weeping. He patted her shoulder.

Then an idea seemed to strike him. He left the cabin hurriedly and went to the lounge. There was a little scrap of paper left unburnt in an ash-tray. Just a few words were distinguishable:

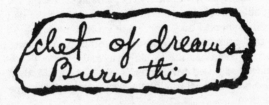

'Now, that's interesting,' said Mr Parker Pyne.

Mr Parker Pyne sat in the room of a prominent Cairo official. 'So that's the evidence,' he said thoughtfully.

'Yes, pretty complete. Man must have been a damned fool.'

'I shouldn't call Sir George a brainy man.'

'All the same!' The other recapitulated: 'Lady Grayle wants a cup of Bovril. The nurse makes it for her. Then she must have sherry in it. Sir George produces the sherry. Two hours later, Lady Grayle dies with unmistakable signs of strychnine poisoning. A packet of strychnine is found in Sir George's cabin and another packet actually in the pocket of his dinner jacket.'

'Very thorough,' said Mr Parker Pyne. 'Where did the strychnine come from, by the way?'

'There's a little doubt over that. The nurse had some – in case Lady Grayle's heart troubled her – but she's contradicted herself once or twice. First she said her supply was intact, and now she says it isn't.'

'Very unlike her not to be sure,' was Mr Parker Pyne's comment.

'They were in it together, in my opinion. They've got a weakness for each other, those two.'

'Possibly; but if Miss MacNaughton had been planning murder, she'd have done it a good deal better. She's an efficient young woman.'

'Well, there it is. In my opinion, Sir George is in for it. He hasn't a dog's chance.'

'Well, well,' said Mr Parker Pyne, 'I must see what I can do.'

He sought out the pretty niece.

Pamela was white and indignant. 'Nunks never did such a thing – never – never – never!'

'Then who did?' said Mr Parker Pyne placidly.

Pamela came nearer. 'Do you know what I think? *She did it herself.* She's been frightfully queer lately. She used to imagine things.'

'What things?'

'Queer things. Basil, for instance. She was always hinting that Basil was in love with her. And Basil and I are – we are –'

'I realize that,' said Mr Parker Pyne, smiling.

'All that about Basil was pure imagination. I think she had a down on poor little Nunks, and I think she made up that story and told it to you, and then put the strychnine in his cabin and in his pocket and poisoned herself. People have done things like that, haven't they?'

'They have,' admitted Mr Parker Pyne. 'But I don't think that Lady Grayle did. She wasn't, if you'll allow me to say so, the type.'

'But the delusions?'

'Yes, I'd like to ask Mr West about that.'

He found the young man in his room. Basil answered his questions readily enough.

'I don't want to sound fatuous, but she took a fancy to me. That's why I daren't let her know about me and Pamela. She'd have had Sir George fire me.'

'You think Miss Grayle's theory a likely one?'

'Well, it's possible, I suppose.' The young man was doubtful.

'But not good enough,' said Mr Parker Pyne quietly. 'No, we must find something better.' He became lost in meditation for a minute or two. 'A confession would be best,' he said briskly. He unscrewed his fountain pen and produced a sheet of paper. 'Just write it out, will you?'

Basil West stared at him in amazement. 'Me? What on earth do you mean?'

'My dear young man' – Mr Parker Pyne sounded almost paternal – 'I know all about it. How you made love to the good lady. How she had scruples. How you fell in love with the pretty, penniless niece. How you arranged your plot. Slow poisoning. It might pass for natural death from gastroenteritis – if not, it would be laid to Sir George's doing, since you were careful to let the attacks coincide with his presence.

'Then your discovery that the lady was suspicious and had talked to me about the matter. Quick action! You abstracted some strychnine from Miss MacNaughton's store. Planted some of it in Sir George's cabin, and some in his pocket, and put sufficient into a cachet which you enclosed with a note to the lady, telling her it was a "cachet of dreams."'

'A romantic idea. She'd take it as soon as the nurse had left her, and no one would know anything about it. But you made one mistake, my young man. It is useless asking a lady to burn letters. They never do. I've got all that pretty correspondence, including the one about the cachet.'

Basil West had turned green. All his good looks had vanished. He looked like a trapped rat.

'Damn you,' he snarled. 'So you know all about it. You damned interfering Nosey Parker.'

Mr Parker Pyne was saved from physical violence by the appearance of the witnesses he had thoughtfully arranged to have listening outside the half-closed door.

Mr Parker Pyne was again discussing the case with his friend the high official.

'And I hadn't a shred of evidence! Only an almost indecipherable fragment, with '*Burn this!*' on it. I deduced the whole story and tried it on him. It worked. I'd stumbled on the truth. The letters did it. Lady Grayle had burned every scrap he wrote, but *he didn't know that.*

'She was really a very unusual woman. I was puzzled when she came to me. What she wanted was for me to tell her that her husband was poisoning her. In that case, she meant to go off with young West. But she wanted to act fairly. Curious character.'

'That poor little girl is going to suffer,' said the other.

'She'll get over it,' said Mr Parker Pyne callously. 'She's young. I'm anxious that Sir George should get a little enjoyment before it's too late. He's been treated like a worm for ten years. Now, Elsie MacNaughton will be very kind to him.'

He beamed. Then he sighed. 'I am thinking of going incognito to Greece. I really *must* have a holiday!'

The Oracle at Delphi

'The Oracle at Delphi' was first published in the USA in *Cosmopolitan*, April 1933, and then in *Nash's Pall Mall*, July 1933.

Mrs Willard J. Peters did not really care for Greece. And of Delphi she had, in her secret heart, no opinion at all.

Mrs Peters' spiritual homes were in Paris, London and the Riviera. She was a woman who enjoyed hotel life, but her idea of a hotel bedroom was a soft-pile carpet, a luxurious bed, a profusion of different arrangements of electric light, including a shaded bedside lamp, plenty of hot and cold water and a telephone beside the bed, by means of which you could order tea, meals, mineral waters, cocktails and speak to your friends.

In the hotel at Delphi there were none of these things. There was a marvellous view from the windows, the bed was clean and so was the whitewashed room. There was a chair, a wash-stand and a chest of drawers. Baths took place by arrangement and were occasionally disappointing as regarded hot water.

It would, she supposed, be nice to say that you had been to Delphi, and Mrs Peters had tried hard to take an interest in Ancient Greece, but she found it difficult. Their statuary seemed so unfinished; so lacking in heads and arms and legs. Secretly, she much preferred the handsome marble angel complete with wings which was erected on the late Mr Willard Peters' tomb.

But all these secret opinions she kept carefully to herself, for fear her son Willard should despise her. It was for Willard's sake that she was here, in this chilly and uncomfortable room, with a sulky maid and a disgusted chauffeur in the offing.

For Willard (until recently called Junior – a title which he hated) was Mrs Peters' eighteen-year-old son, and she worshipped him to distraction. It was Willard who had this strange passion for bygone art. It was Willard, thin, pale, spectacled and dyspeptic, who had dragged his adoring mother on this tour through Greece.

They had been to Olympia, which Mrs Peters thought a sad mess. She had enjoyed the Parthenon, but she considered Athens a hopeless city. And a visit to Corinth and Mycenae had been agony to both her and the chauffeur.

Delphi, Mrs Peters thought unhappily, was the last straw. Absolutely nothing to do but walk along the road and look at the ruins. Willard spent long hours on his knees deciphering Greek inscriptions, saying, 'Mother, just listen to this! Isn't it splendid?' And then he would read out something that seemed to Mrs Peters the quintessence of dullness.

This morning Willard had started early to see some Byzantine mosaics. Mrs Peters, feeling instinctively that Byzantine mosaics would leave her cold (in the literal as well as the spiritual sense), had excused herself.

'I understand, Mother,' Willard had said. 'You want to be alone just to sit in the theatre or up in the stadium and look down over it and let it sink in.'

'That's right, pet,' said Mrs Peters.

'I knew this place would get you,' said Willard exultantly and departed.

Now, with a sigh, Mrs Peters prepared to rise and breakfast.

She came into the dining-room to find it empty save for four people. A mother and daughter, dressed in what seemed to Mrs Peters a most peculiar style (not recognizing the peplum as such), who were discoursing on the art of self-expression in dancing; a plump, middle-aged gentleman who had rescued a suitcase for her when she got off the train and whose name was Thompson; and a newcomer, a middle-aged gentleman with a bald head who had arrived on the preceding evening.

This personage was the last left in the breakfast room, and Mrs Peters soon fell into conversation with him. She was a friendly woman and liked someone to talk to. Mr Thompson had been distinctly discouraging in manner (British reserve, Mrs Peters called it), and the mother and daughter had been very superior and highbrow, though the girl had got on rather well with Willard.

Mrs Peters found the newcomer a very pleasant person. He was informative without being highbrow. He told her several interesting, friendly little details about the Greeks, which made her feel much more as though they were real people and not just tiresome history out of a book.

Mrs Peters told her new friend all about Willard and what a clever boy he was, and how Culture might be said to be his middle name. There was something about this benevolent and bland personage which made him easy to talk to.

What he himself did and what his name was, Mrs Peters did not learn. Beyond the fact that he had been travelling and that he was having a complete rest from business (what business?) he was not communicative about himself.

Altogether, the day passed more quickly than might have been anticipated. The mother and daughter and Mr Thompson continued to be unsociable. They encountered the latter coming out of the museum, and he immediately turned in the opposite direction.

Mrs Peters' new friend looked after him with a little frown.

'Now I wonder who that fellow is!' he said.

Mrs Peters supplied him with the other's name, but could do no more.

'Thompson – Thompson. No, I don't think I've met him before and yet somehow or other his face seems familiar. But I can't place him.'

In the afternoon Mrs Peters enjoyed a quiet nap in a shady spot. The book she took with her to read was not the excellent one on Grecian Art recommended to her by her son but was, on the contrary, entitled *The River Launch Mystery*. It had four murders in it, three abductions, and a large and varied gang of dangerous criminals. Mrs Peters found herself both invigorated and soothed by the perusal of it.

It was four o'clock when she returned to the hotel. Willard, she felt sure, would be back by this time. So far was she from any presentiment of evil that she almost forgot to open a note which the proprietor said had been left for her by a strange man during the afternoon.

It was an extremely dirty note. Idly she ripped it open. As she read the first few lines her face blanched and she put out a hand to steady herself. The handwriting was foreign but the language employed was English.

Lady (it began), – This to hand to inform you that your son is being held captive by us in place of great security. No harm shall happen to honoured young gentleman if you obey orders of yours truly. We demand for him ransom of ten thousand English pounds sterling. If you speak of this to hotel proprietor or police or any such person your son will be killed. This is given you to reflect. Tomorrow directions in way of paying money will be given. If not obeyed the honoured young gentleman's ears will be cut off and sent you. And following day if still not obeyed he will be killed. Again this is not idle threat. Let the Kyria reflect again – above all – be silent.
Demetrius the Black Browed

It were idle to describe the poor lady's state of mind. Preposterous and childishly worded as the demand was, it yet brought home to her a grim atmosphere of peril. Willard, her boy, her pet, her delicate, serious Willard.

She would go at once to the police; she would rouse the neighbourhood. But perhaps, if she did – she shivered.

Then, rousing herself, she went out of her room in search of the hotel proprietor – the sole person in the hotel who could speak English.

'It is getting late,' she said. 'My son has not returned yet.'

The pleasant little man beamed at her. 'True. Monsieur dismissed the mules. He wished to return on foot. He should have been here by now, but doubtless he has lingered on the way.' He smiled happily.

'Tell me,' said Mrs Peters abruptly, 'have you any bad characters in the neighbourhood?'

Bad characters was a term not embraced by the little man's knowledge of English. Mrs Peters made her meaning plainer. She received in reply an assurance that all around Delphi were very good, very quiet people – all well disposed towards foreigners.

Words trembled on her lips, but she forced them back. That sinister threat tied her tongue. It might be the merest bluff. But suppose it wasn't? A friend of hers in America had had a child kidnapped, and on her informing the police, the child had been killed. Such things did happen.

She was nearly frantic. What was she to do? Ten thousand pounds – what was that? – between forty or fifty thousand dollars! What was that to her in comparison with Willard's safety? But how could she obtain such a sum? There were endless difficulties just now as regarded money and the drawing of cash. A letter of credit for a few hundred pounds was all she had with her.

Would the bandits understand this? Would they be reasonable? Would they *wait*?

When her maid came to her, she dismissed the girl fiercely. A bell sounded for dinner, and the poor lady was driven to the dining-room. She ate mechanically. She saw no one. The room might have been empty as far as she was concerned.

With the arrival of fruit, a note was placed before her. She winced, but the handwriting was entirely different from that which she had feared to see – a neat, clerkly English hand. She opened it without much interest, but she found its contents intriguing:

> *At Delphi you can no longer consult the oracle* (so it ran), *but you can consult Mr Parker Pyne.*

Below that there was a cutting of an advertisement pinned to the paper, and at the bottom of the sheet a passport photograph was attached. It was the photograph of her bald-headed friend of the morning.

Mrs Peters read the printed cutting twice.

Are you happy? If not, consult Mr Parker Pyne.

Happy? Happy? Had anyone ever been so unhappy? It was like an answer to prayer.

Hastily she scribbled on a loose sheet of paper she happened to have in her bag:

Please help me. Will you meet me outside the hotel in ten minutes?

She enclosed it in an envelope and directed the waiter to take it to the gentleman at the table by the window. Ten minutes later, enveloped in a fur coat, for the night was chilly, Mrs Peters went out of the hotel and strolled slowly along the road to the ruins. Mr Parker Pyne was waiting for her.

'It's just the mercy of heaven you're here,' said Mrs Peters breathlessly. 'But how did you guess the terrible trouble I'm in. That's what I want to know.'

'The human countenance, my dear madam,' said Mr Parker Pyne gently. 'I knew at once that *something* had happened, but what it is I am waiting for you to tell me.'

Out it came in a flood. She handed him the letter, which he read by the light of his pocket torch.

'H'm,' he said. 'A remarkable document. A most remarkable document. It has certain points –'

But Mrs Peters was in no mood to listen to a discussion of the finer points of the letter. What was she to do about Willard? Her own dear, delicate Willard.

Mr Parker Pyne was soothing. He painted an attractive picture of Greek bandit life. They would be especially careful of their captive, since he represented a potential gold mine. Gradually he calmed her down.

'But what am I to *do*?' wailed Mrs Peters.

'Wait until tomorrow,' said Mr Parker Pyne. 'That is, unless you prefer to go straight to the police.'

Mrs Peters interrupted him with a shriek of terror. Her darling Willard would be murdered out of hand!

'You think I'll get Willard back safe and sound?'

'There is no doubt of that,' said Mr Parker Pyne soothingly. 'The only question is whether you can get him back without paying ten thousand pounds.'

'All I want is my boy.'

'Yes, yes,' said Mr Parker Pyne soothingly. 'Who brought the letter, by the way?'

'A man the landlord didn't know. A stranger.'

'Ah! There are possibilities there. The man who brings the letter tomorrow might be followed. What are you telling the people at the hotel about your son's absence?'

'I haven't thought.'

'I wonder, now.' Mr Parker Pyne reflected. 'I think you might quite naturally express alarm and concern at his absence. A search party could be sent out.'

'You don't think these fiends –?' She choked.

'No, no. So long as there is no word of the kidnapping or the ransom, they cannot turn nasty. After all, you can't be expected to take your son's disappearance with no fuss at all.'

'Can I leave it all to you?'

'That is my business,' said Mr Parker. Pyne.

They started back towards the hotel again but almost ran into a burly figure.

'Who was that?' asked Mr Parker Pyne sharply.

'I think it was Mr Thompson.'

'Oh!' said Mr Parker Pyne thoughtfully.

'Thompson, was it? Thompson – hm.'

Mrs Peters felt as she went to bed that Mr Parker Pyne's idea about the letter was a good one. Whoever brought it *must* be in touch with the bandits. She felt consoled, and fell asleep much sooner than she could ever have believed possible.

When she was dressing on the following morning she suddenly noticed something lying on the floor by the window. She picked it up – and her heart missed a beat. The same dirty, cheap envelope; the same hated characters. She tore it open.

Good-morning lady. Have you made reflections? Your son is well and unharmed – so far. But we must have the money. It may not be easy for you to get this sum, but it has been told us that you have with you a necklace of diamonds. Very fine stones. We will be satisfied with that, instead. Listen, this is what you must do. You, or anyone you choose to send must take this necklace and bring it to the Stadium. From there go up to where there is a tree by a big rock. Eyes will watch and see that only one person comes. Then your son will be exchanged for necklace. The time must be tomorrow six o'clock in the morning just after sunrise. If you put police on us afterwards we shoot your son as your car drives to station.

This is our last word, lady. If no necklace tomorrow morning your son's ears sent you. Next day he die.

With salutations, lady,

Demetrius

Mrs Peters hurried to find Mr Parker Pyne. He read the letter attentively.

'Is this true,' he asked, 'about a diamond necklace?'

'Absolutely. A hundred thousand dollars my husband paid for it.'

'Our well-informed thieves,' murmured Mr Parker Pyne.

'What's that you say?'

'I was just considering certain aspects of the affair.'

'My word, Mr Pyne, we haven't got time for aspects. I've got to get my boy back.'

'But you are a woman of spirit, Mrs Peters. Do you enjoy being bullied and cheated out of ten thousand dollars? Do you enjoy giving up your diamonds meekly to a set of ruffians?'

'Well, of course, if you put it like that!' The woman of spirit in Mrs Peters wrestled with the mother. 'How I'd like to get even with them – the cowardly brutes! The very minute I get my boy back, Mr Pyne, I shall set the whole police of the neighbourhood on them, and, if necessary, I shall hire an armoured car to take Willard and myself to the railway station!' Mrs Peters was flushed and vindictive.

'Ye – es,' said Mr Parker Pyne. 'You see, my dear madam, I'm afraid they will be prepared for that move on your part. They know that once Willard is restored to you nothing will keep you from setting the whole neighbourhood on the alert. Which leads one to suppose that they have prepared for that move.'

'Well, what do you want to do?'

Mr Parker Pyne smiled. 'I want to try a little plan of my own.' He looked around the dining-room. It was empty and the doors at both ends were closed. 'Mrs Peters, there is a man I know in Athens – a jeweller. He specializes in good artificial diamonds – first-class stuff.' His voice dropped to a whisper. 'I'll get him by telephone. He can get here this afternoon, bringing a good selection of stones with him.'

'You mean?'

'He'll extract the real diamonds and replace them with paste replicas.'

'Why, if that isn't the cutest thing I've ever heard of!' Mrs Peters gazed at him with admiration.

'Sh! Not so loud. Will you do something for me?'

'Surely.'

'See that nobody comes within earshot of the telephone.'

Mrs Peters nodded.

The telephone was in the manager's office. He vacated it obligingly, after having helped Mr Parker Pyne to obtain the number. When he emerged, he found Mrs Peters outside.

'I'm just waiting for Mr Parker Pyne,' she said. 'We're going for a walk.'

'Oh, yes, madam.'

Mr Thompson was also in the hall. He came towards them and engaged the manager in conversation.

Were there any villas to be let in Delphi? No? But surely there was one above the hotel?

'That belongs to a Greek gentleman, monsieur. He does not let it.'

'And are there no other villas?'

'There is one belonging to an American lady. That is the other side of the village. It is shut up now. And there is one belonging to an English gentleman, an artist – that is on the cliff edge looking down to Itéa.'

Mrs Peters broke in. Nature had given her a loud voice and she purposely made it louder. 'Why,' she said, 'I'd just adore to have a villa here! So unspoilt and natural. I'm simply crazy about the place, aren't you, Mr Thompson? But of course you must be if you want a villa. Is it your first visit here? You don't say so.'

She ran on determinedly till Mr Parker Pyne emerged from the office. He gave her just the faintest smile of approval.

Mr Thompson walked slowly down the steps and out into the road where he joined the highbrow mother and daughter, who seemed to be feeling the wind cold on their exposed arms.

All went well. The jeweller arrived just before dinner with a car full of other tourists. Mrs Peters took her necklace to his room. He grunted approval. Then he spoke in French.

'*Madame peut être tranquille. Je réussirai.*' He extracted some tools from his little bag and began work.

At eleven o'clock Mr Parker Pyne tapped on Mrs Peters' door. 'Here you are!'

He handed her a little chamois bag. She glanced inside.

'My diamonds!'

'Hush! Here is the necklace with the paste replacing the diamonds. Pretty good, don't you think?'

'Simply wonderful.'

'Aristopoulous is a clever fellow.'

'You don't think they'll suspect?'

'How should they? They know you have the necklace with you. You hand it over. How can they suspect the trick?'

'Well, I think it's wonderful,' Mrs Peters reiterated, handing the necklace back to him. 'Will you take it to them? Or is that asking too much of you?'

'Certainly I will take it. Just give me the letter, so that I have the directions clear. Thank you. Now, good-night and *bon courage*. Your boy will be with you tomorrow for breakfast.'

'Oh, if only that's true!'

'Now, don't worry. Leave everything in my hands.'

Mrs Peters did not spend a good night. When she slept, she had terrible dreams. Dreams where armed bandits in armoured cars fired off a fusillade at Willard, who was running down the mountain in his pyjamas.

She was thankful to wake. At last came the first glimmer of dawn. Mrs Peters got up and dressed. She sat – waiting.

At seven o'clock there came a tap on the door. Her throat was so dry she could hardly speak.

'Come in,' she said.

The door opened and Mr Thompson entered. She stared at him. Words failed her. She had a sinister presentiment of disaster. And yet his voice when he spoke was completely natural and matter-of-fact. It was a rich, bland voice.

'Good-morning, Mrs Peters,' he said.

'How dare you sir! How dare you –'

'You must excuse my unconventional visit at so early an hour,' said Mr Thompson. 'But you see, I have a matter of business to transact.'

Mrs Peter leaned forward with accusing eyes. 'So it was you who kidnapped my boy! It wasn't bandits at all!'

'It certainly wasn't bandits. Most unconvincingly done, that part of it, I thought. Inartistic, to say the least of it.'

Mrs Peters was a woman of a single idea. 'Where's my boy?' she demanded, with the eyes of an angry tigress.

'As a matter of fact,' said Mr Thompson, 'he's just outside the door.'

'Willard!'

The door was flung open. Willard, sallow and spectacled and distinctly unshaven, was clasped to his mother's heart. Mr Thompson stood looking benignly on.

'All the same,' said Mrs Peters, suddenly recovering herself and turning on him, 'I'll have the law on you for this. Yes, I will.'

'You've got it all wrong, Mother,' said Willard. 'This gentleman rescued me.'

'Where were you?'

'In a house on the cliff point. Just a mile from here.'

'And allow me, Mrs Peters,' said Mr Thompson, 'to restore your property.'

He handed her a small packet loosely wrapped in tissue paper. The paper fell away and revealed the diamond necklace.

'You need not treasure that other little bag of stones, Mrs Peters,' said Mr Thompson, smiling. 'The real stones are still in the necklace. The chamois bag contains some excellent imitation stones. As your friend said, Aristopoulous is quite a genius.'

'I just don't understand a word of all this,' said Mrs Peters faintly.

'You must look at the case from my point of view,' said Mr Thompson. 'My attention was caught by the use of a certain name. I took the liberty of following you and your fat friend out of doors and I listened – I admit it frankly – to your exceedingly interesting conversation. I found it remarkably suggestive, so much so that I took the manager into my confidence. He took a note of the number to which your plausible friend telephoned and he also arranged that a waiter should listen to your conversation in the dining-room this morning.

'The whole scheme worked very clearly. You were being made the victim of a couple of clever jewel thieves. They know all about your diamond necklace; they follow you here; they kidnap your son, and write the rather comic "bandit" letter, and they arrange that you shall confide in the chief instigator of the plot.

'After that, all is simple. The good gentleman hands you a bag of imitation diamonds and – clears out with his pal. This morning, when your son did not appear, you would be frantic. The absence of your friend would lead you to believe that he had been kidnapped too. I gather that they had arranged for someone to go to the villa tomorrow. That person would have discovered your son, and by the time you and he had put your heads together you might have got an inkling of the plot. But by that time the villains would have got an excellent start.'

'And now?'

'Oh, now they are safely under lock and key. I arranged for that.'

'The villain,' said Mrs Peters, wrathfully remembering her own trustful confidences. 'The oily, plausible villain.'

'Not at all a nice fellow,' agreed Mr Thompson.

'It beats me how you got on to it,' said Willard admiringly. 'Pretty smart of you.'

The other shook his head deprecatingly. 'No, no,' he said. 'When you are travelling incognito and hear your own name being taken in vain –'

Mrs Peters stared at him. 'Who are you?' she demanded abruptly.

'*I am Mr Parker Pyne*,' explained that gentleman.

Problem at Pollensa Bay

'Problem at Pollensa Bay' was first published in *Strand Magazine*, November 1935, and then in the USA as 'Siren Business' in *Liberty*, 5 September 1936.

The steamer from Barcelona to Majorca landed Mr Parker Pyne at Palma in the early hours of the morning – and straightaway he met with disillusionment. The hotels were full! The best that could be done for him was an airless cupboard overlooking an inner court in a hotel in the centre of the town – and with that Mr Parker Pyne was not prepared to put up. The proprietor of the hotel was indifferent to his disappointment.

'What will you?' he observed with a shrug.

Palma was popular now! The exchange was favourable! Everyone – the English, the Americans – they all came to Majorca in the winter. The whole place was crowded. It was doubtful if the English gentleman would be able to get in anywhere – except perhaps at Formentor where the prices were so ruinous that even foreigners blenched at them.

Mr Parker Pyne partook of some coffee and a roll and went out to view the cathedral, but found himself in no mood for appreciating the beauties of architecture.

He next had a conference with a friendly taxi driver in inadequate French interlarded with native Spanish, and they discussed the merits and possibilities of Soller, Alcudia, Pollensa and Formentor – where there were fine hotels but very expensive.

Mr Parker Pyne was goaded to inquire how expensive.

They asked, said the taxi driver, an amount that it would be absurd and ridiculous to pay – was it not well known that the English came here because prices were cheap and reasonable?

Mr Parker Pyne said that that was quite so, but all the same what sums *did* they charge at Formentor?

A price incredible!

Perfectly – but WHAT PRICE EXACTLY?

The driver consented at last to reply in terms of figures.

Fresh from the exactions of hotels in Jerusalem and Egypt, the figure did not stagger Mr Parker Pyne unduly.

A bargain was struck, Mr Parker Pyne's suitcases were loaded on the taxi in a somewhat haphazard manner, and they started off to drive round the island, trying cheaper hostelries en route but with the final objective of Formentor.

But they never reached that final abode of plutocracy, for after they had passed through the narrow streets of Pollensa and were following the curved line of the seashore, they came to the Hotel Pino d'Oro – a small hotel standing on the edge of the sea looking out over a view that in the misty haze of a fine morning had the exquisite vagueness of a Japanese print. At once Mr Parker Pyne knew that this, and this only, was what he was looking for. He stopped the taxi, passed through the painted gate with the hope that he would find a resting place.

The elderly couple to whom the hotel belonged knew no English or French. Nevertheless the matter was concluded satisfactorily. Mr Parker Pyne was allotted a room overlooking the sea, the suitcases were unloaded, the driver congratulated his passenger upon avoiding the monstrous exigencies of 'these new hotels', received his fare and departed with a cheerful Spanish salutation.

Mr Parker Pyne glanced at his watch and perceiving that it was, even now, but a quarter to ten, he went out onto the small terrace now bathed in a dazzling morning light and ordered, for the second time that morning, coffee and rolls.

There were four tables there, his own, one from which breakfast was being cleared away and two occupied ones. At the one nearest him sat a family of father and mother and two elderly daughters – Germans. Beyond them, at the corner of the terrace, sat what were clearly an English mother and son.

The woman was about fifty-five. She had grey hair of a pretty tone – was sensibly but not fashionably dressed in a tweed coat and skirt – and had that comfortable self-possession which marks an Englishwoman used to much travelling abroad.

The young man who sat opposite her might have been twenty-five and he too was typical of his class and age. He was neither good-looking nor plain, tall nor short. He was clearly on the best of terms with his mother – they made little jokes together – and he was assiduous in passing her things.

As they talked, her eye met that of Mr Parker Pyne. It passed over him with well-bred nonchalance, but he knew that he had been assimilated and labelled.

He had been recognized as English and doubtless, in due course, some pleasant non-committal remark would be addressed to him.

Mr Parker Pyne had no particular objection. His own countrymen and women abroad were inclined to bore him slightly, but he was quite willing to pass the time of day in an amiable manner. In a small hotel it caused constraint if one did not do so. This particular woman, he felt sure, had excellent 'hotel manners', as he put it.

The English boy rose from his seat, made some laughing remark and passed into the hotel. The woman took her letters and bag and settled herself in a chair facing the sea. She unfolded a copy of the *Continental Daily Mail*. Her back was to Mr Parker Pyne.

As he drank the last drop of his coffee, Mr Parker Pyne glanced in her direction, and instantly he stiffened. He was alarmed – alarmed for the peaceful continuance of his holiday! That back was horribly expressive. In his time he had classified many such backs. Its rigidity – the tenseness of its poise – without seeing her face he knew well enough that the eyes were bright with unshed tears – that the woman was keeping herself in hand by a rigid effort.

Moving warily, like a much-hunted animal, Mr Parker Pyne retreated into the hotel. Not half an hour before he had been invited to sign his name in the book lying on the desk. There it was – a neat signature – C. Parker Pyne, London.

A few lines above Mr Parker Pyne noticed the entries: Mrs R. Chester, Mr Basil Chester – Holm Park, Devon.

Seizing a pen, Mr Parker Pyne wrote rapidly over his signature. It now read (with difficulty) Christopher Pyne.

If Mrs R. Chester was unhappy in Pollensa Bay, it was not going to be made easy for her to consult Mr Parker Pyne.

Already it had been a source of abiding wonder to that gentleman that so many people he had come across abroad should know his name and have noted his advertisements. In England many thousands of people read the *Times* every day and could have answered quite truthfully that they had never heard such a name in their lives. Abroad, he reflected, they read their newspapers more thoroughly. No item, not even the advertisement columns, escaped them.

Already his holidays had been interrupted on several occasions. He had dealt with a whole series of problems from murder to attempted blackmail. He was determined in Majorca to have peace. He felt instinctively that a distressed mother might trouble that peace considerably.

Mr Parker Pyne settled down at the Pino d'Oro very happily. There was a larger hotel not far off, the Mariposa, where a good many English people stayed. There was also quite an artist colony living all round. You could walk along by the sea to the fishing village where there was a cock-tail bar where people met – there were a few shops. It was all very peaceful and pleasant. Girls strolled about in trousers with brightly coloured handkerchiefs tied round the upper halves of their bodies. Young men in berets with rather long hair held forth in 'Mac's Bar' on such subjects as plastic values and abstraction in art.

On the day after Mr Parker Pyne's arrival, Mrs Chester made a few conventional remarks to him on the subject of the view and the likelihood of the weather keeping fine. She then chatted a little with the German lady about knitting, and had a few pleasant words about the sadness of the political situation with two Danish gentlemen who spent their time rising at dawn and walking for eleven hours.

Mr Parker Pyne found Basil Chester a most likeable young man. He called Mr Parker Pyne 'sir' and listened most politely to anything the older man said. Sometimes the three English people had coffee together after dinner in the evening. After the third day, Basil left the party after ten minutes or so and Mr Parker Pyne was left tete-a-tete with Mrs Chester.

They talked about flowers and the growing of them, of the lament-able state of the English pound and of how expensive France had become, and of the difficulty of getting good afternoon tea.

Every evening when her son departed, Mr Parker Pyne saw the quickly concealed tremor of her lips, but immediately she recovered and discoursed pleasantly on the above-mentioned subjects.

Little by little she began to talk of Basil – of how well he had done at school – 'he was in the First XI, you know' – of how everyone liked him, of how proud his father would have been of the boy had he lived, of how thankful she had been that Basil had never been 'wild'. 'Of course I always urge him to be with young people, but he really seems to prefer being with me.'

She said it with a kind of nice modest pleasure in the fact.

But for once Mr Parker Pyne did not make the usual tactful response he could usually achieve so easily. He said instead:

'Oh! well, there seem to be plenty of young people here – not in the hotel, but round about.'

At that, he noticed, Mrs Chester stiffened. She said: Of course there were a lot of *artists*. Perhaps she was very old-fashioned – *real* art, of course, was different, but a lot of young people just made that sort of thing an excuse for lounging about and doing nothing – and the girls drank a lot too much.

On the following day Basil said to Mr Parker Pyne:

'I'm awfully glad you turned up here, sir – especially for my mother's sake. She likes having you to talk to in the evenings.'

'What did you do when you were first here?'

'As a matter of fact we used to play piquet.'

'I see.'

'Of course one gets rather tired of piquet. As a matter of fact I've got some friends here – frightfully cheery crowd. I don't really think my mother approves of them –' He laughed as though he felt this ought to be amusing. 'The mater's very old-fashioned . . . Even girls in trousers shock her!'

'Quite so,' said Mr Parker Pyne.

'What I tell her is – one's got to move with the times . . . The girls at home round us are frightfully dull . . .'

'I see,' said Mr Parker Pyne.

All this interested him well enough. He was a spectator of a miniature drama, but he was not called upon to take part in it.

And then the worst – from Mr Parker Pyne's point of view – happened. A gushing lady of his acquaintance came to stay at the Mariposa. They met in the tea shop in the presence of Mrs Chester.

The newcomer screamed:

'Why – if it isn't Mr Parker Pyne – the one and only Mr Parker Pyne! And Adela Chester! Do you know each other? Oh, you do? You're staying at the same hotel? He's the one and only original wizard, Adela – the marvel of the century – all your troubles smoothed out while you wait! Didn't you *know*? You must have *heard* about him? Haven't you read his advertisements? "*Are you in trouble? Consult Mr Parker Pyne.*" There's just nothing he can't do. Husbands and wives flying at each other's throats and he brings 'em together – if you've lost interest in life he gives you the most thrilling adventures. As I say the man's just a *wizard*!'

It went on a good deal longer – Mr Parker Pyne at intervals making modest disclaimers. He disliked the look that Mrs Chester turned upon him. He disliked even more seeing her return along the beach in close confabulation with the garrulous singer of his praises.

The climax came quicker than he expected. That evening, after coffee, Mrs Chester said abruptly,

'Will you come into the little salon, Mr Pyne? There is something I want to say to you.'

He could but bow and submit.

Mrs Chester's self-control had been wearing thin – as the door of the little salon closed behind them, it snapped. She sat down and burst into tears.

'My boy, Mr Parker Pyne. You must save him. *We* must save him. It's breaking my heart!'

'My dear lady, as a mere outsider –'

'Nina Wycherley says you can do *anything*. She said I was to have the utmost confidence in you. She advised me to tell you everything – and that you'd put the whole thing right.'

Inwardly Mr Parker Pyne cursed the obtrusive Mrs Wycherley.

Resigning himself he said:

'Well, let us thrash the matter out. A girl, I suppose?'

'Did he tell you about her?'

'Only indirectly.'

Words poured in a vehement stream from Mrs Chester. 'The girl was dreadful. She drank, she swore – she wore no clothes to speak of. Her sister lived out here – was married to an artist – a Dutchman. The whole set was most undesirable. Half of them were living together without being married. Basil was completely changed. He had always been so quiet, so interested in serious subjects. He had thought at one time of taking up archaeology –'

'Well, well,' said Mr Parker Pyne. 'Nature will have her revenge.'

'What do you mean?'

'It isn't healthy for a young man to be interested in serious subjects. He ought to be making an idiot of himself over one girl after another.'

'Please be serious, Mr Pyne.'

'I'm perfectly serious. Is the young lady, by any chance, the one who had tea with you yesterday?'

He had noticed her – her grey flannel trousers – the scarlet handkerchief tied loosely around her breast – the vermilion mouth and the fact that she had chosen a cocktail in preference to tea.

'You saw her? Terrible! Not the kind of girl Basil has ever admired.'

'You haven't given him much chance to admire a girl, have you?'

'I?'

'He's been too fond of *your* company! Bad! However, I daresay he'll get over this – if you don't precipitate matters.'

'You don't understand. He wants to marry this girl – Betty Gregg – they're *engaged*.'

'It's gone as far as that?'

'Yes. Mr Parker Pyne, you *must* do something. You must get my boy out of this disastrous marriage! His whole life will be ruined.'

'Nobody's life can be ruined except by themselves.'

'Basil's will be,' said Mrs Chester positively.

'I'm not worrying about Basil.'

'You're not worrying about the *girl*?'

'No, I'm worrying about *you*. You've been squandering your birthright.'

Mrs Chester looked at him, slightly taken aback.

'What are the years from twenty to forty? Fettered and bound by personal and emotional relationships. That's bound to be. That's living. But later there's a new stage. You can think, observe life, discover something about other people and the truth about yourself. Life becomes real – significant. You see it as a whole. Not just one scene – the scene you, as an actor, are playing. No man or woman is actually himself (or herself) till after forty-five. That's when individuality has a chance.'

Mrs Chester said:

'I've been wrapped up in Basil. He's been *everything* to me.'

'Well, he shouldn't have been. That's what you're paying for now. Love him as much as you like – but you're Adela Chester, remember, a person – not just Basil's mother.'

'It will break my heart if Basil's life is ruined,' said Basil's mother.

He looked at the delicate lines of her face, the wistful droop of her mouth. She was, somehow, a lovable woman. He did not want her to be hurt. He said:

'I'll see what I can do.'

He found Basil Chester only too ready to talk, eager to urge his point of view.

'This business is being just hellish. Mother's hopeless – prejudiced, narrow-minded. If only she'd let herself, she'd *see* how fine Betty is.'

'And Betty?'

He sighed.

'Betty's being damned difficult! If she'd just conform a bit – I mean leave off the lipstick for a day – it might make all the difference. She seems to go out of her way to be – well – modern – when Mother's about.'

Mr Parker Pyne smiled.

'Betty and Mother are two of the dearest people in the world, I should have thought they would have taken to each other like hot cakes.'

'You have a lot to learn, young man,' said Mr Parker Pyne.

'I wish you'd come along and see Betty and have a good talk about it all.'

Mr Parker Pyne accepted the invitation readily.

Betty and her sister and her husband lived in a small dilapidated villa a little way back from the sea. Their life was of a refreshing simplicity. Their furniture comprised three chairs, a table and beds. There was a cupboard in the wall that held the bare requirements of cups and plates. Hans was an excitable young man with wild blond hair that stood up all over his head. He spoke very odd English with incredible rapidity, walking up and down as he did so. Stella, his wife, was small and fair. Betty Gregg had red hair and freckles and a mischievous eye. She was, he noticed, not nearly so made-up as she had been the previous day at the Pino d'Oro.

She gave him a cocktail and said with a twinkle:

'You're in on the big bust-up?'

Mr Parker Pyne nodded.

'And whose side are you on, big boy? The young lovers – or the disapproving dame?'

'May I ask you a question?'

'Certainly.'

'Have you been very tactful over all this?'

'Not at all,' said Miss Gregg frankly. 'But the old cat put my back up.' (She glanced round to make sure that Basil was out of earshot) 'That woman just makes me feel mad. She's kept Basil tied to her apron strings all these years – that sort of thing makes a man look a fool. Basil isn't a fool really. Then she's so terribly *pukka sahib*.'

'That's not really such a bad thing. It's merely "unfashionable" just at present.'

Betty Gregg gave a sudden twinkle.

'You mean it's like putting Chippendale chairs in the attic in Victorian days? Later you get them down again and say, "Aren't they marvellous?"'

'Something of the kind.'

Betty Gregg considered.

'Perhaps you're right. I'll be honest. It was Basil who put my back up – being so anxious about what impression I'd make on his mother. It drove me to extremes. Even now I believe he might give me up – if his mother worked on him good and hard.'

'He might,' said Mr Parker Pyne. 'If she went about it the right way.'

'Are you going to tell her the right way? She won't think of it herself, you know. She'll just go on disapproving and that won't do the trick. But if you prompted her –'

She bit her lip – raised frank blue eyes to his.

'I've heard about you, Mr Parker Pyne. You're supposed to know something about human nature.

Do you think Basil and I could make a go of it – or not?'

'I should like an answer to three questions.'

'Suitability test? All right, go ahead.'

'Do you sleep with your window open or shut?'

'Open. I like lots of air.'

'Do you and Basil enjoy the same kind of food?'

'Yes.'

'Do you like going to bed early or late?'

'Really, under the rose, early. At half past ten I yawn – and I secretly feel rather hearty in the mornings – but of course I daren't admit it.'

'You ought to suit each other very well,' said Mr Parker Pyne.

'Rather a superficial test.'

'Not at all. I have known seven marriages at least, entirely wrecked, because the husband liked sitting up till midnight and the wife fell asleep at half past nine and vice versa.'

'It's a pity,' said Betty, 'that everybody can't be happy. Basil and I, and his mother giving us her blessing.'

Mr Parker Pyne coughed.

'I think,' he said, 'that that could possibly be managed.'

She looked at him doubtfully.

'Now I wonder,' she said, 'if you're double-crossing me?'

Mr Parker Pyne's face told nothing.

To Mrs Chester he was soothing, but vague. An engagement was not marriage. He himself was going to Soller for a week. He suggested that her line of action should be non-committal. Let her appear to acquiesce.

He spent a very enjoyable week at Soller.

On his return he found that a totally unexpected development had arisen.

As he entered the Pino d'Oro the first thing he saw was Mrs Chester and Betty Gregg having tea together. Basil was not there. Mrs Chester looked haggard. Betty, too, was looking off colour. She was hardly made-up at all, and her eyelids looked as though she had been crying.

They greeted him in a friendly fashion, but neither of them mentioned Basil.

Suddenly he heard the girl beside him draw in her breath sharply as though something had hurt her. Mr Parker Pyne turned his head.

Basil Chester was coming up the steps from the sea front. With him was a girl so exotically beautiful that it quite took your breath away. She was dark and her figure was marvellous. No one could fail to notice the fact since she wore nothing but a single garment of pale blue crêpe. She was heavily made-up with ochre powder and an orange scarlet mouth – but the unguents only displayed her remarkable beauty in a more pronounced fashion. As for young Basil, he seemed unable to take his eyes from her face.

'You're very late, Basil,' said his mother. 'You were to have taken Betty to Mac's.'

'My fault,' drawled the beautiful unknown. 'We just drifted.' She turned to Basil. 'Angel – get me something with a kick in it!'

She tossed off her shoe and stretched out her manicured toenails which were done emerald green to match her fingernails.

She paid no attention to the two women, but she leaned a little towards Mr Parker Pyne.

'Terrible island this,' she said. 'I was just dying with boredom before I met Basil. He is rather a pet!'

'Mr Parker Pyne – Miss Ramona,' said Mrs Chester.

The girl acknowledged the introduction with a lazy smile.

'I guess I'll call you Parker almost at once,' she murmured. 'My name's Dolores.'

Basil returned with the drinks. Miss Ramona divided her conversation (what there was of it – it was mostly glances) between Basil and Mr Parker Pyne. Of the two women she took no notice whatever. Betty attempted once or twice to join in the conversation but the other girl merely stared at her and yawned.

Suddenly Dolores rose.

'Guess I'll be going along now. I'm at the other hotel. Anyone coming to see me home?'

Basil sprang up.

'I'll come with you.'

Mrs Chester said: 'Basil, my dear –'

'I'll be back presently, Mother.'

'Isn't he the mother's boy?' Miss Ramona asked of the world at large. 'Just toots round after her, don't you?'

Basil flushed and looked awkward. Miss Ramona gave a nod in Mrs Chester's direction, a dazzling smile to Mr Parker Pyne and she and Basil moved off together.

After they had gone there was rather an awkward silence. Mr Parker Pyne did not like to speak first. Betty Gregg was twisting her fingers and looking out to sea. Mrs Chester looked flushed and angry.

Betty said: 'Well, what do you think of our new acquisition in Pollensa Bay?' Her voice was not quite steady.

Mr Parker Pyne said cautiously:

'A little – er – exotic.'

'Exotic?' Betty gave a short bitter laugh.

Mrs Chester said: 'She's terrible – terrible. Basil must be quite mad.'

Betty said sharply: 'Basil's all right.'

'Her toenails,' said Mrs Chester with a shiver of nausea.

Betty rose suddenly.

'I think, Mrs Chester, I'll go home and not stay to dinner after all.'

'Oh, my dear – Basil will be so disappointed.'

'Will he?' asked Betty with a short laugh. 'Anyway, I think I will. I've got rather a headache.'

She smiled at them both and went off. Mrs Chester turned to Mr Parker Pyne.

'I wish we had never come to this place – never!'

Mr Parker Pyne shook his head sadly.

'You shouldn't have gone away,' said Mrs Chester. 'If you'd been here this wouldn't have happened.'

Mr Parker Pyne was stung to respond.

'My dear lady, I can assure you that when it comes to a question of a beautiful young woman, I should have no influence over your son whatever. He – er – seems to be of a very susceptible nature.'

'He never used to be,' said Mrs Chester tearfully.

'Well,' said Mr Parker Pyne with an attempt at cheerfulness, 'this new attraction seems to have broken the back of his infatuation for Miss Gregg. That must be some satisfaction to you.'

'I don't know what you mean,' said Mrs Chester. 'Betty is a dear child and devoted to Basil. She is behaving extremely well over this. I think my boy must be mad.'

Mr Parker Pyne received this startling change of face without wincing. He had met inconsistency in women before. He said mildly:

'Not exactly mad – just bewitched.'

'The creature's a Dago. She's impossible.'

'But extremely good-looking.'

Mrs Chester snorted.

Basil ran up the steps from the sea front.

'Hullo, Mater, here I am. Where's Betty?'

'Betty's gone home with a headache. I don't wonder.'

'Sulking, you mean.'

'I consider, Basil, that you are being extremely unkind to Betty.'

'For God's sake, Mother, don't jaw. If Betty is going to make this fuss every time I speak to another girl a nice sort of life we'll lead together.'

'You *are* engaged.'

'Oh, we're engaged all right. That doesn't mean that we're not going to have any friends of our own. Nowadays people have to lead their own lives and try to cut out jealousy.'

He paused.

'Look here, if Betty isn't going to dine with us – I think I'll go back to the Mariposa. They did ask me to dine . . .'

'Oh, Basil –'

The boy gave her an exasperated look, then ran off down the steps.

Mrs Chester looked eloquently at Mr Parker Pyne.

'You see,' she said.

He saw.

Matters came to a head a couple of days later. Betty and Basil were to have gone for a long walk, taking a picnic lunch with them. Betty arrived at the Pino d'Oro to find that Basil had forgotten the plan and gone over to Formentor for the day with Dolores Ramona's party.

Beyond a tightening of the lips the girl made no sign. Presently, however, she got up and stood in front of Mrs Chester (the two women were alone on the terrace).

'It's quite all right,' she said. 'It doesn't matter. But I think – all the same – that we'd better call the whole thing off.'

She slipped from her finger the signet ring that Basil had given her – he would buy the real engagement ring later.

'Will you give him back this Mrs Chester? And tell him it's all right – not to worry . . .'

'Betty dear, don't! He *does* love you – really.'

'It looks like it, doesn't it?' said the girl with a short laugh. 'No – I've got some pride. Tell him everything's all right and that I – I wish him luck.'

When Basil returned at sunset he was greeted by a storm.

He flushed a little at the sight of his ring.

'So that's how she feels, is it? Well, I daresay it's the best thing.'

'Basil!'

'Well, frankly, Mother, we don't seem to have been hitting it off lately.'

'Whose fault was that?'

'I don't see that it was mine particularly. Jealousy's beastly and I really don't see why *you* should get all worked up about it. You begged me yourself not to marry Betty.'

'That was before I knew her. Basil – my dear – you're not thinking of marrying this other creature.'

Basil Chester said soberly:

'I'd marry her like a shot if she'd have me – but I'm afraid she won't.'

Cold chills went down Mrs Chester's spine. She sought and found Mr Parker Pyne, placidly reading a book in a sheltered corner.

'You must *do* something! You *must* do something! My boy's life will be ruined.'

Mr Parker Pyne was getting a little tired of Basil Chester's life being ruined.

'What can I do?'

'Go and see this terrible creature. If necessary buy her off.'

'That may come very expensive.'

'I don't care.'

'It seems a pity. Still there are, possibly, other ways.'

She looked a question. He shook his head.

'I'll make no promises – but I'll see what I can do. I have handled that kind before. By the way, not a word to Basil – that would be fatal.'

'Of course not.'

Mr Parker Pyne returned from the Mariposa at midnight. Mrs Chester was sitting up for him.

'Well?' she demanded breathlessly.

His eyes twinkled.

'The Señorita Dolores Ramona will leave Pollensa tomorrow morning and the island tomorrow night.'

'Oh, Mr Parker Pyne! How did you manage it?'

'It won't cost a cent,' said Mr Parker Pyne. Again his eyes twinkled. 'I rather fancied I might have a hold over her – and I was right.'

'You are wonderful. Nina Wycherley was quite right. You must let me know – er – your fees –'

Mr Parker Pyne held up a well-manicured hand.

'Not a penny. It has been a pleasure. I hope all will go well. Of course the boy will be very upset at first when he finds she's disappeared and left no address. Just go easy with him for a week or two.'

'If only Betty will forgive him –'

'She'll forgive him all right. They're a nice couple. By the way, I'm leaving tomorrow, too.'

'Oh, Mr Parker Pyne, we shall miss you.'

'Perhaps it's just as well I should go before that boy of yours gets infatuated with yet a third girl.'

Mr Parker Pyne leaned over the rail of the steamer and looked at the lights of Palma. Beside him stood Dolores Ramona. He was saying appreciatively:

'A very nice piece of work, Madeleine. I'm glad I wired you to come out. It's odd when you're such a quiet, stay-at-home girl really.'

Madeleine de Sara, alias Dolores Ramona, alias Maggie Sayers, said primly: 'I'm glad you're pleased, Mr Parker Pyne. It's been a nice little change. I think I'll go below now and get to bed before the boat starts. I'm such a bad sailor.'

A few minutes later a hand fell on Mr Parker Pyne's shoulder. He turned to see Basil Chester.

'Had to come and see you off, Mr Parker Pyne, and give you Betty's love and her and my best thanks. It was a grand stunt of yours. Betty and Mother are as thick as thieves. Seemed a shame to deceive the old darling – but she *was* being difficult. Anyway it's all right now. I must just be careful to keep up the annoyance stuff a couple of days longer. We're no end grateful to you, Betty and I.'

'I wish you every happiness,' said Mr Parker Pyne.

'Thanks.'

There was a pause, then Basil said with somewhat overdone carelessness:

'Is Miss – Miss de Sara – anywhere about? I'd like to thank her, too.'

Mr Parker Pyne shot a keen glance at him.

He said:

'I'm afraid Miss de Sara's gone to bed.'

'Oh, too bad – well, perhaps I'll see her in London sometime.'

'As a matter of fact she is going to America on business for me almost at once.'

'Oh!' Basil's tone was blank. 'Well,' he said. 'I'll be getting along . . .'

Mr Parker Pyne smiled. On his way to his cabin he tapped on the door of Madeleine's.

'How are you, my dear? All right? Our young friend has been along. The usual slight attack of Madeleinitis. He'll get over it in a day or two, but you are rather distracting.'

The Regatta Mystery

'The Regatta Mystery' was first published as 'Poirot and the Regatta Mystery' in the USA in the *Chicago Tribune*, 3 May 1936, and then in *Strand Magazine*, June 1936. It first appeared in its current form in the American book *The Regatta Mystery and Other Stories*, published by Dodd, Mead, June 1939.

Mr Isaac Pointz removed a cigar from his lips and said approvingly:
'Pretty little place.'

Having thus set the seal of his approval upon Dartmouth harbour, he replaced the cigar and looked about him with the air of a man pleased with himself, his appearance, his surroundings and life generally.

As regards the first of these, Mr Isaac Pointz was a man of fifty-eight, in good health and condition with perhaps a slight tendency to liver. He was not exactly stout, but comfortable-looking, and a yachting costume, which he wore at the moment, is not the most kindly of attires for a middle-aged man with a tendency to embonpoint. Mr Pointz was very well turned out – correct to every crease and button – his dark and slightly Oriental face beaming out under the peak of his yachting cap. As regards his surroundings, these may have been taken to mean his companions – his partner Mr Leo Stein, Sir George and Lady Marroway, an American business acquaintance Mr Samuel Leathern and his schoolgirl daughter Eve, Mrs Rustington and Evan Llewellyn.

The party had just come ashore from Mr Pointz' yacht – the *Merrimaid*. In the morning they had watched the yacht racing and they had now come ashore to join for a while in the fun of the fair – Coconut shies, Fat Ladies, the Human Spider and the Merry-go-round. It is hardly to be doubted that these delights were relished most by Eve Leathern. When Mr Pointz finally suggested that it was time to adjourn to the Royal George for dinner hers was the only dissentient voice.

'Oh, Mr Pointz – I did so want to have my fortune told by the Real Gypsy in the Caravan.'

Mr Pointz had doubts of the essential Realness of the Gypsy in question but he gave indulgent assent.

'Eve's just crazy about the fair,' said her father apologetically. 'But don't you pay any attention if you want to be getting along.'

'Plenty of time,' said Mr Pointz benignantly. 'Let the little lady enjoy herself. I'll take you on at darts, Leo.'

'Twenty-five and over wins a prize,' chanted the man in charge of the darts in a high nasal voice.

'Bet you a fiver my total score beats yours,' said Pointz.

'Done,' said Stein with alacrity.

The two men were soon whole-heartedly engaged in their battle.

Lady Marroway murmured to Evan Llewellyn:

'Eve is not the only child in the party.'

Llewellyn smiled assent but somewhat absently.

He had been absent-minded all that day. Once or twice his answers had been wide of the point.

Pamela Marroway drew away from him and said to her husband:

'That young man has something on his mind.'

Sir George murmured:

'Or someone?'

And his glance swept quickly over Janet Rustington.

Lady Marroway frowned a little. She was a tall woman exquisitely groomed. The scarlet of her fingernails was matched by the dark red coral studs in her ears. Her eyes were dark and watchful. Sir George affected a careless 'hearty English gentleman' manner – but his bright blue eyes held the same watchful look as his wife's.

Isaac Pointz and Leo Stein were Hatton Garden diamond merchants. Sir George and Lady Marroway came from a different world – the world of Antibes and Juan les Pins – of golf at St Jean-de-Luz – of bathing from the rocks at Madeira in the winter.

In outward seeming they were as the lilies that toiled not, neither did they spin. But perhaps this was not quite true. There are diverse ways of toiling and also of spinning.

'Here's the kid back again,' said Evan Llewellyn to Mrs Rustington.

He was a dark young man – there was a faintly hungry wolfish look about him which some women found attractive.

It was difficult to say whether Mrs Rustington found him so. She did not wear her heart on her sleeve. She had married young – and the marriage had ended in disaster in less than a year. Since that time it was difficult to know what Janet Rustington thought of anyone or anything – her manner was always the same – charming but completely aloof.

Eve Leathern came dancing up to them, her lank fair hair bobbing excitedly. She was fifteen – an awkward child – but full of vitality.

'I'm going to be married by the time I'm seventeen,' she exclaimed breathlessly. 'To a very rich man and we're going to have six children and Tuesdays and Thursdays are my lucky days and I ought always to wear green or blue and an emerald is my lucky stone and –'

'Why, pet, I think we ought to be getting along,' said her father.

Mr Leathern was a tall, fair, dyspeptic-looking man with a somewhat mournful expression.

Mr Pointz and Mr Stein were turning away from the darts. Mr Pointz was chuckling and Mr Stein was looking somewhat rueful.

'It's all a matter of luck,' he was saying.

Mr Pointz slapped his pocket cheerfully.

'Took a fiver off you all right. Skill, my boy, skill. My old Dad was a first class darts player. Well, folks, let's be getting along. Had your fortune told, Eve? Did they tell you to beware of a dark man?'

'A dark woman,' corrected Eve. 'She's got a cast in her eye and she'll be real mean to me if I give her a chance. And I'm to be married by the time I'm seventeen . . .'

She ran on happily as the party steered its way to the Royal George.

Dinner had been ordered beforehand by the forethought of Mr Pointz and a bowing waiter led them upstairs and into a private room on the first floor. Here a round table was ready laid. The big bulging bow-window opened on the harbour square and was open. The noise of the fair came up to them, and the raucous squeal of three roundabouts each blaring a different tune.

'Best shut that if we're to hear ourselves speak,' observed Mr Pointz drily, and suited the action to the word.

They took their seats round the table and Mr Pointz beamed affectionately at his guests. He felt he was doing them well and he liked to do people well. His eye rested on one after another. Lady Marroway – fine woman – not quite the goods, of course, he knew that – he was perfectly well aware that what he had called all his life the *crème de la crème* would have very little to do with the Marroways – but then the *crème de la crème* were supremely unaware of his own existence. Anyway, Lady Marroway was a damned smart-looking woman – and he didn't mind if she *did* rook him at Bridge. Didn't enjoy it quite so much from Sir George. Fishy eye the fellow had. Brazenly on the make. But he wouldn't make too much out of Isaac Pointz. He'd see to that all right.

Old Leathern wasn't a bad fellow – longwinded, of course, like most

Americans – fond of telling endless long stories. And he had that disconcerting habit of requiring precise information. What was the population of Dartmouth? In what year had the Naval College been built? And so on. Expected his host to be a kind of walking Baedeker. Eve was a nice cheery kid – he enjoyed chaffing her. Voice rather like a corncrake, but she had all her wits about her. A bright kid.

Young Llewellyn – he seemed a bit quiet. Looked as though he had something on his mind. Hard up, probably. These writing fellows usually were. Looked as though he might be keen on Janet Rustington. A nice woman – attractive and clever, too. But she didn't ram her writing down your throat. Highbrow sort of stuff she wrote but you'd never think it to hear her talk. And old Leo! *He* wasn't getting younger or thinner. And blissfully unaware that his partner was at that moment thinking precisely the same thing about him, Mr Pointz corrected Mr Leathern as to pilchards being connected with Devon and not Cornwall, and prepared to enjoy his dinner.

'Mr Pointz,' said Eve when plates of hot mackerel had been set before them and the waiters had left the room.

'Yes, young lady.'

'Have you got that big diamond with you right now? The one you showed us last night and said you always took about with you?'

Mr Pointz chuckled.

'That's right. My mascot, I call it. Yes, I've got it with me all right.'

'I think that's awfully dangerous. Somebody might get it away from you in the crowd at the fair.'

'Not they,' said Mr Pointz. 'I'll take good care of that.'

'But they *might*,' insisted Eve. 'You've got gangsters in England as well as we have, haven't you?'

'They won't get the Morning Star,' said Mr Pointz. 'To begin with it's in a special inner pocket. And anyway – old Pointz knows what he's about. Nobody's going to steal the Morning Star.'

Eve laughed.

'Ugh-huh – bet I could steal it!'

'I bet you couldn't.' Mr Pointz twinkled back at her.

'Well, I bet I could. I was thinking about it last night in bed – after you'd handed it round the table, for us all to look at. I thought of a real cute way to steal it.'

'And what's that?'

Eve put her head on one side, her fair hair wagged excitedly. 'I'm not telling you – now. What do you bet I couldn't?'

Memories of Mr Pointz's youth rose in his mind.

'Half a dozen pairs of gloves,' he said.

'Gloves,' cried Eve disgustedly. 'Who wears gloves?'

'Well – do you wear nylon stockings?'

'Do I not? My best pair ran this morning.'

'Very well, then. Half a dozen pairs of the finest nylon stockings –'

'Oo-er,' said Eve blissfully. 'And what about you?'

'Well, I need a new tobacco pouch.'

'Right. That's a deal. Not that you'll get your tobacco pouch. Now I'll tell you what you've got to do. You must hand it round like you did last night –'

She broke off as two waiters entered to remove the plates. When they were starting on the next course of chicken, Mr Pointz said:

'Remember this, young woman, if this is to represent a real theft, I should send for the police and you'd be searched.'

'That's quite OK by me. You needn't be quite so lifelike as to bring the police into it. But Lady Marroway or Mrs Rustington can do all the searching you like.'

'Well, that's that then,' said Mr Pointz. 'What are you setting up to be? A first class jewel thief?'

'I might take to it as a career – if it really paid.'

'If you got away with the Morning Star it would pay you. Even after recutting that stone would be worth over thirty thousand pounds.'

'My!' said Eve, impressed. 'What's that in dollars?'

Lady Marroway uttered an exclamation.

'And you carry such a stone about with you?' she said reproachfully. 'Thirty thousand pounds.' Her darkened eyelashes quivered.

Mrs Rustington said softly: 'It's a lot of money . . . And then there's the fascination of the stone itself . . . It's beautiful.'

'Just a piece of carbon,' said Evan Llewellyn.

'I've always understood it's the "fence" that's the difficulty in jewel robberies,' said Sir George. 'He takes the lion's share – eh, what?'

'Come on,' said Eve excitedly. 'Let's start. Take the diamond out and say what you said last night.'

Mr Leathern said in his deep melancholy voice, 'I do apologize for my offspring. She gets kinder worked up –'

'That'll do, Pops,' said Eve. 'Now then, Mr Pointz –'

Smiling, Mr Pointz fumbled in an inner pocket. He drew something out. It lay on the palm of his hand, blinking in the light.

'A diamond . . .'

Rather stiffly, Mr Pointz repeated as far as he could remember his speech of the previous evening on the *Merrimaid*.

'Perhaps you ladies and gentlemen would like to have a look at this? It's an unusually beautiful stone. I call it the Morning Star and it's by

way of being my mascot – goes about with me anywhere. Like to see
it?'

He handed it to Lady Marroway, who took it, exclaimed at its beauty
and passed it to Mr Leathern who said, 'Pretty good – yes, pretty good,'
in a somewhat artificial manner and in his turn passed it to Llewellyn.

The waiters coming in at that moment, there was a slight hitch in the
proceedings. When they had gone again, Evan said, 'Very fine stone,' and
passed it to Leo Stein who did not trouble to make any comment but
handed it quickly on to Eve.

'How perfectly lovely,' cried Eve in a high affected voice.

'Oh!' She gave a cry of consternation as it slipped from her hand. 'I've
dropped it.'

She pushed back her chair and got down to grope under the table.
Sir George at her right, bent also. A glass got swept off the table in the
confusion. Stein, Llewellyn and Mrs Rustington all helped in the search.
Finally Lady Marroway joined in.

Only Mr Pointz took no part in the proceedings. He remained in his
seat sipping his wine and smiling sardonically.

'Oh, dear,' said Eve, still in her artificial manner, 'How dreadful! Where
can it have rolled to? I can't find it anywhere.'

One by one the assistant searchers rose to their feet.

'It's disappeared all right, Pointz,' said Sir George smiling.

'Very nicely done,' said Mr Pointz, nodding approval. 'You'd make a
very good actress, Eve. Now the question is, have you hidden it somewhere or have you got it on you?'

'Search me,' said Eve dramatically.

Mr Pointz' eye sought out a large screen in the corner of the room.

He nodded towards it and then looked at Lady Marroway and Mrs
Rustington.

'If you ladies will be so good –'

'Why, certainly,' said Lady Marroway, smiling.

The two women rose.

Lady Marroway said, 'Don't be afraid, Mr Pointz. We'll vet her
properly.'

The three went behind the screen.

The room was hot. Evan Llewellyn flung open the window. A news
vendor was passing. Evan threw down a coin and the man threw up a
paper.

Llewellyn unfolded it.

'Hungarian situation's none too good,' he said.

'That the local rag?' asked Sir George. 'There's a horse I'm interested
in ought to have run at Haldon today – Natty Boy.'

'Leo,' said Mr Pointz. 'Lock the door. We don't want those damned waiters popping in and out till this business is over.'

'Natty Boy won three to one,' said Evan.

'Rotten odds,' said Sir George.

'Mostly Regatta news,' said Evan, glancing over the sheet.

The three young women came out from the screen.

'Not a sign of it,' said Janet Rustington.

'You can take it from me she hasn't got it on her,' said Lady Marroway.

Mr Pointz thought he would be quite ready to take it from her. There was a grim tone in her voice and he felt no doubt that the search had been thorough.

'Say, Eve, you haven't swallowed it?' asked Mr Leathern anxiously. 'Because maybe that wouldn't be too good for you.'

'I'd have seen her do that,' said Leo Stein quietly. 'I was watching her. She didn't put anything in her mouth.'

'I couldn't swallow a great thing all points like that,' said Eve. She put her hands on her hips and looked at Mr Pointz. 'What about it, big boy?' she asked.

'You stand over there where you are and don't move,' said that gentleman.

Among them, the men stripped the table and turned it upside down. Mr Pointz examined every inch of it. Then he transferred his attention to the chair on which Eve had been sitting and those on either side of her.

The thoroughness of the search left nothing to be desired. The other four men joined in and the women also. Eve Leathern stood by the wall near the screen and laughed with intense enjoyment.

Five minutes later Mr Pointz rose with a slight groan from his knees and dusted his trousers sadly. His pristine freshness was somewhat impaired.

'Eve,' he said. 'I take off my hat to you. You're the finest thing in jewel thieves I've ever come across. What you've done with that stone beats me. As far as I can see it must be in the room as it isn't on you. I give you best.'

'Are the stockings mine?' demanded Eve.

'They're yours, young lady.'

'Eve, my child, where *can* you have hidden it?' demanded Mrs Rustington curiously.

Eve pranced forward.

'I'll show you. You'll all be just mad with yourselves.'

She went across to the side table where the things from the dinner table had been roughly stacked. She picked up her little black evening bag –

'Right under your eyes. Right . . .'

Her voice, gay and triumphant, trailed off suddenly.

'Oh,' she said. '*Oh* . . .'

'What's the matter, honey?' said her father.

Eve whispered: 'It's gone . . . it's *gone* . . .'

'What's all this?' asked Pointz, coming forward.

Eve turned to him impetuously.

'It was like this. This pochette of mine has a big paste stone in the middle of the clasp. It fell out last night and just when you were showing that diamond round I noticed that it was much the same size. And so I thought in the night what a good idea for a robbery it would be to wedge your diamond into the gap with a bit of plasticine. I felt sure nobody would ever spot it. That's what I did tonight. First I dropped it – then went down after it with the bag in my hand, stuck it into the gap with a bit of plasticine which I had handy, put my bag on the table and went on pretending to look for the diamond. I thought it would be like the Purloined Letter – you know – lying there in full view under all your noses – and just looking like a common bit of rhinestone. And it was a good plan – none of you *did* notice.'

'I wonder,' said Mr Stein.

'What did you say?'

Mr Pointz took the bag, looked at the empty hole with a fragment of plasticine still adhering to it and said slowly: 'It may have fallen out. We'd better look again.'

The search was repeated, but this time it was a curiously silent business. An atmosphere of tension pervaded the room.

Finally everyone in turn gave it up. They stood looking at each other.

'It's not in this room,' said Stein.

'And nobody's left the room,' said Sir George significantly.

There was a moment's pause. Eve burst into tears.

Her father patted her on the shoulder.

'There, there,' he said awkwardly.

Sir George turned to Leo Stein.

'Mr Stein,' he said. 'Just now you murmured something under your breath. When I asked you to repeat it, you said it was nothing. But as a matter of fact I heard what you said. Miss Eve had just said that none of us noticed the place where she had put the diamond. The words you murmured were: "I wonder." What we have to face is the probability that one person *did* notice – that that person is in this room now. I suggest that the only fair and honourable thing is for every one present to submit to a search. The diamond cannot have left the room.'

When Sir George played the part of the old English gentleman, none could play it better. His voice rang with sincerity and indignation.

'Bit unpleasant, all this,' said Mr Pointz unhappily.

'It's all my fault,' sobbed Eve. 'I didn't mean –'

'Buck up, kiddo,' said Mr Stein kindly. 'Nobody's blaming you.'

Mr Leathern said in his slow pedantic manner:

'Why, certainly, I think that Sir George's suggestion will meet with the fullest approval from all of us. It does from me.'

'I agree,' said Evan Llewellyn.

Mrs Rustington looked at Lady Marroway who nodded a brief assent. The two of them went back behind the screen and the sobbing Eve accompanied them.

A waiter knocked on the door and was told to go away.

Five minutes later eight people looked at each other incredulously.

The Morning Star had vanished into space . . .

Mr Parker Pyne looked thoughtfully at the dark agitated face of the young man opposite him.

'Of course,' he said. 'You're Welsh, Mr Llewellyn.'

'What's that got to do with it?'

Mr Parker Pyne waved a large, well-cared-for hand.

'Nothing at all, I admit. I am interested in the classification of emotional reactions as exemplified by certain racial types. That is all. Let us return to the consideration of your particular problem.'

'I don't really know why I came to you,' said Evan Llewellyn. His hands twitched nervously, and his dark face had a haggard look. He did not look at Mr Parker Pyne and that gentleman's scrutiny seemed to make him uncomfortable. 'I don't know why I came to you,' he repeated. 'But where the Hell *can* I go? And what the Hell can I *do*? It's the powerlessness of not being able to do anything at all that gets me . . . I saw your advertisement and I remembered that a chap had once spoken of you and said that you got results . . . And – well – I came! I suppose I was a fool. It's the sort of position nobody can do anything about.'

'Not at all,' said Mr Parker Pyne. 'I am the proper person to come to. I am a specialist in unhappiness. This business has obviously caused you a good deal of pain. You are sure the facts are exactly as you have told me?'

'I don't think I've left out anything. Pointz brought out the diamond and passed it around – that wretched American child stuck it on her ridiculous bag and when we came to look at the bag, the diamond was gone. It wasn't on anyone – old Pointz himself even was searched – he suggested it himself – and I'll swear it was nowhere in that room! *And nobody left the room –*'

'No waiters, for instance?' suggested Mr Parker Pyne.

Llewellyn shook his head.

'They went out before the girl began messing about with the diamond, and afterwards Pointz locked the door so as to keep them out. No, it lies between one of us.'

'It would certainly seem so,' said Mr Parker Pyne thoughtfully.

'That damned evening paper,' said Evan Llewellyn bitterly. 'I saw it come into their minds – that that was the only way –'

'Just tell me again exactly what occurred.'

'It was perfectly simple. I threw open the window, whistled to the man, threw down a copper and he tossed me up the paper. And there it is, you see – the only possible way the diamond could have left the room – thrown by me to an accomplice waiting in the street below.'

'Not the *only* possible way,' said Mr Parker Pyne.

'What other way can you suggest?'

'If you didn't throw it out, there *must* have been some other way.'

'Oh, I see. I hoped you meant something more definite than that. Well, I can only say that I *didn't* throw it out. I can't expect you to believe me – or anyone else.'

'Oh, yes, I believe you,' said Mr Parker Pyne.

'You do? Why?'

'Not a criminal type,' said Mr Parker Pyne. 'Not, that is, the particular criminal type that steals jewellery. There are crimes, of course, that you might commit – but we won't enter into that subject. At any rate I do not see you as the purloiner of the Morning Star.'

'Everyone else does though,' said Llewellyn bitterly.

'I see,' said Mr Parker Pyne.

'They looked at me in a queer sort of way at the time. Marroway picked up the paper and just glanced over at the window. He didn't say anything. But Pointz cottoned on to it quick enough! I could see what they thought. There hasn't been any open accusation, that's the devil of it.'

Mr Parker Pyne nodded sympathetically.

'It is worse than that,' he said.

'Yes. It's just suspicion. I've had a fellow round asking questions – routine inquiries, he called it. One of the new dress-shirted lot of police, I suppose. Very tactful – nothing at all hinted. Just interested in the fact that I'd been hard up and was suddenly cutting a bit of a splash.'

'And were you?'

'Yes – some luck with a horse or two. Unluckily my bets were made on the course – there's nothing to show that that's how the money came in. They can't disprove it, of course – but that's just the sort of easy lie a fellow would invent if he didn't want to show where the money came from.'

'I agree. Still they will have to have a good deal more than that to go upon.'

'Oh! I'm not afraid of actually being arrested and charged with the theft. In a way that would be easier – one would know, where one was. It's the ghastly fact that all those people believe I took it.'

'One person in particular?'

'What do you mean?'

'A suggestion – nothing more –' Again Mr Parker Pyne waved his comfortable-looking hand. 'There *was* one person in particular, wasn't there? Shall we say Mrs Rustington?'

Llewellyn's dark face flushed.

'Why pitch on her?'

'Oh, my dear sir – there is obviously someone whose opinion matters to you greatly – probably a lady. What ladies were there? An American flapper? Lady Marroway? But you would probably rise not fall in Lady Marroway's estimation if you had brought off such a coup. I know something of the lady. Clearly then, Mrs Rustington.'

Llewellyn said with something of an effort,

'She – she's had rather an unfortunate experience. Her husband was a down and out rotter. It's made her unwilling to trust anyone. She – if she thinks –'

He found it difficult to go on.

'Quite so,' said Mr Parker Pyne. 'I see the matter is important. It must be cleared up.'

Evan gave a short laugh.

'That's easy to say.'

'And quite easy to do,' said Mr Parker Pyne.

'You think so?'

'Oh, yes – the problem is so clear cut. So many possibilities are ruled out. The answer must really be extremely simple. Indeed already I have a kind of glimmering –'

Llewellyn stared at him incredulously.

Mr Parker Pyne drew a pad of paper towards him and picked up a pen.

'Perhaps you would give me a brief description of the party.'

'Haven't I already done so?'

'Their personal appearance – colour of hair and so on.'

'But, Mr Parker Pyne, what can that have to do with it?'

'A good deal, young man, a good deal. Classification and so on.'

Somewhat unbelievingly, Evan described the personal appearance of the members of the yachting party.

Mr Parker Pyne made a note or two, pushed away the pad and said:

'Excellent. By the way, did you say a wine glass was broken?'

Evan stared again.

'Yes, it was knocked off the table and then it got stepped on.'

'Nasty thing, splinters of glass,' said Mr Parker Pyne. 'Whose wine glass was it?'

'I think it was the child's – Eve.'

'Ah! – and who sat next to her on that side?'

'Sir George Marroway.'

'You didn't see which of them knocked it off the table?'

'Afraid I didn't. Does it matter?'

'Not really. No. That was a superfluous question. Well' – he stood up – 'good morning, Mr Llewellyn. Will you call again in three days' time? I think the whole thing will be quite satisfactorily cleared up by then.'

'Are you joking, Mr Parker Pyne?'

'I never joke on professional matters, my dear sir. It would occasion distrust in my clients. Shall we say Friday at eleven-thirty? Thank you.'

Evan entered Mr Parker Pyne's office on the Friday morning in a considerable turmoil. Hope and scepticism fought for mastery.

Mr Parker Pyne rose to meet him with a beaming smile.

'Good morning, Mr Llewellyn. Sit down. Have a cigarette?'

Llewellyn waved aside the proffered box.

'Well?' he said.

'Very well indeed,' said Mr Parker Pyne. 'The police arrested the gang last night.'

'The gang? What gang?'

'The Amalfi gang. I thought of them at once when you told me your story. I recognized their methods and once you had described the guests, well, there was no doubt at all in my mind.'

'Who are the Amalfi gang?'

'Father, son and daughter-in-law – that is if Pietro and Maria are really married – which some doubt.'

'I don't understand.'

'It's quite simple. The name is Italian and no doubt the origin is Italian, but old Amalfi was born in America. His methods are usually the same. He impersonates a real business man, introduces himself to some prominent figure in the jewel business in some European country and then plays his little trick. In this case he was deliberately on the track of the Morning Star. Pointz' idiosyncrasy was well known in the trade. Maria Amalfi played the part of his daughter (amazing creature, twenty-seven at least, and nearly always plays a part of sixteen).'

'Not Eve!' gasped Llewellyn.

'Exactly. The third member of the gang got himself taken on as an extra waiter at the Royal George – it was holiday time, remember, and they would need extra staff. He may even have bribed a regular man to stay away. The scene is set. Eve challenges old Pointz and he takes on the bet. He passes round the diamond as he had done the night before. The waiters enter the room and Leathern retains the stone until they have left the room. When they do leave, the diamond leaves also, neatly attached with a morsel of chewing gum to the underside of the plate that Pietro bears away. So simple!'

'But I *saw* it after that.'

'No, no, you saw a paste replica, good enough to deceive a casual glance. Stein, you told me, hardly looked at it. Eve drops it, sweeps off a glass too and steps firmly on stone and glass together. Miraculous disappearance of diamond. Both Eve and Leathern can submit to as much searching as anyone pleases.'

'Well – I'm –' Evan shook his head, at a loss for words.

'You say you recognized the gang from my description. Had they worked this trick before?'

'Not exactly – but it was their kind of business. Naturally my attention was at once directed to the girl Eve.'

'Why? I didn't suspect her – nobody did. She seemed such a – such a *child.*'

'That is the peculiar genius of Maria Amalfi. She is more like a child than any child could possibly be! And then the plasticine! This bet was supposed to have arisen quite spontaneously – yet the little lady had some plasticine with her all handy. That spoke of premeditation. My suspicions fastened on her at once.'

Llewellyn rose to his feet.

'Well, Mr Parker Pyne, I'm no end obliged to you.'

'Classification,' murmured Mr Parker Pyne. 'The classification of criminal types – it interests me.'

'You'll let me know how much – er –'

'My fee will be quite moderate,' said Mr Parker Pyne. 'It will not make too big a hole in the – er – horse racing profits. All the same, young man, I should, I think, leave the horses alone in future. Very uncertain animal, the horse.'

'That's all right,' said Evan.

He shook Mr Parker Pyne by the hand and strode from the office.

He hailed a taxi and gave the address of Janet Rustington's flat.

He felt in a mood to carry all before him.

Part Four

Hercule Poirot:
Belgian Detective

Editor's note

Hercule Poirot was Agatha Christie's most prolific detective. He starred in her first novel, *The Mysterious Affair at Styles*, her first book of short stories, *Poirot Investigates*, and her first original play, *Black Coffee*. The Poirot tales were published weekly in *The Sketch* from March 1923, collectively as 'The Grey Cells of M. Poirot', and set the precedent for all of Agatha Christie's stories appearing in magazines ahead of being collected in books. More than 50 Poirot short stories were written over the next 20 years, and are now collected together in the book *Hercule Poirot: The Complete Short Stories*. However, four published stories were omitted from that volume, because each of them had been expanded by Agatha Christie, and it was felt inappropriate to include similar versions of the same story in one book. Here, therefore, are those Poirot rarities, the four original stories before they were rewritten.

The Submarine Plans

'The Submarine Plans' was first published in *The Sketch*, 7 November 1923.
It was later expanded into 'The Incredible Theft' for the book
Murder in the Mews (Collins, March 1937).

A note had been brought by special messenger. Poirot read it, and a gleam of excitement and interest came into his eyes as he did so. He dismissed the man with a few curt words and then turned to me.

'Pack a bag with all haste, my friend. We're going down to Sharples.'

I started at the mention of the famous country place of Lord Alloway. Head of the newly formed Ministry of Defence, Lord Alloway was a prominent member of the Cabinet. As Sir Ralph Curtis, head of a great engineering firm, he had made his mark in the House of Commons, and he was now freely spoken of as *the* coming man, and the one most likely to be asked to form a ministry should the rumours as to Mr David MacAdam's health prove well founded.

A big Rolls-Royce car was waiting for us below, and as we glided off into the darkness, I plied Poirot with questions.

'What on earth can they want us for at this time of night?' I demanded. It was past eleven.

Poirot shook his head. 'Something of the most urgent, without doubt.'

'I remember,' I said, 'that some years ago there was some rather ugly scandal about Ralph Curtis, as he then was – some jugglery with shares, I believe. In the end, he was completely exonerated; but perhaps something of the kind has arisen again?'

'It would hardly be necessary for him to send for me in the middle of the night, my friend.'

I was forced to agree, and the remainder of the journey was passed in silence. Once out of London, the powerful car forged rapidly ahead, and we arrived at Sharples in a little under the hour.

A pontifical butler conducted us at once to a small study where Lord

Alloway was awaiting us. He sprang up to greet us – a tall, spare man who seemed actually to radiate power and vitality.

'M. Poirot, I am delighted to see you. It is the second time the government has demanded your services. I remember only too well what you did for us during the war, when the Prime Minister was kidnapped in that astounding fashion. Your masterly deductions – and may I add, your discretion? – saved the situation.'

Poirot's eyes twinkled a little.

'Do I gather then, milor', that this is another case for – discretion?'

'Most emphatically. Sir Harry and I – oh, let me intoduce you – Admiral Sir Harry Weardale, our First Sea Lord – M. Poirot and – let me see, Captain –'

'Hastings,' I supplied.

'I've often heard of you, M. Poirot,' said Sir Harry, shaking hands. 'This is a most unaccountable business, and if you can solve it, we'll be extremely grateful to you.'

I liked the First Sea Lord immediately, a square, bluff sailor of the good old-fashioned type.

Poirot looked inquiringly at them both, and Alloway took up the tale.

'Of course, you understand that all this is in confidence, M. Poirot. We have had a most serious loss. The plans of the new Z type of submarine have been stolen.'

'When was that?'

'Tonight – less than three hours ago. You can appreciate perhaps, M. Poirot, the magnitude of the disaster. It is essential that the loss should not be made public. I will give you the facts as briefly as possible. My guests over the week-end were the Admiral, here, his wife and son, and Mrs Conrad, a lady well known in London society. The ladies retired to bed early – about ten o'clock; so did Mr Leonard Weardale. Sir Harry is down here partly for the purpose of discussing the construction of this new type of submarine with me. Accordingly, I asked Mr Fitzroy, my secretary, to get out the plans from the safe in the corner there, and to arrange them ready for me, as well as various other documents that bore upon the subject in hand. While he was doing this, the Admiral and I strolled up and down the terrace, smoking cigars and enjoying the warm June air. We finished our smoke and our chat, and decided to get down to business. Just as we turned at the far end of the terrace, I fancied I saw a shadow slip out of the french window here, cross the terrace, and disappear. I paid very little attention, however. I knew Fitzroy to be in this room, and it never entered my head that anything might be amiss. There, of course, I am to blame. Well, we retraced our steps along the terrace and entered this room by the window just as Fitzroy entered it from the hall.

'"Got everything out we are likely to need, Fitzroy?" I asked.

'"I think so, Lord Alloway. The papers are all on your desk," he answered. And then he wished us both good night.

'"Just wait a minute," I said, going to the desk. "I may want something I haven't mentioned."

'I looked quickly through the papers that were lying there.

'"You've forgotten the most important of the lot, Fitzroy," I said. "The actual plans of the submarine!"

'"The plans are right on top, Lord Alloway."

'"Oh no, they're not," I said, turning over the papers.

'"But I put them there not a minute ago!"

'"Well, they're not here now," I said.

'Fitzroy advanced with a bewildered expression on his face. The thing seemed incredible. We turned over the papers on the desk; we hunted through the safe; but at last we had to make up our minds to it that the papers were gone – and gone within the short space of about three minutes while Fitzroy was absent from the room.'

'Why did he leave the room?' asked Poirot quickly.

'Just what I asked him,' exclaimed Sir Harry.

'It appears,' said Lord Alloway, 'that just when he had finished arranging the papers on my desk, he was startled by hearing a woman scream. He dashed out into the hall. On the stairs he discovered Mrs Conrad's French maid. The girl looked very white and upset, and declared that she had seen a ghost – a tall figure dressed all in white that moved without a sound. Fitzroy laughed at her fears and told her, in more or less polite language, not to be a fool. Then he returned to this room just as we entered from the window.'

'It all seems very clear,' said Poirot thoughtfully. 'The only question is, was the maid an accomplice? Did she scream by arrangement with her confederate lurking outside, or was he merely waiting there in the hope of an opportunity presenting itself? It was a man, I suppose – not a woman you saw?'

'I can't tell you, M. Poirot. It was just a – shadow.'

The admiral gave such a peculiar snort that it could not fail to attract attention.

'M. l'Amiral has something to say, I think,' said Poirot quietly, with a slight smile. 'You saw this shadow, Sir Harry?'

'No, I didn't,' returned the other. 'And neither did Alloway. The branch of a tree flapped, or something, and then afterwards, when we discovered the theft, he leaped to the conclusion that he had seen someone pass across the terrace. His imagination played a trick on him; that's all.'

'I am not usually credited with having much imagination,' said Lord Alloway with a slight smile.

'Nonsense, we've all got imagination. We can all work ourselves up to believe that we've seen more than we have. I've had a lifetime of experience at sea, and I'll back my eyes against those of any landsman. I was looking right down the terrace, and I'd have seen the same if there was anything to see.'

He was quite excited over the matter. Poirot rose and stepped quickly to the window.

'You permit?' he asked. 'We must settle this point if possible.'

He went out upon the terrace, and we followed him. He had taken an electric torch from his pocket, and was playing the light along the edge of the grass that bordered the terrace.

'Where did he cross the terrace, milor'?' he asked.

'About opposite the window, I should say.'

Poirot continued to play the torch for some minutes longer, walking the entire length of the terrace and back. Then he shut it off and straightened himself up.

'Sir Harry is right – and you are wrong, milor', he said quietly. 'It rained heavily earlier this evening. Anyone who passed over that grass could not avoid leaving footmarks. But there are none – none at all.'

His eyes went from one man's face to the other's. Lord Alloway looked bewildered and unconvinced; the Admiral expressed a noisy gratification.

'Knew I couldn't be wrong,' he declared. 'Trust my eyes anywhere.'

He was such a picture of an honest old sea-dog that I could not help smiling.

'So that brings us to the people in the house,' said Poirot smoothly. 'Let us come inside again. Now, milor', while Mr Fitzroy was speaking to the maid on the stairs, could anyone have seized the opportunity to enter the study from the hall?'

Lord Alloway shook his head.

'Quite impossible – they would have had to pass him in order to do so.'

'And Mr Fitzroy himself – you are sure of him, eh?'

Lord Alloway flushed.

'Absolutely, M. Poirot. I will answer confidently for my secretary. It is quite impossible that he should be concerned in the matter in any way.'

'Everything seems to be impossible,' remarked Poirot rather drily. 'Possibly the plans attached to themselves a little pair of wings, and flew away – comme ça!' He blew his lips out like a comical cherub.

'The whole thing is impossible,' declared Lord Alloway impatiently. 'But I beg, M. Poirot, that you will not dream of suspecting Fitzroy.

Consider for one moment – had he wished to take the plans, what could have been easier for him than to take a tracing of them without going to the trouble of stealing them?'

'There, milor',' said Poirot with approval, 'you make a remark *bien juste* – I see that you have a mind orderly and methodical. *L'Angleterre* is happy in possessing you.'

Lord Alloway looked rather embarrassed by this sudden burst of praise. Poirot returned to the matter in hand.

'The room in which you had been sitting all the evening –'

'The drawing-room? Yes?'

'That also has a window on the terrace, since I remember your saying you went out that way. Would it not be possible for someone to come out by the drawing-room window and in by this one while Mr Fitzroy was out of the room, and return the same way?'

'But we'd have seen them,' objected the Admiral.

'Not if you had your backs turned, walking the other way.'

'Fitzroy was only out of the room a few minutes, the time it would take us to walk to the end and back.'

'No matter – it is a possibility – in fact, the only one as things stand.'

'But there was no one in the drawing-room when we went out,' said the Admiral.

'They may have come there afterwards.'

'You mean,' said Lord Alloway slowly, 'that when Fitzroy heard the maid scream and went out, someone was already concealed in the drawing-room, and that they darted in and out through the windows, and only left the drawing-room when Fitzroy had returned to this room?'

'The methodical mind again,' said Poirot, bowing.

'You express the matter perfectly.'

'One of the servants, perhaps?'

'Or a guest. It was Mrs Conrad's maid who screamed. What exactly can you tell me of Mrs Conrad?'

Lord Alloway considered for a minute.

'I told you that she is a lady well known in society. That is true in the sense that she gives large parties, and goes everywhere. But very little is known as to where she really comes from, and what her past life has been. She is a lady who frequents diplomatic and Foreign Office circles as much as possible. The Secret Service is inclined to ask – why?'

'I see,' said Poirot. 'And she was asked here this week-end –'

'So that – shall we say? – we might observe her at close quarters.'

'*Parfaitement!* It is possible that she has turned the tables on you rather neatly.'

Lord Alloway looked discomfited, and Poirot continued: 'Tell me, milor', was any reference made in her hearing to the subjects you and the Admiral were going to discuss together?'

'Yes,' admitted the other. 'Sir Harry said: "And now for our submarine! To work!" or something of that sort. The others had left the room, but she had come back for a book.'

'I see,' said Poirot thoughtfully. 'Milor', it is very late – but this is an urgent affair. I would like to question the members of this house-party at once if it is possible.'

'It can be managed, of course,' said Lord Alloway. 'The awkward thing is, we don't want to let it get about more than can be helped. Of course, Lady Juliet Weardale and young Leonard are all right – but Mrs Conrad, if she is not guilty, is rather a different proposition. Perhaps you could just state that an important paper is missing, without specifying what it is, or going into any of the circumstances of the disappearance?'

'Exactly what I was about to propose myself,' said Poirot, beaming. 'In fact, in all three cases. Monsieur the Admiral will pardon me, but even the best of wives –'

'No offence,' said Sir Harry. 'All women talk, bless 'em! I wish Juliet would talk a little more and play bridge a little less. But women are like that nowadays, never happy unless they're dancing or gambling. I'll get Juliet and Leonard up, shall I, Alloway?'

'Thank you. I'll call the French maid. M. Poirot will want to see her, and she can rouse her mistress. I'll attend to it now. In the meantime, I'll send Fitzroy along.'

Mr Fitzroy was a pale, thin young man with pince-nez and a frigid expression. His statement was practically word for word what Lord Alloway had already told us.

'What is your own theory, Mr Fitzroy?'

Mr Fitzroy shrugged his shoulders.

'Undoubtedly someone who knew the hang of things was waiting his chance outside. He could see what went on through the window, and he slipped in when I left the room. It's a pity Lord Alloway didn't give chase then and there when he saw the fellow leave.'

Poirot did not undeceive him. Instead he asked: 'Do you believe the story of the French maid – that she had seen a ghost?'

'Well, hardly, M. Poirot!'

'I mean – that she really thought so?'

'Oh, as to that, I can't say. She certainly seemed rather upset. She had her hands to her head.'

'Aha!' cried Poirot with the air of one who has made a discovery. 'Is that so indeed – and she was without doubt a pretty girl?'

'I didn't notice particularly,' said Mr Fitzroy in a repressive voice.

'You did not see her mistress, I suppose?'

'As a matter of fact, I did. She was in the gallery at the top of the steps and was calling her – "Léonie!" Then she saw me – and of course retired.'

'Upstairs,' said Poirot, frowning.

'Of course, I realize that all this is very unpleasant for me – or rather would have been, if Lord Alloway had not chanced to see the man actually leaving. In any case, I should be glad if you would make a point of searching my room – and myself.'

'You really wish that?'

'Certainly I do.'

What Poirot would have replied I do not know, but at that moment Lord Alloway reappeared and informed us that the two ladies and Mr Leonard Weardale were in the drawing-room.

The women were in becoming negligees. Mrs Conrad was a beautiful woman of thirty-five, with golden hair and a slight tendency to *embonpoint*. Lady Juliet Weardale must have been forty, tall and dark, very thin, still beautiful, with exquisite hands and feet, and a restless, haggard manner. Her son was rather an effeminate-looking young man, as great a contrast to his bluff, hearty father as could well be imagined.

Poirot gave forth the little rigmarole we had agreed upon, and then explained that he was anxious to know if anyone had heard or seen anything that night which might assist us.

Turning to Mrs Conrad first, he asked her if she would be so kind as to inform him exactly what her movements had been.

'Let me see . . . I went upstairs. I rang for my maid. Then, as she did not put in an appearance, I came out and called her. I could hear her talking on the stairs. After she had brushed my hair, I sent her away – she was in a very curious nervous state. I read awhile and then went to bed.'

'And you, Lady Juliet?'

'I went straight upstairs and to bed. I was very tired.'

'What about your book, dear?' asked Mrs Conrad with a sweet smile.

'My book?' Lady Juliet flushed.

'Yes, you know, when I sent Léonie away, you were coming up the stairs. You had been down to the drawing-room for a book, you said.'

'Oh yes, I did go down. I – I forgot.'

Lady Juliet clasped her hands nervously together.

'Did you hear Mrs Conrad's maid scream, milady?'

'No – no, I didn't.'

'How curious – because you must have been in the drawing-room at the time.'

'I heard nothing,' said Lady Juliet in a firmer voice.

Poirot turned to young Leonard.

'Monsieur?'

'Nothing doing. I went straight upstairs and turned in.'

Poirot stroked his chin.

'Alas, I fear there is nothing to help me here. Mesdames and monsieur, I regret – I regret infinitely to have deranged you from your slumbers for so little. Accept my apologies, I pray of you.'

Gesticulating and apologizing, he marshalled them out. He returned with the French maid, a pretty, impudent-looking girl. Alloway and Weardale had gone out with the ladies.

'Now, mademoiselle,' said Poirot in a brisk tone, 'let us have the truth. Recount to me no histories. Why did you scream on the stairs?'

'Ah, monsieur, I saw a tall figure – all in white –'

Poirot arrested her with an energetic shake of his forefinger.

'Did I not say, recount to me no histories? I will make a guess. He kissed you, did he not? M. Leonard Weardale, I mean?'

'*Eh bien, monsieur,* and after all, what is a kiss?'

'Under the circumstances, it is most natural,' replied Poirot gallantly. 'I myself, or Hastings here – but tell me just what occurred.'

'He came up behind me, and caught me. I was startled, and I screamed. If I had known, I would not have screamed – but he came upon me like a cat. Then came *M. le secrétaire*. M. Leonard flew up the stairs. And what could I say? Especially to a *jeune homme comme ça – tellement comme il faut? Ma foi,* I invent a ghost.'

'And all is explained,' cried Poirot genially. 'You then mounted to the chamber of Madame your mistress. Which is her room, by the way?'

'It is at the end, monsieur. That way.'

'Directly over the study, then. *Bien*, mademoiselle, I will detain you no longer. And *la prochaine fois*, do not scream.'

Handing her out, he came back to me with a smile.

'An interesting case, is it not, Hastings? I begin to have a few little ideas. *Et vous?*'

'What was Leonard Weardale doing on the stairs? I don't like that young man, Poirot. He's a thorough young rake, I should say.'

'I agree with you, *mon ami.*'

'Fitzroy seems an honest fellow.'

'Lord Alloway is certainly insistent on that point.'

'And yet there is something in his manner –'

'That is almost too good to be true? I felt it myself. On the other hand, our friend Mrs Conrad is certainly no good at all.'

'And her room is over the study,' I said musingly, and keeping a sharp eye on Poirot.

He shook his head with a slight smile.

'No, *mon ami*, I cannot bring myself seriously to believe that that immaculate lady swarmed down the chimney, or let herself down from the balcony.'

As he spoke, the door opened, and to my great surprise, Lady Juliet Weardale flitted in.

'M. Poirot,' she said somewhat breathlessly, 'Can I speak to you alone?'

'Milady, Captain Hastings is as my other self. You can speak before him as though he were a thing of no account, not there at all. Be seated, I pray you.'

She sat down, still keeping her eyes fixed on Poirot.

'What I have to say is – rather difficult. You are in charge of this case. If the – papers were to be returned, would that end the matter? I mean, could it be done without questions being asked?'

Poirot stared hard at her.

'Let me understand you, madame. They are to be placed in my hand – is that right? And I am to return them to Lord Alloway on the condition that he asks no questions as to where I got them?'

She bowed her head. 'That is what I mean. But I must be sure there will be no – publicity.'

'I do not think Lord Alloway is particularly anxious for publicity,' said Poirot grimly.

'You accept then?' she cried eagerly in response.

'A little moment, milady. It depends on how soon you can place those papers in my hands.'

'Almost immediately.'

Poirot glanced up at the clock.

'How soon, exactly?'

'Say – ten minutes,' she whispered.

'I accept, milady.'

She hurried from the room. I pursed my mouth up for a whistle.

'Can you sum up the situation for me, Hastings?'

'Bridge,' I replied succinctly.

'Ah, you remember the careless words of Monsieur the Admiral! What a memory! I felicitate you, Hastings.'

We said no more, for Lord Alloway came in, and looked inquiringly at Poirot.

Detectives and Young Adventurers: The Complete Short Stories

'Have you any further ideas, M. Poirot? I am afraid the answers to your questions have been rather disappointing.'

'Not at all, milor'. They have been quite sufficiently illuminating. It will be unnecessary for me to stay here any longer, and so, with your permission, I will return at once to London.'

Lord Alloway seemed dumbfounded.

'But – but what have you discovered? Do you know who took the plans?'

'Yes, milor', I do. Tell me – in the case of the papers being returned to you anonymously, you would prosecute no further inquiry?'

Lord Alloway stared at him.

'Do you mean on payment of a sum of money?'

'No, milor', returned unconditionally.'

'Of course, the recovery of the plans is the great thing,' said Lord Alloway slowly. He looked puzzled and uncomprehending.

'Then I should seriously recommend you to adopt that course. Only you, the Admiral and your secretary know of the loss. Only they need know of the restitution. And you may count on me to support you in every way – lay the mystery on my shoulders. You asked me to restore the papers – I have done so. You know no more.' He rose and held out his hand. 'Milor', I am glad to have met you. I have faith in you – and your devotion to England. You will guide her destinies with a strong, sure hand.'

'M. Poirot – I swear to you that I will do my best. It may be a fault, or it may be a virtue – but I believe in myself.'

'So does every great man. Me, I am the same!' said Poirot grandiloquently.

The car came round to the door in a few minutes, and Lord Alloway bade us farewell on the steps with renewed cordiality.

'That is a great man, Hastings,' said Poirot as we drove off. 'He has brains, resource, power. He is the strong man that England needs to guide her through these difficult days of reconstruction.'

'I'm quite ready to agree with all you say, Poirot – but what about Lady Juliet? Is she to return the papers straight to Alloway? What will she think when she finds you have gone off without a word?'

'Hastings, I will ask you a little question. Why, when she was talking with me, did she not hand me the plans then and there?'

'She hadn't got them with her.'

'Perfectly. How long would it take her to fetch them from her room? Or from any hiding-place in the house? You need not answer. I will tell you. Probably about two minutes and a half! Yet she asks for ten minutes.

Why? Clearly she has to obtain them from some other person, and to reason or argue with that person before they give them up. Now, what person could that be? Not Mrs Conrad, clearly, but a member of her own family, her husband or son. Which is it likely to be? Leonard Weardale said he went straight to bed. We know that to be untrue. Supposing his mother went to his room and found it empty; supposing she came down filled with a nameless dread – he is no beauty that son of hers! She does not find him, but later she hears him deny that he ever left his room. She leaps to the conclusion that he is the thief. Hence her interview with me.

'But, *mon ami*, we know something that Lady Juliet does not. We know that her son could not have been in the study, because he was on the stairs, making love to the pretty French maid. Although she does not know it, Leonard Weardale has an alibi.'

'Well, then, who did steal the papers? We seem to have eliminated everybody – Lady Juliet, her son, Mrs Conrad, the French maid –'

'Exactly. Use your little grey cells, my friend. The solution stares you in the face.'

I shook my head blankly.

'But yes! If you would only persevere! See, then, Fitzroy goes out of the study; he leaves the papers on the desk. A few minutes later Lord Alloway enters the room, goes to the desk, and the papers are gone. Only two things are possible: either Fitzroy did *not* leave the papers on the desk, but put them in his pocket – and that is not reasonable, because, as Alloway pointed out, he could have taken a tracing at his own convenience any time – or else the papers were still on the desk when Lord Alloway went to it – in which case they went into his pocket.'

'Lord Alloway the thief,' I said, dumbfounded. 'But why? Why?'

'Did you not tell me of some scandal in the past? He was exonerated, you said. But suppose, after all, it had been true? In English public life there must be no scandal. If this were raked up and proved against him now – goodbye to his political career. We will suppose that he was being blackmailed, and the price asked was the submarine plans.'

'But the man's a black traitor!' I cried.

'Oh no, he is not. He is clever and resourceful. Supposing, my friend, that he copied those plans, making – for he is a clever engineer – a slight alteration in each part which will render them quite impractible. He hands the faked plans to the enemy's agent – Mrs Conrad, I fancy; but in order that no suspicion of their genuineness may arise, the plans must seem to be stolen. He does his best to throw no suspicion on anyone in the house, by pretending to see a man leaving the window. But there he ran up against the obstinacy of the Admiral. So his next anxiety is that no suspicion shall fall on Fitzroy.'

'This is all guesswork on your part, Poirot,' I objected.

'It is psychology, *mon ami*. A man who had handed over the real plans would not be overscrupulous as to who was likely to fall under suspicion. And why was he so anxious that no details of the robbery should be given to Mrs Conrad? Because he had handed over the faked plans earlier in the evening, and did not want her to know that the theft could only have taken place later.'

'I wonder if you are right,' I said.

'Of course I am right. I spoke to Alloway as one great man to another – and he understood perfectly. You will see.'

One thing is quite certain. On the day when Lord Alloway became Prime Minister, a cheque and a signed photograph arrived; on the photograph were the words: '*To my discreet friend, Hercule Poirot – from Alloway.*'

I believe that the Z type of submarine is causing great exultation in naval circles. They say it will revolutionize modern naval warfare. I have heard that a certain foreign power essayed to construct something of the same kind and the result was a dismal failure. But I still consider that Poirot was guessing. He will do it once too often one of these days.

Christmas Adventure

'Christmas Adventure' was first published as 'The Adventure of the Christmas Pudding' in *The Sketch*, 12 December 1923. It was later expanded for the book *The Adventure of the Christmas Pudding and a selection of Entrées* (Collins, October 1960), appearing first in the USA as 'The Theft of the Royal Ruby' in two parts in *This Week*, 25 September and 2 October 1960.

The big logs crackled merrily in the wide, open fireplace, and above their crackling rose the babel of six tongues all wagging industriously together. The house-party of young people were enjoying their Christmas.

Old Miss Endicott, known to most of those present as Aunt Emily, smiled indulgently on the clatter.

'Bet you you can't eat six mince-pies, Jean.'

'Yes, I can.'

'No, you can't.'

'You'll get the pig out of the trifle if you do.'

'Yes, *and* three helps of trifle, *and* two helps of plum-pudding.'

'I hope the pudding will be good,' said Miss Endicott apprehensively. 'But they were only made three days ago. Christmas puddings ought to be made a long time before Christmas. Why, I remember when I was a child, I thought the last Collect before Advent – "Stir up, O Lord, we beseech Thee . . .' – referred in some way to stirring up the Christmas puddings!'

There was a polite pause while Miss Endicott was speaking. Not because any of the young people were in the least interested in her reminiscences of bygone days, but because they felt that some show of attention was due by good manners to their hostess. As soon as she stopped, the babel burst out again. Miss Endicott sighed, and glanced towards the only member of the party whose years approached her own, as though in search of sympathy – a little man with a curious egg-shaped head and fierce upstanding moustaches. Young people were not what they were, reflected Miss Endicott. In olden days there would have been a mute, respectful circle, listening to the pearls of wisdom dropped by their elders. Instead of which there was all this nonsensical chatter, most of it utterly incomprehensible. All the same, they were dear children! Her eyes softened as she passed them in review – tall, freckled Jean; little Nancy Cardell, with her dark, gipsy beauty; the two younger boys home from school, Johnnie and Eric, and their friend, Charlie Pease; and fair, beautiful Evelyn Haworth ... At thought of the last, her brow contracted a little, and her eyes wandered to where her eldest nephew, Roger, sat morosely silent, taking no part in the fun, with his eyes fixed on the exquisite Northern fairness of the young girl.

'Isn't the snow ripping?' cried Johnnie, approaching the window. 'Real Christmas weather. I say, let's have a snowball fight. There's lots of time before dinner, isn't there, Aunt Emily?'

'Yes, my dear. We have it at two o'clock. That reminds me, I had better see to the table.'

She hurried out of the room.

'I tell you what. We'll make a snowman!' screamed Jean.

'Yes, what fun! I know; we'll do a snow statue of M. Poirot. Do you hear, M. Poirot? The great detective, Hercule Poirot, modelled in snow, by six celebrated artists!'

The little man in the chair bowed his acknowledgements with a twinkling eye.

'Make him very handsome, my children,' he urged. 'I insist on that.'

'Ra-ther!'

The troop disappeared like a whirlwind, colliding in the doorway with a stately butler who was entering with a note on a salver. The butler, his calm re-established, advanced towards Poirot.

Poirot took the note and tore it open. The butler departed. Twice the little man read the note through, then he folded it up and put it in his pocket. Not a muscle of his face had moved, and yet the contents of the note were sufficiently surprising. Scrawled in an illiterate hand were the words: '*Don't eat any plum-pudding.*'

'Very interesting,' murmured M. Poirot to himself. 'And quite unexpected.'

He looked across to the fireplace. Evelyn Haworth had not gone out with the rest. She was sitting staring at the fire, absorbed in thought, nervously twisting a ring on the third finger of her left hand round and round.

'You are lost in a dream, Mademoiselle,' said the little man at last. 'And the dream is not a happy one, eh?'

She started, and looked across at him uncertainly. He nodded reassuringly.

'It is my business to know things. No, you are not happy. Me, too, I am not very happy. Shall we confide in each other? See you, I have the big sorrow because a friend of mine, a friend of many years, has gone away across the sea to the South America. Sometimes, when we were together, this friend made me impatient, his stupidity enraged me; but now that he is gone, I can remember only his good qualities. That is the way of life, is it not? And now, Mademoiselle, what is your trouble? You are not like me, old and alone – you are young and beautiful; and the man you love loves you – oh yes, it is so: I have been watching him for the last half-hour.'

The girl's colour rose.

'You mean Roger Endicott? Oh, but you have made a mistake; it is not Roger I am engaged to.'

'No, you are engaged to Mr Oscar Levering. I know that perfectly. But why are you engaged to him, since you love another man?'

The girl did not seem to resent his words; indeed, there was something in his manner which made that impossible. He spoke with a mixture of kindliness and authority that was irresistible.

'Tell me all about it,' said Poirot gently; and he added the phrase he had used before, the sound of which was oddly comforting to the girl. 'It is my business to know things.'

'I am so miserable, M. Poirot – so very miserable. You see, once we were very well off. I was supposed to be an heiress, and Roger was only a younger son; and – and although I'm sure he cared for me, he never said anything, but went off to Australia.'

'It is droll, the way they arrange the marriages over here,' interpolated M. Poirot. 'No order. No method. Everything left to chance.'

Evelyn continued.

'Then suddenly we lost all our money. My mother and I were left almost penniless. We moved into a tiny house, and we could just manage. But my mother became very ill. The only chance for her was to have a serious operation and go abroad to a warm climate. And we hadn't the money, M. Poirot – we hadn't the money! It meant that she must die. Mr Levering had proposed to me once or twice already. He again asked me to marry him, and promised to do everything that could be done for my mother. I said yes – what else could I do? He kept his word. The operation was performed by the greatest specialist of the day, and we went to Egypt for the winter. That was a year ago. My mother is well and strong again; and I – I am to marry Mr Levering after Christmas.'

'I see,' said M. Poirot; 'and in the meantime, M. Roger's elder brother has died, and he has come home – to find his dream shattered. All the same, you are not yet married, Mademoiselle.'

'A Haworth does not break her word, M. Poirot,' said the girl proudly.

Almost as she spoke, the door opened, and a big man with a rubicund face, narrow, crafty eyes, and a bald head stood on the threshold.

'What are you moping in here for, Evelyn? Come out for a stroll.'

'Very well, Oscar.'

She rose listlessly. Poirot rose also and demanded politely:

'Mademoiselle Levering, she is still indisposed?'

'Yes, I'm sorry to say my sister is still in bed. Too bad, to be laid up on Christmas Day.'

'It is indeed,' agreed the detective politely.

A few minutes sufficed for Evelyn to put on her snow-boots and some wraps, and she and her fiancé went out into the snow-covered grounds. It was an ideal Christmas Day, crisp and sunny. The rest of the house-party were busy with the erection of the snowman. Levering and Evelyn paused to watch them.

'Love's young dream, yah!' cried Johnnie, and threw a snowball at them.

'What do you think of it, Evelyn?' cried Jean. 'M. Hercule Poirot, the great detective.'

'Wait till the moustache goes on,' said Eric. 'Nancy's going to clip off a bit of her hair for it. *Vivent les braves Belges!* Pom, pom!'

'Fancy having a real-live detective in the house!' – this from Charlie – 'I wish there could be a murder, too.'

'Oh, oh, oh!' cried Jean, dancing about. 'I've got an idea. Let's get up a murder – a spoof one, I mean. And take him in. Oh, do let's – it would be no end of a rag.'

Five voices began to talk at once.

'How should we do it?'

'Awful groans!'

'No, you stupid, out here.'

'Footprints in the snow, of course.'

'Jean in her nightie.'

'You do it with red paint.'

'In your hand – and clap it to your head.'

'I say, I wish we had a revolver.'

'I tell you, Father and Aunt Em won't hear. Their rooms are the other side of the house.'

'No, he won't mind a bit; he's no end of a sport.'

'Yes, but what kind of red paint? Enamel?'

'We could get some in the village.'

'Fat-head, not on Christmas Day.'

'No, watercolour. Crimson lake.'

'Jean can be it.'

'Never mind if you *are* cold. It won't be for long.'

'No, Nancy can be it, Nancy's got those posh pyjamas.'

'Let's see if Graves knows where there's any paint.'

A stampede to the house.

'In a brown study, Endicott?' said Levering, laughing disagreeably.

Roger roused himself abruptly. He had heard little of what had passed.

'I was just wondering,' he said quietly.

'Wondering?'

'Wondering what M. Poirot was doing down here at all.'

Levering seemed taken aback; but at that moment the big gong pealed out, and everybody went in to Christmas dinner. The curtains were drawn in the dining-room, and the lights on, illuminating the long table piled high with crackers and other decorations. It was a real old-fashioned Christmas dinner. At one end of the table was the Squire, red-faced and jovial; his sister faced him at the other. M. Poirot, in honour of the occasion, had donned a red waistcoat, and his plumpness, and the way he carried his head on one side, reminded one irresistibly of a robin redbreast.

The Squire carved rapidly, and everyone fell to on turkey. The carcasses of two turkeys were removed, and there fell a breathless hush. Then Graves, the butler, appeared in state, bearing the plum-pudding aloft – a gigantic pudding wreathed in flames. A hullabaloo broke out.

'Quick. Oh! my piece is going out. Buck up, Graves; unless it's still burning, I shan't get my wish.'

Nobody had leisure to notice a curious expression on the face of M. Poirot as he surveyed the portion of pudding on his plate. Nobody observed the lightning glance he sent round the table. With a faint, puzzled frown he began to eat his pudding. Everybody began to eat pudding. The conversation was more subdued. Suddenly the Squire uttered an exclamation. His face became purple and his hand went to his mouth.

'Confound it, Emily!' he roared. 'Why do you let the cook put glass in the puddings?'

'Glass?' cried Miss Endicott, astonished.

The Squire withdrew the offending substance from his mouth.

'Might have broken a tooth,' he grumbled. 'Or swallowed it and had appendicitis.'

In front of each person was a small finger-bowl of water, designed to receive the sixpences and other matters found in the trifle. Mr Endicott dropped the piece of glass into this, rinsed it and held it up.

'God bless my soul!' he ejaculated. 'It's a red stone out of one of the cracker brooches.'

'You permit?' Very deftly, M. Poirot took it from his fingers and examined it attentively. As the Squire had said, it was a big red stone, the colour of a ruby. The light gleamed from its facets as he turned it about.

'Gee!' cried Eric. 'Suppose it's real.'

'Silly boy!' said Jean scornfully. 'A ruby that size would be worth thousands and thousands and thousands – wouldn't it, M. Poirot?'

'Extraordinary how well they get up these cracker things,' murmured Miss Endicott. '*But how did it get into the pudding?*'

Undoubtedly that was the question of the hour. Every hypothesis was exhausted. Only M. Poirot said nothing, but carelessly, as though thinking of something else, he dropped the stone into his pocket.

After dinner he paid a visit to the kitchen.

The cook was rather flustered. To be questioned by a member of the house-party, and the foreign gentleman too! But she did her best to answer his questions. The puddings had been made three days ago – 'The day you arrived, Sir.' Everyone had come out into the kitchen to have a stir and wish. An old custom – perhaps they didn't have it abroad? After that the puddings were boiled, and then they were put in a row on the top shelf in the larder. Was there anything special to distinguish this pudding from the others? No, she didn't think so. Except that it was in an aluminium pudding-basin, and the others were in china ones. Was it the pudding originally intended for Christmas Day? It was funny that he should ask that. No, indeed! The Christmas pudding was always boiled in a big white china mould with a pattern of holly-leaves. But this very morning (the cook's red face became wrathful) Gladys, the kitchen-maid, sent to fetch it down for the final boiling, had managed to drop and break it. 'And of course, seeing that there might be splinters in it, I wouldn't send it to table, but took the big aluminium one instead.'

M. Poirot thanked her for her information. He went out of the kitchen, smiling a little to himself, as though satisfied with the information he had obtained. And the fingers of his right hand played with something in his pocket.

'M. Poirot! M. Poirot! Do wake up! Something dreadful's happened!'

Thus Johnnie in the early hours of the following morning. M. Poirot sat up in bed. He wore a night-cap. The contrast between the dignity of his countenance and the rakish tilt of the night-cap was certainly droll; but its effect on Johnnie seemed disproportionate. But for his words, one might have fancied that the boy was violently amused about something.

Curious sounds came from outside the door, too, suggesting soda-water syphons in difficulty.

'Come down at once, please,' continued Johnnie, his voice shaking slightly. 'Someone's been killed.' He turned away.

'Aha, that is serious!' said M. Poirot.

He arose, and, without unduly hurrying himself, made a partial toilet. Then he followed Johnnie down the stairs. The house-party was clustered round the door into the garden. Their countenances all expressed intense emotion. At sight of him Eric was seized with a violent choking fit.

Jean came forward and laid her hand on M. Poirot's arm.

'Look!' she said, and pointed dramatically through the open door.

'*Mon Dieu!*' ejaculated M. Poirot. 'It is like a scene on the stage.'

His remark was not inapposite. More snow had fallen during the night, the world looked white and ghostly in the faint light of the early dawn. The expanse of white lay unbroken save for what looked like on splash of vivid scarlet.

Nancy Cardell lay motionless on the snow. She was clad in scarlet silk pyjamas, her small feet were bare, her arms were spread wide. Her head was turned aside and hidden by the mass of her clustering black hair. Deadly still she lay, and from her left side rose up the hilt of a dagger, whilst on the snow there was an ever-widening patch of crimson.

Poirot went out into the snow. He did not go to where the girl's body lay, but kept to the path. Two tracks of foot-marks, a man's and a woman's, led to where the tragedy had occurred. The man's footprints went away in the opposite direction alone. Poirot stood on the path, stroking his chin reflectively.

Suddenly Oscar Levering burst out of the house.

'Good God!' he cried. 'What's this?'

His excitement was a contrast to the other's calm.

'It looks,' said M. Poirot thoughtfully, 'like murder.'

Eric had another violent attack of coughing.

'But we must do something,' cried the other. 'What shall we do?'

'There is only one thing to be done,' said M. Poirot. 'Send for the police.'

'Oh!' said everybody at once.

M. Poirot looked inquiringly at them.

'Certainly,' he said. 'It is the only thing to be done. Who will go?'

There was a pause, then Johnnie came forward.

'Rag's over,' he declared. 'I say, M. Poirot, I hope you won't be too mad with us. It's all a joke, you know – got up between us – just to pull your leg. Nancy's only shamming.'

M. Poirot regarded him without visible emotion, save that his eyes twinkled a moment.

'You mock yourselves at me, is that it?' he inquired placidly.

'I say, I'm awfully sorry really. We shouldn't have done it. Beastly bad taste. I apologize, I really do.'

'You need not apologize,' said the other in a peculiar voice.

Johnnie turned.

'I say, Nancy, get up!' he cried. 'Don't lie there all day.'

But the figure on the ground did not move.

'Get up,' cried Johnnie again.

Still Nancy did not move, and suddenly a feeling of nameless dread came over the boy. He turned to Poirot.

'What – what's the matter? Why doesn't she get up?'

'Come with me,' said Poirot curtly.

He strode over the snow. He had waved the others back, and he was careful not to infringe on the other footmarks. The boy followed him, frightened and unbelieving. Poirot knelt down by the girl, then he signed to Johnnie.

'Feel her hand and pulse.'

Wondering, the boy bent down, then started back with a cry. The hand and arm were stiff and cold, and no vestige of a pulse was to be found.

'She's dead!' he gasped. 'But how? Why?'

M. Poirot passed over the first part of the question.

'Why?' he said musingly. 'I wonder.' Then, suddenly leaning across the dead girl's body, he unclasped her other hand, which was tightly clenched over something. Both he and the boy uttered an exclamation. In the palm of Nancy's hand was a red stone that winked and flashed forth fire.

'Aha!' cried M. Poirot. Swift as a flash his hand flew to his pocket, and came away empty.

'The cracker ruby,' said Johnnie wonderingly. Then, as his companion bent to examine the dagger, and the stained snow, he cried out: 'Surely it can't be blood, M. Poirot. It's paint. It's only paint.'

Poirot straightened himself.

'Yes,' he said quietly. 'You are right. It's only paint.'

'Then how –' The boy broke off. Poirot finished the sentence for him.

'How was she killed? That we must find out. Did she eat or drink anything this morning?'

He was retracing his steps to the path where the others waited as he spoke. Johnnie was close behind him.

'She had a cup of tea,' said the boy. 'Mr Levering made it for her. He's got a spirit-lamp in his room.'

Johnnie's voice was loud and clear. Levering heard the words.

'Always take a spirit-lamp about with me,' he declared. 'Most handy thing in the world. My sister's been glad enough of it this visit – not liking to worry the servants all the time you know.'

M. Poirot's eyes fell, almost apologetically as it seemed, to Mr Levering's feet, which were encased in carpet slippers.

'You have changed your boots, I see,' he murmured gently.

Levering stared at him.

'But, M. Poirot,' cried Jean, 'what are we to do?'

'There is only one thing to be done, as I said just now, Mademoiselle. Send for the police.'

'I'll go,' cried Levering. 'It won't take me a minute to put on my boots. You people had better not stay out here in the cold.'

He disappeared into the house.

'He is so thoughtful, that Mr Levering,' murmured Poirot softly. 'Shall we take his advice?'

'What about waking father and – and everybody?'

'No,' said M. Poirot sharply. 'It is quite unnecessary. Until the police come, nothing must be touched out here; so shall we go inside? To the library? I have a little history to recount to you which may distract your minds from this sad tragedy.'

He led the way, and they followed him.

'The story is about a ruby,' said M. Poirot, ensconcing himself in a comfortable arm-chair. 'A very celebrated ruby which belonged to a very celebrated man. I will not tell you his name – but he is one of the great ones of the earth. *Eh bien*, this great man, he arrived in London, incognito. And since, though a great man, he was also a young and a foolish man, he became entangled with a pretty young lady. The pretty young lady, she did not care much for the man, but she did care for his possessions – so much so that she disappeared one day with the historic ruby which had belonged to his house for generations. The poor young man, he was in a quandary. He is shortly to be married to a noble Princess, and he does not want the scandal. Impossible to go to the police, he comes to me, Hercule Poirot, instead. "Recover for me my ruby," he says. *Eh bien*, I know something of this young lady. She has a brother, and between them they have put through many a clever *coup*. I happen to know where they are staying for Christmas. By the kindness of Mr Endicott, whom I chance to have met, I, too, become a guest. But when this pretty young lady hears that I am arriving, she is greatly alarmed. She is intelligent, and she knows that I am after the ruby. She must hide it immediately in a safe place; and figure to yourself where she hides it – in a plum-pudding! Yes, you may well say, oh! She is stirring with the rest, you see, and she pops it into a pudding-bowl of aluminium that is different from the others. By a strange chance, that pudding came to be used on Christmas Day.'

The tragedy forgotten for the moment, they stared at him open-mouthed.

'After that,' continued the little man, 'she took to her bed.' He drew out his watch and looked at it. 'The household is astir. Mr Levering is a long time fetching the police, is he not? I fancy that his sister went with him.'

Evelyn rose with a cry, her eyes fixed on Poirot.

'And I also fancy that they will not return. Oscar Levering has been sailing close to the wind for a long time, and this is the end. He and his sister will pursue their activities abroad for a time under a different name. I alternately tempted and frightened him this morning. By casting aside all pretence he could gain possession of the ruby whilst we were in the house and he was supposed to be fetching the police. But it meant burning his boats. Still, with a case being built up against him for murder, flight seemed clearly indicated.'

'Did he kill Nancy?' whispered Jean.

Poirot rose.

'Supposing we visit once more the scene of the crime,' he suggested.

He led the way, and they followed him. But a simultaneous gasp broke from their lips as they passed outside the house. No trace of the tragedy remained; the snow was smooth and unbroken.

'Crikey!' said Eric, sinking down on the step. 'It wasn't all a dream, was it?'

'Most extraordinary,' said M. Poirot, 'The Mystery of the Disappearing Body.' His eyes twinkled gently.

Jean came up to him in sudden suspicion.

'M. Poirot, you haven't – you aren't – I say, you haven't been spoofing us all the time, have you? Oh, I do believe you have!'

'It is true, my children. I knew about your little plot, you see, and I arranged a little counterplot of my own. Ah, here is Mlle. Nancy – and none the worse, I hope, after her magnificent acting of the comedy.'

It was indeed Nancy Cardell in the flesh, her eyes shining and her whole person exuberant with health and vigour.

'You have not caught cold? You drank the tisane I sent to your room?' demanded Poirot accusingly.

'I took one sip and that was enough. I'm all right. Did I do it well, M. Poirot? Oh, my arm hurts after that tourniquet!'

'You were splendid, *petite*. But shall we explain to the others? They are still in the fog, I perceive. See you, *mes enfants*, I went to Mlle. Nancy, told her that I knew all about your little *complot*, and asked her if she would act a part for me. She did it very cleverly. She induced Mr Levering to make her a cup of tea, and also managed that he should be the one chosen to leave footprints on the snow. So when the time came, and he thought that by some fatality she was really dead, I had all the materials to frighten him with. What happened after we went into the house, Mademoiselle?'

'He came down with his sister, snatched the ruby out of my hand, and off they went post-haste.'

'But I say, M. Poirot, what about the ruby?' cried Eric. 'Do you mean to say you've let them have that?'

Poirot's face fell, as he faced a circle of accusing eyes.

'I shall recover it yet,' he said feebly; but he perceived that he had gone down in their estimation.

'Well, I do think!' began Johnnie. 'To let them get away with the ruby –'

But Jean was sharper.

'He's spoofing us again!' she cried. 'You are, aren't you?'

'Feel in my left-hand pocket, Mademoiselle.'

Jean thrust in an eager hand, and drew it out again with a squeal of triumph. She held aloft the great ruby in its crimson splendour.

'You see,' explained Poirot, 'the other was a paste replica I brought with me from London.'

'Isn't he clever?' demanded Jean ecstatically.

'There's one thing you haven't told us,' said Johnnie suddenly. 'How did you know about the rag? Did Nancy tell you?'

Poirot shook his head.

'Then how did you know?'

'It is my business to know things,' said M. Poirot, smiling a little as he watched Evelyn Haworth and Roger Endicott walking down the path together.

'Yes, but do tell us. Oh, do, please! *Dear* M. Poirot, please tell us!'

He was surrounded by a circle of flushed, eager faces.

'You really wish that I should solve for you this mystery?'

'*Yes.*'

'I do not think I can.'

'Why not?'

'*Ma foi*, you will be so disappointed.'

'Oh, do tell us! How *did* you know?'

'Well, you see, I was in the library –'

'Yes?'

'And you were discussing your plans just outside – and the library window was open.'

'Is that all?' said Eric in disgust. 'How simple!'

'Is it not?' said M. Poirot, smiling.

'At all events, we know everything now,' said Jean in a satisfied voice.

'Do we?' muttered M. Poirot to himself, as he went into the house. '*I* do not – I, whose business it is to know things.'

And, for perhaps the twentieth time, he drew from his pocket a rather dirty piece of paper.

'Don't eat any plum-pudding –'

M. Poirot shook his head perplexedly. At the same moment he became aware of a peculiar gasping sound very near his feet. He looked down and perceived a small creature in a print dress. In her left hand was a dust-pan, and in the right a brush.

'And who may you be, *mon enfant*?' inquired M. Poirot.

'Annie 'Icks, please, Sir. Between-maid.'

M. Poirot had an inspiration. He handed her the letter.

'Did you write that, Annie?'

'I didn't mean any 'arm, Sir.'

He smiled at her.

'Of course you didn't. Suppose you tell me all about it?'

'It was them two, Sir – Mr Levering and his sister. None of us can abide 'em; and she wasn't ill a bit – we could all tell that. So I thought something queer was going on, and I'll tell you straight, Sir, I listened at the door, and I heard him say as plain as plain, "This fellow Poirot must be got out of the way as soon as possible." And then he says to 'er, meaning-like, "Where did you put it?" And she answers, "In the pudding." And so I saw they meant to poison you in the Christmas pudding, and I didn't know what to do. Cook wouldn't listen to the likes of me. And then I thought of writing a warning, and I put it in the 'all where Mr Graves would be sure to see it and take it to you.'

Annie paused breathless. Poirot surveyed her gravely for some minutes.

'You read too many novelettes, Annie,' he said at last. 'But you have the good heart, and a certain amount of intelligence. When I return to London I will send you an excellent book upon *le ménage*, also the Lives of the Saints, and a work upon the economic position of woman.'

Leaving Annie gasping anew, he turned and crossed the hall. He had meant to go into the library, but through the open door he saw a dark head and a fair one, very close together, and he paused where he stood. Suddenly a pair of arms slipped round his neck.

'If you *will* stand just under the mistletoe!' said Jean.

'Me too,' said Nancy.

M. Poirot enjoyed it all – he enjoyed it very much indeed.

The Mystery of the Baghdad Chest

'The Mystery of the Baghdad Chest' was first published in *Strand Magazine*, January 1932, and in the USA as 'The Mystery of the Bagdad Chest' in *Ladies' Home Journal* the same month. It was later expanded into 'The Mystery of the Spanish Chest' for the book *The Adventure of the Christmas Pudding and a selection of Entrées* (Collins, October 1960), appearing first in the USA in three parts in *Women's Illustrated*, 17 and 24 September and 1 October 1960.

The words made a catchy headline, and I said as much to my friend, Hercule Poirot. I knew none of the parties. My interest was merely the dispassionate one of the man in the street. Poirot agreed.

'Yes, it has a flavour of the Oriental, of the mysterious. The chest may very well have been a sham Jacobean one from the Tottenham Court Road; none the less the reporter who thought of naming it the Baghdad Chest was happily inspired. The word "mystery" is also thoughtfully placed in juxtaposition, though I understand there is very little mystery about the case.'

'Exactly. It is all rather horrible and macabre, but it is not mysterious.'

'Horrible and macabre,' repeated Poirot thoughtfully.

'The whole idea is revolting,' I said, rising to my feet and pacing up and down the room. 'The murderer kills this man – his friend – shoves him into the chest, and half an hour later is dancing in that same room with the wife of his victim. Think! If she had imagined for one moment –'

'True,' said Poirot thoughtfully. 'That much-vaunted possession, a woman's intuition – it does not seem to have been working.'

'The party seems to have gone off very merrily,' I said with a slight shiver. 'And all that time, as they danced and played poker, there was a dead man in the room with them. One could write a play about such an idea.'

'It has been done,' said Poirot. 'But console yourself, Hastings,' he added kindly. 'Because a theme has been used once, there is no reason why it should not be used again. Compose your drama.'

I had picked up the paper and was studying the rather blurred reproduction of a photograph.

'She must be a beautiful woman,' I said slowly. 'Even from this, one gets an idea.'

Below the picture ran the inscription:

A recent portrait of Mrs Clayton,
the wife of the murdered man

Poirot took the paper from me.

'Yes,' he said. 'She is beautiful. Doubtless she is of those born to trouble the souls of men.'

He handed the paper back to me with a sigh.

'*Dieu merci*, I am not of an ardent temperament. It has saved me from many embarrassments. I am duly thankful.'

I do not remember that we discussed the case further. Poirot displayed no special interest in it at the time. The facts were so clear, and there was so little ambiguity about them, that discussion seemed merely futile.

Mr and Mrs Clayton and Major Rich were friends of fairly long-standing. On the day in question, the tenth of March, the Claytons had accepted an invitation to spend the evening with Major Rich. At about seven-thirty, however, Clayton explained to another friend, a Major Curtiss, with whom he was having a drink, that he had been unexpectedly called to Scotland and was leaving by the eight o'clock train.

'I'll just have time to drop in and explain to old Jack,' went on Clayton. 'Marguerita is going, of course. I'm sorry about it, but Jack will understand how it is.'

Mr Clayton was as good as his word. He arrived at Major Rich's rooms about twenty to eight. The major was out at the time, but his manservant, who knew Mr Clayton well, suggested that he come in and wait. Mr Clayton said that he had no time, but that he would come in and write a note. He added that he was on his way to catch a train.

The valet accordingly showed him into the sitting-room.

About five minutes later Major Rich, who must have let himself in without the valet hearing him, opened the door of the sitting-room, called his man and told him to go out and get some cigarettes. On his return the man brought them to his master, who was then alone in the sitting-room. The man naturally concluded that Mr Clayton had left.

The guests arrived shortly afterwards. They comprised Mrs Clayton,

Major Curtiss and a Mr and Mrs Spence. The evening was spent dancing to the phonograph and playing poker. The guests left shortly after midnight.

The following morning, on coming to do the sitting-room, the valet was startled to find a deep stain discolouring the carpet below and in front of a piece of furniture which Major Rich had brought from the East and which was called the Baghdad Chest.

Instinctively the valet lifted the lid of the chest and was horrified to find inside the doubled-up body of a man who had been stabbed to the heart.

Terrified, the man ran out of the flat and fetched the nearest policeman. The dead man proved to be Mr Clayton. The arrest of Major Rich followed very shortly afterward. The major's defence, it was understood, consisted of a sturdy denial of everything. He had not seen Mr Clayton the preceding evening and the first he had heard of his going to Scotland had been from Mrs Clayton.

Such were the bald facts of the case. Innuendoes and suggestions naturally abounded. The close friendship and intimacy of Major Rich and Mrs Clayton were so stressed that only a fool could fail to read between the lines. The motive for the crime was plainly indicated.

Long experience has taught me to make allowance for baseless calumny. The motive suggested might, for all the evidence, be entirely non-existent. Some quite other reason might have precipitated the issue. But one thing did stand out clearly – that Rich was the murderer.

As I say, the matter might have rested there, had it not happened that Poirot and I were due at a party given by Lady Chatterton that night.

Poirot, whilst bemoaning social engagements and declaring a passion for solitude, really enjoyed these affairs enormously. To be made a fuss of and treated as a lion suited him down to the ground.

On occasions he positively purred! I have seen him blandly receiving the most outrageous compliments as no more than his due, and uttering the most blatantly conceited remarks, such as I can hardly bear to set down.

Sometimes he would argue with me on the subject.

'But, my friend, I am not an Anglo-Saxon. Why should I play the hypocrite? *Si, si,* that is what you do, all of you. The airman who has made a difficult flight, the tennis champion – they look down their noses, they mutter inaudibly that "it is nothing". But do they really think that themselves? Not for a moment. They would admire the exploit in someone else. So, being reasonable men, they admire it in themselves. But their training prevents them from saying so. Me, I am not like that. The talents that I possess – I would salute them in another. As it happens, in my own particular line, there is no one to touch me. *C'est dommage!* As it is, I admit freely and without hypocrisy that I am a great man. I have the order, the method and the psychology in an unusual degree. I am, in fact, Hercule Poirot! Why should I turn red and stammer and mutter into my chin that really I am very stupid? It would not be true.'

'There is certainly only one Hercule Poirot,' I agreed – not without a spice of malice of which, fortunately, Poirot remained quite oblivious.

Lady Chatterton was one of Poirot's most ardent admirers. Starting from the mysterious conduct of a Pekingese, he had unravelled a chain which led to a noted burglar and housebreaker. Lady Chatterton had been loud in his praises ever since.

To see Poirot at a party was a great sight. His faultless evening clothes, the exquisite set of his white tie, the exact symmetry of his hair parting, the sheen of pomade on his hair, and the tortured splendour of his famous moustaches – all combined to paint the perfect picture of an inveterate dandy. It was hard, at these moments, to take the little man seriously.

It was about half-past eleven when Lady Chatterton, bearing down upon us, whisked Poirot neatly out of an admiring group, and carried him off – I need hardly say, with myself in tow.

'I want you to go into my little room upstairs,' said Lady Chatterton rather breathlessly as soon as she was out of earshot of her other guests. 'You know where it is, M. Poirot. You'll find someone there who needs your help very badly – and you will help her, I know. She's one of my dearest friends – so don't say no.'

Energetically leading the way as she talked, Lady Chatterton flung open a door, exclaiming as she did so, 'I've got him, Marguerita darling. And he'll do anything you want. You *will* help Mrs Clayton, won't you, M. Poirot?'

And taking the answer for granted, she withdrew with the same energy that characterized all her movements.

Mrs Clayton had been sitting in a chair by the window. She rose now and came toward us. Dressed in deep mourning, the dull black showed up her fair colouring. She was a singularly lovely woman, and there was about her a simple childlike candour which made her charm quite irresistible.

'Alice Chatterton is so kind,' she said. 'She arranged this. She said you would help me, M. Poirot. Of course I don't know whether you will or not – but I hope you will.'

She had held out her hand and Poirot had taken it. He held it now for a moment or two while he stood scrutinizing her closely. There was nothing ill-bred in his manner of doing it. It was more the kind but searching look that a famous consultant gives a new patient as the latter is ushered into his presence.

'Are you sure, madame,' he said at last, 'that I can help you?'

'Alice says so.'

'Yes, but I am asking you, madame.'

A little flush rose to her cheeks.

'I don't know what you mean.'

'What is it, madame, that you want me to do?'

'You – you – know who I am?' she asked.

'Assuredly.'

'Then you can guess what it is I am asking you to do, M. Poirot – Captain Hastings' – I was gratified that she realized my identity – 'Major Rich did *not* kill my husband.'

'Why not?'

'I beg your pardon?'

Poirot smiled at her slight discomfiture.

'I said, "Why not?"' he repeated.

'I'm not sure that I understand.'

'Yet it is very simple. The police – the lawyers – they will all ask the same question: Why did Major Rich kill M. Clayton? I ask the opposite. I ask you, madame, why did Major Rich *not* kill Mr Clayton.'

'You mean – why I'm so sure? Well, but I *know*. I know Major Rich so well.'

'You know Major Rich so well,' repeated Poirot tonelessly.

The colour flamed into her cheeks.

'Yes, that's what they'll say – what they'll think! Oh, I know!'

'*C'est vrai.* That is what they will ask you about – how well you knew Major Rich. Perhaps you will speak the truth, perhaps you will lie. It is very necessary for a woman to lie, it is a good weapon. But there are three people, madame, to whom a woman should speak the truth. To her Father Confessor, to her hairdresser and to her private detective – if she trusts him. Do you trust me, madame?'

Marguerita Clayton drew a deep breath. 'Yes,' she said. 'I do. I must,' she added rather childishly.

'Then, how well do you know Major Rich?'

She looked at him for a moment in silence, then she raised her chin defiantly.

'I will answer your question. I loved Jack from the first moment I saw him – two years ago. Lately I think – I believe – he has come to love me. But he has never said so.'

'*Épatant!*' said Poirot. 'You have saved me a good quarter of an hour by coming to the point without beating the bush. You have the good sense. Now your husband – did he suspect your feelings?'

'I don't know,' said Marguerita slowly. 'I thought – lately – that he might. His manner has been different . . . But that may have been merely my fancy.'

'Nobody else knew?'

'I do not think so.'

'And – pardon me, madame – you did not love your husband?'

There were, I think, very few women who would have answered that question as simply as this woman did. They would have tried to explain their feelings.

Marguerita Clayton said quite simply: 'No.'

'*Bien*. Now we know where we are. According to you, madame, Major Rich did not kill your husband, but you realize that all the evidence points to his having done so. Are you aware, privately, of any flaw in that evidence?'

'No. I know nothing.'

'When did your husband first inform you of his visit to Scotland?'

'Just after lunch. He said it was a bore, but he'd have to go. Something to do with land values, he said it was.'

'And after that?'

'He went out – to his club, I think. I – I didn't see him again.'

'Now as to Major Rich – what was his manner that evening? Just as usual?'

'Yes, I think so.'

'You are not sure?'

Marguerita wrinkled her brows.

'He was – a little constrained. With me – not with the others. But I thought I knew why that was. You understand? I am sure the constraint or – or – absent-mindedness perhaps describes it better – had nothing to do with Edward. He was surprised to hear that Edward had gone to Scotland, but not unduly so.'

'And nothing else unusual occurs to you in connection with that evening?'

Marguerita thought.

'No, nothing whatever.'

'You – noticed the chest?'

She shook her head with a little shiver.

'I don't even remember it – or what it was like. We played poker most of the evening.'

'Who won?'

'Major Rich. I had very bad luck, and so did Major Curtiss. The Spences won a little, but Major Rich was the chief winner.'

'The party broke up – when?'

'About half-past twelve, I think. We all left together.'

'Ah!'

Poirot remained silent, lost in thought.

'I wish I could be more helpful to you,' said Mrs Clayton. 'I seem to be able to tell you so little.'

'About the present – yes. What about the past, madame?'

'The past?'

'Yes. Have there not been incidents?'

She flushed.

'You mean that dreadful little man who shot himself. It wasn't my fault, M. Poirot. Indeed it wasn't.'

'It was not precisely of that incident that I was thinking.'

'That ridiculous duel? But Italians do fight duels. I was so thankful the man wasn't killed.'

'It must have been a relief to you,' agreed Poirot gravely.

She was looking at him doubtfully. He rose and took her hand in his.

'I shall not fight a duel for you, madame,' he said. 'But I will do what you have asked me. I will discover the truth. And let us hope that your instincts are correct – that the truth will help and not harm you.'

Our first interview was with Major Curtiss. He was a man of about forty, of soldierly build, with very dark hair and a bronzed face. He had known the Claytons for some years and Major Rich also. He confirmed the press reports.

Clayton and he had had a drink together at the club just before half-past seven, and Clayton had then announced his intention of looking in on Major Rich on his way to Euston.

'What was Mr Clayton's manner? Was he depressed or cheerful?'

The major considered. He was a slow-spoken man.

'Seemed in fairly good spirits,' he said at last.

'He said nothing about being on bad terms with Major Rich?'

'Good Lord, no. They were pals.'

'He didn't object to – his wife's friendship with Major Rich?'

The major became very red in the face.

'You've been reading those damned newspapers, with their hints and lies. Of course he didn't object. Why, he said to me: "Marguerita's going, of course."'

'I see. Now during the evening – the manner of Major Rich – was that much as usual?'

'I didn't notice any difference.'

'And madame? She, too, was as usual.'

'Well,' he reflected, 'now I come to think of it, she was a bit quiet. You know, thoughtful and faraway.'

'Who arrived first?'

'The Spences. They were there when I got there. As a matter of fact, I'd called round for Mrs Clayton, but found she'd already started. So I got there a bit late.'

'And how did you amuse yourselves? You danced? You played the cards?'

'A bit of both. Danced first of all.'

'There were five of you?'

'Yes, but that's all right, because I don't dance. I put on the records and the others danced.'

'Who danced most with whom?'

'Well, as a matter of fact the Spences like dancing together. They've got a sort of craze on it – fancy steps and all that.'

'So that Mrs Clayton danced mostly with Major Rich?'

'That's about it.'

'And then you played poker?'

'Yes.'

'And when did you leave?'

'Oh, quite early. A little after midnight.'

'Did you all leave together?'

'Yes. As a matter of fact, we shared a taxi, dropped Mrs Clayton first, then me, and the Spences took it on to Kensington.'

Our next visit was to Mr and Mrs Spence. Only Mrs Spence was at home, but her account of the evening tallied with that of Major Curtiss except that she displayed a slight acidity concerning Major Rich's luck at cards.

Earlier in the morning Poirot had had a telephone conversation with Inspector Japp of Scotland Yard. As a result we arrived at Major Rich's rooms and found his manservant, Burgoyne, expecting us.

The valet's evidence was very precise and clear.

Mr Clayton had arrived at twenty minutes to eight. Unluckily Major Rich had just that very minute gone out. Mr Clayton had said that he couldn't wait, as he had to catch a train, but he would just scrawl a note. He accordingly went into the sitting-room to do so. Burgoyne had not actually heard his master come in, as he was running the bath, and Major Rich, of course, let himself in with his own key. In his opinion it was about ten minutes later that Major Rich called him and sent him out for cigarettes. No, he had not gone into the sitting-room. Major Rich had stood in the doorway. He had returned with the cigarettes five minutes later and on this occasion he had gone into the sitting-room, which was then empty, save for his master, who was standing by the window smoking. His master had inquired if his bath were ready and on being told it was had proceeded to take it. He, Burgoyne, had not mentioned Mr Clayton, as he assumed that his master had found Mr Clayton there and let him out himself. His master's manner had been precisely the same as usual. He had taken his bath, changed, and shortly after, Mr and Mrs Spence had arrived, to be followed by Major Curtiss and Mrs Clayton.

It had not occurred to him, Burgoyne explained, that Mr Clayton might have left before his master's return. To do so, Mr Clayton would have had to bang the front door behind him and that the valet was sure he would have heard.

Still in the same impersonal manner, Burgoyne proceeded to his finding of the body. For the first time my attention was directed to the fatal chest. It was a good-sized piece of furniture standing against the wall next to the phonograph cabinet. It was made of some dark wood and plentifully studded with brass nails. The lid opened simply enough. I looked in and shivered. Though well scrubbed, ominous stains remained.

Suddenly Poirot uttered an exclamation. 'Those holes there – they are curious. One would say that they had been newly made.'

The holes in question were at the back of the chest against the wall. There were three or four of them. They were about a quarter of an inch in diameter and certainly had the effect of having been freshly made.

Poirot bent down to examine them, looking inquiringly at the valet.

'It's certainly curious, sir. I don't remember ever seeing those holes in the past, though maybe I wouldn't notice them.'

'It makes no matter,' said Poirot.

Closing the lid of the chest, he stepped back into the room until he was standing with his back against the window. Then he suddenly asked a question.

'Tell me,' he said. 'When you brought the cigarettes into your master that night, was there not something out of place in the room?'

Burgoyne hesitated for a minute, then with some slight reluctance he replied, 'It's odd your saying that, sir. Now you come to mention it, there was. That screen there that cuts off the draught from the bedroom door – it was moved a bit more to the left.'

'Like this?'

Poirot darted nimbly forward and pulled at the screen. It was a handsome affair of painted leather. It already slightly obscured the view of the chest, and as Poirot adjusted it, it hid the chest altogether.

'That's right, sir,' said the valet. 'It was like that.'

'And the next morning?'

'It was still like that. I remember. I moved it away and it was then I saw the stain. The carpet's gone to be cleaned, sir. That's why the boards are bare.'

Poirot nodded.

'I see,' he said. 'I thank you.'

He placed a crisp piece of paper in the valet's palm.

'Thank you, sir.'

'Poirot,' I said when we were out in the street, 'that point about the screen – is that a point helpful to Rich?'

'It is a further point against him,' said Poirot ruefully. 'The screen hid the chest from the room. It also hid the stain on the carpet. Sooner or later the blood was bound to soak through the wood and stain the carpet. The screen would prevent discovery for the moment. Yes – but there is something there that I do not understand. The valet, Hastings, the valet.'

'What about the valet? He seemed a most intelligent fellow.'

'As you say, most intelligent. Is it credible, then, that Major Rich failed to realize that the valet would certainly discover the body in the morning? Immediately after the deed he had no time for anything – granted. He shoves the body into the chest, pulls the screen in front of it and goes through the evening hoping for the best. But after the guests are gone? Surely, then is the time to dispose of the body.'

'Perhaps he hoped the valet wouldn't notice the stain?'

'That, *mon ami*, is absurd. A stained carpet is the first thing a good servant would be bound to notice.

And Major Rich, he goes to bed and snores there comfortably and does nothing at all about the matter. Very remarkable and interesting, that.'

'Curtiss might have seen the stains when he was changing the records the night before?' I suggested.

'That is unlikely. The screen would throw a deep shadow just there, No, but I begin to see. Yes, dimly I begin to see.'

'See what?' I asked eagerly.

'The possibilities, shall we say, of an alternative explanation. Our next visit may throw light on things.'

Our next visit was to the doctor who had examined the body. His evidence was a mere recapitulation of what he had already given at the inquest. Deceased had been stabbed to the heart with a long thin knife something like a stiletto. The knife had been left in the wound. Death had been instantaneous. The knife was the property of Major Rich and usually lay on his writing table. There were no fingerprints on it, the doctor understood. It had been either wiped or held in a handkerchief. As regards time, any time between seven and nine seemed indicated.

'He could not, for instance, have been killed after midnight?' asked Poirot.

'No. That I can say. Ten o'clock at the outside – but seven-thirty to eight seems clearly indicated.'

'There *is* a second hypothesis possible,' Poirot said when we were back home. 'I wonder if you see it, Hastings. To me it is very plain, and I only need one point to clear up the matter for good and all.'

'It's no good,' I said. 'I'm not there.'

'But make an effort, Hastings. Make an effort.'

'Very well,' I said. 'At seven-forty Clayton is alive and well. The last person to see him alive is Rich –'

'So we assume.'

'Well, isn't it so?'

'You forget, *mon ami*, that Major Rich denies that. He states explicitly that Clayton had gone when he came in.'

'But the valet says that he would have heard Clayton leave because of the bang of the door. And also, if Clayton had left, when did he return? He couldn't have returned after midnight because the doctor says positively that he was dead at least two hours before that. That only leaves one alternative.'

'Yes, *mon ami*?' said Poirot.

'That in the five minutes Clayton was alone in the sitting-room, someone else came in and killed him. But there we have the same objection. Only someone with a key could come in without the valet's knowing, and in the same way the murderer on leaving would have had to bang the door, and that again the valet would have heard.'

'Exactly,' said Poirot. 'And therefore –'

'And therefore – nothing,' I said. 'I can see no other solution.'

'It is a pity,' murmured Poirot. 'And it is really so exceedingly simple – as the clear blue eyes of Madame Clayton.'

'You really believe –'

'I believe nothing – until I have got proof. One little proof will convince me.'

He took up the telephone and called Japp at Scotland Yard.

Twenty minutes later we were standing before a little heap of assorted objects laid out on a table. They were the contents of the dead man's pockets.

There was a handkerchief, a handful of loose change, a pocketbook containing three pounds ten shillings, a couple of bills and a worn snapshot of Marguerita Clayton. There was also a pocketknife, a gold pencil and a cumbersome wooden tool.

It was on this latter that Poirot swooped. He unscrewed it and several small blades fell out.

'You see, Hastings, a gimlet and all the rest of it. Ah! it would be a matter of a very few minutes to bore a few holes in the chest with this.'

'Those holes we saw?'

'Precisely.'

'You mean it was Clayton who bored them himself?'

'*Mais, oui – mais, oui!* What did they suggest to you, those holes? They were not to *see* through, because they were at the back of the chest. What were they for, then? Clearly for air? But you do not make air holes for a dead body, so clearly they were *not* made by the murderer. They suggest one thing – and one thing only – that a man was going to *hide* in that chest. And at once, on that hypothesis, things become intelligible. Mr Clayton is jealous of his wife and Rich. He plays the old, old trick of pretending to go away. He watches Rich go out, then he gains admission, is left alone to write a note, quickly bores those holes and hides inside the chest. His wife is coming there that night. Possibly Rich will put the others off, possibly she will remain after the others have gone, or pretend to go and return. Whatever it is, Clayton will *know*. Anything is preferable to the ghastly torment of suspicion he is enduring.'

'Then you mean that Rich killed him *after* the others had gone? But the doctor said that was impossible.'

'Exactly. So you see, Hastings, he must have been killed *during* the evening.'

'But everyone was in the room!'

'Precisely,' said Poirot gravely. 'You see the beauty of that? "Everyone was in the room." What an alibi! What *sang-froid* – what nerve – what audacity!'

'I still don't understand.'

'Who went behind that screen to wind up the phonograph and change the records? The phonograph and the chest were side by side, remember. The others are dancing – the phonograph is playing. And the man who does not dance lifts the lid of the chest and thrusts the knife he has just slipped into his sleeve deep into the body of the man who was hiding there.'

'Impossible! The man would cry out.'

'Not if he were drugged first?'

'Drugged?'

'Yes. Who did Clayton have a drink with at seven-thirty? Ah! Now you see. Curtiss! Curtiss has inflamed Clayton's mind with suspicions against his wife and Rich. Curtiss suggests this plan – the visit to Scotland, the concealment in the chest, the final touch of moving the screen. Not so that Clayton can raise the lid a little and get relief – no, so that he, Curtiss, can raise that lid unobserved. The plan is Curtiss's, and observe the beauty of it, Hastings. If Rich had observed the screen was out of place and moved it back – well, no harm is done. He can make another plan. Clayton hides in the chest, the mild narcotic that Curtiss had administered takes effect. He sinks into unconsciousness. Curtiss lifts up the lid and strikes – and the phonograph goes on playing "Walking My Baby Back Home".'

I found my voice. 'Why? But why?'

Poirot shrugged his shoulders.

'Why did a man shoot himself? Why did two Italians fight a duel? Curtiss is of a dark passionate temperament. He wanted Marguerita Clayton. With her husband and Rich out of the way, she would, or so he thought, turn to him.'

He added musingly:

'These simple childlike women . . . they are very dangerous. But *mon Dieu!* what an artistic masterpiece! It goes to my heart to hang a man like that. I may be a genius myself, but I am capable of recognizing genius in other people. A perfect murder, *mon ami.* I, Hercule Poirot, say it to you. A perfect murder. *Épatant!'*

The Second Gong

'The Second Gong' was first published in the USA in
Ladies' Home Journal, June 1932, and then in *Strand Magazine*,
July 1932. It was later expanded into 'Dead Man's Mirror' for the
book *Murder in the Mews* (Collins, March 1937).

Joan Ashby came out of her bedroom and stood a moment on the landing outside her door. She was half turning as if to go back into the room when, below her feet as it seemed, a gong boomed out.

Immediately Joan started forward almost at a run. So great was her hurry that at the top of the big staircase she collided with a young man arriving from the opposite direction.

'Hullo, Joan! Why the wild hurry?'

'Sorry, Harry. I didn't see you.'

'So I gathered,' said Harry Dalehouse dryly. 'But as I say, why the wild haste?'

'It was the gong.'

'I know. But it's only the first gong.'

'No, it's the second.'

'First.'

'Second.'

Thus arguing they had been descending the stairs. They were now in the hall, where the butler, having replaced the gongstick, was advancing toward them at a grave and dignified pace.

'It is the second,' persisted Joan. 'I know it is. Well, for one thing, look at the time.'

Harry Dalehouse glanced up at the grandfather clock.

'Just twelve minutes past eight,' he remarked. 'Joan, I believe you're right, but I never heard the first one. Digby,' he addressed the butler, 'is this the first gong or the second?'

'The first, sir.'

'At twelve minutes past eight? Digby, somebody will get the sack for this.'

A faint smile showed for a minute on the butler's face.

'Dinner is being served ten minutes later tonight, sir. The master's orders.'

'Incredible!' cried Harry Dalehouse. 'Tut, tut! Upon my word, things are coming to a pretty pass! Wonders will never cease. What ails my revered uncle?'

'The seven o'clock train, sir, was half an hour late, and as –' The butler broke off, as a sound like the crack of a whip was heard.

'What on earth –' said Harry. 'Why, that sounded exactly like a shot.'

A dark, handsome man of thirty-five came out of the drawing room on their left.

'What was that?' he asked. 'It sounded exactly like a shot.'

'It must have been a car backfiring, sir,' said the butler. 'The road runs quite close to the house this side and the upstairs windows are open.'

'Perhaps,' said Joan doubtfully. 'But that would be over there.' She waved a hand to the right. 'And I thought the noise came from here.' She pointed to the left.

The dark man shook his head.

'I don't think so. I was in the drawing room. I came out here because I thought the noise came from this direction.' He nodded his head in front of him in the direction of the gong and the front door.

'East, west, and south, eh?' said the irrepressible Harry. 'Well, I'll make it complete, Keene. North for me. I thought it came from behind us. Any solutions offered?'

'Well, there's always murder,' said Geoffrey Keene, smiling. 'I beg your pardon, Miss Ashby.'

'Only a shiver,' said Joan. 'It's nothing. A what-do-you-call-it walking over my grave.'

'A good thought – murder,' said Harry. 'But, alas! No groans, no blood. I fear the solution is a poacher after a rabbit.'

'Seems tame, but I suppose that's it,' agreed the other. 'But it sounded so near. However, let's come into the drawing room.'

'Thank goodness, we're not late,' said Joan fervently. 'I was simply haring it down the stairs thinking that was the second gong.'

All laughing, they went into the big drawing room.

Lytcham Close was one of the most famous old houses in England. Its owner, Hubert Lytcham Roche, was the last of a long line, and his more distant relatives were apt to remark that 'Old Hubert, you know, really ought to be certified. Mad as a hatter, poor old bird.'

Allowing for the exaggeration natural to friends and relatives, some truth remained. Hubert Lytcham Roche was certainly eccentric. Though a very fine musician, he was a man of ungovernable temper and had an almost abnormal sense of his own importance. People staying in the house had to respect his prejudices or else they were never asked again.

One such prejudice was his music. If he played to his guests, as he often did in the evening, absolute silence must obtain. A whispered comment, a rustle of a dress, a movement even – and he would turn round scowling fiercely, and goodbye to the unlucky guest's chances of being asked again.

Another point was absolute punctuality for the crowning meal of the day. Breakfast was immaterial – you might come down at noon if you wished. Lunch also – a simple meal of cold meats and stewed fruit. But dinner was a rite, a festival, prepared by a *cordon bleu* whom he had tempted from a big hotel by the payment of a fabulous salary.

A first gong was sounded at five minutes past eight. At a quarter past eight a second gong was heard, and immediately after the door was flung open, dinner announced to the assembled guests, and a solemn procession wended its way to the dining room. Anyone who had the temerity to be late for the second gong was henceforth excommunicated – and Lytcham Close shut to the unlucky diner forever.

Hence the anxiety of Joan Ashby, and also the astonishment of Harry Dalehouse, at hearing that the sacred function was to be delayed ten minutes on this particular evening. Though not very intimate with his uncle, he had been to Lytcham Close often enough to know what a very unusual occurrence that was.

Geoffrey Keene, who was Lytcham Roche's secretary, was also very much surprised.

'Extraordinary,' he commented. 'I've never known such a thing to happen. Are you sure?'

'Digby said so.'

'He said something about a train,' said Joan Ashby. 'At least I think so.'

'Queer,' said Keene thoughtfully. 'We shall hear all about it in due course, I suppose. But it's very odd.'

Both men were silent for a moment or two, watching the girl. Joan Ashby was a charming creature, blue-eyed and golden-haired, with an impish glance. This was her first visit to Lytcham Close and her invitation was at Harry's prompting.

The door opened and Diana Cleves, the Lytcham Roches' adopted daughter, came into the room.

There was a daredevil grace about Diana, a witchery in her dark eyes and her mocking tongue. Nearly all men fell for Diana and she enjoyed her conquests. A strange creature, with her alluring suggestion of warmth and her complete coldness.

'Beaten the Old Man for once,' she remarked. 'First time for weeks he hasn't been here first, looking at his watch and tramping up and down like a tiger at feeding time.'

The young men had sprung forward. She smiled entrancingly at them both – then turned to Harry. Geoffrey Keene's dark cheek flushed as he dropped back.

He recovered himself, however, a moment later as Mrs Lytcham Roche came in. She was a tall, dark woman, naturally vague in manner, wearing floating draperies of an indeterminate shade of green. With her was a middle-aged man with a beaklike nose and a determined chin – Gregory Barling. He was a somewhat prominent figure in the financial world and, well-bred on his mother's side, he had for some years been an intimate friend of Hubert Lytcham Roche.

Boom!

The gong resounded imposingly. As it died away, the door was flung open and Digby announced:

'Dinner is served.'

Then, well-trained servant though he was, a look of complete astonishment flashed over his impassive face. For the first time in his memory, his master was not in the room!

That his astonishment was shared by everybody was evident. Mrs Lytcham Roche gave a little uncertain laugh.

'Most amazing. Really – I don't know what to do.'

Everybody was taken aback. The whole tradition of Lytcham Close was undermined. What could have happened? Conversation ceased. There was a strained sense of waiting.

At last the door opened once more; a sigh of relief went round only tempered by a slight anxiety as to how to treat the situation. Nothing must be said to emphasize the fact that the host had himself transgressed the stringent rule of the house.

But the newcomer was not Lytcham Roche. Instead of the big, bearded, viking-like figure, there advanced into the long drawing room a very small man, palpably a foreigner, with an egg-shaped head, a flamboyant moustache, and most irreproachable evening clothes.

His eyes twinkling, the newcomer advanced toward Mrs Lytcham Roche.

'My apologies, madame,' he said. 'I am, I fear, a few minutes late.'

'Oh, not at all!' murmured Mrs Lytcham Roche vaguely. 'Not at all, Mr –' She paused.

'Poirot, madame. Hercule Poirot.'

He heard behind him a very soft 'Oh' – a gasp rather than an articulate word – a woman's ejaculation. Perhaps he was flattered.

'You knew I was coming?' he murmured gently. '*N'est ce pas, madame?* Your husband told you.'

'Oh – oh, yes,' said Mrs Lytcham Roche, her manner unconvincing in the extreme. 'I mean, I suppose so. I am so terribly unpractical, M. Poirot. I never remember anything. But fortunately Digby sees to everything.'

'My train, I fear, was late,' said M. Poirot. 'An accident on the line in front of us.'

'Oh,' cried Joan, 'so that's why dinner was put off.'

His eye came quickly round to her – a most uncannily discerning eye.

'That is something out of the usual – eh?'

'I really can't think –' began Mrs Lytcham Roche, and then stopped. 'I mean,' she went on confusedly, 'it's so odd. Hubert never –'

Poirot's eyes swept rapidly round the group.

'M. Lytcham Roche is not down yet?'

'No, and it's so extraordinary –' She looked appealingly at Geoffrey Keene.

'Mr Lytcham Roche is the soul of punctuality,' explained Keene. 'He has not been late for dinner for – well, I don't know that he was ever late before.'

To a stranger the situation must have been ludicrous – the perturbed faces and the general consternation.

'I know,' said Mrs Lytcham Roche with the air of one solving a problem. 'I shall ring for Digby.'

She suited the action to the word.

The butler came promptly.

'Digby,' said Mrs Lytcham Roche, 'your master. Is he –'

As was customary with her, she did not finish her sentence. It was clear that the butler did not expect her to do so. He replied promptly and with understanding.

'Mr Lytcham Roche came down at five minutes to eight and went into the study, madam.'

'Oh!' She paused. 'You don't think – I mean – he heard the gong?'

'I think he must have – the gong is immediately outside the study door.'

'Yes, of course, of course,' said Mrs Lytcham Roche more vaguely than ever.

'Shall I inform him, madam, that dinner is ready?'

'Oh, thank you, Digby. Yes, I think – yes, yes, I should.'

'I don't know,' said Mrs Lytcham Roche to her guests as the butler withdrew, 'what I would do without Digby!'

A pause followed.

Then Digby re-entered the room. His breath was coming a little faster than is considered good form in a butler.

'Excuse me, madam – the study door is locked.'

It was then that M. Hercule Poirot took command of the situation.

'I think,' he said, 'that we had better go to the study.'

He led the way and everyone followed. His assumption of authority seemed perfectly natural, he was no longer a rather comic-looking guest. He was a personality and master of the situation.

He led the way out into the hall, past the staircase, past the great clock, past the recess in which stood the gong. Exactly opposite that recess was a closed door.

He tapped on it, first gently, then with increasing violence. But there was no reply. Very nimbly he dropped to his knees and applied his eye to the keyhole. He rose and looked round.

'Messieurs,' he said, 'we must break open this door. Immediately!'

As before no one questioned his authority. Geoffrey Keene and Gregory Barling were the two biggest men. They attacked the door under Poirot's directions. It was no easy matter. The doors of Lytcham Close were solid affairs – no modern jerry-building here. It resisted the attack valiantly, but at last it gave before the united attack of the men and crashed inward.

The house party hesitated in the doorway. They saw what they had subconsciously feared to see. Facing them was the window. On the left, between the door and the window, was a big writing table. Sitting, not at the table, but sideways to it, was a man – a big man – slouched forward in the chair. His back was to them and his face to the window, but his position told the tale. His right hand hung limply down and below it, on the carpet, was a small shining pistol.

Poirot spoke sharply to Gregory Barling.

'Take Mrs Lytcham Roche away – and the other two ladies.'

The other nodded comprehendingly. He laid a hand on his hostess's arm. She shivered.

'He has shot himself,' she murmured. 'Horrible!' With another shiver she permitted him to lead her away. The two girls followed.

Poirot came forward into the room, the two young men behind him.

He knelt down by the body, motioning them to keep back a little.

He found the bullet hole on the right side of the head. It had passed out the other side and had evidently struck a mirror hanging on the left-hand wall, since this was shivered. On the writing table was a sheet of paper, blank save for the word *Sorry* scrawled across it in hesitating, shaky writing.

Poirot's eyes darted back to the door.

'The key is not in the lock,' he said. 'I wonder –'

His hand slid into the dead man's pocket.

'Here it is,' he said. 'At least I think so. Have the goodness to try it, monsieur?'

Geoffrey Keene took it from him and tried it in the lock.

'That's it, all right.'

'And the window?'

Harry Dalehouse strode across to it.

'Shut.'

'You permit?' Very swiftly, Poirot scrambled to his feet and joined the other at the window. It was a long French window. Poirot opened it, stood a minute scrutinizing the grass just in front of it, then closed it again.

'My friends,' he said, 'we must telephone for the police. Until they have come and satisfied themselves that it is truly suicide nothing must be touched. Death can only have occurred about a quarter of an hour ago.'

'I know,' said Harry hoarsely. 'We heard the shot.'

'*Comment?* What is that you say?'

Harry explained with the help of Geoffrey Keene. As he finished speaking, Barling reappeared.

Poirot repeated what he had said before, and while Keene went off to telephone, Poirot requested Barling to give him a few minutes' interview.

They went into a small morning room, leaving Digby on guard outside the study door, while Harry went off to find the ladies.

'You were, I understand, an intimate friend of M. Lytcham Roche,' began Poirot. 'It is for that reason that I address myself to you primarily. In etiquette, perhaps, I should have spoken first to madame, but at the moment I do not think that is *pratique*.'

He paused.

'I am, see you, in a delicate situation. I will lay the facts plainly before you. I am, by profession, a private detective.'

The financier smiled a little.

'It is not necessary to tell me that, M. Poirot. Your name is, by now, a household word.'

'Monsieur is too amiable,' said Poirot, bowing. 'Let us, then, proceed. I receive, at my London address, a letter from this M. Lytcham Roche. In it he says that he has reason to believe that he is being swindled of large sums of money. For family reasons, so he puts it, he does not wish to call in the police, but he desires that I should come down and look into the matter for him. Well, I agree. I come. Not quite so soon as M. Lytcham Roche wishes – for after all I have other affairs, and M. Lytcham Roche, he is not quite the King of England, though he seems to think he is.'

Barling gave a wry smile.

'He did think of himself that way.'

'Exactly. Oh, you comprehend – his letter showed plainly enough that he was what one calls an eccentric. He was not insane, but he was unbalanced, *n'est ce pas?*'

'What he's just done ought to show that.'

'Oh, monsieur, but suicide is not always the act of the unbalanced. The coroner's jury, they say so, but that is to spare the feelings of those left behind.'

'Hubert was not a normal individual,' said Barling decisively. 'He was given to ungovernable rages, was a monomaniac on the subject of family pride, and had a bee in his bonnet in more ways than one. But for all that he was a shrewd man.'

'Precisely. He was sufficiently shrewd to discover that he was being robbed.'

'Does a man commit suicide because he's being robbed?' Barling asked.

'As you say, monsieur. Ridiculous. And that brings me to the need for haste in the matter. For family reasons – that was the phrase he used in his letter. *Eh bien*, monsieur, you are a man of the world, you know that it is for precisely that – family reasons – that a man does commit suicide.'

'You mean?'

'That it looks – on the face of it – as if *ce pauvre* monsieur had found out something further – and was unable to face what he had found out. But you perceive, I have a duty. I am already employed – commissioned – I have accepted the task. This "family reason", the dead man did not want it to get to the police. So I must act quickly. I must learn the truth.'

'And when you have learned it?'

'Then – I must use my discretion. I must do what I can.'

'I see,' said Barling. He smoked for a minute or two in silence, then he said, 'All the same I'm afraid I can't help you. Hubert never confided anything to me. I know nothing.'

'But tell me, monsieur, who, should you say, had a chance of robbing this poor gentleman?'

'Difficult to say. Of course, there's the agent for the estate. He's a new man.'

'The agent?'

'Yes. Marshall. Captain Marshall. Very nice fellow, lost an arm in the war. He came here a year ago. But Hubert liked him, I know, and trusted him, too.'

'If it were Captain Marshall who was playing him false, there would be no family reasons for silence.'

'N-No.'

The hesitation did not escape Poirot.

'Speak, monsieur. Speak plainly, I beg of you.'

'It may be gossip.'

'I implore you, speak.'

'Very well, then, I will. Did you notice a very attractive looking young woman in the drawing room?'

'I noticed two very attractive looking young women.'

'Oh, yes, Miss Ashby. Pretty little thing. Her first visit. Harry Dalehouse got Mrs Lytcham Roche to ask her. No, I mean a dark girl – Diana Cleves.'

'I noticed her,' said Poirot. 'She is one that all men would notice, I think.'

'She's a little devil,' burst out Barling. 'She's played fast and loose with every man for twenty miles round. Someone will murder her one of these days.'

He wiped his brow with a handkerchief, oblivious of the keen interest with which the other was regarding him.

'And this young lady is –'

'She's Lytcham Roche's adopted daughter. A great disappointment when he and his wife had no children. They adopted Diana Cleves – she was some kind of cousin. Hubert was devoted to her, simply worshipped her.'

'Doubtless he would dislike the idea of her marrying?' suggested Poirot.

'Not if she married the right person.'

'And the right person was – you, monsieur?'

Barling started and flushed.

'I never said –'

'*Mais, non, mais, non!* You said nothing. But it was so, was it not?'

'I fell in love with her – yes. Lytcham Roche was pleased about it. It fitted in with his ideas for her.'

'And mademoiselle herself?'

'I told you – she's the devil incarnate.'

'I comprehend. She has her own ideas of amusement, is it not so? But Captain Marshall, where does he come in?'

'Well, she's been seeing a lot of him. People talked. Not that I think there's anything in it. Another scalp, that's all.'

Poirot nodded.

'But supposing that there had been something in it – well, then, it might explain why M. Lytcham Roche wanted to proceed cautiously.'

'You do understand, don't you, that there's no earthly reason for suspecting Marshall of defalcation.'

'*Oh, parfaitement, parfaitement!* It might be an affair of a forged cheque with someone in the household involved. This young Mr Dalehouse, who is he?'

'A nephew.'

'He will inherit, yes?'

'He's a sister's son. Of course he might take the name – there's not a Lytcham Roche left.'

'I see.'

'The place isn't actually entailed, though it's always gone from father to son. I've always imagined that he'd leave the place to his wife for her lifetime and then perhaps to Diana if he approved of her marriage. You see, her husband could take the name.'

'I comprehend,' said Poirot. 'You have been most kind and helpful to me, monsieur. May I ask of you one thing further – to explain to Madame Lytcham Roche all that I have told you, and to beg of her that she accord me a minute?'

Sooner than he had thought likely, the door opened and Mrs Lytcham Roche entered. She floated to a chair.

'Mr Barling has explained everything to me,' she said. 'We mustn't have any scandal, of course. Though I do feel really it's fate, don't you? I mean with the mirror and everything.'

'*Comment* – the mirror?'

'The moment I saw it – it seemed a symbol. Of Hubert! A curse, you know. I think old families have a curse very often. Hubert was always very strange. Lately he has been stranger than ever.'

'You will forgive me for asking, madame, but you are not in any way short of money?'

'Money? I never think of money.'

'Do you know what they say, madame? Those who never think of money need a great deal of it.'

He ventured a tiny laugh. She did not respond. Her eyes were far away.

'I thank you, madame,' he said, and the interview came to an end.

Poirot rang, and Digby answered.

'I shall require you to answer a few questions,' said Poirot. 'I am a private detective sent for by your master before he died.'

'A detective!' the butler gasped. 'Why?'

'You will please answer my questions. As to the shot now –'

He listened to the butler's account.

'So there were four of you in the hall?'

'Yes, sir; Mr Dalehouse and Miss Ashby and Mr Keene came from the drawing room.'

'Where were the others?'

'The others, sir?'

'Yes, Mrs Lytcham Roche, Miss Cleves and Mr Barling.'

'Mrs Lytcham Roche and Mr Barling came down later, sir.'

'And Miss Cleves?'

'I think Miss Cleves was in the drawing room, sir.'

Poirot asked a few more questions, then dismissed the butler with the command to request Miss Cleves to come to him.

She came immediately, and he studied her attentively in view of Barling's revelations. She was certainly beautiful in her white satin frock with the rosebud on the shoulder.

He explained the circumstances which had brought him to Lytcham Close, eyeing her very closely, but she showed only what seemed to be genuine astonishment, with no signs of uneasiness. She spoke of Marshall indifferently with tepid approval. Only at mention of Barling did she approach animation.

'That man's a crook,' she said sharply. 'I told the Old Man so, but he wouldn't listen – went on putting money into his rotten concerns.'

'Are you sorry, mademoiselle, that your – father is dead?'

She stared at him.

'Of course. I'm modern, you know, M. Poirot. I don't indulge in sob stuff. But I was fond of the Old Man. Though, of course, it's best for him.'

'Best for him?'

'Yes. One of these days he would have had to be locked up. It was growing on him – this belief that the last Lytcham Roche of Lytcham Close was omnipotent.'

Poirot nodded thoughtfully.

'I see, I see – yes, decided signs of mental trouble. By the way, you permit that I examine your little bag? It is charming – all these silk rosebuds. What was I saying? Oh, yes, did you hear the shot?'

'Oh, yes! But I thought it was a car or a poacher, or something.'

'You were in the drawing room?'

'No. I was out in the garden.'

'I see. Thank you, mademoiselle. Next I would like to see M. Keene, is it not?'

'Geoffrey? I'll send him along.'

Keene came in, alert and interested.

'Mr Barling has been telling me of the reason for your being down here. I don't know that there's anything I can tell you, but if I can –'

Poirot interrupted him. 'I only want to know one thing, Monsieur Keene. What was it that you stooped and picked up just before we got to the study door this evening?'

'I –' Keene half sprang up from his chair, then subsided again. 'I don't know what you mean,' he said lightly.

'Oh, I think you do, monsieur. You were behind me, I know, but a friend of mine he says I have eyes in the back of my head. You picked up something and you put it in the right hand pocket of your dinner jacket.'

There was a pause. Indecision was written plainly on Keene's handsome face. At last he made up his mind.

'Take your choice, M. Poirot,' he said, and leaning forward he turned his pocket inside out. There was a cigarette holder, a handkerchief, a tiny silk rosebud, and a little gold match box.

A moment's silence and then Keene said, 'As a matter of fact it was this.' He picked up the match box. 'I must have dropped it earlier in the evening.'

'I think not,' said Poirot.

'What do you mean?'

'What I say. I, monsieur, am a man of tidiness, of method, of order. A match box on the ground, I should see it and pick it up – a match box of this size, assuredly I should see it! No, monsieur, I think it was something very much smaller – such as this, perhaps.'

He picked up the little silk rosebud.

'From Miss Cleve's bag, I think?'

There was a moment's pause, then Keene admitted it with a laugh.

'Yes, that's so. She – gave it to me last night.'

'I see,' said Poirot, and at the moment the door opened and a tall fair-haired man in a lounge suit strode into the room.

'Keene – what's all this? Lytcham Roche shot himself? Man, I can't believe it. It's incredible.'

'Let me introduce you,' said Keene, 'to M. Hercule Poirot.' The other started. 'He will tell you all about it.' And he left the room, banging the door.

'M. Poirot –' John Marshall was all eagerness '– I'm most awfully pleased to meet you. It is a bit of luck your being down here. Lytcham Roche never told me you were coming. I'm a most frightful admirer of yours, sir.'

A disarming young man, thought Poirot – not so young, either, for there was grey hair at the temples and lines in the forehead. It was the voice and manner that gave the impression of boyishness.

'The police –'

'They are here now, sir. I came up with them on hearing the news. They don't seem particularly surprised. Of course, he was mad as a hatter, but even then –'

'Even then you are surprised at his committing suicide?'

'Frankly, yes. I shouldn't have thought that – well, that Lytcham Roche could have imagined the world getting on without him.'

'He has had money troubles of late, I understand?'

Marshall nodded.

'He speculated. Wildcat schemes of Barling's.'

Poirot said quietly, 'I will be very frank. Had you any reason to suppose that Mr Lytcham Roche suspected you of tampering with your accounts?'

Marshall stared at Poirot in a kind of ludicrous bewilderment. So ludicrous was it that Poirot was forced to smile.

'I see that you are utterly taken aback, Captain Marshall.'

'Yes, indeed. The idea's ridiculous.'

'Ah! Another question. He did not suspect you of robbing him of his adopted daughter?'

'Oh, so you know about me and Di?' He laughed in an embarrassed fashion.

'It is so, then?'

Marshall nodded.

'But the old man didn't know anything about it. Di wouldn't have him told. I suppose she was right. He'd have gone up like a – a basketful of rockets. I should have been chucked out of a job, and that would have been that.'

'And instead what was your plan?'

'Well, upon my word, sir, I hardly know. I left things to Di. She said she'd fix it. As a matter of fact I was looking out for a job. If I could have got one I would have chucked this up.'

'And mademoiselle would have married you? But M. Lytcham Roche might have stopped her allowance. Mademoiselle Diana is, I should say, fond of money.'

Marshall looked rather uncomfortable.

'I'd have tried to make it up to her, sir.'

Geoffrey Keene came into the room. 'The police are just going and would like to see you, M. Poirot.'

'*Merci*. I will come.'

In the study were a stalwart inspector and the police surgeon.

'Mr Poirot?' said the inspector. 'We've heard of you, sir. I'm Inspector Reeves.'

'You are most amiable,' said Poirot, shaking hands. 'You do not need my co-operation, no?' He gave a little laugh.

'Not this time, sir. All plain sailing.'

'The case is perfectly straightforward, then?' demanded Poirot.

'Absolutely. Door and window locked, key of door in dead man's pocket. Manner very strange the past few days. No doubt about it.'

'Everything quite – natural?'

The doctor grunted.

'Must have been sitting at a damned queer angle for the bullet to have hit that mirror. But suicide's a queer business.'

'You found the bullet?'

'Yes, here.' The doctor held it out. 'Near the wall below the mirror. Pistol was Mr Roche's own. Kept it in the drawer of the desk always. Something behind it all, I daresay, but what that is we shall never know.'

Poirot nodded.

The body had been carried to a bedroom. The police now took their leave. Poirot stood at the front door looking after them. A sound made him turn. Harry Dalehouse was close behind him.

'Have you, by any chance, a strong flashlight, my friend?' asked Poirot.

'Yes, I'll get it for you.'

When he returned with it Joan Ashby was with him.

'You may accompany me if you like,' said Poirot graciously.

He stepped out of the front door and turned to the right, stopping before the study window. About six feet of grass separated it from the path. Poirot bent down, playing the flashlight on the grass. He straightened himself and shook his head.

'No,' he said, 'not there.'

Then he paused and slowly his figure stiffened. On either side of the grass was a deep flower border. Poirot's attention was focused on the right hand border, full of Michaelmas daisies and dahlias. His torch was directed on the front of the bed. Distinct on the soft mould were footprints.

'Four of them,' murmured Poirot. 'Two going toward the window, two coming from it.'

'A gardener,' suggested Joan.

'But no, mademoiselle, but no. Employ your eyes. These shoes are small, dainty, high-heeled, the shoes of a woman. Mademoiselle Diana mentioned having been out in the garden. Do you know if she went downstairs before you did, mademoiselle?'

Joan shook her head.

'I can't remember. I was in such a hurry because the gong went, and I thought I'd heard the first one. I do seem to remember that her room door was open as I went past, but I'm not sure. Mrs Lytcham Roche's was shut, I know.'

'I see,' said Poirot.

Something in his voice made Harry look up sharply, but Poirot was merely frowning gently to himself.

In the doorway they met Diana Cleves.

'The police have gone,' she said. 'It's all – over.'

She gave a deep sigh.

'May I request one little word with you, mademoiselle?'

She led the way into the morning room, and Poirot followed, shutting the door.

'Well?' She looked a little surprised.

'One little question, mademoiselle. Were you tonight at any time in the flower border outside the study window?'

'Yes.' She nodded. 'About seven o'clock and again just before dinner.'

'I do not understand,' he said.

'I can't see that there is anything to "understand", as you call it,' she said coldly. 'I was picking Michaelmas daisies – for the table. I always do the flowers. That was about seven o'clock.'

'And afterward – later?'

'Oh, that! As a matter of fact I dropped a spot of hair oil on my dress – just on the shoulder here. It was just as I was ready to come down. I didn't want to change the dress. I remembered I'd seen a late rose in bud in the border. I ran out and picked it and pinned it in. See –' She came close to him and lifted the head of the rose. Poirot saw the minute grease spot. She remained close to him, her shoulder almost brushing his.

'And what time was this?'

'Oh, about ten minutes past eight, I suppose.'

'You did not – try the window?'

'I believe I did. Yes, I thought it would be quicker to go in that way. But it was fastened.'

'I see.' Poirot drew a deep breath. 'And the shot,' he said, 'where were you when you heard that? Still in the flower border?'

'Oh, no; it was two or three minutes later, just before I came in by the side door.'

'Do you know what this is, mademoiselle?'

On the palm of his hand he held out the tiny silk rosebud. She examined it coolly.

'It looks like a rosebud off my little evening bag. Where did you find it?'

'It was in Mr Keene's pocket,' said Poirot dryly. 'Did you give it to him, mademoiselle?'

'Did he tell you I gave it to him?'

Poirot smiled.

'When did you give it to him, mademoiselle?'

'Last night.'

'Did he warn you to say that, mademoiselle?'

'What do you mean?' she asked angrily.

But Poirot did not answer. He strode out of the room and into the drawing room. Barling, Keene, and Marshall were there. He went straight up to them.

'Messieurs,' he said brusquely, 'will you follow me to the study?'

He passed out into the hall and addressed Joan and Harry.

'You, too, I pray of you. And will somebody request madame to come? I thank you. Ah! And here is the excellent Digby. Digby, a little question, a very important little question. Did Miss Cleves arrange some Michaelmas daisies before dinner?'

The butler looked bewildered.

'Yes, sir, she did.'

'You are sure?'

'Quite sure, sir.'

'*Très bien*. Now – come, all of you.'

Inside the study he faced them.

'I have asked you to come here for a reason. The case is over, the police have come and gone. They say Mr Lytcham Roche has shot himself. All is finished.' He paused. 'But I, Hercule Poirot, say that it is not finished.'

As startled eyes turned to him the door opened and Mrs Lytcham Roche floated into the room.

'I was saying, madame, that this case is not finished. It is a matter of the psychology. Mr Lytcham Roche, he had the *manie de grandeur*, he was a king. Such a man does not kill himself. No, no, he may go mad, but he does not kill himself. Mr Lytcham Roche did not kill himself.' He paused. 'He was killed.'

'Killed?' Marshall gave a short laugh. 'Alone in a room with the door and window locked?'

'All the same,' said Poirot stubbornly, 'he was killed.'

'And got up and locked the door or shut the window afterward, I suppose,' said Diana cuttingly.

'I will show you something,' said Poirot, going to the window. He turned the handle of the French windows and then pulled gently.

'See, they are open. Now I close them, but without turning the handle. Now the window is closed but not fastened. Now!'

He gave a short jarring blow and the handle turned, shooting the bolt down into its socket.

'You see?' said Poirot softly. 'It is very loose, this mechanism. It could be done from outside quite easily.'

He turned, his manner grim.

'When that shot was fired at twelve minutes past eight, there were four people in the hall. Four people have an alibi. Where were the other three? You, madame? In your room. You, Monsieur Barling. Were you, too, in your room?'

'I was.'

'And you, mademoiselle, were in the garden. So you have admitted.'

'I don't see –' began Diana.

'Wait.' He turned to Mrs Lytcham Roche. 'Tell me, madame, have you any idea of how your husband left his money?'

'Hubert read me his will. He said I ought to know. He left me three thousand a year chargeable on the estate, and the dower house or the town house, whichever I preferred. Everything else he left to Diana, on condition that if she married her husband must take the name.'

'Ah!'

'But then he made a codicil thing – a few weeks ago, that was.'

'Yes, madame?'

'He still left it all to Diana, but on condition that she married Mr Barling. If she married anyone else, it was all to go to his nephew, Harry Dalehouse.'

'But the codicil was only made a few weeks ago,' purred Poirot. 'Mademoiselle may not have known of that.' He stepped forward accusingly. 'Mademoiselle Diana, you want to marry Captain Marshall, do you not? Or is it Mr Keene?'

She walked across the room and put her arm through Marshall's sound one.

'Go on,' she said.

'I will put the case against you, mademoiselle. You loved Captain Marshall. You also loved money. Your adopted father he would never have consented to your marrying Captain Marshall, but if he dies you are fairly sure that you get everything. So you go out, you step over the flower border to the window which is open, you have with you the pistol which you have taken from the writing table drawer. You go up to your victim talking amiably. You fire. You drop the pistol by his hand, having wiped it and then pressed his fingers on it. You go out again, shaking the window till the bolt drops. You come into the house. Is that how it happened? I am asking you, mademoiselle?'

'No,' Diana screamed. 'No – no!'

He looked at her, then he smiled.

'No,' he said, 'it was not like that. It might have been so – it is plausible – it is possible – but it cannot have been like that for two reasons. The first reason is that you picked Michaelmas daisies at seven o'clock, the second arises from something that mademoiselle here told me.' He turned toward Joan, who stared at him in bewilderment. He nodded encouragement.

'But yes, mademoiselle. You told me that you hurried downstairs because you thought it was the second gong sounding, having already heard the first.'

He shot a rapid glance round the room.

'You do not see what that means?' he cried. 'You do not see. Look!

Look!' He sprang forward to the chair where the victim had sat. 'Did you notice how the body was? Not sitting square to the desk – no, sitting sideways to the desk, facing the window. Is that a natural way to commit suicide? *Jamais, jamais!* You write your apologia "sorry" on a piece of paper – you open the drawer, you take out the pistol, you hold it to your head and you fire. That is the way of suicide. But now consider murder! The victim sits at his desk, the murderer stands beside him – talking. And talking still – fires. Where does the bullet go then?' He paused. 'Straight through the head, through the door if it is open, and so – hits the gong.

'Ah! you begin to see? That was the first gong – heard only by mademoiselle, since her room is above.

'What does our murderer do next? Shuts the door, locks it, puts the key in the dead man's pocket, then turns the body sideways in the chair, presses the dead man's fingers on the pistol and then drops it by his side, cracks the mirror on the wall as a final spectacular touch – in short, "arranges" his suicide. Then out through the window, the bolt is shaken home, the murderer steps not on the grass, where footprints must show, but on the flower bed, where they can be smoothed out behind him, leaving no trace. Then back into the house, and at twelve minutes past eight, when he is alone in the drawing room, he fires a service revolver out of the drawing room window and dashes out into the hall. Is that how you did it, Mr Geoffrey Keene?'

Fascinated, the secretary stared at the accusing figure drawing nearer to him. Then, with a gurgling cry, he fell to the ground.

'I think I am answered,' said Poirot. 'Captain Marshall, will you ring up the police?' He bent over the prostrate form. 'I fancy he will be still unconscious when they come.'

'Geoffrey Keene,' murmured Diana. 'But what motive had he?'

'I fancy that as secretary he had certain opportunities – accounts – cheques. Something awakened Mr Lytcham Roche's suspicions. He sent for me.'

'Why for you? Why not for the police?'

'I think, mademoiselle, you can answer that question. Monsieur suspected that there was something between you and that young man. To divert his mind from Captain Marshall, you had flirted shamelessly with Mr Keene. But yes, you need not deny! Mr Keene gets wind of my coming and acts promptly. The essence of his scheme is that the crime must seem to take place at 8:12, when he has an alibi. His one danger is the bullet, which must be lying somewhere near the gong and which he has not had time to retrieve. When we are all on our way to the study he picks that up. At such a tense moment he thinks no one will notice.

But me, I notice everything! I question him. He reflects a little minute and then he plays the comedy! He insinuates that what he picked up was the silk rosebud, he plays the part of the young man in love shielding the lady he loves. Oh, it was very clever, and if you had not picked Michaelmas daisies –'

'I don't understand what they have to do with it.'

'You do not? Listen – there were only four footprints in the bed, but when you were picking the flowers you must have made many more than that. So in between your picking the flowers and your coming to get the rosebud someone must have smoothed over the bed. Not a gardener – no gardener works after seven. Then it must be someone guilty – it must be the murderer – the murder was committed before the shot was heard.'

'But why did nobody hear the real shot?' asked Harry.

'A silencer. They will find that and the revolver thrown into the shrubbery.'

'What a risk!'

'Why a risk? Everyone was upstairs dressing for dinner. It was a very good moment. The bullet was the only contretemps, and even that, as he thought, passed off well.'

Poirot picked it up. 'He threw it under the mirror when I was examining the window with Mr Dalehouse.'

'Oh!' Diana wheeled on Marshall. 'Marry me, John, and take me away.'

Barling coughed. 'My dear Diana, under the terms of my friend's will –'

'I don't care,' the girl cried. 'We can draw pictures on pavements.'

'There's no need to do that,' said Harry. 'We'll go halves, Di. I'm not going to bag things because Uncle had a bee in his bonnet.'

Suddenly there was a cry. Mrs Lytcham Roche had sprung to her feet.

'M. Poirot – the mirror – he – he must have deliberately smashed it.'

'Yes, madame.'

'Oh!' She stared at him. 'But it is unlucky to break a mirror.'

'It has proved very unlucky for Mr Geoffrey Keene,' said Poirot cheerfully.

Postscript

The Christmas Stories

Editor's note

The Christmas stories collected in the book *Star Over Bethlehem and other stories* (a slightly misleading title, as it contained poems as well as stories) represent Agatha Christie's only venture into writing for children. The title story was first published in December 1946 in *Woman's Journal*, but it is not known when she wrote the other five – it appears to have been specifically for the book in 1965. Agatha's husband, Max Mallowan, thought the stories were his wife's 'most charming and among the most original of her works' and said, 'These sweet tales . . . may fairly be styled "Holy Detective Stories".'

Because *Star Over Bethlehem and other stories* was not in the crime genre, Agatha chose to follow the convention set by her earlier volume of memoirs, *Come, Tell Me How You Live*, and publish it under her full married name of Agatha Christie Mallowan.

Star Over Bethlehem

'Star Over Bethlehem' was first published in *Woman's Journal*, December 1946.

Mary looked down at the baby in the manger. She was alone in the stable except for the animals. As she smiled down at the child her heart was full of pride and happiness.

Then suddenly she heard the rustling of wings and turning, she saw a great Angel standing in the doorway.

The Angel shone with the radiance of the morning sun, and the beauty of his face was so great that Mary's eyes were dazzled and she had to turn aside her head.

Then the Angel said (and his voice was like a golden trumpet):

'Do not be afraid, Mary . . .'

And Mary answered in her sweet low voice:

'I am not afraid, O Holy One of God, but the Light of your Countenance dazzles me.'

The Angel said: 'I have come to speak to you.'

Mary said: 'Speak on, Holy One. Let me hear the commands of the Lord God.'

The Angel said: 'I have come with no commands. But since you are specially dear to God, it is permitted that, with my aid, you should look into the future . . .'

Then Mary looked down at the child and asked eagerly:

'Into *his* future?'

Her face lit up with joyful anticipation.

'Yes,' said the Angel gently. 'Into *his* future . . . Give me your hand.'

Mary stretched out her hand and took that of the Angel. It was like touching flame – yet flame that did not burn. She shrank back a little and the Angel said again:

'Do not be afraid. I am immortal and you are mortal, but my touch shall not hurt you . . .'

Then the Angel stretched out his great golden wing over the sleeping child and said:

'Look into the future, Mother, and see your Son . . .'

And Mary looked straight ahead of her and the stable walls melted and dissolved and she was looking into a Garden. It was night and there were stars overhead and a man was kneeling, praying.

Something stirred in Mary's heart, and her motherhood told her that it was her son who knelt there. She said thankfully to herself: 'He has become a good man – a devout man – he prays to God.' And then suddenly she caught her breath, for the man had raised his face and she saw the agony on it – the despair and the sorrow . . . and she knew that she was looking on greater anguish than any she had ever known or seen. For the man was utterly alone. He was praying to God, praying that this cup of anguish might be taken from him – and there was no answer to his prayer. God was absent and silent . . .

And Mary cried out:

'Why does not God answer him and give him comfort?'

And she heard the voice of the Angel say:

'It is not God's purpose that he should have comfort.'

Then Mary bowed her head meekly and said: 'It is not for us to know the inscrutable purposes of God. But has this man – my son – has he no friends? No kindly human friends?'

The Angel rustled his wing and the picture dissolved into another part of the Garden and Mary saw some men lying asleep.

She said bitterly: 'He needs them – my son needs them – and they do not care!'

The Angel said: 'They are only fallible human creatures . . .'

Mary murmured to herself: 'But he is a *good* man, my son. A good and upright man.'

Then again the wing of the Angel rustled, and Mary saw a road winding up a hill, and three men on it carrying crosses, and a crowd behind them and some Roman soldiers.

The Angel said: 'What do you see now?'

Mary said: 'I see three criminals going to execution.'

The left-hand man turned his head and Mary saw a cruel crafty face, a low bestial type – and she drew back a little.

'Yes,' she said, 'they are criminals.'

Then the man in the centre stumbled and nearly fell, and as he turned his face, Mary recognized him and she cried out sharply:

'No, no, it cannot be that my son is a *criminal*!'

But the Angel rustled his wing and she saw the three crosses set up, and the figure hanging in agony on the centre one was the man she knew to be her son. His cracked lips parted and she heard the words that came from them:

'*My God, my God, why hast thou forsaken me?*'

And Mary cried out: 'No, no, it is not true! He cannot have done anything really wrong. There has been some dreadful mistake. It can happen sometimes. There has been some confusion of identity; he has been mistaken for someone else. He is suffering for someone else's crime.'

But again the Angel rustled his wing and this time Mary was looking at the figure of the man she revered most on earth – the High Priest of her Church. He was a noble-looking man, and he stood up now and with solemn hands he tore and rent the garment he was wearing, and cried out in a loud voice:

'This man has spoken Blasphemy!'

And Mary looked beyond him and saw the figure of the man who had spoken Blasphemy – and it was her son.

Then the pictures faded and there was only the mudbrick wall of the stable, and Mary was trembling and crying out brokenly:

'I cannot believe it – I *cannot* believe it. We are a God-fearing straight-living family – all my family. Yes, and Joseph's family too. And we shall bring him up carefully to practise religion and to revere and honour the faith of his fathers. A son of ours could never be guilty of Blasphemy – I cannot believe it! All this that you have shown me cannot be true.'

Then the Angel said: 'Look at me, Mary.'

And Mary looked at him and saw the radiance surrounding him and the beauty of his Face.

And the Angel said: 'What I have shown you is Truth. For I am the Morning Angel, and the Light of the Morning is Truth. Do you believe now?'

And sorely against her will, Mary knew that what she had been shown was indeed Truth . . . and she could not disbelieve any more.

The tears raced down her cheeks and she bent over the child in the manger, her arms outspread as though to protect him. She cried out:

'My child . . . my little helpless child . . . what can I do to save you? To spare you from what is to come? Not only from the sorrow and the pain, but from the evil that will blossom in your heart? Oh indeed it would have been better for you if you had never been born, or if you had died with your first breath. For then you would have gone back to God pure and unsoiled.'

And the Angel said: 'That is why I have come to you, Mary.'

Mary said: 'What do you mean?'

The Angel answered: 'You have seen the future. It is in your power to say if your child shall live or die.'

Then Mary bent her head, and amidst stifled sobs she murmured:

'The Lord gave him to me . . . If the Lord now takes him away, then I see that it may indeed be mercy, and though it tears my flesh I submit to God's will.'

But the Angel said softly:

'It is not quite like that. God lays no command on you. The choice is *yours*. You have seen the future. Choose now if the child shall live or die.'

Then Mary was silent for a little while. She was a woman who thought slowly. She looked once at the Angel for guidance, but the Angel gave her none. He was golden and beautiful and infinitely remote.

She thought of the pictures that had been shown her – of the agony in the garden, of the shameful death, of a man who, at the hour of death, was forsaken of God, and she heard again the dreadful word *Blasphemy* . . .

And now, at this moment, the sleeping babe was pure and innocent and happy . . .

But she did not decide at once, she went on thinking – going over and over again those pictures she had been shown. And in doing so a curious thing happened, for she remembered little things that she had not been aware of seeing at the time. She saw, for instance, the face of the man on the right-hand cross . . . Not an evil face, only a weak one – and it was turned towards the centre cross and on it was an expression of love and trust and adoration . . . And it came to Mary, with sudden wonder – 'It was at *my son* he was looking like that . . .'

And suddenly, sharply and clearly, she saw her son's face as it had been when he looked down at his sleeping friends in the garden. There was sadness there, and pity and understanding and a great love . . . And she thought: 'It is the face of a *good* man . . .' And she saw again the scene of accusation. But this time she looked, not at the splendid High Priest, but at the face of the accused man . . . and in his eyes was no consciousness of guilt . . .

And Mary's face grew very troubled.

Then the Angel said:

'Have you made your choice, Mary? Will you spare your son suffering and evildoing?'

And Mary said slowly:

'It is not for me, an ignorant and simple woman, to understand the High Purposes of God. The Lord gave me my child. If the Lord takes him away, then that is His will. But since God has given him life, it is not for me to take that life away. For it may be that in my child's life there are things that I do not properly understand . . . It may be that I have seen only *part* of a picture, not the whole. My baby's life is his own, not mine, and I have no right to dispose of it.'

'Think again,' said the Angel. 'Will you not lay your child in my arms and I will bear him back to God?'

'Take him in your arms if it is God's command,' said Mary. 'But *I* will not lay him there.'

There was a great rustling of wings and a blaze of light and the Angel vanished.

Joseph came in a moment later and Mary told him of what had occurred. Joseph approved of what Mary had done.

'You did right, wife,' he said. 'And who knows, this may have been a lying Angel.'

'No,' said Mary. 'He did not lie.'

She was sure of that with every instinct in her.

'I do not believe a word of it all,' said Joseph stoutly. 'We will bring our son up very carefully and give him good religious instruction, for it is education that counts. He shall work in the shop and go with us to the Synagogue on the Sabbath and keep all the Feasts and the Purifications.'

Looking in the manger, he said:

'See, our son is smiling . . .'

And indeed the boy was smiling and holding out tiny hands to his mother as though to say 'Well Done.'

But aloft in the vaults of blue, the Angel was quivering with pride and rage.

'To think that I should fail with a foolish, ignorant woman! Well, there will come another chance. One day when *He* is weary and hungry and weak . . . Then I will take him up to the top of a mountain and show him the Kingdoms of this World of mine. I will offer him the Lordship of them all. He shall control Cities and Kings and Peoples . . . He shall have the Power of causing wars to cease and hunger and oppression to vanish. One gesture of worship to me and he shall be able to establish peace and plenty, contentment and good will – know himself to be a Supreme Power for Good. He can never withstand *that* temptation!'

And Lucifer, Son of the Morning, laughed aloud in ignorance and arrogance and flashed through the sky like a burning streak of fire down to the nethermost depths . . .

In the East, three Watchers of the Heavens came to their Masters and said:

'We have seen a Great Light in the Sky. It must be that some great Personage is born.'

But whilst all muttered and exclaimed of Signs and Portents a very old Watcher murmured:

'A Sign from God? God has no need of Signs and Wonders. It is more likely to be a Sign from Satan. It is in my mind that if God were to come amongst us, he would come very quietly . . .'

But in the Stable there was much fun and good company. The ass brayed, and the horses neighed and the oxen lowed, and men and women crowded in to see the baby and passed him from one to the other, and he laughed and crowed and smiled at them all.

'See,' they cried. 'He loves everybody! There never was such a Child . . .'

The Naughty Donkey

'The Naughty Donkey' was first published in the book
Star Over Bethlehem and other stories (Collins, November 1965).

Once upon a time there was a very naughty little donkey. He *liked* being naughty. When anything was put on his back he kicked it off, and he ran after people trying to bite them. His master couldn't do anything with him, so he sold him to another master, and that master couldn't do anything with him and also sold him, and finally he was sold for a few pence to a dreadful old man who bought old worn-out donkeys and killed them by overwork and ill treatment. But the naughty donkey chased the old man and bit him, and then ran away kicking up his heels. He didn't mean to be caught again so he joined a caravan that was going along the road. 'Nobody will know who I belong to in all this crowd,' thought the donkey.

These people were all going up to the city of Bethlehem, and when they got there they went into a big *Khan* full of people and animals.

The little donkey slipped into a nice cool stable where there was an ox and a camel. The camel was very haughty, like all camels, because camels think that they alone know the hundredth and secret name of God. He was too proud to speak to the donkey. So the donkey began to boast. He loved boasting.

'I am a very unusual donkey,' he said, 'I have foresight *and* hindsight.'
'What is that?' said the ox.

'Like my forelegs – in front of me – and my hind legs – behind me. Why, my great great, thirty-seventh time great grandmother belonged to the Prophet Balaam, and saw with her own eyes the Angel of the Lord!'

But the ox went on chewing and the camel remained proud.

Then a man and a woman came in, and there was a lot of fuss, but the donkey soon found out that there was nothing to fuss about, only a woman going to have a baby which happens every day. And after the baby was born some shepherds came and made a fuss of the baby – but shepherds are very simple folk.

But then some men in long rich robes came.

'V.I.P.s,' hissed the camel.

'What's that?' asked the donkey.

'Very Important People,' said the camel, 'bringing gifts.'

The donkey thought the gifts might be something good to eat, so when it was dark he began nosing around. But the first gift was yellow and hard, with no taste, the second made the donkey sneeze and when he licked the third, the taste was nasty and bitter.

'What stupid gifts,' said the donkey, disappointed. But as he stood there by the Manger, the baby stretched out his little hand and caught hold of the donkey's ear, clutching it tight as very young babies will.

And than a very odd thing happened. The donkey didn't want to be naughty any more. For the first time in his life he wanted to be good. And *he* wanted to give the baby a gift – but he hadn't anything to give. The baby seemed to like his ear, but the ear was part of *him* – and then another strange idea came to him. Perhaps he could give the baby *himself* . . .

It was not very long after that that Joseph came in with a tall stranger. The stranger was speaking urgently to Joseph, and as the donkey stared at them he could hardly believe his eyes!

The stranger seemed to dissolve and in his place stood an Angel of the Lord, a golden figure with wings. But after a moment the Angel changed back again into a mere man.

'Dear, dear, I'm seeing things,' said the donkey to himself. 'It must be all that fodder I ate.'

Joseph spoke to Mary.

'We must take the child and flee. There is no time to be lost.' His eye fell on the donkey. 'We will take this donkey here, and leave money for his owner whoever he may be. In that way no time will be lost.'

So they went out on the road from Bethlehem. But as they came to a narrow place, the Angel of the Lord appeared with a flaming sword, and the donkey turned aside and began to climb the hillside. Joseph tried to turn him back on to the road, but Mary said:

'Let him be. Remember the Prophet Balaam.'

And just as they got to the shelter of some olive trees, the soldiers of King Herod came clattering down the road with drawn swords.

'Just like my great grandmother,' said the donkey, very pleased with himself. 'I wonder if I have foresight as well.'

He blinked his eyes – and he saw a dim picture – a donkey fallen into a pit and a man helping to pull it out . . . 'Why, it's my Master, grown up to be a man,' said the donkey. Then he saw another picture . . . the same man, riding on a donkey into a city . . . 'Of course,' said the donkey. 'He's going to be crowned King!'

But the Crown seemed to be, not Gold, but Thorns (the donkey loved thorns and thistles – but it seemed the wrong thing for a Crown) and there was a smell he knew and feared – the smell of blood; and there was something on a sponge, bitter like the myrrh he had tasted in the stable . . .

And the little donkey knew suddenly that he didn't want foresight any more. He just wanted to live for the day, to love his little Master and be loved by him, and to carry Him and his mother safely to Egypt.

The Water Bus

'The Water Bus' was first published in the book *Star Over Bethlehem and other stories* (Collins, November 1965).

Mrs Hargreaves didn't like people.

She tried to, because she was a woman of high principle and a religious woman, and she knew very well that one ought to love one's fellow creatures. But she didn't find it easy – and sometimes she found it downright impossible.

All that she could do was, as you might say, to go through the motions. She sent cheques for a little more than she could afford to reputable charities. She sat on committees for worthy objects, and even attended public meetings for abolishing injustices, which was really more effort than anything else, because, of course, it meant close proximity to human bodies, and she hated to be touched. She was able easily to obey the admonitions posted up in public transport, such as: 'Don't travel in the rush hour'; because to go in trains and buses, enveloped tightly in a sweltering crowd of humanity, was definitely her idea of hell on earth.

If children fell down in the street, she always picked them up and bought them sweets or small toys to 'make them better.' She sent books and flowers to sick people in Hospital.

Her largest subscriptions were to communities of nuns in Africa, because they and the people to whom they ministered, were so far away that she would never have to come in contact with them, and also because she admired and envied the nuns who actually seemed to *enjoy* the work they did, and because she wished with all her heart that she were like them.

She was willing to be just, kind, fair, and charitable to people, so long as she did not have to see, hear or touch them.

But she knew very well that that was not enough.

Mrs Hargreaves was a middle-aged widow with a son and daughter who were both married and lived far away, and she herself lived in a flat in comfortable circumstances in London – and she didn't like people and there didn't seem to be anything she could do about it.

She was standing on this particular morning by her daily woman who was sitting sobbing on a chair in the kitchen and mopping her eyes.

'– never told me nothing, she didn't – not her own Mum! Just goes off to this awful place – and how she heard about it, I don't know – and this wicked woman did things to her, and it went septic – or what ever they call it – and they took her off to Hospital and she's lying there now, *dying* . . . Won't say who the man was – not even now. Terrible it is, my own daughter – such a pretty little girl she used to be, lovely curls. I used to dress her ever so nice. Everybody said she was a lovely little thing . . .'

She gave a gulp and blew her nose.

Mrs Hargreaves stood there wanting to be kind, but not really knowing how, because she couldn't really *feel* the right kind of feeling.

She made a soothing sort of noise, and said that she was very, very sorry. And was there anything she could do?

Mrs Chubb paid no attention to this query.

'I s'pose I ought to have looked after her better . . . been at home more in the evenings . . . found out what she was up to and who her friends were – but children don't like you poking your nose into their affairs nowadays – and I wanted to make a bit of extra money, too. Not for myself – I'd been thinking of getting Edie a slap-up gramophone – ever so musical she is – or something nice for the home. I'm not one for spending money on *myself* . . .'

She broke off for another good blow.

'If there is anything I can do?' repeated Mrs Hargreaves. She suggested hopefully 'A private room in the Hospital?'

But Mrs Chubb was not attracted by that idea.

'Very kind of you, Madam, but they look after her very well in the ward. And it's more cheerful for her. She wouldn't like to be cooped away in a room by herself. In the ward, you see, there's always something going on.'

Yes, Mrs Hargreaves saw it all clearly in her mind's eye. Lots of women sitting up in bed, or lying with closed eyes; old women smelling of sickness and old age – the smell of poverty and disease percolating through the clean impersonal odour of disinfectants. Nurses scurrying along, with trays of instruments and trolleys of meals, or washing apparatus, and finally the screens going up round a bed . . . The whole picture made her shiver – but she perceived quite clearly that to Mrs Chubb's daughter there would be solace and distraction in 'the ward' because Mrs Chubb's daughter liked people.

Mrs Hargreaves stood there by the sobbing mother and longed for the gift she hadn't got. What she wanted was to be able to put her arm round the weeping woman's shoulder and say something completely fatuous like 'There, there, my dear' – and *mean it*. But going through the motions would be no good at all. Actions without feeling were useless. They were without content . . .

Quite suddenly Mrs Chubb gave her nose a final trumpet-like blow and sat up.

'There,' she said brightly. 'I feel better.'

She straightened a scarf on her shoulders and looked up at Mrs Hargreaves with a sudden and astonishing cheerfulness.

'Nothing like a good cry, is there?'

Mrs Hargreaves had never had a good cry. Her griefs had always been inward and dark. She didn't quite know what to say.

'Does you good talking about things,' said Mrs Chubb. 'I'd best get on with the washing up. We're nearly out of tea and butter, by the way. I'll have to run round to the shops.'

Mrs Hargreaves said quickly that she would do the washing up and would also do the shopping and she urged Mrs Chubb to go home in a taxi.

Mrs Chubb said no point in a taxi when the 11 bus got you there just as quick; so Mrs Hargreaves gave her two pound notes and said perhaps she would like to take her daughter something in Hospital? Mrs Chubb thanked her and went.

Mrs Hargreaves went to the sink and knew that once again she had done the wrong thing. Mrs Chubb would have much preferred to clink about in the sink, retailing fresh bits of information of a *macabre* character from time to time, and then she could have gone to the shops and met plenty of her fellow kind and talked to *them*, and *they* would have had relatives in hospitals, too, and they all could have exchanged stories. In that way the time until Hospital visiting hours would have passed quickly and pleasantly.

'Why do I always do the wrong thing?' thought Mrs Hargreaves, washing up deftly and competently; and had no need to search for the answer. '*Because I don't care for people.*'

When she had stacked everything away, Mrs Hargreaves took a shopping bag and went to shop. It was Friday and therefore a busy day. There was a crowd in the butcher's shop. Women pressed against Mrs Hargreaves, elbowed her aside, pushed baskets and bags between her and the counter. Mrs Hargreaves always gave way.

'Excuse me, *I* was here before you.' A tall thin olive-skinned woman infiltrated herself. It was quite untrue and they both knew it, but Mrs

Hargreaves stood politely back. Unfortunately, she acquired a defender, one of those large brawny women who are public spirited and insist on seeing justice is done.

'You didn't ought to let her push you around, luv,' she admonished, leaning heavily on Mrs Hargreaves' shoulder and breathing gusts of strong peppermint in her face. 'You was here long before she was. I come in right on her heels and I know. Go on now.' She administered a fierce dig in the ribs. 'Push in there and stand up for your rights!'

'It really doesn't matter,' said Mrs Hargreaves. 'I'm not in a hurry.'

Her attitude pleased nobody.

The original thruster, now in negotiation for a pound and a half of frying steak, turned and gave battle in a whining slightly foreign voice.

'If you think you get here before me, why not you say? No good being so high and mighty and saying' (she mimicked the words) '"*it doesn't matter!*" How do you think that makes *me* feel? *I* don't want to go out of my turn.'

'Oh no,' said Mrs Hargreaves' champion with heavy irony. 'Oh no, of course not! We all know that, don't we?'

She looked round and immediately obtained a chorus of assent. The thruster seemed to be well known.

'We know her and her ways,' said one woman darkly.

'Pound and a half of rump,' said the butcher thrusting forth a parcel. 'Now then, come along, who's next, please?'

Mrs Hargreaves made her purchases and escaped to the street, thinking how really awful people were!

She went into the greengrocer next, to buy lemons and a lettuce. The woman at the greengrocer's was, as usual, affectionate.

'Well, ducks, what can we do for you today?' She rang up the cash register; said 'Ta' and 'Here you are, dearie,' as she pressed a bulging bag into the arms of an elderly gentleman who looked at her in disgust and alarm.

'She always calls me that,' the old gentleman confided gloomily when the woman had gone in search of lemons. '"Dear," and "Dearie" and "Love." I don't even know the woman's name!'

Mrs Hargreaves said she thought it was just a fashion. The old gentleman looked dubious and moved off, leaving Mrs Hargreaves feeling faintly cheered by the discovery of a fellow sufferer.

Her shopping bag was quite heavy by now, so she thought she would take a bus home. There were three or four people waiting at the bus stop, and an ill-tempered conductress shouted at the passengers.

'Come along now, hurry along, please – we can't wait here all day.' She scooped up an elderly arthritic lady and thrust her staggering into the bus where someone caught her and steered her to a seat, and seized Mrs Hargreaves by the arm above the elbow with iron fingers, causing her acute pain.

'Inside, only. Full up now.' She tugged violently at a bell, the bus shot forward and Mrs Hargreaves collapsed on top of a large woman occupying, through no fault of her own, a good three-quarters of a seat for two.

'I'm so sorry,' gasped Mrs Hargreaves.

'Plenty of room for a little one,' said the large woman cheerfully, doing her best without success to make herself smaller. 'Nasty temper some of these girls have, haven't they? I prefer the black men myself. Nice and polite *they* are – don't hustle you. Help you in and out quite carefully.'

She breathed good temper and onions impartially over Mrs Hargreaves.

'I don't want any remarks from you, thank you,' said the bus conductress who was now collecting fares. 'I'd have you know we've got our schedule to keep.'

'That's why the bus was idling alongside the curb at the last stop but one,' said the large woman. 'Fourpenny, please.'

Mrs Hargreaves arrived home exhausted by recrimination and unwanted affection, and also suffering from a bruised arm. The flat seemed peaceful and she sank down gratefully.

Almost immediately however, one of the porters arrived to clean the windows and followed her round telling her about his wife's mother's gastric ulcer.

Mrs Hargreaves picked up her handbag and went out again. She wanted – badly – a desert island. Since a desert island was not immediately obtainable (indeed, it would probably entail a visit to a travel agency, a passport office, vaccination, possibly a foreign visa to be obtained and many other human contacts) she strolled down to the river.

'A water bus,' she thought hopefully.

There were such things, she believed. Hadn't she read about them? And there was a pier – a little way along the Embankment; she had seen people coming off it. Of course, perhaps a water bus would be just as crowded as anything else . . .

But here she was in luck. The steamer, or water bus, or whatever it was, was singularly empty. Mrs Hargreaves bought a ticket to Greenwich. It was the slack time of day and it was not a particularly nice day, the wind being distinctly chilly, so few people were on the water for pleasure.

There were some children in the stern of the boat with a weary adult in charge, and a couple of nondescript men, and an old woman in rusty black. In the bow of the boat there was only a solitary man; so Mrs Hargreaves went up to the bow, as far from the noisy children as possible.

The boat drew away from the pier out into the Thames. It was peaceful here on the water. Mrs Hargreaves felt soothed and serene for the first time today. She had got away from – from *what* exactly? 'Away from it all!' that was the phrase, but she didn't know exactly what it meant . . .

She looked gratefully around her. Blessed, blessed water. So – so *insulating*. Boats plied their way up and down stream, but they had nothing to do with *her*. People on land were busy with their own affairs. Let them be – she hoped they enjoyed themselves. Here she was in a boat, being carried down the river towards the sea.

There were stops, people got off, people got on. The boat resumed its course. At the Tower of London the noisy children got off. Mrs Hargreaves hoped amiably that they would enjoy the Tower of London.

Now they had passed through the Docks. Her feeling of happiness and serenity grew stronger. The eight or nine people still on board were all huddled together in the stern – out of the wind, she supposed. For the first time she paid a little more attention to her fellow traveller in the bows. An Oriental of some kind, she thought vaguely. He was wearing a long cape-like coat of some woollen material. An Arab, perhaps? Or a Berber? Not an Indian.

What beautiful material the cloth of his coat was. It seemed to be woven all in one piece. So finely woven, too. She obeyed an almost irresistible impulse to touch it . . .

She could never recapture afterwards the feeling that the touch of the coat brought her. It was quite indescribable. It was like what happens when you shake a kaleidoscope. The parts of it are the same parts, but they are arranged differently; they are arranged in a new pattern . . .

She had wanted when she got on the water bus to escape from herself and the pattern of her morning. She had not escaped in the way she had meant to escape. She was still herself and she was still in the pattern, going through it all over again in her mind. But it was different this time. It was a different pattern because *she* was different.

She was standing again by Mrs Chubb – poor Mrs Chubb – She heard the story again only this time it was a different story. It was not so much what Mrs Chubb said, but what she had been feeling – her despair and – yes, her guilt. Because, of course, she was secretly blaming herself, striving to tell herself how she had done everything for her girl – her lovely little girl – recalling the frocks she had bought her and the sweets – and how she had given in to her when she wanted things – she had gone out to work, too – but of course, in her innermost mind, Mrs Chubb knew that it was not a gramophone for Edie she had been working for, but a washing machine – a washing machine like Mrs Peters had down the road (and so stuck up about it, too!). It was her own fierce house-pride that had set her fingers to toil. True, she had given Edie things all her life – plenty of them – but had she *thought* about Edie enough? Thought about the boy friends she was making? Thought about asking her friends to the house – seeing if there wasn't some kind of party at home Edie could have? Thinking about Edie's character, her life, what would be best for her? Trying to find out more about Edie because after all, Edie was *her* business – the real paramount business of her life. And she mustn't be stupid about it! Good will wasn't enough. One had to manage not to be stupid, too.

In fancy, Mrs Hargreaves' arm went round Mrs Chubb's shoulder. She thought with affection: 'You poor stupid dear. It's not as bad as you think. *I* don't believe she's dying at all.' Of course Mrs Chubb had exaggerated, had sought deliberately for tragedy, because that was the way Mrs Chubb saw life – in melodramatic terms. It made life less drab, easier to live. Mrs Hargreaves understood so well . . .

Other people came into Mrs Hargreaves' mind. Those women enjoying their fight at the butcher's counter. Characters, all of them. Fun, really! Especially the big red-faced woman with her passion for justice. She really liked a good row!

Why on earth, Mrs Hargreaves wondered, had she minded the woman at the greengrocer's calling her 'Luv'? It was a kindly term.

That bad-tempered bus conductress – why? – her mind probed, came up with a solution. Her young man had stood her up the evening before. And so she hated everybody, hated her monotonous life, wanted to make other people feel her power – one could so easily feel like that if things went wrong . . .

The kaleidoscope shook – changed. She was no longer *looking* at it – she was inside it – *part of it* . . .

The boat hooted. She sighed, moved, opened her eyes. They had come at last to Greenwich.

Mrs Hargreaves went back by train from Greenwich. The train, at this time of day, the lunch hour, was almost empty.

But Mrs Hargreaves wouldn't have cared if it had been full . . .

Because, for a brief space of time, she was at one with her fellow beings. *She liked people*. Almost – she loved them!

It wouldn't last, of course. She knew that. A complete change of char-acter was not within the bounds of reality. But she was deeply, humbly, and comprehendingly grateful for what she had been given.

She knew now what the thing that she had coveted was like. She knew

the warmth of it, and the happiness – knew it, not from intelligent observation from without, but from within. From *feeling* it.

And perhaps, knowing now just what it was, she could learn the
beginning of the road to it . . . ?

She thought of the coat woven in the harmony of one piece. She had
not been able to see the man's face. But she thought she knew who He
was . . .

Already the warmth and the vision were fading. But she would not
forget – she would never forget!

'Thank you,' said Mrs Hargreaves, speaking from the depths of a
grateful heart.

She said it aloud in the empty railway carriage.

The mate of the water bus was staring at the tickets in his hand.

'Where's t'other one?' he asked.

'Whatchermean?' said the Captain who was preparing to go ashore
for lunch.

'Must be someone on board still. Eight passengers there was. I counted
them. And I've only got seven tickets here.'

'Nobody left on board. Look for yourself. One of 'em must have got
off without your noticing 'im – either that or he walked on the water!'

And the Captain laughed heartily at his own joke.

4

In the Cool of the Evening

'In the Cool of the Evening' was first published in the book
Star Over Bethlehem and other stories (Collins, November 1965).

The church was fairly full. Evensong, nowadays, was always better attended than morning service.

Mrs Grierson and her husband knelt side by side in the fifth pew on the pulpit side. Mrs Grierson knelt decorously, her elegant back curved. A conventional worshipper, one would have said, breathing a mild and temperate prayer.

But there was nothing mild about Janet Grierson's petition. It sped upwards into space on wings of fire.

'God, help him! Have mercy upon him. Have mercy upon *me*. Cure him, Lord. Thou hast all power. Have mercy – have mercy. Stretch out Thy hand. Open his mind. He's such a sweet boy – so gentle – so innocent. Let him be healed. Let him be *normal*. Hear me, Lord. Hear me . . . Ask of me anything you like, but stretch out Thy hand and make him whole. Oh God, *hear* me. *Hear* me. With Thee all things are possible. My faith shall make him whole – I *have* faith – I believe. I *believe*! Help me!'

The people stood. Mrs Grierson stood with them. Elegant, fashionable, composed. The service proceeded.

The Rector mounted the steps of the pulpit, gave out his text.

Part of the 95th psalm; the tenth verse. Part of the psalm we sing every Sunday morning. 'It is a people who do err in their hearts, for they have not known my ways.'

The Rector was a good man, but not an eloquent one. He strove to give to his listeners the thought that the words had conveyed to him. A people that erred, not in what they *did*, not in *actions* displeasing to God, not in overt sin – but a people not even knowing that they erred. A people who, quite simply, did not know God . . . They did not know what God was, what he wanted, how he showed himself. They could know. That was the point the Rector was striving to make. Ignorance is no defence. They *could* know.

He turned to the East.

'And now to God the Father . . .'

He'd put it very badly, the Rector thought sadly. He hadn't made his meaning clear at all . . .

Quite a good congregation this evening. How many of them, he wondered, really *knew* God?

Again Janet Grierson knelt and prayed with fervour and desperation. It was a matter of will, of concentration. If she could get through – God was all powerful. If she could reach him . . .

For a moment she felt she was getting there – and then there was the irritating rustle of people rising; sighs, movements. Her husband touched her arm. Unwillingly she rose. Her face was very pale. Her husband looked at her with a slight frown. He was a quiet man who disliked intensity of any kind.

In the porch friends met them.

'What an attractive hat, Janet. It's new, isn't it?'

'Oh no, it's terribly old.'

'Hats are so difficult,' Mrs Stewart complained. 'One hardly ever wears one in the country and then on Sunday one feels odd. Janet, do you know Mrs Lamphrey – Mrs Grierson. Major Grierson. The Lamphreys have taken Island Lodge.'

'I'm so glad,' said Janet, shaking hands. 'It's a delightful house.'

'Everyone says we'll be flooded out in winter,' said Mrs Lamphrey ruefully.

'Oh no – not *most* years.'

'But *some* years? I knew it! But the children were mad about it. And of course they'd adore a flood.'

'How many have you?'

'Two boys and a girl.'

'Edward is just the same age as our Johnnie,' said Mrs Stewart. 'I suppose he'll be going to his public school next year. Johnnie's going to Winchester.'

'Oh, Edward is much too much of a moron ever to pass Common Entrance, I'm sure,' sighed Mrs Lamphrey. 'He doesn't care for anything but games. We'll have to send him to a crammer's. Isn't it terrible, Mrs Grierson, when one's children turn out to be morons?'

Almost at once, she felt the chill. A quick change of subject – the forthcoming fête at Wellsly Park.

As the groups moved off in varying directions, Mrs Stewart said to her friend:

'Darling, I ought to have warned you!'

'Did I say something wrong? I thought so – but what?'

'The Griersons. Their boy. They've only got one. And *he's* subnormal. Mentally retarded.'

'Oh how awful – but I couldn't know. Why does one always go and put one's foot straight into things?'

'It's just that Janet's rather sensitive . . .'

As they walked along the field path, Rodney Grierson said gently, 'They didn't mean anything. That woman didn't know.'

'No. No, of course she didn't.'

'Janet, can't you try –'

'Try what?'

'Try not to mind so much. Can't you accept –'

Her voice interrupted him, it was high and strained.

'No, I can't *accept* – as you put it. There must be *something* that could be done! He's physically so perfect. It must be just some gland – some perfectly simple thing. Doctors will find out some day. There must be something – injections – hypnotism.'

'You only torture yourself, Janet. All these doctors you drag him round to. It worries the boy.'

'I'm not like you, Rodney. I don't give up. I prayed *again* in church just now.'

'You pray too much.'

'How can one pray "too much"? I believe in God, I tell you. I *believe* in him. I have faith – and faith can move mountains.'

'You can't give God orders, Janet.'

'What an extraordinary thing to say!'

'Well –' Major Grierson shifted uncomfortably.

'I don't think you know what faith is.'

'It ought to be the same as trust.'

Janet Grierson was not listening.

'Today – in church, I had a terrible feeling. I felt that God wasn't there. I didn't feel that there was no God – just that He was somewhere else . . . But where?'

'Really, Janet!'

'Where could He be? Where could I find Him?'

She calmed herself with an effort as they turned in at the gate of their own house. A stocky middle-aged woman came out smiling to meet them.

'Have a nice service? Supper's almost ready. Ten minutes?'

'Oh good. Thank you, Gertrude. Where's Alan?'

'He's out in the garden as usual. I'll call him.'

She cupped her mouth with her hands.

'A–lan. A–lan.'

Suddenly, with a rush, a boy came running. He was fair and blue-eyed. He looked excited and happy.

'Daddy – Mummy – look what I've found.'

He parted his cupped hands carefully, showing the small creature they contained.

'Ugh, horrible.' Janet Grierson turned away with a shudder.

'Don't you like him? Daddy!' He turned to his father. 'See, he's partly like a frog – but he isn't a frog – he's got feathers and sort of wings. He's quite new – not like any other animal.'

He came nearer, and dropped his voice.

'I've got a name for him. I call him Raphion. Do you think it's a nice name?'

'Very nice, my boy,' said his father with a slight effort.

The boy put the strange creature down.

'Hop away, Raphion, or fly if you can. There he goes. He isn't afraid of me.'

'Come and get ready for supper, Alan,' said his mother.

'Oh yes, I'm hungry.'

'What have you been doing?'

'Oh, I've been down at the end of the garden, talking to a friend. He helps me name the animals. We have such fun.'

'He's happy, Janet,' said Grierson as the boy ran up the stairs.

'I know. But what's going to become of him? And those horrible things he finds. They're all about everywhere nowadays since the accident at the Research station.'

'They'll die out, dear. Mutations usually do.'

'Queer heads – and extra legs!' She shuddered.

'Well, think of all the legs centipedes have. You don't mind them?'

'They're natural.'

'Perhaps everything has to have a first time.'

Alan came running down the stairs again.

'Have you had a nice time? Where did you go? To church?' He laughed, trying the word out. 'Church – church – that's a funny name.'

'It means God's house,' said his mother.

'Does it? I didn't know God lived in a house.'

'God is in Heaven, dear. Up in the sky. I told you.'

'But not always? Doesn't He come down and walk about? In the evenings? In summer? When it's nice and cool?'

'In the Garden of Eden,' said Grierson, smiling.

'No, in this garden, here. He'd like all the funny new animals and things like I do.'

Janet winced.

'Those funny animals – darling.' She paused. 'There was an accident, you know. At the big Station up on the downs. That's why there are so many of these queer – *things* about. They get born like that. It's very sad!'

'Why? I think it's exciting! Lots of new kinds of things being born all the time. I have to find names for them. Sometimes I think of lovely names.'

He wriggled off his chair.

'I've finished. Please – can I go now? My friend is waiting for me in the garden.'

His father nodded. Gertrude said softly: 'All children are the same. They always invent a "friend" to play with.'

'At five, perhaps. Not when they're thirteen,' said Janet bitterly.

'Try not to mind, dear,' said Gertrude gently.

'How can I help it?'

'You may be looking at it all the wrong way.'

Down at the bottom of the garden, where it was cool under the trees, Alan found his friend waiting.

He was stroking a rabbit who was not quite a rabbit but something rather different.

'Do you like him, Alan?'

'Oh yes. What shall we call him?'

'It's for you to say.'

'Is it really? I shall call him – I shall call him – Forteor. Is that a good name?'

'All your names are good names.'

'Have you got a name yourself?'

'I have a great many names.'

'Is one of them God?'

'Yes.'

'I thought it was! You don't really live in that stone house in the village with the long thing sticking up, do you?'

'I live in many places . . . But sometimes, in the cool of the evening, I walk in a garden – with a friend and talk about the New World –'

Promotion in the Highest

'Promotion in the Highest' was first published in the book
Star Over Bethlehem and other stories (Collins, November 1965).

They were walking down the hill from the little stone church on the hillside.

It was very early in the morning, the hour just before dawn. There was no one about to see them as they went through the village, though one or two sleepers sighed and stirred in their sleep. The only human being who saw them that morning was Jacob Narracott, as he grunted and sat up in the ditch. He had collapsed there soon after he came out of the *Bel and Dragon* last night.

He sat up and rubbed his eyes, not quite believing what he saw. He staggered to his feet and shambled off in the direction of his cottage, made uneasy by the trick his eyes had played him. At the crossroads he met George Palk, the village constable, on his beat.

'You'm late getting home, Jacob. Or should I say early?' Palk grinned.

Jacob groaned, and rocked his head in his hands.

'Government's been and done something to the beer,' he affirmed. 'Meddling again. I never used to feel like this.'

'What'll your Missus say when she sees you rolling home at this hour?'

'Won't say anything. She's away to her sister's.'

'So you took the opportunity to see the New Year in?'

Jacob grunted. Then he said uneasily: 'You seen a lot of people just now, George? Coming along the road?'

'No. What sort of people?'

'Funny people. Dressed odd.'

'You mean Beats?'

'Nah, not Beats. Sort of old-fashioned like. Carrying things, some of 'em was.'

'What sort of things?'

'Ruddy great wheel, one had – a woman. And there was a man with a gridiron. And one rather nice looking wench, dressed very rich and fancy with a great big basket of roses.'

'Roses? This time of year? Was it a sort of procession?'

'That's right. Lights on their heads they had, too.'

'Aw, get on, Jacob! Seeing things – that's what's the matter with you. Get on home, put your head under the tap, and sleep it off.'

'Funny thing is, I feel I've seen 'em before somewhere – but for the life of me I can't think where.'

'Ban the bomb marchers, maybe.'

'I tell you they was dressed all rich and funny. Fourteen of them there was. I counted. Walking in pairs mostly.'

'Oh well, some New Year's Eve party coming home maybe: but if you ask me, I'd say you did yourself too well at the *Bel and Dragon*, and that accounts for it all.'

'Saw the New Year in proper, we did,' agreed Jacob. 'Had to celebrate special, seeing as it wasn't only "Out with the Old Year, and in with the New." It's out with the Old Century and in with the New one. January 1st A.D. 2000, that's what today is.'

'Ought to mean something,' said Constable Palk.

'More compulsory evacuation, I suppose,' grumbled Jacob. 'A man's home's not his castle nowadays. It's out with him, and off to one of these ruddy new towns. Or bundle him off to New Zealand or Australia. Can't even have children now unless the government says you may. Can't even dump things in your back garden without the ruddy Council coming round and saying it's got to go to the village dump. What do they think a back garden's *for*? What it's come to is, nobody treats you like you were *human* any more . . .'

His voice rumbled away . . .

'Happy New Year,' Constable Palk called after him . . .

The Fourteen proceeded on their way.

St Catherine was trundling her Wheel in a disconsolate manner. She turned her head and spoke to St Lawrence who was examining his Gridiron.

'What can I *do* with this thing?' she asked.

'I suppose a wheel always comes in useful,' said St Lawrence doubtfully.

'What for?'

'I see what you mean – it was meant for torture – for breaking a man's body.'

'Broken on the wheel.' St Catherine gave a little shudder.

'What are you going to do with your gridiron?'

'I thought perhaps I might use it for cooking something.'

'Pfui,' said St Cristina as they passed a dead stoat.

St Elizabeth of Hungary handed her one of her roses.

St Cristina sniffed it gratefully. St Elizabeth fell back beside St Peter.

'I wonder why we all seem to have paired up,' she said thoughtfully.

'Those do, perhaps, who have something in common,' suggested Peter.

'Have we something in common?'

'Well, we're both of us liars,' said Peter cheerfully.

In spite of a lie that would never be forgotten, Peter was a very honest man. He accepted the truth of himself.

'I know. I know!' Elizabeth cried. 'I can't bear to remember. How could I have been so cowardly – so weak, that day? Why didn't I stand there bravely and say, "I am taking bread to the hungry?" Instead, my husband shouts at me, "What have you got in that basket?" And I shiver and stammer out "Nothing but roses . . ." And he snatched off the cover of the basket –'

'And it *was* roses,' said Peter gently.

'Yes. A miracle happened. Why did my Master do that for me? Why did he acquiesce in my lie? Why? Oh why?'

St Peter looked at her.

He said:

'So that you should never forget. So that pride could never lay hold of you. So that you should know that you were weak and not strong.

'I, too –' He stopped and then went on.

'I who was so sure that I could never deny him, so certain that I, above all the others, would be steadfast. I was the one who denied and spoke those lying cowardly words. Why did he choose *me* – a man like me? He founded his Church on me – Why?'

'That's easy,' said Elizabeth. 'Because you loved him. I think you loved him more than any of the others did.'

'Yes, I loved him. I was one of the first to follow him. There was I, mending the nets, and I looked up, and there he was watching me. And he said, "Come with me." And I went. I think I loved him from the very first moment.'

'You are so nice, Peter,' said Elizabeth.

St Peter swung his keys doubtfully.

'I'm not sure about that Church I founded . . . It's not turned out at all as we meant . . .'

'Things never do. You know,' Elizabeth went on thoughtfully, 'I'm sorry now I put that leper in my husband's bed. It seemed at the time a fine defiant Act of Faith. But really – well, it wasn't very *kind*, was it?'

St Appolonia stopped suddenly in her tracks.

'I'm so sorry,' she said. 'I've dropped my tooth. That's the worst of having such a small emblem.'

She called: 'Anthony. Come and find it for me.'

They were in the Land of the Saints now, and as they breathed its special fragrance St Cristina cried aloud in joy. The Holy Birds sang, and the Harps played.

But the Fourteen did not linger. They pressed forward to the Court of Assembly.

The Archangel Gabriel received them.

'The Court is in Session,' he said. 'Enter.'

The Assembly Chamber was wide and lofty. The walls were made of mist and cloud.

The Recording Angel was writing in his Golden Book. He laid it aside, opened his Ledger and said, 'Names and addresses, please.'

They told him their names and gave their address. St Petrock-on-the-Hill. Stickle Buckland.

'Present your Petition,' said the Recording Angel.

St Peter stepped forward.

'There is unrest amongst us. We ask to go back to Earth.'

'Isn't Heaven good enough for you?' asked the Recording Angel. There was, perhaps, a slight tinge of sarcasm in his voice.

'It is too good for us.'

The Recording Angel adjusted his Golden Wig, put on his Golden Spectacles, and looked over the top of them with disapprobation.

'Are you questioning the decision of your Creator?'

'We would not dare – but there was a ruling –'

The Archangel Gabriel, as Mediator and Intermediary between Heaven and Earth, rose.

'If I may submit a point of law?'

The Recording Angel inclined his head.

'It was laid down, by Divine decree, that in the Year A.D. 1000 and in every subsequent 1000th Year, there should be fresh Judgments and Decisions on such points as were brought to a special Court of Appeal. Today is the Second Millennium. I submit that every person who has ever lived on earth has today a right of Appeal.'

The Recording Angel opened a large Gold Tome and consulted it. Closing it again, he said:

'Set out your Case.'

St Peter spoke.

'We died for our Faith. Died joyfully. We were rewarded. Rewarded far beyond our deserts. We –' he hesitated and turned to a young man with a beautiful face and burning eyes.

'You explain.'

'It was not enough,' said the young man.

'Your reward was not enough?' The Recording Angel looked scandalised.

'Not our reward. Our service. To die for the Faith, to be a Saint, is not enough to merit Eternal Life. You know my story. I was rich. I obeyed the Law. I kept the Commandments. It was not enough. I went to the Master. I said to him: '"Master, what shall I do to inherit Eternal Life?"''

'You were told what to do, and you did it,' said the Recording Angel.

'It was not enough.'

'You did more. After you had given all your possessions to the poor, you joined the disciples in their mission. You suffered Martyrdom. You were stoned to death in Ephesus.'

'It was not enough.'

'What more do you want to do?'

'We had Faith – burning Faith. We had the Faith that can move mountains. Two thousand years have taught us that we could have done more. We did not always have enough Compassion . . .'

The word came from his lips like a breath from a summer sea. It whispered all round the Heavens . . .

'This is our petition: Let us go back to Earth in Pity and Compassion to help those who need help.'

There was a murmur of agreement from those around him.

The Recording Angel picked up the Golden Intercom on his desk. He spoke into it in a low murmur.

He listened . . .

Then he spoke – briskly, and with authority.

'Promotion Granted,' he said. 'Approval in the Highest.'

They turned to go, their faces radiant.

'Hand in your Crowns and Halos at the door, please.'

They surrendered their Crowns and Halos and went out of the Court. St Thomas came back.

'Excuse me,' he said politely. 'But what you said just now – was it *Permission* Granted? Or was it *Promotion* Granted?'

'Promotion. After two thousand years of Sainthood, you are moving up to a higher rank.'

'Thank you. I *thought* it was promotion you said. But I wanted to make *sure*.'

He followed the others.

'He always had to make sure,' said Gabriel. 'You know – sometimes – I can't help wondering what it would be like to have an immortal soul . . .'

The Recording Angel looked horrified.

'Do be careful, Gabriel. You know what happened to Lucifer.'

'Sometimes I can't help feeling a little sorry for Lucifer. Having to rank below Adam upset him terribly. Adam wasn't much, was he?'

'A poor type,' agreed the Recording Angel. 'But he and all his descendants were created in the image of God with immortal souls. They *have* to rank above the Angels.'

'I've often thought Adam's soul must have been a very small one.'

'There has to be a beginning for everything,' the Recording Angel pointed out severely.

Mrs Badstock heaved and pulled. The smell of the village dump was not agreeable. It was an unsightly mass of old tyres, broken chairs, ragged quilts, old kerosene tins, and broken bedsteads. All the things that nobody could possibly want. But Mrs Badstock was tugging hopefully. If that old pram was any way repairable – She heaved again and it came free . . .

'Drat!' said Mrs Badstock. The upper portion of the pram was not too bad, but the wheels were missing.

She threw it down angrily.

'Can I help you?' A woman spoke out of the darkness.

'No good. Blasted thing's got no wheels.'

'You want a wheel? I've got one here.'

'Ta, ducks. But I need four. And anyway, yours is much too big.'

'That's why I thought we could make it into four – with a little adjustment.' The woman's fingers strayed over it pushing, pulling.

'There! How's that?'

'Well, I never! However did you – Now, if we'd got a nail or two – or a screw. I'll get my hubby –'

'I think I can manage.' She bent over the pram. Mrs Badstock peered down to try and see what was happening.

The other woman straightened up suddenly. The pram stood on four wheels.

'It will want a little oil, and some new lining.'

'I can see to that easy! *What* a boon it will be. You're quite a little home mechanic, aren't you, ducks? How on earth did you manage it?'

'I don't know really,' said St Catherine vaguely. 'It just – happens.'

The tall woman in the brocade dress said with authority: 'Bring them up to the house. There's plenty of room.'

The man and the woman looked at her suspiciously. Their six children did the same.

'The Council are finding us somewhere,' said the man sullenly.

'But they're going to separate us,' said the woman.

'And you don't want that?'

'Of course we don't.'

Three of the children began to cry.

'Shut your bloody mouths,' said the man, but without rancour.

'Been saying they'd evict us for a long time,' said the man. 'Now they've done it. Always whining about their rent. I've better things to do with my money than pay rent. That's Councils all over for you.'

He was not a nice man. His wife was not very nice either, St Barbara thought. But they loved their children.

'You'd better all come up to my place,' she said.

'Where is it?'

'Up there.' She pointed.

They turned to look.

'But – that's a *Castle*,' the woman exclaimed in awestruck tones.

'Yes, it's a Castle all right. So you see, there will be lots of room . . .'

St Scoithín stood rather doubtfully on the seashore. He wasn't quite sure what to do with his Salmon.

He could smoke it, of course – it would last longer that way. The trouble was that it was really only the rich who liked smoked salmon, and the rich had quite enough things already. The poor much preferred their salmon in tins. Perhaps –

The Salmon writhed in his hands, and St Scoithín jumped.

'Master,' said the Salmon.

St Scoithín looked at it.

'It is nearly a thousand years since I saw the sea,' said the Salmon pleadingly.

St Scoithín smiled at him affectionately. He walked out on the sea, and lowered the Salmon gently into the water.

'Go with God,' he said.

He walked back to the shore, and almost immediately stumbled over a big heap of tins of salmon with a purple flower stuck on top of them.

St Cristina was walking along a crowded City street. The traffic roared past her. The air was full of diesel fumes.

'This is terrible,' said St Cristina, holding her nose. 'I must do something about this. And why don't they empty the dustbins oftener? It's very bad for people.' She pondered. 'Perhaps I had better go into Parliament . . .'

St Peter was busy setting out his Loaf and Fish stall.

'Old Age Pensioners first,' he said. 'Come on, Granddad.'

'Are you National Assistance?' the old man asked suspiciously.

'That kind of thing.'

'Not religious, is it? I'm not going to sing hymns.'

'When the food's all gone, I shall preach,' said Peter. 'But you don't have to stay on and listen.'

'Sounds fair enough. What are you going to preach about?'

'Something quite simple. Just how to attain Eternal Life.'

A younger man gave a hoot of laughter.

'Eternal Life! What a hope!'

'Yes,' said Peter cheerfully, as he shovelled out parcels of hot fish. 'It *is* a hope. Got to remember that. There's always Hope.'

In the Church of St Petrock-on-the-Hill, the Vicar was sitting sadly in a pew, watching a confident young architect examining the old painted screen.

'Sorry, Vicar,' said the young man, turning briskly. 'Not a hope in Hell, I'm afraid. Oh! sorry again. I oughtn't to have put it like that. But it's long past restoring. Nothing to be done. The wood's rotten, and there's hardly any paint left – not enough to see what the original was like. What is it? Fifteenth century?'

'Late fourteenth.'

'What are they? Saints?'

'Yes. Seven each side.' He recited. 'St Lawrence, St Thomas, St Andrew, St Anthony, St Peter, St Scoithin, and one we don't know. The other side: St Barbara, St Catherine, St Appolonia, St Elizabeth of Hungary, St Cristina the Astonishing, St Margaret, and St Martha.'

'You've got it all very pat.'

'There were church records. Not in very good condition. Some we had to make out by their emblems – St Barbara's castle for instance, and St Lawrence's gridiron. The original work was done by Brother Bernard of the Benedictines of Froyle Abbey.'

'Well, I'm sorry about my verdict. But everything has got to go sometime. I hear your rich parishioner has offered you a new screen with modern symbolical figures on it?'

'Yes,' said the Vicar without enthusiasm.

'Seen the big new Cathedral Centre at New Huddersfield? Coventry was good in its time, but this is streets ahead of it! Takes a bit of getting used to, of course.'

'I am sure it would.'

'But it's taken on in a big way! Modern. Those old Saints,' he flicked a hand towards the screen. 'I don't suppose anyone knows who half of them are nowadays. I certainly don't. Who was St Cristina the Astonishing?'

'Quite an interesting character. She had a very keen sense of smell.

At her funeral service the smell of her putrefying body affected her so much that she levitated out of her coffin up to the roof of the Chapel.'

'Whew! Some Saint! Oh well, it takes all sorts to make a world. Even your old Saints would be very different nowadays, I expect . . .'

The Island

'The Island' was first published in the book *Star Over Bethlehem and other stories* (Collins, November 1965).

There were hardly any trees on the island. It was arid land, an island of rock, and the goats could find little to eat. The shapes of the rocks were beautiful as they swept up from the sea, and their colour changed with the changing of the light, going from rose to apricot, to pale misty grey, deepening to mauve and to stern purple, and in a last fierceness to orange, as the sun sank into that sea so rightly called wine-dark. In the early mornings the sky was a pale proud blue, and seemed so high up and so far away that it filled one with awe to look up at it.

But the women of the island did not look up at it often, unless they were anxiously gazing for signs of a storm. They were women and they had to work. Since food was scarce, they worked hard and unceasingly, so that they and their children should live. The men went out daily in the fishing boats. The children herded the goats and played little games of their own with pebbles in the sun.

Today the women with great jars of fresh water on their heads, toiled up the slope from the spring in the cleft of the cliff, to the village above.

Mary was still strong, but she was not as young as most of the women, and it was an effort to her to keep pace with them.

Today the women were very gay, for in a few days' time there was to be a wedding. The girl children danced round their elders and chanted monotonously:

'I shall go to the wedding . . . I shall go to the wedding . . . I shall have a ribbon in my hair . . . I shall eat roseleaf jelly . . . roseleaf jelly in a spoon . . .'

The mothers laughed, and one child's mother said teasingly:

'How do you know I shall take you to the wedding?'

Dismayed, the child stared.

'You *will* take me – you will – you *will* . . .' And she clung to Mary, demanding: 'She will let me go to the wedding? Say she will!'

And Mary smiled and said gently: 'I think she will, sweetheart!'

And all the women laughed gaily, for today they were all happy and excited because of the wedding.

'Have you ever been to a wedding, Mary?' the child asked.

'She went to her own,' laughed one of the women.

'I didn't mean your own. I meant a wedding party, with dancing and sweet things to eat, and roseleaf jam, and honey?'

'Yes. I have been to weddings.' Mary smiled. 'I remember one wedding . . . very well . . . a long time ago.'

'With roseleaf jam?'

'I think so – yes. And there was wine . . .'

Her voice trailed off as she remembered.

'And when the wine runs out, we have to drink water,' one of the women said. 'That always happens!'

'We did not drink water at this wedding!'

Mary's voice was strong and proud.

The other women looked at her. They knew that Mary had come here with her son from a long way away, and that she did not often speak of her life in earlier days, and that there was some very good reason for that. They were careful not to ask her questions, but of course there were rumours, and now suddenly one of the older children piped up and spoke like a parrot.

'They say you had a son who was a great criminal and was executed for his crimes. Is that true?'

The women tried to hush her down, but Mary spoke, her eyes looking straight ahead of her.

'Those that should know said he was a criminal.'

'But you didn't think so?' the child persisted.

Mary said after a pause:

'I do not know of myself what is right or wrong. I am too ignorant. My son loved people – good and bad equally . . .'

They had reached the village now and they divided to go to their own homes. Mary had farthest to go, to a stone croft at the very end of the cluster of sprawling buildings.

'How is your son? Well, I hope?' asked one of the women politely.

'He is well, thanks be to God.'

To erase the memory of what had been said before, the woman said kindly:

'You must be proud of this son of yours. We all know that he is a Holy Man. They say he has visions and walks with God.'

'He is a good son,' said Mary. 'And, as you say, a very Holy Man.'

She left them to go her own way and they stood looking after her for a moment or two.

'She is a good woman.'

'Yes. It is not her fault, I am sure, that her other son went wrong.'

'Such things happen. One does not know why. But she is lucky in this son. There are times when he is animated by the Spirit, and then he prophesies in a loud voice. His feet, they say, rise off the ground – and then he lies like one dead for a while.'

They all nodded and clucked in wonder and pleasure to have such a Holy Man amongst them.

Mary went to the little stone cottage, and stood the jar of water down. She glanced towards where a man sat at a rudely-fashioned table. There was a scroll of parchment in front of him and he bent over it, writing with a pen, pausing now and then, whilst his eyes half closed as he lost himself in the ardours of the spirit . . .

Mary was careful not to disturb him. She busied herself in getting together the midday meal.

The man was a man of great beauty, though no longer young. He had great delicacy of feature, and the far-away eyes of a soul to whom spiritual life is as real as the life of the body. Presently his hand slackened on the pen, and he seemed almost to pass into a trance, neither moving nor speaking, and indeed hardly breathing.

Mary put the dishes on the table.

'Your meal is ready, my son.'

As one who hears a faint sound from very far away, he shook his head impatiently.

'The vision . . . so near . . .' he muttered, 'so near . . . When – oh when?'

'Come, my son, eat.'

He waved the food away.

'There is another hunger, another thirst! The food of the spirit . . . The thirst for righteousness . . .'

'But you must eat. To please me. To please your mother.'

Gently she coaxed and scolded – and at last he came down from that high exaltation, and smiled at her with a human half-teasing look.

'Must I then eat to satisfy you?'

'Yes. Or else I shall be made unhappy.'

So he ate to please her, hardly noticing what the food was.

Then he bethought himself to ask:

'How is it with you, dear mother? You have all you need?'

'I have all I need,' said Mary.

He nodded, satisfied, and took up his pen once more.

When Mary had cleared all away, she went out and stood looking out over the sea.

Her hands clasped together, she bowed her head and spoke softly under her breath.

'Have I done all I could? I am such an ignorant woman. I do not always know how to serve and minister to one who is assuredly a Saint of God. I wash his linen, and prepare his food, and bring him fresh water, and wash his feet. But more than that I know not how to do.'

As she stood there, her anxiety passed. Serenity came back to her worn face.

On the shore beneath, a boat had drawn into the little stone pier. It was not an ordinary fishing boat, but one that stood high in the water, and had a big curving prow of richly carved wood. Two men landed from it, and some old men who were mending fishing nets came to accost the strangers.

Politely the two men made known their business.

'We seek amongst the islands hereabouts for an island on which is said to dwell the Queen of Heaven.'

The old fishermen shook their heads.

'What you seek is certainly not here. We have no shrine such as you describe.'

'Perhaps your women have knowledge of such a shrine?' one of the strangers suggested. 'Women are often secretive about such matters.'

'Inquire if you wish. One of us will go up and show you the village.'

The strangers went up with their guide. The women came clustering out of their houses. They were excited and interested, but they all shook their heads.

'No Goddess has her Shrine here, alas! Neither by our Spring nor elsewhere.'

They told him of other shrines reported from other places, but none of them were what the strangers sought.

'But we have a Holy Man here,' said one of the women proudly. 'He is skin and bone, and fasts all the time when his old mother will let him.'

But the strangers were not looking for a Holy Man, however great his sanctity.

'At least inquire of him,' one of the women insisted. 'He might know of such a thing as you seek.'

So they went to the Holy Man's croft; but he was lost in his Vision and for some time did not even hear what they were saying to him.

Then he was angry and said:

'Do not go astray after heathen Goddesses. Not after the Scarlet

Woman of Babylon, nor after the Abominations of the Phoenicians. There is only one Redeemer, and that is the Living Son of God.'

So the strangers went away, but the Holy Man's mother ran secretly after them.

'Do not be angry,' she begged. 'My son was not meaning to be discourteous to you; but he is so pure and so holy himself that he lives in a region far above this earth. He is a good man and a good son to me.'

The strangers spoke kindly to her.

'We are not offended. You are a good woman, and have a good son.'

'I am a very ordinary woman,' she said. 'But I must tell you that you should not believe in all these Aphrodites and Astartes and whatever their heathen names are. There is only one God, our Father in Heaven.'

'You say you are only an ordinary woman,' said the older of the two strangers. 'But although your face is old and ravaged with the lines of sorrow, yet to my mind you have a face of great beauty – and I in my time was apprenticed to a great sculptor, so I know what beauty is.'

Mary, amazed, cried out: 'Once, perhaps, when I wove the coloured tapestry in the Temple, or when I poured my husband's wine in the shop, and held my first-born son in my arms. But *now!*'

But the old sculptor shook his head.

'Beauty lies beneath the skin,' he insisted. 'In the bone. Yes, and beneath that again – in the heart. So I say that you are a beautiful woman, perhaps more beautiful now than you were as a young girl. Farewell – and may you be blessed.'

So the strangers rowed away in their boat, and Mary went slowly back to the croft and to her son.

The coming of the strangers had made him restless. He was walking up and down and his hands clasped his head in suffering.

Mary ran to him and held him in her arms.

'What is it, dear son?'

He groaned out: 'The spirit has gone out of me . . . I am empty . . . empty . . . I am cut off from God – from the joy of his Presence.'

Then she comforted him – as she had comforted him many times before, saying: 'From time to time, this has to be – we do not know why. It is like the wave of the sea. It goes out from the shore, but it returns, my son, it returns.'

But he cried out:

'You do not *know*. You cannot understand . . . You do not know what it is to be caught up in the Spirit, to be exalted with the great glory of God!'

And Mary said humbly:

'That is true. *That*, I have not felt. For me, there has been only memory . . .'

'Memory is not enough!'

But Mary said fiercely: 'It is enough for me!'

And she went to the door and stood there, looking out over the sea where the strangers had gone away . . .

As she stood there, she felt a strange expectancy rising in her; a fluttering hopeful joy. Almost, she went down to the shore again, but she restrained herself, for she knew that her son would soon need her. And so it was. He began to shake all over, and his body jerked, and at last his limbs stiffened and he fell to the ground and lay like one dead. Then she covered him over for warmth and placed a fold of the cloak between his lips, in case the convulsions should come back. But he lay there motionless, and there was no sign, even, that he breathed.

Mary knew from experience that he would not stir for many hours, and she walked out again on to the hillside. It was growing dark now and the moon was rising over the sea.

Mary stood there savouring the welcome coolness of the evening. Her mind was full of memories of the past, of a hurried flight into Egypt, of the carpenter's shop, and of a marriage in Cana . . .

And again that joyous expectancy rose in her.

'Perhaps,' she thought, 'perhaps at last the time has come.'

Presently, very slowly, she began to walk down to the sea . . .

The moon rose in the sky, and it made a silvery path across the water, and as the light grew stronger, Mary saw a boat approaching.

She thought: 'The strangers are coming back again . . .'

But it was not the strangers . . . She could see now that it was not the handsome carved boat of the strangers. This was a rough fishing boat – the kind of boat that had been familiar to her all her life . . .

And then she knew – quite certainly . . . It was *his* boat and he had come for her at last . . .

And now she ran, slipping and stumbling over the rough stones of the beach. And as she reached the water's edge, half sobbing and half panting, she saw one of the three men step out of the boat onto the sea and walk along the moonlit path towards her.

Nearer and nearer he came . . . and then – and then . . . she was clasped in his arms . . . Words poured from her, incoherently, trying to tell so much.

'I have done as you asked me – I have looked after John – He has been as a son to me. I am not clever – I cannot always understand his high thoughts and his visions, but I have made him good food, and washed his feet, and tended him and loved him . . . I have been his mother and he has been my son . . . ?'

She looked anxiously up into his face, asking him a question.

'You have done all I asked you,' he said gently. 'Now – you are coming home with me.'

'But how shall I get to the boat?'

'We will walk together on the water.'

She peered out to sea.

'Are those – yes, they are – Simon and Andrew, are they not?'

'Yes, they wanted to come.'

'How happy – Oh! how happy we are going to be,' cried Mary. 'Do you remember the day of the marriage in Cana . . . ?'

And so, walking together on the water, she poured out to her son all the little events and happenings of her life, and even how two strangers had come that very day looking for the Queen of Heaven. And how ridiculous it was!

'They were quite right,' said her Son. 'The Queen of Heaven was here on the island, but they did not know her when they saw her . . .'

And he looked into the worn, ravaged, beautiful face of his mother, and repeated softly:

'No, they did not know her when they saw her!'

In the morning, John awoke and rose from the ground.

It was the Lord's Day, and at once he knew that this was to be the great day of his life!

The Spirit rushed into him . . .

He took up his pen and wrote:

I saw a new heaven and a new earth . . . And behind me I heard a great voice as of a trumpet . . . Saying:

I am Alpha and Omega, the first and the last . . . I am he that liveth and was dead; and behold, I am alive for evermore, Amen; and have the keys of hell and of death . . . Behold, I come quickly; and my reward is with me, to give every man according as his work shall be . . .

Appendix
Short Story Chronology

This table aims to present all Agatha Christie's short stories published between 1923 and 1971, starting with her series of Hercule Poirot cases for *The Sketch* magazine and ending with her last contributions to the genre, the stories for children in *Star Over Bethlehem* and, finally, *The Harlequin Tea Set*. It should be noted that a number of stories that first appeared in weekly or monthly magazines were subsequently re-worked in book form, where they became simply chapters in a larger work, no longer independent short stories. In *Partners in Crime*, for example, some short stories were subdivided into smaller chapters, while 13 separate stories were re-worked into the episodic novel, *The Big Four*, and are not generally regarded as individual stories in their own right. There are also a handful of stories which were rewritten so substantially that they appear separately in different books, for example *The Mystery of the Baghdad/Spanish Chest*. This all makes counting up the stories very difficult indeed!

However, excluding *The Big Four* (for the reason stated above) and including the published variants, there are a total of 159 stories published in book form in the UK:

Hercule Poirot – 56
Miss Marple – 20
Tommy & Tuppence – 14
Harley Quin – 14
Parker Pyne – 14
Non-series stories – 35
Children's stories – 6

Titles are listed in order of traced first publication date. Actual first publication details are given where known. It is generally assumed that practically everything Christie wrote – novels, short stories, poetry – appeared first in a magazine or newspaper, prior to the hardback edition. However, despite exhaustive research, it has not always been possible to trace a magazine appearance for every story, in which case the first hardback publication is given.

Whilst most stories first appeared in British magazines or newspapers, a number premiered in America, and these are duly noted. Where both 'firsts' were close together, or where a subsequent publication gave rise to an interesting variation in title for the story, both are given.

KARL PIKE
2008

DATE	CHARACTER	STORY (BOOK TITLE)	PUBLICATION	PUBLISHED AS (IF DIFFERENT)	FIRST BOOK APPEARANCE
			1923		
Agatha Christie's first batch of 12 published short stories appeared as a series: 'The Grey Cells of M. Poirot I.'...					
7 Mar	Poirot	The Affair at the Victory Ball	UK: The Sketch, 1571		Poirot's Early Cases (UK)
Sep			USA: Blue Book Magazine, Vol. 37, No. 6		The Under Dog (US)
14 Mar	Poirot	The Jewel Robbery at the Grand Metropolitan	UK: The Sketch, 1572	The Curious Disappearance of the Opalsen Pearls	Poirot Investigates
Oct			USA: Blue Book Magazine, Vol. 37, No. 6	Mrs Opalsen's Pearls	
21 Mar	Poirot	The King of Clubs	UK: The Sketch, 1573	The Adventure of the King of Clubs	Poirot's Early Cases (UK)
Nov			USA: Blue Book Magazine, Vol. 38, No. 1		The Under Dog (US)
28 Mar	Poirot	The Disappearance of Mr Davenheim	UK: The Sketch, 1574		Poirot Investigates
Dec			USA: Blue Book Magazine, Vol. 38, No. 2	Mr Davenby Disappears	
4 Apr	Poirot	The Plymouth Express	UK: The Sketch, 1575	The Mystery of the Plymouth Express	Poirot's Early Cases (UK)
Jan 1924			USA: Blue Book Magazine, Vol. 38, No. 3	The Plymouth Express Affair	The Under Dog (US)

DATE	CHARACTER	STORY (BOOK TITLE)	PUBLICATION	PUBLISHED AS (IF DIFFERENT)	FIRST BOOK APPEARANCE
11 Apr	Poirot	The Adventure of the Western Star	UK: The Sketch, 1576		Poirot Investigates
Feb 1924			USA: Blue Book Magazine, Vol. 38, No. 4	The Western Star	
18 Apr	Poirot	The Tragedy at Marsdon Manor	UK: The Sketch, 1577		Poirot Investigates
Mar 1924			USA: Blue Book Magazine, Vol. 38, No. 5	The Marsdon Manor Tragedy	
25 Apr	Poirot	The Kidnapped Prime Minister	UK: The Sketch, 1578	The Kidnaped Prime Minister	Poirot Investigates
Jul 1924			USA: Blue Book Magazine, Vol. 39, No. 3		
2 May	Poirot	The Million Dollar Bond Robbery	UK: The Sketch, 1579		Poirot Investigates
Apr 1924			USA: Blue Book Magazine, Vol. 38, No. 6	The Great Bond Robbery	
9 May	Poirot	The Adventure of the Cheap Flat	UK: The Sketch, 1580		Poirot Investigates
May 1924			USA: Blue Book Magazine, Vol. 39, No. 1		
16 May	Poirot	The Mystery of Hunter's Lodge	UK: The Sketch, 1581		Poirot Investigates
Jun 1924			USA: Blue Book Magazine, Vol. 39, No. 2	The Hunter's Lodge Case	

DATE	CHARACTER	STORY (BOOK TITLE)	PUBLICATION	PUBLISHED AS (IF DIFFERENT)	FIRST BOOK APPEARANCE
23 May	Poirot	The Chocolate Box	UK: The Sketch, 1582	The Clue of the Chocolate Box	Poirot's Early Cases (UK)
Feb 1925			USA: Blue Book Magazine, Vol. 40, No. 4		Poirot Investigates (US edition only)
May		The Actress	The Novel Magazine, No. 218	A Trap for the Unwary	While the Light Lasts (UK)
					The Harlequin Tea Set (US)
...followed by 12 more stories – 'The Grey Cells of M. Poirot II.'					
26 Sep	Poirot	The Adventure of the Egyptian Tomb	UK: The Sketch, 1600		Poirot Investigates
Aug 1924			USA: Blue Book Magazine, Vol. 39, No. 4	The Egyptian Adventure	
3 Oct	Poirot	The Veiled Lady	UK: The Sketch, 1601	The Case of the Veiled Lady	Poirot's Early Cases (UK)
Mar 1925			USA: Blue Book Magazine, Vol. 40, No. 5		Poirot Investigates (US edition only)
10 Oct	Poirot	The Adventure of Johnny Waverly	UK: The Sketch, 1602	The Kidnapping of Johnnie Waverly	Poirot's Early Cases (UK)
Jun 1925			USA: Blue Book Magazine, Vol. 41, No. 2		Three Blind Mice (US)

DATE	CHARACTER	STORY (BOOK TITLE)	PUBLICATION	PUBLISHED AS (IF DIFFERENT)	FIRST BOOK APPEARANCE
17 Oct 1925	Poirot	The Market Basing Mystery	UK: The Sketch, 1603		Poirot's Early Cases (UK)
May 1925			USA: Blue Book Magazine, Vol. 41, No. 1		The Under Dog (US)
24 Oct	Poirot	The Adventure of the Italian Nobleman	UK: The Sketch, 1604		Poirot Investigates
Dec 1924			USA: Blue Book Magazine, Vol. 40, No. 2	The Italian Nobleman	
31 Oct	Poirot	The Case of the Missing Will	UK: The Sketch, 1605		Poirot Investigates
Jan 1925			USA: Blue Book Magazine, Vol. 40, No. 3	The Missing Will	
7 Nov	Poirot	The Submarine Plans	UK: The Sketch, 1606	*Later expanded into*	Poirot's Early Cases (UK)
Jul 1925			USA: Blue Book Magazine, Vol. 41, No. 3	The Incredible Theft (1937)	The Under Dog (US)
14 Nov	Poirot	The Adventure of the Clapham Cook	UK: The Sketch, 1607		Poirot's Early Cases (UK)
Sep 1925			USA: Blue Book Magazine, Vol. 41, No. 5	The Clapham Cook	The Under Dog (US)
21 Nov	Poirot	The Lost Mine	UK: The Sketch, 1608		Poirot's Early Cases (UK)
Apr 1925			USA: Blue Book Magazine, Vol. 40, No. 6		Poirot Investigates (US edition only)
28 Nov	Poirot	The Cornish Mystery	UK: The Sketch, 1609		Poirot's Early Cases (UK)
Oct 1925			USA: Blue Book Magazine, Vol. 41, No. 6		The Under Dog (US)

DATE	CHARACTER	STORY (BOOK TITLE)	PUBLICATION	PUBLISHED AS (IF DIFFERENT)	FIRST BOOK APPEARANCE
5 Dec	Poirot	The Double Clue	UK: The Sketch, 1610		Poirot's Early Cases (UK)
Aug 1925			USA: Blue Book Magazine, Vol. 41, No. 4		Double Sin (US)
Dec	Poirot	The Adventure of the Christmas Pudding *A.k.a.* Christmas Adventure	UK: The Sketch, 1611	*Later expanded into* The Theft of the Royal Ruby (1960)	While the Light Lasts (UK)
12 Dec	Tommy & Tuppence	The Clergyman's Daughter/The Red House	Grand Magazine, No. 226	The First Wish	Partners in Crime
Christmas	Poirot	The Lemesurier Inheritance	UK: The Magpie	The Le Mesurier Inheritance	Poirot's Early Cases (UK)
Nov 1925			USA: Blue Book Magazine, Vol. 42, No. 1		The Under Dog (US)
1924					
		This series of 12 stories was subsequently reworked by Agatha Christie into The Big Four (1927), and are therefore not considered to be independent stories. They are included here for the sake of completeness.			
2 Jan	Poirot	The Unexpected Guest	The Sketch, 1614		The Big Four
9 Jan	Poirot	The Adventure of the Dartmoor Bungalow	The Sketch, 1615		The Big Four
16 Jan	Poirot	The Lady on the Stairs	The Sketch, 1616		The Big Four

DATE	CHARACTER	STORY (BOOK TITLE)	PUBLICATION	PUBLISHED AS (IF DIFFERENT)	FIRST BOOK APPEARANCE
23 Jan	Poirot	The Radium Thieves	The Sketch, 1617		The Big Four
30 Jan	Poirot	In the House of the Enemy	The Sketch, 1618		The Big Four
6 Feb	Poirot	The Yellow Jasmine	The Sketch, 1619		The Big Four
13 Feb	Poirot	A Chess Problem	The Sketch, 1620	The Chess Problem	The Big Four
20 Feb	Poirot	The Baited Trap	The Sketch, 1621		The Big Four
27 Feb	Poirot	The Adventure of the Peroxide Blonde	The Sketch, 1622		The Big Four
5 Mar	Poirot	The Terrible Catastrophe	The Sketch, 1619		The Big Four
12 Mar	Poirot	The Dying Chinaman	The Sketch, 1624		The Big Four
19 Mar	Poirot	The Crag in the Dolomites	The Sketch, 1625		The Big Four
Feb		The Girl in the Train	Grand Magazine, No. 228		The Listerdale Mystery (UK) / The Golden Ball (US)
Mar	Mr Quin	The Coming of Mr Quin	Grand Magazine, No. 229	The Passing of Mr Quinn	The Mysterious Mr Quin
Apr		While the Light Lasts	Novel Magazine, No. 229		While the Light Lasts (UK) / The Harlequin Tea Set (US)

DATE	CHARACTER	STORY (BOOK TITLE)	PUBLICATION	PUBLISHED AS (IF DIFFERENT)	FIRST BOOK APPEARANCE
Jun		The Red Signal	Grand Magazine, No. 232		The Hound of Death (UK) The Witness for the Prosecution (US)
Jul		The Mystery of the Blue Jar	Grand Magazine, No. 233		The Hound of Death (UK) The Witness for the Prosecution (US)
Aug		Jane in Search of a Job	Grand Magazine, No. 234		The Listerdale Mystery (UK) The Golden Ball (US)
Aug	Poirot	Mr Eastwood's Adventure *A.k.a.* The Mystery of the Spanish Shawl	The Novel Magazine, No. 233	The Mystery of the Second Cucumber	The Listerdale Mystery (UK) The Witness for the Prosecution (US)
These next 12 stories were subsequently worked into the Tommy & Tuppence book, Partners in Crime (1929):					
24 Sep	Tommy & Tuppence	A Fairy in the Flat/A Pot of Tea	The Sketch, 1652	Publicity	Partners in Crime
1 Oct	Tommy & Tuppence	The Affair of the Pink Pearl	The Sketch, 1653		Partners in Crime
8 Oct	Tommy & Tuppence	Finessing the King/The Gentleman Dressed in Newspaper	The Sketch, 1654	Finessing the King	Partners in Crime

DATE	CHARACTER	STORY (BOOK TITLE)	PUBLICATION	PUBLISHED AS (IF DIFFERENT)	FIRST BOOK APPEARANCE
15 Oct	Tommy & Tuppence	The Case of the Missing Lady	The Sketch, 1655		Partners in Crime
22 Oct	Tommy & Tuppence	The Adventure of the Sinister Stranger	The Sketch, 1656		Partners in Crime
29 Oct	Tommy & Tuppence	The Sunningdale Mystery	The Sketch, 1657	The Sunninghall Mystery	Partners in Crime
5 Nov	Tommy & Tuppence	The House of Lurking Death	The Sketch, 1658		Partners in Crime
12 Nov	Tommy & Tuppence	The Ambassador's Boots	The Sketch, 1659	The Matter of the Ambassador's Boots	Partners in Crime
19 Nov	Tommy & Tuppence	The Crackler	The Sketch, 1660	The Affair of the Forged Notes	Partners in Crime
26 Nov	Tommy & Tuppence	Blindman's Buff	The Sketch, 1661	Blind Man's Buff	Partners in Crime
3 Dec	Tommy & Tuppence	The Man in the Mist	The Sketch, 1662		Partners in Crime
10 Dec	Tommy & Tuppence	The Man Who Was No.16	The Sketch, 1663	The Man Who Was Number Sixteen	Partners in Crime
Oct	Mr Quin	The Shadow on the Glass	Grand Magazine, No. 236		The Mysterious Mr Quin

DATE	CHARACTER	STORY (BOOK TITLE)	PUBLICATION	PUBLISHED AS (IF DIFFERENT)	FIRST BOOK APPEARANCE
Nov		Philomel Cottage	Grand Magazine, No. 237		The Listerdale Mystery (UK)
					The Witness for the Prosecution (US)
Dec		The Manhood of Edward Robinson	Grand Magazine, No. 238	The Day of His Dreams	The Listerdale Mystery (UK)
					The Golden Ball (US)
1925					
31 Jan		The Witness for the Prosecution	USA: Flynn's Weekly	Traitor Hands	The Hound of Death (UK)
					The Witness for the Prosecution (US)
Jun	Mr Quin	The Sign in the Sky	USA: The Police Magazine		The Mysterious Mr Quin
Jul			UK: Grand Magazine, No. 245	A Sign in the Sky	
Sep/Oct		Wireless *A.k.a.* Where There's a Will	Sunday Chronicle Annual 1925		The Hound of Death (UK)
					The Witness for the Prosecution (US)
Oct		Within a Wall	Royal Magazine, No. 324		While the Light Lasts (UK)
					The Harlequin Tea Set (US)

DATE	CHARACTER	STORY (BOOK TITLE)	PUBLICATION	PUBLISHED AS (IF DIFFERENT)	FIRST BOOK APPEARANCE
Nov	Mr Quin	At the 'Bells and Motley'	Grand Magazine, No. 249	A Man of Magic	The Mysterious Mr Quin
Dec		The Listerdale Mystery	Grand Magazine, No. 250	The Benevolent Butler	The Listerdale Mystery (UK)
					The Golden Ball (US)
Dec		The Fourth Man	Pearson's Magazine, No. 360		The Hound of Death (UK)
					The Witness for the Prosecution (US)
1926					
Jan		The House of Dreams	The Sovereign Magazine, Vol. 11, No. 74		While the Light Lasts (UK)
					The Harlequin Tea Set (US)
Feb		S.O.S.	Grand Magazine, No. 252		The Hound of Death (UK)
					The Witness for the Prosecution (US)
Mar		Magnolia Blossom	Royal Magazine, No. 329		Problem at Pollensa Bay (UK)
					The Golden Ball (US)
1 Apr	Poirot	The Under Dog	USA: Mystery Magazine, Vol. 8, No. 6		The Adventure of the Christmas Pudding (UK)
					The Under Dog (US)

DATE	CHARACTER	STORY (BOOK TITLE)	PUBLICATION	PUBLISHED AS (IF DIFFERENT)	FIRST BOOK APPEARANCE
Jul		The Lonely God	Royal Magazine, No. 333		While the Light Lasts (UK)
					The Harlequin Tea Set (US)
30 Jul		The Rajah's Emerald	Red Magazine		The Listerdale Mystery (UK)
					The Golden Ball (US)
Sep		Swan Song	Grand Magazine, No. 259		The Listerdale Mystery (UK)
					The Golden Ball (US)
30 Oct	Mr Quin	The Love Detectives	USA: Flynn's Weekly, Vol. 19, No. 3	At the Cross Roads	Problem at Pollensa Bay (UK)
Dec			UK: Storyteller, 236	The Magic of Mr Quin No. 1: At the Cross Roads	Three Blind Mice (US)
Nov		The Last Séance	USA: Ghost Stories magazine		The Hound of Death (UK)
Mar 1927			UK: The Sovereign Magazine, No. 87	The Stolen Ghost	Double Sin (US)
13 Nov	Mr Quin	The Soul of the Croupier	USA: Flynn's Weekly, Vol. 19, No. 5		The Mysterious Mr Quin
Jan 1927			UK: Storyteller magazine, No. 237	The Magic of Mr Quin No. 2: The Soul of the Croupier	

DATE	CHARACTER	STORY (BOOK TITLE)	PUBLICATION	PUBLISHED AS (IF DIFFERENT)	FIRST BOOK APPEARANCE
20 Nov	Mr Quin	The World's End	USA: Flynn's Weekly, Vol. 19, No.6	World's End	The Mysterious Mr Quin
Feb 1927			UK: Storyteller magazine, 238	The Magic of Mr Quin No. 3 : The World's End	
4 Dec	Mr Quin	The Voice in the Dark	USA: Flynn's Weekly, Vol. 20, No. 2		The Mysterious Mr Quin
Mar 1927			UK: Storyteller magazine, 239	The Magic of Mr Quin No. 4	
1927					
Feb		The Edge	Pearson's Magazine, Vol. 63, No. 374		While the Light Lasts (UK) The Harlequin Tea Set (US)
Apr	Mr Quin	The Face of Helen	The Storyteller, No. 240	The Magic of Mr Quin No. 5	The Mysterious Mr Quin
May	Mr Quin	Harlequin's Lane	Storyteller, No. 241	The Magic of Mr Quin No. 6	The Mysterious Mr Quin
Dec	Poirot	The Enemy Strikes	USA: Blue Book, Vol. 46, No. 2	Part of the novel The Big Four	The Big Four
Dec	Miss Marple	The Tuesday Night Club	UK: Royal Magazine, No. 350		The Thirteen Problems (UK)
2 Jun 1928			USA: Detective Story Magazine	The Solving Six	The Tuesday Night Club (US)

DATE	CHARACTER	STORY (BOOK TITLE)	PUBLICATION	PUBLISHED AS (IF DIFFERENT)	FIRST BOOK APPEARANCE
			1928		
Jan	Miss Marple	The Idol House of Astarte	UK: Royal Magazine, No. 351		The Thirteen Problems (UK)
9 Jun			USA: Detective Story Magazine	The Solving Six and the Evil Hour	The Tuesday Night Club (US)
Feb	Miss Marple	Ingots of Gold	UK: Royal Magazine, No. 352		The Thirteen Problems (UK)
16 Jun			USA: Detective Story Magazine	Solving Six and the Golden Grave	The Tuesday Night Club (US)
Mar	Miss Marple	The Blood-Stained Pavement	UK: Royal Magazine, No. 353		The Thirteen Problems (UK)
23 Jun			USA: Detective Story Magazine	Drip! Drip!	The Tuesday Night Club (US)
Apr	Miss Marple	Motive v. Opportunity	UK: Royal Magazine, No. 354		The Thirteen Problems (UK)
30 Jun			USA: Detective Story Magazine	Where's the Catch?	The Tuesday Night Club (US)
May	Miss Marple	The Thumb Mark of St. Peter	UK: Royal Magazine, No. 35	The Thumb-Mark of St. Peter	The Thirteen Problems (UK)
7 Jul			USA: Detective Story Magazine		The Tuesday Night Club (US)

DATE	CHARACTER	STORY (BOOK TITLE)	PUBLICATION	PUBLISHED AS (IF DIFFERENT)	FIRST BOOK APPEARANCE
11 Aug		A Fruitful Sunday	Daily Mail		Listerdale Mystery (UK) The Golden Ball (US)
23 Sep	Poirot	Double Sin	Sunday Dispatch	By Road or Rail	Poirot's Early Cases (UK) Double Sin (US)
1 Dec	Tommy & Tuppence	The Unbreakable Alibi	Holly Leaves No. 2880 (pub by Illustrated Sporting and Dramatic News)		Partners in Crime
20 Nov	Poirot	Wasps' Nest	Daily Mail, No. 10164	The Wasps' Nest	Poirot's Early Cases (UK) Double Sin (US)
1929					
Jan	Poirot	The Third Floor Flat	UK: Hutchinson's Story Magazine, Vol. 21, No. 1		Poirot's Early Cases (UK) Three Blind Mice (US)
5 Jan			USA: Detective Story Magazine, Vol. 106, No.6	In the Third Floor Flat	
Mar	Mr Quin	The Dead Harlequin	Grand Magazine, No. 288		The Mysterious Mr Quin
5 Aug		The Golden Ball	Daily Mail	Playing the Innocent	The Listerdale Mystery (UK) The Golden Ball (US)

DATE	CHARACTER	STORY (BOOK TITLE)	PUBLISHED AS (IF DIFFERENT)	PUBLICATION	FIRST BOOK APPEARANCE
22 Sep		Accident	The Uncrossed Path	The Sunday Dispatch	The Listerdale Mystery (UK) The Witness for the Prosecution (US)
Sep		Next to a Dog		Grand Magazine, No. 295	Problem at Pollensa Bay (UK) The Golden Ball (US)
Oct	Mr Quin	The Man from the Sea		Britannia & Eve, Vol. 1, No. 6	The Mysterious Mr Quin
Dec	Miss Marple	The Blue Geranium		The Christmas Story-Teller, Vol. 46, No. 272	The Thirteen Problems (UK) The Tuesday Night Club (US)
2 Dec		Sing a Song of Sixpence		Holly Leaves No. 2932 (pub by Illustrated Sporting and Dramatic News)	The Listerdale Mystery (UK) The Witness for the Prosecution (US)

DATE	CHARACTER	STORY (BOOK TITLE)	PUBLICATION	PUBLISHED AS (IF DIFFERENT)	FIRST BOOK APPEARANCE
			1930		
Jan	Miss Marple	The Four Suspects	USA: Pictorial Review, Vol. 31, No. 4	Four Suspects	The Thirteen Problems (UK)
Apr			UK: Storyteller magazine, No. 276		The Tuesday Night Club (US)
Jan	Miss Marple	A Christmas Tragedy	Storyteller, Vol. 46, No. 273	The Hat and the Alibi	The Thirteen Problems (UK)
					The Tuesday Night Club (US)
Feb	Miss Marple	The Companion	UK: Storyteller, Vol. 46, No. 274	The Resurrection of Amy Durrant	The Thirteen Problems (UK)
Mar			USA: Pictorial Review	Companions	The Tuesday Night Club (US)
Mar	Miss Marple	The Herb of Death	Storyteller, Vol. 46, No. 275		The Thirteen Problems (UK)
					The Tuesday Night Club (US)
Apr	Mr Quin	The Bird with the Broken Wing	The Mysterious Mr Quin (Collins 1930). No pre-hardback appearances found		The Mysterious Mr Quin

DATE	CHARACTER	STORY (BOOK TITLE)	PUBLICATION	PUBLISHED AS (IF DIFFERENT)	FIRST BOOK APPEARANCE
May	Miss Marple	The Affair at the Bungalow	Storyteller, Vol. 46, No. 277		The Thirteen Problems (UK) The Tuesday Night Club (US)
23–28 May		Manx Gold	The Daily Dispatch		While the Light Lasts (UK) The Harlequin Tea Set (US)
1931					
Nov	Miss Marple	Death by Drowning	Nash's Pall Mall, Vol. 88, No. 462		The Thirteen Problems (UK) The Tuesday Night Club (US)
1932					
Jan	Poirot	The Mystery of the Baghdad Chest	UK: Strand Magazine, No. 493	*Later expanded into* The Mystery of the Spanish Chest (1960)	While the Light Lasts (UK) The Regatta Mystery (US)
			USA: Ladies' Home Journal, Vol. 49, No. 1	The Mystery of the Bagdad Chest	
Jun	Poirot	The Second Gong	USA: Ladies' Home Journal, Vol. 49, No 6	*Later expanded into* Dead Man's Mirror (1937)	Problem at Pollensa Bay (UK)
Jul			UK: Strand Magazine, No 499		The Witness for the Prosecution (US)

DATE	CHARACTER	STORY (BOOK TITLE)	PUBLICATION	PUBLISHED AS (IF DIFFERENT)	FIRST BOOK APPEARANCE
Aug	Parker Pyne	The Case of the Rich Woman	USA: Cosmopolitan	The Rich Woman Who Wanted Only To Be Happy	Parker Pyne Investigates (UK)
					Mr Parker Pyne, Detective (US)
Aug	Parker Pyne	The Case of the Distressed Lady	USA: Cosmopolitan	The Pretty Girl Who Wanted a Ring	Parker Pyne Investigates (UK)
22 Oct			UK: Woman's Pictorial	Faked!	Mr Parker Pyne, Detective (US)
Aug	Parker Pyne	The Case of the Discontented Soldier	USA: Cosmopolitan	The Soldier Who Wanted Danger	Parker Pyne Investigates (UK)
15 Oct			UK: Woman's Pictorial	Adventure – By Request	Mr Parker Pyne, Detective (US)
Aug	Parker Pyne	The Case of the Discontented Husband	USA: Cosmopolitan	The Husband Who Wanted To Keep His Wife	Parker Pyne Investigates (UK)
29 Oct			UK: Woman's Pictorial	His Lady's Affair	Mr Parker Pyne, Detective (US)
Aug	Parker Pyne	The Case of the City Clerk	USA: Cosmopolitan	The Clerk Who Wanted Excitement	Parker Pyne Investigates (UK)
Nov			UK: Strand Magazine, No. 503	The £10 Adventure	Mr Parker Pyne, Detective (US)

DATE	CHARACTER	STORY (BOOK TITLE)	PUBLICATION	PUBLISHED AS (IF DIFFERENT)	FIRST BOOK APPEARANCE
8 Oct	Parker Pyne	The Case of the Middle-aged Wife	Woman's Pictorial	The Woman Concerned	Parker Pyne Investigates (UK) / Mr Parker Pyne, Detective (US)
1933					
Feb		The Call of Wings	The Hound of Death (Odhams 1933). No pre-hardback appearances found		The Hound of Death (UK) / The Golden Ball (US)
		The Gipsy			The Hound of Death (UK) / The Golden Ball (US)
		The Hound of Death			The Hound of Death (UK) / The Golden Ball (US)
		The Lamp			The Hound of Death (UK) / The Golden Ball (US)
		The Strange Case of Sir Arthur Carmichael			The Hound of Death (UK) / The Golden Ball (US)

DATE	CHARACTER	STORY (BOOK TITLE)	PUBLICATION	PUBLISHED AS (IF DIFFERENT)	FIRST BOOK APPEARANCE
Apr	Parker Pyne	Death on the Nile	USA: Cosmopolitan		Parker Pyne Investigates (UK)
Jul			UK: Nash's Pall Mall, Vol. 91, No. 482		Mr Parker Pyne, Detective (US)
Apr	Parker Pyne	The Oracle at Delphi	USA: Cosmopolitan		Parker Pyne Investigates (UK)
Jul			UK: Nash's Pall Mall, Vol. 91, No. 482		Mr Parker Pyne, Detective (US)
Apr	Parker Pyne	The House at Shiraz	USA: Cosmopolitan		Parker Pyne Investigates (UK)
Jun			UK: Nash's Pall Mall, Vol. 91, No. 481	In the House at Shiraz	Mr Parker Pyne, Detective (US)
Apr	Parker Pyne	Have You Got Everything You Want?	USA: Cosmopolitan		Parker Pyne Investigates (UK)
Jun			UK: Nash's Pall Mall, Vol. 91, No. 481	On the Orient Express	Mr Parker Pyne, Detective (US)
Jun	Parker Pyne	The Gate of Baghdad	Nash's Pall Mall, Vol. 91, No. 481	At the Gate of Baghdad	Parker Pyne Investigates (UK)
					Mr Parker Pyne, Detective (US)

DATE	CHARACTER	STORY (BOOK TITLE)	PUBLICATION	PUBLISHED AS (IF DIFFERENT)	FIRST BOOK APPEARANCE
Jul	Parker Pyne	The Pearl of Price	Nash's Pall Mall, Vol. 91, No. 482	The Pearl	Parker Pyne Investigates (UK)
					Mr Parker Pyne, Detective (US)
1934					
28 Jul		In a Glass Darkly	USA: Collier's, Vol. 94, No. 4		Miss Marple's Final Cases (UK)
Dec			UK: Woman's Journal		The Regatta Mystery (US)
1935					
25 May	Miss Marple	Miss Marple Tells a Story	Home Journal	Behind Closed Doors	Miss Marple's Final Cases (UK)
					The Regatta Mystery (US)
Jun	Poirot	How Does Your Garden Grow?	USA: Ladies' Home Journal, Vol. 52, No. 6		Poirot's Early Cases (UK)
Aug			UK: Strand Magazine, No. 536		The Regatta Mystery (US)
Nov	Parker Pyne	Problem at Pollensa Bay	UK: Strand Magazine, No. 539		Problem at Pollensa Bay (UK)
5 Sep 1936			USA: Liberty	Siren Business	The Regatta Mystery (US)

DATE	CHARACTER	STORY (BOOK TITLE)	PUBLICATION	PUBLISHED AS (IF DIFFERENT)	FIRST BOOK APPEARANCE
			1936		
12 Jan	Poirot	Problem at Sea	USA: This Week		Poirot's Early Cases (UK)
Feb			UK: Strand Magazine, No. 542	Poirot and the Crime in Cabin 66	The Regatta Mystery (US)
2 Feb	Poirot	Triangle at Rhodes	USA: This Week		Murder in the Mews (UK)
May			UK: Strand Magazine, No. 545	Poirot and the Triangle at Rhodes	Dead Man's Mirror (US)
3 May	Poirot / Parker Pyne	The Regatta Mystery	USA: Chicago Tribune		Problem at Pollensa Bay (UK)
Jun			UK: Strand Magazine, No. 546	Poirot and the Regatta Mystery	The Regatta Mystery (US)
Sep/Oct	Poirot	Murder in the Mews	USA: Redbook Magazine, Vol. 67, Nos. 5–6		Murder in the Mews (UK)
Dec			UK: Woman's Journal	Mystery of the Dressing Case	Dead Man's Mirror (US)
			1937		
Mar	Poirot	Dead Man's Mirror	Murder in the Mews (Collins, 1937). No pre-hardback appearance found.	*Expanded version of* The Second Gong (1932)	Murder in the Mews (UK)
					Dead Man's Mirror (US)

DATE	CHARACTER	STORY (BOOK TITLE)	PUBLICATION	PUBLISHED AS (IF DIFFERENT)	FIRST BOOK APPEARANCE
6–12 Apr	Poirot	The Incredible Theft	Daily Express	*Expanded version of* The Submarine Plans (1923). *Adapted by Leslie Stokes as a radio play, broadcast by BBC National Programme, 10 May 1938.*	Murder in the Mews (UK) Dead Man's Mirror (US)
Jul	Poirot	Yellow Iris	UK: Strand Magazine, No. 559	*Later expanded into* Sparkling Cyanide (Collins 1945)	Problem at Pollensa Bay UK)
25 Jul			USA: Chicago Tribune		The Regatta Mystery (US)
23 Oct	Poirot	The Dream	USA: Saturday Evening Post, Vol. 210, No. 17		The Adventure of the Christmas Pudding (UK)
Feb 1938			UK: Strand Magazine, No. 566		The Regatta Mystery (US)
1939					
3 Sep	Poirot	The Lernean Hydra	USA: This Week	Invisible Enemy	The Labours of Hercules
Dec			UK: Strand Magazine, No. 588		
10 Sep	Poirot	The Girdle of Hyppolita	USA: This Week	The Disappearance of Winnie King	The Labours of Hercules
Jul 1940			UK: Strand Magazine, No. 595	The Girdle of Hyppolyte	

DATE	CHARACTER	STORY (BOOK TITLE)	PUBLICATION	PUBLISHED AS (IF DIFFERENT)	FIRST BOOK APPEARANCE
17 Sep	Poirot	The Stymphalean Birds	USA: This Week	The Vulture Women	The Labours of Hercules
Apr 1940			UK: Strand Magazine, No. 592	Birds of Ill-Omen	
24 Sep	Poirot	The Cretan Bull	USA: This Week	Midnight Madness	The Labours of Hercules
May 1940			UK: Strand Magazine, No. 593		
Nov	Poirot	The Nemean Lion	UK: Strand Magazine, No. 587		The Labours of Hercules
?			USA: This Week	The Case of the Kidnapped Pekinese	
1940					
Jan	Poirot	The Arcadian Deer	UK: Strand Magazine, No. 589		The Labours of Hercules
19 May			USA: This Week	Vanishing Lady	
Feb	Poirot	The Erymanthian Boar	UK: Strand Magazine, No. 590		The Labours of Hercules
5 May			USA: This Week	Murder Mountain	
Mar	Poirot	The Augean Stables	Strand Magazine, No. 591		The Labours of Hercules

DATE	CHARACTER	STORY (BOOK TITLE)	PUBLICATION	PUBLISHED AS (IF DIFFERENT)	FIRST BOOK APPEARANCE
12 May Sep	Poirot	The Apples of the Hesperides	USA: This Week UK: Strand Magazine, No. 597	The Poison Cup	The Labours of Hercules
26 May Aug	Poirot	The Flock of Geryon	USA: This Week UK: Strand Magazine, No. 596	Weird Monster	The Labours of Hercules
June ?	Poirot	The Horses of Diomedes	Strand Magazine, No. 594 USA: This Week	The Case of the Drug Peddler	The Labours of Hercules
9 Nov	Poirot	Four-and-Twenty Blackbirds	USA: Collier's, Vol. 106, No.19		The Adventure of the Christmas Pudding (UK)
Mar 1941			UK: Strand Magazine, No. 603	Poirot and the Regular Customer	Three Blind Mice (US)
1941					
2 Nov Jul 1944	Miss Marple	Strange Jest	USA: This Week UK: Strand Magazine, No. 643	A Case of Buried Treasure	Miss Marple's Final Cases (UK) Three Blind Mice (US)
16 Nov Feb 1942	Miss Marple	Tape-Measure Murder	USA: This Week UK: Strand Magazine, No. 614	The Case of the Retired Jeweller	Miss Marple's Final Cases (UK) Three Blind Mice (US)

DATE	CHARACTER	STORY (BOOK TITLE)	PUBLICATION	PUBLISHED AS (IF DIFFERENT)	FIRST BOOK APPEARANCE
			1942		
Jan	Miss Marple	The Case of the Caretaker	UK: Strand Magazine, No. 613		Miss Marple's Final Cases (UK)
5 Jul			USA: Chicago Sunday Tribune		Three Blind Mice (US)
Apr	Miss Marple	The Case of the Perfect Maid	UK: Strand Magazine, No. 616	The Perfect Maid	Miss Marple's Final Cases (UK)
13 Sep			USA: Chicago Sunday Tribune	The Maid Who Disappeared	Three Blind Mice (US)
			1946		
Dec		Star Over Bethlehem	Woman's Journal		Star Over Bethlehem
			1947		
16 Mar	Poirot	The Capture of Cerberus	USA: This Week	Meet Me in Hell	The Labours of Hercules
Sep			UK: The Labours of Hercules (Collins 1947)	Replacement for original 12th Labour rejected by the Strand Magazine in 1940	

DATE	CHARACTER	STORY (BOOK TITLE)	PUBLICATION	PUBLISHED AS (IF DIFFERENT)	FIRST BOOK APPEARANCE
1948					
May		Three Blind Mice	USA: Cosmopolitan, No. 743		Three Blind Mice (US)
31 Dec 1948 – 21 Jan 1949			UK: Woman's Own	*In 4 weekly parts. Developed from the radio play of 30 May 1947. Forms the basis of the play The Mousetrap.*	For contractual reasons, this story has never been published in book form in the UK.
1954					
12&19 Sep	Miss Marple	Sanctuary	USA: This Week	Murder at the Vicarage	Miss Marple's Final Cases (UK)
Oct			UK: Woman's Journal		Double Sin (US)
1956					
3–7 Dec	Miss Marple	Greenshaw's Folly	Daily Mail		The Adventure of the Christmas Pudding (UK)
					Double Sin (US)
1958					
Dec		The Dressmaker's Doll	Woman's Journal		Miss Marple's Final Cases (UK)
					Double Sin (US)

DATE	CHARACTER	STORY (BOOK TITLE)	PUBLICATION	PUBLISHED AS (IF DIFFERENT)	FIRST BOOK APPEARANCE
			1960		
17&24 Sep, 1 Oct	Poirot	The Mystery of the Spanish Chest	Woman's Illustrated	*In 3 parts. Expanded version of* The Mystery of the Baghdad Chest (1932)	The Adventure of the Christmas Pudding (UK) / The Harlequin Tea Set (US)
25 Sep & 2 Oct	Poirot	The Adventure of the Christmas Pudding *A.k.a.* The Theft of the Royal Ruby	USA: This Week	The Theft of the Royal Ruby, *in 2 parts*	Miss Marple's Final Cases (UK)
24&31 Dec and 7 Jan 1961			UK: Woman's Illustrated	*In 3 parts. Expanded version of* Christmas Adventure (1923)	Double Sin (US)
			1965		
Nov		In the Cool of the Evening	Star Over Bethlehem (Collins, 1965)		Star Over Bethlehem
		The Island			Star Over Bethlehem
		The Naughty Donkey			Star Over Bethlehem
		Promotion in the Highest			Star Over Bethlehem
		The Water Bus			Star Over Bethlehem
			1971		
?	Mr Quin	The Harlequin Tea Set	Winter's Crimes, No. 3 (Macmillan)		Problem at Pollensa Bay (UK) / The Harlequin Tea Set (US)

ALSO IN THIS SERIES

Agatha Christie

HERCULE POIROT:
The Complete Short Stories

At last – the complete collection of over 50 Hercule Poirot short stories in a single volume!

Hercule Poirot had a passion for order, for rational thought, and had a justified confidence in his deductive genius. No matter what the provocation, he always remained calm.

The shrewd little detective with the egg-shaped head and the enormous black moustache was created by one of the world's greatest storytellers, Agatha Christie, who excelled at the art of short story writing. Only she could have devised the cases worthy of Poirot's skill, the ingenious mysteries that challenge the reader as well as the detective.

There is a spectacular diversity in the plots and themes of these cases, ranging from very brief tales to full-length novellas. Violent murders, poisonings, kidnappings and thefts, all are solved or thwarted with Poirot's usual panache – and the characteristic application of his 'little grey cells'.

'Little masterpieces of detection – Poirot and Agatha Christie at their inimitable best.'   *Sunday Express*

Agatha Christie

POIROT in the ORIENT

There is nothing exotic about murder, no matter where it takes place. Away from home, Hercule Poirot finds that he cannot escape death, even when travelling across the Mesopotamia, the Nile and Petra.

MURDER IN MESOPOTAMIA

At the Hassanieh dig deep in the Iraqi desert, the wife of a celebrated archaeologist is suffering from terrifying hallucinations. Apparent madness – until a murderer strikes.

DEATH ON THE NILE

The tranquillity of a Nile cruise is shattered by the discovery that a young girl has been shot through the head. Stylish and beautiful, she had everything – even enemies.

APPOINTMENT WITH DEATH

And among the towering red cliffs of Petra sits the corpse of Mrs Boynton. A tiny puncture mark on her wrist is the only sign of the fatal injection that killed her.

Based on Agatha Christie's own experiences in the 1930s travelling with her husband, archaeologist Sir Max Mallowan, this trilogy of bestselling novels represents crime fiction at its very best.

Agatha Christie

POIROT: The WAR Years

It seems Hitler's Luftwaffe aren't the only ones responsible for the deaths of innocent people as World War II rages – it seems there are plenty of murderers willing to help them reduce Britain's war-torn population further. And it's up to Hercule Poirot to stop them . . .

ONE, TWO, BUCKLE MY SHOE

A dentist lies dead in his Harley Street surgery, a pistol lying on the floor near his out-flung right hand – but was it suicide or murder? Poirot finds his investigation isn't exactly child's play . . .

FIVE LITTLE PIGS

Hell hath no fury like a woman scorned, so they say – and beautiful Caroline Crale's husband found that out the hard way. He was poisoned after flaunting his mistress in front of his wife – but was Caroline truly '*deadlier than the male*'?

TAKEN AT THE FLOOD

When the wealthy Gordon Cloade is killed in the blitz, his new, young wife inherits everything, much to the anger of the Cloade family. Hercule Poirot receives a message from the 'spirits' – which confirms his suspicion that Mrs Cloade's position is a dangerous one.

This trilogy of bestselling novels represents a time in Agatha Christie's life during which her writing was at its most prolific and, many would argue, its most ingenious.

Agatha Christie

POIROT: The FRENCH Collection

It seems Hercule Poirot can never escape murder. Crimes, motives and killers followed him across the Orient and now they have found him again – but this time much closer to home . . .

MURDER ON THE LINKS

An urgent cry for help brings Poirot to France. But he arrives too late to save his client, whose brutally stabbed body now lies face downwards in a shallow grave on a golf course. As Poirot struggles to match the pieces of the puzzle, a second identically murdered corpse is found.

THE MYSTERY OF THE BLUE TRAIN

When the luxurious Blue Train arrives at Nice, a guard attempts to wake serene Ruth Kettering from her slumbers. But she will never wake again – for a heavy blow has killed her, disfiguring her features almost beyond recognition.

DEATH IN THE CLOUDS

From seat number 9 Hercule Poirot is ideally placed to observe and enjoy the antics of his fellow air passengers. What he fails to observe, however, is the dead woman slumped in the seat behind him.

Three bestselling novels that all radiate the Queen of Crime's flawless plotting and certain '*je ne sais quoi*'.

Agatha Christie

POIROT:
The Complete Battles of
HASTINGS

VOLUME I

Captain Arthur Hastings OBE, veteran of the First World War and former private secretary to a Member of Parliament, became well-known as Hercule Poirot's trusty sidekick and confidante, the perfect foil for the great detective and his 'little grey cells'.

Yet although Agatha Christie wrote 33 novels about her famous Belgian detective, only eight of them actually feature Captain Hastings. Considered to be some of the very best Christie stories, the distinctive Hastings novels are distinguished by being recounted in the first person, just as Dr Watson's were for Holmes.

This omnibus volume brings together the first four Poirot and Hastings novels, including the very first book, *The Mysterious Affair at Styles*, the international adventures *The Murder on the Links* and *The Big Four*, and the ingenious Cornish mystery *Peril at End House*.

Agatha Christie

The
MARY WESTMACOTT
Collection

VOLUME ONE

Agatha Christie is known throughout the world as the Queen of Crime. It was her sharp observations of people's ambitions, relationships and conflicts that added life and sparkle to her ingenious detective novels. When she turned this understanding of human nature away from the crime genre, writing anonymously as Mary Westmacott, she created bittersweet novels, love stories with a jagged edge, as compelling and memorable as the best of her work.

GIANT'S BREAD

When a gifted composer returns home after being reported killed in the war, he finds his wife has already remarried...

UNFINISHED PORTRAIT

On the verge of suicide after a marriage break up, a young novelist unburdens herself on an unsuspecting young man...

ABSENT IN THE SPRING

Unexpectedly stranded in Iraq, a loyal wife and mother tries to come to terms with her husband's love for another woman...

'I've not been so emotionally moved by a story since the memorable *Brief Encounter. Absent in the Spring* is a *tour de force* which should be recognized as a classic.' *New York Times*

Agatha Christie

The
MARY WESTMACOTT
Collection

VOLUME TWO

Agatha Christie is known throughout the world as the Queen of Crime. It was her sharp observations of people's ambitions, relationships and conflicts that added life and sparkle to her ingenious detective novels. When she turned this understanding of human nature away from the crime genre, writing anonymously as Mary Westmacott, she created bittersweet novels, love stories with a jagged edge, as compelling and memorable as the best of her work.

THE ROSE AND THE YEW TREE

When an aristocratic young woman falls for a working-class war hero, the price of love proves to be costly for both sides...

A DAUGHTER'S A DAUGHTER

Rejecting personal happiness for the sake of her daughter, a mother later regrets the decision and love turns to bitterness...

THE BURDEN

With childhood jealousy behind them, the growing bond between two sisters becomes dangerously one-sided and destructive...

'Miss Westmacott writes crisply and is always lucid. Much material has been skilfully compressed within little more than 200 pages.'   *Times Literary Supplement*

Agatha Christie Mallowan

COME, TELL ME
HOW YOU LIVE

Agatha Christie was already well known as a crime writer when she accompanied her husband, Max Mallowan, to Syria and Iraq in the 1930s. She took enormous interest in all his excavations, and when friends asked what her strange life was like, she decided to answer their questions in this delightful book.

First published in 1946, *Come, Tell Me How You Live* gives a charming picture of Agatha Christie herself, while also giving insight into some of her most popular novels, including *Murder in Mesopotamia* and *Appointment with Death*. It is, as Jacquetta Hawkes concludes in her introduction, 'a pure pleasure to read'.

'A pure pleasure to read.'
JACQUETTA HAWKES, *from the Introduction*

'Perfectly delightful ... colourful, lively and occasionally touching and thought-provoking.'
CHARLES OSBORNE, *Books & Bookmen*

'Good and enjoyable ... she has a delightfully light touch.'
MARGHANITA LASKI, *Country Life*